ALYRIA

TREACHERY. BEASTS. AND TREASURE

SNRL ROCKY

Borra
Borra
THE KURZAN EMPIRE
Emperor's Rest
Lordalu
Kurza Proper
Anvil Harbor
Brova
Atarra
Star Ocean
Rafik
N
W
E
S
HERA
0 200 400 600 800 1000
Hindra

FJORAN SEA
Lai-Man
THE DYONIAN EMPIRE
Isle De Morta
Port De Morta
Hohto
The Mouse Isles
Spirus
NORTHERN AMARANTHINE OCEAN
Jai Nyng Dyona
Livera
The Storm Tide
SOUTHERN AMARANTHINE OCEAN
Tad'Vong
ALLAN
ANTILE
Bagwham
Maj'Xalla
Luxon

Blue Shades Publishing Inc.

380 Redwood Lane NW, Unit C

Concord, North Carolina 28027

www.blueshadespublishing.com

Paperback ISBN: 979-8-9887958-0-3

eBook ISBN: 979-8-9887958-2-7

Book cover design and map design by Ellie Bockert Augsburger of CreativeDigitalStudios.com

Stock Images from Adobe Stock Include:

Hand drawn ink sketch of bamboo leaves and branches. Vector illustration By Artem

Set of isolated sketched coconut or queen palm trees with leaves. Beach and rainforest, desert coco flora By ilonitta

Map elements illustration, drawing, engraving, ink, line art, vector By jenesesimre

Sasquatch, Yeti, Bigfoot walking vector illustration black and white By Michael Hinkle

A painting of a man in a pirate costume By tilialucida

Pirate ship at night with large moon By Sunshower Shots

a painting of a skeleton in a pirate costume, skeleton pirate, dark fantasy art By vvalentine

Golden skull illustration By Alguien

In Memoriam, A Dedication

We are a singular link in an endless chain. But without what came before us we would not exist. I dedicate this to the links of yesterday, to the ones that forged me, and the God that cast me into this life. At times, I am resentful, but always, I am grateful.

I dedicate this book to Stephanie Vernice Conway-Thomas, my beloved mother. Born November 20th, 1958, and passed on to glory on September 24th, 2020. I wanted to make you a queen of the earth, like you'd always been, but I ran out of time. Instead, God made you a queen in heaven, where you always belonged. This book wouldn't exist without you. For how can a story be told if its teller is never born? I owe you everything, and I am more sorry than words can express that I never lived up to the promises I made you.

I dedicate this book also to my beloved sister, Stesha Amara Thomas. In life, our relationship was stormy on a good day, and fractious on a bad one. We fought and bickered as siblings do, and there were many days where I couldn't stand you. But tragedy gave me new eyes for old issues, and I am so very happy that our last months together were not spent at war. I am sorry, so terribly sorry, that I could not take your pain away. But I am thankful that God gave me the chance to make amends. Your story began on October 12th, 1990, but it was cut so painfully short on February 23rd, 2021. If you're listening, Stesha, I love you and I miss you all the time. Rest well.

This is for you.

FOREWORD

Come with me into a world that is so alike and unalike our own. Where fear is made manifest, and where heroes and villains are forged in the crucible of fate, and overwhelming odds. Where God is not a watchmaker, starting the clock of creation and leaving it to its own inexorable designs, but is one of many active players in the game of destiny. Where dragons and demons are as real as the air you breathe, and the pages of this book, or screen, or the sound waves that make up the audio playing into your ears right now.

Join me in the world of Hera, in these tales of Alyria. Where pirates prowl, battling men of honor and monsters of the deep in conquest for the high seas, and all its horrors and bounties. Where kings, queens, and Emperors vie for control in a deceptive and secretive game of thrones.

Great men and women are born and die, here. Wars rage, and tear the world asunder, leaving broken, malleable souls in their wake. And the gods plot and observe, watching the struggles of men, laughing and scheming for their own apotheosis. This is the world of Alyria: Treachery, Beasts, and Treasure.

Enjoy, and I hope that you have even half the joy reading this as I did making it.

I

THE EL'WA PRIZE

Gormas patrolled the deck of the Lumaril, surveying her features with a practiced gaze. He had lost count of how many times he lapped the ship this patrol. He typically stopped counting after the twelfth lap. He cupped his gauntleted hand over his helmet visor and observed the other ships in their fleet formation. He admired their beauteous fin-shaped sails with royal purple fabric billowing in the ocean breeze. The symbol of the House of the Sun, a fiery yellow orb, was emblazoned on all their sails. He looked up at the sails of his own ship, an exact copy of the sails of the other three. It always filled him with pride to see the symbol of the House, of which he was descendant. On calm, sunny days such as this, he often thought of the homeland.

Sai'Haluud, the Imperium of the El'wa, the true inheritors of Hera.

Yes, he was proud to be an El'wa. Though the Book of the Celestials spoke ill of pride and its vices, he was proud of everything he did. Surely to be proud of your people was not a sin, however? How could one wear the golden armor of the Sun Knights and not feel pride? How could he live two-hundred years on this earth, surrounded by his people's marvelous works and feats, and not feel proud of their combined achievement? He blinked as light reflected off the sea into his eyes.

"Did you see something, fal'ren?" Another of his kind, this one wearing plain naval clothes with floral designs on them, asked.

The guard bowed his head in deference. "No, sul'ren, it was naught but the reflection of the sun on the water."

The man nodded. "Very well. Remain sharp. There are reports of pirates in the area. We'd do well not to be caught unawares."

The guard held in a chuckle. "Pirates, sul'ren? To attack us is to invite death. We have crushed their kind before. Should they show their face, this time will be no different. The Alyria cannons will see that their ships are destroyed long before they could hope to fell us."

The plain-clothed El'wa frowned. "You have faced small-time thugs, bandits in boats, more like. A pirate is a much greater threat than a petty criminal." He turned and started walking away. ""You would do well to remember that, fal'ren."

"As you say, sul'ren," the armored man said respectfully. He saw no danger, not from pirates. Pirates were but kith, mortal and weak. Against the might of their guard ships, they stood no chance. No, their treasures would be safe, as they had always been. The man squinted at the glint of light once more, a nuisance now. He didn't bother to pull out his spyglass. He would continue his—

He paused, hearing a scraping sound coming from the side of the ship. He leaned over the railing to check and got a knife through the eye for his trouble. His body hit the deck as his killer climbed over and removed the knife from his shocked face.

The killer, a youthful man with spiraling tattoos, honey-colored skin, a short afro and fierce, chestnut eyes looked briefly at the dead El'wa before whistling and summoning his companions. "He's dead. Plant the nullifier, quickly," he whispered, watching the deck for more. The killer wore a black vest with a brown, short-sleeved button-up shirt and a black bandana tied around one arm. Tucked in his tan sash was one of his pistols, he wiped the blood on his black trousers, and tucked the blade back into his boot. Upon him was a bandoleer covered in more pistols. He pulled one out before loading it.

The others climbed aboard, twelve men in all, soaked to the bone from the sea, carrying swords, pistols, axes, and spears.

"Hide them well, if they destroy them, the cannons will burn Azura to driftwood in minutes," the killer instructed.

"Aye, Siris, we know the drill," another of the men, this one a tall, angry-looking blonde man, said.

"Ye say that Cutter, but considerin' ye barely know how to spell your own name, I don't really believe you."

Cutter opened a sack slung over his back and pulled out a large, black piece of metal with glass that shined an ominous blue color from within. He planted the nullifier, then pulled the pin. The device made a loud thrumming noise, before projecting a bubble of see-through blue energy. He nodded, then looked at Siris, or Osiris, as was his full name. "Fuck you. How's that for a response?"

Osiris smirked. "Typical."

"Where do I place mine?" The youngest member of the boarding party asked. His name was Hanover.

"Nowhere, give it to Flint and have him plant it further down the deck," Osiris responded sharply.

"I can plant it myself," Hanover replied.

Flint, the tallest of the group, reached for the device, but Hanover moved away and began creeping up the deck toward where Osiris pointed.

"Why'd ye bother to bring the kid if ye won't use him?" Flint asked.

"I didn't; he did," Osiris responded, nodding to the horizon.

"Aye," Flint responded.

"Over there! Humans!" An armored guard shouted. He clenched Hanover's wrist in his arm.

"Shit, they've found us! Hurry it up!" Osiris ordered as he charged at the guard, who was sounding an alarm chime. He sprinted at the man, sword out as several more guards took up rank next to him.

"Shoot them!" The alarm guard ordered.

The others fell into a firing formation, pulling out their rifles.

"Get outta the way!" Osiris shouted, then leaped high into the air, dodging the gunfire before landing on the first guard and knocking him to the deck, slashing his throat, and freeing Hanover.

"Get back to the group!" Osiris ordered in the middle of the melee.

"I'll not leave you!" Hanover shouted.

"That's an order!" Osiris shouted as he kicked another El'wa in the side, knocking him overboard, then grappled with another who slammed him against the railing. The metal of the El'wa's gauntlets dug into Osiris' throat as he stared the man in his angry, glowing green eyes.

Hanover swung a mace at the back of the El'wa's helmeted head. The mace bounced off the helmet, momentarily distracting the El'wa. Osiris threw the man off him, then snatched the mace from Hanover's hands.

"This is how you do it, boy," Osiris grunted, then crushed the man's face with an overhead swing of the mace. Hanover winced slightly, watching as the man's legs kicked, then went still.

The other guards, having charged at Flint, Cutter, and the others, were cut down immediately.

Osiris picked up the nullifier and planted it behind a crate before turning it on.

"When I give an order, you follow it, understand me?" Osiris looked Hanover in his eyes.

Hanover blinked, his hair in his eyes. "Yes, sir."

"Good. Stay put and stay hidden. When the rest of them get here, you get ghost. Understand me?"

"But—"

"Do you understand me?"

Hanover sighed, then nodded. "Aye, sir."

"Stay put. The rest of ye, get ready."

The group watched as dozens of blue bubbles appeared across all four ships. The nullifiers had been planted and activated. Osiris, Flint, and Cutter smiled at one another. The easy part had been completed.

"We've got company," Cutter said, pointing to their left as a dozen El'wa in leather and cloth armor appeared.

"Kill the pirates!" One of them shouted, then charged.

The pirates charged back at them.

*****

"The nullifiers have been set, we can come 'round, now, Cap'n," a stout Half-Duwa man named Frederick Moary, said.

The captain, a sturdy, older-looking man with a well-kempt black beard and bicorn hat, nodded. He stood at the nose of the ship, overlooking the infiltration of the El'wa ships from afar through his spyglass. "All hands, make ready! Man the top guns and angle at seventy-five degrees. Prepare for fire."

The crew did as he bid, like clockwork they completed their tasks, repeating his orders so that all could hear and follow suit. The captain folded up his spyglass as the top guns fired, then walked down the steps from the foredeck. "Gun Master, tell the gun crews to get ready for a raking strike. We're going to put holes in their sails so they can't run, but when we get in close, we need to destroy their broadsides. We're going to go between the first two ships to disable them, then board from there."

"Aye, Cap'n, I'll relay your orders."

A dark-skinned man covered in ritual scars on his arms, chest, and face, approached. Yaman Huasca.

"What of the other two ships? They will try to box us in and fire at our fore and aft," he warned.

"Not if we capture their guns first. Each ship is laden with enough treasure and provisions to make a healthy sum back at the Storm Tide and last us till we arrive. We only need capture one prize, two maximum. The other two can go up in flames and we'll still turn a profit. I doubt it will come to that, however. The nullifiers will render their guns useless and a few shots to their sails will ensure they're too busy refitting them to give chase. By time they're sea ready again we will be long gone."

Huasca nodded his approval. "A sound strategy, Captain Morgan."

The captain, Morgan, smiled and nodded. "I've taken a few El'wa prizes in my day."

Huasca chuckled, a rumble in his throat. "I would know; I've seen a fair amount of them."

The two surveyed the deck and paused as they came across a grumbling, blonde haired crewman who was laboring away loading a top gun. They paused for several moments watching him and listening as he loaded the cannon, cursed, then fired it at the enemy's sails.

"Is there a problem, Mr. Yager?" Morgan asked, having heard the man grumble his name several times.

Yager froze a moment before looking at Morgan and Huasca. His green eyes settled squarely on Morgan, and he shook his head.

"Nay, sir. Thinkin' out loud, is all."

"Thinking of me, evidently. You mentioned my name several times amid your mutterings. Would you like to share with the congregation?" Morgan asked.

"Aye, uh, nay, sir. Was nothing of note, sir."

Yager quickly set back to loading his cannon, this time being careful to keep his lips sealed and focus on his work. The top guns were substantially lighter than the lower guns, and so they could be maneuvered, laboriously, and fired by a single operator. Yager was experienced at loading them, it used to be one of his duties to oversee, in fact.

Used to be.

He fired the cannon again, watching as the shot sailed in an arc and struck the upper topsails of one of the El'wa ships. It was a perfect shot, tearing the sail canvas and breaking the topsail itself in the process.

"A perfect shot. Your skill with a cannon never fails to impress." Morgan nodded.

"Thank you, sir," Yager replied, proudly.

"If only you had stayed this course, you would still be an officer," Huasca said with a shake of his head.

Morgan scowled, nodded, and the two walked away. Yager grumbled to himself again, shook his head, now turning bright red, and set back to his work.

*****

"The cannons won't fire, sul'ren! The nullifiers have disrupted them!" The gunner reported to Hal'ren.

"Ful'karin! It all makes sense, now! The pirates sent infiltrators to board the ship and nullify the Alyria cannons to stop us from obliterating them on the spot!" Hal'ren turned to address the guards standing behind him, "Guards, find those nullifiers and destroy them! We can't destroy the pirate ship without the Alyria cannons!"

"It will be done, sul'ren! We will alert the other ships!" The guard leader said, and marched above deck.

Just as the guards left, the door on the far side of the gun deck opened, and an El'wa woman fell to the deck, dead. Immediately after, Flint, Cutter, and several other pirates stormed into the cabin.

"Pira—" Hal'ren barely got the word out of his mouth before a bullet shaved off his cheek and sent him sprawling on the floor.

Cutter pulled out his blunderbuss. "Stand back!" he ordered, the pirates hit the floor behind him and covered their ears as he fired the weapon. The flared muzzle of the blunderbuss belched out a wave of fire and burning shrapnel, momentarily blinding him to everything in front of him. When the smoke cleared, a dozen plus El'wa lay in pieces on the floor and many others scattered in horror, injured by the shrapnel. His ears rang, so he couldn't hear them screaming, but he could see the screams on their faces as they fled.

"Clear!" he shouted at the top of his lungs.

The pirates chased after the fleeing El'wa.

Flint, having stayed back, fired a bullet into the back of the lone El'wa that made it to the stairs on the other side of the gun deck. He hit the man in his spine, and he fell down the stairs, unable to move.

"Good shot, mate," Cutter patted him hard on the back, now speaking at a normal tone.

Flint nodded, then reloaded his rifle before charging into the fray with Cutter.

The El'wa who weren't attempting to flee were cut down to the man, as were the stragglers. The ship's gun deck was completely disabled.

"We've got one still alive," someone shouted.

Flint and Cutter stood over Hal'ren, who was gasping for air on the floor. Flint rolled him over with his foot and both men grimaced at the side of his face. The bullet had shaved the flesh of his cheek and face off across the right side of his head. The bone and gristle showed, and his tongue lolled out the raw, bloody hole that used to be his cheek.

"End his misery," Cutter said.

Flint pulled out his flintlock pistol and shot Hal'ren in the head, ending his suffering.

"Deck's cleared. Let's see how Siris 'n the others faired up top." Flint walked to the stairs, past the El'wa he'd paralyzed—whom he promptly slit the throat of—and went above deck, followed by the others.

*****

Osiris slammed into a mast, then dodged as his attacker brought her longsword down where his head had been a moment prior.

"Your days are numbered, pirate filth!" his attacker, an El'wa knight, threatened. The woman was tall and imposing in her golden armor. She cut down every pirate that got in her path with ease. Her gaze focused on Osiris, never letting him slip from her sight as he dodged her attacks. He bumped into a pirate fighting one of the crew and fell to the deck as the knight cut down the pirate to get to him. Thinking fast, Osiris pulled out a pistol and fired at a clasp overhead, holding a net in place. The net fell onto the knight and several others, entangling them and giving Osiris time to recover.

On a gamble, he pulled out a hand grenade and lit it as the knight freed herself from the net, cutting it open.

"Clever, for a ver'mak. Unfortunate that I'll have to—" She froze as Osiris tossed the grenade at her.

"Catch!" he laughed, then took cover to escape the blast.

The knight watched as the wick burned down before grabbing the grenade and chucking it right before it detonated. It went off midair, spraying hot projectiles at the knight and everyone in range. She hissed as it bit into her armor and a stray shard struck the exposed skin of her neck.

Where did he go?

She wondered as she looked around. He'd fled the chaos, of course. Did he really think that a simple grenade would be enough to take down a mighty knight of Sai'Haluud? That he, a lowly ver'mak pirate would—

A weight slammed into her back as a hand grabbed hold of her helmet and pulled it back to expose her throat. She barely had time to react, but she swung her fist back and punched her attacker in the jaw.

Osiris grunted as he struggled with the knight. She slammed him against a crate to dislodge him from her back and avoid the knife he was attempting to kill her with. He sprawled out on the crate and kicked her in the head. She brought her blade down on the crate, missing his crotch by an inch as he pulled out another pistol and fired it at her face. The gun misfired, missing her entirely and striking a random El'wa as Hanover sprung out from his hiding place and rushed to save him.

"Stay back, boy! I told you!" Osiris screamed, alerting the knight to the surprise attack.

She spun to see Hanover charging her with a sword. She immediately disarmed him and grappled him to the deck.

"**NO!**" Osiris growled, his eyes turning bright turqouise as his pitch lowered dramatically and he leapt at the woman, the tattoos covering his body lit up and he felt a surge of energy. He tackled the El'wa knight, charging her across the deck and slamming her into a mast.

"How did you—" she froze again as she saw the glow of the pirate's tattoos and the fierce light coming from his eyes. "An Alyrian?! The pirates have an Alyrian! Kill him!" she shouted, gathering the attention of several El'wa, who charged at Osiris, weapons drawn.

Osiris drew both his swords and quickly parried the attacks coming at him, disarming one attacker before beheading another and shoving his sword through the chest of a third. The first El'wa, crawling towards his discarded sword was stabbed through the throat by one of Osiris' blades before he brought it to bare to overwhelm his last two attackers. None of the El'wa could keep up with his speed and ferocity. He stood over their corpses, covered in blood and panting in rage as he turned his gaze back to the El'wa knight, who now held Hanover hostage.

Both she and Hanover gazed at him with terrified eyes as he glared in their direction. He said nothing as he cracked his neck and stalked towards them, bloodied swords raised.

"Come any closer pirate and I'll slit this whelp's neck, as Aeradin is my witness!" she threatened, unable to hide the fear in her voice.

Osiris smirked and nodded his head before turning his back on her. Seizing the opportunity, she threw Hanover to the side before raising her blade to the sky. A beam of light struck the blade as she prepared to swing it. The knight sliced the blade downward as an arc of orange light swept towards Osiris. He reacted immediately, twisting his core as he turned around and launched his sword at her and dodged the arc of energy that scorched the deck as it travelled. Surprised, the knight was defenseless as the sword flew into her shoulder.

"Ful'karin…damn…pirate…" She spat blood as it sprayed from her shoulder wound onto the sword. She fell to her knees, unable to raise her shield arm as he closed the gap.

Osiris stood over her, the unnatural light leaving his eyes as he regarded her defeated form. "Ye put up a good fight, El'wa. Your Stars will be pleased."

He pulled out his last pistol and aimed at her forehead. She closed her eyes. He fired.

She fell to the deck.

Osiris turned and looked at Hanover, who was scrambling to his feet. He grabbed him by the shirt collar and dragged him over to a barrel before opening the lid.

"Wait, don't—" Hanover stammered as Osiris dropped him into the barrel and closed the lid.

"Stay. Put. I'll knock on the barrel when it's time for you to come out and I swear to the dead sea gods that I'll shoot you myself if you come out beforehand."

"Yes…sir," Hanover replied angrily.

"Good."

*****

Azura closed the distance, having disabled all four ships before they could muster a defense, now, all that remained was to subdue them. To make his point, Morgan brought Azura's guns to bare and raked the gun decks of two El'wa ships as she passed by them, then came around behind the ships to fire at the remaining two, damaging them.

"We've subdued them, Captain," Huasca reported.

Morgan frowned as he looked through his spyglass at one of the ship decks that his officers had yet to overtake. "No, not quite."

A nullifier powered down as a cannon port slid open, and an Alyria cannon took aim at Azura.

"Brace for impact! One of the nullifiers has been disabled!" Morgan roared, ducking in cover as the cannon charged up, then fired.

A slow-moving ball of bright red energy arced through the air as it came crashing down near Azura, grazing her. The ball exploded in the water, rocking the ship and knocking men to the deck.

"Destroy those cannons! If we take a direct hit, we'll be aflame!" Morgan ordered.

Yager took aim with his cannon and fired at the offending cannon, destroying its barrel just as it powered up to fire. The cannon misfired with spectacular effect, blowing a hole in the side of the El'wa ship and lighting it ablaze as the other cannons began to detonate. The men cheered and patted Yager on the back as Morgan watched with bittersweet relief as the ship went up. Several of his men were aboard the ship and he was watching as they were consumed by the explosions and flames. He folded up the spyglass with a nod and a sigh.

"What's that over there?!" A pirate shouted as Morgan turned his gaze to one of the El'wa ships. It was one they'd raked with cannon fire.

"What in the Stars' names is…" Morgan paused, as did Huasca, who stood next to him, watching.

*****

"Pirate filth!" The El'wa captain shouted as he stood on the foredeck. He pointed to a group of men the El'wa had managed to take captive on their ship, having failed to subdue all the crew. "You think that because you have taken us unawares and destroyed our Alyria cannons that you have evaded our wrath?!

Tis not so! We El'wa have many tricks up our sleeves, as even nature itself can be bent to our will!" The El'wa captain declared.

He was a tall man, as was common of the El'wa men. He towered over the captives kneeling before him as he spoke, wielding an ornate knife in his hand. He knelt before one of the men, who looked at him defiantly. "Are you ready, ver'mak? Are you ready to die for your sins?"

The pirate looked deep into the El'wa's glowing yellow eyes before spitting in his face, then laughing, as did many of the other captive pirates. "Piss on you, piss on my sins. Let the Gods judge me."

The captain grinned at the pirate's savage display. "I'm going to enjoy this." He looked to one of his subordinates. ""Bring out the beast, fal'ren."

"As you say, sul'ren," the subordinate replied, giving an almost sorrowful look at the pirate as he and several others went below deck.

Less than a minute later, a heavy thumping, followed by low growling came from below as something large and spirited was dragged up from below deck. The captive pirates, Morgan, Huasca, and the men above deck on the Azura all strained to see what it was that had been brought on deck.

"What's that?" the pirate who spat on the El'wa captain asked.

The captain grinned toothily as he let the spit run down his cheek. "Your executioner."

He grabbed the pirate's restrained hands and cut one of the palms open, making him hiss in pain. The El'wa captain held the bloodied blade up for all to see as it dripped onto the deck—and the creature was let loose.

It took flight, then landed on the foredeck, causing every El'wa and pirate on the deck to shout in alarm as the captain dropped the blade and watched the creature come to investigate, sniffing and grunting loudly.

Standing on four legs, towering over even the El'wa captain, was a beast of fable. It had the head of an overly large and toothy lion, with blood red eyes and a wild mane of black fur. Its wings were powerful, leathery bat wings wide enough to encompass a horse in their embrace. The beast's hind legs were scaly, and hook clawed, ending in a thick, long serpent tail with a hissing serpent's head at the end of it. The serpent, large enough to swallow a man whole, flicked its tongue and came close to the bleeding man's face as he closed his eyes and hyperventilated. It flicked a bead of sweat off his face as it came well within striking distance and paused, staring at him. The other men huddled in fear, murmuring to themselves as they beheld the towering monster in front of them.

"A Chimera…no! No! Please no! Oh God, no!" The pirate pleaded as the lion's head of the beast licked his blood from the deck. It licked its chops, briefly exposing its fangs as the deck grew quiet, and even the din of gunfire and swords clashing in the distance seemed to cease for a moment.

The man opened his eyes, staring directly into the yellow orbs of the serpent head.

"Please…no—"

The jaws of the serpent opened wide, exposing bright pink flesh as it encompassed the man's head and shoulders and swallowed him whole, kicking and screaming all the while. The frightened pirates watched as the muffled, wailing bulge travelled down the length of the serpent tail and disappeared into the body of the Chimera. Suddenly, the lion-end of the beast came round and roared at the men, who screamed in turn as it descended upon them, tearing them apart with tooth and claw.

"Kill them all, Chimera! Devour them all!" The El'wa captain cheered maniacally as the serpent tail reared at him and sprayed a cloud of poison at him. The man screeched like an animal as the mist melted him to the bone.

"Bloody fools! They've unleashed a monster! All hands, shoot that beast before it kills us all!" Morgan ordered. They fired at the creature, but the bullet did little to it from their distance as it tore apart the rest of the captive pirates and took flight again. It sailed through the air, dodging gunfire as it headed for the ship that Osiris, Hanover, Flint, and Cutter were on.

II

THE CHIMERA

"What in Sheolhenna is that?!" Cutter shouted as he ducked out of the way of the swooping Chimera. It crashed on top of several men, and began tearing into them after it landed, flailing its serpent-head tail at any who came near. It ripped four men apart in less than as many seconds, tossing chunks of flesh and limbs as it fed on what it wanted, soaking its fur in blood.

"A fucking Chimera, here?!" Osiris raised his blades, panting from the previous skirmish. He was in the middle of fighting off three El'wa, but now everyone had stopped to behold the terrifying arrival.

"They loosed the beast! The day is lost! Scramble for the lifeboats!" An El'wa shouted and made for a boat. The Chimera, perhaps sensing his attempt to escape, or perhaps just drawn by his cries, leapt at him, dislodging several lifeboats and taking flight again.

Osiris watched in shock as the creature tore the man apart midair, using its tail to rip chunks out of him before it dropped the remains into the sea and flew back towards the ship.

"Kill the beast before it kills us all!" Cutter shouted, taking aim with his blunderbuss as it swooped back down and bayed at them, prowling back and forth as it sized them up. He fired the blunderbuss at the creature's side, eliciting a yowl as it flopped onto its side momentarily and swung its tail at him.

Knowing what came next, Cutter lunged out of the way as the serpent belched a cloud of corrosive poison from its maw. The cloud ate away at the wood where he'd just stood, and an El'wa had his leg partially melted trying to escape the spew, crippling him.

The El'wa and the pirates charged the beast, slashing, stabbing, and hacking at it as it flailed on the ground. It rose back to its feet and began slashing and biting in turn, maiming and killing several as it fought them back. His tattoos and eyes aglow once more, Osiris looked for an opening as the beast turned away from him, distracted momentarily as Cutter fired a rifle bullet at the serpent head, piercing it.

"Now's your chance!" Flint shouted as he took off running and kicked open a door, narrowly escaping the jaws of the enraged Chimera as it tried and failed to force its broad frame through the cabin door.

Seeing the opportunity Flint gave him, Osiris charged past the mob of combatants trying to get at the creature and went straight for the tail. He struck the serpent head, which was coughing up blood from the bullet wound. He stabbed it with both of his swords, spearing the blades through its head and sealing the deadly orifice shut. He grabbed onto the tail as the beast turned back around and held tight as it took to the air again. He pulled out his knife and began stabbing over and over into the tail as the Chimera kicked at him and flailed, trying to get him off.

The creature crashed into the top of a mast, and he suffered a blow to the head, nearly letting go of the creature as his world spun. His legs remained locked around the whipping tail as his upper body swayed in the slipstream of its ascent. It was trying to dislodge him. The ships began to shrink as it neared the clouds before a rifle bullet through the wings brought it crashing back down towards the ships. The Chimera howled as it tried to control the landing. Osiris regained control and wrapped his upper body back onto the tail before crawling towards the lion's head of the beast. He braced himself as the monster fell into the netting of another of the ships, and he was knocked off its back, becoming entangled in the ropes.

He looked in alarm at the congregating El'wa, who were now focused on he and the Chimera, rather than the pirates they'd been fighting. "Don't shoot! Don't shoot!" he shouted, attempting to free himself from the ropes, sawing like mad with his knife as one of the El'wa took aim at him. He cut a hole in the ropes and fell through, getting caught in another section of the netting. He closed his eyes as the El'wa took aim, but the bullet went wide as a pirate shoved the man, stopping him from shooting him.

Meanwhile, the Chimera was furiously gnawing and slicing its way free of the ropes as several men shot at it. It rained blood down on the deck as it fought its way free and dropped down, landing on a man and crushing his skull. The El'wa went from firing at the creature to running from it. Osiris freed himself shortly after, dropping to the deck and landing on his back, gasping. He stumbled to his feet as two pirates helped him up, then watched the Chimera as it slaughtered men left and right just a few yards away. Already it was beginning to heal from the wounds he'd inflicted upon it. He watched the blades fall from the serpent head as it regenerated.

"It's unstoppable!" A pirate cried as they watched the creature feast on a still screaming El'wa and heal all its wounds. The bullet hole in its wing sealed, the cuts and scrapes it had sustained to its head and neck closed and scabbed over, and a knife wound it'd sustained to its eye immediately healed, pushing out the knife and then scabbing over as the eye opened wide, glaring at Osiris.

"…Shit."

Osiris leapt overboard as the Chimera charged at him, taking out the men who'd helped him to his feet, narrowly missing him.

*****

"How do we kill the Chimera?" Huasca asked as he and Morgan watched the El'wa, and their men fruitlessly attempt to kill it. The bullets that struck it either bounced off its hide or was healed almost as quickly as they struck.

"So long as the creature has bodies to devour, its healing abilities will allow it to regenerate whatever damage is done to it. We need a decisive blow to kill it before it can heal itself," Morgan explained, smoking his pipe. An idea formed in his head, and he pulled out his spyglass. Most of the El'wa on the ship he'd sent Osiris and the others onto were already slain. Which meant…

"Grab Mr. Stone, he should be overseeing the crews on the second gun deck. I've a job for him."

*****

He dove underwater.

He didn't know where the Chimera was, but he knew his best chance of evading its clutches was to swim. He prayed to any God that would listen that there weren't any sharks prowling nearby, drawn by the sound of cannon fire and the smell of corpses in the water. That hope was immediately dashed, however, when he watched a body launch into the water and begin to sink, dying the water around the corpse red. Something came up from the deep blue and took a bite from the corpse. It was a cobalt-colored shark with a large, jagged fin.

And it wasn't alone.

15

A shiver of them came up from the depths, blending with the blue of the ocean until their white underbellies showed, or when the light from above reflected off them.

Bladefins. A whole fucking shiver of bladefins.

Osiris cursed internally and damned the Dead Sea Gods for the trouble. Most sharks, save for a few, didn't tend to pay sailors too much mind. Too small, not enough meat to be worth the meal. Bladefins were one of those few. They thrive in the open ocean, and will often follow ships whenever fighting starts, waiting to feast on the remains.

Or any bastard dumb or unlucky enough to be in the water…

He corrected himself.

He saw a boat a few meters away and started swimming towards it, Chimera be damned. He stood a chance against the creature on solid footing but stood next to none against a shiver of bladefins. He kicked for the surface as he saw one bee-lining towards him, slashing a body in its path in half with its razor-sharp fin. He broke the surface and grabbed onto the edge of the boat. It held three, startled-looking El'wa.

Get on the boat first. Worry about them second.

He pulled himself up, adrenaline running through his veins as he felt the shark on his heels. He flopped onto the boat as the first El'wa made up his mind to dispose of Osiris.

"Back into the sea, pirate!" The El'wa said as he attempted to stab Osiris.

"Wrong choice, mate!" Osiris spat back, wrestling the blade from the man and kicking him away as the bladefin breached the water and slammed into the man, taking him back into the sea with it. Startled, the other two El'wa, another El'wa male and an El'wa female, huddled together on the opposite end of the boat. They glared daggers at him, then pointed skyward and spoke in their native tongue.

He heard the roar before he even looked over his shoulder to see the Chimera approaching. It made straight for the boat. Osiris looked around, seeing another boat a few meters away, its occupants taking aim at the Chimera.

There we go!

He leapt back into the water as the beast landed on the boat and set upon the now screaming El'wa.

He took stock of where the bladefin that had been chasing him was. It was preoccupied with feasting on the corpse of his would-be attacker. The others were too far away and more interested in feasting on the bevy of corpses dropping into the water, either from the fighting aboard the ships or from the Chimera dropping its half-eaten meals into the water. For now, he was in no immediate danger.

He came up for air next to the boat he was about to board, listening to the occupants. They were reloading, having already shot at the Chimera.

Why isn't it attacking them, then?

He heard the flap of its wings and watched as it sailed high into the air again, carrying a new victim, likely one of the unfortunate occupants of the other boat.

They'll be distracted, now's my time.

He climbed silently up onto the boat, still holding the knife he'd taken from the dead El'wa. There were three of them, and they were looking skyward, facing away from him. He threw the knife at the neck of one. The blade found its target as he tackled the second, pushing him into the water before grappling with the third, who'd just finished reloading his rifle. The El'wa barely had time to register the attack before Osiris was on him, ripping the reloaded rifle from his hands and bashing him in the head with the ornate metal stock. The blow sent him reeling back and he fell overboard as well.

The threats neutralized, Osiris looked around, surveying the area. There was at least a dozen more boats. Maybe twenty total. He looked and saw that a rope ladder was hanging from the ship he'd boarded with Flint, Cutter, and Hanover.

He'd better still be in that damned barrel, for both our sakes.

Osiris cleared the thought from his mind. The boy would have to fend for himself, right now he was competing with bladefins, a Chimera, and El'wa that wanted him dead.

I could head straight for the ladder. The beastie seems to avoid the water. The bladefins, though. Longer I'm in the water, longer they have to scent me. I can't outswim them, the boats are the only safe haven and that's assuming they don't leap out of the water or capsize the whole thing.

He thought that as he watched several bladefins rush a lifeboat and flip it over.

No, gotta risk it. The longer I'm in the water the longer these things have to catch me.

His mind made up, Osiris took a deep breath and leapt back into the water, headed straight for the ladder. He paused for a moment as he recognized the Azura sidling up next to the ship but kept swimming as he realized he still had ample space to mount and climb onto the El'wa ship.

*****

The El'wa crowded the end of the gangplank as a pirate with grey hair and a beard as well as a blonde-haired, wild-looking, shirtless pirate, covered in tattoos lead the charge to board the El'wa ship. The grey-haired pirate, Stone, fired his two dragon guns into the El'wa barring their path, scorching them with a blast of flame and a spray of hot metal. Those that weren't scorched and ripped to pieces ran howling, their clothes aflame.

"Path's clear, ye know what to do! Move out!" Stone ordered as he stepped on the deck of the ship. He spotted Flint stepping out of the cabin the Chimera had tried to grab him from, the frame warped and splintered from its attempts. "Mr. Flint, where's Mr. Cutter?" Stone asked.

Flint thumbed behind him. "Down there, he took several with him to clear below deck and secure the cargo."

"Good. That means the gun deck'll be clear, ay?" Stone asked.

"Aye. Was the first thing we cleared when we set the nullifiers."

"Good. Now disable them. I need the cannons workin'."

Flint quirked a brow. "Pardon?"

"Cap'n's orders, mate," Stone said, pressing past Flint, followed by several men.

Flint pointed to the blonde, shirtless pirate that boarded with Stone. "Ye brought the madman, ay?"

Stone laughed as he stepped down the stairs. "Ye thought he'd just stay on the Azura 'n hide from the fightin? When's a Northman ever turned down bloodshed?"

With that, he disappeared below deck, the men he came with following shortly.

Flint leaned against the ruined doorframe and lit a cigarette. "My jobs done, then." He shook his head as he watched the shirtless pirate pant and whoop, then start beating his chest as some of the remaining El'wa tentatively approached him.

"Steven Cage!" Flint called. The shirtless pirate turned his head in his direction, training an eye on him. "We don't need any prisoners, not from this ship."

The shirtless pirate, Steven Cage, smiled toothily. "Good! Their souls can go to Irkalla, then."

He refocused on the El'wa. Some of them had grown bold and were coming toward him, weapons ready.

"Pompous El'wa. Your souls belong to de Dark Mother, now!" Cage declared.

He charged headlong, wielding two hatchets.

Flint watched with macabre interest as Cage took on the first two attackers, hamstringing one, then braining the other before using the hamstrung El'wa as a shield, who absorbed several pistol shots for him before being shoved forward into the group and leaving an opening for Cage to attack.

Flint took a long drag from the cigarette as Steven Cage tore the group apart. His animalistic movements and growling evoked the image of the Chimera in his mind.

He looked around, seeing the creature was still circling in the air. The El'wa and pirates had stopped shooting at it to refocus on the immediate threat—each other.

"What are you waitin' for, beast?" he asked aloud to no one in particular. The creature had momentarily ceased its rampage, but why? It seems all but unstoppable. It was picking people off left and right. Why, now, was it just circling in the air? As if on cue, he heard someone heave themselves up onto the deck. It was Osiris.

"Siris, you're still alive!" Flint rushed over and helped the man to his feet. The glow having left his eyes and tattoos, his energy clearly spent.

"Somehow…where's the monster?" he panted, spotting it circling above.

It saw him, too.

The Chimera dived toward the ship.

"Shit," Flint said.

"Fucking whoreson!" Osiris shouted in exhaustion.

The Chimera's rampage had resumed.

*****

"Cage! Look out!" Flint shouted before being pushed into the spare cabin by Osiris.

The Chimera was back at the doorframe a split second later, this time, however, the doorframe was coming apart. The pair watched, frozen in horror for a moment as the raging beast glared daggers at them for a moment before opening its maw wide, exposing its fangs and the pink of its mouth as it let loose a deafening roar. They clutched their ears as the beast disoriented them with its howl.

Stone helped them to their feet. "Are the nullifiers disabled?"

The pair looked at him, then at the cannon that several men were painstakingly dragging up the stairs.

"Morgan is a fucking madhat," Flint said, rubbing his bald head.

Outside, Cage ducked behind a crate as the serpent tail of the Chimera sprayed acid mist at the men attacking it. He looked to his side to see Hanover crawling out of the barrel he'd been hiding in, wild-eyed and confused. Cage looked at him, then the nullifier sitting on the deck next to the barrel and pointed at it.

Hanover, realizing what was being asked of him, climbed out of the barrel and grabbed hold of the nullifier before disabling it, smashing it against the deck and releasing its energies with a whine, destroying its bubble of influence.

Back in the cabin, the Chimera managed to fit its shoulder through the doorframe and was moments away from forcing its arms through when the cannon hummed to life, illuminating the cabin with oceanic blue light.

"Stand back," Stone ordered.

Everyone, save for Osiris, cleared the path as he loaded a charged crystal into the bore of the cannon.

"Goodbye, beastie." Osiris smirked as its gaze bore through him—and he dodged out of the way.

The Chimera stared into the blinding light of the El'wa cannon as it fired.

The blast momentarily deafened and blinded everyone in the cabin. The ball of pure Alyria energy ejected from the cannon crashed into the Chimera's body, wedged into the doorframe.

And obliterated it.

The blast turned the torso of the Chimera into a blue and red mist as it tore through the beast, sending its flaming hindquarters sprawling out onto the deck as the ball of energy shot forward across the deck, igniting or destroying anything that happened to be in its path. It crashed through the other side of the main deck, blowing a large, burning blue crater into what used to be the aft section of the ship.

As the smoke settled and the flames spread, signaling the end of the battle, the remaining El'wa surrendered. The Azuran pirates had won the day, and the El'wa ships were seized, overtaken by the lone pirate ship.

III

FOLLY

The Azura, and the two prize vessels they'd taken found harborage a mile off the coast of an islet about a half-day's sailing from where they'd ambushed the El'wa ships. The islet, pristine and covered in long stretches of white sand bars and jungle greenery, was open, but ideal for them to rest, take stock of the wounded, and prepare for the long journey ahead to the Storm Tide. Yet and still, the pirates remained on their ships. A seahawk landed on the stern deck railing and took stock of its surroundings as the officers planned their next move below, in the captain's cabin.

"The men wonder why we have weighed anchor so far from the beach, Cap'n?" Stone asked as the officers and captain stood over a large map of the known world, sitting on Morgan's desk.

Morgan toked from his pipe. "Because while we may have taken two prizes, we are still in unfamiliar territory in an untamed stretch of sea. If the men wish to make merry, be my guest, but I would advise they do it on the safety of the ship. The jungle could hold untold dangers, and we haven't the time nor reason to scout them for it."

"Have the Mygredo no enclaves in the Golden Ocean?" Osiris asked, folding his arms. "I was under the impression wherever monsters may lurk, they plied their trade. The Golden Ocean is rife with them."

"The Mygredo hunt where there is gold and favors to be won. Unless the Imperium wishes to break its coffers on paying Mygredorians to clear out the thousands of islands in their waters, I doubt this little no-name island will be free of things that want to kill us," Morgan replied.

He let the smoke out with a sigh. "Speaking of things that need killing, what rations have we from the captured El'wa ships?"

"The pompous knife-ears? They've left us a veritable banquet. Must've been transporting for a royal feast or the like. Salted meat, alcohol, even fruit, stored in Alyria-infused containers," Cutter proudly announced.

"Enough to last us to the Storm Tide, then?" Morgan asked with a pleased expression.

"Enough to bloody last us to the Star Ocean and back, if need be, Cap'n!" Cutter replied.

"Good. We can rest easy, then. The men will burn through half of it before we reach Dyonian waters."

"Won't Lady Krait be taking a pittance, seein' as how we took prey from her waters?" Flint chuckled.

All the officers laughed in unison.

"Lady Krait can subtract whatever pittance she thinks is owed from the sum she's gained bandying my name around to curry fear and men. The Brethren Court feasts and languishes under the shadow we cast, and I've been a member longer than the current lords have been living!" Morgan laughed.

"What of the wounded?" he continued.

"Sir, the sawbones says that outside the forty we lost, another seventeen wait at the gates of the Aethera from injury," Stone answered, somberly.

The men fell silent, and Morgan nodded. "Aye, I'd feared as much. I trust he'll do what he can to ease the dying and save the living. What of our munitions stock?"

The gunner, Frederick Moary, stepped forth. The Half-Duwa stood a head shorter than most but pushed past them easily to stand before the captain.

Moary cleared his throat. "Sir, we'd spent over two-thirds of our cannonballs and powder in the fightin'. Since the El'wa use Alyria crystals for their cannons, we can't utilize their munition stores for the Azura's guns. The added firepower from the captured ships will more than make up for our lost munitions, however."

"I'd figured as much. Are you familiar with the workings of Alyria cannons, gunner? They're a great deal different from traditional powder cannons," Morgan asked, knowing the answer.

Moary released a low grumble from his chest, "I know human cannons, I know the difference 'tween Dyonian rocket guns 'n Xallan spray cannons. Between Duwa volcans 'n yes, even El'wa Alyria cannons. I'll have the men blowin' apart Chimeras with 'em in no time, Cap'n."

Morgan gave a smirk and nod at the mention of his plan to lure and kill the Chimera. "Very good, Mr. Moary. Next, we must speak of shares." He looked to the quartermaster. "Mr. Stone?"

Stone stepped forward as the officers waited with pricked ears. "Usual shares, two for meself, Mr. Huasca, and the Cap'n. One 'n a quarter fer all at present, includin' the sawbones, Claude Humris, the bosun 'n carpenter—"

"And de cooper, of course—" Steven Cage butted in. As he was an officer, he was privy to the information given in these meetings, though he seldom sat in on them. Save for when shares were involved.

"Yes, northman, ye'll get yer tranche 'o gold fer the blood ye've spilled fer yer Dark Mother, ay?" Stone responded, his Sarxian accent coming out thick.

Steven Cage nodded. "Good. I've whores to fuck 'n beer to drink."

Seemingly satisfied with the information he'd heard he turned towards the door. "Is there anything you would ask of me, Captain?"

"We'll need barrels to store the rations divvied between the ships. Will you be able to fashion twenty by our departure on the morrow?" Morgan asked. This, too, he knew the answer to.

"I could warp wood and make barrels in my sleep, Captain. It will be done by midday, if not sooner," Cage replied.

Morgan nodded, taking another puff of his pipe. "That will be all, Mr. Cage."

With that, the now-shirted Steven Cage left the cabin.

"Siris, I know you are recovering from your injuries, so I'll not have you scaling the crow's nest today. I rather think it's time for the boy to learn how to spot on his own," Morgan said, looking back at the map. He could feel Osiris' questioning gaze on him.

"Aye, Cap'n, it will be done. I'll work the deck, then," Osiris responded, holding his tongue.

"You'll do nothing of the sort. Rest, and give your body time to heal, Second Mate. That is an order," Morgan answered calmly.

Osiris again bit his tongue and nodded. "As you say, Cap'n."

"And Mr. Huasca, I assume you've already charted our course for the Storm Tide?" Morgan finished.

"Of course, Captain. We are an ocean away, but we should arrive in the Southern Amaranthine in three months, provided we are unmolested by doldrums, sea creatures, or misfortune," Huasca answered.

"Very good, sir."

Morgan nodded, having gone through his mental checklist of orders. The bosun and carpenter, Ryker and Sarkad, would be tending the ship. He'd search them out later in the day personally.

"Before we adjourn I would speak plain with you," Morgan said, sensing the officers' eagerness to adjourn.

They looked among themselves, knowing what was to come.

"A few short weeks ago, before we found our prize, an event occurred aboard Azura, one of some precedence. Mr. Yager and several of our brethren attempted a mutiny…" Morgan said.

The room fell silent.

"You know me. I am not one to bear grudges against my own men. We are brothers, and brothers quarrel as is their tendency. And, as no blood was spilled, I saw no need for dire measures to be enacted," Morgan said, making eye contact with Stone, whose face was unreadable. "When we deliver our prizes to the Storm Tide and settle accounts, the Azura will be in harborage for some time. She is in need of an upgrade in firepower, and it will take some time for her to be refitted and reinforced. Those of you who have sailed long with me know what this entails Men will leave, joining other crews with the prestige of having sailed with the 'Immortal' Captain Morgan. If, in that time, any of you wish to bid farewell, know that you will do so with my blessings."

The men nodded solemnly. It was unlikely that many of the officers would leave. Most of them had been sailing with Morgan for several years, some well over a decade plus. All, save for perhaps Stone.

Reece Stone, the ship's quartermaster—and the man that Morgan had been looking at all the while when he spoke of the mutiny and bidding farewell when they made port. Stone had been party to the mutiny, as well as it's chief co-conspirator, along with Yager.

"On the high seas is where we belong, and we'd ne'er forsake it, Cap'n," Stone said.

"You're Sarxian, Mr. Stone. Your lot seldom stay on land for a fortnight unless your wives anchored you to the shore!" Morgan joked.

The men erupted into laughter.

Sarx was a seafaring kingdom in the Kurzan Empire, relying on their fishery skills and naval prowess to eke out a living. It was often said that Sarxians were descended from merfolk, born with salt water in their veins and fins for feet. While that part of the legends was patently false, it was rare that a Sarxian existed that couldn't swim like a fish and catch them too. Unsurprisingly, they were legendary sailors, and Reece Stone was no different. While he was the quartermaster of Azura, it was easy for him to steer and navigate as well, often functioning as a helmsman during storms, or during the most difficult of voyages. He was also a skilled fighter, a competent leader in battle, and none too bad a cook, neither. Perhaps it was this versatility that saved his position, where Yager had lost his.

"Sarxians 'n water is like trolls 'n bridges; one can't exist without the other!" Cutter said between belts of laughter.

"Aye, and you 'n ugly are like pigs 'n shit. One can't exist without the other!" Stone said snidely, causing the other officers, even Osiris, to erupt in laughter as Cutter took in the remark.

The men adjourned after a few more light-hearted jokes and set to the tasks before them.

*****

"Your plan for overtaking the El'wa, it was quite ingenious," a voice said.

"As they often are. I seldom move without thought," Morgan responded briskly.

"I am aware. For some time, I was the one who gave you those ingenious ideas," the voice responded.

Huasca re-entered the cabin and saw Morgan holding a glowing amulet in his palm, pulsing a bright blue light.

"Yaman Huasca, a pleasure, as always," the voice announced, coming from the glowing amulet.

Huasca bowed his head. "Abbal, greetings. You have been remarkably talkative of late."

The amulet pulsed slowly for several moments before responding, "Ah, so you've noticed as well? I… slept for long periods before. Now, I am awake more than I slumber…"

Morgan thought back to a warning that Abbal had given him many, many years ago. "So, it's almost time, then."

"All good things come to an end, Morgan. Our deal is reaching its conclusion, I believe."

"You believe? You're not certain?" Morgan asked, raising a brow. "Before you talked as though it was an exact science."

"It is not. It is signs, omens, feelings, and inclinations. It is enigmatic dreams and portents, like those a prophet or sybil may have," Abbal explained.

"Another century then," Morgan chuckled. "Wonderful."

"Were it only so far gone. No, I give it another year, perhaps two at the maximum," Abbal guessed.

"You speak of this event, but you never describe what will come to pass, merely that it will. What is going to happen?" Huasca asked, leaning against Morgan's desk, now.

"Of that, Yaman Huasca, I am not sure. The gods offer me no such clarity, merely the portent that we've a part to play in what is to come. It is our destiny."

"To the hells with destiny! Each man's fate is decided by his own actions, and mine is no different!" Morgan said, his voice rose sharply.

"Be angry, be indignant, be willful—it matters not, Morgan. I gave you a century to sail these seas and see this world. I can give you no longer, soon I will not be able to protect you from death, and the pull of time will drag you into the grave!"

"I fear not the grave, for all men go to it. What I take umbrage with is this notion that I must do some lofty gesture for gods that give not one squirt of piss for me or any living, breathing creature etching out a living on this earth!" Morgan gripped the amulet tightly in annoyance.

"We are all beholden to the whims of another. Though we may not always see the ripple that set us on our path, one was made, and its effects were felt."

Morgan mocked the amulet's words with a laugh, "Tell the gods that I care not for their games. They would not entertain my desires, so I'll not entertain theirs."

"Of that, old friend, I fear we will have no choice…" Abbal said, falling silent. The glow died, leaving the orb Morgan had been clutching a dark, lightless blue.

Morgan shook his head, brushing off the cryptic words. "To business, then."

✶✶✶✶✶

"I'm to man the crow's nest alone? I'm honored you have such faith in me," Hanover said in disbelief.

Osiris rolled his eyes and winced. He'd suffered a head injury, rope burn, splinters, cuts and bruises from his brush with the Chimera, and every one of them ached. Most of the cuts had closed, he'd removed the splinters, and while his head hadn't ever really been in a good place (random ringing in his ears and various head blows he'd taken over the years saw to that) the mind-splitting headache he'd had shortly after the battle had gone.

But damn, did it still hurt. His body ached like he'd taken it far past its limit. He could still man the crow's nest, though. All he had to do was sit and watch the horizon.

So why is he manning the Crow's nest?

"While I like your optimism, I'm not the one who made the call. That was the Cap'n, again," Osiris answered.

Hanover's shoulders slumped a bit. "Captain's orders, then. One wonders why anyone else ever has a say if Captain Morgan is the only one who makes decisions."

"Cap'n makes the calls he thinks are necessary. He thinks you're ready to man the crow's nest alone, and so we'll trust his judgement."

"And what do *you* think, Siris? Have you no thoughts of your own?"

Osiris shrugged, holding his tongue once more. "I think it's time to quit whining and man the crow's nest. I'm goin' to go rest, as the cap'n ordered. If you see trouble on the horizon, ye know what to do. Ring the alarm and warn the officers."

With that, Osiris turned and walked away.

"I know how to man the crow's nest!" Hanover shouted after him. Osiris cast a thumbs up over his shoulder.

*****

Flint, Cutter, Moary, and a crowd of pirates sat in the galley around a table covered in full bottles of alcohol. The men drank merrily from the bottles, laughing and joking by candlelight as the officers wagered amongst themselves.

"Heads or tails?" Flint asked as he held the copper coin in his hand. On the heads side was the face of some rich-piss Emperor or another. Probably one of the current Emperor's inbred ancestors. On the tail side was the imperial seal.

"I like ass, so tails," Cutter answered, eliciting a giggle from the other pirates surrounding them.

Flint nodded. "Fair enough. Let's see what's what, then?"

Flint flicked the coin that was resting on the crook of his pointer finger with his thumb and watched the coin sail into the air, flipping end-over-end for a split second before landing on his open palm and being slapped onto the back of his hand. Heads.

"Fuck me!" Cutter groaned, kicking the table they sat around.

"Should've played a game of Delilah, laddie! Hahahaha!" Moary laughed heartily, clapping Cutter on the back with a hand.

"Why would I do that? You'd have won automatically 'n still wouldn't be cookin' shit," Cutter grumbled.

"I like my stew with carrots, ay? 'N them El'wa left us plenty to add to the pot. Salt, seasonings, damn near every meat ye can think of. I want to eat like a king, savvy?" Flint stated.

"Aye, and if the broth ain't right I'm leavin' a crab in your hammock, got me?" Moary added.

"Yeah, yeah, yeah. Dupont, Simmons, grab the others 'n tell 'em I'm head chef tonight…fuck!" Cutter said as he downed the rest of his cup of wine.

The other officers stood up as well, and Moary grabbed a bottle El'wa moon spirits.

"Takin' the good stuff for yourself, eh?" Flint asked.

Moary shook his bearded head. "Nay, this'n is for the boy. He'll be on watch through the day 'n I figure he deserves a pick me up for helpin' to slay the Chimera."

"So yer givin' 'em moon spirits? He'll be off his ass all day 'n night," a pirate said with a hearty laugh, joined in by several others.

"Just as well. Today is a day of celebration, ay? The lad deserves a might treat for playin' his part. He's owed that much," Moary said.

"You're too soft on 'em, ye ask me," Flint shrugged. He didn't think much of Hanover, or 'the boy' as most of them called him, as he was the youngest—and newest—member of the crew. Younger than Osiris, who'd previously been the youngest crewman on the ship, by several years.

"He's but a boy of eighteen years. What was you like his age, I wonder?" Moary asked reflectively before climbing the stairs to the above deck, leaving the galley.

"I'd already killed men, for starters…" Flint breathed, shaking his head. "Have fun cookin', Cutter. Don't fuck it up or you'll never hear the end of it, haha!"

"You'd do me like that, brother? Not gonna help your old partner in crime?" Cutter begged with mock hurt.

"I've done better men worse. You just happen to be one of the only breathers on this ship I happen to call friend," Flint shrugged as he lit a cigarette. "'Sides, I gotta go 'n oversee one of the El'wa merchant brigs we took. Stone has one, I've got the other."

Flint sighed internally. He hated captaining ships, all the men sat around doe-eyed and expectant, and he basically had to grow eyes in the back of his head to watch everyone and everything. It was exhausting. And this time, he wouldn't have Cutter watching his back.

"He gonna have Yager with 'em, then?" Cutter asked in a low voice as the other pirates dispersed.

Flint paused, pondering a moment. "I don't rightfully know. I didn't ask, and the Cap'n didn't tell. Ye don't think…"

"I don't put anythin' past anybody, brother. Keep your head on a swivel," Cutter replied, nodding to him.

Flint did the same and left the galley.

"Alright, you sad sods. I need meat chopped, I need water to simmer it, vegetables chopped, and somebody bring me a damn bottle of that moon ether, I know we've got more 'round here! Hop the fuck to it!" Cutter ordered with a clap of his hands. The remaining men, his kitchen staff for the night, jumped to their tasks.

*****

Reece Stone stepped out of Morgan's office and covered his eyes from the midday sun as he surveyed the deck. His eyes focused on a bird taking flight from above deck atop the stern. Puzzled, he climbed the stairs to see where it had perched. He saw Yager, leaning over the railing, gazing at the bird as it took flight. The man gave him a sideways glance Before flicking his eyes back to the bird.

"A seahawk? You a druid now? Whispering to the birds 'n such? Heh," Stone chortled.

"I can barely speak to other people anymore, seems like. The thoughts of a bird are of no use to me," Yager said, his face turning red with irritation again.

"Nobody's stoppin' ye from talkin' to the crew, mate," Stone responded, trying to smooth things over.

"Ye say that, but you ain't the one getting' dirty looks every time ye enter a room. Funny, that, considering you was right there next to me plottin' the mutiny. But I've been knocked down to deckhand, 'n you still get to be quartermaster. How is that?" Yager asked, the question burning in his cheeks and mind.

"I don't rightfully know. Would that please ye, then? Seein' me swab the deck with ye, rather than servin' the crew as I do?"

Yager sneered, Stone was good at framing his questions to make the answerer look all the fool for asking.

"It'd certainly make my sleep a little bit sounder, knowin' I wasn't the only one with a black spot in me palm."

Stone shook his head, whistling between his teeth.

"Misery loves company, and ye sure have become a miserable sod, ain't ye, Yager?"

Yager spat on the deck. "Don't ye have a fuckin' ship to oversee? Piss off."

"For one, we don't depart till the 'morn. For two, cap'n put you in my crew, so when we do make ready, you'll be takin' my orders. 'N thirdly, last I checked, Daniel Yager, ye don't get a say whether I come or go."

Yager's sneer deepened as he walked away.

Stone watched him go, taking note of the bloody holes in his shirt by his shoulder. Then, he watched the seahawk as it flapped away into the horizon.

*****

Hanover took a swig of the bottle of moon spirits. It had a sweet, but sharp flavor. He wasn't sure whether that was normal of alcohol or not. He'd never drank before now, in truth.

"Ye ever had spirits afore, boy?" Moary asked as he handed the boy the bottle, all for him.

"Back in Spirus? All the time, sir!" Hanover replied with a smile.

He'd lied through his teeth.

Still, he sipped at the strong liquid and kept his gaze on the horizon. He momentarily regarded the seahawk flying away from the ship, but lost track of it as well as his train of thought as the moon spirits took hold. It was a bright, sunny, beautiful day. He could hear gulls chirping, the men singing, and that ever-present aroma of the salty sea air accosted his nose. He'd hated it when he first came aboard. Now, he honestly couldn't imagine life without it.

His lids grew heavy as his world began to tilt. The alcohol was taking effect. Propped up against the flagpole in the crow's nest, Hanover rested his chin on his chest, and drifted off to sleep…

An explosion of sound broke his slumber.

"We have ships off the port and starboard! Five north and three more north, noreast!" Huasca shouted as the alarms sounded.

Hanover nearly fell from the crow's nest as his heart tried to do the same from his chest. The ships were close enough that he could see their shapes, and even make out their sails…and flags.

"Imperial Navy ships approaching! They are raising their signal flags, captain!" Huasca shouted, running a hand over his bald head in confusion.

"What in Sheolhenna are the fuckin' Bluecoats doin' way out here?" A pirate asked.

"Why didn't the lookout tell us we had blues on our ass?!" Another shouted.

Morgan came from his office and glanced at Hanover, as did many of the pirates on deck.

"The fucking boy is lookin' out, that's why!" The first pirate shouted.

Hanover's face drained of all color. He'd drank himself to slumber and may have just doomed the entire crew in the process.

"We're far outside of their jurisdiction. What are the Imperials doing here?!" Morgan whispered into Huasca's ear.

"I do not know, captain. But if we deny parlay with them, with their numbers and our compromised position, they will be upon us within the hour, and we will be too busy scrambling to put up a proper fight."

"Surely you don't mean…" Morgan began, scarcely believing the words.

"I do not believe we have a choice, Morgan," Huasca answered frankly. "We are outgunned and outmaneuvered. We need to play our hand carefully…"

"Aye…" Morgan sighed. "Raise the white flag 'n signal them. The blues want to parlay…and we shall honor them."

The men looked at him like he'd just sprouted a new head. But the realization quickly donned on them as well. They had no other choice. They were dead to rights.

IV

An Irrefutable Offer

Three and A Half Months Later…

"Morgan Sarron, I am Hendrick Viceroy, Commander of the Imperial Guard of Kurza. You have been summoned by His Imperial Majesty, Emperor Varryn Kurza. We have travelled many thousands of miles to bring you before him. You and your crew will come with us to Emperor's Rest to meet with him." Viceroy had said.

"And if I refuse?" Morgan had asked him.

"This is an Then I am ordered to bring your head, as well as the remainder of your crew to Emperor's Rest to be tried for high-seas piracy. Are we clear?" Viceroy had responded, calmly.

"I see…and why is it that I am summoned by His Imperial Majesty?"

"That is for the two of you to discuss. This is an irrefutable offer."

Morgan rolled those words through his head at least two hundred times since then. He'd had plenty of time to think, in the three months it had taken them to reach the port city Oceanus, and then the two weeks it took them to reach Emperor's Rest.

Now, Azura sat sequestered in a seaside cave some twenty-five miles down the channel, to avoid being seen near the capital. Her crew, guarded by over a hundred Bluecoats sailors and imperial guardsmen.

"An irrefutable offer…"

He said the words aloud as he rode in the carriage procession that took himself, Second Mate Osiris, Viceroy, and a cavalcade of armed and armored guardsmen through the streets of Emperor's Rest. Next to him, Osiris fretted with the collar of the vest and dress clothes he'd been given. Both pirates had been given the attire to hide their true identities. Morgan was quite comfortable in his new dress. This was not the first time he'd been forced to dress like a pompous ass for nobility. Osiris, however, was not taking kindly to it.

"This collar's tight, and this doublet's stifling. What the hell do we have to wear these noisome clothes for?" he complained.

"Because if we rode through Emperor's Rest with two pirates in a carriage with the commander of the Imperial Guard, it would be a bigger scandal than the queen of Brova fucking in a brothel. The city has enough issues and scandals to go around, I'll not contribute to it, pirate."

Osiris scowled in annoyance. The commander was right, as much as he hated to admit it. There were enough Bluecoats in this city to sink Azura ten times over, and even Morgan's skills as a captain and the Azura's weaponry couldn't hope to beat them all. While they would never attempt to attack them in broad daylight, they would most certainly come after them under the cover of darkness. There were plenty of places to ambush a ship along the Amaranthine-Fjora channel.

"Fascinating. The last time I walked these streets they were under siege. That was almost a century ago, now. Now, the city's grown twice its size. Everything I knew from that era's been buried under the new. It would seem even utter destruction cannot stop mankind's growth," Morgan mused, smoking from his pipe once more.

"The empire will survive the test of time because the Stars will it and our resourcefulness knows no bounds. Praise be to the Emperor!" Viceroy responded dogmatically.

Osiris couldn't help but chuckle and roll his eyes. It evoked a glare from Viceroy, as well as one of the carriage drivers, who looked over his shoulder into the carriage before spitting over the side in disgust.

"You dare mock the empire and its ruler, Xallan pirate?!" Viceroy accused, the veins in his neck bloating with irritation.

"Me? Mock one of the most powerful men in the world? In the midst of his lapdogs? Nay, I'm not so foolish." Osiris shook his head, a smirk still plastered on his face. His brown eyes looked unflinchingly into Viceroy's steel-grey ones as he spoke.

"Then why did you laugh at the mention of his name?!"

Osiris shrugged, folding his arms. *The empire will survive the test of time because the Stars will it'*. That's what you said, right? Do ye honestly believe that some gods of a long-gone era give two fucks about us? About our petty squabbles 'n plights? When a dragon awakens and goes on a range, destroying towns, villages, and lives, do you think the gods care? Pfft." He looked out the window. "The only ones that care is us. The only ones that can be relied on are us."

"Careful, pirate. The Church of the Stars has deep roots in this city, and those words sound dangerously close to heresy," Viceroy warned, nodding to a church as they passed by. It had a thin, five-pointed star surrounded by a ring upon it. A classical sign of the Church of the Stars.

Morgan watched the city roll past as the two men argued. He took note of all the little details that someone like Commander Viceroy likely overlooked. In the lowtown, there was filth, trash, prostitutes, drunks, and gangers standing out in the street in broad daylight. The guards stood at street corners or in alleys, hands on their swords, ready to strike. He could only imagine what went on when Viceroy wasn't watching.

When they reached the high town, he didn't even need to read the signs to know they'd reached the wealthy part of town. The street's cobbles were white and clear of filth and trash. The prostitutes were courtesans, dressed in stately attire, bodies covered. Nobles busied along the streets in carriages of their own, and those who stood roadside were well-dressed. The guards walked amongst them, even conversing with them. Some of the townsfolk even waved, and Viceroy waved back.

The haves still have, the have nots still have not.

"Some things never change," Morgan said aloud.

Osiris and Viceroy momentarily paused their argument, having just remembered that Morgan was even in the carriage.

"Pardon?" Viceroy asked, still agitated.

"I asked if we should be expecting a bath and a shave before we meet with his Imperial Majesty?" Morgan covered. It was a valid question. He knew from experience that cleanliness was often a requirement when meeting with royalty. He found it hard to imagine that the Emperor was any different.

Viceroy sighed and shook his head. "While ordinarily such filthy rabble as yourselves would be required to be *cleansed* before appearing in His Grace's presence, I have been told that, as you will be departing shortly, it will not be required."

Morgan could feel the disgust rolling out of Viceroy's lips. He suddenly remembered why he killed men like him. They were too mouthy, too pompous. Unfortunately, that would not be an option this time around.

"And here I was hoping for a trim. My beard's been getting unruly these past few months," Morgan replied.

"Yes, well. Perhaps you could appropriate a razor in your near travels…" Viceroy scoffed.

The men sat in silence for another half hour as they approached the gates of the palace. As they approached the checkpoint outside the gates, Osiris' eyes fell on several men in bright purple tunics and tattoos chatting with the guards. He tapped Morgan's arm, discreetly, and nodded in their direction. Morgan nodded. He'd noticed them as well.

The two pirates silently watched the men for several moments as the carriage came to a stop at the checkpoint and the guards took notice of them. He saw a guard clap one of the men in purple tunics on the back before shaking his hand as they departed. The men in purple turned and left. The man whose hand the guard had shook cast a sidelong glance at the carriage, the other occupants, and then Osiris. The men's eyes crossed for a moment before the group of purple-clothed men passed the carriage and continued leisurely down the street.

Morgan watched the two lock eyes, then raised a puzzled look at Osiris, who shook his head and turned his gaze back to scanning the guards, who now spoke with Viceroy.

"Tell no one, as per usual. If anybody comes inquiring, you know nothing—and inform me. Are we clear?" Viceroy asked in a calm but serious tone.

"Aye, commander," a guard responded nervously.

"Good. Now open the damned gate, time is of the essence." Viceroy waved his hand.

The guards obliged, immediately.

As they passed through the outer gates of the palace and rode toward the courtyard, Viceroy turned his attention back to the matter at hand.

"Captain, you will come with me to meet the Emperor. Your bodyguard is to remain in the courtyard. Make sure that he understands that should he act foolish, he will be shot. Understood?"

Osiris smiled at the obvious hatred Viceroy already had for him but remained quiet.

"My Second Mate is perhaps the sharpest man in my crew. There is a reason I chose him as my companion. He'll behave himself just fine. See that your men do him the same kindness, however. For their own sakes," Morgan said casually.

The guard who'd spat over the side of the carriage looked back inside again at those words. Osiris locked eyes with him, and for the briefest of moments, no longer than the blink of an eye, Osiris' eyes glowed.

The man's eyes went wide, and he rubbed them, but Osiris had already gone back to looking out the carriage window, ignoring him.

*****

The inner courtyard of the imperial palace was a large, open area with arches and walkways overlooking it, and the entrance to a verdant garden to one side. The pirates took in the majesty of it for a moment as they exited the carriage and fixed their clothes. Osiris immediately looked to the garden. He'd never been in a garden, before.

"I would walk the garden while you have your audience, Cap'n," Osiris said, more of an announcement than a request.

Morgan looked to Viceroy, who looked at Osiris, then the garden, likely trying to think of all the ways he could potentially find a weapon and attack from within.

"You will have a guard escort you…but yes, it should be fine. You may," Viceroy said, turning towards the ponderous stairway leading up to the palace throne room. "Come, Captain. The Emperor awaits."

Morgan nodded to Osiris, then followed Viceroy and a group of imperial guardsmen up the stairs.

Osiris turned and looked at his guard escort, who handed the horses pulling the carriage apples from a basket before facing him. Osiris tilted his head back and observed the man a moment. It was the guard who'd been eyeing him.

Osiris stood about a head taller than him, though he eyed the pistol and sword on the man's hips warily, as well as the metal shield on his back. The guard was too well-armed and armored for Osiris to take on unarmed. Not that he could, at any rate.

There were lookouts on the walkways overhead, and guards posted at the stairs leading to the throne room as well. He was vastly outnumbered, even if he was armed. He noticed a faint tremble in the guard's hand as it rested at his side.

You've got me outnumbered and outgunned; still, you're afraid? Pathetic.

Osiris turned his back on the guard wordlessly and walked toward the overgrown archway leading into the garden.

These men would never make it out at sea.

*****

The garden was perfectly maintained. Every rose bush, every lily, every flower, and shrub were immaculately pruned and kept. As he walked, he saw groundskeepers trimming the hedges. They gave him a glance, but otherwise ignored him. Without his weapons or his regular clothes, apparently, he blended quite well. He paused and bent over to inspect a vibrant blue rose bush. As he gazed at the peculiar roses, he took notice that there were trace lines of bright, glowing blue covering them, like veins almost. No, like—

"They're blue Alyria roses, a rarity here, in the heartlands of the empire. These are perhaps the only blue Alyrias in all Kurza Proper," a dusky female voice said.

He jerked upright and turned reflexively to face the source of the pleasant voice. His breath caught in his throat; she was the most stunning woman he'd ever seen.

Before him stood a regally dressed maiden, perhaps twenty years of age. She wore a deep, royal blue dress that dove modestly at the neckline and contrasted with her almost snow-white complexion and charcoal-black lipstick. Her hair was raven tresses, tucked behind her ears, with a few delicate curls hanging near her eyes.

Her eyes.

The most entrancing he'd ever seen. They were sharp, hooded orbs with clashing ice blue and deep purple irises, split at the middle of each. He'd never seen eyes like hers in his entire life, and they drew him in like a siren's song drew in wayward sailors at sea.

"Ma'am?" he said, finding his voice after his momentary lapse.

She drew closer, and the guard who watched him crossed the distance between them and drew his blade.

"Stay away from the Imperial Princess, cur!"

Osiris, so struck by the princess' sudden appearance, didn't even react when the blade was held at his throat. His eyes were still locked on hers.

38

"That is quite enough, Ser Roderick," she said, calm but stern. ""This man has done no wrong. If anything, I believe I am the one to have erred. He was taken by the roses, and I intruded on his appreciation, did I not?" the grand princess asked.

Osiris nodded, ever aware of the blade at his throat. "I uh, I believe that to be correct, ma'am—your Highness—I" he stumbled. Why in all the hells of Sheolhenna was he stumbling?

"Please, you may call me Odessa," she stopped him, chuckling. "You are dismissed, Ser Roderick."

Ser Roderick's jaw hung a moment. "My lady, I am ordered by Knight-Commander Viceroy to—"

"Is your duty to your lady first or to the commander?" she asked.

Ser Roderick closed his mouth and nodded. "As you wish, my lady. I will wait over yonder."

Ser Roderick bowed politely before giving Osiris the evil eye and walking away. Osiris once again held in a smirk at the guardsman's displeasure.

She offered him her hand. Her nails were polished black, like her lipstick.

He took her hand. He could hear the guard, Ser Roderick, she'd called him, gasp from afar.

Her hand was soft as silk. He kissed it.

"I am Osiris. Pleased to meet you, ma'am—Odessa," he corrected himself.

He felt a crackle of energy where their hands connected. He saw a faint trace of light in her eyes.

Is she…

"I'm pleased to make your acquaintance, Osiris." She redirected her gaze to the flower. ""The blue Alyria roses have powerful alchemical properties. They are often used as a stimulant for the humors. It can enhance one's senses. The Mygredo like to include it in their elixirs before they go on hunts. It is quite powerful when mixed with wisp amanita and ghoul secretions—" Odessa smiled then covered her mouth. "Oh! Apologies, I spend so much time discussing alchemy and the like with my tutors, it can be hard not to talk shop with new acquaintances."

Osiris smiled in turn. When was the last time a beautiful woman spoke to him, rather than running away in horror?

When was the last time you didn't give them every reason to?

"I've never seen you on the palace grounds before. Are you new to the court, Osiris?" she asked.

He suddenly realized he hadn't been speaking. "I am…not of the court, My Lady. I was summoned here along with my captain at the behest of your father. My captain meets with him as we speak while I observe your beautiful garden."

Osiris motioned all around them, quickly sorting out what to say and what to withhold as he spoke.

Odessa nodded curtly. "Well, I hope that the garden pleases you. Have you an eye for alchemy?"

"It pleases me very well, but no, my skills are of a more…pragmatic sort. Weapons and munitions and the like."

Odessa's eyes lit up. "Oh? Are you a soldier, then?"

"Of a sort to be considered. Though I don't imagine you'll find me serving in a lord's army."

"A mercenary, then?" her eyes played over his features, then paused when she noticed a skull and bones tattoo behind his ear. "No. you're a pirate."

He froze, wondering how she'd managed to figure out how—he remembered the tattoo behind his left ear. His expression dropped.

Here comes the screaming.

"…That I am."

*****

Morgan watched as the guards lined outside on the steps leading to the throne room stood in formation, raising their weapons to salute Viceroy and his men as they escorted Morgan to the throne. The double-doors that lead to the throne room were pushed open as the men crossed into the theatre-sized room that served as the seat of power in the empire. Pillars, thick and painstakingly carved from the fine dark grey marble held the sealing up, and stained-glass windows with intricate artistry cut into them let in the light from outside. Morgan took note that not a single courtesan or noble was in the room. Only the guards, likely sworn to secrecy, were present.

Down that long chamber, sitting in a ponderous throne of steel, silk, and gold, was the man who had summoned him.

Varryn Kurza. The most powerful man in all six realms of the empire.

Morgan regarded the man as they stopped at the foot of the throne. Next to him stood the imperial advisor, a man whose name escaped Morgan now, but he wore an insignia that demarked him from House Trinitian, one of the strongest noble houses in Kurza Proper. The man looked at them a moment, then began writing in a thick tome in his hands.

Viceroy pushed Morgan down to his knee as they prostrated before the Emperor. "Your imperial majesty, I brought the pirate captain, as you requested."

Both Morgan and Viceroy kept their heads low, facing the ground as he spoke. Morgan could feel the Emperor's gaze upon him.

"Excellent, Commander. You, and the pirate, may rise," Varryn said, motioning with his hand.

The two stood.

"Now, take your leave. I would speak with this man in private, and I am told that the new paladin has been spotted in the city," he continued.

"As you wish, your excellency, but in private? He is a dangerous—"

"That is an order, Commander. I have Vexyn with me, he will ensure that our guest behaves himself. Besides, he sits in the very heart of the dragon's den. I doubt very much that he would be so bold—or foolish—to act out of turn, here. Am I correct, Captain Sarron?" Varryn asked, looking directly at Morgan, now.

His were imposing, deep purple eyes that seemed to bore through Morgan. He held back a smile. He'd met far too many men in his lifetime with eyes like those.

"Just Morgan. And I am many things, your majesty, but a fool is not one. You do not go far in my line of work acting as one," Morgan replied.

The imperial advisor finally spoke, lifting his head, "This is His Imperial Majesty Varryn Kurza, Slayer of Wuhlven, Repeller of the El'wa Imperium, and Master of the Six Realms. You will refer to him with respect, or you will not refer to him at all, lest you pay with your head. Is that understood, pirate?"

The man had an angular, regal face. Reminiscent of an El'wa, but not quite as inhuman. He spoke with a calm, noble voice, even in his indignation.

"At ease, Vexyn. The good captain is of a swarthy lot. One cannot expect one such as he to fully appreciate the etiquette of the court," Varryn soothed.

Vexyn bowed. "As you wish, your grace."

"That will be all, Viceroy," Varryn finished.

"As you wish, your excellency," Viceroy said. "When you are finished here, pirate, wait for me by the carriage. I've matters to sort first."

His peace said, the Knight-Commander bowed to the Emperor and left.

"Now, Captain. I have brought you here under such peculiar circumstances for a very critical matter." Varryn rose to his feet. "Come with me."

The Emperor stepped down gracefully from his throne and went off through a side doorway, followed by Morgan and then Vexyn. Morgan noted the dagger on Vexyn's hip but discarded the thought as quick as it came. No matter what happened next, he was in no position to bargain.

*****

"A century ago, now, you stood in this city. You even made it into these very halls at one point. You and your comrades of the day were the sole destroyers of the Continental Navy of old, prior to the reformation of the realms into the empire we have today."

"I recall it well, yes. Though I recall standing in this city, not as a destroyer, but as a savior," Morgan said as he followed Varryn through the palace halls.

"Yes, I recall. You saved my father's father from a terrible fate and solidified our place in the empire to come. It is for that reason that until today, the empire has been rather lax in its efforts to apprehend you. The Immortal Captain... You have cost us millions of gold over the years." Varryn cast a leer over his shoulder.

Morgan again held in his smirk.

"Not much of a feat, considering you likely make a hundred times what I've stolen in a single year."

"Yes, but with the combined weight of your efforts, as well as every other pirate the world over that decides to steal our cargo, we have lost progressively more capital over time. The trading companies are growing more desperate, and soon my hand will be forced."

They stopped at a door, and the Emperor pulled a key from his pocket, unlocking it. They all stepped inside, and Morgan's eyes scanned the room as they stood around a table covered in open and unopen missives and maps.

"Half of these are requests from trading companies. The Grand Amaranthine Trading Company, the Golden Hand Trading Company, Baradin Merchant Guild—the list goes on. They want naval escorts to protect their goods and an increased Mygredo presence because the spring is upon us, and the hydras are spawning in the south. In addition, we have the ever-present issue of piracy. Now, we have culled a lot of pirates from our waters..."

Varryn nodded to a nearby wall covered in crossed-out pictures of pirates, many of which Morgan had known, or at least known of. He also saw one for which he was unfamiliar with personally but had heard the name of. A man named Edward Patron.

"But like flesh worms, more of them dig out of the mud each time we kill one. We hang fifty pirates out in the squares, we have fifty-five more running rampant out along the coastline. Add onto that the increase in Valkar raiders razing towns and villages from Borra down to Sarx and—well, I rather think I've painted you a clear enough picture. A change is coming. The wolves are being let off their leash. As a favor to my ancestors, I am offering you an opportunity to get out of the storm before it sweeps away you and everyone and everything you've ever known!"

Varryn's voice rose to emphasize his point. He came within striking distance of Morgan and glared hard at him.

"...Were this a curtain call, I'd already be hanging bug-eyed at the palace gates. You wouldn't have wasted the energy concealing my appearance in civilian attire, and you certainly wouldn't have talked this long, your excellence. I assume this is for another matter?"

Varryn's harsh expression eased as he held up an envelope. A thick envelope, sealed with his insignia.

"Letters of pardon. One for every man in your crew. Your records, expunged. All warrants, dismissed. All past crimes...forgiven. There is even a letter of marque authorizing your continued existence as privateers under my employ."

Morgan could hear the disgust in those words.

"In exchange for...what?"

"When you destroyed the Continental Navy, you did not do it by ordinary means. No, legends tell that you used a certain artifact of great historical importance: the Eye of Atla. I would have it. You will retrieve it for me."

Morgan felt the amulet light up. He heard Abbal's voice in his head.

"The Eye? It is lost to the sea. He asks an impossible request."

"The Eye of Atla was lost at sea along with Thunderbolt Colt and his flagship, Storm Rider. Where it fell, no man knows, and through all these years its entirely plausible that the merfolk came and retrieved it. If that occurred, then your odds went from impossible to inconceivable, your grace," Morgan dismissed. He folded his arms behind his back and observed a map sitting on the table, heavily used, and drawn over.

"The stories said as much, and I had all but given up on such a notion—until a report crossed my desk a few months ago. Reports of a discovery of a Dyonian fishing vessel. Allegedly, a large, beautifully colored pearl the size of a fist was dredged up in the haul of one of the fishers. The fishermen, unaware of what they'd found, sold it to a jeweler in an island town. The jeweler contacted the Dyonian Imperial treasury, and had an appraiser come and look over the pearl. The appraiser, so taken by the pearl, sent word to the Empress Kagura herself."

Morgan's eyebrows raised as Varryn's story continued.

"The Empress sent a lone trade vessel to retrieve this very special pearl on its route back home. A trade vessel, laden with gold and cargo, deviated from its course at her behest to retrieve a pearl that 'glowed with the light of the ocean.' Now, while that does not guarantee that this mysterious pearl is the Eye of Atla, it certainly does beg the question as to why the empress of Dyona wants this pearl so badly. She even went through the trouble of having a chest made for it. I want you to intercept this trade ship and bring me this pearl. Do this within two months, and you and your men will be free to go."

"And if this pearl isn't the Eye? What then?" Morgan asked.

"Then I'll consider our business concluded, regardless. This is not a request, captain. You have two months to retrieve the Eye and bring it to me in person. Should you dally, I will send my Seekers after you to retrieve it—and your head. Are we clear?"

Morgan's blood ran cold at the mention of the Seekers. They were powerful Alyrian warriors controlled by the Emperor himself. Each one wielded terrible magick, capable of felling scores of men before even one could be put down.

"For what reason does he ask this of you, I wonder? Surely he has no shortage of men to send for the task."

Abbal was right. Why did he need Morgan for this?

"You have Bluecoats, you have Seekers, you have imperial guardsmen, assassins, informants, and all manner of men and women at your disposal. Why go through the trouble of finding one old pirate and his crew to retrieve an artifact that may not even exist any longer?" Morgan asked.

Varryn paused a moment, turning his back to Morgan. "…Because the Stars themselves have spoken to me and declared that only *you* can accomplish this task, Captain. Idallon has said it so."

Morgan felt the amulet warm against his chest.

"Idallon? Spoke to this human Emperor? But why? Something is amiss…"

"If I send one of my agents and they are discovered, the empress of Dyona will have the truth ripped out of their dying breaths. That will mean war, Captain. But no one will ever believe that I would stoop so low as to employ pirates. I have heard tell of your escapades. Indeed, you exist as a sort of folk hero *and* villain to the people of the empire. The 'Immortal Captain', the man who has faced insurmountable odds and survived.

"The pirate that felled the Dread Captain of old and saved Emperor's Rest and, indeed, the empire at large from being subjugated by an undead madman. You have fought men, monsters, and even stood against armadas. You are, it would seem, a man that cannot be bested. Indeed, Captain, many men fear you because of that. They see you as a force of nature, a tide of rebellion, freedom, and mankind's capricious spirit."

Morgan couldn't help but smile sarcastically. "One wonders, then, how you so easily captured me? Were I the man you think I am, surely, you'd need a flotilla with at least a half dozen dreadnoughts to take me down, never mind take me alive."

Varryn laughed. "I said many men fear you—not all. Viceroy is an ambitious and shrewd man. Should the drums of war sound, he will make a phenomenal battlefield general. He is of low birth, but he has proven himself an asset of some value. Because of his feat of capturing you and your men, in fact, he has earned himself a sizeable tract of land deserving of his station. Do not be humbled by that. He is cut from a different cloth than most."

Morgan nodded satisfactorily. He could tell even at a glance that Viceroy had some measure more cunning than the average sycophant.

There is still the matter of his informant.

Morgan was no fool. Someone had been feeding information to Viceroy, and somehow managed to hide it from him. But who?

"Be that as it may, there is still the matter of time. Two months is a pipe dream. At sea, circumstances can change at a moment's notice, one moment the water is calm, the next a storm comes on the horizon. As you said before, the hydras will be spawning this time of year, which means they'll be active—and in numbers. Should we find ourselves combating one, or several, we may be waylaid at sea, forced to land in order to commit repairs. We could be attacked by other pirates, hell, the winds of Alyria could rear their chaotic heads and cause all manner of vagaries.

"Two isn't enough to account for that, even if we'd only need that time to make it here and back, on paper."

Varryn's face twisted in annoyance. "Two months is your allotted time, and you will make do. Lest my Seekers come for you."

Morgan dragged a hand down his face in exasperation. This was bad. "Shall I assume these pardons are only valid should we deliver?" he asked, holding up the thick, weighty envelope.

"The pardons are valid as soon as you walk out of these halls. Any guard or officer you should run across will be forced to honor them. My Seekers, however, will not. So, I ask once more, are we *clear*, Captain Morgan?" Varryn stressed, his gaze hard once more.

Morgan nodded, extending a calloused palm. "Yes, your grace. It will be done."

Varryn examined the hand a moment, his curiosity evident. Vexyn, having remained quiet up until this moment, stepped forward.

"To touch His Imperial Majesty, Emperor Varryn Kurza is to—"

Varryn took his hand and shook it. His grip was that of a warrior, matching the firmness of Morgan's as they shook.

"Good; see it done. There will be an envoy at the port of Oceanus, awaiting your return. Today is the 21st of Gofannyn. It will take roughly two weeks to reach Oceanus, further down the river. You have until the 4th of Thalla."

Morgan turned and walked away, pausing at the door as Varryn spoke up once more.

"And captain? Leave no survivors."

Morgan turned, looking Varryn deep in his dark purple eyes with his own dark blue ones. He nodded sharply once, then shut the door behind him as the guards outside escorted him away.

*****

As Morgan descended toward the carriage, he caught a glimpse of Odessa leaving the courtyard through the garden, and Osiris walking back toward the carriage, irate guard in toe.

"Was that the princess?" Morgan asked, confused.

"Yes, it was—and your impudent bodyguard laid hands upon her!" Ser Roderick growled.

"Oh, go to the pub 'n drown it. I kissed her hand at her behest and made polite conversation, is all," Osiris dismissed. "If she really took issue with it I'd be on my way to the stockade, by now."

"Stockade? I imagine Ser Roderick here as well as all the guards watching us would have just shot you on the spot and called it a day," Morgan said.

He was right; the guards were plainly glaring at them.

"Where's Viceroy?" Osiris asked.

"On his way down. We've much to discuss in the meantime, however." Morgan's face hardened.

Osiris folded his arms. "Go on…"

V

A New Arrival

A man in gray gambeson clothes knelt before the altar of the Stars. The altar was a tall statue of a beautiful woman in robes, cradling her bosom as though holding a babe to it. She held nothing but air and had the deepest look of loving concern painstakingly etched into her beauteous features by the mason who carved her. To his side was his armor, blessed by the bishops of the Order of the Stars, and forged from gold-steel alloy. His great sword sat in its sheath, to the right of him.

The man pulled out a golden-beaded rosary necklace with a hanging, thin, nine-pointed star with a ring around it. He held the star of the necklace up before the altar of the melancholy woman, and a shaft of light from the stained-glass window above the altar shown down upon him. His reddish blonde hair hung in his face as he cast his head down to the base of the altar and bathed in the light.

He shut his eyes, then picked up his sword, still sheathed and held it before the altar.

"I give to you my blade, Ideal Mercy, to be used to smite your enemies. The demonick, the wicked, the worshippers of darkness and suffering. To be used to protect your children, the innocent and valorous."

He sat the blade down as a shaft of light from the skylight above the altar cast a bright beam down on the blade. It hummed with energy.

He grabbed his armor and sat it before the altar.

"I give to you my armor, that it may shield me from the blades and onslaughts of the occult, the abhorrent, the godless and the deviant. That no weapon formed against me shall prosper, until the day you deem fit that my time has come, and my duties done."

The armor, bathed in the light of the altar, began to crackle with energy as lines of bright yellow Alyria snaked across and covered it in a sheen of blessed protection.

"Where others flee, I charge and fight. No evil will escape me, under the dark of night. In the darkest of nights, or the dawn of day, I will save the weak to keep doom at bay. Gods of the light, of what is good and right, bless me with your holy might."

He felt an effervescent peace wash over him. Energy surged through his body, and he felt that he could shoulder the very weight of the world with ease.

"Idallon, my Patron. Guide my way as I walk this path. We begin a new duty, a new dawn, a new day. Praise be the Stars, who watch over me," the man finished.

He opened his eyes, and for a moment a brilliant yellow light flashed within them, before they returned to their hazel brown color. He stood, clasping the rosary around his neck for a moment before releasing it and donning his armor and blade.

"You recite your vow from memory, paladin? And so elegantly, too. I must confess, when they told me of your coming, I thought naught of it. I pray that I was mistaken," a nun said, having watched the paladin commit his vows at the altar, and arm himself.

"Sister Minerva, yes? I am pleased to make your acquaintance. I am Paladin Immanel Corinth, at your service, sister." He bowed, dipping low before the nun whom he towered over. She placed a hand upon his shoulder pauldron, running a hand over the gold eagle upon it.

"And polite? How rare. You may rise, Ser Corinth."

He did so, noticing her hand lingering on his shoulder a moment before releasing.

"Have you made communion at the Cathedral of the Stars in High Town? Archbishop Kalen will want to see you and brief you on your duties prior to going before the Emperor."

Corinth shook his head. "Nay, this was my first stop upon entering the city proper. I'm to meet with Knight-Commander Viceroy at my new office chamber, however. I'd rather have that in order before the bureaucracy commences."

Minerva couldn't help but laugh. "Well, at least you understand the way of the land. And here I was afraid they'd sent a fool into the fire."

Corinth analyzed Minerva as she spoke. She was a young nun, but remarkably spirited and improper. He found that surprisingly comforting.

"I was told the city would be trying to navigate. I see I was not misinformed," he said as he walked toward the front doors to the small church.

"No, you were not. Though I imagine the Knight-Commander will sure that up for you. Good luck, Ser Corinth. I look forward to serving with you!" Minerva said with a curt bow. Corinth gave a warm nod over his shoulder before pushing open the doors and stepping out into the sun.

*****

"This is your desk, mine is in the corner over there," Viceroy said hurriedly as he directed Corinth around. He could tell the man was in a rush, as he quickly came across the palace outer courtyard to meet him. He'd quickly nodded, pushed open the door and climbed the tower's stairs to begin his impromptu tour.

Corinth nodded, his desk, cabinets, drawers, as well as a space for him to set up his mementos all sat neatly in a corner by a window, the light beaming in. He ran a gauntleted hand over the fine wood of the desk before opening the window and looking out. The tower they were stationed in was one of the outer guard towers of the palace, on the northeast side of the walls, overlooking the prayer district of High Town, the market district of Low Town, and the docks, nestled in the distance. He could even see the great lake, Emperor's Cup, from his vantage point. It was beautiful. He could hear the bustle of the city and the chiming of church bells below.

"It's beautiful," Corinth commented.

Viceroy, having ignored him and been prattling on for the past several moments paused. "I beg pardon, paladin?"

Corinth nodded to the open window and the view outside. "It's beautiful. You can see the entire city out there, almost."

Viceroy nodded after a moment. "Yes, yes, it is. Spend enough time here, however, and believe me when I say the view grows stale. Now, as I was saying. We begin first muster just before daybreak at 0500 hours. Second comes at noon, and final is at 1900 hours, around sunset. The musters are on Mundus, Apus, and Farengus. Weekend musters are infrequent, but you will be expected to preside over training for Prince Gundyr and any others who join him on any given day. Obviously, your duty to the prince comes first, clergy duties second,

50

and your duty to the guard third. I ask that you be transparent and communicative, however, so that we may all complete our tasks and duties with as little inconvenience as possible.

"That was a lot of information, do you have any questions for me, Ser?"

Corinth listened, but he already knew what was expected of him. "I believe I understand well, Knight-Commander."

Viceroy nodded, pleased. He'd been worried he'd be dealing with a buffoon, perhaps this 'Ser Corinth' wouldn't be so bad after a—

"Do you walk the block often, Knight-Commander?"

Viceroy furrowed his brow. "Walk the block?"

Corinth nodded. "It is common practice for a commander of a city's watch to walk the block to keep abreast of how his men conduct themselves in the street, amongst the people. Do you not?" he asked, earnestly.

"The city is vast and bustling. My duties are many and all-consuming. I leave it to my subordinates to handle such frivolities—I've more important matters to attend, as you likely will as well," Viceroy argued.

Corinth nodded, running a hand through the stubble on his chin. At twenty-five years, he had seen a lot since he'd taken his vows. He'd met good men and bad men, but he wasn't quite sure where the man before him stood. He'd heard of the rampant corruption in the city watch, but he wondered if that corruption rotted from the top-down, or from some place more insidious.

"If you never walk among your men in the street, how can you trust that what your captains report to you is true?" Corinth probed, leaning on his desk.

"My men do as I say, when I say. I have personally trained every sergeant, every captain, and every lieutenant of the city watch AND the imperial guard. I would think, Ser Corinth, that I would notice if my men were acting untoward," Viceroy said defensively.

Corinth shook his head. "You know just as well as I that men lie, Knight-Commander. At best, if one of your men were found in err, they'd be court marshalled. At worst? They'd be executed. I very much doubt that one of them would admit to treachery were that the case."

"So, you've been here for half a day and already you believe to my men better than I? Well, I was not aware that when you took your vows, they also gave you the power to read minds!" Viceroy said, his voice raising.

"I am merely saying, Knight-Commander, that vigilance and prudence is key! I was brought here for three reasons: to train the heir-apparent to the throne, to aid the archbishop, and to act as peacekeeper for the city. I cannot do that without the utmost confidence and cooperation of my cohort in office!" Corinth responded, his own voice raising, now.

"Well, paladin. Perhaps before jumping the gun, you should take a few days to take stock of your environment and learn what situation it is that you've found yourself in. This is Emperor's Rest! A city where what ought be often isn't, and what ought not be, is! Remember this first lesson well, if you intend to keep your station, here," Viceroy said, shaking his head in disappointment. "I must away, I've business to attend to. While I am gone, since you think it so prudent, perhaps you should 'walk the block'."

"I must meet with the archbishop, first," Corinth replied, coarsely.

"Oh? Well, welcome to the way of office, Ser Corinth. You'll be stretched thin and still be found wanting," Viceroy snubbed as he shut the door behind him.

Corinth sighed and looked out the window. Why on Hera did he think that would play out any different?

"Off to a great start, here, Immanel. Grand Marshall Ludus would be proud."

Stars, he missed the monastery.

VI

A New Heading

"So, way I figure it, yeah? We all take a piss on one fucker 'n greasem' up real good so's he can slip out of the cuffs n—"

"I'm gonna stop you right there, Cutter, because I don't wanna hear how the rest of that thought was goin' to play out. The cap'n's here!" Flint said, stopping whatever awful idea was about to come out of Cutter's mouth.

Flint and Cutter turned and looked up at Captain Morgan, Second Mate Osiris, and Commander Viceroy as they talked to the guard captain who'd been watching over their bondage since they departed the day before, Captain Davis.

"They're free to go. Release them all so that they may depart and be out of my sight and away from the Emperor's city."

Davis frowned. "All of them? The Bluecoats caught wind of them, sir, and I don't believe they—"

Viceroy put up an arm and scowled. "I don't give a horse's ass about what the Bluecoats and Admiral Lucatial wants. These pirates have been given marque by the Emperor and all men of arms will honor it! Are we understood, Captain?"

Davis nodded, visibly pained by the response. "Yes, commander. Your orders are understood perfectly. Unshackle them! We depart!"

The guardsmen collectively groaned as they freed the loud, vulgar, and cantankerous pirates.

Cutter smiled in Davis' face as he was set free.

"It's been real fun, Davy boy, but now the fun's over. Chop chop!"

Captain Davis grumbled in contained anger as he unshackled Flint, then Cutter. Cutter spat at his feet, narrowly missing his boots. Davis pulled out a dagger and held it to Cutter's neck as the man grinned still, looking him in the eyes.

"You are free today, pirate. But tomorrow? I will have your head on a pike."

"I do hope you try, bleeder. I'll be waiting for ye, out on the open water!" Cutter promised.

Davis bit his lip in anger as he walked off, and glared daggers at Cutter before he departed.

"I would lie and say this has been a pleasure, captain, but it would be just that." Viceroy waved his hand as he departed. "May we never meet again."

"Were we both so fortunate, Knight-Commander," Morgan said, equally unenthusiastic.

The guards departed, leaving the pirates alone on Azura. They'd sank the El'wa ships, and commandeered all their hard-earned treasure, shortly after apprehending them. Now, the pirates were back to square one.

"You're safe. I had thought the Knight-Commander would be bringing back your severed head, considering how poorly you two got along," Huasca said to Osiris as they approached.

Osiris gave him a sidelong glance and scoffed, "Were it so easy, old man. It'll take a lot more than some posh knight to lay me down."

"I didn't mean—" Huasca began, but Osiris had already walked past and greeted the other officers. He sighed.

Everytime...

*****

"So, what sort of shit storm are we in, now, cap'n?" Stone asked, breaking the ice.

The officers, all ten of them, including Morgan himself, crowded into the captain's cabin and stood before him as he leaned against his desk.

Morgan lit his pipe, then nodded to Huasca. "Mr. Huasca, what have you learned?"

Yaman Huasca shook his head. "Whomever the turncoat is, they've been in communication with the imperials for quite some time. They knew our heading. They knew we were low an ammunition. They knew we would not be vigilant because we had recently taken prizes. They *knew* we had taken prizes. The perfect time, the perfect place, the perfect opportunity. Even a blind shaman can see that we have been betrayed."

The officers, disgusted at the prospect of a traitor in their midst, looked at one another with uncertainty. Who among them had turned their back on their brothers? Who had gone against the black?

"Are they among us?" Osiris asked, his anger building.

"I do not know. Every man is accounted for, all of us who were on the ship the day we were captured are here now. That traitor is still among us," Huasca declared.

"Which one of you bastards went against the black, ay?" The ship's bosun, Ryker, asked.

"Hold on, then! How do we know it's even a man what's in this room?!" Ryker's brother and the ship's carpenter, Sarkad, asked.

"How do we know it ain't? How do we know it weren't a group that turned on us, ay?" Flint said, looking over everyone.

"How do we know half the damn officers in this fucking room aren't bloody turncoats? Huh?!" Cutter accused, reaching for his pistol. But a knife to his throat stopped him dead in his tracks. He slowly looked to his left at Steven Cage, who gave him a look that could spoil milk.

"You would pull a gun on your fellow officers? Turncoat or no, among Valkar, that is a death sentence," Cage tutted.

"Enough!" Morgan shouted, slamming his hand on his desk and breaking the officers from their frenzy. "This ship has withstood mutinies, boardings, and firing formations. She will not be undone because of the suspicions of one turncoat! Not today! Not ever, are we clear?!"

The men fell silent.

"Every man in this room I have known for no less than five years. In this life, five years is a lifetime. At the mercy of the unforgiving ocean, and all the horrors that lurk within her womb. Hunted by men, El'wa, Duwa, and even Wuhlven. You are some of the finest pirates this world has ever seen, and I know it to be true, for I have seen many of them and fought with them. The turncoat, we will find in due time, and give him black justice. For now, we have another, more pressing matter to discuss."

Morgan put down his pipe, breathing the last of the smoke out as he laid a map out before the men and dropped the thick envelope full of pardons upon it. Jaws dropped and eyes went wide.

"Is that…" Cutter began.

"Couldn't be, no…" Flint finished.

Morgan smiled furtively and opened the envelope, the octopus seal of the Emperor already broken. He pulled out several of the pardons within, as well as the letter of marque.

"The Emperor, it would seem, has given you all a choice. You can work as privateers for the empire, or walk away from piracy as free men. What you choose is entirely up to you. You may choose to continue the account, working for the crown. Or you may choose to put this life we live behind you."

He paused for several moments. The weight of that decision felt heavy in the air.

"…What's the catch?" Stone asked after stepping forward and holding a pardon in a trembling hand.

"We are to hunt a Dyonian trade ship for the Emperor," Morgan said, leaning back in his chair.

"One ship? For the pardon of two hundred pirates? This a trick, cap'n?" Stone asked skeptically.

Morgan shook his head. "Nay. I've been told that the ship is without escort. The Emperor was adamant that it be captured, however."

"What's on the ship, then?" Flint asked.

Morgan's eyes flitted at Osiris and Huasca.

"A grave danger. Tell them." Abbal instructed.

"Allegedly an object of myth is upon this ship, gentlemen. The Eye of Atla," Morgan said, skeptically.

A laugh broke out in the cabin. All save for Morgan, Huasca, and Osiris.

"The Eye of Atla? We're hunting legends, now? Stars above, the Emperor of Kurza really has flown the coup, ay." Cutter laughed.

"While we're at it, why don't we wrestle a hydra and tame a dragon?" Sarkad joked.

"I assure you, gentlemen, the Eye is very real," Morgan said, annoyedly.

"And how would ye know that cap'n? Have ye ever even seen the damned thing before?" Stone asked.

"Seen it? Mr. Stone, I've held it in my own two hands and gazed into it. I was there when Thunderbolt Colt used its power to bring down the Continental Navy at Red Holm. And I watched it disappear into the sea after Colt went up in a flash of lightning."

The men stopped laughing. They could see that Morgan was dead serious.

"Ye mean ye were actually there? At Red Holm? Shite, cap'n, I thought that story was all a drunken sailor's tale," Stone admitted.

This time, Morgan laughed, as did Huasca.

"Did you think the name 'Immortal Captain' came from telling tall tales at the tavern? No. Every story, I've lived it. Every deed? I've done it. The Eye of Atla is very real, and according to the Emperor's sources, is on its way to the hands of the Dyonians."

"And why do we give a rat's ass about that? Dyonians get it, empire gets it—all the same, really. Some rich twat gets more power, and it all goes to their head," Stone shrugged.

"Because this rich twat is offering you all freedom—and a choice. Something most men never get in all their years, in this world."

Stone and the other officers looked among themselves, considering the offer.

"If we do not retrieve the Eye from the Dyonians, then the Emperor will NOT take that defiance lightly. He *will* send the Seekers after us. They will come in numbers, they will come prepared, and they will not stop until they hunt us down and kill us to the last," Morgan warned.

The pirates were alarmed, now. They'd all heard of the Imperial Seekers, and what terrible things they do to those who earn the Emperor's wrath. They could not afford to have that kind of trouble.

"I hope I have your attention, now. We have been given two months to complete our task. The Dyonian trade ship, Empress' Bounty, will be travelling close to the Chain Lands, here, about seven hundred nauts off the coast." Morgan explained. Nauts, the shortened term for nautical miles, is how seamen measured distance between two points.

"She will be approaching a string of small islands, the Mouse Isles. We will arrive, with favorable winds, about a day and a half ahead of her. From there, we will find an ideal place to berth and lay our trap. All we need is for her to get close, the Azura will outpace her, and we'll clip her sails to ensure she cannot escape. From there, we will board her and claim her treasures. I am told that she is laden with gold and spices from the Shimmer Isles, so mayhap we'll make back what we lost when the imperials took our haul."

"They took the provisions and sank the ships..." Steven Cage muttered bitterly.

"Any questions?" Morgan asked.

Moary stepped forward. "Aye, cap'n. What do we know of their firepower and manpower?"

Morgan shook his head. "Not much, Mr. Moary. As it is a trade ship, it's cannons are likely weak. I wouldn't expect anything much bigger than a twelve-pounder cannon. As for who's aboard it. Well, your guess is as good as mine. Any more questions?"

Osiris raised his hand.

Morgan, perplexed, nodded to him. "Siris?"

"What of the turncoat?" Osiris asked coolly. His gaze was hard and intent.

"Be vigilant, be observant, and keep your eyes and ears open. We *will* find him. But for now, we must bide our time and embark on our mission."

Osiris, as well as Steven Cage and several others, nodded.

"Claude Humris, you've been quiet. Have you any questions, sir?" Morgan asked.

Standing in the back of the room, flitting through one of the captain's books, was the sawbones of the crew, Claude Humris. He was a reserved, soft-spoken Atarran man. He shook his head. "No, capitaine, I have no questions. I will keep an ear to the men. See if perhaps, a softer approach is necessary." He nodded. His accent thick and pronounced.

Morgan nodded. Claude was not one for violence or impassioned speech. He would help, but as was his nature, Morgan knew it would not be in a direct manner.

Morgan clapped his hands together. "Very good. We must make ready for departure. I'd rather not stay here long enough to find out how much information our captors gave to the Bluecoats, and we're in no position to fight them right now. Dismissed!"

The men, save for Huasca, made for the door.

"Oh, and gentlemen? The Emperor had one more very stringent request: we are to leave no survivors…"

"Stars above…" Stone sighed.

They left.

✶✶✶✶✶

Azura was a pirate frigate, larger than most of her class. She had two separate gun decks that ran the whole length of the ship, as well as a storage compartment that covered the same distance beneath the gun decks. She also had several different rooms used to store provisions and livestock from a stairway at midship. Just above the provisions deck was a galley large enough to hold about a hundred and fifty men at a time, and beneath that was a spare compartment just above the waterline where the crew slept. Below the storage, running the whole bottom of the ship, was the bilge, a large, cavernous section of empty space where the base of the bilge pump sat, and all the runoff emptied during storms and the like. Osiris had learned, over the years, every nook and cranny of Azura. So, when he saw the barrel conspicuously sitting a few feet from Morgan's cabin door, he understandably was suspicious.

He flipped the top open and sighed at what he saw inside. "A barrel? You thought you could hide in a barrel to eavesdrop? How the hell did you even get it up here without anyone noticing?!"

Hanover popped up out of the barrel, flustered.

"Everybody else was either below deck, or in the captain's office," he explained.

"Why were all the men below deck?" Osiris asked, leading Hanover back down to the main deck. As he grabbed the boys wrist and lead him, he took note of the tattoo on his wrist. Two serpent heads, one black, and one a skin tone outline, with odd markings coming off them at the corners, top, and bottom. He'd always been meaning to ask him about that.

"They're enraged, sir! They've realized that the only way we could have been found out is if someone told the imperials, and now they're all arguing below about who the traitor is."

Osiris sighed and called over Flint and Cutter. The two approached, eyeing Hanover like one might look at a mosquito sucking blood from their arm.

"What is it, Siris? We finally throwing the boy overboard?" Cutter asked, hopefully.

Hanover's eyes widened, but he kept silent. He deserved that. It was his fault they'd been caught off-guard by the imperials in the first place.

"Nay, he says that the men have started witch-hunting each other below deck. See to it that they don't wind up killing each other before we get underway, ay?"

Cutter groaned, "Fuckin' hell, already? At this rate we'll be a crew divided before we even set sight on the damn merchant ship." He looked to Flint. "Let's handle it. Get Stone, he'll set 'em straight."

Flint nodded wordlessly before addressing Hanover. "Ye cocked up real bad a few months back, boy. What with all the mayhem bein' detained by the damn imperials 'n the cap'n coverin' your ass, you've been spared the type of punishment ye'd normally get. Don't think he'll be coverin' for ye much longer, though." He leaned in, filling Hanover's view with his cold, hard blue eyes, and the stink of his breath. "This is the first—and last—warning you'll ever get from me, ye hear? Shape up before ye catch *real* trouble."

With that, the two set off.

Hanover stood firm, but Osiris could see the sweat beading at his brow. "I…I deserved that."

Osiris folded his arms. "Yes. Yes, you did. I told ye before this life ain't for most folk. Its dangerous, its ugly, and it requires the utmost attention. You'd normally get thirty lashes for getting us caught like that. You'd be bleeding for hours and hurting for weeks. The cap'n saved ye from that. He won't be able to save ye again."

Hanover nodded. "I understand, sir."

"Good. Now go find Moary, he'll be needing ye below deck, soon enough."

*****

Morgan and Huasca sat in the captain's cabin. Azura had well and truly set sail, now. She was making her way down the rivers of the Fjora-Amaranthine channel, and now he watched the comparatively calm waters of the channel sail by as they made their way toward Oceanus. It would be at least two weeks before they reached her, however.

"You did not tell them the true danger that they are in, captain. That may very well cost us all," Abbal admonished.

"As a captain, it is my job not only to inform my crew of their situation, but also maintain morale. We go into an uncertain storm. I need those men as focused and driven as possible to ensure we come out of it in one piece," Morgan explained matter-of-factly.

"If we are in danger of being hunted by the Seekers, should we not be trying to find shelter to weather the storm? Captain, I do not see a scenario where the Emperor keeps his word. We are pirates. He will suffer no consequences for betraying and killing us. We should make for the Storm Tide. The Seekers will not be able to penetrate the storm walls to reach us."

"And if we do so, we will never be able to leave. Should the Seekers discover the location of the Storm Tide, they will blockade it for months, years if they must, until either we meet them with force or surrender. Thousands will die all because we chose to hide. I cannot allow that!" Morgan said.

"If this human Emperor gets hold of the Eye of Atla, Morgan Sarron, a lot more people will die than just pithy pirates. You have seen its power. You have seen what damage it can do in the hands of a capable wielder! The knowledge it can give! If this human gets ahold of it, he will use it to gain supremacy over his enemies, the balance of power between the empires of men will crumble!" Abbal shouted back.

"Then so be it."

Morgan said as he watched a small sailing boat pass behind the ship. He saw two fishermen, a father and a son, by the looks of them, casting their lines now that the mighty frigate had passed them. They had hidden their colors, so the pair likely had no idea that a small army of pirates had just sailed past them. How close they had come to death…

"My duty is not to the empire, the mercantile, or the dynasty. I care not for these people who would hunt me and mine to death for our audacity not to live by their rules. The Emperor can have his Eye. And if he chooses to destroy the empire in the process? Then the Brethren Court can loot the remains and live like royalty for generations to come."

"Such callous disregard for life. You have grown cold in your old age, Morgan," Abbal noted.

"I have grown *tired*."

"You know nothing of true exhaustion, human. But I see that you are too learned even for I…" Abbal said disappointedly. The bright blue glow of the amulet faded as Abbal went dormant once more.

Huasca sighed, opening a cabinet and pulling out a bottle of alcohol. Bagwham Black Rum. He grabbed two glasses and sat the bottle on the desk, then poured the rum in both.

"Dark, heady, and strong: just how I like my women." Morgan chuckled; Huasca joined in.

"Ha, I not seen you with a woman for quite some time, old friend. I'm surprised ya still remember what they look like."

Morgan shrugged, taking a long gulp from his glass before slamming it down and taking in its strong flavor.

"That's because none of the women I meet ever can compare to the ones I've lost," Morgan mused, slurring his words a bit.

"Not many women can compare to *her*, Morgan," Huasca said, nodding to the portrait on the wall.

He sighed longingly, then pulled out his pistol. It was made entirely of silver-steel, with sharp rose vines elegantly molded around her barrel. It was a long piece, the barrel just over a foot in length, and given a powerful enchantment so that her bullets struck with the ferocity of a cannonball and tore through damn near anything that was unfortunate enough to be in its path. He'd named it after her. He called it Bullet Rose. He took another sip of the rum.

"Let us not speak of her, now. I'd rather not drain the whole bottle of such fine rum. Let us toast on the matter at hand. We have escaped the headman's block once more. And now the men's gaze is set on a new prize."

Huasca nodded and toasted as well. "To new prospects and a brighter tomorrow."

Morgan raised his glass. "Cheers, old friend." The two drank as a knock came at the door. "You may enter," Morgan called.

VII

The Derelict

Three weeks passed. The Azura made it through the sea gates at Oceanus with minimal issue. The Bluecoats that inspected every ship that came in and out of the gates were wary, but they were forced to let the pirates go as Morgan showed them several pardons and the letter of marque for clearance. Now, they were truly out on the open ocean once more. The pirates rejoiced briefly at their return to the sea but settled in as their voyage well and truly began.

The first few days on the open ocean were uneventful. The weather, fair and tame. Hanover, one of the only crewmen who could play an instrument, had started playing his guitar for the crowd to break up the monotony. And so, it was on the fourth day, as Hanover played his guitar on the main deck, that Osiris would call out the ship on the horizon.

"Vessel to starboard! Noreast!" he called, pointing to the northeastern horizon.

The men stopped and looked. Morgan, having been on the wheel, pulled out his spyglass to observe the vessel.

"What is it?" Huasca asked as he came to the steering deck.

Morgan paused a moment, then let the glass down from his eye. "It's a derelict…"

Everyone stood and watched as they drifted close to the ship and got a better look. She looked awful. Even from afar they could see the bodies littering the deck as seagulls and other scavengers circled the ship. As they came around, Steven Cage came up to the steering deck and requested Morgan's spyglass.

He peered through it. "It has been raided by Valkar, captain," he said with certainty. "I do not know which clan the attackers hail from, however."

"Do you think they may still be around?" Morgan asked concernedly. The idea of being ambushed by Valkar did not sit well with him.

Valkar were savage raiders, hailing from Borra, a kingdom in the far north of the Kurzan Empire. A faction of cult warriors who love to wage war and fight, Valkar were a threat to all who found themselves in their midst, civilian, navy, or pirate. It mattered not, for the Valkar would happily kill all who were not of their ranks.

"Unlikely. My kin are not known to lie in wait at sea. They prefer direct assaults, to chase down prey like wolves hunting deer. We should be safe to approach. Moving forward, we should be cautious. They may still be in the area," Cage warned.

"I see." Morgan nodded. "Let's see what's become of her, then. Perhaps we can at least figure out what we're up against."

Azura sidled next to the derelict ship, and the sound of cawing birds and buzzing flies was so pervasive that Hanover had no choice but to stop playing his guitar. In its place was the drone of death, leaving all men on the deck uneasy.

"I don't like this," Flint warned Cutter and Moary.

The trio were observing the ship from the foredeck.

"Me neither. Whole ship reeks of death, looks like a damn slaughterhouse," Cutter said.

Moary climbed off the crate he'd been sitting on. "Aye, I feel it too. Tell the cap'n I'm readyin' the cannons, just in case."

The bulky Half-Duwa hurried off the foredeck and went below. Flint and Cutter looked at one another, knowing they'd likely be the ones to scout the ship. They went across the main deck to where Morgan, Huasca, Steven Cage, and now Osiris stood.

"Gunner says he's goin' to prime the cannons in case things get dodgy. Orders, cap'n?" Flint asked.

"Good. I want you two, Siris, and Cage, to lead a party aboard. Search the ship from top to bottom 'n tell me what you find. If you find anything that might tell us what happened to these poor bastards, let me know. Savvy?" Morgan ordered.

"Aye, cap'n, we'll keep our eyes peeled." Flint nodded,and then the pair made for the armory to gear up.

"Tell Mr. Stone to arm some men to guard the ship in case something or someone tries to board us. And we need another lookout to watch the horizon." Morgan nodded to Osiris, who nodded in return.

"Aye. I'll have Hanover redeem himself," Osiris said.

*****

Osiris kicked open the door and looked down the long throat of the stairwell. His eyes, able to pick out shapes in low light, struggled to make out anything in the darkness.

"Gonna need a torch," he called.

Flint came up behind him and handed him a lit lantern. He took the lantern and used it to illuminate a few feet ahead of him. "I think this leads to the bilge. We'll check there last," Osiris said before shutting the door. They opened another door and looked inside. This one lead to a crew compartment.

"Hermalla, have mercy," Cutter muttered, then wretched as he saw what was in front of them—and smelled it.

The crew compartment of the ship had been turned into a butcher shop. Human remains were littered about like discarded pieces of meat. Several mangled corpses were nailed to the walls, and entrails were strewn all over the floor. Flies and maggots ate at the eyes and mouths of the corpses, and the smell of voided bowels and decaying flesh assaulted the men's nostrils in a fog of rot that tasted as bad as it smelled.

Steven Cage pushed past Cutter and several others who stood stunned at the entrance and inspected the corpses up close. Runic symbols had been etched into their flesh, and he saw a circle with a large rune drawn in blood in the cleared-out middle of the room.

"What were they summoning?" Osiris asked, leaning next to him.

"Not summoning, they were offering the souls of these men to the Gods. If I had to guess, I would say that they were offering them to Urdrot, the Mother of Pestilence. But I cannot be sure. The ritual circle was left unfinished. They stopped very suddenly," Cage said, standing up and shaking his head. "This is very bad. My kin are raiding further and further south each year. I fear that something much bigger, and much worse is on the way."

"Like what?" Osiris asked.

Cage looked at him for a moment, analyzing him. "It does not matter, now. We need to investigate the rest of this ship," he said in his accented Kurzan.

Cutter walked up to one of the bodies nailed to the walls and grimaced. "I've killed a lot of people, but I've never done anything like this. These fuckers tortured these people before they killed them."

The faces of the men on the walls were twisted in expressions of agony and horror. Some of them still had their eyes wide open, though they were being eaten by flies and maggots now.

"Well, I think we know what to expect on the rest of the ship, ay? Brace yourselves, brothers. This is about to be ugly," Osiris announced.

*****

Hanover sat in the crow's nest, eyes peeled and sweeping over the horizon. He nearly jumped when he heard someone climbing the ladder to get into the crow's nest with him but calmed down when he saw it was the gunner, Frederick Moary.

"How ye holdin' up, son?" Moary asked as he made it into the crow's nest.

Hanover nodded, momentarily looking away from the horizon. "I'm doing fine, I suppose. Just trying to keep vigilant."

And trying not to fuck everything up like I did last time.

"I see that. Ye whip your head around any harder and you're liable to spin it around like an owl's!" Moary laughed warmly.

Hanover cracked a smile at the joke. Moary had been hard on him since he'd joined the crew over half a year ago, but he'd grown accustomed to him over that time. Now, he could practically load a cannon by himself, blindfolded. He learned how to fill powder bags, clean the bore of a cannon, and secure them during a storm. Without him, Hanover realized, he probably would have been left at port months ago.

"Well, at least if I could turn my head like an owl's I'd likely never miss a bloody navy ship on the horizon again…" Hanover said quietly.

"That eats at ye, does it?" Moary asked, already knowing the answer.

"I've…gotten more than a few dirty looks because of it, yeah. Perhaps a threat or two."

"Ha! A threat or two? Way I hear it, Thomas Cole had to pull a man away from ye. He wanted to box your ears because of it!" Moary cackled.

Hanover sighed. He remembered that day very well. A mate named Louis had gotten in his face and yelled at him after they started sailing for Emperor's Rest. He'd blamed him for the situation they were in and suggested that it was his fault that the imperials had found them in the first place. The man was piss drunk, and no matter what Hanover told him, he simply didn't care. Thomas Cole stepped in when Louis had pushed him to the floor and went to hit him.

"I remember, yeah," Hanover replied, growing quiet. He glared at one of the bodies, so far below him on the deck of the derelict ship. "Do you think they'll find anything on that ship? Besides bodies, I mean?"

Moary abruptly stopped laughing before following Hanover's gaze to the bodies on the deck of the dead ship. He whistled and shook his head. "Dark stuff, that. We've come across deserted ships before but it's rare we see somethin' quite like this, lemme tell ye," he said.

He sounded unnerved.

"It's just, I've heard…stories, like," Hanover mumbled, his mind going back into memory. "Stories 'bout abandoned ships at sea. Ghost stories, and all that."

"Oh, laddie. I think we've all heard stories, but let me tell ye, some of the ones I've heard'll make your skin crawl. Make ye want to swim for land and ne'er touch the sea again…" Moary said, mirthlessly. His expression turned hard and dark.

"Like what, sir?" Hanover asked slowly.

Moary rocked his jaw and ran a hand through his beard, looking hard at one of the bodies on the deck of the derelict as a flock of seagulls crowded around it. They pecked the eyes and the tongue out as he thought back onto a dark tale, one that was very near to the crew. He looked at Captain Morgan, who stood still, talking to Huasca and scanning the horizon.

"Ye ever heard the story of the Dread Captain, son?"

Hanover blinked, trying to remember if he had. "Dread Captain, sir?"

Moary scratched at the scar running across his cheek. "Aye. It's a story that's well-known among sailors. Hell, ye can scarcely be one without hearin' it. Might as well tell ye then, I figure. The story of Felix Helregal, and his Armada of the Damned…"

The gulls pecked at the corpse as Moary told Hanover a story that made his blood run cold…

*****

Osiris reluctantly turned to the last door, the door to bilge. He'd been putting this one off since the beginning. One, because there was basically no chance that anything of value or importance was down there, two, because after they'd seen what abhorrent things had been done in just about every other room and cabin in the barrack, he was honestly wary of what they might find down

67

there. And third, and most importantly, they'd found a large hole in the side of the ship leading into the cargo compartment, above the waterline. As well as a secondary hole in the floor of the cargo hold, which of course, lead right down into the bilge. Osiris *knew* that *something* was in the bilge. And he really, really didn't want to find out what.

But, in the name of diligence, they were about to open the door.

"I'll go first. Guns ready, just in case," Osiris sighed, quieting the anxiety in his gut.

This is a bad idea, I can feel it.

He strained his eyes, forcing the barest fraction of Alyria into them to enhance his sight, held up the lantern, pulled out his pistol, and tread down the stairs.

Even with the light of the lantern, he couldn't see far. It clashed with his night vision, weakening it, and he'd thought to toss it, but felt more secure with it in hand. As though keeping a light source with him would somehow deter whatever might be down here.

Maybe it's gone.

He hoped, vainly.

He knew he wasn't that fortunate, however.

As soon as he got to the point where the stairs opened out into the bilge, however, he froze. The smell had hit him. Something resembling spoiled fish and brine water.

What is that?

He couldn't make it out exactly, but he swore he'd seen something move in the far corner. Outside of the rays of the small amount of light leaking in from the hole in the ceiling. The hairs on his arms and neck stood on end, begging him not to go further down. Osiris was not a stupid man. You didn't survive over a decade at sea being foolish. If he had a bad feeling about something, he tended to follow his intuition.

I still need to figure out what's down here.

He threw the lantern at the corner where he'd seen movement…

It shattered against something large, making a pronounced crunch as it was smashed against whatever it had struck.

Then, the shadows moved.

His eyes went wide as he saw something surge past the weak light leaking from above and immediately turned around.

"Get up those stairs NOW!"

He pushed and shoved the men up the stairs until everyone got the message and stormed back up to the deck. He could hear it right behind him, however. He cleared the opening where the stairwell opened into the bilge just in time to escape something large crashing down where he'd been a moment prior, smashing the stairs. He didn't bother to look to see what he'd escaped.

The pirates emptied out onto the main deck as something chittered from below and the sound of something sharp scraping against the wood echoed up to their ears. He slammed the door shut.

"Get across the gangplank! Everybody get off this starsdamned ship right fucking now!" he barked.

"What is it?! What did ye see?!" Cutter asked, alarmed.

Back on the Azura, Morgan and Huasca watched the alarmed men surge onto the deck, as did Stone from his vantage point, who motioned for the men to raise their guns.

"What's got them spooked?" Morgan asked.

Huasca shook his head. "I do not know, but he would not be this alarmed if it was not something bad!" Huasca said in alarm, running down the stairs to meet them.

"No time! Get back on Azura—it's coming!"

"What's comi—"

Cutter's words were cut short as an explosion of sound and wood grabbed their attention. A black, barnacled claw had exploded out of the deck and grabbed hold of an unsuspecting pirate. Everyone stood frozen in horror as the man screamed briefly. His cries were cut short as he was pulled down into the crater. There was stunned silence for several moments as the sound of loud chewing and crunching bones filled the air, and the seagulls took flight, startled by the commotion.

Then the first leg came.

Then the second.

Then the fourth.

And the last four, as the claws and body of the creature revealed themselves in the light. Eye stalks the size of watermelons gazed at the pirates as the body of an enormous, armored black crab rose to greet them, clicking together claws big enough to slice a man in two. Its mouth parts opened, and it regurgitated a foam of bubbles.

"Widow Crab! Open fire!" Stone shouted as he fired his rifle at the creature, as did the two dozen men he'd armed in case of such an event.

The creature rubbed its claws together, producing a stridulating chatter as it retreated from the gunfire. Most of the bullets simply bounced off its thick chitinous hide, but a few had struck its joints, and Stone had even landed a shot on one of its eyes, eliciting jittering dance of the creature's legs as it charged at the men still onboard the derelict.

Osiris leapt onto the gangplank and ran like hell, as did Flint and Cutter, escaping the wrath of the widow crab. Several of the other men, however, were not so fortunate. As he dove onto the Azura, Osiris heard the screams of several men who were set upon by the crab and looked over his shoulder in horror.

Two men were held in its claws as two front legs impaled two more men onto the deck, and one unfortunate soul was stuck headfirst in the creature's maw, Osiris looked on in horror as the creature bit the man's head off, slicing it at the neck with its blade-like mouth parts. Another volley of bullets pelted the widow crab and it cut the men in its claws in half as it clacked them together in irritation.

He broke from his shock as Huasca helped him to his feet.

"Get off me!" Osiris spat and ran to a nearby top gun as Yager was rapidly loading in the shot and took aim. "Aim for the face!" he yelled as he pushed the man fumbling with the cannon next to Yager to the side and began loading the weapon meticulously by himself.

Yager nodded. "Aye!" And maneuvered the cannon to aim at the beast.

The remaining men on the derelict had either abandoned it or were in the clutches of the crab as it feasted on another poor man. This one, having seen the horrific fate of the last men the beast had swallowed, pull out his pistol and fired into its open mouth. The beast slammed the man to the deck, stunning him, before sidestepping towards him and smashing his head into the deck with a claw. Then, it set its sights on Flint and Cutter, who were ushering the last of the pirates back across the gangplank.

"Shit; bad news!" Cutter said, pointing at the beast as it scuttled slowly towards them.

Flint gritted his teeth and pulled out his sword and pistol, taking aim at the widow crab. He fired at its good eye, and the creature thrashed about as the bullet hit the eye stalk, narrowly missing the eye itself. It slammed a claw at the pair, forcing them to split up to dodge out of the way, then turned toward Flint, ready to kill.

"Say goodbye, crab legs!" Yager shouted, firing the cannon at the creature's carapace. The cannonball punched a hole through the crab, and a gout of blue, bloody fluids spurted from the wound. The creature retreated as Osiris fired his cannon at it as well, striking it in the base of its claw. The claw exploded from the force of the cannonball, and the creature quickly retreated into the hole in the ship, escaping the gunfire that peppered it, and sparing Flint and Cutter.

"It's retreated into the belly of the ship!" Stone announced.

"Not for long it hasn't!" Morgan shouted. "Fire the cannons and blow that monster to bottom of the sea!"

Moary, who'd come down from the crow's nest along with Hanover, nodded and called down below deck to the gun crews. "Open fire!"

The ship shook as the cannons let loose at near point-blank range, over penetrating the derelict and ripping it apart inside and out. One of the shots struck the powder room, igniting it and sparking a roaring blaze that quickly began to consume the ship.

The sails were unfurled, and Morgan manned the wheel as Azura pulled away from the blazing ship. The stern-mounted cannons fired at the ship, a last goodbye from Azura's crew as the hulk was consumed in flame, and all the horror visited upon it and its unfortunate crew was cleansed with flame.

*****

All told, nine men had been killed by the widow crab. Those that survived the derelict were visibly shaken, not just from the widow crab attack, but from the mutilation they'd witnessed.

"The Valkar who killed those men were likely scared off by the crab. It would have been drawn to the ship by the scent of blood and by other scavengers, come to feast on the remains. Still, the fact that they came this far south, captain—it is concerning," Steven Cage said as the officers gathered on the steering deck.

"Was it World Reavers? I've heard tell that they've begun raiding south to avoid the other clans that prefer raiding further north up the coast," Morgan said.

"The World Reavers are not afraid of the Deathwatch or the Pestilent Skalds—they have come to the south because they know that the villages and harbors here are ripe for plunder," Cage revealed. "But if they have begun raiding the southeast then the Watch and the Skalds will soon follow. Grim tides will be upon us all if that happens."

"He speaks truth. Even in Xalla, these Valkar have begun to garner a reputation. I have heard stories of some of their ships being spotted off the northern coast of Bagwham. What they do to those they've captured is the stuff of nightmares," Huasca said.

"If that's so, then we may very well have the beginning of another reave on our hands. All the more reason we need to finish our business for the Emperor and return to the Storm Tide. It may be time that the Brethren Court began paying closer attention to the Valkar," Morgan said as he steered the ship.

"I am afraid, captain, that the Brethren Court alone cannot hope to cull the combined might of the Valkar. What you see in the south is but a sample of what goes on up north. There is a reason the Warden never leaves. Were he to step foot outside of it for but a day, the Valkar and the warring lords of the north would tear Borra apart."

Morgan didn't like the sound of that. The Valkar raped, pillaged, and enslaved wherever they tread. Whole villages disappeared when they raided up and down the coasts of the empire. That meant that the pirates had less to loot themselves.

"Do you think we'll run into them? The men who slaughtered that ship?" Morgan asked.

Cage shrugged. "Hard to say. If not them, then someone like them. We need to be careful; we're not the only hunters out here in these waters. And my kin have no mercy in their hearts, especially for anyone who would deny them plunder."

None of them liked the sound of that.

"Right then, we need watchmen all hours of the night, going forward. Siris, I want you to setup a rotation throughout the day. Men we know to have good eyes. We cannot afford to be caught unaware by Valkar. I don't think any of us want to end up like those poor sods," Morgan said with a grimace.

"It'll be done, sir. I'll have a list by the evening," Osiris responded.

"Very good. Mr. Moary, I need the cannons ready at all hours. Have the boy make powder bags in preparation for any skirmish we may find ourselves in. We'll need them regardless for the Bounty, when we find her."

Moary nodded. "Aye, cap'n. Givem' somethin' to do, ay?"

"Other than waste space and sell us out to the imps? Aye, givem' somethin' to do that ain't fuckin' us in the ass," Flint said dismissively.

Moary paused, looking hard at him. "The boy nodded off cause of liquor *I* gave 'em. But he's a stalwart sort so he didn't send me up the river, ay? So leavem' be. If anyone's the turncoat in that scenario it's me. And I'd die before I sold out my brothers."

Flint ground his teeth but remained silent.

"We're a few days removed from the ambush point. When the time comes, we need to act as one. Are we clear?" Morgan asked, looking at Flint, now.

Flint nodded. "Yes, of course cap'n. Just lookin' out for the crew, is all," he said, looking towards Hanover, who sat perched in the crow's nest up above, still watching the horizon.

"Good. Dismissed."

The men dispersed back to their duties, and Huasca made to leave before Morgan grabbed his shoulder to stop him. "Man the wheel a spell, I would walk the deck."

Huasca nodded wordlessly, and Morgan descended the stairs from the steering deck, past his quarters, and down to the main deck. He walked calmly, surveying the men, and watching as many of them stopped to gaze at the shrinking image of the burning wreck.

They lost their brothers, all because we decided to investigate a derelict…

Morgan let the weight of that loss rest on him. Though they would never say it, it was his fault that those men died. This was nothing new, he'd lost many, many men over these long years, whole crews worth. Still, he could not dismiss the weight of that loss.

Stars, forgive my foolishness.

As the horizon scrolled and the burning derelict faded away, and the widow crab succumbed to the flames of its feeding ground turned tomb, a pall was cast over Azura. Morgan could feel it. The silence that made every knock of wood and every wave slapping against the side of the ship sound loud and ominous. As the men dispersed back to their duties, their prayers for their fallen brethren said, Morgan glanced at the burning orange speck in the distance.

"What terrible thing have I wrought upon us?"

"Only the Stars know what lies ahead, Morgan Sarron," Abbal answered.

"Now you speak? But when my men were dying you said nothing!" Morgan growled.

"What words would I have offered that you would have heeded? You are a stubborn man, Morgan Sarron. As I said before, you are too learned even for I."

"Speak sense and I will respond in kind. You speak of duties, prophecies, and sundry! I care not for such dribble, amulet!"

"You have seen what extraordinary things exist in this world. You have fought with and beside great and powerful men and women, yet still you doubt your role in fate? How is one as clever as you so blind?"

Morgan shook his head. "I see far better than can be believed. I see the madness behind it all."

"You have killed a thousand men for gold and legacy. Why do you balk, now?" Abbal asked, confused.

"Every man that I killed I killed because he would have killed me were the roles reversed. Every gold I took I took to aid my cause!"

"Is that what you believe? You are a pirate, Morgan. You have no cause, no loyalty but to yourself."

"I am the leader of the Brethren Court—"

"You are the leader of thieves, and there is no honor among them."

Morgan leaned against the railing. How many times had they had this very same conversation? How long would he fight it until he admitted his worst fear?

"Be gone, spirit. I wish to be alone."

"So you ask, so you shall have, Morgan Sarron..."

The amulet's light faded away, and he was alone. For now. He watched the twinkle of flame on the horizon, and reminisced on days gone...

VIII

Bounty in Blood

Sailing southeast toward the Mouse Isles, the Empress' Bounty's crew milled about the ship in preparation to weigh anchor. The merchant ship's master, Ayumu Jahiro, stood with his chief and deck officers, going over the assignment listings for the day.

"Has all of the goods on the storage deck been secured and accounted for?" Jahiro asked, reading off the scroll of paper he'd written the checklist on.

"Yes, master. Everything is where it should be," an officer, Donzu, replied.

"Including the…*other* cargo?" Jahiro asked in a hushed tone.

Donzu nodded and whispered, "Yes, the samurai are guarding it as we speak."

"Good. Soon we will deliver them to port and be done with this whole mess," Jahiro exhaled. He could see that the others agreed. "I see that the main deck has been scrubbed. What of the crew deck and galley?"

Another officer, Yushi, spoke up this time. "The crew deck is being scrubbed as we speak, they should be finishing shortly—"

The conversation was cut short as a commotion starts on the main deck. Jahiro and the officers descended from the steering deck to see a group of crew members crowding around someone.

"Get out of my way! I must see it!" A man shouted at the top of his lungs as Jahiro parted the crowd. He froze as he saw a standoff between one of the crew and a samurai. The warrior stared down the agitated crewman, his fist around the hilt of his blade.

"Get back, or I will be forced to draw my blade," the samurai warned.

The crewman, a man Jahiro recognized as Botan, was panting in anger, staring daggers at the armed man barring his path. "Botan! What are you doing? Step away from the samurai!" Jahiro ordered, trying to hide his alarm.

"Be silent, Jahiro! You wish to keep it from me, but I will have it! The Eye is mine!" Botan growled maniacally.

Jahiro inched forward, his hand on his pistol. "Botan! Do not listen to it! It lies to you! It will be your death!" he gave a pleading look to the samurai. "Please, do not kill this fool! I will calm him!"

The samurai looked at Botan, still glaring madly at him, then at Jahiro. He shrugged. "Control him, or I will be forced to, captain."

Jahiro strode toward Botan, who jolted at his approach and pulled out a dagger from his hip. Jahiro placed a warding hand in front of him. "Do not do this, Botan! Fight it!"

Botan shook his head violently. "Fight what? You covet it for yourself, it tells me so! You wish to steal it! Have it for yourself! But I was there when we loaded it onto the ship! It told me to watch over it, to hold it! Protect it!" he said in a trembling voice. His eyes looked around wildly, like a scared animal.

Jahiro inched closer still, wary of the dagger. Behind Botan, he could see the samurai silently approaching on the balls of his feet, ready to strike. The samurai looked at Jahiro, waiting for the signal. Jahiro didn't react, knowing that if he did, it would mean death.

"Botan, the Eye is trying to control you. It does not need to be protected from us. No, we need to be protected from it! That is why the samurai are here! To protect *us*..." Jahiro pleaded, trying his hardest to speak sense into the man.

Botan laughed. "It said you would say that—that you would tell me more lies, try to turn me against it. But it will not work, Jahiro. Your lies will be silenced!"

Botan charged at Jahiro, swiping his dagger at him and slashing open Jahiro's palm. Jahiro scrambled back, thumbing his pistol, but Botan already closed the distance. He grabbed hold of Jahiro's shoulder, ready to bury the dagger in his gut. The samurai was faster, however, and stabbed Botan through the heart with his katana. Botan gasped and dropped the dagger as the samurai ripped the blade from his back and sheathed it in a smooth motion. Botan fell to his knees as Jahiro sighed in resignation. The madness in Botan's eyes died away, and naked reality took its place. The voice was gone.

The samurai looked at the rest of the crew, his expression a calm mask. "If you hear anything, a voice, a noise that sounds of place—anything, do not heed it. It is an illusion, a trick meant to compel you. If anyone, save for the captain approaches trying to get to the Eye of Atla, I will be forced to kill you." The samurai knelt over the dying body of Botan and said a quick prayer, eulogizing the man before two men approached and carried away the body.

Jahiro shook his head.

That made three.

Three of his men who had succumb to the whispers and walked to their deaths. He wondered how many more would die before their voyage was over.

"…Return to your duties. We must prepare for the night watch," Jahiro said, shooing the men off as he and his officers returned to their checklist.

"…Back to the matters at hand…" Jahiro began, exhaustedly.

*****

Jahiro entered his cabin as the sunset was in full view from his cabin window. He set his paperwork on his desk, lit several lanterns around the cabin, and then several candles in front of his shrine. He disrobed and changed into his evening attire before pausing and looking at the portrait of his wife and beaming infant daughter. He rubbed a longing thumb over their picture before wiping away a tear and facing the shrine. A pillow sat at the base of it, and he knelt upon it. He gazed at the large, framed picture of Empress Kagura, and prostrated before it, pressing the tip of his nose to the floor.

He prayed to her, as was the tradition of all merchants of Dyona who sought safe travels. In the middle of his prayer, however, he paused. He heard a faint voice coming from outside. He turned toward the sound coming from outside his bedroom window. But of course, nothing was there.

He turned back to the altar and said a prayer for the souls of his dead crewmates. That their souls would find peace with the ancestors, and that the empress would watch over their souls. As he rose from the altar, he walked to his desk and settled into his seat. He took a deep breath and gathered his thoughts before opening his captain's log. He grabbed his quill, dipped it in ink, and began to write.

Captain's Log:

Apus, Thirteenth of Xallha, 2995 AS

Another death today. Botan, a deck hand who often worked in the galley. He said he heard it too, the call of the Eye. I tried to speak reason into him, to make him see the terrible trap set before him. He would not listen. He was struck down by a samurai guarding the Eye, same as the others. He tried to kill me. The samurai saved my life by ending his. The men live in terror. They hear voices and see shadows on the wall without a source. I have heard and seen much the same, and only through diligent prayer to the empress have I managed to stay sane.

My dreams are hazy, feverish, and frightful. I see things, terrible things, and hear the siren song of the Eye. I feel that something terrible is on the horizon. As we approach the Mouse Isles, the voices grow more feverish. I approached the Eye earlier, checking upon it, as is my duty each day. The voices sounded...different. Calm, where once they were frantic. Though their words were still unintelligible to me, as they always are, their tone was sedate. As if they were...waiting for something.

But I do not know what...

Jahiro closed his logbook and looked out the window behind him once more. The sun was nearly gone, it would be night when they found harborage in the isles. As he looked at his own reflection in the glass, he saw an ugly figure behind him, he quickly spun around, whipping out his dagger and shouting in surprise.

Nothing.

He took deep breaths to calm himself as he surveyed the room.

We need to reach Kanto as soon as possible.

*****

As Azura sat in the dying light, hidden in the shadow of a cove looking out into a waterway between the high peaks of the Mouse Isle's interior, Morgan stood at the railing of the steering deck and looked down at his crew, illuminated by lanterns and torches.

"We're sure that this is where she'll end up?" he asked, looking at Huasca.

"These coves offer the best cover to a passing ship. It allows easy access back out to sea and is far enough into the interior to avoid casual observation. If they try to weigh anchor at any of the other caves around the isles, they will have to contend with narrower waterways or exposure from facing out to the open ocean. It is the most likely place for them to hide," Huasca explained.

"And if they anchor in this cave, instead of either of the other three across from us, they'll be dead to rights either way," Morgan noted with a pleased smirk. "Clever."

Huasca nodded. "You're not the only one who's ambushed a few prizes, Captain."

Morgan turned to address the crew, who stood eagerly on the main deck, silent and expectant. On the eve of every battle, before they attacked their prey, the captain would stand on the steering deck and address the crew. And he wouldn't be breaking tradition now.

"Good evening, gentlemen. These past few months have seen us in strange times. When last I addressed you in this manner, it was the morning before we brought down the El'wa merchant ships," Morgan began.

The crewmen grumbled at the mention of their stolen prizes, taken by the imperials shortly before they reached Emperor's Rest. There was nearly an uprising that day.

"Now, we are on the eve of battle. You have all heard by now the details of our target, from myself as well as the officers. We are to take this prize, loot it, and sink it—no survivors. Do this, and every man aboard this ship will have a pardon from the Emperor of Kurza himself. Freedom to go off the account and renounce the black, to take his shares of our victory, this night, and begin himself anew.

"All that stands between you and a new life, pirate, is the Dyonians aboard that ship, and the will to do what must be done. Do this, not for the bloody imperials and their pernicious motives, but for yourself, and the new beginning it will bring. Look to your left and your right. Beside you is your brother in black. Together, you have plundered dozens of prizes, and together, you will set yourselves free. This life, it is free; but it is deadly. The sea takes as much as it gives, sometimes more. Before, you committed piracy as necessity. Because your family was too poor to have you, because the corrupt laws of the *civilized* folk were weaponized against you. Or perhaps you did it to escape being thrown into the meatgrinder of war. Now, you have become a warrior apart. One who breathes the salty sea air and bleeds brine. One who makes men shiver at the mention of your name. Pirate.

"Regardless of why you're here, now you have something that was denied to you all your life: the freedom to choose your own fate. Do this, and the life you want is yours. Do this, and the horrors of your past are forgotten. Do this, and pirate or no, you are a free man, once more…"

Morgan pointed out the mouth of the cove, but in his mind, he was pointing at the Empress' Bounty.

"Plunder them; kill them, and all your hearts' desires are yours."

The men looked out the mouth of the cove. The hunt was about to begin.

"Like wolves to slaughter…" Abbal mused.

*****

Osiris opened the door to the armory and went immediately to his stash as the others filed in. He opened the chest where he stored his favorite weapons and pulled out two spadroons—double-edged, light straight swords used for slashing and thrusting. He fixed their sheathes around his hips and sheathed the blades. Then, he grabbed a bandoleer of flintlock holders. He meticulously loaded and holstered each pistol on the bandolier. To finish his gear, he wrapped a holster around his leg, just below the knee, and sheathed a dagger within. He tied his skull and bones bandana around his head. He was ready.

Flint, Cutter, and Stone did the same, arming themselves for the battle to come. All of them grabbed swords and knives, as well as their own preferred firearms of choice. As he was their best sniper, Flint grabbed a flintlock rifle, fitted with a custom sight he'd made himself. Cutter, preferring to spot for Flint and work as his flank, grabbed two pistols and a blunderbuss.

"I'm takin' the deck sweeper again," Cutter said to Stone as he grabbed and loaded the gun.

"Knock yerself out. I'm goin' with the dragons again!" Stone said eagerly, grabbing the guns in question from his chest. The dragons, shortened blunderbusses with flared muzzles, were carved with the depictions of dragons along the metal of the barrel, ending in a dragon's head at the muzzle. They were short, weighty, and utterly devastating at short range. Stone could already hear the ringing in his ears.

"Both of you stay far away from me, then. I'd rather not go deaf in the middle of a fight," Osiris said.

As they spoke, Steven Cage entered the armory, cutting through the crowd of pirates lined up to arm themselves.

"They let your crazy ass into the armory, Northman?" Cutter asked, getting a laugh from the other officers.

Cage smirked as he grabbed two axes and sheaths for them. "I am Valkar. To hide from battle is not our way. Let the gunner and his crews fight from afar. I will fight and die gloriously in the heart of battle!" he shouted in his thick Borran accent.

The men in the hallway cheered at Cage's words. If the Northman was in the fight, then that meant that half the battle would be fought by him alone, saving their necks from the chopping block.

"Just don't grab any explosives, ye know the cap'n don't like you usin' em," Osiris said.

Cage chuckled and nodded. "No fun, you lot are no fun."

He finished arming himself by grabbing a spear and resting it on his shoulder.

"No gun? Are ye fuckin' mental?" Stone asked.

Cage shook his head. "I hear the Dyonians are relentless fighters. They would rather die than submit to defeat. I want to see the truth to these words."

Flint nodded. "He's right. I talked to Yang down on the gun deck, he said he'd rather die than go toe-to-toe with his kin. Said soon as they saw one of their own was in our ranks they'd single 'em out 'n kill em. Said that they'll fight us all to the death before they surrendered."

Osiris had heard much the same. The Dyonian pirates he'd met back in the Storm Tide were deadly fighters. They were polite and honorable to strangers, but to cross one of them was to invoke a wrath that few men could withstand. They would challenge you to a duel, and if you refused or fought unfairly, all of them would descend upon you and cut you to pieces. Their leader, the Lotus King, was a fighter without reproach. He wondered, now, if that same ferocity was endemic of him and his pirates, or to his people as well.

Osiris grabbed a grenade and tucked it in his pocket. He had a feeling he would need it.

*****

"Everyone knows their part to play?" Morgan asked as the officers, armed and ready, convened on the main deck.

"Aye. Flint, Cutter, Stone, Cage, and I will direct the boarding party for the attack. We're to take out as many men on the main deck as we can before we're discovered. When the fighting begins, send up the flares to alert Azura," Osiris said.

"When the flairs go up, Ryker 'n Sarkad will pull Azura out onto the open water, 'n me gun crews will provide supportin' fire for the boardin' party," Moary said. He handed each officer a flare gun.

"Aim all shots at the whip staff and rudder, if possible. We don't want any shots to penetrate her body because we risk killing our own men and blowing the whole thing to kingdom come if we hit the magazines," Morgan added.

"Aye, cap'n. Disablin' shots only," Moary corrected.

"Mr. Huasca and myself will be overseeing deck operations during the battle, we'll have men ready for the main boarding and coordinate coming about the Bounty when she's disabled. Boarding party, we need those cannons to be disabled before we do. The Dyonians like to use rocket guns, and I'd rather not be lit on fire if they have them," Morgan said.

"If we rush them hard enough, they'll be too overwhelmed to put up a proper offensive," Osiris noted.

"Precisely. The goal is to shock them into focusing on deck combat rather than waste time and manpower focusing on a ship battle with us. Go in fast and silent, and when the cover's blown, go hard and loud. Do that, and we'll have them dead to rights in short order. Even the Dyonians can't argue with a broadside pressed against them," Morgan said confidently.

The officers voiced their agreement.

"Good. Give them hell, gentlemen," Morgan finished.

As the officers broke away, Stone paused as he saw Yager approach, pushing past several men.

"Again? You've got me on the *fucking* ship again. Why the hell ain't I goin' over there to help take the Bounty like everybody else?!" Yager complained as he stood face to face with Stone.

"Because you're our best top gunner and we've got a full detail for the deck boarding as is," Stone responded, irritated.

Here we go again.

"So, remove someone from the detail and add me to it! I've been on dozens of boardings with this crew, I've more than proved my competence!" Yager said, his anger building.

"And so has every other man in the boardin' party, all of them deserve a position just as much as you, but *none* of 'em can fire a top gun like you, see the problem?" Stone said, folding his arms.

"So, because I can hit the broadside of a barn with a cannon I'm to be punished, rather than teachin' someone else how to do it? Hogwash, 'n you know it, Reece!" Yager said, shoving Stone.

Stone's cheeks warmed as a crowd began to form. He could feel Morgan's eyes on him as the other officers watched the situation unfold.

"Daniel Yager, the only reason ye care about boardin' the Bounty is so ye can have first choice of the loot," Stone said, evoking a grumble of agreement from the crowd. "Every other man has just as much right to it as ye. So let it be done, get to yer post 'n get ready for the battle!"

The pirates jeered at Yager, whose rage dwindled as he realized he was outmatched. He backed away.

"And Yager?" Stone called after him.

Yager paused and turned his head.

Stone gave him a hard, cold look. "If ye ever put hands on me like that again, I won't lash ya." He pulled out his flintlock pistol, pulled back the hammer and aimed it at Yager, who stood like a deer blinded by a bright light. "I'll shoot ya—understand me?"

Yager nodded and skulked off silently.

*****

Osiris leaned over the edge of the boat as the men rowed. There were four boats, filled with about a dozen men each, and his was the first, where all the officers who were boarding sat. He watched the guards walking the deck of the Empress' Bounty, their lanterns forming a sphere of light around them in the darkness. He watched, noting their pace and predicting when it would be best to strike. He counted the time it took for one patrolman to leave the area before another guard took his place. He nodded to Stone.

Five…

"Get ready. When they clear out, throw the rope hook over the railing, and secure it. We need to get up, over, and hidden before the guards come. I'll take point." Osiris whispered.

Four…

"It's a tight shift. Ye gotta move like hell's at your heels, Siris." Cutter warned.

Three…

"Trust me, mate. Ye shouldn't worry about whether *I* can do it. Worry about what's goin' to happen to this poor fool if he sees me." Osiris grinned.

Two…

"Check your pistols. Wet powder doesn't kill them; it kills you," Flint reminded.

The men began cocking their pistol hammers and checking their guns. They were near the side of the ship, now.

"Irkalla, their souls will be yours," Cage menaced, a dark twinkle in his eye.

"Rise 'n shine, boys," Flint announced.

The guard left the area as they sidled next to the boat and stopped. Osiris swung his hook before throwing it up. It caught. He took a deep breath.

One…

IX

BOARDING PARTY

Osiris climbed as quietly as he could. He listened for the sound of footsteps as he reached the railing. He peered over and clambered to hide in a gap between two cargo crates. He saw a guard approaching from the left.

Here they come.

Osiris closed his eyes and steadied his breath. He pulled out his spadroons.

Get ready.

He crouched and waited as the footsteps stopped in front of him, and a shadow overtook his vision. The man was facing seaward, smoking a cigarette as he gazed into the darkness, unaware of the man standing behind him. Osiris squinted. The light from the guard's lantern was nearly blinding against the dark of the moonless night. He struck.

One blade plunged through the man's back, poking out of his stomach. He gurgled a noise between a gasp of surprise and a groan of pain. The second blade followed almost immediately after, nearly severing his head from his body before he could finish his shout of pain. He slumped forward, falling onto the railing as the pirates climbed past him. The man's head twisted around on a flap of skin, his face frozen in shock as Steven Cage climbed up the rope.

Cage clucked, "Oh sorry, I didn't see you there, matey," before climbing up and pushing the body overboard into the water. The corpse splashed down next to the longboat. It sprayed the pirates still in the boat as well as the ones climbing up.

"Ye fuckin' moron!" Cutter growled as several men called out from nearby. They were coming.

*****

Several patrollers rushed to the sound of the splash. They shouted in Dyonian, likely sounding off that a man had fallen overboard.

From the shadows, Osiris, Stone, Flint, Cutter, and Steven Cage all sat silently, lying in wait. As the guardsmen came into view, Cage grabbed his axe, ready to strike. Cutter held him down, putting his hand over his mouth and shooshing him. There were at least six patrollers in front of them. They looked at one another, silently debating whether to strike or not. Osiris looked warily at the rope hook anchored on the railing. A patrolman had taken notice.

Fuck.

Osiris cursed internally.

He grabbed Stone and Flint by the shoulders and nodded. It was time to strike. The guards looked over to see the pirates scaling the side of the ship and shouted in alarm. One pirate was just below the railing—and suffered a bullet to the head because of it. The shot rang out.

Their cover was blown.

Fucking fuck!

He cursed again and sprang forward. He ran both blades through the man in front of him.

Stone ran his cutlass through a second patrolman.

Cutter slit the throat of a third patrolman.

Flint ran his straight sword through the fourth man.

The fifth and sixth quickly spun to meet them, aiming their pistols dead in their faces, and the four pirates froze.

The men shouted at them in Dyonian and were abruptly cut off. Steven Cage launched himself from the shadows, swinging his axes. One patrolman jumped out of the way—narrowly, the other felt the slash of the axes. Steven Cage cackled as the last patrolman attempted to run, but the four pirates blocked him. He aimed his pistol at them, shouting again. He was silenced with an axe to the back of his head. The man fell to his knees, and the blood-covered Steven Cage grinned as he put his foot on the man's back and ripped the axe blade from his cleaved head.

"Now *dat's* how you kill, boys!" he howled boisterously as the pirates climbed aboard the boat.

Cutter looked past Cage to see more patrollers approaching and huffed. "Ye alerted the whole fuckin' ship, ye idiot! 'N ye missed one." He pointed at the man lying on the deck.

Steven Cage furrowed his brow and turned around as the men scattered about the deck. He crouched down over the dying man. The man breathed heavy, labored breaths and mumbled in his native tongue, perhaps a prayer, possibly begging for mercy. "You made me look yellow, little man," Cage said, furrowing his brow.

The patrolman had been slashed twice and was bleeding profusely. He raised his arm, tears streaming from his eyes as he gasped in pain.

"Please…" He finally managed to stammer a word in Kurzan.

"May the rime of Neðri claim you," Steven Cage growled. He raised an axe and severed the man's head from his body in one grizzly swipe. Steven Cage picked up the dead man's head by the hair and looked it over before smiling and tossing it overboard.

"This will be fun!" he cackled.

*****

Jahiro burst out of his chambers, hearing the alarm bell and the sound of gunfire. Donzu and Yushi were already on the deck, clashing with their attackers.

"Pirates! We've been boarded!" Jahiro announced. ""Where are the samurai—"

Just as the words were uttered from his lips, the door to the lower deck at the front of the ship opened, and five samurai poured out of it. He recognized the samurai who'd saved his life in their ranks and watched in momentary awe as the five made their presence on the deck known. Each of them killed pirates as they entered the fray, slashing, stabbing, disarming, and maiming. The samurai who saved him, he believed his name was Renzo, killed three pirates in less than ten seconds as he charged to the aid of the men on the deck. Jahiro climbed down the stairs and pulled out a yawara—a small, hand-gripped metal rod with a blunt stabbing end, used for melees, as well as a short, two-and-a-half-foot katana.

If we're to be assaulted, I'll not stand by idly!

Jahiro swore to himself. He was powerless to save Botan and the others, but pirates? He could deal with them handily.

A pirate with his back to him, fending off two crewmen, was his first target. He came up behind the man and jammed the blunted point of the yawara into the man's shoulder, stunning him momentarily and making his sword arm drop. The pirate cried out in pain as the yawara dug into a pressure point and sent a jolt of pain through his arm. The pirate turned to face Jahiro as the katana ran him through. The pirate hit the deck as Jahiro nodded to his men to press on. He carried on, disabling, disarming, and cutting down several pirates in his path as he made his way towards the samurai.

They must not reach the artifact! We are all lost if they do!

Fear strengthening his resolve, Jahiro cut his way through the main deck, calling upon all his years of service and training to carry him through the bloodbath on the deck. He saw several of the pirates cutting their own bloody swathes through his men. A blonde-haired pirate with strange runic tattoos covering his body, wielding two hatchets like they were extensions of his own arms. He knew instantly that this man was one of the yaban-senshi, or Valkar, as they called themselves. He bypassed the rampaging Valkar and turned his attention to the samurai, who were dueling with several of the pirates. He went to attack one of them from behind, a tan-skinned man with a bandana on his head. This one also had tattoos, though they were primarily on his arms, from what Jahiro could see.

Attack the pressure points, then strike...

He raised his yawara in his left hand and moved in for the attack.

The pirate, seeming to sense his presence, spun around.

*****

It was a quick twitch of the head of the samurai in front of him that tipped Osiris off to the man approaching from behind. He felt the hairs on the back of his neck rise, and, in the same instant, he spun to face his ambusher. He could tell that the man was surprised he'd noticed him. Osiris didn't give Jahiro time to ponder, swinging a spadroon at him and nearly cleaving his head from his shoulders.

Jahiro ducked beneath the swing, losing a few hairs in the process. It was followed up with a stab from Osiris' other sword, but Jahiro dodged away, bringing his katana around for a backward swipe and clashing with Osiris. He likely would have caught the other blade had the samurai engaging him not intervened. The samurai brought his sword down on Osiris' back, and both Jahiro and the samurai were shocked when he blocked the blow from behind.

"How is he deflecting our swings?!" Jahiro gasped. The samurai grunted as Osiris broke free from the blade lock and distanced himself from the two attackers. The samurai watched as Osiris' eyes began to glow as the realization set in.

"He is Alyrian. It runs through his veins!" The samurai said, gripping his blade two-handed and holding it in front of him as he locked eyes with Osiris.

Osiris raised his spadroons and beckoned the two men forth. "C'mon, then. Let's see who's the better swordsman. I've heard about you lot, they say Dyonian samurai are some of the best fighters in the world. Let's put that claim to the test!"

Jahiro and the samurai looked at one another, confused. They understood little to no Kurzan, so Osiris' words were nothing but gibberish to them. "Go, captain. Secure the Eye, Koga awaits below deck." The samurai nodded. "This one is mine."

Jahiro nodded. "May the empress empower you, Sojin."

The samurai, Sojin, nodded quickly to Jahiro as he departed, leaving the two to battle one another. He took a quick stock of his surroundings In the few minutes these pirates had been aboard the ship, they had caused utter havoc. Bodies were mounting on the main deck as the pirates slaughtered the ill-prepared merchant sailors. These men were not warriors, not like Sojin, or Renzo, or Koga, or the other samurai onboard. But they were Dyonian, and so he knew they would fight to the death regardless. "Let us see who the better warrior is, Alyrian pirate!"

Sojin launched himself at Osiris as the pirate came sprinting at him. The two fighters clashed blades for a moment before breaking away and attacking again. Blades swung as one tried to get an edge over the other. Sojin would strike high, while Osiris went low. Osiris landed a glancing blow on Sojin's shoulder, but his armor deflected the blow. He landed another, this time on the samurai's leg, then another on his arm. Each time, however, the riveted armor ate the blow, stopping each hit from lethally cutting Sojin.

Osiris had no such armor, however.

He suffered a cut to his shoulder and arm. One swipe even cut through his clothes to his chest. He couldn't afford to eat hits like the samurai, who would routinely let a blow strike his shoulder or body to get in close for a counter. Realizing this, Osiris feinted a strike, baiting Sojin and getting in close. A helmet protected the samurai's head, and a red mask resembling a scowling man covered his face. Osiris headbutted Sojin, surprising him and forcing him back. He smiled as he felt the energy inside him building and welling to the surface as the samurai recovered from the attack.

Osiris was bought a moment's reprieve as two pirates bumped into Sojin, and he cut them down as quickly as they approached. When he turned to face Osiris again, the pirate's eyes and tattoos glowed a ghostly blue-green.

What kind of Alyrian are you?

Sojin wondered. He had never seen an Alyrian pirate, though he knew that sometimes their kind employed Alyrians in their ranks as a fear tactic. An Alyrian was capable of unpredictable things. One never knew what magick they may have at their disposal. Yet he had not seen this one sling a single spell, mutter an incantation, or draw any marks on the ground that might be used for summoning. He was, as far as Sojin could tell, an ordinary pirate, albeit a bit quicker and sharper than the others. As Sojin watched, two other crewmen ran upon the pirate, and he killed them swiftly, spinning around and slashing the legs out from under one before nearly detaching the arm of the other in one swing.

A metallic roar echoed from behind him, like a gun's discharge.

Now is my time!

Sojin took that as his cue and gripped the handle of his sword, feeling his ancestors' will rush through him. If he were to die, he would do so, bringing this pirate down with him, this he promised. He sprinted, moving at twice his normal speed and bringing the blade down on Osiris, who barely had time to register the attack.

Osiris was forced to block the attack with both swords, and he felt them strain under the pressure of the katana.

If I keep this up, he's going to break my guard, and one of those swings is going to cleave through my collarbone.

Osiris thought with certainty.

These samurai were heavily armored and well-trained. If they weren't taken out, the deck boarding would be a failure. He watched as Stone approached, however, and saw his opportunity. He made eye contact with the approaching pirate. Stone had already dispatched one of the samurai, his smoking body lay just behind him as he came toward Osiris and Sojin.

Stone nodded, and Osiris broke the clash before throwing himself back and away from the samurai. Sojin raised his sword in a final strike against the now defenseless Osiris—and was enveloped in a gout of flame as a second metallic roar broke through the air. Osiris grinned in triumph as Sojin stumbled forward, and Osiris rose to his feet.

He brought both spadroons down on Sojin's shoulders, burying them deep into the openings around his collar. Sojin fell to his knees, flames licking off his back where he'd been shot. Osiris looked the samurai in his eyes as he planted a foot on his chest and pushed him off the blades. Blood spurted from the samurai's neck.

Sojin was slain.

"Thanks for the save, brother," Osiris said.

"Think nothin' of it. These bastards are tough, only me dragons seemed to be able to pierce that armor of theirs," Stone noted.

Osiris looked behind Stone, seeing another of the samurai approaching from behind in ambush.

"Stone!" he shouted, pushing the man out of the way, thinking fast. He ripped the flare gun Moary had given him from his sash and fired it at the Samurai. The flare struck him square in the chest and lit his armor aflame as the wooden and leather sections went up. He burned a fierce, luminescent red that illuminated the whole of the main deck and made everyone freeze momentarily.

Stone, realizing that Osiris had just saved his life, clapped him on the shoulder. "Smart thinkin'."

As the first shots from Azura rang out, Osiris nodded his agreement; smart indeed.

He turned his gaze to the doorway he'd seen Jahiro disappear into. "We need to find out where their captain went. My gold's on him being the one who'll lead us to the Eye of Atla."

Stone nodded. "Aye, let's go before those other samurai turn on us. The two looked around, seeing one samurai fighting Cage and another one going after Flint and Cutter. "They can handle 'em. Let's go!"

*****

"Keep coming! Send your best! Send your strongest! Send them all! The Dark Goddesses hunger! I will feed them your souls! Frelsi í dauðanum!" Cage howled the last words in Borran as the samurai approached him. Around him were the bodies of his last challengers, cut to pieces as offerings to the Dark Mother. She whispered her hunger into his ears like a siren song that filled his heart with bloodlust. He pointed an axe at the approaching samurai as the other Dyonians crowded around them, frightened by the savagery of the pirate but also in honor of the samurai who came to slay him.

"Kill him, Renzo! He has slain our kin for sport!" A man in the crowd, officer Yushi, shouted.

"It will be done. This pirate will feel the wrath of Dyona before he takes his last breath!" Renzo promised as he stood in front of Cage. He pulled out his katana, as well as his second blade, a tach—a blade similar to a katana but longer and more curved. "Pray to your gods, savage. You will be meeting them soon."

Cage spat on the deck as he readied himself for battle. His shirt had already been tattered from where others had grabbed or cut it, so he slammed his blades into the deck and tore the remainder of it off, exposing the myriad of scars and runic tattoos adorning his body. He was ready.

The two warriors looked at one another wordlessly before charging. Renzo dodged Cage's first swings before slicing his side and giving him another wound to add to his collection. Cage grunted, the pain barely even registering as he turned around to face him again.

"You are fast, honorable one, but speed can only get you so far," Cage complimented as they came in for another pass.

This time, Cage deflected the initial swings and kicked Renzo in the gut, knocking him back before swiping with the axes. The blades slashed across his chest armor, damaging it.

"He broke through the armor?! How?!" Yushi shouted in disbelief. It shouldn't have been possible for the pirate to cut through the samurai's armor, not with those axes. Yet Renzo bled, and Cage laughed at the shocked crowd.

"Armor cannot save you from me!" Cage clashed his axes together and charged at Renzo again.

Renzo ducked his head and leaned into his own charge, dragging his swords across the deck before swinging them upward at Cage. Cage stopped short, dipping away from the blades and swinging. The axes narrowly missed Renzo's faceguard, and he knew that if they struck, he would have lost his eyes— and much worse.

Steven Cage pressed the assault, swinging wildly at Renzo, who was forced to back away. A man in the crowd suffered a fatal blow to the head as Cage raged and chased after Renzo, who ran up several stairs on the foredeck before turning around and leaping at Cage. Cage hit the deck, was knocked down by the force, and narrowly avoided Renzo's blades coming down on his crotch. He kicked Renzo harshly in the head, knocking him back before rolling to his feet and charging again, barreling into the samurai before he could recover. Renzo hit the stairs again, and Cage ripped his helmet and mask from his head.

Cage growled like an animal and punched Renzo in the face, dropping his axes and brawling with the samurai, punching him again and again as Renzo reached for a hatchet, and Cage grabbed his wrist. Renzo punched Cage with his free hand and sent him stumbling back before he rose, hatchet in hand. He swung and whiffed. Cage elbowed him in the face before ripping the weapon from Renzo's hands and slamming him in the face with the flat of the hatchet head. Renzo sprawled on the deck, delirious from the blow.

"No! Honor-less filth! You will pay!" Yushi shouted, breaking through the crowd and picking up one of Renzo's discarded swords. He swung at Cage, slashing him across the back. Cage roared in anger as he turned around and knocked the blade from Yushi's hands.

"Fool! Die like the coward you are!" Cage spat as he sliced the hatchet across Yushi's face, killing him.

The crowd dispersed as another cannon shot rang out, splintering a yardarm of the Bounty and sending it crashing down onto the deck. Cage turned his attention back to Renzo, who was still reeling from the head injury.

"You fought well, samurai. Your ancestors are proud," Cage said, honestly. He had heard tales of the samurai of Dyona. Honorable, ferocious warriors who valued strength and discipline above all else. It was an honor to have fought one.

"Die well."

He pulled out his knife and thrust it under Renzo's chin, killing him instantly.

*****

Osiris and Stone stepped down the stairs into the compartment. The room was long and well-lit with lanterns but was almost entirely empty, aside from simple mats stacked in the corner, likely for the samurai who evidently slept in the room. Across the room, standing by the door, was Jahiro, who looked at the pirates in disgust.

"You bloodthirsty killers will not have the Eye of Atla," he said simply, knowing they would not be able to understand him.

The two looked at one another. "Right then, Dyonian. Open the door 'n we can finish this off quick, ay?" Stone said, stepping forward.

Osiris grabbed his shoulder, stopping him, then nodded to the unlit corner next to Jahiro. From behind a support beam stepped a figure. He wore armor reminiscent of the samurai from above but different. His was made almost entirely of metal, and he wore no helmet, just a blue, horned mask with a grinning demon's face carved into it. The demon's fangs were long, curving below and above its lips and giving it a sinister smile. Osiris believed it was a depiction of what the Dyonians called an 'oni.'

"This one's different," Stone said warily.

Osiris nodded. "Aye…I can feel it. This'll get ugly."

The samurai looked at Jahiro. "Captain, go above deck and rally the men to repel the invaders. I will handle these two."

Jahiro nodded. "Empress watch over you, Koga," and walked towards the pirates to leave.

Osiris and Stone pulled out their swords, barring Jahiro's path.

"Let the captain go, pirates. Your fight is with me, if you wish to have the Eye, that is," Koga said in heavily accented Kurzan, unsheathing his weapons. In one hand, he wielded a fist weapon with large, serrated claws on it. In the other, he held a blade almost as long as Osiris was tall. He sat the spine of it upon his shoulder spaulder.

Stone placed a hand on one of his holstered dragon guns. "Ugly, indeed."

The two let Jahiro pass, and he left the three to their duel. He cursed them as he left.

Osiris charged in first, sprinting towards Koga and dragging his spadroons across the floor, digging trails into the wood before he thrust them up at Koga. The samurai blocked both blades with his absurdly long katana, barely moving an inch from the impacts. Osiris' eyes went wide with shock.

Koga followed up with a claw slash that Osiris nearly evaded, catching him across the forearm. He hissed in pain as blood ran from his forearm, and Stone came to intervene, shooting at Koga with a pistol. The bullet ricocheted off the armor, and Koga turned his focus on him, charging at him. Stone sidestepped a vertical sword slash, then swung with his own blade. Koga dodged the swing as Osiris attempted to backstab him, missing entirely and bumping into Stone.

"Watch it!" Stone griped as the tip of the spadroon just missed him.

Osiris suddenly tackled Stone, saving him from a sweep that would have cut him in two. The two rolled away from each other on the floor as Koga sliced the sword down over and over, just missing his target with each cut. He stepped on Osiris' vest, pinning him to the floor as he raised his sword.

Stone slammed into him, knocking his head into a wall-mounted lantern and shattering it. It snuffed the flame, but Koga's mask protected his face from serious damage. Osiris got to his feet as Koga and Stone fought. Stone narrowly evades getting sliced, trying to find a way around the samurai's claw. Whenever he came close enough to bypass the reach of the katana, Koga would swing his claw.

Seeing an opening, Osiris broke up the two as he brought his swords down on Koga's claw arm. The metal protected it from being severed by the swords, but the force behind the blow still stunned him, making him drop the weapon. Stone saw the opening and bit his sword into Koga's other arm, cutting between the openings at an armor joint. Koga grunted in pain before shoulder-slamming Stone and stabbing him in the side with his blade.

Stone gasped, then howled in pain as the blade ripped out of his side, and he was left bleeding on the floor. He fell on his back and closed his eyes as the samurai closed in for the kill. Osiris charged at Koga, slashing at him again and again with his swords, but he shrugged off the blows. He grabbed Osiris by the throat and slammed him up against a wall as he brought his sword to bear. Osiris looked around him for anything to give him an edge and stopped on the busted lantern, briefly noting the pool of shadow it left in its wake. An idea formed in his head as he shifted out of the way of the Koga's slash. He swung the pummel of his sword into Koga's head, knocking him away and releasing his grip. Then, Osiris began systematically shattering each lantern and snuffing its flame as Koga chased after him. The two dueled as Osiris led the fight towards every lantern in the room, breaking it. Soon, there was but one lantern left, and the samurai paused, looking around the dark room.

"Clever pirate. But how will you kill what you can't see?" Koga asked.

Osiris grinned darkly as he shattered the last lantern and plunged the room into darkness. His eyes glowed as the Alyria in his body flooded into them and illuminated his vision, casting everything in a faint, turquoise hue and illuminating the dark room. The samurai inched across the room slowly, listening for his quarry. Osiris moved the injured Stone to one wall, hushing him quietly, pain twisting the man's face.

"I'm going to finish him," Osiris whispered.

"Use the dragon," Stone whispered back, handing him one.

Osiris nodded, checking that the gun was loaded, then tucking it partially beneath the sash of his pants as he crept away from Stone. Koga was on the far side of the room, searching. The samurai had found his claw.

His armor's too thick to shoot outright. I need to weaken it before I shoot him.

He remembered the grenade he'd stuffed in his pocket earlier and beamed. He knew exactly what to do next. He charged at Koga, knowing all too well that the samurai would hear his approach. He was right, Koga spun around immediately to face him and swung his sword. The blade missed the mark, and he swung wildly with his claw, slashing the air where he thought Osiris was. He was dangerously close to the mark. Osiris rolled out of the way and slashed behind Koga's leg, cutting him. The samurai fell to one knee, weapons still ready.

He realized then that his opponent was no ordinary man. "You are gifted, pirate? I should have known. I sensed something was off about you as soon as I saw you. Two can play this game, however!" Koga said, rising to his feet.

What are you…

Koga froze in place and listened, his ears hyper-focused. He heard creaking footsteps and pinpointed their direction and distance, waiting. As Osiris closed in, Koga lashed out, slashing him across the chest with his katana. Osiris gasped in surprise, falling back.

How did he see me?

Koga laughed. "I do not need my eyes to sense you, pirate. I have been trained to fight my enemy blind, deaf, and with an arm tied behind my back. The mongoose does not fear the serpent. Come forth and face me. Let steel decide our fates!"

X

OMEN

Hanover carefully filled the powder bags, covering his face with a tied-up cloth to filter out the lingering powder in the air. Moary told him that if enough of the stuff got into his lungs over a long enough period, it would give him a terrible cough that could kill him. He'd asked Moary how he learned that, and Moary told him how his mentor had died from the stuff.

"It's a curse all us gunners seem to succumb to, eventually. If it isn't an exploding cannon or an accident, it's the damned powder powering all of it that gets us. Ironic, really."

He shook the memory from his head as he loaded the last bag with powder and ran out of the room with an armful of them and ran up the stairs to the gun deck. He elbowed the door open, then began passing them out to the gun crews to load their cannons with.

"Just in time, laddie! Whole starboard side of the deck's fired her load!" Moary said, clapping him on the back.

"I learned from the best," Hanover said as he loaded a cannon with powder and then helped load a cannonball into the bore.

The ship had been taking shots from the starboard gun ports, aiming at the Bounty's sails and rudder. So far, not a single shot had struck the body of the ship, and the Bounty sat idle. Taken by surprise, her captain and crew were too busy trying to repel the boarders to sail. Now that her sails were in tatters, however, it didn't matter. She was dead in the water.

"Are all crews on the starboard ports ready?" Moary asked aloud. He looked down at the side of the gun deck, checking the sergeants in charge of the guns. They gave the affirmative, and he nodded.

"Rolling fire!"

Hanover covered his ears with his hands and closed his eyes as the concussive boom of over twenty cannons shook the ship and deafened the room, rolling out over ten thunderous seconds. His ears rang, and he felt nauseous, his organs having jostled in place from the vibrations of the cannons. Moary laughed loudly as he patted him on the back, but Hanover couldn't hear it. All he could hear was the ringing.

"Ye get used to it. Well, ye start ta go deaf, 'n so ye can't hear it—but ye get used to it! Hahahaha!" Moary laughed at his own joke.

*****

Koga moved like a diving hawk, striking at Osiris over and over. He struck high, he struck low, from the left, the right, and every angle in between. Each blow was harsher than the last. Though he couldn't see, he countered every maneuver that Osiris made against him. Koga's right leg was cut open, but the injury barely even gave him pause.

Osiris panted. He was losing energy, and his enemy didn't even seem to be phased. This samurai was much tougher than the other one he'd fought, and without Stone to tip the scale, he was on his own. The samurai had more armor than him, was a more seasoned fighter than him, and had a longer reach than him. He thumbed the handle of the dragon gun.

This is it. If this fails, then he'll kill me before I can reload it.

He holstered a sword and pulled his grenade from his pocket. He threw the other sword across the room, and it made a loud clang as it struck a lantern and hit the floor. Koga charged at the sound, taking the bait. He threw the unlit grenade, and it skidded across the deck toward Koga. Then he pulled out a pistol from his bandolier as Koga turned and listened to the sound of the grenade. Osiris fired at it just as Koga attempted to dive away, and the explosion rocked the cabin, deafening the occupants, releasing a momentary flash of light, and blowing a hole through the floor where it detonated.

Koga groaned. The shrapnel from the blast had punched through his armor and mask. He struggled to reach his feet as Osiris closed in on him and pulled out his dragon gun.

"You have killed me, but you have not won. You hold a trigger, but you are not the one behind the gun. You have lit a bomb, pirate, but you all are too blind to see it."

Osiris raised a brow, confused by the samurai's riddle. It didn't matter, though.

"You finished?" Osiris asked.

"See you in Jigoku," Koga said.

BOOM!

A flash of flame and an explosion of shrapnel enveloped the wounded samurai, and he fell to the ground, his head blown apart by the dragon gun.

*****

As Azura approached the immobile Empress' Bounty, Morgan and Huasca stood ready to lead the secondary boarding party aboard the deck. Standing ready by the chase guns, Yager watched on, disgruntled but silent. The two paid him no mind as the remainder of the secondary boarding party gathered.

"We're nearly upon her, cap'n," Ryker said.

Sarkad was ordering the remaining pirates on deck as they drew the sails to decrease speed.

"Very good, Mr. Ryker," Huasca nodded. He leaned over to Morgan. "He is fuming with rage. Why do we entertain him still?"

Morgan checked his guns as he cast a look over in Yager's direction, who was leaning against a top gun, smoking a cigarette. He was looking at the approaching Bounty. Morgan could see the anger in his eyes.

"We do not kill our own if we can avoid it. We're better than that," Morgan responded.

"He tried to mutiny, captain. Better men have been executed for less!" Huasca said, trying to keep his voice low.

The two watched as the men filed in, a steady group of thirty men aligning behind them. The Bounty was only a few dozen yards away now. The sound of gunfire and sword fighting was getting louder.

"As did Mr. Stone. He kept his position and has proved quite handy still," Morgan replied.

"Reece Stone is a natural-born sailor. His skills easily vouch for him, and most importantly, he backed down when you spoke with him."

"Perhaps Yager would have done the same. Unfortunately, that night, he did not have the opportunity."

"That is his fault, *not* ours," Huasca insisted.

"Innocent until proven guilty. We need to focus on surviving this battle. He has done no ill since then, though he fumes like a petulant child. Unless you've any proof to back your claim?" Morgan asked.

Huasca sighed and ran a hand across his bald scalp. "There are no leads. We have no clue who this turncoat is, captain."

Morgan sighed as several men lowered the boarding planks. "To arms!"

Morgan, Huasca, and thirty men charged across the gangplanks.

*****

"Kill the bastard!" Cutter shouted as the samurai cut through two men to get at him. Flint was kneeling at the top of the stairs behind him, lining up a shot. He ducked out of the way as the samurai pulled a pistol, fired at the would-be sniper, then swung his katana at Cutter, who deflected it. He'd already fired his blunderbuss and didn't have the time or the space to refill it. Sword swipes did fuck all, and the bastard was cutting men down left and right. Ever since their captain came back on the deck, the Dyonians had been putting up an organized retaliation, sending men to encircle the pirates, but it had all come crumbling down around them as the cannon fire from Azura brought down a mast, causing utter chaos on the deck. Now, instead of being encircled, the last remaining samurai was hunting them.

"KILL HIM NOW!" Cutter shouted at the top of his lungs as the samurai slowly overpowered him.

He gazed up into the facemask of his killer, taking notice of the smiling mask he was wearing, and gritted his teeth as he fought with all his might not to be cut in half. He'd already sustained a slash to his right arm, so it was struggling to hold its own weight.

"Say goodbye, asshole," Flint said, firing at the samurai.

The bullet rattled in the rifle barrel and went off the mark, glancing off the side of his helmet rather than striking him square in the head as intended. The samurai looked up at Flint, and Cutter used the opportunity to push him off him.

"Fuck! Misfire!" Flint cursed loudly.

Cutter panted, exhausted from the fighting. "Of all the times you had to be a bad shot, why'd it have to be now, Flint?" he asked. The samurai was occupied by a group of pirates trying to wrestle him to the ground, but already he was fighting them off.

"How the hell is he still going?!" Cutter asked. He'd been fighting for nearly ten minutes now. His body was worn out, his adrenaline was flagging, and he knew that if he didn't take a break soon, he would fall out on the deck.

The samurai killed the last of his attackers and slowly made his way towards Flint and Cutter. "Almost got the rifle loaded! Keep him busy!" Flint instructed.

Cutter gave Flint a smoldering look. "When we die, I'm beating your ass in Sheolhenna."

Cutter rose to his feet, legs unsteady. "Come here 'n get me, you tenacious cunt."

Just as he prepared himself for what was sure to be a grizzly end, an explosion of gunfire drew their attention as a horde of pirates landed on the deck and reinforced the flagging boarding party. Captain Morgan jumped off the gangplank and sighted them, charging across the deck as Huasca backed him. The Xallan pirate pulled out a sickle-shaped sword and began slashing men left and right as Morgan pushed through several, cutting them down with his cutlass. The samurai ignored Cutter and faced Morgan, both hands on his blade.

Morgan wasted no time, clashing with the samurai with one arm and firing into his gut with his pistol in the other. The gun let out a thunderous bang as it punched clean through the samurai's armor and left a gaping hole in his back. He fell to the ground as Morgan approached the exhausted officers.

"Oh thank fuck…" Cutter sighed in relief.

He had evaded death yet again.

*****

It was cold.

Cold as the grave.

"Ye feel that?" Osiris held out a trembling hand. "It's freezing in here. Like all the energy's been sucked out."

Stone nodded. "Aye, I feel it too. Look at the walls."

Osiris looked around, noticing that the walls had been painted with Dyonian word characters. He couldn't read any of it, however. The very lanterns that lit the room seemed to shrink from what sat in its center. A black chest sat in the middle of a circle chalked onto the ground.

"I'm no magister, but I know a warding circle when I see one, Stone," Osiris said. Some of the storybooks Huasca had him read as a child spoke of such things. Warding circles were made for one thing and one thing only: to keep something trapped inside.

"What were they tryin' to contain, I wonder?" Stone asked, stepping closer and stopping at the edge of the circle. His gut and every fiber of his being warned him not to step over its threshold.

Osiris leaned against a support beam. "I think we both know the answer to that."

Stone nodded mirthlessly. That they did.

"*...you are about to ignite a bomb, and you're too blind to see it...*" Koga's words echoed in their minds. What was it that they were about to bring aboard their ship?

"I got a right terrible feelin' about this, Siris," Stone confessed, folding his arms.

"You 'n me both, mate. This stinks like halghoul shit."

Osiris took a deep breath and crossed the threshold of the warding circle. He felt a drop in his gut as he placed a hand on the chest. The wood that comprised it was black, as was the metal that reinforced it. It blended with the shadows of the room and sat in stark contrast to the white chalk of the warding circle surrounding it.

"Come on. We've got to move it..."

Stone muttered a prayer to himself, making a nine-pointed star on his chest. "Hermalla, have mercy for what I'm about to do." He doubted the goddess of priests and mercy gave much of a fuck about a murdering, marauding bastard like himself. But he still held out hope.

"Let's do this, then."

*****

"Death before dishonor!" Jahiro shouted as his men charged at the resurging pirates. He watched as their captain boarded the ship and coordinated his men's slaughter. The two locked eyes, and Jahiro pointed his blade at him in a challenge. The pirate captain nodded and pushed his men aside as the two confronted one another.

Morgan appraised the merchant ship's captain. He was a dignified and hard man. He could see blood on the man's blade and knew that he did not shy from pitched battle. He carried a short katana blade as well as a peculiar weapon that looked like a metal stake but severely dulled at the tip and fitted with a hand grip. Morgan tried to recall the last time he'd seen someone wield one of those. A yawara, he believed it was called, typically used for close-quarters combat. He wondered then if this captain had martial skills, as many Dyonians he'd fought over the years had.

"He does not wish to fight you. He knows that he cannot win." Abbal said telepathically.

"Then he will die as foolish as he lived," Morgan responded in kind.

"You have invaded my ship. You have slaughtered my men, and you have slain the honorable men sent to protect us. I have been raided by pirates before, but never ones so cold, callous, and savage as you! If I am to die today, let it be defending the people of Hera from a villain!" Jahiro pointed to the flag billowing over the Azura. "I know that flag! They call you the Immortal Pirate, Captain Morgan! They spoke of you as a legend, a dangerous man, but never cruel! You kill these men! You do not offer quarter! You do not offer mercy! All you offer is bloodshed! I did not know your pirate code was a code of butchery!"

Morgan looked at Jahiro. He could not understand the words he said, but he knew that they were spirited. "What does he say?" he asked the amulet aloud.

"In essence, he says that you have lost your way. That instead of giving them quarter, you have chosen to butcher them. He says you defile the pirate code," Abbal translated.

Morgan looked around at the dead and dying littering the deck. He saw Steven Cage leaning against a railing, shirtless and drenched in blood, wiping his axes clean with the shirt of a dead man. Though he couldn't concede it, the man was right. This was a wholesale slaughter, and the Emperor made sure that he was the one with blood on his hands.

"I do this not because I desire to. We kill not for sport. The gun that is pressed against our backs demands that we leave no survivors, and I will not sacrifice my men for yours. I am sorry, captain. I am sure that you are an honorable and worthy man. I guess the Stars will have to judge me for what I do this day, as they judge me for every sin I commit in the name of freedom."

Morgan pulled out Blade Rose, the cutlass sword he'd named after his wife, as well as Bullet Rose. He handed Bullet Rose to Huasca, who stood beside him and folded an arm behind him. If he were to kill this man, he would do it with honor.

"Let what is to be done next be done with some semblance of honor..." Morgan nodded.

Jahiro shook his head in disgust and dropped his yawara, holding his katana in both hands.

The two captains circled one another, then stepped forward to joust. Their blades crossed, and Morgan dodged each blow that Jahiro made for his body. He gauged his opponent, judging his speed and reflexes. Jahiro left little opening for a counter. Morgan pressed on him, slapping away several light blows before thrusting his cutlass at Jahiro, who took a light nick to the shoulder but was otherwise unphased.

Jahiro countered, attempting to disarm Morgan several times in succession, but Morgan simply backed away and evaded the blows.

The crowd of onlookers grew as the fighting slowed. The combatants were tired, the battle having carried on for over fifteen minutes now. They watched each other but also watched their captains' duel. They knew that the winner would decide the fate of the battle.

Morgan sidestepped a sweep from Jahiro but was caught by a backhand swipe and suffered a cut on his arm, slicing open his coat and bleeding him a bit. He smiled. His first blood.

Jahiro pressed his advantage, slashing and thrusting, forcing Morgan back toward the stairs leading to the steering deck. Morgan pivoted and ran up several stairs as Jahiro gave chase—and fell for the bait. Morgan spun back around and slashed at Jahiro in rapid succession, nearly causing the man to fall backward off the stairs. Jahiro pivoted and backed off, realizing he now had the low ground. Morgan leaped off the stairs and plunged his sword down, breaking Jahiro's guard and sending him stumbling backward. Jahiro deflected three near-fatal blows before Morgan feinted a throat slice and swept at Jahiro's legs, slashing them.

Jahiro cried out in pain, blood leaking from his cut shins, and Morgan disarmed him, knocking the katana from his hands and pressing the tip of the cutlass against Jahiro's throat.

The two looked at one another. The battle was decided. Morgan thought to compliment the man's swordsmanship but didn't get the opportunity.

Jahiro thrust his throat forward, spearing it on the end of Blade Rose, then pulling away violently, slicing his own throat open. He gurgled blood and looked at the stunned men standing around him.

"Death before dishonor; do what must be done…"

He sputtered those last words as he fell to the deck in a pool of blood and asphyxiated.

Morgan stood, stunned by the suicidal gesture. He looked around as the crew of the Empress' Bounty followed their captain's lead. Scores of the remaining crew raised their weapons and slit their own throats or plunged their blades into their own stomachs.

They were committing mass suicide.

XI

THE PLUNDERED BOUNTY

Morgan walked the deck. Bodies littered almost every foot of it. He sighed and pulled his pipe from his pocket, lighting it.

"Any stragglers, finish them quickly. Gentlemen, as you have borne the scars of this battle, you are owed first prizes. Take what you want from this deck. Leave the treasures below for the quartermaster to sort and distribute. Fan out but be careful. There could still be traps aboard this ship," he ordered.

"Aye aye, cap'n!" They shouted in agreement as they set about finding their prizes.

Morgan turned and holstered his gun after Huasca handed it back to him. "You fought well," he applauded.

Morgan shook his head. "I fought someone who had no intention of winning. He knew the score, he knew his odds, he just wanted to save his men from dishonor."

Huasca nodded. "True. The captain had no intention of winning that duel. These men, they fought hard, but they are not fighters; they are merchants and workers."

"Makes you wonder, then, why no one else came and got them," Morgan noted as he smoked.

"If samurai were aboard this ship, then it is very likely that the empress would have ensured that false information and confusion was spread about their whereabouts. False records of their route and destination, forged documentation of their cargo—anything to throw a potential informant off their trail."

"Then how did Emperor Varryn-fucking-Kurza manage to get hold of it? Are his spies so omniscient that they could read the minds of misinformed sailors? Hell, I wonder if these men even knew where their true heading was."

"What are you suggesting?" Huasca asked, a knowing look in his eyes.

"The same thing you probably suspect. The information was fed to the Emperor's spies. They wanted this ship to be found, else we would have never heard of it."

"But why?" Huasca asked. "I cannot understand *why*."

Morgan threw up his arms. "That, I still can't figure out."

"Perhaps the captain's logbooks will shed light," Huasca offered. "Come."

The two men made their way toward the aft of the ship and the captain's quarters. Morgan paused as he saw a dying man on the deck before him. The man was feigning death but couldn't help but take in a breath when Morgan stepped on his hand. The man looked up, face smeared with blood and eyes pleading for life. It was Dozu, the last remaining officer of the Empress' Bounty.

Morgan frowned. He didn't want to do this.

"Another sin to a mountain of sins."

Abbal said, indifferent.

Morgan pulled his gun and wordlessly shot the man's head before holstering it again and carrying on his way. A trail of smoke followed him.

*****

As Morgan and Huasca exited the captain's cabin, documents and maps in hand, Osiris and Stone came topside, a black chest in toe.

"This is it…" Abbal said.

"So, it would seem," Morgan responded.

The four pirates converged, Morgan and Huasca nodding to Osiris and Stone. The quartermaster and second mate were drenched in blood and sweating in exhaustion. They looked around the corpse-littered deck. In the lantern lights illuminating the deck, the corpses cast ugly shadows. As long as they lived, the stench of death would never cease to disgust them.

"I take it we won, ay?" Stone asked.

"After their leader killed himself on my blade, the rest followed suit," Morgan answered, running a hand over the chest and stopping at the keyhole. "And the key?"

"Dunno, the samurai leader only had the key to the door. We assumed the key for the chest was with the captain," Osiris said.

Morgan nodded slowly. It made as much sense as any.

Huasca walked over to the body of Jahiro and gently checked it for a key. He found it hanging around his neck, tucked beneath his clothes. He closed the dead man's defiant eyes as he lifted it from him. "I found it."

He handed it to Morgan, who looked it over before fitting it into the keyhole as Flint, Cutter, and Steven Cage approached, having pilfered what they wanted from the dead.

Morgan pocketed his pipe, then crouched in front of the chest and ran a hand over the top of it. He noticed the blood on his hand and gazed at it thoughtfully. It was shaking. He clutched his wrist before turning the key and clicking open the lock. He flung open the chest. The dimly lit deck was bathed with piercing, bright purple light. Morgan covered his eyes, as did the other officers gathered around him and the chest.

Everyone who was above deck, whether on the Empress' Bounty or Azura, momentarily paused and looked toward the light. Yager, having moved from his perch on the foredeck, paused and gazed at it, a fresh cigarette falling from his lips. Hanover, who had just come above deck, stumbled to the top of the stairs coming up from the first gun deck and stared in fascination at the blinding light.

Everyone was still. Silent, for but a moment.

Morgan placed a hand upon the source of the light. A bright purple orb the size of a fist. As he raised it aloft, he exhaled the smoke he'd been holding in his lungs and felt himself leaving his own body. His mind traveled back to a vivid memory, one that he had long since tried to forget…

*****

"How could you?!"

A man asked, his hand clutching Morgan's wrist. Morgan gazed into his tortured eyes. The eyes of an old friend. Ones that he had gazed upon the horrors of war with, now looking back at him in fear.

"I trusted you—this is how you repay me?!"

They stood on a mountain of gold and treasure big enough to climb on, but it was crumbling around them as the stalactites of the cavern ceiling crashed down around them, and men fled in panic, diving into the water and swimming towards the entrance of the cave. Morgan turned to leave, but the hand gripped tighter.

"Wait!" The man shouted as Morgan tore his hand free and fled down the slopes of gold. "Don't leave me here, please! Not here!" the man called after him, pleading.

Morgan ignored him, diving into the water and swimming toward the cave mouth, narrowly escaping being crushed and skewered by the collapsing cavern.

"Please! PLEAAASE!!!"

The man howled a rage-filled howl that died into a sob of defeat.

The vision ended.

*****

"Felix!" Morgan shouted as he came to.

Huasca was shaking his shoulder as the other officers crowded around him.

Why am I on the floor?

Morgan pondered as they helped him to his feet. He realized he was gasping for air, and a cold sweat had covered his skin. He threw the Eye of Atla back into its chest and slammed it shut.

"Captain, are you—" Huasca began.

"This is it. This is the Eye. We have what we came for. Let's load the cargo onto Azura and get out of here," Morgan said, cutting Huasca off and collecting himself. "Grab the documents. We need to see what the captain logged prior to our boarding. See if we can't find more trade routes to attack after our business with the Emperor is concluded."

Morgan didn't give anyone any time to respond as he grabbed hold of a side of the chest and looked at Osiris, who grabbed the other side. The two men carried the chest back to Azura as the others prepared for departure.

"What just happened?" Cutter asked.

"Not sure. Maybe nothin', maybe somethin'," Stone responded non-committally. "Flint, Cutter, take some men down below 'n check out what our dearly departed friends left us."

The duo looked at one another and shrugged. "Aye, sir," he said as he left.

Stone walked over to Steven Cage, who was tying a tourniquet around one of his wounds, ignoring the gash in his side and the ugly slice through his back.

"Aeradin's breath, ye look like shite, Cage. How do ye feel?" Stone asked rhetorically.

Steven Cage laughed loudly as he tied the tourniquet taught around his leg. "I am living, and my enemies are dead. So, I am doing well, Mr. Stone," he replied in his Borran-accented kurzan. "Though I will be having an unpleasant session with the sawbones and his tools, I fear."

Stone winced, feeling the stab wound in his own side. He knew it would need cleansing—and that would hurt worse than getting the wound in the first place.

"Aye, I know the feelin'. Claude's gonna have me howlin' for me mother by midday."

Cage chuckled, much lower now, and picked up his axes, having discarded them on the deck to dress his wound.

"Ye saw it, then? The Dyonians killin' themselves?"

Cage nodded, sheathing his axes and then digging a finger into his ear to pull out the wax. "Aye, I did, yes. Quite the spectacle, that," he said indifferently.

"'N it didn't bother ye at all? Everyone else seems right shook about it," Stone noted, a bit unsettled.

Cage shrugged. "I am Valkar, Reece Stone. In my culture, we enslave those we pillage, and we sometimes skin their warriors alive in front of the enslaved to demoralize them. When I was a little barn, my far took me out to watch my older brødre beat each other to shit, practicing for raiding. If I cried or complained, I was beaten just the same. I learned from a very young age that life is cruel. The strong will always prevail over the weak, and the weak will always be beholden to de strong. So no, watching those men kill themselves rather than fight bloodthirsty pirates did not phase me."

Cage looked Stone directly in the eyes, his expression calm and unconcerned. "The only part that upset me was that I did not get to offer their souls to the Dark Mother!" he laughed at that as though he'd heard the funniest joke in the world. "But there will be many more battles yet. The Mother will have her blood!"

Stone nodded. There were few people he'd met in his life who were more violent and desensitized than the Valkar. Steven Cage, while he was his brother in black, was more savage animal than man. He couldn't help but wonder what it said about him that he called such a demon-in-the-flesh a brother. He pushed the thought from his mind and went below deck.

*****

Morgan and Osiris opened the door to the spare compartment and dropped the chest inside. The men stood a moment, collecting their breaths.

"Ye saw somethin' when you picked up that glass ball, didn't you, cap'n?" Osiris asked as he leaned against the doorframe.

Morgan caught his breath and wiped the sweat from his brow. Was it really that obvious, or did Osiris know how to read people? He supposed it was both.

"Of a sort, aye," he replied, neutral.

"Was it bad?"

"Why do you ask, second mate?"

Osiris shrugged. "I've never seen you look so shaken before, and I've been sailing with you for nigh on ten years. I've seen you fight men, I've seen you fight monsters, I've seen you battle the sea itself—and I don't think I've ever even seen you shed a tear in nearly ten years. Just a few minutes ago, you looked like you saw death. I could feel the dread weeping out your pores, even without the Alyria runnin' through me."

Morgan was taken aback. Osiris was rarely so candid. Honestly, it seemed as though he was disconnected from everyone around him most of the time. And in all of thirty seconds, he'd just dissected Morgan's thoughts and emotions.

"Ye can be honest with me, cap'n. Ye know I won't tell a soul. Not Huasca, not Stone, not the boy—nobody. What in Sheolhenna have we just brought on our ship?"

Morgan turned and looked him in the eyes. "Something more dangerous than anything we've ever faced. Something that I can't protect any of you from." He placed a hand on Osiris' shoulder. The shoulder was hard as a rock. "I will need your skills more than ever on this voyage, Siris. I see a bad moon rising, and I need a sentinel to guard the men against it."

Osiris held his gaze for several tense moments before nodding. What was he hiding? "Aye, cap'n."

Morgan nodded and walked a few feet down the hall before turning his head. "We'll discuss this further later. Right now, I…need to collect my thoughts," he said and walked off.

Osiris stayed in the doorframe for a few moments, looking at the black chest. He could *feel* that it was off.

What the fuck does the Emperor want with you?

He shut the door.

*****

As Azura departed from the cove, she left the Empress' Bounty with a final parting gift. Several grenades were wrapped around her mainmast in a chain, and Flint fired at them, detonating the explosives and starting a fire aboard the ship. The Bounty and her dead occupants were slowly consumed by flames, illuminating the cove she rested in as Azura sailed away several tons heavier with gold and provisions.

The men stood and watched as she faded around a bend, and some of them cheered at their successful hunt. But most were silent. Like the derelict, they had left part of themselves behind on that sinking vessel. Over two dozen men lost their lives aboard it, and though they had robbed it of its riches, it felt as though its ghost would haunt them.

"Ye feel that?" Osiris asked Hanover as the crowd dispersed.

Hanover blinked, his eyes still searching for the Bounty, and his ears still shot from the cannon fire. "Feel what?" he asked after a silence.

"The air… it feels even heavier now than it did before," Osiris noted, looking around the ship and noticing how quiet it had become. Normally, they'd all be cheering and celebrating right now.

Hanover cocked his head, looking around as well. "I suppose so."

"Suppose so? You're normally entuned with these things," Osiris said.

"Entuned?" Hanover asked.

"You hard of hearing?"

"Well, my ears *are* still ringing."

Osiris dragged a hand down his face.

"You know what I meant."

"You asked if I was hard of hearing, and I responded that I am, in fact, hard of hearing at the moment, yes," Hanover deadpanned.

"The fuck is spoiling your milk?"

He was getting irritated, now.

"Well, it could be the fact that I was, once again, stuck with powder duty. The fact that everyone still treats me like a child, and several men have approached me accusing me of treachery, so now I have that mark upon me. A great many things, Siris. It could be a great many things," Hanover listed off on his fingers. His expression was stoic.

"Well, boy, you *are* the youngest on this ship, add to that you have almost no experience as a seaman, let alone as a pirate—and we're in this mess because you nodded off on your duties—and well, I think ye can see where the issue might have arisen."

"Do you think it too? That I'm a traitor? That I wanted this to happen?!" Hanover accused, his voice rising.

"As a matter of fact, I don't, surprisingly."

"Well, then, what do you want from me?!" Hanover shouted.

Osiris scowled and grabbed him by the shoulder, slamming him up against the railing and fixing him with a stare that could curdle milk. "What do I want from you? Well, for starters, I want you to stop whining like a pissy little bitch because people are holding ye accountable for your actions! For two, I want ye to stop coming to me to be your only friend, then throwing a fit when I tell ye the shit you don't want to hear! And I want ye to finally get it through your thick little skull that this life we live—I live—the men who *died* today lived—isn't a fucking game!" Osiris growled, garnering the attention of the others on the deck. His eyes had turned, now blazing with turquoise light.

Hanover sat pinned against the mast, eyes wide in some marriage of fear and hurt. "I…I understand—"

"Do you?! Because where I'm standing, all I've seen in you in six months since you first set foot on this ship is a child trying to play pirate!"

"I am a pirate—"

"You are a **boy**! Barely eighteen summers have you seen and not yet one of them spent at sea—and you believe yourself worthy to call yourself *pirate*?! Do you even know what that word means? Do ye know that it means death when uttered in the company of the wrong people?" Osiris shouted, his tone harsh and passionate.

He pushed Hanover away and growled, kicking a barrel. "I've spent my whole *life* as a pirate, boy! I didn't get to choose! So why the *fuck* are you wasting yours?!"

Hanover backed away, stumbling backward and falling over before running below deck.

Osiris watched him go, a grimace of anger and disgust plain on his face. He looked around the deck, fuming. He exhaled a shudder of emotion and walked the opposite direction, toward the crow's nest.

I see a bad moon rising, and I need a sentinel to guard the men against it.

He took his anger, his confusion, and his concern and stuffed it back down inside the bottomless chest he stored his heart and emotions in. And as he hunkered down atop the crow's nest, high above the ship and far away from people, he watched the horizon.

A sentinel.

That was what was needed, and that was what he would be. He wondered what the word meant. He wondered why he felt it in the depths of his soul, like a forgotten piece of a puzzle. Then, as he drained a bottle of rum he'd stowed in his pocket, he wondered why he ever cared in the first place.

*****

In the spare room of the belly of Azura, the black chest sat in darkness. It was one with the shadows. But every shadow needed a figure to cast it. Every puppet needs a master to control it, whose pain it can pantomime in silence. Disembodied voices broke that silence, whispering and muttering to themselves as the air in the small room turned electric.

The chest quaked slightly, and its lock clicked open. The lid of the chest creaked wide like the jaws of an alligator waiting for its prey. Then, a flash of light and a zap of energy exited it, phasing through the door and the walls of the ship as something sinister began to unfold. The bolt of purple energy arched like lightning streaks into the blackness of the midnight sea and traveled far toward its destination, deep within its treacherous depths…

XII

BAD MOON RISING

"In this world, there is no shortage of evil men. Men—and women who prey upon the weak and the misfortunate because it suits them. There are some things, however, for which even evil men fear. Beings so vile that the coldest winds do not blow their way, for fear of their ire…" – Thaddeus Mora, When the Cold Winds Blow

Far away from the Azura in a cold stretch of the Amaranthine Ocean, a schooner ship trailed beneath a full moon and a cloudless sky. The schooner, Ruby's Prize, was a small vessel with only a few cannons to point with and a modest crew of forty men to man them and navigate. A few of them were holding watch as their brothers and captain slept, meandering about the ship in lax patrols, chatting amongst themselves in earnest.

Two of them, Ricken and Baker, were walking the ship and doing just that. The two carried unlit torches with them, the moon's light easily illuminating their path. "It's been almost a month since we last touched land. 'Fore too long, we'll be back in Livera," Ricken said eagerly.

"Thank the fuckin' Stars for that. Tired of drinkin' rum 'n eatin' bread hard as a damned rock. I need real food 'n real drink real fuckin' quick before I lose my mind and put a bullet in someone!" Baker groaned.

"You're preachin' to the converted, mate. My knuckles still hurt from that scuff with Bran the other day," Ricken said as he shivered and pulled his fur coat tight around himself. "Cold as a witch's tit tonight. Can't wait to get to warm waters. No man should have to huddle together with twelve other men to keep warm through the night."

"Amen to that. The cold is enough to drive a man mad. Makes me wanker freeze when I have to take a piss—speakin' of which, walk a piece, I've gotta spring one over the side," Baker said as he stopped at the portside railing and fished in his pants.

"Aye. Try not to piss all over yourself again—the wind'll freeze it on ye within the hour."

"It was the wind, ye bastard. Now shove off!"

Ricken cackled and kept walking as Baker let loose.

As the pirate began to release his bladder, he took notice of the subtle change taking over the moon. Its color, once pale blue, had shifted to bright red. The color deepened to a blood-red intensity by the time his stream ran dry. Beneath him in the watery depths, clusters of bubbles rose to the surface as something began to surface. He happened to look down and watched as the bubbles rose from the night-blackened depths of the sea. He squinted his eyes.

What is that down there? It looks like…no…couldn't be.

A long pole shot up from the rising froth of bubbles, and following it was a blank-faced, blindfolded, naked woman made of gold, with her arms clasped around herself and her body chained and mounted to the nose of a ship that rose up from the depths. The water seemed to boil as the ship rose. The great vessel, much, much larger than the tiny schooner, Ruby's Prize, righted itself on the water, shadowing the ship with its vast size.

Baker stood frozen in disbelief, pants still open as the Ruby's Prize rocked from the waves caused by the mysterious ship's appearance. He stumbled and fell back, grabbing hold of the railing to avoid being tossed from his feet as the schooner shook, bobbing back and forth for several moments before calming.

"By the fucking Stars and the Dead Sea Gods, what the fuck is that?!" Ricken shouted as he came back around.

He looked at Baker. His form was obscured in shadow, only his rough outline could be seen in the shadow of the ship, and he was silent. Ricken raised the lantern he'd been carrying and lit it with a match, illuminating Baker's face, who was gazing at him now. His face was twisted in a mix of disbelief and fear.

Ricken jumped in place and cursed, "Angydra's breath!"

Baker blinked, his face returning to normal as he looked at the ship in front of them. He could see the gun ports all along its side and prayed to whatever god would listen—living or dead—that they did not flip open.

"Where…where in Sheolhenna did this thing come from?" Ricken asked.

Baker shook his head in disbelief. "I-i-it came right outta the f-fuckin' sea, Ricken! Shot up like a breachin' whale!"

"Shot up outta the sea? Ye smokin' hemestra in yer cigarettes again, mate? That ain't possible," Ricken shook his head.

"As the day I was born 'n on my mother's fuckin' grave, it did! I can scarce believe it but it did!" Baker clutched a shaking hand on Ricken's shoulder. "We gotta tell the cap'n, we gotta—"

Just as he was about to finish his words, the alarm bells began to ring across the deck as the other sentries saw the ship and alerted one another. The door to the captain's cabin swung open, and he bolted out, lantern in hand.

"What in the fuck? All hands-on deck! We've got a damn galleon or ship-of-the-line or summing off port! Ready for boarding!" The captain, a weasel-like man named Amry, shouted in his nasal voice. "Officers Kemper and Temper, rally the men for battle!"

The officers, who rushed up the stairs toward his quarters, nodded and ran back down, yelling at the men as they went. "Arm yourselves! We don't know what we're up against!"

*****

As the seconds ticked by, it became evident that nobody was on the mystery ship. No warnings were called, no flags were raised, and not even a footstep could be heard from its decks. Realizing the ship was derelict, the crew of Ruby's Prize threw up grappling lines and set up ladders onto the massive ship so that all could board it. Then, they began to check through it, room by room, deck by deck…

Baker kicked open a door, lantern in hand, and aimed his flintlock inside. It didn't take long for him to realize nobody was inside.

"Clear!" he called out loud enough for all on the deck to hear, then walked in and looked around the room, taking note of its condition, despite it being water-logged.

The damn thing was spotless. Damp, but spotless. No coral, or seaweed, or even barnacles were in it. Not a crab—nothing. It was perfectly clean. But how?

"How is a ship that was waterlogged for Stars know how long, in this good of condition?" Ricken asked.

"Dunno, was wonderin' the same thing. Seems odd, donnit?" Baker replied, scratching his chin.

As the two men walked back out onto the deck from the empty cabin, they looked out over the deck. The ship's wood was black, perhaps ebonwood or some other dark lumber. Its trim, however, was gold. Everything was lined with it. The railing toppers, the clasps holding the lines in place, the edgings around the ship itself. The bowsprit was made of solid gold, as was the statue that sat

117

beneath it. Even the shrouds, which were made of rope on every ship he'd ever seen, were made of golden chains. To the eyes of the pirates, it was enchanting. And in the light of the blood moon, everything glittered and shined with a haunting beauty.

Across the deck from Ricken and Baker, Captain Amry and the two officers, Kemper, and Temper, opened the doors to the captain's cabin. As they headed into the cabin, they paused in appreciation of its grandeur. It was a large room, and the light of the blood moon poured in from outside, framed by the cabin's large, sectioned window bay. The walls were lined with bookshelves and artwork, pieces depicting people of some import, clearly, judging by their dress and the fact that a portrait was even made of them in the first place. The middle of the room had a large, gold-furnished map table with gold measurement and navigation tools and a large map depicting much of the known world. From the Star Ocean to the far west of the Kurzan Empire, to the edge of northern straits, to the Sai'Haluud Imperium to the far east, and the Southern Ocean to the far south, beneath the Xallan Mercantile Empire.

"Nice map. Didn't know they made 'em this big," Kemper noted as they stood around the table.

"Look at these. They've got trade routes on them," Amry said, looking over several maps at the edge of the table.

Most of them were old as dirt and dated back at least fifty years or more. Some, however, were quite new. Only a few months old, in fact.

How are maps as recent as the beginning of the year mixed in with maps from years and decades past?

Amry wondered. Something wasn't adding up.

"This one's dated the 3rd of Hermora, 2995 AS. That's this year!" Temper said in disbelief, holding the map for the others to see.

Amry's brows furrowed.

But that means…

Amry walked over to the captain's chair and looked over its desk. He opened the drawers and pulled out envelopes wrapped in twine and sealed with an indigo octopus' emblem. An octopus? What house used an octopus as its seal? None that he was aware of. Perhaps one from Dyona or Xalla? His hair stood on end. Something was very wrong. It made him recall a story he'd been told when he was just a boy. A dark story. A—

"Captain! We've searched every cabin above the deck. All of them are empty. No hammocks, no furnishings, nothing!" Ricken called out, startling the officers and Amry, breaking his train of thought.

"Dammit, Ricken, ye fuckin' twit, what'd I tell you about walkin' in unannounced, ay?!" Amry shouted. His heart had slammed against his chest.

"Apologies, sir," Ricken grumbled.

"Anyway, let's go. This is a big ship 'n we need to scour the rest of it. Have the men start delving below deck."

Ricken nodded. "I'll pass the word, sir."

Amry, Kemper, and Temper stepped out of the captain's cabin, but Amry's suspicions were still high.

A thought occurred to him. "Let's go to the steering, I wanna see what colors this ship is flyin'."

"Aye, sir," Temper responded as the trio made their way up the stairs to the steering deck.

Amry and the others looked around, immediately taking note of the golden steering wheel. The entire apparatus seemed to be made of it.

If all else fails, we can certainly dig the gold out of this ship.

"See that railing topper over there? Dig it out with your knife. If there's no treasure aboard this ship, we can certainly make a healthy profit from the gold in it."

Kemper nodded and walked over to one of the railing toppers. It was carved into the shape of the naked woman statue beneath the bowsprit.

Meanwhile, Amry took a closer look at the flags mounted at the aft of the ship.

Ordinarily, there would be three flags mounted here on a pirate ship: a skull and crossbones, the universal symbol for piracy; the ship's flag, unique to each pirate ship, depicting its own heraldry; and a white flag of surrender. Another set of the three would be mounted on the main mast to be raised so that those afar or those outside of the smoke of battle could see them as well. But there were only two flags mounted here. A skull and crossbones. But what was this red flag? He couldn't quite make it out.

"Hoist the flag," Amry instructed.

"Aye, sir." Temper replied.

The two men pulled on the gold chains to hoist the flags up, and as both rose to prominence and the wind caught them, Amry—and Temper—froze in place.

"Oh, no..." Amry rasped, his voice having left him along with the air in his lungs.

Before them was a red flag with a black skull emblazoned upon it. A gold-toothed, screaming skull. Gold chains were positioned behind the skull like the crossbones of a jolly roger.

"It's the Pain...it's the Pain!" Amry began, his voice raising to a shout. He ran to the railing overlooking the main deck. "Everybody! GET OFF THIS SHIP RIGHT NOW! ANATHANE'S PAIN! THIS SHIP IS ANATHANE'S PAIN, IT'S—"

Kemper dug his knife into the wood of the railing and pulled the figurehead off. He appraised it for a moment, admiring its immaculate detail...and then it screamed. A scream so loud and piercing it sounded like it came from everywhere. He looked around wildly, then cursed as the gold figurehead bit into the skin between his thumb and pointer finger, tearing it loose. He howled, throwing the cursed thing away and clutching his bleeding hand.

Everyone aboard the ship went into chaos, some falling to the deck, covering their ears, others making for the ladders to disembark. Ricken and Baker made their way up from below as the screaming deafened them.

"What in the fuck is going on?!" Ricken shouted, but he could barely hear himself over the noise.

So loud was the noise that they didn't hear the rattling coming from below...

Baker happened to look down and placed a hand on Ricken's shoulder as his eyes went wide. Ricken looked at him, puzzled, then followed his gaze. It was too late.

A golden link of chains snaked up the stairs slowly towards them, then struck when they laid eyes on it. Baker dodged out of its path, but it wrapped itself around Ricken's arm. Ricken howled in pain as it tightened its grip, crushing the bones in his hand as it pulled him down. Baker grabbed Ricken's other hand as the man pleaded with him not to let go, his words muffled by the constant screaming of the ship. Baker held firm, but his grip was slipping as sweat greased his palm, and Ricken began to pull away.

He couldn't hear Ricken's scream of pain, but he could see it etched into his features as he was pulled steadily into the darkness below deck, his lantern having already fallen from his hand and landed at the base of the stairs, illuminating many more golden chains, slithering up from below.

"I've got you!"

Baker jerked with all his might, and by a stroke of pure luck, the chains relented, releasing Ricken's arm. Ricken looked at Baker gratefully before nodding to the right. "We need to go!"

The two men ran, looking all around them as more men met the same fate. Gold chains slipped out from every grate, every open door, and even the shrouds and sails of the ship and descended upon the pirates. The screaming of the ship stopped abruptly, but it was immediately replaced by the terrified howls and screams of the crew as the chains got hold of them. The duo ran toward the ladders as they saw men get ripped away mid-stride by the chains and yanked below deck or up into the canopy of black sails above. In the light of the blood moon, they couldn't be sure if the liquid covering the deck now was water or blood. But as a man was torn apart above them, and his entrails rained down upon them, their doubts were all but abolished.

The ship was drenched in blood.

The two made for the ladder, then veered away as they looked down to see chains leaking out of the gunports on the side of the massive ship and binding men to the ladders, kicking and screaming. Ricken locked eyes with one—Bran, the man whom he'd fought with a few days prior. He raised his arm, begging for help—before it was wrapped in chains and snapped out of place. Baker vomited as they watched Bran's fingers get snapped backward at a nauseating angle, and the man's face contorted in abject agony.

"I'm sorry, brother…" Ricken sighed, and then they ran up the stairs toward the steering deck, the only place, it seemed, that was not covered in these murderous living chains, their gold now streaked red with the blood of their slain brethren.

"Captain! The ship has come alive! It's attacking us, its—" Baker shouted, then froze as he saw a sea of chains encircling Amry, Kemper, and Temper.

"Fuck," Ricken cursed, and they turned back, only to see more chains snaking towards them.

They ran back up the stairs and leaped into the circle the others stood in, and they all pressed against one another as the chains swirled around them in a tornado of metal. The men shivered and huddled together on the deck, cold and terrified as the tornado abated and the chains settled around them. Amry rose to his feet and took a step toward the edge of the circle but froze as the chains twitched.

Then the footsteps came.

Slow, leisurely steps up the stairs below them. The footsteps paused a moment, long enough for them to wonder if they'd simply imagined the sound. Then, they saw the top of a head, followed by the body of a man, approach from the stairs and stop a few feet away from them in the mesh of chains surrounding them. The man, tall and imposing, looked them over silently for a moment.

He wore the attire of a distinguished captain. Gold link chains looped around his neck and held a ponderous red orb around his neck. It looked like a perfectly spherical ruby, but its surface was cloudy, its colors shifting to different hues of red. His pale hands were covered in ruby gemmed gold rings, one upon each finger. His tricorn hat, large and wickedly curved, drew their eyes, but they quickly settled on his face. It was covered by a mask.

A gold, grinning skull mask, its eye holes revealing inhuman, blood-red eyes that glowed eerily in the moon's light. At some point, the screaming had died away, and the ship became silent as the grave. Amry released a breath he didn't even know he was holding.

The masked man focused on him.

"Well, well, well, what have we here? Pirates snooping over my ship, oh dear. Tell me, little pirate, why are you here? Choose your words carefully."

Amry shivered and cleared his throat, looking at his companions, Temper, Kemper, and the blood-soaked Baker and Ricken. "We saw your ship come up out the water. We came to investigate," Amry offered.

"Come you did, investigate you have." He looked at Kemper, who shuddered under his gaze. "You attempted to steal from me."

Kemper's lips went dry as he tried to find his voice, "I…"

"Silence!" The man shouted.

A chain, whip-fast flew at Kemper and wrapped around his throat, raising him high into the air. He bleated and clutched at his throat as the chain tightened.

"Kemper, no! Let 'em go, you rat bastard!" Temper growled, finding his voice.

He stood up, and the chains came alive, rearing up like cobras and rattling in front of him. He stopped dead in his tracks.

"Be quiet, mate, or you'll be joining him," the man warned, his voice pure ice.

The men watched in resignation as Kemper hung, flailing and grabbing at his throat. His veins bulged, as did his eyes as they tightened, and his face changed color. He flailed like that, slowly strangulating in front of them, chains dancing around him as he died.

"Now, tell me. Do you know who I am?" The man asked, leaning against the railing, his gaze never leaving Amry.

"You're…you're the Dread Captain, sir. Felix Helregal."

The man chuckled, but even his laugh sounded menacing. "Astute one, you are! That I am. Shall I assume you know what happens next, then?"

Amry shivered and mumbled to himself, sobbing. Temper, Ricken, and Baker were still staring at the dying Kemper, body dancing in place, but the chain holding him was like the arms of a gallows, unmoving.

His lips frothed, and his tongue poked out as he spat and sputtered for breath.

"You…please, no…" Amry begged, falling on his knees clasping his hands together, begging. "Please, Stars above, no!"

Temper, Baker, and Ricken looked at each other, then at Amry, shaking their heads in disgust. Even facing death, Amry was a coward.

"How the hell did you become captain, cowardly as you are?" Temper asked.

And why the fuck did I follow him?

He wondered. He supposed it didn't matter now.

"Listen to your officer, Amry. Begging will get you nowhere with me, hahahaha!" Helregal cackled. "I can tell you won't be much use. You're all yellow." He looked at the chains. "Take him."

"No! No, not me, please! I can be useful, I swear! Take them! Y-y-you need me! You can use me, I swear! I SWEAR!" Amry pleaded as the chains shot up and grabbed hold of him, lifting him into the air to gaze at the still-choking Kemper before pulling him away.

"In pieces, please," Helregal ordered.

Amry gibbered in terror, whimpering like a child as the chains tightened, then let loose a bone-rattling scream as they ripped his arms from their sockets and blood gushed from the stumps. They did the same with his legs.

Helregal turned and looked at him, cocking his head to the side. "You're a worm, Captain Amry. Now die like one."

Amry's howls trailed away as a grated hatch opened wide, and he was dragged down into it. Temper and Baker trained their focus on Helregal now. Kemper had gone limp, his tongue half bitten off, his face purple, and his eyes nearly popped out of their sockets. They couldn't bear to gaze at him any longer.

"Just you three and us, now, gentlemen," Helregal said with a clap. "Let's talk."

"Us?" Baker asked, finally speaking.

"These ones may prove useful to me. We may not need to kill them. At least, not all of them…" A hissing voice said.

The three men looked at the glowing red amulet around Helregal's neck, now. From within, two jaundiced yellow eyes looked at them, and they could see a disembodied set of fanged teeth smiling at them. It made their skin crawl.

"W-w-what is that?" Ricken asked.

"I am the reason you yet live. But all gifts demand a price. My name is Caine since you deigned to ask. Two men will survive this night. For those lucky souls, I have a task! Captain, explain their plight!" The vile thing within the red orb rhymed.

"Two…of us?" Baker asked, his gut sinking.

Helregal nodded slowly. "Only two. I have a reputation to keep."

He pulled out an envelope wrapped in twine and sealed in wax with an indigo octopus' insignia. "I need a message delivered. Who delivers it, I will leave for you to decide."

With his other hand, he pulled out three knives from his pockets, tossing each to a man. The face in the amulet, Caine, smiled darkly.

"You know what to do," Helregal said with a chuckle.

Ricken and Baker looked at one another, then at Temper, who backed away, knife at the ready. "Two against one? Really?"

"I'm so fucking sorry, mate. We'll be quick about it, yeah?" Baker said.

"Fuck the both of you. Come and die!" Temper spat.

He was taller and stronger than either of them, but it didn't matter so long as numbers were on their side. The two men dodged his knife swipes. Then

Baker stuck him in the side. He gasped as Ricken followed up with a stab to the gut after he exposed it, clutching his side. He hitched his breath and swung his knife again, slashing open Ricken's shirt and bleeding him before Baker came behind him and stabbed him in the back repeatedly. Temper coughed, the wind leaving his body from the sharp, burning stabs, and fell to his knees.

"May the Stars protect your soul, brother," Ricken eulogized as he slit Temper's throat. The man gurgled blood, eyes wide, then fell down face first.

Ricken and Baker drenched in a fresh coat of blood, looked at one another in shame and disgust. They had survived the night, but at what cost? Helregal gave a slow clap, and both men turned to look at him in a mix of fear and hatred.

"Very good. Except…there is one small detail I forgot to mention. You see, my friends, my reputation demands that I leave just one man alive. Not two."

Their hearts sank as they looked at one another and dropped their knives. They couldn't do it. Not to each other.

"Now, I know this is a very hard decision. I get the sense that the two of you are very close. So, in lieu of just killing one of you outright at random, let's make a game of it, ay?"

Helregal pulled out a gold coin and held it for both men to see. On one side was the face of Emperor Vagryn I, the very first Emperor of the Kurzan Empire. On the other side was a sword and shield. He looked at Ricken. "Heads or tails?"

Ricken swallowed a lump down his throat before looking at Baker, who nodded. "…Tails…"

Helregal nodded his head once, then looked at Baker. "Heads for you, then, mate."

He placed the coin on the crook of his pointer finger, then flicked it. The coin flipped high into the air, flickering in the moonlight as it came down. Ricken and Baker closed their eyes, dreading what was to come. The sight of Kemper's bulging features was staring at them from the back of their eyelids.

The coin landed in Helregal's palm, and he quickly slapped it onto the back of his other hand. He looked at the two men, his expression unreadable behind his golden mask, and he lifted his hand, revealing the outcome.

"Heads it is, then."

Baker breathed a sigh of relief. It was over.

He was dead, but it was over.

"Be good, brother."

Ricken hugged Baker, a genuine, brotherly hug. He tried to remember the last time he'd willingly hugged another man. The cold nights huddled together didn't count. He did that to survive. This, however, came from the heart.

"When this is all over, find my sister, Tellarya. Tell her I love her and tell her I'm sorry I wasn't able to buy her the horse she always wanted. Chestnut mare, her favorite. She wanted to name it Mocha," Baker laughed.

The two men laughed at the terrible name. They knew it was the last laugh they would have together.

"Find a good woman and settle down, brother. This life is naught but death and destruction. I grow tired of it, anyway," Baker finished.

"I promise, brother. I fucking promise I will," Ricken said, his voice hoarse.

Baker looked at Helregal. His smile turned to a scowl of pure hate. Hate for all he'd taken from him; hate for all he would take still. "Do it, you bastard."

Helregal leaned off the railing and pulled out a gun that looked like it was carved from solid gold. "Tell me, do you know how Vagryn the First died?"

Ricken furrowed his brow. "How?"

Helregal cocked his gun and aimed it at Baker. "He was shot in the head by his own brother."

Baker closed his eyes.

BANG!

The rapport of the gun cracked out and broke the hush that fell over the sea, echoing through the air.

Baker opened his eyes, his lip quivering.

Ricken hit the deck, the back of his head hollowed out from the force of the gunshot.

"No! No! NOOOOOOOOOOOOO!" Baker howled. His voice was raw as he held his dead friend's head in his hands.

The bullet hole was the size of a peach pit, square in the middle of his forehead. Ricken's eyes were hooded but open. The look of shock was still frozen on his face.

Helregal holstered his pistol and stretched before pulling out the envelope and tossing it onto the deck next to the grieving Baker. "Listen to me, and listen to me closely," he said, hovering over the sobbing man. "Deliver this letter to Sel'Thamman, the patriarch of the House of Umbra in the City of Leaves. You will get into the rowboat left for you on the starboard side of the ship; within it will be a map. The boat and the map will lead you directly to the port to deliver my message. Are we clear?"

Baker nodded his head, tears still streaking down his cheeks.

"Good. Do not fail me, Mr. Baker or you will suffer a fate far worse than the one that I gave your friend here. Now begone, I have work to do," Helregal instructed.

Baker slowly lifted himself up, peeling his eyes away from Ricken. He looked at the corpse of Temper on the deck, staring blankly into the sky. He looked at the hanging body of Kemper, who was staring blankly at nothing, and then at Ricken, whose eyes he'd shut for the final time.

He had lost everything in less than a half hour. His friends, his crew, everything. He cast one smoldering look at Helregal, who looked indifferently at him as the chains carried off the remains of his crewmates.

"If the stories are true, then he'll come for you. I hope he sends you straight to the bottom of Sheolhenna—for good this time."

Helregal laughed as he grabbed hold of the steering wheel. "I have seen the hells and all their horrors. It holds no surprises for me, neither does he. But I do hope so! I know I'll be coming for him. Run along now, boy. And do not tarry..."

Baker climbed onto the raft, picking up the map inside as it lowered itself into the water and set sail toward its destination. As the boat drifted away, the gun ports of Anathane's Pain, the mystery ship that had destroyed his life, slid open. It opened fire on Ruby's Prize, blowing it to pieces in seconds. He watched the last remnants of his old life go up in flames as he sailed away...

*****

Helregal turned back to the deck of the ship. The tepid silence was broken as the grates reopened, and new noises echoed from below. Unearthly groans and growls came from below as rotted, sea-soaked hands gripped the lips of the grates and climbed from the darkness. Where once there was life, there was only deathless hatred and hunger.

They were his, now. They were Damned.

"Summon the chosen! We sail for the Blasphemous Isle!" Helregal bid. Caine illuminated and let loose a shrill, unearthly rattle, a sound so loud that it would easily have deafened a living man.

Memories of times passed flashed through Helregal's dark mind, and he smiled. "Ahh... tis good to be back in the land of the living, atop the water rather than forty fathoms deep... hoist the sails, gentlemen. We be off to warmer waters. I have an appointment to keep with some friends of mine."

The Damned howled in agreement, a foul cacophony piercing the night. As the blood moon rose ever higher into the night sky, a terrible force was set loose upon the sea...

XIII

Old Wounds

"Gentlemen, we really must stop meeting under these circumstances. People will talk," Claude Humris said dryly.

Osiris, Steven Cage, Stone, and Cutter all sat in his examination room, unamused at his joke.

"Funny. Let's just get this over with, then?" Osiris said.

"Ye got any whitestar syrup? I'd rather not do this lucid," Cutter asked.

Whitestar syrup was a powerful numbing and healing agent, often used by alchemists and surgeons to numb and sedate patients prior to surgery. Claude kept a generous supply of it locked away to mend the crew after major battles and ease their pain if their wounds were too grievous to be fixed.

"I am running low on mon approvisionnement—eh, supply. I need to save it for le most…egregious injury, yes?" Claude spoke in a heavy Atarran accent and often had to pause to order his words in Kurzish, the standard language of the empire.

"Fuck. Ye mean I gotta take these stitches raw?" Cutter groaned.

Claude shook his head, pulling out a thick needle filled with a clear brownish liquid. "Non, you will have a lesser anathema injection."

Cutter winced. "That…that needle for me?"

Claude nodded. "Step into my parlor, monsieur Cutter."

Cutter looked at the other men warily. "A-a-any of you boys wanna go fi—"

"Get on with it 'n quit bitchin' like a maid, Cutter," Osiris waved. "none of us like the needle, either."

Cage snickered. "Is the little loudmouth afraid of a wee needle? I had thought you made of thicker skin than that, Volld Cutter!"

"Can it, Northman! Do they even have medicine where you're from, or do ye just fuck goats and rub shit on your wounds?" Cutter spat.

"I am not a Kurzan highland farmer, I do not fuck animals for pleasure or otherwise. We Valkar have skalds that use the power of the Dark Goddesses to heal our wounds. Perhaps if your faith was stronger, little pirate, your wounds would not need medicine to heal," Cutter retorted.

"If you're so in tune with your goddesses, then why is your smelly ass here? Go pray your wounds away, Valkar!" Cutter shot back as Claude injected the needle into his arm. He hissed, "Fuck!"

"I am not a skald. My injuries will not be healed by my prayers alone," Cage grunted.

"Ladies, ladies—you're both ugly. Shut up so Claude can focus 'n we can all get the fuck outta here, ay?" Stone cut in, rubbing his temples. Between Cutter's shouting and Cage's naturally loud and blunt nature, he wasn't sure he would be able to take much more of this. The pain in his side where that damned samurai had cut him already smarted bad enough.

"Aye aye to that. Shut the fuck up and let the man work. We need to start putting a damn muzzle on you," Osiris added.

He winced as the slash through his arm Koga had given him burned and throbbed. It left three long, deep tracks in his arm. It cut to the bone, and even his own above-average healing abilities simply weren't going to be able to mend this type of injury alone. He'd wrapped it in cloth after the fight, but it'd been throbbing ever since. He was pretty sure it was getting infected.

"Put a muzzle on him, and he'd probably just rip it off." Stone pointed out. Cutter loved opening his mouth almost as much as he loved killing people that pissed him off, drinking, and whoring.

"That's why ye get it enchanted, so every time he tries to take it off, his dick shrinks an inch," Osiris chuckled.

"Ye have to have an inch to shrink an inch!" Stone guffawed, slapping his knee.

Osiris, Stone, and Cage all burst into laughter. Claude Humris was completely expressionless, fully absorbed in his work of stitching Cutter's arm closed from where it'd been slashed open.

Cutter winced and scowled. "When all of you die, I'm pissing on your graves."

"Make sure ye squat when ye do, brother!" Stone cackled, causing a further uproar from his companions.

The men carried on, making fun of each other as they all had their wounds stitched and were sent on their way until only Osiris remained.

"Try not to take too long, brother. There's ale to be had below. We're crackin' into the provisions we took from the Dyonians," Stone said on his way out.

"Aye, I'll be along shortly, Stone." Osiris nodded as the older pirate nodded to him and Claude and left the operation room.

As the two sat in silence for several minutes, Osiris finally broke the quiet. "Has anybody made mention of him, Claude?" Osiris asked, now solemn and serious.

Claude Humris was silent for several moments as he worked. He stuck the needle into the side of Osiris' arm, just above where the three rents in his arm began. Osiris didn't flinch, the pain of the needle barely registering over the burning of the wound. Then, he unwrapped the cloth he'd put over it. It pulled away with a wet, sticky peel as clear sap-like fluid held onto the cloth in threads.

"Curious. Normally, this wound would be infected by now," Claude noted. His eyebrow was raised in surprise.

"Mean to tell me it isn't? Sure feels like it."

"What you feel is the inflammation, so of course it hurts. It probably feels like a low flame is being held over it, no?"

"All the damn time." Osiris nodded.

"I was expecting pus, foul odor, discoloration—the usual signs of infection. Instead, it would appear the wound is closing and healing itself. All I have to do here is clean and stitch the wound, but even that would not be necessary in a few days' time, I am sure."

Osiris braced himself and looked at his arm. He was surprised to see that while it looked gross, covered in strange fluid, and looking generally wet and nasty, it wasn't discolored, and even the flesh had grown back over the exposed bone.

Well, that's a new development.

"How the hell is this possible, doc?" Osiris asked.

Claude shrugged. "You are an Alyrian, are you not?"

Osiris froze. Huasca had told him many times to avoid ever going by that word. Huasca. He hated talking about him.

"I'm just different, is all," he offered weakly.

Claude looked him dead in the eyes silently. The two sat for a tense moment before Claude turned back to the wound and grabbed a rag to clean it. He pulled out a bottle of strong-smelling spirits and doused the cloth in it.

"I am far from a fool, Second Mate Osiris. I have seen much in my life, Alyrians included."

Osiris bit his lower lip.

"I understand that First Mate Huasca has instructed you n'en parle à personne—do not tell anybody. But I am a doctor, disgraced as I may be."

Osiris exhaled.

"Even without these injuries, your differences are plain to see. These tattoos on your arms, they are Alyria tattoos. I have seen them before. You are stronger, faster, and more resilient than le average pirate can ever hope to be. Your eyes glow in the dark, and when you are angered, your tattoos glow as well. Everyone knows what you are—but no one will say it."

"What are ye gettin' at, sawbones? Say it plain," Osiris said with an edge.

"Ordinarily, you would be le first person people here expect to turn against us. Alyrians, unregulated by le Consortium often fall victim to the wiles of demons and spirits. But you are different. You care about ces gens—these people—very much. So, I must confess that my first inquiries were all directed towards suspicions of your intent. You will be pleased to know that no one believes it is you. They all believe it to be young Hanover, or even Stone, or Yager, or the person they hate most on a given day. I've heard at least fifty different names in these past weeks."

"If not me, then who do *you* think it is, Claude?" Osiris asked as the first stitch was made.

Claude worked for several moments, silent and contemplative. Osiris thought to ask again and opened his mouth just as he spoke.

"This life necessitates a certain type of personality in a man, I think. One has to be strong of will and loyal—but not necessarily to leurs frères—eh, their *brothers*. One must be able to do whatever black deed need be done, and still believe oneself to be above the consequence. To a pirate, the ends must always justify the means," he said as he sewed Osiris' arm shut.

"You're saying that anybody could be the turncoat because everybody is in it for themselves. No honor among thieves, as it were," Osiris said, connecting the dots.

"I am. But we know that it was not just anybody, and I do not believe it to be a group. Were that the case, I believe they would have made a move by now."

Osiris nodded; it made sense.

"So, it's not a mutiny, then."

"No, the person who did this is not seeking to become captain. I think that thought is long behind them now. They feel strongly enough that they did not leave when we were brought to the imperial capital, either. I counted every man, and not one turned up missing. Curious. No, I believe the turncoat did what they did as un crime passionnel. A crime of passion."

Osiris rolled the thought over in his head. A crime of passion? Who hated the crew badly enough to do this out of passion? His mind scrolled through everyone who was at odds or had ever been at odds with the crew. There was Hanover, but he knew the boy, and even on his worst day, he would not dare turn against them in such a way—and definitely wouldn't get away with it.

Yager was too stupid.

At one point in time, Cage was the most hated man on the ship. Hell, people still hate him because of his heritage. Many of the men aboard the ship had lost family to the Valkar. But Cage was too proud and too single-minded to be so deceptive. All he cared about was raiding, pillaging, and fighting.

Maybe that's why we get along so well.

Osiris mused.

It wasn't Cage.

He thought back to how they laughed together when they were ribbing at Cutter and each other. Him, Cage and—

Could it be? No…

"It's—"

"All done," Claude cut him off, having finished sewing the wound together. He lightly patted Osiris on the arm, signaling for him to get up.

"Thank you, uh…thank you, Claude," Osiris mumbled, lost in thought.

It can't be him. He wouldn't dare…would he?

"I am sorry that I could not give you a specific name, Osiris. But I hope I have at least given you an idea as to what to look for," Claude said as he stood up and put away his supplies.

"Aye, sawbones. Ye've given me plenty," Osiris said as he abruptly stood and started walking toward the door.

"Good. And Second Mate Osiris?"

Osiris paused, looking back at Claude.

"We do not ask to be born as we are. But we can choose what we become. I see in you great potential, but you lack control. First Mate Huasca was a shaman before he was our navigator. He raised you like his own son, and I know that he has talked to you about your gifts. Perhaps you should try listening to him, I know that your relationship is strained but…"

Osiris tipped his head, thinking back to when Huasca had saved him, all those years ago. He wondered for just a moment when he had started to hate the man. He pushed the thought aside as quickly as it came.

"Aye." He shut the door behind him.

*****

"Well, what do we do with a drunken sailor? What do we do with a drunken sailor? What do we do with a drunken sailor earlay in the mornin?" Cutter sang drunkenly.

"Way hay 'n up she rises! Way hay 'n up she rises! Way hay 'n up she rises earlay in the mornin!" A cavalcade of drunken pirates sang.

Meanwhile, others still brawled drunkenly with one another, either because they were bored, and this was what constituted fun for them or because they were settling old grudges. Or more recently, because they suspected each other of treachery.

"Damn, they sound better drunk 'n they do sober!" Moary laughed as he slammed his tankard down on the table.

"Cutter can only hold a bloody tune when he's besotted, that's why!" Flint yammered, already deep into his own cup. "Bastard sings like a dyin' troll otherwise."

"Ay laddie, now that's just rude to trolls!" Moary remarked.

Both men peeled into fits of laughter, slapping each other on the back as Cutter and a choir of drunken pirates sang to their hearts' content.

"I miss all the fun, then?" Stone asked as he sat down next to the other officers at one of the only tables in the galley. Moary passed him an untouched tankard as the two still tittered pleasantly.

"Nay, brother, merely a light ribbin' on Cutter's account, is all," Moary said, clapping him on the shoulder in greeting.

Stone flinched. Moary's hands were nearly the size of bear paws, due to his Duwa blood, and sometimes the stout man forgot his own strength.

"Easy, Moary, ye clap almost as hard as me ol' man used to hit me!" Stone laughed, sipping from his cup.

"Aye, apologies Stone, I forget me own strength at times, ay? Poor Hanover nearly fell on his ass when a patted him this morn'. Boy's been a right sulk of late," Moary answered, still giddy from the drink.

Stone nodded. He'd seen Hanover earlier in the day as well. He was broody, though he tried to hide it. "Aye, heard he 'n Siris got into it after the battle. The boy spoke outta turn 'n Siris gavem' what for."

"Serves the little pissant right; s'his fault we's in this mess like, far as I'm concerned," Flint chimed in.

Moary defended Hanover. "Ye ne'er liked the boy at all, Flint. Ne'er gave 'em a chance. How's that fair to do to a child, ay?"

Flint drank long from his cup and shook his head as he swallowed. "Boy like him got no place on a pirate ship. Too young 'n on top 'o that he ain't never sailed 'fore he came aboard with us. He needs to take his ass back to land and stay there."

"Oh, piss off! Ye ne'er liked the boy from the moment he set foot on the ship 'n ye been lookin' for every reason to oust him ever since!" Moary said, his irritation plain.

Flint folded his arms, not looking at Moary. "I care about the protection of me brothers. We're pirates, not babysitters. The boy is goin' to get one of us killed savin' his sorry ass and I'll not be part of it." He looked directly into Moary's eyes, now. "You 'n Siris spend too much time babyin' the brat. Ye care too much. How long until he's thrown into the middle of battle and has to show out? What if he chokes? Who's goin' to save em? Not me, that's for damn sure."

He took a draw from his cup. "But you, Moary? I know ye will. 'N you'll die for it. All 'cause of him. So yer damn right I don't like that boy. He's a walkin' death note for my brothers."

Moary laughed it off. "I always knew ye had a heart somewhere in that chasm of a chest of yours. The boy is less a threat than ye fancy, 'n he'll prove his gumption in due time. I put the safety of me crew—especially me gun crews over everythin'. If I am to die, brother, know that I'll die in fire 'n glory, not defending the lad. By the Dead Sea Gods 'n me ancestors, Duwa *and* human, this I swear, 'n I never break an oath!"

Moary thumped his huge fist against his chest.

Flint chuckled mirthlessly, then nodded.

"We'll see."

Stone sat, drinking from his mug and watching the two bickering pirates. "Ye gonna kiss 'n make up, then? I always hate when lovers spat like this, ay?" he laughed. His two companions did as well.

"How was the good doctor? Ye offer 'em to come down for a cup?" Moary asked with a wry smirk.

"The day Claude Humris gets drunk with us is the day we're all well 'n truly fucked—mark me words. Stitches still hurt, though," he said, rubbing a hand over his side where that damnable samurai sliced him open.

"You have killed me, but you haven't won. You hold a trigger, but you are not the one behind the gun."

He reflected on the samurai's cryptic words.

"You've lit a bomb, pirate, but you all are too blind to see it."

Too blind to see what?

Stone pondered. He thought back to finding the chest with the Eye of Atla inside. A cold chill ran down his spine as a raucous broke out across the galley, and the men began to whoop and holler, crowding around someone.

"Shite on a stick—another fuckin' brawl?" Stone groaned, running a hand through his thick salt and pepper hair.

Cutter stopped singing and looked from the table he'd been standing on to see Yager's blonde head bobbing in the middle of the crowd, as well as another crewman with brown hair. Louis, perhaps?

"Stars dammit, Yager, again?!" Cutter yelled as he hopped off the table and joined the other officers pushing through the crowd. They broke through in time to see Yager landing a heavy cross on Louis' cheek, making the taller, burlier pirate stumble.

"Mac truamhéileach soith! You will show me respect, ye bastard!" Yager growled, slipping into his native Sarxian tongue as his rage rose.

Louis began lying into him, swinging at his head. Yager blocked the headshots but took a punch to the gut that knocked the wind out of him. He grabbed at his gut reflexively and left his face open. Louis then punched him square in the nose, causing a loud snap and ushering a gush of blood from his nostrils. Yager stumbled back, clutching at his nose and falling on his ass. His coin pouch fell from his pocket, as well as a knife and several other odds and ends.

The crowd cheered at the first blood and goaded the two men on as the officers stepped in to break up the fight.

"Settle down, boys, that's enough. What's this all about, then?" Stone said as he came between the two and pushed Louis back, narrowly stopping him from stomping on Yager.

Yager removed his hand from his bleeding, likely broken nose. "Bastard's makin' light 'o me! He spoke ill 'o me mother 'n goaded me into a fight!"

Stone looked at Louis. "This true?"

Louis smiled. "All I said, quartermaster, was that his mother must be proud that her son's a would-be pirate captain who couldn't even finish what he started, is all!"

He laughed, as did many of the other men. To them, Yager and Stone's failed mutiny was a laughing matter. As it was deathless and amounted to nothing more than a few bruised egos and bloodied noses, it was looked upon as yet another story of high-seas, high-jinx.

"As memory serves, Louis, ye were one 'o the men what did the mutinyin'," Stone remarked.

Louis' smirk disappeared.

When everything broke down and Stone dismantled the mutiny he'd started with Yager, he kept the names of those who'd stood with them secret. Arguing that it was best that the blame rests squarely on his own shoulders. Stone knew that the only way to navigate that storm and come out the other side alive and with his position still intact was to head straight into it, own up to it, and handle it personally. This had saved him much face in the eyes of the crew—and captain.

But, if one of his former co-mutineers was going to throw another under the wagon, then far be it from him to let them throw a stone and hide their hand.

"Nothin' to say, matey? I mean, we all know what parts we had to play, don't we? There was me, and you, and Yager. Whole lot of us good ol' boys that conspired together. Now, I'm not the type of man to finger a brother to the law—but I'll damn sure call 'em out when he's quick to throw one of his own under the cart amongst his kin," Stone said.

Louis sobered quickly, his mocking posture and tone crumbling under the scrutiny of his peers.

They all knew who had a hand in the mutiny, but none dared speak of them for fear of digging into the old wound. Now, though, a name had been uttered, and the shame that it carried would be felt.

Louis looked around. His allies faltered, distancing themselves from him, and now the crowd was turning against him, whispering ugly things about him. His blood began to boil, and his face turned red.

"You've made me," he said.

"Ye made yerself—now clear out. Ye're cut off for the night." Stone waved his hand, dismissing him as he crouched down to help up Yager.

Louis grumbled and turned to leave—then spun around and charged at Stone, knife in his hand.

"Stone!" Cutter shouted, but it was too late.

No one even had time to process and react before he was on him. But Stone was quicker.

The quartermaster turned around just in time and grabbed Louis' wrist, directing it away from his body, then disarming him by twisting it. Louis cried out in pain as Stone elbowed him sharply across the face and made him stumble backward, clutching his wrist. Before he could even defend himself, Reece Stone pulled out the lash that he kept curled up on his waist and unfurled it, lashing Louis across the arms and torso and even slapping him twice in the face. The man hit the deck, bloody welts forming on his exposed skin, moaning in pain.

The whip, a cat-o-nine with nine thin, tightly bound leather cords splaying out from a leather handle, was a fearsome disciplinary weapon in the right hands, and Stone had all the experience needed to make it deadly. He stood over Louis, who moaned and whimpered in pain before kneeling next to him.

"Ye know what the punishment is for attemptin' to murder an officer, Louis?" Stone asked evenly. His voice was low and cool.

Louis blubbered, the pain rendering him incapable of forming sentences.

"A walk on the plank into the depths 'o the sea. Throw 'em in the brig. Cap's gonna wanna hear about this." Stone nodded to Cutter and Flint, who raised the moaning Louis to his feet before dragging him up the stairs.

The men had quieted down considerably, the show having come to an end.

"Carry on, brothers. But mind yer manners—and check yer weapons," Stone said casually before going to help up Yager, who sat stunned on the floor. The pirate blinked, then accepted his hand as he pulled him to his feet and the crowd dispersed. Yager and Stone exchanged knowing glances.

"Go raibh maith agat...deartháir," Yager said.

"Thank you, brother."

Stone smiled. "Tá fáilte romhat, a dheartháir."

"You're welcome, brother."

"Get a pint, then head to the sawbones. Yer nose is fucked," Stone instructed, patting the man on the shoulder.

Yager groaned, gripping the busted nose and clenching his eyes in pain. "Aye, I'll need it. Goddamn, that hurts!" he mumbled, then spat blood onto the deck as it flowed down his sinuses.

Stone laughed as Yager walked away, then paused as he noticed the items he'd dropped on the floor. "Oi, ye dropped the—" The words died in his throat as he inspected the dropped items.

The coin pouch had a red dragon embroidered into it. And there were trace amounts of a grainy substance on the floor. He touched it with a finger and looked over to see where Yager was, but in the returning roar of the crowd, he didn't hear Stone calling after him. He touched his finger to his nose, smelling the grainy substance. It had a strong scent to it, smelling faintly of fruit but also grain seed. He tasted it.

Is that…

A large palm clapped down on his shoulder, and Stone startled, turning his head to see Moary standing behind him.

"Ye handled that scuff well, Stone! I remember why the cap'n made ye quartermaster!" Moary congratulated.

Stone nodded, his heart rate returning to normal as he picked up the items left on the floor and scooped up a good amount of the grainy substance in a cloth from his pocket.

"Cap's gonna wanna hear about this too," he muttered to Moary, who looked at him perplexedly as he showed him the coin purse.

Understanding donned on the jolly Half-Duwa's face as his granite features settled into a scowl. "Aye."

As the two stood, Stone caught sight of Hanover, leaning against a wall and silently nursing a cup. He was watching them.

"Go talk to the boy, I'll go and handle the cap'n," Stone said.

Moary nodded. "Keep this under wraps, ay?"

"My thoughts exactly." Moary walked toward Hanover, his jovial nature returning as he laughed and greeted the brooding teen.

Stone put his findings in his pocket, gazed around the room, and spied Yager holding a rag to his nose as he nursed a cup. Stone sighed and shook his head before heading above deck.

XIV

Call of the Grave

She traveled beneath the tide.

Deep in the dark of the ocean, she traversed its expanse. No creature dared to face her, speeding from her path long before she reached them. Even the monsters of the deep feared her. Anathane's Pain was the flagship of Sheolhenna. She sped through the water at unnatural speed, more akin to a shark giving chase than a cumbersome ship trailing through water.

In her belly, there was a grand atrium, running the length of her bilge, where water never touched. In the atrium were many candles illuminating its interior, as well as the lavish paintings upon its walls. At an altar at the far corner of the atrium was a portrait of a beautiful woman and a man holding hands. Beneath this portrait was a king's throne, and on the throne sat Felix Helregal. Tubes lining the ceiling of the compartment amplified and funneled the acoustics from the atrium out into the ship and surrounding sea.

Helregal played a large, silver cello with golden strings. He played it with a maestro's skill and emotion, lost in a trance as he played a somber piece from memory. And there he sat, playing a song into the void. Only the fish and the dead could hear his music.

*****

"We're nearly there. I can sense them."

Caine hissed.

He ceased his playing.

"Will they kneel?" Helregal asked.

"It is the will of the Gravefather. They will yield."

"Good. I would hate to have to destroy them. It is rare such powerful souls walk this world."

The ship neared its destination and broke through the waves. It sat before an island, strange and unnatural in its formation. Helregal surfaced from below deck. His new crew stood silent, inanimate like statues, their heads cast down. He walked past them as the ship came close to their meeting place.

"Let us see who has answered his call."

*****

Helregal stepped onto the black sand of the isle. He could feel the trembling souls tethered to it. He could hear their screams of anguish. They called this place by many names, but it was most infamous as Blasphemous Island. He had heard stories of it, of what horrid things resided upon it. He wondered if they would show themselves.

He was a revenant, his soul unbound to his flesh. They could not feed on him. He wondered if his new acquaintances could say the same. He saw them standing on the sand in a circle, looking amongst themselves. As he approached, however, they focused on him.

He met the group on the blood-moonlit beach and looked across them with a growing smile hidden behind his mask. Before him stood his new officers, those who would lead his crew and enact his plans.

"Well, well, well. What have we here?" he asked.

To the far left of the circle was the tallest and broadest of the party. A chalk-white skinned creature with a black skull tattooed over its toothy, ferocious face. It was a Drakkari that much Helregal knew. Theirs was an old and extinct race, feared in ages past as some of the most formidable and savage warriors this world had ever seen. So feared were they that the Duwa wiped their race out millennia ago, though on occasion, a rare rumor or sighting of the creatures was reported. He knew they were big, but the stories simply didn't do this brute justice. The beast towered over the tallest of men by well over a head and was built like the strongest Duwa colossi he'd ever seen. The monster, wearing black, armored leg guards and claw-toed sabatons and naught else, looked bred for war.

It looked at him with intelligent, bright yellow eyes set far back in its robust head and regarded him with a fanged, bloodthirsty smile.

To the brute's left was a tall (by human standards), curvaceous woman. She wore white bandage wrappings that bound her frame and gold armor on her shoulders, hands, hips, knees, and shins. She moved with the ease of a dancer. Her unbandaged feet dug into the sand, and she tilted her head from side to side as though she were catching a breeze or a rhythm. A gold mask covered her face.

It had an ancient script scrawled upon it. Her movements were silent and meditative, though Helregal could sense that she was focused on him.

To the right of her was a figure drenched in vaporous shadows. His boots seemed to hover over the sand, though it was hard to differentiate the two in the moonlight. His eyes were glowing white pinpoints in a skeletal face. The man looked thin enough to be blown away in the wind, as he was too thin to have anything other than skin and bone to his body beneath his shadow-shrouded pirate clothes. His gaze was vacant but squarely set on Helregal.

The last member of the party was rather mundane in appearance in comparison to her inhuman and questionably human—or living—companions. Though the Dread Captain could sense Alyria dripping off her. She wore a black cloak and hood, masking much of her body, and she was average in height in comparison to the bandaged woman. However, easily a head shorter than her. She raised a singular palm, and a ball of green flames materialized in it. Helregal's smile widened as he walked directly toward her and peered into the hood covering her face.

"This one is strong with the Alyria of death. She holds much promise…" Caine said aloud.

The talking amulet glowed that fearsome red, framing Helregal's masked face and illuminating the woman's.

Her irises were an unnaturally bright, electric green color. He saw the edges of similarly colored tattoos around what showed of her neck, all but confirming what he already knew.

"You're a necromancer, child. I can *smell* it," Helregal said, breathing deeply of the fetid air. "You heard the call of the Gravefather?"

The woman raised her head and let her hood fall from it, revealing a beautiful, deathly pale face.

"He speaks to me always, but many moons ago, he screamed into my dreams of a destined meeting. He bid me come to the Isle of Black Oaths. He tells me that you are his avatar, that your words are his. Is this true, master?" she asked in a refined, dusky voice.

He placed a calloused hand on her shoulder. "I am risen from death, blessed with its icy touch. The Gravefather gave unto me this gift so that I may enact my revenge and herald his reign." He turned to the others. "Follow me, and he shall bless you too. You walk the path of undeath, but you have not seen its true power. I will make you powerful beyond measure. Fight for me, and you will have our master's favor and all the gifts it brings. Turn against me, and you turn against him. I need not tell you what that brings."

The group all faced him. They could see the aura of dread around him, a thick, maroon-tinged mass of black energy, wicking off him like flames. If they thought to speak, it was interrupted by the sound of heavy movement behind them.

They all turned as they heard a wail from the trees, and a tall, abhorrent creature emerged. It was huge, easily four meters in height. It lumbered forth on fleshy legs, its feet nothing but stumps. It raised its arms toward them and clacked the teeth of its many mouths that covered its arms, shoulders, head, and torso. It had jaundiced eyes, mad with an insatiable hunger. Its head was nothing more than a raised dome, reminiscent of a human's but much larger and half sunken into its mass. It opened its main mouth, a gaping, toothy tunnel fused to its neck and chest. It unleashed that horrible wail once more and charged at the group, shaking the ground with its weight.

The assembled strangers all drew their weapons, ready to attack as it bounded from afar.

"Ah, a target. Excellent," Helregal said nonchalantly.

He pushed past the others and walked calmly towards the charging giant. He pulled out a long, black, and gold metal pistol with a skull at the muzzle. It hummed with power as he fired it at the monster. Its rapport was a thunderous roar of the damned as it gushed that same, maroon-tinged energy. It came in a torrent, faster than sound, headed by a large metal shot ball. It punched through the sprinting horror and stopped it dead in its tracks as the energy washed over—and through—it. Its head was gone entirely, and its body was aflame with the Dread Captain's energy, quickly succumbing to it. It unleashed a cacophony of agonized wails from its many mouths. The sound of trapped souls freeing themselves from the abomination echoed in the wind.

It burned away before their eyes, felled in one swift attack. The party was in awe and faced the Dread Captain as he spun back around to address them. They knelt before him. They needed no more proof.

"Master, what is your will?" The goliath Drakkari asked as he bowed his head to the much shorter Dread Captain.

"Come, brothers and sisters. We have much work to do..."

The party rose and followed the Dread Captain back to his ship. The island howled as they left; it wanted no part of them.

XV

What Must Be Done

When the knock came to his door, Huasca had been preparing a decoction over a flame. He raised an eyebrow. He rarely got visitors, and Morgan's knock was quite distinct. He stood and stretched before walking toward the door and cracking it open to see a familiar—and unexpected set of eyes glaring back at him.

"…Come in…" He offered, letting him into the room.

As Osiris walked around the room, he found a spot to sit and took it promptly, without words or much to do. Huasca reclaimed his seat by the burner, taking his decoction off the flame and mixing it with a spoon.

"To what do I owe the pleasure, child?"

"Ye know I don't like it when ye call me that, First Mate," Osiris said matter-of-factly.

Huasca settled back in his chair. "My apologies, Osiris."

Osiris nodded, folding his arms. "These powers that I have. Whenever I ask ye where they came from, you're vague with me. Why?"

Huasca looked at him for a moment, still mixing the decoction liquid into a creamy consistency, before putting it down and folding his arms. "What sparked the curiosity? Every time I'd tried to give you council in the past, you ignored me."

"Spoke to Claude Humris as he was examining me. Let's just say he gave me food for thought."

"Well, I should take notes from him, then," Huasca said pleasantly. Claude was a brief speaker, a soft speaker, but his words often struck a chord that others wouldn't.

"You no doubt have noticed that every time that you use your powers, your eyes, and those tattoos covering your body glow, yes? Most likely after you get angry or distressed?"

Osiris rubbed a hand over a tattooed arm. He wasn't surprised that he knew.

"Aye…"

"Tell me, have any of the people you've fought ever called you any strange names—other than pirate, pirate filth, pirate bastard—you get the picture."

Osiris thought back to when he'd fought the El'wa knight. She called him an 'Alyrian'. As did the samurai aboard the Bounty. They were not the first, nor would they be the last. "They say I'm an Alyrian. But I've never cast a spell in me life," Osiris said.

Huasca nodded. "I thought as much. I suppose it is time that I started explaining what you are and why it is you have lived almost your entire life at sea…"

*****

The captain's cabin was the most well-furnished room on the ship, though it was still sparse in comparison to what no doubt would be found on a merchant or naval ship or even some other pirate ships. Morgan kept his quarters simple. A bookshelf sat on the wall to the right of the doorway, several yards from his desk. To the left wall was a coat rack, as well as a chest where Morgan stored his weaponry when not in use. And then, beside his hammock, which was slung between two posts near the large, multi-sectioned bay windows that framed the sea aft of the ship, was his liquor cabinet. It was filled with almost every alcohol Morgan had ever collected and had not drunk, and it was commonplace for him to share in its bounty in celebration with his officers. In fact, a bottle from the cabinet sat on Morgan's desk beside him.

He gazed at his guest with tired, puzzled eyes.

Stone sat down in front of Morgan. This was the first time in a long time that it had just been the two of them speaking.

First time since…

Stone pushed the memory from his mind. That would come later. Morgan looked at him perplexedly and leaned back in his chair, toking his pipe.

"Are we to sit and gaze longingly at one another for several more awkward minutes, or are you going to tell me why it is you felt the need to interrupt the few brief hours of sleep I get in a given day?" Morgan asked, dark circles apparent beneath his weathered eyes.

Stone nodded apprehensively and cleared his throat. "Y-yes cap'n, apologies, sir," he excused as he composed himself and took a deep breath.

"Whatever it is you wish to say, speak it, and speak it plain. It is just the two of us now," Morgan urged with a nod. "Anything you tell me, I promise on my name and my honor to keep it between us."

Stone looked thoughtfully at Morgan for a moment, weighing the truth in those words. It mattered not. What he had to say needed to become public knowledge, and it needed to be done right.

"Bill Louis attempted to stab me tonight after I broke up a fight between him 'n Yager."

A scowl settled into the worn lines of Morgan's face. "Attempted murder of an officer? That's a black penalty. He'll walk for that."

Stone nodded. "With yer permission, sir, I'd have 'em do just that."

Morgan nodded and took another puff of his pipe. "It is granted. Have him walk the plank at sunrise. The sharks will have their breakfast."

Stone nodded slowly. "Aye, sir."

Due to the constant stream of waste that a ship trails behind it—animal bones, feces, scraps of meat that were undesirable for human consumption—it was all too common for fish to begin trailing after the ships, especially during the day, when the cooks would be most likely to throw their food refuse overboard. This, of course, would attract the things that ate the fish as well. Usually, nothing bigger than a barracuda. On occasion, however, especially after large meals and feasts, like they were having tonight, the fish would school together around the ship. This inevitably attracted sharks in their wake. Bladefins, great maws, prowlers, and the like. All of them were known and eager maneaters. If he were lucky, Bill Louis would be ended by them quickly.

If he's not, however.

Stone didn't want to ponder what would become of the man if he was left to sit in the water, especially till nightfall. There were terrible things that lurked in the depths at night, things that did not always kill their prey outright.

"Was that all, Mr. Stone? If so, I'd like to go back to my slumber," Morgan said impatiently.

He'd had troubled sleep for the past several nights, and Stone had come in just when he was in the middle of a restful sleep.

"There's one more matter, sir," Stone finally said, his hand squeezing tightly around the pouch in his pocket.

Morgan studied Stone's expression and put out his pipe, releasing the last plume of its bitter tobacco smoke into the air and putting it into his coat pocket. "Speak."

Stone's larynx bobbed up and down in his neck as he swallowed. "Durin' the fight, Yager dropped his belongings on the floor and left 'em there afterward. I went to gather 'em, to give 'em back to 'em. Then I found *this*."

He dropped the coin pouch on the desk, and Morgan looked at it a moment before grabbing it and dragging it back across the table to inspect it further. He noted the red dragon insignia upon it, and he gave a furtive smirk.

"This is an imperial coin purse. The kind nobles and the like handout to each other. No man on this ship would have access to one of these, and I don't recall any of them being of noble blood, either. Especially not Daniel Yager," Morgan said.

He looked Stone in the eyes. "And you believe this is his? Perhaps he picked it up from someone else."

Stone paused a moment, then shook his head.

Stars, do I wish that was the case.

"Early before, 'fore we set sail from Emperor's Rest, I came into the cabin to speak with ye. I told ye I had a notion of who was the turncoat, but I didn't want to give a name at the time 'cause I didn't want to alert them, remember?" Stone said.

"I recall. I was more than a little unhappy with that declaration, but I understood its reasoning 'n respected it," Morgan said.

"'N I thank ye, sir, and well…I had hoped the same. That Yager just stole the purse off some fool 'n kept it fer himself, sure—but me gut says otherwise. So does this." He dropped the cloth with the fruity and grainy-smelling powder on it.

Morgan took it, looked at the multi-colored substance therein, and sniffed it. "This is birdseed."

Stone nodded. "The day we was boarded, I saw a seahawk fly over the ship and depart in the direction where the imperials came from. Coulda been nothin' I thought, but I happened to find Yager standin' where the bird had just flewn from. So's I asked 'em about it. He played cagey, brushed it off, 'n so did I. Then, when I found that seed it all came rushin' back to me. Now, I'm thinkin' that the way the Imps managed to get the drop on us is cause that seahawk flew over 'n warned 'em. If a man were to, say, lure the bird with seed, then attach a message to it 'n send it off to deliver it to its handlers, then we'd be none the wiser. Seahawks, gulls 'n the like, all common birds ye see at sea from time to time.

"'Cept them birds only travel about twenty miles or so off the coast to feed. We was well over that from land, at least fifty or more. Again, odd, but easy to dismiss. Birds get lost, they go further out to sea if food's scarce 'n they'll sit atop the water to feed 'n rest a spell—all makes sense, really. Till I start to think about the circumstances that lead to us gettin' captured. That bird took flight no more than an hour or two 'fore we was found. Too close to be a coincidence. Then I recalled seein' a seahawk, flyin' round the ships when we was sailin' to Emperor's Rest…"

Morgan connected the dots and leaned forward on his desk, his furtive smile turning back into a scowl. His eyes narrowed as realization dawned on them.

"The hawk takes flight shortly before we're boarded. I see Yager standin' where it flew from. Then, tonight, I find a coin purse, the kind the Imps would definitely use to pay someone of import. And, if that wasn't damnin' enough, we have the birdseed. Why would Yager need seed to draw the hawk in? Why would he want to catch the hawk, period? Well, cap'n…you tell me, because where it stands, it seems plenty obvious."

"Daniel Yager was given birdseed to lure the seahawk to relay our location. He wrote a message, lured the hawk while we were preoccupied and while the men would be reveling, and sent it off before he could draw too much attention. The hawk delivered his message to the imperials, waiting beyond the horizon. Then, the imperials closed in on us. His job done, they paid him for his services, but as he knew that he could not evade suspicion, was he to up and leave—or perhaps because he was instructed to carry on with us to relay information to his handlers, he remained. A bit too close to the flame, but in keeping with Yager's modus operandi," Morgan said.

"My thoughts exactly. If it were me, I'd be long gone by now. I'd have jumped ship at Oceanus soon as we weighed anchor 'n made for the hills 'n the brothels with a pocket full uh gold. But I know Yager, he's a risk-taker, and he's got an axe to grind here. It would eat at 'em not to set the record straight. What he wants is vindication from the shadow cast o'er 'em. He's been a pirate most of his adult life. This life is all he knows 'n he's a Sarxian through 'n through. We Sarx need the sea air to stay stable. To turn against the Black would put a mark on 'em. He'd never be able to sail with another crew again. Every pirate would know of his treachery, 'n he'd have a price on his head," Stone explained.

"So here he remains. Biding his time, trying to win back what he's lost, or at least find a way to reconcile it. A pity it will cost him his life."

Stone sighed. He'd sailed with Yager for as long as he'd been a pirate. Now, he would be the one responsible for his demise. How cruel this life could be.

"So, how do we proceed? The men need to know who the turncoat is, or they'll be tearin' each other apart until someone's thumbed for it."

Morgan folded his arms. "Whom have you told?"

Stone shook his head. "None, though Moary was there with me when I found the pouch. Whether he put together what I did is another story, though."

Morgan nodded slowly. "Good. Soon, we are going to come upon a lone isle, I've spoken with the Tannis brothers, and they recommend we run Azura aground for repairs. When we do, we're going to take what we've found, inform the other officers, and formally accuse Yager of treachery. From there, we will let the men decide what his fate will be."

"They'll have him keeled. Ye know that don't ye?" Stone said, his heart speeding up in his chest.

"If that is their wish, then so be it."

*****

Huasca drank the decoction he'd been mixing, taking slow, heavy gulps of the syrupy liquid. When he finished, he wiped his lips with the back of his hand and gritted his teeth. Osiris watched as the man's ritual scars and eyes began to glow. They glowed the same bright turquoise color as Osiris'. Osiris watched reservedly; he'd seen this before. Huasca often partook of strong alchemical substances to aid his navigation. He said that they helped him see the stars, even on cloudy nights, and that they gave him a preternatural sense of location. He could tell their geographic position without the need for ordinary measurement tools like Morgan or Stone would resort to.

They also let him speak to the voices in his head.

Osiris mused.

Back in Xalla, Huasca was a shaman, or so he'd been told. An Alyrian medicine man who could use his powers to divine people's fates and manipulate the elements. Now, however, all he could do was give directions and sit catatonic, talking to the voices in his head. He didn't know what to make of that. If the old man was so powerful, why was it that he hadn't ever seen him actually *do* anything powerful? Throw a fireball or a bolt of lightning. Or turn his skin to stone.

Why can't I do that?

"Our world is overflowing with a strange and powerful energy. An energy as old as time and more powerful than any man, woman, or monster in this world. A force that shapes the ground beneath our feet and the waves of the sea. We call this energy, this force, by many names. The changing winds, the ephemeral ether, the blood of Hera, but you know it as Alyria. Alyria exists in every living thing in this world, child. From the mightiest dragon to the smallest and meekest mouse, all of them have Alyria inside of them. All are capable of manipulating Alyria, but they do so with great difficulty and limited success. It took the combined efforts of thousands of generations of El'wa for them to gain their limited mastery over Alyria, and still, to this day, they only have a weak understanding of what precisely it is," Huasca explained.

"But Alyrians are different?" Osiris said, already seeing where the explanation was going.

Huasca nodded. "Yes. What requires immense training and effort for a normal mortal to accomplish, an Alyrian can do naturally. The energies that flow through our world are attracted to an Alyrian like lightning to a mountain peak. This energy, however, requires an outlet. As Alyrians, we use tattoos to channel this energy to the surface and release it into the world. This energy can be used in many ways, expressing itself in many forms. An Alyrian can do great good with this gift…but they can also cause great destruction. That is why the Alyrian Consortium exists."

Osiris had heard of the Consortium. They were every apostate Alyrian's worst nightmare. Their magisters hunt them down with fanatical zeal, either trapping them and bringing them back to the Consortium or killing them. For Alyrians, there was no escaping the Consortium, forcing them to go into hiding, secluding themselves from the world to escape subjugation.

Or out at sea…

"I'd imagine the Consortium doesn't have much jurisdiction on the high seas, then?" Osiris asked.

Huasca nodded. "Yes, I found that high-seas life was a much easier alternative than living in Xalla any longer."

Osiris cocked his head. "So it'd be easier to be a pirate than just live in the middle of the mountains?"

Huasca gave a slow blink. "Have you ever lived in the mountains or spoken to anyone who does?"

Osiris threw his hands up. "If they lived in the mountains, I'd imagine they'd have no interest or cause for talking to a pirate."

"Well, having lived in the mountains for several years, I can tell you that it is not a fun existence. You live in isolation, so you are an easy target for predators. The mountain I lived on had a population of whiteheads living in its caves and mines, which meant that I had to routinely put up warding barriers at night to avoid being eaten."

Osiris scratched his head. "What the fuck is a whitehead?"

"They are spiders, roughly the size of a man, but with a torso attached, arms, and a spider's head on its shoulders."

Osiris shivered. "That sounds like a nightmare."

"It was. I did not sleep much."

Osiris looked at his arms. The tattoos that lined them were dark, inert. When the Alyria surged through him, he felt positively electric. Fearless. It was a sensation he could get drunk from.

"So, I am fated to be seabound forever? Hiding from some hitherto unseen threat?" Osiris gave a mock laugh. "I face death damn near every day. This is no different, old man."

Huasca sighed. "In time when you learn to control your powers, you may yet be able to return to land. *True* land, not the Storm Tide or a brief repose at port. One day, you may yet return home. But you are not ready—"

"Not ready? Fifteen years at sea isn't enough? Will I sail every sea on this world before I am to be strong enough to decide my own fate?"

"You could sail for an eternity and not get anywhere with that impenetrable ego of yours, boy!" Huasca spat.

"My ego is—"

A sharp knock at the door broke their argument. The two agitated men looked at one another before Huasca spoke.

"Enter."

Captain Morgan opened the door and came into the room, shutting it behind him. "Mr. Huasca, we've a matter to discuss regarding Daniel Yager..." he paused, noticing Osiris sat in the chair across from Huasca.

Osiris sat, arms folded, looking inquisitively at Morgan. "Cap'n."

Morgan nodded. "Siris." He looked between the two men. He could sense the tension in the air. Huasca was standing, his glowing eyes furrowed in irritation.

"Did I interrupt something? I apologize. I will return later," Morgan said, turning for the door.

"Nay, cap'n, we're done here. Why don't we discuss this matter of Mr. Yager?" Osiris asked with interest.

Morgan looked back at Huasca, then Osiris, and weighed his options. Siris was a good and loyal mate. He would not speak of what was said unless expressly given permission to.

"Aye, have a seat." Morgan looked at Huasca, who nodded sharply, then sat back down. "We have new information regarding our turncoat and potentially an end to this ugly business," he began.

*****

Osiris stepped out of the cabin and into the cool night air. As he walked the main deck and looked up at the crow's nest, he saw an unexpected sight; Armen Hanover was there. He scaled the ladder, pondering his next words.

"See anythin'?" Osiris asked, standing next to the teen.

Hanover didn't respond for several long moments, gazing out at the horizon through a spyglass.

"I saw a whale and its calf breach the water not too long ago. Looked like a blue breacher. It broke the surface and sprayed a geyser of water into the air, as did the babe before they went back down."

Osiris whistled. "I 'member when we sailed up north in the Boreal Sea we saw a pod ofem'. They grow bigger up there, for some reason. One of 'em breached the water and launched straight up into the air, easily twenty feet up."

Osiris lit up with awe, and he spread his arms wide. "Big as the damn ship, just about. When it went back under, it sent up a wave nearly big enough to capsize us. When the ship settled 'n we managed to get everything secured again, I remember just sittin' there, stunned, like." He bit his lip, trying to find the words to describe the sheer humbling majesty of what he'd seen.

"Couldn't have been much older 'n ten, maybe? Ye live at sea, you see all kinds of strange things. But up till that point I'd never seen somethin' so big as that. 'N there was hundreds of 'em! Far as the eye could see!" Osiris fanned his arms out, trying to imitate the vastness of the pod of blue breacher whales.

Hanover put the spyglass down, watching Osiris' expression light up. "How did you survive? A ten-year-old at sea. How?"

Osiris shrugged. "For years, I stayed land-bound in the Storm Tide. Livera was my home, and I got all my learning from there. Eventually, though, Huasca took me on my first voyage out to sea. Some small, no-name sloop ship. Can't remember the captain's name and barely remember the crew. When the fightin' came, Huasca'd hide me below deck, have me sit in a cabin with the door locked. Told me never to open it, less he told me to."

Hanover was shocked. A ten-year-old child at sea? In the middle of a ship battle?

No wonder he's so callous.

The things he must have seen as a child. Words couldn't begin to describe it. It made him think back to his own childhood on the streets of Spirus. The squalor, the loneliness, the hunger…

"When did you become a pirate?"

Osiris leaned against the opposite railing, looking up at the moon as he searched his memories. "When I was fifteen, I took the Black."

"Fifteen? That's two years younger than I! How did you get recruited at fifteen years?!" Hanover flubbed, unable to hide his surprise.

Osiris fixed him with a blank gaze. "I wasn't recruited into bein' a pirate. A Storm Tide pirate is not the same as some random fuck with a boat and a bunch of men with guns. We're a society. And to become one of us—to truly take up the Black Code of Piracy—ye have to be blooded in. Ye must kill someone."

Hanover held his gaze. "Then I will kill. Give me a blade and be done with it. When next we board, I will go with the boarding party and prove my worth!"

Osiris leaned forward and put a hand on Hanover's shoulder. "This will be the last warning ye hear from me, boy. The path ye wish to tread I have spared ye from for as long as I can. Once you're out there in the fray, it's kill or be killed. Remember that, and do not hesitate. Do ye hear me?"

The look Osiris gave him was not one of anger, disgust, or disdain but concern.

You'll regret this, boy.

Osiris knew. But if this was his choice, then so be it.

"I will spill blood for my brothers in black, and seal my fate, never to turn back!" Hanover shouted for all to hear.

Osiris blinked slowly, looking down below them at the deck of the ship. "Then so be it, boy. When next we sail into battle, ye will board with us, and ye will have your first blood."

He held out a hand for Hanover, not in camaraderie, but in promise. Hanover took it.

XVI

Bad Meets Evil

Far north of Azura, a battle raged between a fleet of human pirates, the Hail Mary pirates, and a fleet of Duwa merchants, Lokan 'n Sons Trading Company. The pirates had chased their prey for several hours, but now, as the night ushered in, they closed in on their targets.

"Signal for Jackson 'n Smith to come around and fire upon the western flank!" The leader of the pirates, a man named Captain Pate said. He was manning the wheel of his ship.

"If we mean to board her, then broadsiding the ship will hamper our efforts!" Pate's second-in-command, Brunt, said.

Pate shouted orders to the men controlling the sails before turning back to Brunt. "The only ships worth boarding in this whole fleet are the two in the center. The other three are guard ships. Take them out and the two in the center are vulnerable and ripe for plunder. Now get him on that ship before they can form a firing line! I'll signal for Andrews 'n Franklin to bring up the east. If we can outmaneuver 'em, we may be able to surround 'em and kill their cannonade before it starts!"

Brunt nodded, then set off to signal the other ships.

Pate knew that if the Duwa got into a broadside formation they would obliterate any ship that was caught in the firing range. Their ships were bigger and bulkier than most human ships, but their cannons far outclassed even the best human-made ones. They would turn their ships to driftwood in minutes at best.

Force them to choose. Us or the merchants?

Pate strategized.

He pulled out signal flags from his coat pocket and flashed them to his two ships to the east. They signaled back. They were moving forward to assault the guard ship. Pate nodded, then returned to the wheel.

The Duwa had too few gunships to split their focus, and if they failed to lockdown a target, they risked compromising the merchant ships they meant to protect, as well as their own flanks. They would either lose the merchant ships or lose the whole fleet.

Or die fighting.

Pate knew the chances of the Duwa peacefully surrendering, especially to humans, was almost non-existent. The Duwa were a proud, stout people who would sooner die than submit to an aggressor. Unlike men, it was unlikely that they would be bribed or scared to surrender. No, absolute victory or crushing defeat were the only ends to this conflict. And Pate knew his men wouldn't even consider retreating, not after they'd fully committed to the attack.

"We've got all cannons loaded 'n ready for a broadside, cap'n!" The ship's gunner reported.

Pate swept his gaze over the middle ship guarding the merchants, their target. Andrews and Franklin, Jackson and Smith would be tackling the western and eastern ships, respectively. It was the flagship, Hail Mary's job to take out the center ship.

"Prepare to fire on my command, when we come within two-hundred meters we'll volley," Pate instructed, guesstimating how long it would take to reach the appropriate angle and distance. Less than a minute, perhaps.

"Aye, cap'n!" The gunner responded before heading back below deck.

Pate watched as Andrews and Franklin moved in on the western gunship and saw Jackson and Smith coming for the east. His other ships, Mary Minor the First, Second, Third, and Fourth, were all smaller, faster ships than Hail Mary, but had less firepower as a result.

"They're scrambling. They don't know whether to engage us in a firing line or attempt to surround the merchant's vessels," Brunt observed.

"They don't have enough ships to surround them and face us. They'd have been better off trying to blast as many of us as they could in a broadside formation even if it cost them a trade ship. Now, they'll lose everything."

Pate and Brunt congratulated themselves as the Hail Mary's broadside came to bear against their target. The ship had turned its broadside to face them.

"Fire!" Pate yelled.

BOOM!

Hail Mary unleashed her cannons on the ship in a series of explosions. Its target faltered, only managing to fire several of its cannons as Hail Mary's cannonade rained upon it, blowing apart the foe's gun decks and obliterating the side of the ship facing Hail Mary.

Pate could hear their screams from here as their ship began to crumble from the barrage. The Duwa guard ship would not sail again, and it was too damaged now to put up a fight. The day was most assuredly won.

"Cap'n, look to the east! A fog bank is upon us!" Brunt warned.

Pate looked east in confusion. How had he not noticed fog rolling in? It was coming in fast. He knew that it would be upon them in minutes at best.

"No matter. The lieutenants will scupper the other two guard ships before the fog overtakes us. The merchants have nowhere to run," Pate dismissed, though a creeping chill ran up his spine at the sight of the fog.

At some point in the heat of battle, the moon had shifted from blue to red. In the red moonlight, the fog looked downright ominous. Pate shrugged it off, however. He was no stranger to sudden weather changes, it was part and parcel of being a seaman. He had more pressing concerns. He trained his spyglass on the western flank as he heard the boom of cannon fire. Lieutenants Jackson and Smith, the captains of Mary Minor the First and Second, respectively, had closed in and fired on the western guard ship, which had turned to face them for a broadside.

The ship was unable to fire at both ships, so it fired at Smith's ship. The damage was evident. Duwa cannons were much stronger than human-made ones, and so even their smallest ships packed a deadly punch in comparison to their size.

Something about their powder.

He recalled.

The stuff explodes like a mountain of dynamite.

It had certainly done so on Smith's ship. It was positively gutted on its starboard side. It had done considerable damage to the Duwa ship as well, however. Its broadside was aflame, evidence that one of the cannonballs had struck the magazines. The ship was done for, as were its men. Smith and his crew would be forced to abandon ship, however.

"Good shootin' boys," Pate said with a nod of approval.

"Aye. It cost them their ship, but they may have just killed all hope for a turnaround as well. Two ships destroyed means even if the third manages to sink Andrews *and* Franklin, it will never be able to recover in time to stop us from blowing them to Aethera," Brunt said. "That fog, though…"

Pate looked back at the fog. It was only a few dozen meters away from Andrews and Franklin's ships. He watched as the fog swallowed them just as they closed in on the last remaining Duwa gunship. He heard cannons discharge and saw sparks of light in the red haze of fog, then nothing as the fog rolled toward his own vessel.

"Fog's rollin' in, boys. Keep sharp! We're still in the heat of battle!" Pate instructed.

The men watched the fog as it passed over the ship, blanketing it. Pate could tell that they were also uneasy about it.

As the red cloud consumed their ship and their sight, an ice-cold sensation froze into Pate's spine.

A blood moon 'n fog. Where have I heard that story before?

"What are the odds that we get a blood moon 'n fog all in the same night within minutes of each other?" Pate wondered aloud.

"Not exactly impossible, but still slim to none," Brunt replied.

"Where's that damn Alyrian? Can't he dispel this fog?"

"Just because I can harness Alyria, doesn't mean I can snap my fingers and make all your troubles disappear good captain," a bookish, curt voice answered.

Pate hitched his breath as a figure materialized before him and he gazed into the unwelcome, but familiar features of the Alyrian in question.

"Mr. Oculeth, good to see that ye've decided to join us when the battle's nye over. I hope ye weren't expecting any shares for attendance?" Pate greeted him sarcastically.

Oculeth flashed a disingenuous smirk before returning to his normal, unconcerned expression. "I've no need for the poultry sum you call a share, captain, I assure you. I came to observe this strange phenomenon that has befallen us. A blood moon *and* a fog wall, all in the same evening? Quite the rarity. We're surely fortunate to witness it."

"Fortunate? Perhaps you haven't noticed, friend, but we're in the middle of a battle. Visibility is paramount to victory. Now, we've no idea whether Lieutenants Andrews and Franklin have destroyed their mark or been destroyed by it!" Pate griped.

"Considering that we only saw one set of flashes in the fog at the position they would have been in, I think it fair to assume that only one set of volleys was exchanged. So at worst, the first ship to come about on the gunship was destroyed. At best, Mr. Andrews was successful in his attack and the gunship is taking on water as we speak," Oculeth dissected, pushing the spectacles sitting on the edge of his nose back up to his eyes.

"Then why haven't we heard any screamin'?" Brunt asked warily.

The three men stood silent for a moment, taking note of the lack of noise. Following every cannonade was the inevitable sound of wood splintering and men screaming their last, dying breaths. Now, however, there was silence. And that didn't sit well with any of them.

As if in answer to their curiosity, a series of rapid, explosive rapports sounded off in the direction of the eastern flank, roughly where Andrews, Franklin, and the remaining Duwa gunship would be. The sound was simultaneously from splintering wood, falling lumber, and screaming men.

Pate, having heard the sound of his ships' cannons more times than could be counted, noted the peculiar sound of the cannon fire.

"That wasn't one of ours what fired," Pate said grimly.

Brunt nodded. "Aye. Those must've at least been twenty-six pounders. Too weighty to have been Andrews or Franklin's shot."

That wasn't good. Only the Duwa would use cannons that big. Which meant they had fired first, which meant that at least one of his ships was all but destroyed.

"That means..." Pate trailed off.

The night lit up as a hail of cannon fire followed, and the trio watched as a great blaze emerged where the ships were. Pate could see, now, what was happening at the eastern flank, and it made his jaw drop.

"What in the name of Aeradin, Goffanyn, and Idallon, is that?" Oculeth asked aloud.

"I don't know...but it isn't good," Pate said, quietly.

*****

"Ancestor's take me! What in the ironclad *fuck* is *that*?" Lorkan, the captain of the Ironfist, or as Pate simply knew it the last Duwa gunship, shouted.

"I dunno, but it turned those two pirate ships to kindlin', it did!" Lorkan's second, Gromly, exclaimed.

The Duwa sailors all cheered in awe at the devastation that had just befallen their would-be killers. The pirates had come in fast and hot, baring down on them as they struggled to bring their lug of a ship to bear. One ship might have been surmountable, so long as they could point the cannons at it, but the two that came upon them were too much to handle in one maneuver. The pirates positioned themselves to shoot them from the portside and the nose of the ship. An attack that would have seen their ship gutted by cannon fire.

Lorkan had seen what these cagey pirates had done to the other two ships he'd been deployed with. He'd been mumbling a prayer to the ancestors as he saw their fate come for him.

But then the mystery ship came.

It materialized seemingly out of nowhere, shooting up from below the surface and almost immediately firing on the two pirate ships on either side of it, striking them true and igniting them. Now, the pirates were too busy abandoning ship, screaming for their lives, and preparing for their watery graves. Lorkan and the Ironfist had been spared.

But still, an unsettling feeling was weighing in his gut. He ran a hand through his long beard that hung to his waist. Who were these mysterious saviors? Why had they come when they did? And why had they slain the pirates, rather than siding with them? He could tell the ship was not of Duwa make. It bore no heraldry of such, from what he saw, and it was not as broad as his kin liked to make their vessels.

Even so, it was a massive ship. From his limited knowledge of human ships, he'd guess it was between a galleon and a ship-of-the-line in terms of size. So large was it that it had a statue mounted beneath the bowsprit, a naked woman, blindfolded and wrapped in chains.

"Look, cap'n! It's comin' about us! Our saviors've come to greet us, boys!" Gromly cheered, as did the other sailors.

They're just grateful to be alive.

Lorkan thought.

As the ship neared, however, and he could fully appreciate her size and features, his heart began to sink. The Duwa cheered and waved at their saviors, silent shadows standing on the decks and hanging off the masts and yardarms of the ship. But their cheers fell silent as their benefactors came close. Through the red haze of fog, and the smoke that billowed from the burning pirate ships, Lorkan could see that their saviors were neither human nor Duwa.

No, they were…

"Man your stations and ready the cannons! This fight's not over, kin!" Lorkan shouted.

Gromly looked confused a moment but saw what his captain was staring at. He echoed his command and pulled out his weapons.

"Ancestors, give us strength!" Lorkan shouted.

A red-eyed figure, standing on the steering deck of the mystery ship laughed maliciously as golden chains erupted from it and attacked the Ironfist.

*****

"Reload the cannons 'n ready for an engagement! That bastard killed Andrews, Franklin, and all their crews!" Pate barked.

"Aye, aye, cap'n!" The Hail Mary pirates shouted as they readied for their next strike.

Pate turned the wheel and angled the ship toward the east, looking over to the west to see that Jackson had begun to turn around to join his attack on the mystery ship. He nodded. Though they may lose the merchant ships, they would make damn sure that whoever these bastards were, they paid for killing their brothers and sisters.

As they approached, Pate watched in confusion as he heard a cacophony of rattling chains and screaming men.

"What is that strange noise? It sounds like rattling chains," Oculeth said.

"Aye, that's what I thought," Brunt added.

"The fuck are they doing with chains? Are they slavers?" Pate wondered.

"I feel ill tidings, captain. I know that you'll not accept it, but I would be remiss if I did not suggest we forfeit the field," Oculeth whispered in Pate's ear. Pate looked at him as though he'd just been shot.

"They killed my men and may have just cost us our prize. If I were to walk away now, at best I'd be done as a captain, at worst I'd be killed for cowardice. Do I look like a man where either of those would be acceptable to me?"

Oculeth scowled and looked at Brunt, who was loading a bullet into his flintlock. Brunt noticed his gaze and shrugged.

"He's right. To turn away now is career suicide. Look at those men, they want blood," Brunt pointed to the main deck.

Oculeth could see the anger and determination in their eyes. The look that men gave when they'd made up their minds and would not be turned from it. They reminded him of Pate.

"Ye wanted to observe the phenomena, well now you're about to get some hands-on experience with one. That ship shot up out the water and blew our boys to smithereens. How's that for a phenomenon?" Brunt finished.

He put his pistol away and looked through his spyglass once more.

Oculeth looked back at the ship and clenched his fist. Like the tensing of a muscle, he could feel the Alyria tattoos tense on his skin and thrum energy through him. He could sense something was very abnormal about this ship. As they drew closer, he could see an *aura* around it. It was black and maroon, and it smelled of death.

"Cap'n…you'll…you'll want to see this…" Brunt said in a low voice.

Pate paused and let Brunt take the wheel, perplexed. Brunt pointed to the mystery ship, and Pate aimed the spyglass at it. Through the fog, it was hard to make out the finite details.

"What am I lookin' for?"

"The sails, Pate. Look at the bloody sails."

Pate looked up and froze.

He dropped the spyglass.

"Can't be…"

"Cap'n! There's somethin' knockin' around on the side of the ship!" Phillip, a deckhand, as Pate recalled, said.

Pate walked down the stairs to the main deck, listening for the knocking sound. Several of the men had paused working, listening as well. He waited, listening, for several moments. He opened his mouth to speak just as the noise happened again.

Knock.

Knock.

Drag.

Pate cocked his head, trying to position where the sound came from.

Knock.

Knock.

Drag.

It sounded like somebody tapping a sword on wood, then dragging their foot along it, or at least that's the best he'd describe it.

Knock.

Knock.

Drag.

Starboard. It's coming from the starboard side.

Pate realized.

He looked at Phillip who nodded. He wordlessly approached the starboard railing and looked over.

Phillip twitched once, a hard, jerky movement. Then, he stumbled backward.

"What the—" Pate mouthed.

A jagged, golden knife was stuck in his eye.

All eyes turned to the railing as the killer dragged themselves over it.

"What in Sheolhenna is *that*?!" Someone shouted as the figure came stood up.

Before them was a waterlogged, lipless corpse. Its teeth glittered with gold caps, and it had a gemstone pressed into its forehead. Pate realized that the corpse was carrying two axes with gold handles, as well. They glittered in the foggy, blood-moonlit night. It regarded the men with sunken, jaundiced eyes. A trembling man dropped his weapon on the deck, and the noise sparked the creature into action. It attacked immediately with startling speed for a ragged bone corpse. It swung at the man, splitting his throat open messily with the axe and making his head cock back, gushing blood all over as he fell. It crouched over him and began to gnaw at his throat.

It was eating him.

"Stars above, kill it!" Pate shouted.

He aimed his double-barrel pistol and fired at the monster, as did a dozen other men, lighting up the creature and the body of the man in its clutches with bullets for several moments.

The creature released the body and stumbled backward as the bullets impacted it. Pate landed a telling blow to its head, emptying both barrels of his gun and punching holes through it as it fell backward over the railing.

"Gods…" Brunt gasped as he placed a hand on Pate's shoulder. He'd been drawn down by the sound of gunfire and came just in time to see the horrible corpse monster stumble backward over the railing.

"That was but one of what awaits us, brethren. The enemy that sank the Third and the Fourth is no ordinary foe. It is a nightmare made reality. Behold," Pate said as he pointed at the mysterious ship.

Many of the men froze in place, the fight and the anger drained from them as they beheld the flags of their adversary.

A red flag with a black, gold-toothed, screaming skull. Gold chains sat behind it like the crossbones of a jolly roger.

"Anathane's Pain…the stories were true…" Brunt mumbled. He'd been hoping that his eyes were playing tricks on him when he looked through the spyglass. They weren't.

"Steel yourselves, pirates. We be in the midst of a ghost story, tonight," Pate announced.

He pulled out his sword. They were in range.

"Unload on that ship and send it back to the watery depths it came from!" Pate commanded.

Just then, the men on deck screamed as a wave of waterlogged, jeweled corpses boarded the ship and began attacking the crew.

"We're boarded!" Brunt announced.

Several of the undead creatures scrambled up to the steering deck to attack them, and Pate moved from the steering wheel to meet them. He swung his sword and clashed with the sword of one of the foes. He broke the clash, shoving the attacker forward and nearly cutting its arm off with his second swing. He watched in horror as the creature ripped the destroyed limb off entirely and began battering him with it, smacking him in the head and face with the arm before discarding it. In its place, a new one surged forth, a skeletal arm, made entirely of gold. The creature flexed the new arm and looked at Pate, smiling.

"What unholy Alyria is this?"

He looked around, uncertain how to proceed. To his right, Brunt was being pressed against a railing by his attacker.

Where's that cowardly Alyrian? I'll skin him alive if he's abandoned us!

Pate never trusted Oculeth. Too prim and proper, too posh to engage in the 'drudgery of manual labor' as he called it. Now, was it any wonder that he'd abandoned them in their hour of need? That he'd—

"Watch out, captain!" Oculeth shouted from behind.

Pate felt the hair on his neck stand on end and knew that he was about to cast a spell of some sort. He leapt out of the way and turned just in time to see his attacker's confused expression as Oculeth attacked. He was levitating a spear in the air, likely the weapon of his fallen opponent, who lay dismembered on the deck. His eyes glowed and his tattoos flared like blue auroras on his skin as he launched the spear at the undead—and impaled it to a mast. Pate and Oculeth watched the creature twitch violently for several moments before Pate emptied his gun into its head. It sprayed liquid gold from its destroyed head, and the duo turned their attention to Brunt and the creature attempting to bite into his neck.

"Get offem', bugger!" Pate yelled as he charged at them and grabbed the thing in a chokehold, pulling it off Brunt.

It fought hard, jerking left and right and elbowing Pate in the ribs, breaking his grapple. The two stood, and Pate sized the creature up, but paused when he realized it wasn't assuming a combat stance. He lowered his blade and cocked his head as he watched it. His adversary was also adorned in gold, with a chain dangling from its rotted ear to what remained of its nose. The foe charged at him with its sword, and Pate parried the blow. He went to counter it but was thwarted when the creature was suddenly enveloped in a translucent blue mist and was propelled over the main deck, slamming harshly into a mast, then a railing before falling into the sea. Pate looked at Oculeth, who nodded.

"Not so useless, now, am I?" Oculeth asked.

Pate scoffed and helped up Brunt, who was rubbing his neck where the undead had been trying to strangle him.

"We've got bigger problems, I fear." Brunt coughed, then pointed as several figures leapt from Anathane's Pain, including a man wearing a captain's garb.

"More boarders! Look sharp!" Pate warned as he stormed down the stairs to the main deck.

XVII

HAIL MARY

"Fall to your knees 'n pray!" A Damned officer screamed as they jumped aboard Hail Mary.

Helregal moved wordlessly as he fell upon the pirates. Many of them were too stunned by the terrors amidst them to act. He cut them down with ease. Some mustered themselves to fight but quickly scattered as Helregal felled each man with a slash of his cutlass, Bloodletter. It lived up to its name, spraying their essence out from vicious slash wounds and humming as it drank of their blood.

"Is this the best ye can muster? Will no man face the Dread Captain in battle?" he challenged as every man either ran from him or was preoccupied fighting with his crew.

"I'll answer yer challenge, goldie. Stories or no, ye killed my men 'n that can't go unanswered," Pate said as he pushed through the fray.

His men were being slaughtered around him. He knew Jackson would be upon them soon, a minute or two at most. He just needed to hold out until then.

Fight the Dread Captain of Anathane's Pain, Sheolhenna's Flagship, himself. If I die, at least mine will be one for the ages!

Pate mused.

He dropped into a dueling stance.

"Ha! Do ye know who I am, mortal?"

"Once, ye were the hero of every pirate on Hera. Then, ye became the scourge of every pirate on Hera, 'n the Immortal Captain put ye in the dirt himself. He should've sent ye in pieces, I aim to correct that mistake," Pate promised, swiping his sword at the ready.

"Is that so? Well, ye've nothing if not spunk. I like that."

"I'll keep that in mind after I tear that mask off your face and use it for a codpiece!" Pate spat and charged at Helregal.

The Dread Captain laughed and clashed his blade with Pate's, waiting until the last possible moment to defend himself. Pate's eyes were wide.

How the bloody hell did he move that fast?

"Is that *all*? You'll need more than that to kill me, boy. Now get on with it!" Helregal yelled, knocking the blade away and pushing Pate back with his own jabs and slashes.

He assumed an honor duelist's pose: sword arm forward, offhand tucked behind his back. Pate clutched is sword in both hands, assuming the fighter's stance. He used the added control from gripping the blade with both hands to help deflect the force of Helregal's mammoth strikes that battered his blade.

Pate attempted to parry a swing, but the power of Helregal's strike killed the maneuver, barely even redirecting the force of the blade. Pate clenched his teeth in concentration.

"I know ye must be scared, pirate. Most men do not survive the first strike, let alone the twelfth. Ye have my respect, hahahaha!" Helregal mocked.

"I don't need the respect of you, betrayer! You're a plague, and I'll purge you for what you've done!" Pate growled as he blocked another harsh strike. Bloodletter slid uncomfortably close to his shoulder, and he could *feel* the cursed sword attempting to cut into him.

"Plague? I am the very reason you salty seadogs get to sail as free men! I am the reason kings and Emperors alike fear the jolly roger! I made all of you, boy, and don't you ever forget it!" Helregal spat back as Pate forced the blade away from him.

Suddenly a series of gunshots broke up their fight as a horde of pirates stormed onto Hail Mary's deck.

"Cap'n! The cavalry has arrived!" Lieutenant Jackson shouted as he charged onto the deck and cut the legs out from under a Damned before chopping its head off.

Several pirates charged Helregal, breaking up their duel and leaving Pate time to retreat back to Jackson.

"What's the status of the merchant ships?" Pate asked, shouting over the scream of men and the din of battle. The Pain's massive bulk blocked out much of his sightline to the west.

"Smith and several of his men took long boats to board a merchant ship!" Jackson reported.

Pate nodded his agreement. If Smith could take a ship, then even if the other escaped, they'd still have a prize to claim.

"What the fuck are these abominations, and why are they covered in gold?!" Jackson gasped as he watched one of the Damned cut down three of his men. The creature was feasting on the head of one that it had just beheaded.

"Our enemy! Kill them with extreme prejudice!" Pate answered, charging back into the fight. Even now, he could see his men were losing. The bodies were piling up, and most of them were his own men.

If I'm to die today, I'll die as I lived—like a bloody menace to anyone who gets in my way!

✻✻✻✻✻

"Set a course for Anvil Harbor! We need to get out 'o here and back to port as soon as possible!" Captain Brogdan commanded as his officials stood in his office, solemn and somber.

"What of the Ironfist and the other brother ships? Are we to leave 'em to die?" Officer Duggar asked.

"The Ironfist, the Erabis, and the Ghammol were assigned to protect us at all costs. They knew their role, and they played it admirably. When we return to the mountains, we'll honor them and bring news of their heroism for the shamans to memorialize. But right now, we need to get back home in order for that to even be a possibility!" Brogdan explained.

Duggar sighed, as did Grimgy, Hogan, and Tilda. This was not the Duwa way. To abandon one's kin at sea, far from the safety of the mother mountains, was unthinkable. But Brogdan knew that if they went with their toothless ships into the battle, they'd be overtaken just as quickly as their guardsmen had. No, retreat was their only option. What few soldiers were aboard his ship would have to suffice, and they'd have to pray to the ancestors that nothing else barred their path on the voyage back home, as they had not the manpower or the firepower to contend with the hydras that would be teeming in the south, now. Or anything else that might notice them, for that matter.

"What should we tell the militiamen? Many of their own platoon mates were aboard those ships!" Hogan asked.

"Tell them that their brothers 'n sisters died to leave us an openin' to get back home, 'n that squanderin' it would spit on their memory 'n their sacrifice, that's what," Brogdan answered.

"Me battle sisters won't like any of this, merchant captain. I hope you're prepared for the reckonin' awaitin' you back at the cave port," Guard Officer Tilda warned. She was the only ranking service officer aboard the ship now. All her superiors had gone and presumedly died aboard the Erabis.

"Yer battle sisters should thank me fer gettin' one 'o theirs back home 'n one piece, Officer Tilda. But I kannae begrudge 'em their anger." Brogdan sighed. "You're all dismissed. We need to get underway while the pirates are distracted."

The officers began to disperse, but Hogan spoke up, "What of that strange ship, then?"

They all stopped, waiting to hear Brogdan's response.

Brogdan cleared his throat. "We all heard the stories, ay? We don't move off stories 'n fables. What e'er that thing is, it'll not be our concern much longer. Dismissed."

The officers left. Brogdan looked out his window at the receding battlefield. The other merchant ship had broken off, likely to return to Anvil as well, or perhaps not. They were two different trade guilds, so it didn't particularly concern him now. It was eerie, the sea. Duwa was afeared of it just as much as any other sane mortal ought be. But on nights such as this, under such terrible circumstances, it seemed to come alive with its own murderous hunger. Already he could see the fins of sharks headed toward the carnage. A lot of men, good and bad, would be dying tonight. It was his job to make sure that his weren't of their number.

He frowned.

He saw the shape of a rowboat moving just out of view, going towards the side of his ship. He almost didn't notice it for the blazing spectacle that was the remains of the ships felled in the battle, but he *had* seen it.

"Just couldn't leave us be, could ye?" he grunted.

The fight had come to them.

*****

"Sisters! The cutthroats are upon us! Prepare to—" Tilda's words were cut short when a bullet punched through the back of her head and blew her eye out in a gush of blood. She thumped onto the deck as the pirate who killed her stepped over her corpse, and his men followed.

"Good evening, ladies and gentlemen! I am Lieutenant Bronson Smith, and I will be commandeering your ship. Any disagreements can be taken up with the quartermaster here." He patted Tims, his quartermaster, on the shoulder.

Tims gave a cough and a noncommittal smile.

The Duwa looked at the pirate, then at his men. "Ye made a terrible mistake boardin' our ship, manóg. That'll cost ye. Kill 'em, kin!" a woman in the hoard shouted as they charged the pirates.

So much for that.

Smith hefted the mace of the woman he'd shot through the eye and braced himself when he did. It was heavy as a log and cumbersome to swing. He used it to bash the heads of two attackers before he dropped it in favor of his sword.

He dodged out of the way as a Duwa battle sister charged at him, then slammed into Tims, running him through with a poleaxe.

"Tims! Dammit!" Smith cursed, pulling out another pistol and firing at the battle sister. The bullet glanced off her shoulder armor, and she leered at him as she pulled the spike of her poleaxe out of Tims' chest.

The Duwa were a short, stocky people, about the height of an average ten-year-old child but built broader than a grown human man, with the strength and musculature of an ape. This one, Smith observed, was a comely lass.

Shame she's going to have to die.

He lamented.

"Ye killed our mistress, Tilda, manóg. I figured I'd return the favor!" she spat in a thick Duwa accent.

"Don't worry, lovely, you'll be joining her shortly, I assure you!" Smith promised.

The two charged at each other but halted as a terrified wail pierced the din of battle.

"It's got him!"

The two paused, inches away from clashing with one another as they looked in the direction of the screams. A crowd had formed.

A Duwa man was wrestling with a human-sized figure. Its clothes were hanging off its thin, soaked frame, and its face was covered with gold nuggets, seemingly growing out of its head. It slammed the man against a railing and began biting into him.

"It's…eating him…" One of the onlookers gasped.

"There's more of them!" Smith shouted, pointing to the railing the creature was leaning against as numerous undead climbed aboard the ship and entered the fight. They left them no room to process as the creatures charged headlong into the fray, tearing apart pirates and Duwa alike with indiscriminate savagery.

Smith looked at the battle sister, who looked at him. They nodded, then turned to face the new foe. Though they were most certainly not allies, their new enemy took precedence. The two charged, side-by-side, into the horde of gathering Damned, slashing and swinging at them in a coordinated attack. The other pirates and Duwa took their cue and began working together, attacking their hideous new adversaries.

They fought valiantly as the boat was overwhelmed by the Damned.

*****

I'm going to kill you.

I promise I'm going to kill you.

Pate swore.

Oculeth kicked open the door.

"This way! Hurry!"

Pate entered the doorway with Brunt leaning on his shoulder. Oculeth slammed the door behind them and barred it as Pate hurried down the corridor. It was dark, but a bright blue light at the end of the hall illuminated their path and beckoned them from the darkness. They could hear the Damned screaming at them and banging on the door.

Pate hobbled along, practically dragging Brunt with each step. Brunt moaned, unable to hide the pain he felt.

"Hang on, brother! We're almost there, dammit!"

"Leave me…" Brunt said almost pitiably.

"Infernals as me witness, I'll drag ye to heaven before I leave ye in this hell, you understand me?!" Pate said.

Halfway there.

The door splintered open, and the horde of Damned clogged the doorway, fighting themselves to get through before they eventually began guttering out into the hall in pursuit. Their bodies, covered in gold, glittered in the light from the portal.

"They're here! Get through the portal. I'll take up the rear!" Oculeth commanded as he shot a spear of energy into the swarm and cut several in half. The horde surged over the dismembered corpses.

Pate halted at the portal. He didn't trust Oculeth further than he could throw him, but he knew this was their only chance.

"Take Brunt and go! I'll hold them back!" Pate said as the horde bore down at them.

Oculeth grabbed Brunt and turned to go through the portal. "It's been an honor, captain."

"Die well, Mr. Oculeth."

Pate pulled out his reloaded double-barrel pistol as well as his sword. He gritted his teeth and wiped a smear of blood from his face with the crook of his arm.

He faced the horde, unafraid.

Oculeth pushed Brunt through the portal.

Then, he grabbed Pate by the scruff of his collar and dove through. Pate howled, flailing his sword and firing his gun into the crowd as the horde bore down on them. The last thing he saw was a hulking, chalk-white figure charging through the Damned, beelining straight for him. Its eyes were yellow flames of bloodthirst, and then they were gone as he fell through the portal.

Coward.

*****

Helregal looked over his victory with indifference.

The battlefield was littered with sinking, broken ships, and the merchant's vessels were claimed as his own. They would come in handy soon. The battle had been short and violent, lasting less than an hour, but in that time, he had gained much. The Hail Mary pirates, as they called themselves, put up a strong fight, considering that they were ambushed. The Duwa were found wanting, however. By the time he'd entered the fray, most of their gunships were already destroyed. The one he'd attacked was too slow on the draw to put up a real fight, either. He used the chains of Anathane's Pain to lock the ships together, and they were quickly overcome before they could even fire on her.

Even now, a hanging garden of corpses was before him, dangling from the golden chains that made up the shrouds and rigging of Anathane's Pain. He basked in his success for but a moment before turning to his officers kneeling before him.

"What have you to report?"

"The captain of the Hail Mary fleet escaped through a portal with the help of an Alyrian, captain," the beast grunted.

"A pity. But do not despair, Officer Black, there will be many more opportunities for bloodshed in the future," Helregal assured him.

"Good. I hunger for slaughter," Black responded, his voice a deep, quaking baritone, much deeper than any man would be able to muster.

"We have survivors, master. If it pleases, I would experiment on them, after interrogation, of course," the electric green-eyed necromancer, Byzarra, reported.

"Retrieve them," Helregal said.

Byzarra bowed curtly and walked away.

He looked at the tall, masked woman. "Lady Volldah, I have a task that requires your expertise, dear."

The woman rose silently and stepped forth to his side as he turned to look back over the ravaged seascape.

"There is a man that I wish for you to track for me. He wears an amulet like mine, but blue. A pirate captain. Upon his ship is what we seek. Find him, and you will find it. Bring him, and it, to me. Do you understand?"

The woman nodded once. Helregal placed a hand on her golden mask, and she froze as the image of her target flooded her mind. Like a bloodhound on a trail, she could sense him. But he was so very far away.

"Good. Go, now."

She turned and walked to the nose of the ship before stepping onto the railing and leaping overboard, disappearing into the black water. Her pursuit had begun.

"Mr. Shade, were you able to retrieve the shipping lane maps from the trade ships you and Byzarra boarded?" Helregal asked.

The last of them stood, the ghostly black skeleton. "Yes, captain," he responded, handing the maps over to the Dread Captain with a skeletal hand.

Helregal nodded, looking them over a moment before handing them back. "Put them in my study. I will look them over later."

Just then, Byzarra returned with the prisoners in question. Helregal watched as the assortment of men and Duwa shuffled forward and lined up.

Many of them looked shell-shocked and were still streaked in blood. He took note of two of them, a human man with an eyepatch and an armored Duwa woman. They were all lined up before him.

"Kneel!" A Damned Officer said, lashing at the captives with a wicked cord of whip. They knelt.

Helregal walked the line, inspecting each of the survivors as he went. He paused at one man, who was gibbering to himself. Helregal squatted down to eye level with him.

"Do you know who I am?" Helregal asked.

The man whimpered, nodding his head.

"Do you know what is to come?"

The man froze, still gibbering to himself and sobbing.

"Look at me, boy."

The man slowly raised his gaze and looked at Helregal's masked face. The gold skull smiled at him as Helregal's blood-red eyes looked into his soul.

"I ask again: Do you know what is to come?"

The man snuffled, sucking in snot and fear, "Y-y-yes…"

"I can offer you respite, a second chance at life, and an escape from the fate that waits for you."

"An…escape?"

"My master wields the power of life after death. I am his vessel. I offer you a chance to escape judgment for your sins."

"He offers ye nothin' but lies! Dae not fall for this revenant's schemes!" The battle sister warned.

Helregal looked at her sharply and walked over to her, this time standing tall rather than squatting down.

"And who might you be, battle sister?"

The woman spat at his boots. "Gretke Thromburne. I'll not be made to swear an oath to the Infernals!"

Helregal laughed. "Careful, Sister Gretke. Speak of the devil, and he may very well appear. I see that your mind will not be changed, however. Would you like to join your sisters?"

She knew exactly what he meant.

Gretke stared defiantly at him. "I'd join 'em in death before I served ye in life."

Helregal shook his head. "Then be done with it."

He pulled out his pistol and pressed it into her forehead.

"Any last words for the choir?"

She looked to her right at Smith, then to her left at the other pirates and her crewmates who'd been captured.

"Nothin' lives forever," Gretke warned.

"Noted."

He shot her there, and she slumped to the deck. The other Duwa wept for her, chanting prayers for her soul to return to the ancestors in the earth. Helregal regarded her for a moment, then stepped over her and walked to Smith, who was gazing at her corpse. He knelt at eye level with him.

Smith was covered in blood and the liquid gold that filled the veins of the Damned.

"You're quite the fighter, aren't you? Ye even managed to fell a few of my Damned. Admirable. What is your name, pirate?"

"The name is Lieutenant Bronson Smith. Livin' or dead makes no difference. If it moves it can be made not to. Your Damned can't survive having their heads taken, though I see that just about everything else they can do without," Smith noted.

The first one he'd killed, he'd chopped off its arms. It grew two new ones made of gold. He aimed for the head after that, and the creature was finally felled when he sliced it off.

"Ye have grit, pirate. Most of these men are simperin' like babes in fear of my Damned. You though? Ye seem positively indifferent. And why is that?"

Smith shrugged. "Most of these boys haven't been pirates long. I've been a seaman for nigh on forty years. Ye don't get this old without seein' some things that give you pause. Crabs the size of elephants, sirens that call the unwary to their deaths, and sharks that will leap over a ship to snatch a man. I've seen it all and know well enough about the history of these waters to know that there is much more that I have yet to see."

"The pirate's life is a gift and a curse. In life, ye are free to roam the seas and plunder as a hunter. In death, ye are cursed to walk the bottom of the sea in penance for your sins…"

Smith's good eye went wide.

"Yes…the legends are true. Do ye want to know what awaits a man like you at fifteen hundred fathoms below the surface?" Helregal placed a hand on Smith's shoulder and looked deep into his eye.

Smith swallowed hard.

"Down, down, down in the abyss. The light never shines. You pray for remit. Treading the sands of the lightless wake, gasping for a breath to take. And in those depths, at the gates of hell, are where all pirate souls will dwell. Damned to walk the treacherous waters. Never to see your sons and daughters. Where Dead Sea Gods slumber and wait. Lurking in the darkness, your soul to take," Helregal sang solemnly.

The pirates shivered. They knew this rhyme well.

"The Cold Black. It yawns wide like the maw of a sea serpent, hungering for more souls. If you should refuse my offer, you will walk that plank over yonder, and you will drop into the sea. From there, you will be beholden to the creatures of the deep. And when you die…you will be at the mercy of the Dead Sea Gods."

Smith looked out on the horizon as Helregal pulled away from him and stood. He saw all the lives he had taken, all the gold he had plundered and spent, and all the nights of revelry he'd had afterward. Before, he reminisced on such memories with fondness and joy. Now, however, he was terrified. Each sin was a chain that would drag him down and hold him at the bottom of the sea.

"What do you want?" he asked finally.

Helregal held out a hand. His palm was filled with gold coins. "You lived your life and sealed your fate in the pursuit of this. Men have lived and died for the lust of this. I can make it so that you never want for it. You told yourself you were a hunter of the seas, but in truth, you were but prey. You lived in fear of the day that men in blue would come to kill you, or fever would take you, or the uncaring beasts of the sea would devour you! For what? Damnation is all that awaits. An ugly reward for a hard and ugly life. You were *never* master of your own fate, merely beholden to it. Now, at the end of your life, I offer you a choice. Sail with me, and you will never want for gold. You will never hunger; you will never thirst. You will be resurrected anew as a king of the seas. Do you accept, Bronson Smith? Or do you choose death?"

Smith investigated Helregal's palm of gold. He saw his life before his eyes in the reflection of the coins. He saw his youth, which he spent working on his father's farm. He saw his conscription into the navy. He saw the day he was kicked out after the end of the Lordalus-Sarx war. He remembered the hunger and cold, begging on the streets. Then, he became a pirate. He saw the bloodshed, the fear of death, and the long years of sailing in the unforgiving seas.

He shuddered.

He could hear the drowned screams of the lost souls trapped at the bottom of the sea. He could see them clawing at the sky, grasping at him from far below. They wanted to drag him down, chain him to the sea floor, where the sun never shined. They called his name.

"Bronson Smith, you'll be joining us, soon enough. So have your laughs. When life is past, a nightmare waits for you.."

"No…no!" Smith spat, opening his eye and staring hard into Helregal's. "I accept," he gasped. "I will join you!"

Helregal searched his one good eye, then nodded once.

"Take my hand, Bronson Smith. Make your pact with Anathane's Pain and swear your fealty to her captain!"

Smith clasped his hand with Helregal's gold-covered palm. "I swear!"

A burst of red light erupted from their clasped hands, and Bronson gasped as Helregal released his hand. The coins had vanished from the Dread Captain's palm and Bronson felt a warmth crawl up his arm. His skin turned black as a burnt corpse, and his vision swam. He let loose a wail from deep within himself as he turned. His face rotted away, as did his body. Gold chains and gemmed jewelry materialized on his body, growing out of his skin. His mind emptied, and a single-minded hunger and anger filled him.

The imprisoned men shouted in horror as the transformed Bronson Smith growled at them. He flashed his gold-covered teeth and made to attack them.

"Welcome to the Damned, Lieutenant Smith."

XVIII

New Beginnings

The sea was black as ebony, the sky red like hellfire. Beneath a raging storm of black clouds and red lightning, arms reached up from the sea, clawing at the moon. Hail Mary sailed, flying the banner of the Damned. Her crew meandered her decks, glittering in gold with eyes sunken and hollow. At her helm was Bronson Smith. His skin was black and dead; his eyes were molten pools of gold. He hissed and flashed his teeth, and they glittered like gold doubloons. He sailed into the horizon, a fleet of ships flying the Damned flag in his wake…

Pate awoke to thin beams of sunlight shining on his face. He heard birds chirping and the wind rustling through tree branches outside. There was the smell of grass and hay, as well as a hint of manure. The manure smell became stronger. He looked over and saw a piglet sitting next to him.

A farm? I'm on a farm? But how?

The piglet made little snuffling noises as it sniffed him, then backed up quickly upon realizing he was awake. He sat upright. The piglet twitched its ears, cocking its head at the man sitting in its home. It made oinking noises as Pate stretched and eyed the little creature with intrigue. His ships used to keep farm animals onboard as livestock for food, but he'd not seen a pig in many months. Most pigs he saw when he came to land were roasted on a spit or cut up on a plate. It snuffled inquisitively as it trotted towards him again, coming over to his outstretched hand. He rubbed the chin of the little creature, and it closed its eyes and flattened its ears in appreciation. He groaned as he slowly rose. His body ached something fierce, and he noted bandages in several spots where he'd been cut or scraped in the battle. The battle…

As if on cue, a man came into the barn he was lying in, farming hoe and sickle in hand. He casually regarded the man now standing before him. "Ahh, so the captain lives! You've been out for three days. I'd feared I'd have to bury you soon!" he said with a jovial tone. Pate was at ease now. Having been tense, uncertain as to whether this man meant harm or not.

"Are you the one that bandaged me?" Pate asked, motioning towards the bandages on his arms and sides.

"Nay, t'wasn't me, friend. It was my wife, Lillabelle." He pointed to his house over yonder. Sitting down his tools. "If you're wantin' to thank someone, I'd recommend you go and thank her. Truth be told, I didn't know what to think when I saw a bright flash of light in me fields in the middle of the night and found three bewildered, half-dead men in them. Lillabelle, though. She damn near ordered me to help ya." He nodded to the captain's hat, having been sat next to where Pate rested. The piglet was sniffing it curiously, pushing it with its nose. Pate grabbed the hat, scooting the curious creature out of the way, and holding it ponderously in his hand.

"Aye, we be that…" Pate spoke.

The man nodded in return.

"None of us are entirely what we seem, friend." The farmer said, motioning for the pirate to follow him.

Pate patted the piglet on the head and scratched the underside of its snout. It made a pleasing squeal as he followed the farmer.

*****

The pair entered the backdoor to the kitchen to witness Oculeth and a jovial, plump woman engaging in spirited banter. "Oh, please tell me more. You absolutely must!" The woman squealed.

Oculeth eyed Pate and nodded. He'd been smiling, but it turned somber as he laid eyes on the man. "I *would* tell you more tales of my travels, Misses Lillabelle, but I believe the captain here will wish to see Brunt."

Lillabelle's smile slackened as well as she saw the two men enter and nodded. "How're ye feelin', dear? When ye turned up the other night, ye were out cold. Yer friend, Mr. Brunt, was in such bad shape I plum threw ye in the barn, put a blanket and pillow under ye, and kept after 'em. Sorry, dearie!"

Pate smiled. "Tis of no worry to me, ma'am. I'm quite glad that ye opted to aid us regardless. Not many would, and I am grateful for it. May I see him?"

Lillabelle paused a moment, squeezing a rag she'd been holding in her hand. It was stained red. "Aye, just this way, dearie…"

She led him up the stairs to the second story of the farmhouse. As they walked down the hall, Pate took note of the various odds and ends of the rooms they passed. Stuffed animals and shoes sitting haphazardly on the floor.

"Ye've any children, ma'am?" Pate asked.

Lillabelle sighed. "Once. They've all grown now. Our boys went off to the war some years back. They've written, so we know they yet live, but they've not been home in some time. Our daughter married 'n left the isle as well. Her husband's a good man, but travel to and from the mainland is costly, so we exchange letters. Now, we're a house abandoned, feels like."

"I can but imagine," Pate said as they passed the last room before Brunt's. It was clearly their patrons' room. A man's trousers sat slung over a chair, and there were folded clothes on the bed.

"Have ye any children, captain?" Lillabelle asked finally as they stopped at a closed door.

He looked long in their room a moment, pondering his answer before shaking his head. "Nay. The sea's me wife, but she gives no mortal man her womb," he said with a chuckle.

"There's always time, dearie," she said, placing a hand on his shoulder and squeezing it before opening the door.

They walked into the room, and the smell of sickness hit Pate's nostrils like a taurox bull slamming into a cobblestone wall. A basket of blood-soaked cloths sat at the foot of the bed, and Pate saw flies buzzing around it. He covered his nose and held back the urge to curse and vomit. He looked at the head of the bed at its occupant, and his heart sank deep into his gut.

"Hello, old friend…" Brunt managed weakly.

"William…" Pate said, unable to hide his shock.

William Brunt's face was wrapped in gauze, but the flesh that Pate could see was raw. His pale skin was now swollen, and his eyes were glassy. His arms were likewise wrapped, and his hands looked like they were covered in baby mittens made from cloth. The wrapping, though it was still white in places, was stained thoroughly and turned brown from dried blood. Brunt breathed in slow, labored heaves that ended in muffled whimpers.

"Leave me…"

That was what he'd said, wasn't it?

It would've been kinder to shoot him.

Pate knew.

Birds chirped outside, and the light from the nearby window cast a glow on his ailing frame, but Pate knew that soon only the silence of the grave would be embracing his oldest friend. And it filled him with rage.

"What did they do to you, brother? Stars...what did that *bastard* do?!" Pate gasped, rushing to Brunt's side.

"What? I'm fit as a fiddle, in fightin' shape, really." Brunt chuckled. It turned into a wet cough.

Pate smiled painfully. "You always were a kid. Even in the navy, you git."

"Shame that I didn't have children then, ay? We'd have gotten on right as rain, heh," Brunt said.

He raised a gauze-covered hand and placed it on Pate's shoulder as the man leaned over him, then groaned.

Lillabelle sat down with her supplies and pulled out what appeared to be herbs wrapped in cloth. She also pulled out more bandages.

The bedridden man regarded her with a slight nod. "Good morning, Mrs. Lillabelle," he said with a wet cough, covering his mouth with his wrapped hand.

"Good morning, dearie. Did ye sleep well through the night?"

Brunt shook his head impishly. "Afraid not, Ma'am. More nightmares, it seems."

"One bite on the shoulder did all this?" Pate asked.

Brunt nodded to the spot on his left shoulder, the bandages and cloth soaking through with blood.

The creature had bitten into his shoulder just before Pate knocked it off him. He'd thought nothing of it, then.

"The Damned! Stars curse them all!" Pate grimaced, squeezing his clenched fist in rage at the all too-fresh memory of losing his entire fleet in minutes. The Mary Minors I through IV being destroyed in the battle. "Anathane's Pain..." he whispered.

The injured pirate looked into the eyes of his beleaguered captain. "The ship's statue was a woman bound in chains and blindfolded, Cap'n. The Pain...is all too real. The ghost stories, the massacres, the sunken ships, the tales of entire fleets gettin' decimated in the dead 'o night. The blood moon. All of it..." He said weakly as he leaned into Pate's ear. He coughed profusely, covering his mouth with the gauze on his hand again. Pate looked in alarm as he saw blood forming in the cloth.

You're dying, too...

Pate knew.

"I know, Will. I know…" Pate clenched his fists in suppressed rage.

"He's alive, Edward. I don't know how, I don't know why, but the Dread Captain has returned. And I don't think he's going to be returning to the Dark Depths anytime soon. This isn't the end; it's just the beginning." Brunt clenched his fists, balling up the sheets.

Pate recalled his battle with the Dread Captain. He was outmatched, completely and utterly. The Dread Captain played with him, but even that was too much to combat.

That golden skull mask, those eyes like blood-red hellfire…

He could scarcely believe he'd gone toe-to-toe with one of the most feared pirates of legend. He was more fortunate than most. The Dread Captain was said to devour the souls of those he slew.

Like a demon from Sheolhenna itself.

In his mind, Pate saw visions of torrential rain and water twisters towering high above the sea, touching the sky. He saw a blood-red moon, and he saw the Damned, rising from the blackened depths of the sea, hungry for flesh.

Pate snapped back into the now. A sick Brunt stared him down, eyes imploring—begging him. "Edward Patron, you must tell them! Tell everyone, warn them of what is coming! The Dread Captain will not remain at sea forever. Things will not get better! He must be stopped!" Brunt was coughing now, blood streaking the cloth over his mouth as his cheeks turned bright red. He was fading slowly.

"Tell the Court… tell them." Brunt fell off the bed.

Oculeth lunged and caught the man as he fell. Mrs. Lillabelle had been standing at the foot of the bed, unwrapping fresh cloth to place over the wound. She rushed to his side, checking his temperature with the back of her hand.

She scowled.

"He's even hotter than he was before. Whatever he's got, it's aggressive, and it's working fast. At this rate, he's going to cook before the day's out." She stated. Her tone was flat and matter-of-fact.

Pate groaned, "Is there nothing we can do for him—nothing at all?!"

Lillabelle shook her head slowly. "No, dearie. We've no Alyrians on this isle. Consortium saw to that. Those who didn't get taken by them have either hid or went to the mainland to find refuge there. No doctor on this isle can help him, not when he's this far gone, and we haven't a Priest of the Stars."

Pate despaired. He looked at his ailing brother and realized this very likely would be the last time he saw him in this life.

Another long goodbye…

"I see…then I know what I must do."

He strode out of the room and down the hall, pausing at the top of the stairs to peer into the room with children's toys strewn about one last time. Memory began to surface, but he pressed it down and went down the stairs.

"Captain?" Oculeth greeted him, sensing his mood.

"I must away, come or do not—it makes no difference. Where's the man of the house?" Pate said quickly.

"Mr. Roth? He is in the stables, tending a horse, I believe," Oculeth replied.

"Good, I must speak with him," Pate answered as he stormed out of the backdoor.

Oculeth followed.

*****

"Ye need to ride into town, ay? I can spare a horse for that, easy," Roth said as he brushed down a brown mare. "Ye can use this girl here, Myrtle. She's even of temperament 'n quick to boot. I assume the Alyrian'll need one as well?"

Pate looked to Oculeth, who uncomfortably shifted his collar. The glow of his tattoo peaked out from his sleeve as he fixed it.

"Not to worry, I'm no informant. I hate the Consortium almost as much as I hate the Imperials' taxes, to be frank. One of mine was gifted like you. They took 'em from me. I'll never forget it," Roth sighed and wiped the sweat from his brow.

"The playroom…" Pate whispered under his breath.

"Aye. T'was his. He was but a youngin' when they took Falstead. At any rate, take Myrtle and her stallion, Gunther, over there. Mr. Oculeth may want to wear one of my coats, however. His tattoos are quite bright."

Oculeth nodded. "My thanks." He ran into the house to grab a coat.

"Headed back out to sea, ay?" Roth asked as Oculeth disappeared into the house.

"Aye, how'd ye figure?" Pate asked.

Roth chuckled as he led Myrtle out of the barn. "One look at ye 'n I could tell ye were a man of the sea. Not just any pirate, but a captain, 'n I didn't need the hat to figure that. 'A man of the sea, married to her be' isn't that what they say?"

"She's a fickle mistress with a cruel sense of humor 'n justice…"

"'N yet she calls to ye all the same. The sea air, the sloshing of the waves, the swaying of the timbers beneath your feet. And yet still she calls, and what is a man to the wiles of his beloved but a puppet on a string?"

Pate nodded and patted his coat pocket before digging inside and pulling out a rolled cigar. "Got a light?"

Roth had the lighter to Pate's lips before he could even finish the question. "Always. Keep it, I don't smoke anymore, anyways."

Pate thanked him and took the lighter, inspecting it a moment. It was silver and engraved with two bars and a five-pointed star.

"You were an LTC…"

"Lieutenant Commander, aye. I served in the navy during the Lowland Troubles."

"Sarx, just like your boys…"

"Most of the people here get their heritage from there. When war comes, Sarx looks to us island boys to remember our heritage. Pity it never does when the favor needs returning."

Pate's nostrils flared as he exhaled cigar smoke. "Don't I fuckin' know it. The motherland left me high 'n dry after the last scuff with Lordalus a decade back. I was homeless, jobless, and had night terrors damn near every night."

Roth inhaled the scent of Pate's cigar smoke. "Hemestra? Strong stuff for a seaman to be partaking and still hold water."

Pate shrugged. "No choice. Found out it was the only thing that keeps me from seein' demons and ghosts in me sleep."

The two chatted about their hatred for the service and their salvations afterward for several more minutes before Oculeth returned, and they parted ways.

✶✶✶✶✶

Port De Morta was a modest seaside town. It faced the open ocean, had few cannons, and the ones they did have weren't even manned. Pate barely saw any guardsmen as they rode. Looking at the streets, however, it made sense. The buildings weren't ramshackle, but it was clear this place had no real significance. It was a stopover point from the major trading lanes, nothing more, nothing less. Be that as it may, money was still coming in, that much he knew. It just wasn't being distributed to the people, was all. He could tell as much when they rode in on horses, and everyone stopped to gawk at them.

"There's a crowd. Watch your pockets," Pate warned as the horses slowed up.

"Should we dismount?" Oculeth asked, noting their gazes. He'd made sure to cover his tattoos completely and was thankful for it.

"Here? Nay, these horses'll be gone when we get back if we do. We'll have to keep 'em close…"

As they made their way through the crowd, they were separated. A carriage came through as a line of guardsmen pushed through the crowd, making a path for it to ride through.

"Make your way straight until you reach the docks!" Pate shouted as they broke away, and the carriage came.

He didn't know if Oculeth heard him, but he figured the Alyrian was at least smart enough to realize he had to stay the course. Pate scanned the crowd as the horse slowly pushed through, and men shot him dirty looks. He paid them no heed, motioning for them to move as he went, and with what was easily a thousand pounds of horse backing him, none could argue. He paused, however, when he saw a figure watching him from the side of the street.

He did a double-take as he looked at him.

The man had no face. He hadn't even a mouth. It was just smooth, unnaturally pale skin.

Pate slapped the reigns of the horse, urging it to move quicker and nudging her side.

He has no fucking face, no eyes, nose—nothing! Why the fuck is he looking at me?!

The man raised an arm and pointed at Pate as he moved past, his pale head tracking him perfectly, even without any visible orifice to do so.

Pate looked away, looking for Oculeth after the carriage passed. He saw the back of his head, much further ahead of him now. When he looked back, the man was gone.

A hand grabbed his shoulder.

He grabbed for his sword and cursed at himself as he remembered he'd left it back at the farm. He turned into his attacker and swung with all his—

A hand caught his fist, and he blinked as he realized that he was staring into the spectacled eyes of Oculeth. A flicker of something in his eyes made Pate pause.

Taren…I love you…

An errant thought whistled through his head like a cool breeze.

"Captain! Captain! I've been calling your name for two minutes, now. Are you alright?" Oculeth asked, his voice elevated.

"I'm fi…I'm fine," Pate managed, shaking his head. The thought disappeared as quickly as it came. He looked around again. They were at the docks, but he didn't recall walking the horse all the way there.

"Who did Mr. Roth tell you to look for?" Oculeth asked, hand still on his shoulder.

Pate cleared his throat. "Peter Barlow." He looked past Oculeth and saw a burly man chatting it up with several merchants at the edge of a pier. "I think that's him."

He immediately dismounted and started walking towards the man, ignoring Oculeth's inquiries as to what had just happened to him. "Watch the horses."

The man noticed Pate walking straight towards him and turned to face him, whispering something to one of the merchants. They turned away.

"Pete Barlow?" Pate asked.

"Who's askin'?" The man responded, narrowing his eyes.

"A friend of Roth. He tells me you're the dock master here, and I can speak to ye about procuring a new ship," Pate introduced.

"A whole ship? Roth happen to give ye the gold for it as well?" Pete laughed.

Pate shook his head. "Nay, he didn't."

"Then quit pissin' with me 'n fuck off, mate. I got business to handle 'n time's non-refundable." Pete dismissed him and turned back to the merchants, who'd walked out of earshot.

"I haven't gold but I've somethin' far more valuable!" Pate finally said.

Pete paused, groaned, and turned around.

"'N what's that, then?"

Pate gritted his teeth, briefly glanced at Oculeth, and then went into his pocket. Oculeth gave him a puzzled look.

If Roth's wrong about this, we're dead men, Mr. Oculeth…

Pate pulled a gold coin from his pocket and flicked it toward Pete, who caught it. The big dock master looked at the coin, and his expression changed from annoyance to surprise.

"Well, I'll be a siren's thrall…" Pete chuckled and nodded and walked towards the two men, then past them.

Pate looked at Oculeth again.

"Did you just tell that man what I think you did?" Oculeth asked.

He nodded, biting his lip. "Aye."

"You killed us, didn't you?"

Probably.

"Aye."

"Gentlemen, I believe we have business to discuss." Pete waved them over.

What choice did they really have? They followed him.

XIX

MYTH AND MEMORIAL

"Bold of ye to show your mark in public. Stupid, too," Pete chided as they sat down in his office.

The dock master's office was strewn with paperwork, empty bottles, and several different ashtrays that needed cleansing. He sat his bulky frame down in his leather-padded chair and opened a drawer, pulling out a bottle and sitting it on the desk between them. He popped it open and offered it to his guests.

Pate declined; Oculeth obliged.

"What vintage?" Oculeth asked.

"Not but port ale, I'm afraid. Ain't much in the way of fine alcohol round here."

"So long as it gets me a bit tipsy, I don't particularly care, to be honest," Oculeth admitted.

He took the bottle, popped the top off with his teeth, and spat it before downing half of it in one go. The two pirates watched him, stunned. When he realized they were staring at him, he raised a brow.

"Did I do something wrong?"

"Nay, just…didn't think you'd open the bottle like that, is all," Pate managed. Another thought began to form in his mind and burst like a bubble as Pete started talking.

"We thought you was too soft to pop a bottle like a roughneck, is what he meant to say," Pete said with a chuckle.

"Just because I speak properly and dress more than swarthy doesn't mean I don't know how to open a bottle. I was born in the countryside if you must know," Oculeth explained.

The countryside…

Pate thought of the last time he'd been in the countryside. He couldn't remember. It'd been so long.

He took his seat and nursed his bottle as they returned to the matters at hand.

"At any rate, I was desperate. Still am, to be frank. We need back on the seas—and fast, Mr. Barlow," Pate admitted.

"What happened to your first one? You're clearly a pirate captain. Run afoul of the Imperials, or just some ugly beastie?"

"Neither, I'm afraid. I rather think that would've been preferable," Oculeth said with a shudder and another sip from his bottle.

"What's specs on about?" Pete asked.

Pate leaned forward and held out his hand. Pete stared at it for a moment, chuckled, and then handed him back his gold skull coin.

"Ye know what these coins were originally based off, Mr. Barlow? Who made them?"

Pete thought a moment, then shrugged. "Afraid me memory's a bit spotty. Care to enlighten me?"

Pate rolled the coin between his fingers, staring intently at the skull engraved on its sides. "Ever heard of the story of the Dread Captain, Felix Helregal?"

"Hah! Any sailor worth his salt has."

"I haven't," Oculeth admitted.

The two looked at him again.

Pete scratched his head. "How?"

"I was born in the country, far from the sea. Sailor's tales wouldn't even be part of our local legends."

"Fair enough. We're Sarxian boys, the sea 'n its fables is all we know," Pate explained. "Tell 'em."

Pete sighed, made a five-pointed star on his chest, and pulled out another bottle. This one was a clear decanter.

"I thought all you had was ale?" Oculeth gasped.

"All I had for *you* is ale. If I'm goin' to be tellin' the sort of stories that makes sailors shiver, I'll need somethin' to keep me even..."

*****

"Before he was a monster, he was a man. Felix Helregal and his running mate, Morgan Sarron, were no-name pirates turned leaders, turned heroes in the forge of war. In that era, the first pirate war ravaged the three continents of men, and pirates everywhere fought for survival, hunted relentlessly by the

Continental Navy. Those two men saved us from them and solidified themselves as legends.”

“Morgan Sarron…who is he?”

“He’s the Immortal Pirate, as all kin of the black know him. He is the…*prodigal son* of the Brethren Court. He’s sailed the seas of Hera for longer than most men have been alive and made quite a name for himself in the process.”

“Stars, what I wouldn’t give to shake that bastard’s hand one time,” Pate said.

“Do I sense admiration, captain?” Oculeth asked.

“Finish the story, Pete,” Pate dodged.

“Every shooting star falls to the earth. And when they do, they always leave a crater. In the months followin’ the end of the First Pirate War, the Brethren Court of the Storm Tide began to reconstitute itself. The wealthiest pirates who’d managed to survive the war became the new pirate lords, and Morgan and Helregal wanted to solidify their place in that lot.

“So, an expedition was launched to find a trove of treasure hidden on an island in the Star Ocean. The forgotten treasure of Ceph. When Morgan returned to the Storm Tide after finding the treasure, he told of a terrible curse placed upon it, ‘n how it killed half their men, including Captain Helregal. The Court mourned their loss and hosted a feast in their memory.”

“Then he came back…” Pate grumbled.

“‘N he weren’t alone. He brought with ‘em an army of the dead, tainted with the cursed gold. We call them the Damned. They slew scores of pirates and left the isle in shambles. The Dread Captain was born. He turned his gaze to Kurza, and the Second Pirate War began.”

Oculeth scratched his head. “Why Kurza? He’s a pirate. Why not just set up on an island somewhere and make himself a king there?”

“Because it was his birthright,” Pate answered.

“Birthright?”

“Felix Helregal was originally born Felix Kurza, the first trueborn son of Queen Anathane Kurza. That is until the king’s spies discovered he was the lovechild of Anathane Kurza and Frost Helregal—a known pirate lord and a habitual thorn in the side of the kingdoms of Gransys. He didn’t take too well to that, as one can imagine. Had the queen killed and dogged the young prince across the land to put him to the sword as well.

"Eventually, the boy found his father, and a pirate was he made. But his hatred for Kurza never died. He vowed to bring it to heel one day and claim the throne in honor of his mother. Well, now he had the power to do so. He cut a swathe of destruction across the Amaranthine and destroyed the Seagate at Oceanus, plundering his way towards Emperor's Rest, or King's Rest, as it was called back then. He sieged the city, destroying an army over a thousand strong in the process and raising them into his Army of the Damned. Then, he killed the king and took his crown for himself. Thus, the Dread Captain became the Dread King, and his reign of terror truly began."

"I'm assuming since we don't have an undead Emperor ruling Kurza, that he was defeated?" Oculeth asked.

"Ye were a smart ass in school, weren't ye, specs?" Barlow squeezed the bridge of his nose.

"I did quite well, yes. I was one of the only children to get past the third year."

"Heh, this posh bastard went to school." Pate smirked.

"Must've been nice. I went to the school of hard knocks for ten years, got an education in urchinry, then graduated to piracy." Barlow laughed and nudged Pate, who broke up as well.

"Positively comical, you should've pursued a career as a jester instead of a dock master," Oculeth said, topping off his ale bottle and chucking it into the pile Barlow left in the corner. "Or a barkeep."

"And here I thought you were all paper with no cut," Pete joked.

"At any rate, he sacked the city, took control of the kingdom, and ran it with a no-nonsense policy of killing dissidents and installing his pawns in their stead. Carried on like that for a good while until the Immortal Pirate amassed allies to combat him. Captain Morgan led his forces straight into the heart of the Dread King's Kurza and slew him once and for all."

"Or so everyone thought," Pate said.

Oculeth already knew the answer. "He came back again."

"And again, and again. For brief periods on a blood moon, *always* on a blood moon. He'd come with the night, terrorize, and kill till first light, and disappear for months or years at a time, leaving terror and shipwrecks in his wake. He would leave one witness to his attack so that they could tell of what he'd done. And so, the legend of the Dread Captain grew…"

They sat in silence for several minutes, and Pete drank from his decanter. He even poured Oculeth some of it.

"You didn't ask me to recite that story for shits 'n giggles, Captain Pate. So why did ye ask who made those coins?" Barlow finally asked.

Pate nodded. He'd been leaning back in his chair, flipping the coin over and over the entire time.

"Because each of these coins is one of Helregal's…"

Barlow nearly choked on his liquor. "Come again?"

Pate nodded. "After the end of the Second Pirate War, these coins were plundered from the Dread Captain's ship before it sank in the Amaranthine. One of the most disrespectful things a pirate can do to one of their own is steal their haul. So, they took his gold and gave out a thousand of these coins, one for every captain. They had a sea nymph bless them, and she conjured a mighty storm to surround the isle, ensuring that only those who bore these coins could enter. Thus, Storm Tide Isle was born."

He pocketed the coin.

"I must return to the Storm Tide, and I need a crew 'n ship to do it. Ye know who I am, ye know what I am. Can ye help us, Mr. Barlow?"

Pete sighed, stood up, and corked his decanter before putting it back in its drawer. He pulled out a sheet of paper and grabbed his quill and inkwell. Then, he wrote.

"This is a special writ of consignment. You are to present this to the dock officer by pier five. He'll look at it. Then ye will ask to claim ownership of the Duchess, a galleon that—"

"A bloody galleon? You're yankin' me!"

"Calm down. The galleon is a repurposed freight ship. Not much in the way of heavy cannons, and slow to maneuver. But it can carry a lot of men, and it can carry a lot of cargo. Which you'll be utilizin' to pay me back when ye finish your business at the isle, ay?" Pete emphasized.

"Why you doin' all this?" Pate asked.

"Brethren Court did me a good turn, settin' me up here. I spot prizes for 'em, keep 'em abreast of the comings 'n goings 'n they send me a nice stipend while I collect a paycheck from these nice folk. Good business. This is but a small favor in return," Pete said.

He offered a muscled paw to Pate, and he shook it, revealing both men's wrist tattoos. "For my brothers in black, I'd go to Sheolhenna 'n back."

"For the pirates of old, we will plunder untold."

"Meet me at the pier on the 'morrow. We've a crew to recruit." Pete nodded. "Later Specs. Take this with ye." He pulled out the decanter and gave it to Oculeth, who gladly accepted.

*****

"What the fuck is in that bottle?" Pate asked as they rode out of town. He kept an eye out for the faceless man, but he didn't see him again. He wasn't sure whether that was a good or bad sign.

Oculeth took a swig straight from the bottle, coughed, and laughed. "Considering I'm already seeing double, I think it might be alcosav!" he hiccuped.

Pate whistled. "Bastard's off his ass all day and collects a purse for it. Maybe I need to switch jobs."

"Don't be glum, old friend! We'll be dead *long* before you'll be able to find an honest job that accepts ex-pirates." Oculeth giggled, then clapped a hand over his mouth. "Shit."

Pate ground Myrtle to a stop, and Gunther followed suit immediately. The horses whinnied.

"What do ye mean we'll be dead, Alyrian?"

Oculeth sighed.

He cradled his head and corked the alcosav. "How much do you remember from the other night?" he slurred. "Our escape?"

"I remember running like hell and dragging Brunt with me while a horde of gold-toothed biters chased after us. And I remember preparing to fight them to the death before you pulled me through that damned portal. Then, I woke up with a piglet licking me face in a barn. 'Bout it, really."

"Yes, well, I was conscious of all of it. It wasn't…pleasant. When this business with Mr. Barlow and the ship is settled, we need to discuss the specifics. It's something that you'll…want to sit down for," he warned.

"I'd prefer now, actually," Pate insisted.

"Captain, I'm drunk…HIC!" he hiccupped.

"And I'm a pirate. Half my men are drunk off their arse all damn day."

"Well, that explains the accidents," Oculeth said.

"No, stupidity explains that part. I can be drunk and still run a ship better than most of these rodent brains."

"That's a very rude thing to say about your own men…HIC!" Oculeth leaned forward and held onto Gunther's neck for support. The mottled horse grunted and shook its head, causing Oculeth to slide gracelessly off his side and fall to the ground.

"It seems Gunther has an amazing sense of smell; he can smell your bullshit. We need to get back to the house to check on Brunt, so I can't afford to press ye further right now. But we'll be havin' this conversation shortly, understand?"

Oculeth groaned as he pitifully attempted to remount the horse, who kept sidling away when he attempted to mount its stirrups. "I hate you, Gunther."

Pate beckoned Myrtle forward, and Gunther slowly plodded after them, leaving Oculeth toddling after him.

"Good Gunther, you'll be gettin' an apple when we get back to the house," Pate praised.

*****

When they arrived back at Roth and Lillabelle's farm, it was sunset. As they came to the front of the house, they saw Roth sitting out front in his rocking chair. A lantern sat next to him, illuminating him in the shadows of the porch. He rose as they approached and stepped down the stairs, holding the lantern.

"How did the meetin' with Mr. Barlow go, then?"

"Splendidly. We talked shop 'n he gave me a boat with interest," Pate answered. "Where's Brunt?"

"What boat did he give ye?" Roth pressed.

Pate shrugged. "An old, repurposed galleon. Calls it 'The Duchess.'"

"That's good. She's been languishin' in that harbor for too long, she deserves to spend her final days at sea. Wish ye luck findin' crew though," Roth warned.

"Why's that?" Pate asked as he hitched Myrtle, then Gunther. The horse had made Oculeth jog after it for about a mile before it finally decided to let him back on. If he didn't know better, he'd have thought the horse found it funny, the way it whinnied and flicked its tail.

"The ports are a bit barren these days in this stretch of sea. Ever since that scuff with Lordalus, our boys have been gettin' conscripted for the navy like mad. I fear another war may be on the horizon," Roth explained worriedly.

"Another war? Hah! With who? Empire's got its fingers in enough pies. Valkar is running rampant in the north and along the east coast. Empire's still tryin' to prevent civil war after it stepped in and sided with Lordalus durin' the last war."

"I heard rumors from me old friends in the admiralty, but I like to think that it's just paranoia they speak. They say we're gearin' up for war with the Dyonians again, or preparin' to."

Pate grumbled and spat in the dirt. "Emperor needs to sit his pomp arse down 'n look at his own doorstep, 'fore he starts trackin' mud on someone else's."

"If only his council shared such sentiments," Roth said.

"If their sons 'n daughters died like ours do, I rather think they'd reconsider ever havin' another war again," Pate said.

"In a just world they'd fight themselves, but in this one, we fight for them and suffer for it…" Roth shook his head in disgust.

"He's dead…isn't he?" Pate finally asked after looking at Roth for several long moments.

Roth sighed and put a hand on the pirate's shoulder.

"I'm sorry, son."

Pate nodded slowly and patted Myrtle, rubbing her snout and looking deep into the horse's eyes as she flicked her ears and slowly blinked. He saw a hundred memories flash before his eyes. The day they first met, Pate was begging on the street without a copper kurtz to his name, and Brunt offered him a purse of coins if he sat with him for a beer. Their first beer together; it had been the first drink Pate had had in three months. He remembered the day they set sail on their first ship. The storm that nearly sent them to their makers before their dreams could ever be realized. So many stories, so many shanties sang, so many hardships overcome. He was going to name his next son after Brunt. He'd promised him he would. He'd promised that—

"Just as well."

I'm going to kill you. I promise, in front of the Stars, the Infernals, and Brunt himself—I will destroy you, once and for all.

He felt the hurt burn into a rage in his heart. He kissed the horse on the nose, and she licked his cheek, and he walked out of the stall and kept walking out into the farm pastures. Oculeth called after him as he went, but he ignored him and stormed off. He made to follow, but Roth stopped him and gave him the same terrible, painful news.

"Let him walk. He must process this by himself," Roth said.

"I understand," Oculeth said and leaned deep into the bottle of alcosav, hoping that draining its contents would drain the pain he felt in his heart.

*****

"Seasons change. Grass grows, ripens, then withers. Trees blossom from seeds to saplings, maturing and growing tall and strong before withering to a snag and succumbing to nature's call. When I met you, brother, I had thought that my grass would never grow again, that my seeds would never sprout. I was destitute, without shoes on my feet and without hope in my heart. I was broken, and no one would have me. When I looked in the puddles of mud, I saw the reflection of a broken, disgraced, lonely failure. A man who'd lost his family, his career, and his purpose. That day, though, ye saw somethin' different. Somethin' more than what I ever thought I could be. Ye saw a captain in the makin'. Ye helped forge this useless hunk of iron into a sword that would cut our path to riches. Ye believed in me, William. Ye were a better brother than any of my blood. Nay, our bond ran deeper than blood. It ran black, like the flags we flew and the masks we wore. I know not what the Gods will say to ye, but I know that I'll see ye again one day…

"And when we meet again, know that I will have brought your killer to justice. Know that I will have avenged ye, and our brothers who fell the night our world was set aflame. I promise this to ye, brother, not just as a pirate, but as a friend…"

Pate's voice broke, and he thumped his hand on the bible he was clutching. Oculeth, Roth, and Lillabelle watched quietly as he gathered himself.

"Go on, son," Roth urged supportively.

"This was yer favorite passage from the Book of the Stars…I always found it funny that in the face of all we'd been through ye still held out faith in the gods," he chuckled hoarsely.

"And low is they who forsakes their kin, who would not break bread with them. Though their brother is wretched and their sister destitute, they offered nothing of them. Just as they were miserly in life, they shall find no quarter in death. But he who shepherds his brother, and she who shelters her sister shall find salvation. For we art one body, one spirit, and one soul. One hand will wash the other, and both hands will wash the face. So saith the Stars…Idallon, Book Three, Chapter 14, Verse 32-38."

Pate closed the book.

"Ye shepherded me, brother. May the Stars shepherd you…"

Pate picked up a bottle of alcohol sitting at his feet, uncorked it, then took a sip. He hated its burn, but he swallowed it down for Brunt. He offered it to Oculeth, who took a long sip, then to Roth and Lillabelle, who drank as well. Then, he poured the rest on the rock he used to mark Brunt's grave.

"May the Stars guide you through the long dark, William Brunt. Until we meet again, further on down the road…" Pate finished. He placed the Book of the Stars on the grave, as well as the empty bottle, Brunt's pistol, and sword. His job done, he nodded at his handiwork and ran a hand over the rock in parting, then walked away…

William Brunt resides on a hill, on the outskirts of Roth and Lillabelle Ford's farm, beneath an apple tree. He is survived by no children, no spouse, and no family, though Edward Patron would fight the 'no family' part tooth and nail, as Brunt was family to *him*.

XX

THE PRICE OF FREEDOM

"They're a bit green, mind," Pete warned before they departed. He and Captain Pate were standing at the dock, watching the men file onboard. He'd been introduced to them individually, but it would take quite some time for him to learn all their names.

"I wouldn't expect anything more. I didn't exactly peg this place to have any Kurzan Marauder types here." Pate mused.

"Oh, good. Because you'll be lucky if you find Martin's Scallywags here." the Harbormaster cracked wise.

"Blimey, that bad? This is a bloody seaside town. You mean to tell me there ain't any half-decent sailors 'round here? Or at least a fisherman or two?!" Pate inquired.

"Round here? Nay, mate. Isle De Morta is a stopover point for merchants—and a poor one at that. 'Round this time of year, the water's still warming up. The fish will still be south to breed and spawn, so the fishermen follow suit, heading towards the coastal towns of Sarx to the east for work or down southwest towards Brova for warmer waters and more fish to haul and sell. And the sailors? Pfft. You sign up for the Navy, you really think someone's gonna want to stay in this ass-end-of-nowhere island town? The damn Lord of the Isle barely stays here. Right now, he's abroad, rubbin' elbows and suckin' farts from the cheeks of nobles with deeper pockets than him."

He cawed, laughing with a deep-bellied warble. "Nay, Pate. This is the best you'll be gettin' from here. And trust me when I say that really ain't much."

Pate sighed, shaking his head as a man began to walk up towards them to introduce himself. They regarded him silently, Harbormaster Pete nodding to the man with a familiar smirk.

"Name's Crimp, sir. Crimp Shaw." He introduced politely, carrying a duffel slung over his shoulder and nodding excitedly. He was a plain-looking man, wearing a fisherman's cap and overalls. Crimp had short stubble on his face, and his lips cracked slightly. He looked about thirty years old, almost a decade younger than Pate himself.

Pate looked the man over.

"Crimp, ay? What'd ye do before ye decided to try yer hand at a sailor's life, Mister Crimp?" Pate asked curiously, smoothing a hand over his mustache, then running it through his beard absentmindedly. He wasn't exactly expecting much now.

"I sailed a bit in me father's old boat, y'see. But I made me livelihood as a butcher, sir." Crimp responded proudly.

"A butcher? That's decent livin', Mister Crimp. Why'd ye decide to turn away from that life?" Pate asked, folding his arms behind his back now.

"When I have a son, I wantem' to grow up to be somethin', ye know? Not another butcher. Me father was a butcher, 'n so was his father. I figure a few months at sea, under a real pirate captain, I can make me fortune. Then I'll have my pick of the lasses, 'n the money to make sure my boy, whenever I have 'em, is sittin' pretty 'n has a leg up in life." He confided.

Pate nearly gagged at the naivety in his words. The same dribble every poor soul had filled their ears with before they consigned themselves to a life of crime.

"Honorable aims, Mister Crimp. Mister Pete here tells me that ye have some sailin' experience prior?"

"Aye, sir. I mentioned me father's boat. He owned a little dingy, what with this bein' a seaside town 'n all. He fished for some of our food, 'n he taught me how to do it."

"Ye ever sailed during a storm, Mister Crimp?" he asked pragmatically.

"I have, sir."

"What do ye do when a storm's comin'?" He asked.

"Stow the sails, sir." Crimp replied.

"Stow the sails, sir— Of course, stow the bloody sails, Mister Crimp!" he mimicked, flaring his nostrils. "Which. Sails. Do ye stow first?" he tried again.

"The aft sails, sir." He said, quite serious.

"Mmm. And why is that, mind?"

"The aft sails aren't squared. They're mounted fore to aft, so if all the other sails are facing left to right, the aft sail is facing the front to the back of the ship, sir."

"Aye aye, Mister Crimp." He said with a pleased grin. "And why is that important?"

"When the wind of the storm blows, it will hit the aft sail and cause the boat to spin from the back. This can conflict with the wind pushing the other sails and cause the ship to spin in the water, ceasing all motion with the waves. That's deadly in open water, sir. Durin' a storm, especially. Could leave ye to be swept overboard by a storm squall, or if the different pulls on the sails are strong enough, could tear the sails or break the mast. Sometimes even damage the rest of the ship." He explained.

Pate smiled. Maybe this isle wasn't completely bereft after all. He was pleased.

"Aye, that it is, Mister Crimp. That it is. Welcome aboard." He said, extending a hand, for which Crimp shook gladly. "Mister Henry, our Second Mate, is already aboard. Familiarize yourself with him and Mister Oculeth. They will be your fellow officers aboard the Duchess." He waved, dismissing him.

"Aye, sir," he said, nodding to him and the Harbormaster before departing.

"Brother, ye fool, ye forget about me already?!" A woman shouted from down the pier, running toward the men.

Pate and Pete looked at one another, intrigued.

Crimp froze and turned slowly with a sigh. "Judith, ye dim-witted lass, I told ye this voyage was too dangerous for ye!"

"And it ain't for you? I was the one what saved your arse a thousand times on Pa's boat. Come to think of it, I'm the one who's been watchin' your back since we was littlin's, so why the fuck are ye catchin' an attitude now, when I might finally get off this stars forsaken rock in the ocean?"

Crimp shooshed her hurriedly, looking at Pate and Pete, who were laughing now.

"Well, well, well, Mr. Crimp! Ye didn't tell us ye had a sister! And one with fire in her belly? Taught ye everythin' ye know, she says—fancy that," Pate said, walking over to them and folding his arms. He fixed Crimp in place with a harsh gaze, then glanced at the woman.

"Ms. Judith, is it? Tell me, ma'am. How does a ship sail against the wind?"

Judith looked at Pate. Her eyes were a sharp, stormy blue, and she peeled her top lip back in disgust at his question. "Do ye think me daft, cap'n? Every child who lives on this island from the age of three years knows how to sail into the wind!"

Pate chuckled; she had bollocks, something her brother clearly lacked. "Fair enough, ma'am—but humor me, please. I must make sure all of me sailors are competent, understand?"

Judith rolled her eyes, then nodded conciliatorily.

She cleared her throat. "Well, Cap'n. A ship sails against the wind via tackin' of the sails. Dependin' on the size of the ship, the strength of the wind, 'n the desired angle or destination, a ship may tack in a half-circle, zig-zag pattern, or anythin' in between to fool the winds into takin' 'em in the desired direction. That a good enough answer?"

Pate and Pete shared a surprised glance between them.

He cleared his throat. "Ahem, yes ma'am, that'll do perfectly. Mayhap ye could rub some of that knowledge onto your brother?" he joked.

Judith shrugged as she started toward the ship. "Tried that already. His dome's too smooth for it to stick if ye get my meanin'," she called over her shoulder.

Pate nodded to the woman with a smirk and waved her off. "Well. At least she, Mr. Crimp, and Mr. Henry know how to sail. So that's a start, ay?" he said pragmatically, raising a hand for the dock master to shake.

"Aye. When ye gonna tell 'em the heading? The Storm Tide isn't called the Storm Tide for naught. Tis a dangerous place to sail. Even a vessel this size can easily be pulverized by its waves." Pete pointed out. "And even if those three are competent, the rest of the crew is green. If they don't do what needs to be done when it needs to be done, ye could be sailin' straight into yer doom, Captain."

"Aye. They'll know soon enough." He said.

"Thank ye for yer aid, Mr. Barlow. I'll make sure the Brethren Court knows of how ye helped me this day."

Pete snorted, clapping his mitt onto the man's hand and shaking it like an old friend.

"Think nuffin' of it, Captain. The Court's done me many a good turn. They even helped me get this cushy-arsed job. Beats cuttin' throats any day. This is a pittance by comparison." He dismissed. "You sure about takin' womenfolk in your crew, though? Men get distracted when too many pretty faces are around."

Pate shrugged. "That they do. But I need all the able bodies I can, so if a lady like Miss Judith wants to join me crew, I'll not be turnin' 'em away. Consequences be damned."

"I'll trust your judgment, then," Pete said. He turned to leave—before pausing and turning a serious glance over his shoulder at the captain. "You be careful, though, Edward Patron. I see dark clouds over your future. I don't fancy myself a scryer or a prophet. But I know black waters when I see them. Ye've been warned," he nodded to the man and stalked off. His bulky frame lightly shook the dock as he went.

"Aye… I feel it too." He confided to no one, looking out at the sunny horizon before pulling out his watch, checking it, and walking towards the ship.

His mind wandered to the faceless man in town, but he pushed the thought away as quickly as it came. A gust of wind blew from the sea, and he could've sworn he'd heard someone calling his name out at sea. But when he looked, no one was there.

*****

Pate stood on the foredeck overlooking the ship. They were preparing to set sail, so everyone was busy running about, getting ready for their departure. The Duchess wasn't Hail Mary; she couldn't hold a candle to that beautiful ship. She was big, with a lot of storage and only a few cannons to shoot with. She would do, however. Pate had done far more with far less.

When Brunt was here.

He lit a cigar and took a long draw from it to try and calm his nerves. He couldn't be harsh with these men, not yet. He needed to rally them. Something that Pate simply couldn't do without digging under their skin first. Brunt was better at being kind, but with him gone, it was just Pate and his naturally brash mannerisms.

And the Alyrian.

He shook his head.

The drunk, cagey Alyrian who's hiding a secret from me.

"Right then!" he called out loud and sharply. The men froze, and several turned to look at them. "Listen to me now, listen to me clear, and hold me words dear, understand?"

The remainder turned to face him, as did Henry, Crimp, and Oculeth, who were all chatting amongst themselves at the steering deck.

"You lot want to be pirates, well that's all fine 'n dandy. Bein' a pirate is a whole hell of a lot more than callin' yourselves pirates, however. Were the circumstances different, ye'd all be put through your paces to weed out those of ye who ain't quite cut for this life. But I don't have the time nor the luxury for

203

that, so instead, you'll be going through a trial by fire. Your *first mission* is to sail this ship to the Storm Tide. I'm sure many of ye of heard of it, but I doubt any of ye know where it is. I do. I know what we'll be facin' to reach it, and I know how to reach the isle without dying to the storm."

The men murmured excitedly. The Storm Tide was a place of legend to sailors and those who lived by the sea. An island full of pirates, protected from the world by an impenetrable storm surrounding it. A haven where pirates lived freely and had their own kingdom, unbeholden to the rules of civilized men. A place where the whores, both female and male, were plentiful, beautiful, and loose with their foibles. A place where you could become rich and powerful and live free. A place where a pirate could *be* a pirate and not fear the noose.

"Listen to my every word. It could very well save your life. The sea is a dangerous, unforgiving, and unpredictable place. These waters are treacherous. Make ready, ladies 'n gentlemen. We're about to embark on the grandest adventure many of you are like to see in your entire lives. 'N maybe, just maybe, ye might walk away richer than when ye began, ay?!"

The crew cheered, the prospect of witnessing legends and becoming rich more than filling their hearts with hope. He prayed he could deliver on even a fraction of what he'd promised.

"I see dark clouds over your future."

Stars, he hoped he was wrong.

But as the men and women of his new crew cheered, and The Duchess set sail on her first voyage in years, Pate saw a glimpse of the faceless man in the crowd, and a chill settled in his gut. The man was clinging to a rope tether with one arm while standing on a crate, staring at him. The crew around him seemed oblivious. Pate knew then that what he was seeing only *he* could see. He looked away, and the faceless man was gone.

*****

Pate entered Oculeth's study, now the navigation room for The Duchess. The room was spacious and dark, lit by candles mounted on the support beams casting long shadows into the poorly lit sections of the room. When he entered the study the Alyrian was nose-deep in a book, face scrunched in concentration at the words he was reading. Pate leaned against a beam and watched for several moments as the man read. He'd taken off his coat and rolled up his sleeves, exposing the brilliantly glowing tattoos that covered his arms, a trademark of Alyrians.

Apparently, the tattoos help channel the energy that flows from them, or so he'd been told. He'd also been told that all of them sold their souls to demons and that drinking their piss would give you a longer, stronger erection. He somehow doubted that was true, however. He didn't really know what was and what wasn't true about them, in all honesty. He wasn't much of a reader, and he had a strict, no-Alyrians policy on his old ship. The only reason they'd taken him on was because Brunt insisted, and Brunt only insisted because the hunt they'd been doing at the time required the help of the Alyrian to pull it off.

Pate wanted to put him out immediately after, and perhaps they would've, but the Alyrian had saved them from an ambush laid out for them by the Bluecoats, and it was damn hard to convince several hundred men to turn against the one who'd saved their lives. As Oculeth turned a page in the book he was reading, however, a wrist tattoo caught Pate's attention. It sparked a flash in his memory, something that he could quite parse. He'd seen it before, but where? And why didn't it glow like his other tattoos?

"Do you plan on staring at me forever, or are you going to ask about why I said we were all going to die the other day?" Oculeth asked without looking up from his books.

Pate scowled. "I'm wonderin' what Brunt saw in you, is all. All I see is a drunk and a leech."

"Flattery will get you everywhere, captain. Perhaps you should try it sometime?" Oculeth said without missing a beat.

He closed the book he'd been reading and looked up at Pate. "We're going to need to perform a ritual. Which means I'm going to need you to trust me. Whatever I have to do to prove that in short order, I will do. But you have to put your disbelief and your prejudice to the side to make that happen."

"Hmm, so the impossible, then?" Pate said.

"Mr. Brunt wouldn't consider it impossible. He would simply tell you to remove your head from its position firmly planted up your ass," Oculeth said humorlessly.

Pate frowned, then nodded his agreement. "Aye, think he may have said that once or twice."

Or a hundred times.

"Very good," Oculeth said.

He cleared the other books from his desk and then pulled out one. It was a leatherbound, dark blue book with glowing lettering. It was eye-catching, to say the least.

"Nyalotha: The Gateway of Dimensions…" Pate read the title aloud. The words left an odd, metallic tang in his mouth. He didn't like it. "Did ye just make me utter a spell?"

"No, though the word 'Nyalotha' definitely carries a lot of weight behind it."

"And why is that?"

"Because it is the domain of the Infernal Goddess of Knowledge and Deception, Ma'Thilla."

Pate spat on the floor and made a nine-pointed star on his chest. To utter the name of one of the Profane Powers was to invite their ear.

"We just set sail 'n ye already curse the ship by utterin' the name of an Infernal? Do ye want us to die early, Alyrian?!"

"Quite the opposite. But for you to understand our situation, you need to understand what exactly I did on that ship to save our lives and what it will cost us because of it."

Pate leaned over him at his desk. "What did you do, cursed one?"

Oculeth slit his eyes. That one hurt. "Never call me such a thing again, or I will show you what a true cursed one looks like. Are we clear, pirate?"

Pate leaned off the desk. "What did you do, Mr. Oculeth?"

"I made a deal with devils to save ourselves from certain doom. And now, the devils are coming to collect."

Pate gasped, "…Come again?"

"In order for us to go through that portal and end up where we did, I had to make a deal with the Nyalothan Lords. Otherwise, we would have teleported into the maw of some monster or into the emptiness of space rather than the breathable atmosphere and safety of the Ford Farm. These beings want for one thing and one thing only: souls."

Pate placed a hand over his hammering chest. "S…souls? They want my…"

"Badly. If it weren't so difficult for them to cross over to this world on their own, they'd already have it. But they can't, at least not easily. Unless someone summons them, they are all but stranded in their realm, unable to do much more than watch what goes on in this one."

Pate sighed in relief. "So we're safe then?"

Oculeth shook his head, swiping the curly, sweaty black bangs from his face. "Oh, how I wish we were. No, we are, as far as our souls are concerned, the walking dead. You see, whenever a being passes through Nyalotha, a 'thread' of sorts is attached to them. Like the dragline of a spider's silk, it clings to you, immaterial and imperceptible to you or me, but oh so very real and tangible to them. Slowly but surely, they pull on this 'thread,' drawing your soul in. It takes some time. Days, weeks, sometimes months, but eventually, they reel you in…"

Pate leaned on the desk for support, now. He felt weak.

The faceless man…

"How do ye know when you're gettin' close? Surely there's a sign, a symptom to look out for?"

"It can take many forms. Strange visions, noises, vivid dreams. Eventually, it's as though every waking moment is the worst nightmare you've ever seen, but you never wake from it. Suddenly, the things from your dreams are real, but no one else can see them, but you, and they can *touch* you, *hurt* you…"

Both men paused as a knock came at the door. They looked at one another, wondering if the other had heard what they did. The knock came again, and now they both knew the other could hear it.

"Cap'n? We've pulled away from the port. The men wanted to know who's on meal duty tonight," the voice of Henry asked.

Pate opened the door, hand on his gun, and was relieved to see that it was *just* Henry at the door. "Of course, Mr. Henry. I'll leave you 'n Mr. Crimp to divvy the responsibility. Find the best man who knows how to cook 'n assign 'em four men to aid them. We took two cows, eight chickens, two pigs, and four goats for the journey. Whichever livestock is slain for supper, make sure to escort it away from the others 'n kill it above deck. Scrub the blood off the floorboards, or it'll attract insects. We clear?"

Henry nodded his head anxiously. "Yes, sir. But what if they put up a fuss? None of the men seem too keen on cookin'. They all keep lookin' at the women folk to make the supper, 'n Judith is more likely to stab someone for supper than stir a pot."

Pate blinked slowly.

"Tell 'em that Captain Pate said for ye to choose the cook 'n if they have issue with it, they have issue with *me*. Savvy?"

Henry gulped and nodded. "Yes, sir. I'll tell 'em right away, sir!"

"Good."

Pate shut the door, not bothering to give him room to speak further. "I have demons after me soul 'n spineless imbeciles in me crew. Maybe bein' torn apart by the Damned would've been better."

"I wonder myself. To avoid dying, we might have just found ourselves in an even worse fate," Oculeth admitted.

"Your faith is inspiring, Mr. Oculeth," Pate said.

"I do have some good news, however. Before we departed, I had the notion of procuring several volumes from the local library in Port De Morta. That peculiar blue tome is one such volume. It details a method to safeguard ourselves from our bleak fate, if only for a short time. It will require you to do the one thing that I know you loathe, however."

"There isn't much I can fathom loathing more than losing my soul to a demon or submitting to the Dread Captain."

"You'll need to trust me."

"Bugger all, why don't I just shoot myself while I'm at it?"

"Because if you shoot yourself now, the Dread Captain wins, and the Nyalothans claim your soul, now and forever. A fate that is perhaps a thousand times worse than the fate the Dread Captain would have given you."

Pate sat down across from Oculeth and folded his arms. "I very much doubt that."

"Do you? Tell me, in every fairy tale fable that you've heard involving demons and the like, do they ever go into much detail about what happens when the demon *wins*?" Oculeth asked.

Pate shrugged. "Bad shit."

"*Bad shit* doesn't even begin to describe what will happen if the Nyalothans get to us before we can break the thread, captain. Eternal Damnation has no ending and no respite. You will be driven mad with fear, pain, and forbidden knowledge. You will cease to exist as you know it and be made into something far worse than you can ever comprehend in this blessedly brief and merciful mortal coil. Were I able to describe to you even a fraction of what will happen to us, I rather think you would not sleep ever again and would break down the doors of the closest monastery to beg whatever gods may listen to save your immortal soul," Oculeth said mirthlessly.

Pate sat upright in his seat. He heard a faint voice, far away, as though it was coming from through the walls and out at sea. He gritted his teeth together. He had no choice.

"What do we have to do?"

Oculeth extended a thin hand. "Do you trust me?"

Pate groaned and rolled his eyes before extending his calloused palm. "I don't have much choice, do I?"

Oculeth shook his hand. "Basically none, actually."

Then, he pulled out a glowing blue needle and an inkwell. "Have you ever been tattooed before?"

Pate lifted his sleeve and showed the two tattoos on his inner wrist: skull and crossbones, and the symbol of Hail Mary. "I've got a brand on me back where they marked me as a navy man, as well."

Oculeth wasn't surprised. "Well, it's time to add another tattoo to the collection. This one, perhaps, is the most important one of all."

Oculeth set the needle down and took off his shirt, exposing his torso and arms. He was in better shape than Pate had thought he'd be, though he was still quite thin. He reminded him of a younger him. He picked up the nearby bottle of alcosav (he'd gotten several more from Pete Barlow before they left) and took a long draught from it.

"This is going to hurt. A lot."

"Pain is all I know, Mr. Oculeth. Why would it be any different now?" Pate asked.

He lit a cigar and let the numbing smoke of the hemestra leaf within calm him and dull his nerves. He took a long, deep breath. "Begin."

Oculeth grabbed the needle and heated it over a lantern flame.

XXI

Black Business

Bill Louis shivered as they pushed him toward the plank. He gazed down at the turquoise water below and shook his head rapidly. "No, no, no, please no! I'm sorry! Please, I'll never do it again, I'll—"

Morgan stepped forward as the men barred Louis' path and pushed him to the beginning of the plank. His expression was a blank mask.

"Bill Louise, you stand accused of the attempted murder of a superior officer, and brother in black. May the witnesses to this crime come forth and speak their claim," he announced.

Stone came forth, as did Flint, Cutter, Moary, and several other men, all proclaiming that they witnessed Bill Louis attempt to stab Quartermaster Stone. After they spoke, Morgan nodded, then handed down the sentence.

"For your crimes against your brothers, Bill Louis, you will walk the plank into the drinking deep. May Xalhanna, Holder of the Scales of Judgement, have mercy on your soul. Do ye have any final words for your brothers?"

Bill was moaning and sobbing the whole time, pleading with the men, who were disgusted and unmoved by his pleas.

"I didn't kill him! I just got angry, is all! It was an honest mistake, I swear! It won't never happen again on my life 'n on me mother!" he sobbed.

Morgan sighed exhaustedly. He looked over the crew for a moment, his eyes settling on Yager before passing him by. Yager was watching intently, obviously pleased with how things were playing out.

If only you knew, Mr. Yager.

He cleared his throat as he set his gaze back on Bill Louis, who looked at him with scared, desperate eyes. "Your intent was to kill Reece Stone, your superior officer and brother-in-black. Were he slow in his reaction, you would have. An example must be made; a life must be paid. Go into the sea, and ask *her* for mercy..."

Morgan nodded to the men, and Bill Louis wailed in horror as they forced him to walk the plank, swords, and guns trained on him. He hugged himself and sobbed as he was forced to the edge.

Osiris, who was in the group forcing him down the plank, stepped forward. "Die with some dignity, coward!"

He kicked Bill Louis hard in the back, sending him over the edge, flailing and screaming into the water.

Bill Louis landed in the water with a loud splash. He surfaced immediately after, kicking and waving an arm at the ship.

"Come back! Please! Come back!" he begged, his voice hoarse from shouting already.

The men watched, cheering as the ship slowly pulled away from Louis, who had no hope of catching up with her. They slowly migrated to the steering deck, watching as he flailed and chased after the ship, making pitiful sounds.

As he fell behind the ship's wake, he gasped as he looked around. "T-there's something in the water with me! I felt it brush against me leg!" he shouted. "Come back! There's something in the water with me!"

The men watched as a large, sharp fin cut the surface of the water several dozen yards back and rapidly made its way toward Louis. The men pointed at the fin, their exhilarated cries reaching new levels as it approached Louis. He turned, following their gaze, and froze as the fin closed in on him. He didn't utter another scream, as it died in his throat when the fin launched him up into the air and sliced him open. A gout of blood sprayed around him in a ring as he spun through the air.

Morgan broke through the crowd just in time to catch a glimpse of Louis' terrified face as he fell back into the water, now clouded red with his blood. It was silent for several moments; the spectacle was over. Groans and jeers of disappointment were uttered as the men began to walk away from the railing of the steering deck, their entertainment for the day having ended abruptly.

Suddenly, the water exploded as Bill Louis' screaming body was hoisted out of the water in the jaws of a large bladefin shark. The fish sailed well over ten feet out of the water, and as it reached its apex, Morgan watched as Bill Louis waved his remaining arm in the air, his body already in the toothy maw of the beast. He let out one last terrified shriek. It was a loud, pitiful, ear-splitting sound. They disappeared in a bloody splash.

And did not resurface.

The cheers had died, as had the jeers. All that remained was a pregnant silence. Morgan looked over at Yager, who was leaning against the railing, mouth agape.

Osiris stood nearby, scowling.

Armen Hanover stood next to Osiris, a shocked expression on his face, running his hand absentmindedly over his wrist tattoo.

"A life for a knife. How primitive," Abbal noted bemusedly. "Will you mortals ever know peace?"

"Peace is for the dead. Strife is the province of the living. Goodbye, Mr. Louis—and mind the Depths," Morgan eulogized briefly, then walked away.

*****

In an inlet on the east side of Isle De Morta, Azura's pirates dragged her aground. As they worked, they sang sea shanties to bolster their spirits and take their minds off the heat, the exhaustion, and the arduous task ahead of them.

"Shiver me timbers, shiver me bones, yo ho heave-ho!" Cutter began, growling out the first lines of the song as the men worked. The beach was alive with the sound of pirates heaving and dragging the thick ropes they used to tether the Azura across the beach. They'd careened well enough in a secluded area, not easily visible from the sea, but spacious enough for them to set up for what needed to be done. Now they had the daunting task of cleaning her undercarriage. And by the Stars, did she need it. Azura's bottom teemed with mussels, barnacles, sea squirts, and even some sea slime that'd found its way onto her.

If a man were keelhauled across Azura's spine, he'd be torn to shreds on the very first pass—and that was if he was lucky. She was positively infested with pests and stank to high heaven. The sailors were dragging the ropes, finding the heaviest, sturdiest trees they could, and diligently tying them.

"There are men whose souls are as black as coal, yo ho heave-ho!" The men sang the next line as they worked, tying down the ropes as the ship began to tilt over to starboard. As one group tied down the boat, another hauled the behemoth onto land.

This was a feat in and of itself. Every able-bodied man was either dragging the ship or tying the halyards.

Osiris cursed aloud as he heaved, pulling with all his might to make the massive ship turn over. It felt like he was playing tug of war with a whale—and losing.

"We raised our sails and set out to sea!" Cutter sang.

"A bloodthirsty cap'n, 'n me mates 'n me!" The men chanted in retort, focusing on the song to get through the pain.

Osiris cared not for the shanty. He'd lived the reality that these shanties sang of long enough to know the grim truths behind the words. He didn't need a catchy tune to work. What he needed right now was water.

"Quit your jabberin' 'n throw me a skin!" Osiris shouted through parched lips as they fully turned the Azura to her starboard, exposing her portside undercarriage. He watched as the men behind him secured the ropes, then caught the waterskin that Cutter threw at him, taking parched gulps from it. It was lukewarm, but it was water- and he needed it regardless. As he downed all its contents, he nodded his appreciation and gasped for air. "Thanks."

"Ye interrupted me song, Siris," Cutter stated, sounding annoyed.

"I interrupted ye doing what ye do best—running your big mouth," Osiris said, unapologetic. Cutter huffed in response.

"You're welcome," Cutter responded, nodding to the waterskin.

Osiris rolled his eyes. "Thank you, Mr. Cutter, for giving me the water that I so desperately required," he said half-heartedly.

"Of course, mate," Cutter responded with his cock-sure grin, clapping him on the back. Cutter's hand hurt afterward.

"Right. Well, while you 'n Flint oversees these lot securing the ship, I'm goin' to have a word with the cap'n," Osiris said, walking off in his direction.

"Can I finish me song uninterrupted, now?" Cutter called after him, sarcastically.

"Be my guest. Who needs ears, anyway?"

"Ouch," Flint said with a chuckle, having just come over from the encampment.

"You're an asshole, Flint," Cutter responded casually.

"Yeah, and you're an ass. What a pair are we, ay?"

"Dully noted."

The two laughed before turning their attention back to making sure that the crew didn't unceremoniously fuck everything up.

*****

"How bad is she, truly?" Captain Morgan asked, standing in front of the now upraised portside of the Azura.

213

"Honestly? Pretty bad. It's amazin' that she's as quick as she is with this much drag on her. There are enough barnacles here to make an Atarran buffet-line," Ryker half-joked.

"I never was partial to seafood, to be frank," Captain Morgan responded with a chuckle. "All these years, and I *still* can't stand the taste of tuna."

Ryker and Sarkad both laughed as well. "Remember when we were sailin' up north 'n we had to stock up on provisions? The only thing we could find in that damn haven was salted tuna 'n snow oysters. Yuck!" Sarkad gagged.

"Aye, I remember. This 'n was raisin' a fuss every night cuz the cookie couldn't find 'a way to make the tuna taste better'." They laughed as Ryker quoted the cookie's words. "'*Well, no shit, Cap'n! Tuna's fuckin' tuna, whether ye salt it, pepper it, douse it in alcohol, shit's goin' to taste fishy!*'"

"God, whatever happened to Liam? He was the best cookie we'd had in a while," Sarkad reminisced. The others fell silent.

"Liam? Remember, brother? He died in our last hunt. The Chimera got 'em," Ryker reminded him.

"Oh, fuck. I remember now… damn." Sarkad fell silent as well.

When the Chimera took flight and terrorized the ships, one of the unfortunate souls it had snatched from the decks was Azura's cook, Liam. It ate him, leaving nothing but gore for them to bury at sea.

"We should be able to scrape her clean within 48 hours. Two days. Can we make it?" Ryker asked conspiratorially.

Morgan counted the time in his head, biting his lip. "Nineteen days. Subtract two days for cleaning and reassembly… seventeen days ." He looked at the two in the eyes as he saw Osiris striding towards them from around the nose of the ship. "We have seventeen days to reach the envoy at Oceanus. Are we sure we won't be disturbed on this side of the island? Port De Morta is only a few miles away, through the jungle," Morgan asked as the entourage walked.

"The forest is thick, filled with pitfalls and predators, and the islanders know to steer away from it. The port guards would have no reason to come this far out of the town limits, and I doubt they have the resources to send boat patrols. This place is a near non-existent blip on the map for the Empire. No one cares about Port De Morta," Huasca explained.

"Which makes it the perfect place for us to careen while we clean Azura's hull." Morgan nodded. "Very good, Mr. Huasca."

"I try, Captain," Huasca nodded with a smirk.

They paused a moment, taking note of Osiris walking up the beach toward them.

"The men won't be thrilled to hear that they won't be allowed to parlay on the beach—even more, so that they won't be able to go into town, either," Ryker said.

"Why is that? Port De Morta is a small island town, and the chances of our discovery are slim to none. We have letters of marque; we're free men," Sarkad pointed out.

"Because while we may be free men in the eyes of the Empire, we are not free men in the eyes of the Dynasty or the Mercantile. The Xallans aren't likely to have any agents in the area, but the Dyonians most certainly will. We just stole from the Empress, gentlemen. It is only a matter of time before she's made aware of precisely *who* stole the Eye of Atla. And when she discovers this, the Dyonians will be on our trail.

"About four hundred miles to the east of here is the island of Hohto. Hohto is a naval port—a heavily guarded one. The logbook from the Bounty says that it was to be their next port. They would have reached that port *today*. While they may not know what happened to the Empress' Bounty right now, in a day or two's time, they will be scouring this entire corner of the Amaranthine for a lead and a target. We cannot afford to be discovered by the Dyonians, not when we have this much at stake. *That* is why we can't send them into town. Sailors and pirates alike have loose lips when women and alcohol mix. All it takes is the wrong set of ears hearing the conversation for a Dynastic Man 'O War to be at our heels in a matter of days."

"What's this about Men 'O War?" Osiris asked, catching the end of the statement as he approached.

Morgan nodded. "I'm talking about the *other* threat we have to worry about—besides the Empire and their Seekers, of course."

"How many Seekers will they send, do you figure?" Osiris asked, inspecting the infested hull a moment.

"Enough to make sure that none of us will live to tell of what we've done, more than likely. So, at least five or so."

Osiris' eyes bugged open. "A handful of Seekers is enough to kill all of *us*? This a joke, cap'n?"

Morgan shook his head solemnly. "No, Siris, it isn't. You all have been blessed that you've never encountered a Seeker in combat before. I have. They are powerful; Alyria runs deep in their veins. They can form a shield around their body from their own energy, nearly impenetrable to bullets. They can cast spells, and they know how to use weapons, as well. And two or three of them can easily cut down a hundred of us. They'll come armed to the teeth and prepared for a fight, likely on a naval frigate or better-grade vessel. They'll have the firepower and the manpower to wipe us off the face of Hera."

"Stars, fuck me. So how do we beat them?" Osiris asked.

"Well, unless you have powerful Alyria of your own that we don't know about or a method to silence or rebuke theirs, then there isn't much. A cannonball would likely kill one just as it would you or I, provided you can hit them with it, that is. Explosives, perhaps. But they'll know how to find us. They'll know who we are."

Osiris thought of the nullifiers they'd used to disable the El'wa cannons. The nullifiers only affected objects that had Alyria in them, however, not people. That was fortunate for him. He'd have lost his duel with the El'wa knight otherwise.

"How?"

Morgan pulled the letter of marque out of his pocket and conspiratorially showed the men. He opened the envelope and pulled out the pardons therein. Scribbled on the back of each pardon was a circle with a stylized S at the center of it. It glowed faintly. Osiris cursed.

"Fucking magick..."

"This ain't good, cap'n. Not at all," Ryker warned.

"What if we burn it? They can't track us, then," Osiris offered.

"Burn this, and we burn any chance we have of ever making it out of this alive. When these markers fade out, the Emperor will know that we aim to cross him. When he realizes that, he will send out an NBO, a Naval Black Order. Every Bluecoat in the Amaranthine will have free reign to chase us down to the last man. We'll never see the end of it, and we'll never be able to hunt again. It will be the end of us," Morgan explained.

"So that's it, then? We deliver the Eye, or we die?" Osiris huffed.

"Aye," Morgan confirmed.

"Cheeky bastard's got us where he wants us..." Osiris lamented. He didn't like their lack of options. The Emperor was their enemy, whether they worked for him or not. He would kill them as soon as he no longer needed them. They were pirates, after all.

Morgan nodded wordlessly. "Did you secure the chest?"

"Stone and Yager are guarding it as we speak. Moary is making a rotation listing for guard duty. We've got it locked down," Osiris responded.

"I would gaze upon it," Morgan said, then walked towards the encampment with Huasca in toe, leaving the officers to themselves.

Osiris regarded Ryker and Sarkad. "Tannis Brothers, how fair you this tumultuous day?"

"Like shit, hehe," Ryker chuckled in his gravelly voice.

He was the older of the two brothers. He stood quite tall, over six and a half feet. His body was wiry but strong, and he had scars and tattoos covering his arms. His eyes were weary, though he could have been no older than forty years.

"We're old, we're tired, and we're longing for a day without having to check behind our backs," Sarkad responded, "and my back hurts."

Sarkad was younger and a bit shorter than his brother, standing around six feet in height. He had long reddish-brown hair tied in a bun and a beard. He was more robust than his brother, but he looked just as old in the face.

"Oh, to be old. I wonder if I'll make it that far?" Osiris joked.

"With the way you work? Bah, dead before thirty, mark my words," Sarkad dismissed.

"Why thank you, carpenter, such nice words to hear from a Brother in Black." Osiris rolled his eyes as he took out a knife to try and cut out a particularly large and ugly barnacle he'd been staring at. He grunted as he worked the knife between it and the gross brown substance it produced, gluing it to the wood. He dug into the wood and pried it out with an audible pop and crunch of wood. He inspected its shelly exterior a moment before chucking it over his shoulder.

"It's true, ye know. Ye work yourself like ye've got somethin' to prove, Siris," Ryker said.

"I work myself like I give a damn, Bosun," he responded, digging out another barnacle, straining to tear it free. "Fuck it, I need a scraper for this."

"We all give a damn, Siris. You damn near give your life for this, every day. It's admirable, seein' a youth so passionate about the Black. You've earned your stripes, time 'n again. So what do ye have to prove, then?" Ryker asked.

"I wasn't aware this was a schooling session," Osiris replied.

The two brothers looked at one another and shook their heads. "Bah, forget it. You're too young 'n your skull's too thick." Sarkad waved his hand, and the two set off for the encampment. "Leave some scrapin' for the rest ofem', ay?" Ryker said over his shoulder. Osiris waved an arm dismissively, focusing on the barnacles.

*****

"Did ye lay eyes on it?" Yager asked.

Stone looked at him with a questioning gaze. "On what?"

"The treasure! I heard a few of the boys say they saw it when Morgan opened the chest. Said it was the most beautiful thing they'd ever seen—must be worth a fortune!" he exclaimed.

Stone could see the glitter in his eyes. He shook his head. "I wouldn't call what I saw in that chest beautiful. Glowed brighter 'n any gold I ever saw. It was like a siren's call—invitin', but evil. That artifact, that Eye? T'ain't nothin' but a demon's work."

"Demons? Pfeh, you believe in that hogwash them uppity priests talk about in their sermons? Demons don't exist but in fables, Reece. One hasn't been seen in ages. They're a dead memory, like dragons 'n gryphons," Yager dismissed.

"Just because ye can't see it, doesn't mean it don't exist, Danny. Ye know that well as I do! Stars, 'member when we was boys 'n Paul McAllister went out in the moors at midnight on Zyloth Eve?"

Yager shrugged. "I 'member he didn't come back, s'bout it."

"He did. The elders just didn't say shite about it when they found 'em."

"…Found 'em?" Yager said, confused.

"Aye, when they found what was left ofem'."

"What was left ofem'? Fuck are you on about, Reece?" Yager asked, his eyes wide.

"Bout three weeks after Paulie went missin', some folks went out in the moors after dark. The elder druid said that she'd gotten a vision of ol' Paul. Said he was callin' to 'er out in the moors, beggin' to be found. Said they'd only find 'em after dark. So, they rounded up some folks, hunt hounds, rifles, and torches, and they went lookin' *after dark*. They found 'em in an open stretch in the swamp, hangin' on a snag."

"Hermalla!" Yager gasped, calling out the name of the Goddess of Mercy and Shelter.

"They went through that same span a half dozen times over. Never saw the snag, 'n never saw Paul McAllister, neither. But on this night, when the moon was full again, they found 'em. Or what was left ofem'…"

"So that's why his funeral was on the hush, ay?" Yager whistled. "Gods…"

"The night Paulie disappeared, I had this *feelin'*, like…this cold, dreadful feelin' in me belly. I told the poor bastard not to go. Told 'em that nothin' good would come of it. But soon as he got wrapped up with Ronnie 'n them damn idiots, his goose was cooked. It was just simmerin' till he made his last mistake."

"Ronnie never did say what happened that night, did he?" Yager noted. "Everyone thought him 'n his boys killed 'em, but no one could find nothin' concrete 'n he fled the village soon after."

"I seen what Paul McAllister's corpse looked like, Danny. That weren't no man that did that to 'em. 'N ain't no man that made that shiny marble sittin' in this chest. Cuz, I got that same cold, ugly feelin' in me gut when I stand near this thing. The same feelin' I got when Paulie died."

Yager was stunned; Stone felt his hair standing on end at the memory.

"So no, I don't think this here bauble is beautiful. I think it's wicked as a cold wind blowin' over the moors in the dead of winter. 'N whatever the Emperor wants with it is his business, and nothin' good is goin' to come of it. Nothin' good at all."

Before Yager could find his words, Morgan and Huasca approached and greeted them.

"Mr. Stone, Mr. Yager. Anything to report?" Morgan asked.

Stone shook his head. "Nothin' cap. None of ours are fixin' to take this cursed thing."

"My thoughts exactly, but it's better to be safe than sorry when our futures are on the line, ay?" Morgan said.

"Aye, cap'n."

Morgan pulled out the chest key and twisted it in the lock. The lock mechanisms of the chest sounded like gunshots as they popped open. It made Stone's heart jump. Curiously, it opened smoothly and silently. The Eye didn't glow, this time. It was dull, but when Morgan placed his hand upon it, he could still feel an electric rush pass through him. He didn't like it, not one bit. He placed a hand on his amulet and spoke to it telepathically.

"Would that I could cast this thing into the sea for the last time," Morgan lamented.

"Then do it and spare the world a madman's wrath." Abbal urged.

"I will not sacrifice my men for the world that scorns them."

"But you will sacrifice countless lives for the sake of a few cutthroats?"

"They are more than cutthroats; they are my family."

Morgan ceased his conversation with Abbal. He could see that it would go nowhere. He placed the Eye wordlessly back in the chest, shut it, then locked it.

"Mr. Moary will be along with your relief shortly. Carry on, gentlemen." Morgan nodded. He turned to Huasca, who nodded to the men as well, and the two departed.

Yager cast a leery gaze at the chest. He thought of Paul McAllister, now— the boy that disappeared and the moors that claimed him.

XXII

HONOR AMONG THIEVES

Osiris leaned against the base of a palm tree. He had walked the beach all day, directing and supervising the men to ensure that they cleaned the hull of Azura thoroughly. He did so until Cutter came to relieve him and instructed him to rest.

"Captain's Orders," Cutter said.

He wondered if it'd been true. He didn't care if it had, in truth. It was a long, hot day, and he was tired. His wounds from the fight with the leader of the samurai had healed almost entirely, but they flared from the exertion. He needed to rest.

"You have lit a bomb, pirate, but you are all too blind to see it."

What had the samurai meant by those words? He still wasn't sure. He sat beneath the palm tree, drinking water and contemplating the conversation that he, Morgan, and Huasca had shortly before they beached.

I always knew Yager was yellow.

Osiris growled internally.

There were few things he hated more than a turncoat. Bluecoats, yes. Sea monsters, storms, and running out of rum—all bad things. But turncoats…turncoats set his blood aflame. He wanted to kill Daniel Yager right then and there.

"Mr. Stone wishes to handle this situation. So, we'll let him," Morgan had said.

Stone…

Osiris had mixed feelings about Stone. After the mutiny, he'd put him on the long list of people that he just didn't trust. But he'd proven himself time and again as a competent, dependable, and fearless pirate. He reminded him of himself, though with better people skills.

As though summoned by the Stars themselves, Stone appeared, walking towards him against the yellow-white sand of the beach, his image wavering in the heat of the sweltering sun. Osiris took another parched draught from his water skin.

Stone nodded to him as he came into speaking distance. "Siris."

Osiris nodded. "Mr. Stone."

He offered his waterskin to the man, who thanked him, but declined. "I've my own, thank you," Stone said.

He pulled out his skin and drank from it as he sat down next to Osiris beneath the shade of the palm tree, panting lightly. They sat like that for several quiet minutes, drinking water, hiding from the oppressive heat, and watching the small figures of the men on the beach working away at the underside of the frigate.

"All these years I've worked ships, from the navy till now, ye'd think this shite'd get easier—but it never does," Stone lamented.

"Nay, I guess it doesn't. It's hard, thankless work. Someone's gotta do it though, ay?" Osiris commented.

"Aye. Men need ships to sail, ships need maintenance to sail proper," Stone agreed.

"Sometimes she needs more 'n barnacles scraped off her belly to get right, though," Osiris finally said.

Stone nodded slowly but was silent for a while after that. His eyes were narrowed, his jaw set in a reflective scowl.

"I could handle it for ye, ye know? It's nothin' to me, just a task needs doin', a barnacle needs scrapin'," Osiris offered.

Stone blinked and took a slow, full gulp of water. "There're some tasks, Siris, for which only one will do. This be one such task. I'll do what need be done. Stars spare me soul."

Osiris let out an amused chuckle, nearly spitting the water from his mouth. "After all we done, Reece Stone. Ye really think the Stars give two fucks about our souls?"

Stone looked at Osiris, thoughtfully. He recalled his conversation with Steven Cage, after all the Dyonians had committed suicide. That casual indifference to their suffering, as though he'd merely watched an amusing circus trick rather than the ritual deaths of dozens of men—because of them. He didn't see that indifference in Osiris' eyes, but he did still feel ill-will. A disregard for life that was honestly astonishing.

"I like to think they do, Osiris. Cause if they don't, 'n them books be true? Well, this beach'll feel like a frozen mountaintop by comparison, 'n the sun's oppressive light will seem like a fleetin' fantasy."

Osiris shrugged, and looked back at the men on the beach. "We're all damned, Reece Stone. Most of us just don't know it yet. Go handle your business. Worry about *your* soul. I've got mine."

Osiris emptied the last of the water from his skin, and already his tongue was parched for more. In this heat, even a gallon of water evaporated from the skin like droplets on a hot skillet. He stretched, nodded once to Stone, and set off to look for more.

Stone sat beneath the tree awhile longer, thinking long about what he was about to do. He saw a lone, familiar figure step away from the group and walk slowly down the beach. His opportunity had come. He took a deep breath and suppressed the contrasting thoughts and emotions that bubbled just beneath the surface. Then, he stood up and walked towards the figure. The cut in his side he'd sustained from the samurai burned in anticipation.

*****

He walked away from the men, far enough down the strand that they wouldn't be able to make out who he was, or what it was he was doing. He was relieved, so he knew no one would miss him. Flint and Cutter were eager to let him go, surprisingly. Normally they gave him hell these days. He cupped his mouth and made the bird call several times before he heard a weak, chirping call. He looked around and saw that the bird had in fact been hiding in the trees, past the shoreline.

The Imps sure do train their birds smart.

He agreed.

When the envoy had given him the bird, he was skeptical. It was a sea hawk, so he knew it wouldn't attract much attention, hovering around the ship and flying off into the distance. He worried about being seen giving it messages, however. He always had to go above deck, as there was but a few windows in the crew quarters and far too many eyes and ears to send out a message. The hawk proved resourceful, though. It would perch on the yardarms of the ship, hiding in the shrouds and sails. It seldom made a sound, but when to address him and respond to his calls.

It landed on his shoulders, and he gritted his teeth as its talons dug in. It had a message for him, wrapped around its ankle. He took it, unfurled it and looked around before reading it. The message had but one phrase:

Await further orders.

He nodded. He'd known what it would say. What the orders were, he had no idea. How the bird continued to find him and transmit the messages, he was also uncertain. He saw a figure approaching from the direction of the ship, but they were too far for him to identify them just yet. He made a call, and the bird took flight. He pulled out the waterskin from his hip and drank from it parchedly. It was a struggle, every minute, not to down all its contents. But until the scouts returned with the coordinates for a pool to replenish their stores, he knew he couldn't afford to drain it all.

He sat down at the water's edge, letting the cool saltwater lap at his shoes as the figure approached.

"It's hotter than a dragon's gullet out here," he complained as the figure sat beside him.

"Aye. Makes me long for home, it does. The moors were harsh, but they sure as Sheolhenna didn't get *this* hot," Stone recalled.

"Nay, they didn't. But I'd trade gators, snakes, 'n drowners for a hot beach any day. Most I've gotta worry about here is crabs, 'n right now, I'd love for a crab to come 'n try its luck," Yager said, pulling out his pistol and aiming it at the sea. He made a mock firing motion, and the two laughed heartily.

"I remember Elder Abernathy used to make this right delicious swamp crab stew. Stars, I'd kill for it right now," Stone reminisced.

"Agh, the one with the diced potatoes 'n carrots in it? She used to make a big pot of the stuff in the middle of the village, cook it 'n season it all day till it was simmerin'. She'd put a whole bucket 'o butter in the broth. Crab flesh was so tender it melted on your tongue," Yager moaned longingly.

"Shut up, ye fool. Yer makin' me hungry!" Stone said, slapping him on the back. "Never thought I'd miss that crazy old crone so bad."

"Aye, even though I'm damn sure she placed a hex on Kyle Denny, when he raided her garden that one summer."

"Aww shite! I'd forgotten about that poor bugger. His tongue turned purple 'n swole to the size of a damn apple in his mouth. He couldn't eat, couldn't swallow—could barely breathe for a whole fortnight! His Mum had to force a straw down his throat 'n force feed 'em broth 'n water that way!" Stone made a noise of disgust.

"I gotta give it to 'er. No one went routin' through her garden no more after that," Yager admitted.

"Aye, for true. Kyle weren't thievin' no more after that, neither. He told on all his brothers, though, when his mother made 'em apologize to 'er. Always felt some type of way 'bout that." Stone said.

Told on his brothers…

His mind returned to the present. His smile, and the memories of times past faded away once more.

"I can't find it in meself to blame 'em, though. It took more 'n one man to climb 'er fence, 'n the lock she put on that damn gate was enchanted—couldn't open it without the key, no matter what ye did to it. The boy nearly died all 'cause he was the one what got caught," Yager admitted.

"Doesn't matter, Daniel. He knew the code: never tell on yer brothers. I can't say I don't see why he broke it, but he broke it all the same," Stone said.

"That boy went through hell. His brothers could've helped 'em, told the old crone what they'd done, maybe gotten him some leniency. Nay, instead they was hoopin' 'n hollerin', laughin' at their brother with the rest of us. How do ye make sense 'o that? The boy was sufferin' for a crime *they all* committed together, 'n they left 'em to rot!" Yager said, his voice elevating.

"We all know the score. If we're caught, we don't speak on who did it with us; we stand strong 'n take what's given to us."

"Pfft, easy for you to say, isn't it? Ye managed to skirt on by, while your brother was left in the fire, still burnin'."

"I tried to save you! I told ye that we had to fall back, bide our time 'n wait till we had more men on our side! But ye didn't listen!"

"You went 'n talked to that old bastard after I told ye not to! I *told ye*, Reece! That he's a snake with a silver tongue! That he'll turn ye against us if ye try to argue 'em down!"

"I wanted a peaceful transition 'o power, Daniel! *You* wanted a bloodbath! If we'd done it your way, the Azura would've been destroyed 'n all of us with her!"

"Since we did it *your* way, we lost the only opportunity we had to take her, period!" Yager frothed.

Stone stood up, staring at the red-faced Yager.

"Think about it! A ship 'o legend! One that's fought in countless battles, been in countless stories! The ship 'o the Immortal Pirate Cap'n! We woulda been legends ourselves to control such a vessel! Captain Stone 'n Captain Yager! The men what bested the Immortal Pirate 'n stole his ship! No man would contest us, not with Azura at our command! But instead 'o that, ye contented yerself with bein' her quartermaster, 'n I was regulated to another deck sweepin', barrel rollin' dreg like all the rest!"

Yager was fuming, and he stood inches from Stone's face as he spat his rage. Stone set his jaw and hardened his heart.

"Ye know why I stopped the mutiny, Yager? Because unlike ye I spoke with the cap'n, 'n discovered how it is that ship over yonder has been able to survive so much hell over the years. She's enchanted. The bastard bound his soul to her 'n she's bound to him! One can't exist without the other! The very timber she's comprised of lives and breathes for 'em!"

"Bull-fucking-shite!" Yager spat.

Stone pushed Yager away from him. He stumbled back and fell onto the sand.

"It's the bloody truth! I watched the bastard climb the crow's nest 'n leap from it! The shrouds of the ship caught him in their grasp! They saved 'em, Yager! The fuckin' ship saved 'em! I don't know how, maybe that damn amulet 'round his neck did it, maybe he spoke the truth 'n he really did bind himself to her—it doesn't fuckin' matter! Without 'em, that ship is a floatin' heap of dead wood. She's unclaimable! Yer so blinded by rage, ye can't see the forest fer the fuckin' trees!" Stone sighed in frustration.

Yager scrambled to his feet. "I'm not blind! I see it all! I see the serpent in the grass! I see what Morgan Sarron *really* is! No man can survive that long naturally! He'll be the death of us all, Reece!"

"And how do you know? A blind fool who can't see when he's been bested?!"

"BECAUSE I TOLD THEM!" Yager roared.

Stone heard the words he knew to be true, and he looked at his old friend with a hurt that only bonds thicker than blood could invoke. Yager stood indignant, face beet red with rage, sweat pouring down his brow.

"You sold us out, brother…did ye think that would change the outcome? Yes, what happened after the mutiny was wrong. Ye got sent up the river, 'n I'm damn sorry ye did. I pleaded yer case to the cap'n, told 'em that it was all me what done it. Ye know what he told me, Daniel? Ye know why he demoted ye to crewman? Why I had to beg 'em not to send you off the plank? Because he said of all the men who had a hand in the mutiny, ye were the only one who had murder in yer heart. Ye were the only one willin' to kill yer cap'n 'n brothers, damned be the consequences, fer yer own gain. He said he knew ye were the one to engineer the mutiny. He knew that ye were set on takin' his spot, 'n he knew ye'd betray the rest of us after ye got it…" Stone spat.

Yager growled low in his threat, his face a mask of anger. "You betrayed me, Reece. You left me to rot."

"You betrayed us all, Daniel. You ain't no brother of mine anymore…" Stone shook his head and threw up his hands as he walked away. "I wash my hands of you."

He heard a gun cock behind him, and he paused a few meters away, his back still turned.

"I can't let ye tell 'em what I done, Reece. I'll not go out like Bill Louis did."

Stone looked down the beach at the sunbaked image of Azura, and the small shadows of men working around her. "Put the gun down, 'n come back with me, or they'll do you far worse than they did Bill Louis," he warned. His voice was cold and certain; he didn't fear death.

Yager's hand trembled as he weighed his options, and realized that all roads ended in his demise, if he shot his old friend dead, here.

"Gaaah—fuck it!" He raged like a child in a tantrum, throwing his gun to the sand at Stone's feet.

Stone turned slowly and picked it up before fixing Yager with a hard stare.

"At least ye didn't cross that line."

"I crossed that line miles ago, Reece Stone. What you're seein' is just a mirage in the wind."

The two men walked back to camp, silent and divided.

*****

Morgan walked into the tent and regarded Daniel Yager. He was sitting in a chair, tied down to it with rope. He'd already sustained several blows from the officers after they'd discovered what he'd done.

"How are you feeling, Mr. Yager?" Morgan said as he brought up his own chair and sat in front of the man.

"How do ye think I feel, ye old vulture?" Yager asked, his gaze still hateful, despite one eye being almost completely swollen shut.

Morgan chuckled as he lit his pipe. "I can see you're ready to cooperate, so why don't we begin, then? How did you come in contact with the imperials first?"

"Why would I tell ye a damn thing? I'm a dead man, anyways. If I'm goin', I'll make it as hard for ye as possible."

Morgan leaned back in his chair, a bemused smirk on his lips as he shrugged. "I was hoping you'd ask that. Mr. Cutter, Mr. Flint, come here, please?"

Immediately the two offers came through the tent flaps and stood on either side of Morgan. They stared harshly at Yager.

Yager eyed them warily. Cutter was holding a gun, and Flint, curiously enough, was holding an unlit torch.

"Now, I know you'd like to go out on your own terms, Mr. Yager, but I would advise against that. I don't need to tell you that Mr. Flint and Mr. Cutter are downright sadistic in their treatment of captives when they have reason to be. If I give the word—and I want ye to listen to this very carefully." Morgan leaned forward.

"Mr. Cutter is going to use that dragon gun he's holding. He's going to fire it just below your knee. It will destroy your leg and ensure you can never walk again."

For effect, Cutter raised the gun in question, and aimed the dragon's head of the gun at Yager's legs. He smirked. "Bang."

"Now, that's going to hurt a lot, I would say. And ordinarily, that would kill you pretty quickly, except Mr. Flint's job is to make sure that doesn't happen. No, he's going to take that torch there." Morgan thumbed at Flint. "And he's going to cauterize your wounds. It's going to hurt beyond imagining, and it will staunch the blood flow."

Morgan watched as Yager's hard expression faltered at the mention of the cauterization of his leg stump. "Now, we can do that two times—before we move onto your arms, that is."

"…They approached me when we made port at Theldrin, a few days before we hunted down the El'wa trade ships in the Golden Ocean…" Yager said impishly.

"I knew you'd see reason. Mr. Flint, Mr. Cutter, wait outside, please," Morgan bid.

"Damn. I was hoping ye'd put up more of a fight, traitor," Cutter admitted before the pair stepped out.

"…Where and when?" Morgan asked.

Yager bit his lip and contemplated putting up a fight again. He knew that he'd be losing his legs if he did that.

"When we were at port, I was in the pub, nursin' a beer when a comely lass came 'n tempted me. She offered me arse for free, so of course I took it. We went out back 'n she led me to the beach. I thought nothin' of it—I had me pistol 'n me dagger on me, 'n I knew these posh types weren't goin' to move against me."

"You didn't think it odd that a human prostitute was plying her trade in an El'wa port?" Morgan asked.

"That's the strange thing—she weren't human. She were El'wa, or at least she were half-El'wa."

"A half-El'wa? Interesting. When did she reveal her true intentions?"

"About right when we made it to the beach out of earshot. She smiled, 'n asked me why I was sittin' alone at the bar, when all me brothers was sittin' around me, ignorin' me. I asked her why it mattered. She asked me if I wanted to earn some extra scratch 'n get back at 'em at the same time. At first, I said no. Then she pulled out a pocket pistol 'n aimed it at me balls. She did it faster 'n I could react. Said I could either lose me bollocks or earn some scratch. I says 'fuck it, I'm listenin'' 'n she proceeds to lay it out for me.

"She says she works for the empire, 'n that it's important that they get hold of ye," Yager says, nodding to Morgan.

"Me? Why?" Morgan asks, concerned.

"Says they need yer help. Says they need ye to retrieve somethin' for 'em, 'n only ye can do it—no one else. So they tracked us, 'n had been trackin' us for some time. She told me to keep an eye on ye, 'n then she gave me a trained seahawk to relay messages. The rest is history," Yager said.

"So the imperials tracked us for months to get at me?" Morgan asked, skeptically.

"Ye heard me right, old man. Yer the reason we got shanghaied. They didn't care for us, they didn't want us. They wanted *you...*" Yager smirked, blood dripping down the cuts in his face. "Seems the Imps needed their seadog once more, to go 'n fetch 'em somethin'. I wonder if that little glowin' orb was worth all this trouble? Doesn't matter, I guess. They'll get theirs, in the end. The Emperor always gets what he wants, the posh bastard..."

Morgan stood up. He felt as though his legs were made of jelly. He turned toward the tent flap and grabbed his chair, walking towards it, making sure not to let his surprise show.

"Siris will take you to a secluded spot after dark and turn you loose. I would suggest you use whatever money the Imps gave you to start a new life and stay far away from the sea. You're not a pirate anymore, Daniel Yager. You turned your back on the black, and your name will be cursed by all," Morgan stated before pushing through the flap and leaving the stunned Yager to grapple with what he'd done and mourn what it cost him...

XXIII

KING OF THE WORLD

The imperial palace of Emperor's Rest was perhaps the most lavish structure in all of the eastern kingdoms of the empire. Its halls were lined with royal purple carpets and tapestries displaying the imperial heraldry—a roaring, purple dragon. Every painting, every marble statue at a juncture, and every cup on a table was worth more than the average peasant could hope to see in a month's work, if not years, depending on the item. In these wide, tall, extravagant halls, the Emperor's guardsmen patrolled, constantly, day in and day out.

The imperial family's quarters sat atop it all, in the central castle within the interior of the palace complex. The castle itself was one of the oldest structures in the city. Its halls were narrower and more personal. Varryn preferred it that way, however. In the long, wide corridors of the lower palace and its subsidiary buildings, it always felt too open. His father had taught him well in his youth to be wary of wide-open spaces just as well as he should appreciate them. Space meant maneuverability, freedom of motion and ease of surveillance. It also meant that you had much more room to be outmanned, outmaneuvered, and outplayed.

And in the Emperor's court, being outplayed was a very real and present danger. Varryn knew that the juncture he was at in his plan demanded focus and privacy. And so, he had indefinitely adjourned his small council. The imperial treasurer, the high justice, the archbishop, and even the war master had been instructed in private to return to their respective keeps and castles and await the Emperor's summons once more. Emissaries from the vassal kingdoms of the empire had been similarly frozen. The imperial embassy had not seen a summit in over half a year. Such was the state of the empire, now. A hulking, massive beast with many heads, arms, and legs, wasting away at its core as its heart struggled to pump blood to all its disparate limbs. And the brain of this great, continent-spanning creature, had all but decided to let it hibernate.

For now…

And so, Emperor Varryn Kurza, Son of Vagran the Fifth, Slayer of Wuhlven, Repeller of the El'wa Imperium, and Ruler of the Six Kingdoms…sat in his study reading through paperwork. Alone. As had been his daily routine for nigh on six months. He stared blankly at a missive from Bora. The Warden of the North, Jotunn Wightsbane, had written a plea for aid to the imperial crown.

The North was a savage land by southern standards. Frigidly cold in all but the warmest months, fraught with dangerous wildlife and creatures supernatural, as well as the all-too-common threat of man itself. Borra was a land divided; strife-ridden since mankind first set foot on its frozen soil. Its people were hardy, resourceful, deeply spiritual, and if Varryn was being polite, completely wild and untamable. The most violent of them all, however, was the Valkar. The very scourge that Warden Wightsbane wrote of in his plea for aid.

The Valkar were vile, merciless, and savage raiders, more vicious and cutthroat than any pirate could ever conceive of being. Pirates murdered and stole, yes. But it was a rare day forthat they raided and pillaged the land. The Valkar raided, raped, and pillaged as though it was their Stars-given right to do so. When pirates raided, there were survivors to tell the tale. When Valkar raided, no man, woman, or child remained.

At least not alive.

All that remained were bodies. Burned, skinned, crucified, and depending on the clan, half-eaten.

"I write to you with frank honesty, your grace. The Valkar grow bolder by the day. Entire villages have disappeared overnight, their residents killed or enslaved to be spirited away to the hell pits that the Valkar call home. There they are sacrificed, or else made to endure the cruelest most debased existence as the slaves and livestock of the pitiless Valkar. My warriors tire and dwindle, our battle with the forces of chaos neverending. In each skirmish, we fell a dozen of their warriors and lose two dozen of our own. Each battle they return with foul Alyria and weapons cursed by their Dark Goddesses.

"I write to you in plea, your grace. The summer months will soon be upon us, and the Valkar will commence their reaves once more. They will away from the north and turn their gaze south…"

A knock at the door to his study broke his concentration.

"Enter, Vexyn," Varryn answered.

The door opened, and the imperial advisor, Vexyn Trinitian, entered.

"I apologize for the interruption, my liege, but something terrible has occurred in the city!" Vexyn announced urgently.

Varryn closed the missive from Wightsbane and folded it back in its envelope as he stood. "What has happened?"

"An explosion has lit ablaze one of the storage warehouses on the pier of the Emperor's Cup. Guardsmen had been dispatched to assess the damage and contain the blaze," Vexyn said.

Varryn walked toward the door and began walking hurriedly down the hall, followed by Vexyn.

"What of the casualties? Do we know of the cause? Where is the Knight-Commander?"

"The blaze has been quelled, sire. I came to inform you of such. As soon as the report came, a knight entered the keep, following the guardsmen who had detained the dock workers for questioning, as is protocol, sire. He is…quite irate at their treatment and wishes to speak with you about it…" Vexyn said, somewhat nervously. The pair traveled down a stairwell, flanked by guards, and approached the door leading to the inner castle entrance hall.

Varryn laughed incredulously. "Wishes to speak with me? Just who does he presume to be?"

"Sire, he is—"

A man in gold-steel armor approached, and Varryn recognized him immediately.

I would've known.

He groaned internally.

"Paladin Immanel Corinth," Varryn said, unable to hide his lack of enthusiasm.

"My liege, I would speak with you of the detainment of those poor dock workers! They aided me in fighting the blaze, why then are they being detained like criminals?" Corinth asked immediately, unable to hide his own agitation.

"It is standard protocol to round up witnesses to such crimes, paladin. They could very well be the orchestrators, cleverly hiding themselves from suspicion," Varryn said.

"If they orchestrated the blaze, then *fleeing* would have been their best means of hiding suspicion! A man not seen cannot be blamed," Corinth replied.

"A man is always seen, but in plain sight he can hide his hand. They will be freed when they have been cross-examined and the culprit has been found. We are not savages in the capital, Ser Corinth."

Though you may think us so.

Varryn added internally.

Corinth shook his head. "And who will cross-examine them? That torturer, Axios? Or perhaps Ebonheart, the man who renders his victims screaming and incoherent?"

When Varryn dismissed his small council, he also dismissed the city's judicial officials. He had thought it prudent to restructure them, as allegations of corruption had become prevalent in the previous years. He had been too busy to recruit new ones, however.

"Ebonheart serves the crown well. Every instrument has a purpose, and he serves his. Axios is on an appropriately short leash. Disciple Zaviar will give whomever is responsible a fair sentencing before the people and release the innocent."

"Zaviar? My liege, why do you continue to give the loyals any say in matters of law and order? They are not trained or sanctioned officials," Corinth pressed.

"Why do you question your Emperor on matters that he is decided on?" Varryn asked, his patience running out.

"Because I am—"

A statuesque woman in a regal purple dress and gold crown appeared from the doorway and approached the arguing men.

"Apologies, husband. Brella has prepared the dinner you promised to attend tonight."

Seeing who it was, the guards immediately fell to one knee, as did Corinth, who paused mid-sentence.

"Apologies, My Empress. I did not mean to intrude upon the imperial family's supper," he said before he could even think, then bowed.

Varryn faced her and bowed. "Alessa, my dear, I will be along shortly after Ser Corinth and I finish our discussion."

Empress Alessa pinched the bridge of her nose. "Must you prattle on with the paladin again? Ser Corinth trains your son in the ways of a proper knight, and you reward him with ceaseless bickering. We must *away*, dear."

Varryn's jaw hung open, unable to form a response as Alessa grabbed his hand and pulled him toward the stairwell. Vexyn watched from the doorway, hiding his own mirth as she passed him.

"Apologies, Vexyn, I did not see you! Will you join us tonight for dinner? It has been overlong since Tempeste and I have dined together," Alessa asked warmly.

Vexyn smiled and shook his head. "Not tonight, My Lady. Tempeste wishes to dine with her parents. They've come to visit, and they already complain of my absence."

"Admirable for you to suffer them, dear. Lavvy will not even *speak* to mine," she said, casting a sideways glance at Varryn.

Vexyn held back a chuckle. Lavvy was Alessa's pet name for the Emperor, an abbreviation of his middle name Lavernus.

"We will dine soon, My Lady, I promise it," Vexyn said.

Varryn thought to stop her and press the issue with Ser Corinth but thought better of it as his wife's vice grip dragged him away from the hall and back upstairs.

"I was in the middle of a conversation," he said as they were heading out of earshot.

"You were in the middle of sparking a fire that needed no starting. Paladin Corinth is a good man, perhaps the least serpentine in your court, as a matter of fact, barring Vexyn and the high bishop. In a city of serpents, you would make bones with the one mongoose."

"I am wary of all, Alessa. I have to be; it is the nature of my station."

"Yes, well, in your station it is just important to identify and *commend* friends, as it is to sniff out and punish enemies. Or had you forgotten in these long months of searching?"

Varryn felt her words acutely; they stilled his tongue.

They topped the stairwell and paused at the door leading to the dining hall.

"The children are in the hall. Mind yourself before you greet them, especially Gundyr. I know how you two get…"

They pushed open the door.

*****

The imperial palace had three dining halls: one in the outer court, near the throne room. This hall was for feasts with nobles, dignitaries, and other such guests. The second was the council dining hall, which had been derelict for the past several months. This hall was used for meals with the Emperor's council. The third and final was the inner castle dining hall, where the imperial family ate most of their meals. This evening was no different.

Varryn and Alessa entered the dining hall as several of the servant staff left, having delivered their bounty upon the furnished dining table. The main course, a suckling pig with an apple in its mouth, stared blindly at the Emperor as he sat down at the head of the table and Alessa stood at his side. To Varryn's right stood his wife, Alessa, followed by his youngest son, Andryn, and next to Andryn was his daughter, Odessa. To his left stood his eldest son, Gundyr.

When he saw that everyone was in place, he nodded, said a brief prayer to the Stars, and pulled out his wife's seat, allowing her to sit as the children followed suit. The remaining attendant staff stood, heads bowed in waiting for their masters to request drinks, or other such needs. So silent were they most often, one could almost forget their presence.

Varryn surveyed his family, rubbing a doting thumb over his wife's hand, who squeezed his, he saw little Andryn sitting next to her, his seat mounted high with pillows to prop him up and support him, keeping him stuck in place, should he decide to try and wander (as toddlers often do). Andryn babbled happily, playing with his food.

"Now, now, Andryn, you must eat your vegetables as well so that you may grow big and strong," Varryn directed, gently sticking a leaf of greens, perhaps cabbage, onto his fork and offering it to the toddler's lips. Andryn made a hacking noise.

"No," he grumbled in his high-pitched infantile voice, and took his small hand, barely big enough to wrap around one of Varryn's fingers and halted his advance. The child hated vegetables (as most toddlers do) and would fuss with anyone who tried to feed them to him.

"If you will not eat your greens, child, then how will you grow big as a mountain and protect mommy?" Alessa asked with a smirk.

"Mommy safe?" Andryn asked concernedly, his little face twisting up in concern as he shook with anxious energy.

Odessa leaned over and rubbed her baby brother on the head. He giggled and looked at her and she smiled back at him.

"Mommy is safe and sound. Open wide," she instructed as she gazed at the fork in her father's hand.

It levitated.

Andryn gazed in wonder and awe at her, completely oblivious as the food went in his mouth. He squealed and ate the food. His sister's trick had worked.

"Odessa, child, you know how I feel about you using Alyria at the table," Alessa complained.

Odessa's smile faltered. "My apologies, mother."

She looked down at the table and stabbed at her food with her fork.

Varryn placed a reassuring hand on Alessa's shoulder. "Let her express her gifts, dear. We pay Sage Freke to tutor her for a reason."

Alessa scowled, looking at Varryn harshly. "Yes, I am aware, husband. I am also aware of just how dangerous such *gifts* can be for the gifted and those around them."

Odessa's eyes widened momentarily, then returned to normal as she continued to mess with her food.

I'm not dangerous.

She told herself.

She'd heard it every day of her life since her powers first revealed themselves, shortly after her fourth birthday. She remembered the look of profound disappointment on her mother's face when they told her that her daughter was an Alyrian.

"They'll take her away, then," Alessa said to her father and the magisters, as she clutched Alessa's hands.

"She will be trained in the ways of Alyria, but she will be trained here, under our supervision, as well as Master Erebus and her new teacher, Sage Freke," Varryn tried to reassure her.

She looked down at Odessa, then. Her expression unreadable as her hands clutched hers almost painfully.

Odessa returned to the present as Andryn tugged at her sleeve and waved his fork at her giddily.

"Wywa?" he asked hopefully.

He was too young, and struggled to say 'Alyria', so he said 'wywa'. It was his catch-all term for anything that confounded him, as well as the tricks that Odessa would occasionally perform for him.

She stopped stabbing at her food and gently gripped his small hand, which was swallowed up in her modest ones.

"Not now, Andryn." She leaned over to his ear. "But *later…*" She gave his hand a squeeze.

He squealed and kicked in his seat before grabbing a handful of diced meat and stuffing it in his face. He still struggled with utensils. He'd smeared grease and juices all over his face in the process, and must have dropped half of it on the handkerchief in his lap as he chewed. He pointed across the table to their remaining sibling.

"Baba!" he shouted, waving at his brother.

Across the table, by his lonesome, the middle of the imperial children, Prince Gundyr, sat in silence, eating slowly, watching. He saw his baby brother waving at him, alerted by his cry, 'Baba', his infantile attempt at saying 'brother', or so Gundyr presumed. He smiled at his baby brother and waved back.

"Baba," he said back, though he couldn't muster the same youthful exuberance as his brother.

Varryn, having been chatting with Alessa, turned his gaze towards his eldest son, and saw a figure that so closely resembled himself.

Almost.

Where Varryn had raven hair, as did his daughter, Odessa, and their youngest, Andryn, Gundyr had taken after his mother. His hair was curly, and blonde like golden wheat on a summer's eve. Varryn's eyes were a lighter purple than his. Gundyr's were deep purple like a midnight rose. He was only seventeen years, but he stood as tall as his father and promised to grow a bit taller still when his growing was done.*Now, if only he could put on some muscle,* Varryn thought.

His son was built tall and thin, though he noticed he'd put on a small amount of musculature in the past few weeks.

He had no facial hair yet, but Varryn recalled it took some time before he began to grow his in earnest, and regardless he shaved it. Gundyr also did not have Varryn's pronounced robust jawline as of yet. His closer resembled the more elegant jaw of his mother.

Yes, Varryn saw much of himself in his eldest son. Already he had trained him for years in the ways of a proper ruler: posture, etiquette, how to speak, how to read a man and know his nature, and how to lead. These lessons showed in his every movement. He was not a lazy child. Indeed, he was perhaps almost as ambitious as his father.

"You're most quiet, my son. Such is a rarity for you at the dinner table. Are you feeling well?" Varryn asked.

"Merely pondering, father," Gundyr responded, continuing to eat.

"Pondering what, I wonder?" His father asked casually as he ate, wiping his mouth with a cloth.

The boy stopped chewing and looked around the room at the empty chairs next to his sister and brother and the hollowness of the hall they dined in. "This room is almost always empty. There are no less than forty chairs on either side and yet we still manage to seldom have more than the five of us dining in here at once. Six on the occasion that Vexyn eats with us. Why is that father?" The boy asked, his voice already grabbing a smidge of the baritone gravel and ice that was his father's voice but with a bit more fire.

His father looked around at the empty room, noticing its spacious void for the first time in some time. "Are the six of us not enough?" he asked. Varryn's eldest, his daughter Odessa, the tall and regal maiden she was, sat her utensils down and placed her hands on her temples, her long raven locks fanning out over her face.

"This again?" she groaned, tired of these daily spats.

"Nay, my dear. We shan't begin this again. I know how it upsets you." Varryn assured her, his tone returning to an appeasable one.

"There are five of us, Vexyn has his own family that he eats with, as he should. Why then do they not eat with us? Why do they not dine with the imperial family, as deserving as they are? Why not have the knights, the diplomats, and the clergy also eat with us? Why not the public? At *least* Paladin Corinth should dine with us as a church knight!" Gundyr continued his inquiry, watching his father's expression sour a bit.

He seethed at the mention of Ser Corinth.

"Vexyn and his family are always welcome. No one has told Knight-Commander Viceroy that he is not welcome, nor have the clergy and Archbishop Kalen been told to stay away," Varryn explained, head mounted on a heavy arm and palm. "Would you like to invite them?"

"Now father, you and I both know that does not count as a proper invitation. They would see it as an order and nervously comply. Viceroy himself is a sycophant. They would sit here, trying to make themselves as small as a mouse and as proper as a puppet with a hand up its ass," Gundyr responded sarcastically.

"Manners, child," Varryn corrected him. The boy sighed in exasperation.

"Manners matter little when men die for naught," Gundyr said, having finished all he cared for with his plate, and began staring out a window, done with the conversation. Varryn frowned, then moved on to his daughter, whom he'd yet to formally speak to.

"And how are you, my dear? Are your lessons going as well as your brother's?" Varryn asked, putting on a smile for his beautiful daughter.

Odessa flashed a knowing smirk, her eyes hooded in a calculative manner. "My lessons have gone well father, thus far. Though I do so *bore* of the etiquette of the court. Not fitting of a lady, I know surely," she admitted with an open-mouth smirk, displaying a flash of her pearly, straight teeth. She was twirling a piece of steak on her fork as she spoke. Odessa's eyes were a piercing mix of the bright blue of her mother's, and the signature purple of her father's, splitting in half on either eye to create an entrancing breakup and contrast between the two colors.

She had the most striking and entrancing eyes that Varryn ever saw. Already, she had no less than a thousand bartering suitors, whom he'd kept away with a stern declaration that she would not see a suitor till her twenty-first year. She was two years away.

"I understand, dear. The responsibilities and necessary skills of an imperial princess aren't all glamour. There are things one must learn to bring honor and distinction, even if one's own interest run opposed to it," Varryn agreed, his eyes cast off into the distance, focusing on something in his mind's eye. He blinked it away, focusing back on the here and now. "And how goes your other studies, my dear?"

Her smile broadened. "Quite well, indeed. I could show you, father—after dinner, I mean," she offered eagerly.

Varryn nodded. "It would be my pleasure, child."

He cast a glance once more at his eldest son, and noticed the cold shift in temperament, from one side of the table to the other. To his right was the warmth of life: his wife, his toddler son, and his mystical daughter.

To his left was a cold, iron curtain.

Gundyr looked away out of a window into the moonlight. He tried to recall the last time he'd seen his son smile. He couldn't remember.

XXIV

ARSON

Varryn and Vexyn walked across the inner courtyard of the imperial palace, making their way to a guard tower. At the tower was a thick, steel-framed door that required a key to unlock it. Vexyn pulled out a large, many-keyed ring and fitted the proper key into the lock, opening it. They paused at the entrance and looked down into its torchlit depths, took a glance back out to the moonlit night, and descended into the depths, followed by several guardsmen, including Ser Roderick.

"My liege, Lord Advisor," Roderick addressed them with a bow, the white cloak around him jostling with the effort.

"How fairs the undercroft this day, Ser Roderick?" Vexyn asked jokingly.

"The usual fair. Howling inmates, Axios swearing in anger, and Guardsman Conway swears up and down he saw a shadow opening and shutting doors." Ser Roderick shrugged.

Ser Daven, another guardsman, bowed silently and joined the entourage.

They travelled down, down into the depths of the palace undercroft— a deep, many-pathed labyrinth of dungeons, cells, walkways, and rooms utilized in the early days of Emperor's Rest, back when it was called King's Rest, before the formation of the empire. Many of the undercroft's rooms were vacant, unused for at least a generation or more. And so in their vacancy, rats, spiders, and various nightcrawlers had taken residence in its long, empty corridors.

And ghosts.

Varryn recalled.

There were stories of the undercroft that dated back centuries, and Varryn knew that many of them were true. Numerous enemies of the crown had been brought here and imprisoned, never to see the light of day again. That black energy of death had pervaded the halls, leaving a thick layer of menace that simply never left. Disembodied voices, strange noises, smells, and shadows. No man traveled alone in the halls of the undercroft. Not because of any inherent danger, or at least not because of one that could be measured and identified.

The atmosphere was thick and oppressive, and when one wandered alone through its dark recesses, men swore that they heard footsteps following them, heard voices calling them, and saw *things* that simply couldn't be described. Varryn had never seen anything strange in these halls, but he knew that strangeness lived here—ghosts—lived here.

This place should have been exercised a generation ago.

But that would have to wait. There were much more prescient matters to attend to than a haunted dungeon.

"Has Axios managed to pry any information from the Dyonian?" Varryn asked as they approached a gate leading to the first cell block.

"He has proved difficult, my lord. He does not respond to torture or interrogation like most. He is *remarkably* resilient, and seems unwilling, or unable to answer our questions in Kurzan, Atarran, Sarxian, or any of the imperial languages," Vexyn sighed.

"Perhaps Ebonheart would be better suited, then. The Master Interrogator is fluent in all the languages of men," Varryn suggested.

"Those were my thoughts, yes. Axios was adamant that he could get through to him, however," Vexyn said.

"Axios is a wolf that leaps at any chance to torment a cornered sheep. He would give the same answer whether he was interrogating a common criminal or a Bagwham Druid," Varryn stated.

And he'd kill them both without finding out their full names.

Vexyn wanted to say.

Axios was a young and sadistic torturer who loosely wore the title of *interrogator*. He seldom even asked questions before he started turning the screws on his victims. Vexyn couldn't comprehend why they even kept him, useless as he was as anything but a fear tactic. Master Ebonheart, however, swore by him. In his eyes, he was a tumultuous and willful lump of clay, waiting to be molded. Vexyn saw only a monster waiting to be unleashed, ready to sow terror wherever he went.

"Shall we inform him that his torturing is done for the day, then?" Vexyn asked, frankly.

They were already making their way to his chambers. On their way, they past several occupied cells, and a man reached out, grasping at Varryn's cloak and pleading pitifully.

"...Please, my lord. Water...I ask only for water..." the sad shell of a man begged.

"Insolent cur, you grab at the cloak of His Imperial Majesty! You will lose your head for that!" Ser Roderick spat as he swiftly unsheathed his sword and grabbed the man's head through the bars, bringing it forward to decapitate him.

The man moaned weakly in fear, too weak to scream. "I...didn't...know...I..." he wheezed.

"Ser Roderick, that is enough!" Varryn spat, stopping him dead in his tracks.

Roderick froze, his blade already raised to behead the poor fool. "My lord?"

Varryn shook his head. "This man is broken, already. A cornered animal will do whatever it must to save itself. Inform the guardsmen to bring him water. Bring all of them water, do you understand? I'll not ask again!"

Ser Roderick, momentarily stunned, nodded profusely, and set off to the task. "Yes, your grace, right away, your grace!"

Varryn shook his head in annoyance and nodded to the caged man, prostrate before him. "You will have your water," he said, and walked away.

"Th-thank you, your majesty..." the man said weakly, and leaned back against the wall of his cell, spent.

Varryn felt a nauseating pang run through him as they walked. There was a part of him that was angered by his show of weakness, giving mercy to the condemned. He tried to fight that part of him, every day. But every day, it became harder to fight.

The weak will always be beholden to the strong, Varryn. The condemned must suffer the consequences of their actions.

He admonished himself.

As they neared Axios' interrogation room, they could clearly hear the shouts coming from within. A man speaking an unintelligible language, and Axios, shouting at him to speak in Kurzan.

"I can see he's made progress," Varryn sighed, rubbing his temples as Vexyn opened the door with a chuckle.

"Progress? Axios is the kind of dog to run in a circle, nipping his own tail, then be astounded when he bites it clean off."

They entered the room, and Axios immediately paused his interrogation and greeted them.

"Good evening, your grace, I was working on our spy."

Varryn nodded slowly as he approached the man, strapped down in a chair. Already he had several bleeding cuts and bruises on his body—the first caresses of Axios' bloodthirsty inquest.

"And have you made any progress, other than teaching this man to fear you, more than he fears death?"

Axios paused a moment. The wisdom in Varryn's words already lost in the vacant void of violence that was Axios' mind.

"He will not speak our tongue, Sire. He speaks only the gutter language of the Dyonian filth."

Varryn looked at the man in question and appraised him. He was definitely a Dyonian. He had the almond-shaped eyes, he had the thick black hair, and he had many other subtle features of their kind. Though most tellingly, he had a tattoo of swirling clouds upon his neck. Varryn knew enough about Dyonian heraldry to know that the cloud was a symbol of theirs. He couldn't recall what clan, however.

He towered over the man, holding his gaze. The Dyonian, despite the sorry state they'd found him in, and the tortures he'd been subjected to by the brute, Axios, stared Varryn down defiantly.

"There is much fight in you, I see. Will you tell your secrets to me?" Varryn asked.

The Dyonian muttered, "Watashi wa zettai ni yuzuranai, kuruzan inu."

"I will never yield, Kurzan dog."

Varryn understood none of his words, but he looked in his eyes and knew that his answer was no.

"Very well. Interrogator Axios, you are done with this man. We will be sending him to your master," Varryn stated.

Axios was visibly displeased by this news, but even one as uncouth as he knew to keep his mouth shut when the Emperor gave a direct order.

"Y-yes, Sire. I will bring the captive to him, myself—immediately," Axios stammered out.

Varryn looked to Vexyn, who looked at Axios with a measuring gaze.

"Do hurry, and make sure that when this man arrives at your master's lair, he is *unchanged*. Are we clear?" Vexyn instructed.

Axios nodded immediately. "Yes, M'lord, it will be done! No harm will come to this man, I swear it!"

Vexyn looked to Varryn, who nodded satisfactorily.

"Very good," the Emperor said.

The party departed as Ser Roderick came to meet them and paused at a cell closer to Axios' interrogation chambers. Varryn peered inside the cell, noting the unconscious man inside, clad in fine linen attire.

"What is a nobleman doing in these festering cells?" Varryn asked, confused.

Vexyn looked the man over, then flitted through some notes he had in his log before licking his lips and nodding. "This is the man that Ser Corinth found with the Dyonian. He is, indeed, a nobleman. A merchant, it would seem. Or so his cover was. You are looking at Donivus Ballandry, son of Fontaine Ballandry."

Varryn blinked. Ballandry. That was an Atarran name. His irritation flared. "A spy, then. Why is he sitting in Axios' cells?"

"He is to be interrogated by him, my liege," Vexyn reported.

"No. He will be interrogated by Ebonheart and *myself* personally," Varryn corrected.

Vexyn raised an eyebrow and looked at Varryn. The Emperor never interrogated men himself. He saw the look of barely contained irritation upon the Emperor's face, however, and quickly put his concerns on mute. "It will be done, your excellency. When would you like the interrogation to take place?"

Varryn scowled deeply. "Now."

He snapped his fingers. "Ser Roderick, Ser Daven, grab the prisoner and carry him to Master Ebonheart's chambers. We'll be paying him a prompt visit."

The two knights nodded and opened the gate to grab the unconscious man.

*****

Several Hours Prior, Port of the Emperor's Cup…

On a cool, foggy night, a modest trade ship arrived at port in Emperor's Cup. The dock workers milled about in the early morning darkness, offloading crates of goods as a finely dressed young man spoke to the dock master.

"All of the goods are in order. Some of Atarra's finest wines and cuisine are stored in these crates. Mind that you handle them with care, gentlemen," the young noble said. The dock master nodded as the men unloaded the cargo.

"Very good. I'll inform the necessary persons that the shipment has been delivered. Come with me to my office so that we may finalize the paperwork, and I can hand over your letter of credit and seal it for approval, Lord Ballandry," the dock master said.

"Very well," the young noble said.

The two exchanged a knowing glance, then left for the office, leaving the dock workers to unload the cargo.

*****

The dock master's office was sparsely furnished, lacking much in the way of clutter or characteristics.

"Excusez-moi, but are you new to this position, Dock Master?" Lord Ballandry asked, a hint of Atarran bleeding into his words.

"That I am, Milord. I've been workin' these docks for many a year, working with the sea for many more. But only recently have I become the one givin' the orders, rather than receivin'," the dock master replied, sitting down at his desk after offering the noble a seat and a glass of dark liquor.

"The name is Hedrick Norton, Milord. I forgot to introduce myself," Norton said, bowing his head to the nobleman.

"No offense taken, monsieur. How are you liking your new position?"

Norton shrugged as he pulled out the envelope, flipped it open to verify its contents, then closed it once more. He pulled the stamp out of its spot on his desk, warmed it over a candle, then sealed the envelope with his wax insignia.

"The pay is markedly better than my last position. The responsibility is much higher as well, however."

"What is the phrase again? With great power comes great responsibility?" Lord Ballandry joked.

"That it is. I suppose you would know all about that subject, Milord. Now that you've taken up your father's work, that is," Norton said in a more hushed tone.

Norton handed him the letter of credit.

Lord Ballandry smiled. "Donivus Ballandry doesn't turn down an opportunity. And this work is rife with it. But, now that the open business has been attended to… let us discuss more clandestine matters."

Norton smiled furtively before taking a glance out of his window, making sure no one was around to hear them. He opened his drawer again and pulled out another envelope, this one wrapped in twine. He handed it to Donivus.

"Très bon," Donivus said, running a hand thoughtfully over the envelope before putting it into his coat pocket. "What do you have for me?"

Norton sighed, lighting a cigarette. He shook his head. "Nothing good. The world's gone topsy-turvy, and the Emperor's the one spinning the top. I saw the judges walk out of the Judicial Hall, a few weeks passed. They said nothing, just up and rolled out, complete with a royal entourage, down the front steps, into carriages, and off to parts unknown. Word on the streets is that the Emperor dismissed them all. Dismissed them—like school children bein' dismissed from class. He did the same for his small council."

"Dismissed them? Mais pourquoi, why would the Emperor do such a thing?" Donivus asked, confused.

"The Right to Trial… ye know what that is, Milord?" Norton asked rhetorically. He took another drag from his cigarette. "In practice, that means that every man, no matter his status, may have his day in court. He has a right to a fair, impartial trial, headed by a Justice of the Empire and a jury of his peers. In practice. It is often not so simple. The rich often get off with less severe punishments than the poor. The poor often get severe punishments for minor crimes. A man like myself steals a loaf of bread and loses a hand. A man like yourself gets a slap on the wrist at the very worst, and at best, he suffers no repercussion. The man that accuses him, however, loses his life."

Donivus said nothing, merely looking at the candle flame. He could feel Norton's eyes burning holes through him.

"The system isn't perfect. It never was and likely will never be. But there was a system. A system that generally stopped people from paying with their lives for minor offenses and accusations—now that's gone. The judges haven't returned since. Trials are carried out in mob fashion, with the accused bound in chains or a stockade and judged by folk wearing purple garb, calling themselves the 'Loyals'.

"This is assuming they get a trial at all. If the guards get hold of 'em it's the gallows, through and through. Had you come into the city via the Gold Road, you would have noticed a display of the recently tried, hanging from oak trees and posts all along the road. Like corpsid fruit. The Emperor left them there."

Norton finished his cigarette and stomped it into the floorboards. "That's all I've got, Milord. Nothing good. As for what's in the letter? Haven't a clue. The former Port Master was rather vague about what these envelopes contained and even vaguer about what to expect from who came to collect them."

Donivus nodded. "Thank you, Monsieur Norton."

He stood up, smoothing his coat as a thump shook the room.

The two men looked at one another.

"What was that?" Donivus asked.

Norton shook his head and opened his desk drawer. He pulled out a flintlock pistol. "I don't know. But whoever they are, they shouldn't be here. Stay here, Milord." He stepped outside. The dock was calm and quiet. He couldn't even hear the sound of his men moving the cargo from the Atarran ship.

Wait. Why couldn't he hear them?

He started towards the ship—and then an explosion set him on his back. He reeled for a moment, then stood back up. The boat was aflame and sinking. He saw men dancing around on fire as the ship sank rapidly into the water.

"Stars!" he shouted, making a five-pointed star gesture on his chest before running back towards his office. He pushed the door open. "Lord Ballandry, your ship—"

He saw a blur of motion, and something stung him in the shoulder. He gasped as he slid down the wall and pulled out the projectile. It was a small black dart that disintegrated before his very eyes.

"What…who… you…" Norton fell over, unconscious.

A shadow disappeared through the window, carrying an unconscious Donivus, leaving Norton on the ground, incapacitated. Moments later, a second explosion erupted, burning a warehouse and eliciting more shouts from the scrambling, confused dock workers.

XXV

NO GOOD DEED

He raced down the side alleys, making his way toward the source of the explosion. Already, he could see smoke billowing upward over the building tops. As he neared the source, the sharp scent of burning wood greeted his nostrils. He surged out of the last alleyway onto the pier and raced towards the blaze. Now that he was near, he could clearly see that a warehouse was aflame. Already, men were gathering before it, jumping and shouting for their comrades inside to get out.

The doors have collapsed. They're trapped…

Corinth stopped in his tracks as he nearly ran into several men crowded around one of their own. He pushed them aside and looked over the man they were surrounding. He had minor cuts and scrapes on his body and face and scorch marks on his clothes. Either the man had escaped the blaze—barely, or he'd been caught in the blast wave.

The man bolted upright, coughing and looking around wildly.

"D'ya see who done it?" he asked frantically.

"Nay, I arrived just moments prior," the Paladin replied.

The crowd quickly dispersed to go aid with fighting the fire as Corinth helped the man to his feet, then motioned to the crowd of dock workers, throwing buckets at the flames to no avail. The water evaporated as soon as it touched the burning wood. The flames hissed defiantly at their attempts to contain it. They backed up, and the fire began to edge away from the immolated dock building. It needed to be quelled soon, or Corinth feared that they would spread to the surrounding buildings and immolate the whole port. More men came, carrying more buckets of water as the others began to fill up their buckets from the edge of the pier. Corinth checked his surroundings, and an idea began to formulate.

"Grab the water troughs," he shouted, dragging one towards the well and snatching a filled bucket from a man as he finished hoisting it up. He dumped the water in the trough, directing everyone else to do the same. They began to pick up on his notion, and soon they had a half dozen water troughs lined up at the edge of the dock.

"On my mark, we're going to push them all over. The rest of you with buckets come in after. The cooler we make the flames, the easier it will be to extinguish them," Corinth said, putting his foot on a trough before signaling for the men to kick theirs over.

They all flipped the troughs as close to the flames as they could tolerate and watched as the water spread towards the fire, hissing and evaporating as they made contact. The men followed up with buckets of water, dousing the fire. They carried on for several minutes, rushing to the edge of the dock, passing up water buckets in a chain, and soaking the dock house. After a half-hour, the men managed to extinguish the fire, gasping from exhaustion. They cheered triumphantly, and the man the Paladin had spoken to earlier clapped him on the back.

"Smart thinking, that. You've saved these folk from being out of work," Norton congratulated him.

"It was of no consequence. I merely did what needed to be done," the Paladin explained, watching as the dock smoked.

"Aye, well, in Emperor's Rest, few folks are willing to do what needs to be done, especially folk wearing fancy suits of armor," the man replied, offering a calloused hand to the Paladin, who shook it. "Hedrick Norton, port master of the Emperor's Cup Port, at your service," he introduced with a white-stubbled smile. The Paladin noted the man's disheveled appearance. He looked like he'd just woken up from a dirt nap.

Norton looked to be about fifty or so years of age to him, though a hard life can age even harsher than time.

"Ser Immanel Corinth, Paladin of the Church of the Stars," the Paladin introduced with a slight bow.

"A white knight? In this city? What is a man of conviction doing in a place such as this?" Norton asked. He was intrigued.

"I was sent here by the Church to perform peacekeeping duties. This is my first civilian assignment. Where better to learn how to keep the peace than in a place of unrest?" Corinth asked.

"Ah, the naivety of youth," Norton laughed, as did several of his men upon hearing Corinth's words.

"This city? She is a diamond drenched in blood and dirt. You are fighting the force of the river here," Norton warned and looked past Corinth to see a large squadron of guardsmen jogging toward the burnt-out warehouse. "And here comes the rapids proceeding the storm."

The leader of the guardsmen looked at the burnt-out warehouse, then at the dock workers, who nervously gazed at them, their excitement having quelled. "What have we here? A destroyed warehouse? Did any of you men see the culprit?"

The dock workers all shrugged and gave noncommittal answers. They didn't know.

"Well, I apologize, gentlemen, but it is standard procedure that we have to take you all in. We cannot afford to let an arsonist escape, and we need to make sure that they do not stand amongst you," the guard captain said.

"You would take us in? We have done no crime! We are the victims!" Norton argued irately.

The men spoke up in agreement.

"The guard wants no parts of us when things are going well and the Emperor's precious property is unharmed. Now, when one of his warehouses burns, he cares not for the men what built it 'n worked it. Nay, he punishes them for costing him money," Norton spat.

The guard captain lifted the visor of his helmet, revealing his scowling face. "You stand in the midst of his Imperial Majesty's men, dock worker. Mind your tongue, lest you lose it." He turned to his men. "If they put up a fight, detain them. You lot are coming with us."

Corinth stepped forward, raising his arms in a calming gesture. "Guard Captain, these men have done no wrong! They fought the flames—they did not set them!"

The guard captain eyed Corinth. "Ser Corinth, correct? You're the new liaison from the Church of the Stars. The Knight-Commander told me of you. Are you walking the block now?"

Ser Corinth slid his tongue around behind his lips. Viceroy had already told them of his suspicions. This didn't bode well. If the guard captains and lieutenants felt as though they were being investigated, they would not be compliant and would fight him at every turn.

"I have walked these streets, and I have served these people. These men did no harm. They are not the arsonists," he maintained.

"I'll take that as a no, then," the guard captain said smugly. "Ye have no jurisdiction over us in the field. Yours is a supervisory role, and this is not a matter of the Church. Unless you have a decree from Archbishop Kalen to provide?"

The guard captain held out his hand, waiting.

Ser Corinth frowned. The guard captain was right, stars damn him, he had no jurisdiction here but to observe, record, and report to Viceroy. So, he took out a sheet of paper from his waist pouch and used one broad hand to hold it while he wrote with the other.

"What is your name, guard captain?" he asked sharply.

The guard captain looked at his men, then smirked. "Captain Yates, 23rd Guard Regiment."

Corinth wrote down his name and regiment, underlining the 23rd Guard Regiment. There were thirty-two total regiments. Each of them had between one hundred and one hundred and fifty men. He would be further investigating the 23rd.

"Will that be all, Paladin?" Captain Yates asked dismissively.

"I must once again implore you not to apprehend these innocent men. They are the Emperor's stars-fearing servants and have committed no cri—"

A hand fell on his shoulder guard. He looked to see Norton shaking his head and patting his shoulder.

"Spare your breath, Ser Corinth. The guard captain has already made his decision," Norton sighed.

Captain Yates nodded. "Come with us."

Norton turned to his men, who were clearly uncertain of what was happening. "Come on, boys. Let's take a walk with the captain 'n his men. It'll all be sorted by the morning."

The dock workers nervously followed as the guards led them away. Captain Yates and Ser Corinth regarded each other for a moment.

"See you at muster, Ser Corinth," Yates said.

"Don't be late, Captain Yates," Corinth responded.

Yates smirked devilishly, pivoted on a heel, and walked off. Corinth sneered and turned to inspect the smoking shell of a warehouse. Several guardsmen were still in the area, left to investigate the scene of the crime, more than likely.

He pushed past them abruptly and stepped into the warehouse. He could tell that the flash point had been within the warehouse, as the damage was most extensive within. Beams had been burnt to ashen husks. He attempted to move one to the side, and it crumbled in his grip, turning to powder.

What explosive did they use that burned this wood so thoroughly, so quickly?

The building had been aflame for less than an hour, and already it had turned everything within the interior into ash. Corinth attempted to climb a stairway leading to the remains of the second floor, but the step powdered under his foot instantly, and the rest of the steps fell apart. He cautiously walked around the first floor, knowing that too much commotion would crumble the remainder of the second.

"Find anything?" One of the guards called out.

Corinth shook his head as he stepped over a beam and happened upon a curious sight. Several corpses, nearly completely burned to ash, were piled atop one another beneath some rubble. He inspected them. Their bodies were too destroyed to tell who they were, what they wore, or how they died.

"Corpse husks. I think they were the first victims of the fire," he shouted.

"Corpses?" The guards looked at one another and stepped carefully into the fragile structure.

Corinth and the three guardsmen who'd remained to investigate inspected the burnt corpses and debated what happened to them.

"Could be the dock workers got into some volatile shipping material. Occasionally the pier gets military-grade explosive material delivered to be moved into the barracks," one guard offered.

"Couldn't be. No explosives were scheduled for pickup within the past fortnight," another shot him down.

"Nay, whatever destroyed this warehouse burned very hot, very quickly. I'm not quite sure we even have explosives that can do that," Corinth explained.

He was well-versed in military weaponry, as was required for his paladin training. The only incendiaries the empire used (as far as he was aware, at any rate) were alchemical fire, pitch bombs, and the explosive mixture used to make dead man's hands, which were weapons only naval captains used. The former was reserved for special detachments, as it was quite expensive and time-consuming to produce, requiring the aid of alchemists who were trained in its manufacture. It was not something a civilian would be able to get their hands on.

Dead man's hands were made only on special order. Only one was made per imperial naval captain, and they were quite expensive and time-consuming to make. If a dead man's hand was used, the dock warehouse would have been completely blown to smithereens and damn near everything around it would be ablaze, so powerful it was.

Pitch bombs, on the other hand, were standard fair. Anyone could make them. All it required was a ceramic or glass shell, some pitch to burn, a fuse, and a flame. They were made to spread the burning pitch and immolate whatever it touched. But it would take a long time for a pitch flame to burn hot enough to turn a body into ash. Far longer than it would have taken to extinguish the flames and retrieve the corpses.

No, whatever burned this warehouse was much stronger than conventional incendiaries, and it certainly wasn't a dead man's hand.

A noise from outside broke Corinth's thoughts. He went to investigate, and the guards followed after him. Across the street from the warehouse was a small, abandoned dead-end street with several dilapidated dwellings in it and an alleyway at the far end. Corinth and the guardsmen stood on the street, looking down the street.

"Where'd it come fro—" one of the guards began.

A noise like clattering bottles caught their attention and turned all their gazes to the left. The guards grabbed for their weapons, and Corinth raised an arm to stop them.

"I'll investigate. Stand watch," he said firmly.

None of them even opened their mouths to argue.

Corinth approached the house where the noise came from. The door was ajar, and he clutched the dagger on his hip as he pushed it open. His eyes glossed over the dark interior for a moment before settling on a shape hunched over in a corner.

"Who goes there?" he called out.

No one answered, but he saw the shape move once more. He had an unlit torch that he carried with him, and so he pulled it from the loop on his hip and lit it, illuminating the room and the figures occupying it.

"What do ye see?" A guard asked from behind him.

Corinth looked at the figure hunched in the corner and realized he was looking at a man wrapped in black garb, covering his eyes. A few feet in front of him, face turned away from the light of his torch, was a nobleman judging by his dress.

"We've two men in the shack!" Corinth reported.

He heard movement behind him, as well as the sound of a metal object hitting the ground. He turned around to go back out and check, but the man in the corner immediately bolted towards him, shouting.

"No, do not go! It is a trap!" The man shouted in Dyonian.

Corinth nearly stabbed the man but paused and restrained him as he stared into his wild, frightened eyes.

"Unhand me, stranger! Or I will be forced to take your life!" Corinth shouted, throwing the man against a wall with one arm.

The nobleman stirred slightly.

Sufficiently subdued, the man in the black garb threw his hands up in defeat. "Your funeral," he sighed. His words fell on deaf ears.

Corinth stepped back outside to check on the guards but paused when he saw that they had vanished, leaving discarded swords and torches on the ground. He looked around. Where had they gone? And why had they left their weapons behind?

This isn't good; something isn't right.

He placed his hand on the hilt of Ideal Mercy, his blessed great sword and closed his eyes. He could sense a dark presence nearby. He heard the faintest footsteps, so quiet that they could have been mistaken for a trick of the wind. He felt something close to him—too close, it was—

He opened his eyes and brought his great swordgreat sword to bear. It hummed with holy Alyria and illuminated the area around him. His eyes panned over the dead-end street, looking for the attacker. At first, he didn't see the shadow in the alleyway. His eyes passed it several times without recognizing its significance. But then his eyes fixed on it, and he realized what he saw.

A figure, tall and thin, was standing in the alleyway. Slung over its shoulder with one arm was one of the guardsmen. Dragged on the ground by its other arm was the second.

"Unhand those men and submit yourself to me at once! That is an order!" Corinth belted, his sword pointed at the figure.

The figure regarded him for a moment.

"No, not yet…" it said in a quiet voice. It spoke Dyonian as well.

It dropped the men on the ground and turned away from Corinth. "But, soon…"

The figure walked away, stepping over the third guardsman, who was slumped over behind it, as it made its way down the dark alley.

"I said halt!" Corinth ordered as he charged at the shadowy figure.

Its body seemed to melt into the darkness. When he reached where it walked, it was gone without a trace.

Corinth stood in the dark alley, confused.

What was that?

He didn't know. But he knew that whatever it was, it was trouble. He checked the pulses of the guards; they were all dead. The figure had killed three grown, trained, armed, and armored men in less than a minute—and without a sound.

He turned back to the dead-end street and the ruined warehouse across from it. He didn't sense the dark presence anymore. But he knew that he needed backup.

The thought of dealing with Yates again made his skin crawl, and some unsanctified, angry thoughts crossed his mind.

"*A house divided is a ruin in the making. Chasten thy brother like ye chasten thyself and sharpen steel with steel.*"

Corinth recited scripture to himself, took a ragged, angry breath, and pulled out his guard-issue flare gun.

He loaded in a red flare and shot it into the air. Even on a cloudy night, it would be easy for the guardsmen to see it and rally to him. He would need all the help he could get. He stood under its red glow, keeping his eyes set on the shack that housed the only two leads he had to what transpired that night. His thoughts, however, kept returning to that tall, shadowy figure in the alleyway.

*****

PRESENT TIME…

256

Donivus awoke with a start. He looked around and was confused to see that his environment had changed so drastically. A blinding light from a fire made him reach to cover his eyes—but his arms were restrained. His heart raced, and he began to panic. He realized he was in a wooden chair, and both his arms and legs were restrained within them.

"H-h-hello? Where am I? What is the meaning of this?!" he called aloud. His voice echoed in the empty, brown-bricked room. He heard no response. He looked around more, inspecting his sparse surroundings. It didn't bode well.

The walls were sparsely lined with racks, which housed various implements that Donivus knew all too well were for torture. He was in a torturer's chamber.

Who would torture a Ballandry? Unless…

He heard footsteps behind him, and he strained to turn his head in their direction. "Hello?"

The origin of the footsteps came into view wearing all black, with a leather, skin-tight mask covering his face. He stood side-profiled, looking into the fire before slowly turning to look at Donivus. His motions were slow and methodical, and even the turn of his head was precisely so. It unsettled Donivus.

"Do you know where you are, Donivus Ballandry?" The man asked. His voice was deep, calm, and cold.

Donivus made a show of trying to move his arms and legs. "Considering you're not a buxom maiden with a love for leather-strapped corsets and stockings, I'm going to assume you're a torturer," he said, trying to keep the mood as light as possible, considering his bleak circumstances.

The man chuckled. "A sense of humor, I like that! Most of the people who end up down here are so dour, so serious." The man shook his head disappointedly.

"It ruins the experience."

"I suspect that the experience was ruined long before they found themselves in your parlor, monsieur," Donivus responded.

"Well, that depends on your view of what kind of experience it is. You see, I am a truth seeker by trade," the man said as he walked over to the lone table in the room and grabbed a pair of black gloves from it. "It is my duty and my pleasure to be the instrument of elucidation for my lord. I am but a tool, an object made with a purpose. A purpose that I fulfill with aplomb."

Donivus felt his heart rate increase as the man refocused his gaze on him. It felt like being in a cold vice. He cleared his throat. "You speak as though you're discussing fine art rather than the torture of men to extract confessions."

The man strolled back toward him and cocked his head to the side. "Art is an experience as much as it is a thing to behold. Music is art, and my tools are the instruments that pluck great symphonies from the lips of my subjects. Like a painter, I spray arterial rouge on the canvas of their flesh. But I am a minimalist at heart. A deft stroke, a sharp note—these can express a thousand messages. Why spoil the art with too many conflicting elements when you can convey just as much with less?"

He leaned in close so that his masked face and small, piercing yellow eyes eclipsed Donivus' view. "I can make you sing, Donivus. But will the lyrics be yours or mine?"

Donivus had never known fear before, not like this. He was used to killers and cutthroats, mercenaries for hire, the whole lot. This man was none of those things. He was acutely insane but also aware of what he was doing. Donivus knew that he was staring into the eyes of a true madman.

The door opened behind him, and both he and the torturer looked to see who entered. The torturer bowed deeply and regally. "My liege. Welcome to my workshop," he said graciously but not cravenly.

Donivus' breath hitched in his throat.

It all makes sense, now...

The jewelry of the Emperor's dress reflected the firelight as he stepped into view, followed by a blonde-haired man with a scribe's pad, who Donivus instantly knew was the Imperial Advisor, Vexyn Trinitian.

"Has the subject given you any information yet, Master Ebonheart?" Varryn asked, giving Donivus a sidelong glance.

"He has only just awoken, your grace. We have not begun our work yet," he replied.

"Very good. I would speak with him first," Varryn said, looking fully at Donivus now.

He was every bit as imposing and no-nonsense as his intel had told him. His father had said that he'd met with the Emperor once, along with a coterie of other family members, and remarked that the man was as self-important and proud as they come.

"He thinks himself a god amongst men but fails to understand that gods only have power so long as their subjects worship them." his father said.

"Do you know who I am, boy?" Vexyn asked as he stood before Donivus, towering over him. His arms were folded behind his back.

Donivus cleared his throat. "You are Emperor Varryn Kurza, Slayer of Wuhlven, Repeller of the El'wa Imperium, and Master of the Six Realms. And I must say, you are every bit as imposing as the stories say. Magnifique."

"Do not lump praise on me, now, boy. I know who you are, and I know what you've done. My only question is: Why?" Varryn asked intensely.

Donivus cocked his head. "Why? Why what, your grace?"

"*Your grace*", Pfeh! Do not play coy with me, Atarran—why have you destroyed one of my warehouses and sank the trade ship you arrived on? What game are you playing at?" Varryn asked. He leaned forward and squeezed his thick hands on the armrests.

"I did no such thing, your grace. I did not destroy your warehouse, and I would not be so foolish as to destroy le ship I arrived upon," Donivus said as his Atarran accent began to bleed into his speech.

"Then who? Did?" Varryn asked.

"For that, my liege, I have no answers, I am afraid. I came with the intent to trade Atarran goods for a lettre de credit. Nothing more. L'explosion was not my doing and came as quite a surprise for myself as well," Donivus paused, trying to recollect how long it had been since the transaction and what had happened in the interim.

He could not.

"…I actually do not recall anything after being given my lettre de credit by the dock master…"

"That is because you were found incapacitated—and remarkably unharmed—in a dead-end street across from the blaze, about an hour after the blaze was quelled. Fortuitous, really, that you were found so close to the scene of the crime…"

Donivus raised his brows. "Would it not have been prudent, my liege, for me to s'échapper after the explosion, rather than remain?"

Varryn nodded in agreement.. "Yes, yes, it would. And perhaps you would have had your allies not turned on you and that unfortunate Dyonian spy found with you."

Donivus' eyes widened. "A Dyonian? With me? I have no Dyonians in my crew, your grace. I believe that I have been framed for actions that were not my own."

Varryn looked at Ebonheart, who had been lurking in the background, silently, standing by the fireplace with his back turned to them. "Master Ebonheart, the envelope, if you please?"

Ebonheart pulled an envelope wrapped in twine from his pocket. Donivus' heart sank. Ebonheart pulled out a knife and carefully cut the twine around the envelope before opening it and handing it to Varryn. In the corner, Vexyn sat, transcribing everything that was being said in his notes. He paused and looked at Varryn.

"Shall I, your grace?"

"Yes, Vexyn. This conversation is too private for the annals," Varryn instructed.

Vexyn put down his quill and pad on Ebonheart's table and sat on the edge, watching. Donivus tried to get a read on the imperial advisor's thoughts but could not. The long, blond-haired man wore an unreadable poker face, and he watched the situation unfold with a seemingly indifferent gaze.

Varryn opened the envelope and read off a random excerpt from a page within:

"1st Hermora, 2995 A.S.: Justicars are dismissed from Judgement Hall; Right to Judgement is nullified.

9th Hermora, 2995 A.S.: First instance of Loyals activity is reported in Lowtown.

30th Idollus, 2995 A.S.: First instance of Loyals adjudication is reported.

20th of Gofannyn, 2995 A.S.: Pirate Frigate is sighted off the port of Crown Cup. A pirate is brought into the gates of the Palace. Pirate leaves one hour later... need I go on?"

Donivus looked at the floor.

"You've been spying on me, Donivus Ballandry. Ballandry... that's an Atarran royal name. Why does that not surprise me?" Varryn asked.

Donivus went silent and looked at the floor for several long moments.

Varryn called over his shoulder, "Master Ebonheart, I believe your subject is ready." He placed a hand on Donivus' and squeezed it firmly. "When next I return, it would be in your best interest to provide any and all information Master Ebonheart and I request. I need not explain to you what will happen if you do not," he finished.

Varryn and Vexyn headed for the door.

"Attendez, Monseigneur! Please, wait! Lis is all a misunderstanding!" Donivus called after them as Ebonheart stared sharply at him from next to the fire.

"It will be done, Your Majesty. Donivus Ballandry, our session begins," Ebonheart said as he walked towards his restrained captive.

"Non! Je t'en prie, non! Miséricorde! Aies pitié!" Donivus pleaded.

Varryn slammed the door shut behind them. He glanced over his shoulder at the open peep slot. For a moment, it looked like the opening of an oven with a roaring flame inside. He blinked, and it looked normal once more. A shudder ran through him, and they departed.

XXVI

DRIFTWOOD

Pate made his way below deck, trying to escape the pelting rain. He needed to check on the livestock, the men reported that one of the cows was making strange noises. They wouldn't elaborate further. And so, he'd grabbed a lantern and made his way below deck into the gloom.

He walked the hall that led to the storage compartment where they kept the livestock. Every footstep felt like it was agitating the floorboards, creaking them loudly in protest. In the storm, every creaking timber sounded ominous. A sailor's worst fear was a break in the hull of his ship during a storm. Your odds were bad if the break happened in clear weather. Your odds were non-existent if it happened during a storm, in the dark of night. There was seldom a body to be found afterward, let alone a survivor.

He reached the middle of the hallway before he realized he was being followed. His footsteps echoed, but not precisely and not in perfect sync with his feet. He paused and turned, focusing the light down the hall. It was barren. He wondered idly about the previous owners of the Duchess now.

What did Pete say? Killed at port, or at sea?

He couldn't recall. It seemed irrelevant at the time, and so he'd skimmed past it. He wondered if that was wise, now.

"Edward…" a faint, female voice whispered by his ear.

He whipped around and swung the lantern at the air.

"Who goes there?" he called out.

Silence was his answer.

He shook his head. The voices were playing tricks on him again. Oculeth had warned him to ignore them. As if on cue, the tattoo that the Alyrian had etched into his flesh began to burn dully. He scratched his arm and noticed its glow beneath the sleeve of his coat. He needed to keep moving.

Pate cleared the hallway and unlocked the door but paused as he heard low noises coming from within. He pressed his ear to the door. They didn't sound like livestock noises. He opened it with a hand on his sword hilt, then paused.

The pigs, cows, and goats were all huddled together around something that he couldn't see in the dim light. He aimed his lantern at them, but they were too busy with whatever they were crowding to be bothered. He approached slowly and whistled, trying to draw their attention without spooking them. The last thing he needed was a startled cow goring him to death; the pigs would be halfway done eating him before someone came to check in this storm. He whistled several times, but the only movements were the animals whipping their tails and stamping their feet as they mobbed together in a circle in the corner of the room.

Is that…are they eating something?

He understood the sounds now. They were the sounds of chewing. The animals were snorting, braying, bleating, and chewing on something. He'd known pigs to eat chickens when food was scarce. He didn't know goats and cows would partake as well, however. He made a shooing noise as he got closer, but he paused as the burning in his shoulder intensified.

"*Mmmooooooooo!*" one of the cows uttered as Pate neared the huddled animals. He paused. The noise sounded…off. He'd heard a cows moo a thousand times before, but never like this, never so…

It's the voices. Got to be.

He pulled out his sword and slammed the flat of it against the wall to get the animals' attention. They all started and turned to face him.

He wished they hadn't.

Their faces were bloodied—all of them were. Dark red gore leaked from their mouths. Their eyes were wide enough to show the whites, staring at him fixedly.

"Stars above, what in *Sheolhenna* is this?!" he cried out.

The animals looked at him with intelligence. One of the chewing goats *smiled* at him. He saw what it was they were eating.

On the floor was a body. Who it was, he couldn't say. They'd been eaten so thoroughly that their face was gone, and all that was left was a vacant, gory skull attached to a mangled, gnawed body.

It was a woman.

He could tell by the breasts, still uneaten, hanging from their chest. He approached, shocked and disgusted, his sword ready to behead the first animal that so much as sniffed at him. They looked at his weapon with alarm and moved away from the body, leaving the chickens to peck at it.

They know what a sword is.

He thought. They looked at him with naked fear.

The chickens scattered as he looked down at the body in horror. The livestock had eaten one of his crew. Never in his life had he ever heard of livestock eating people. It was beyond the pale. Apart from the natural order of things, it was—

It moved.

He dropped his sword, fell back on his buttocks, and scooted away as the mangled corpse sat bolt upright and stared blankly at him. Dull purple light emitted from deep in its skull, and the thing looked at him.

"Edward," it stated blankly.

The corpse rose to its feet and reached out toward him, lurching forward. He scrambled backward.

"Stay back!" he warned, fumbling for his double-barrel pistol.

The creature advanced toward him, the purple light emitting from its eye sockets growing brighter and brighter until it was almost blinding. "You were promised to us, Edward. Join us," it bid.

"Shut up and begone!" he shouted.

Where was his pistol? He'd had it just a moment ago, where had it gone?

"Join us. Join us. Join us," it chanted as the gap closed. Its voice grew deeper, darker, and more demonic with each repetition. "You belong to us."

Pate covered his eyes and face as the purple light blinded him, and the corpse closed the distance. He braced himself for the inevitable…

There was a knock at the door.

*****

He gasped as though he'd been drowning and finally got a breath of fresh air. His body was drenched in sweat, and he was thankful that he chose to sleep in his drawers. He fell to the floor, scrambling to get his bearings and clutching at the burning mark on his right arm. He heard the sharp knocking at his door again, and he jumped at the noise. He went for his pistol and slammed his body against the wall next to the door. He cocked it.

"Who goes there?!" he shouted.

"Cap'n? It-it's Henry. I just wanted to tell you that we've found something that we think you should look at…sir…" Henry's confused voice said.

Pate calmed his breathing as he returned to the present.

The livestock didn't eat something, and that something didn't try to eat me. It was all a dream.

He repeated that several times, believing his own words more and more with each repetition.

"Yes." He cleared his throat. "I'll be out in a moment."

He took several unsteady breaths and grabbed a rag to wipe himself down with so that he didn't soak his clothes the moment he threw them on. Several minutes later, he'd composed himself and dressed to face whatever lay outside his door. He spared a glance into his mirror just before he opened the door and was disgusted to see how rundown he looked. His eyes had dark circles beneath them, and his skin was looking paler than usual.

He walked back to his desk and lit a cigarette to calm his nerves and took a few gulps from the rum bottle sitting there to try and revive himself. Satisfied, he smoothed back the hair hanging wildly in his face and pushed open the door after putting his captain's hat on.

*****

Pate stepped out onto the balcony and looked first at the crew below him, who gazed starboard, and then at the sea to starboard.

"Dead Sea Gods, spare us all…" Pate murmured.

Oculeth sidled up next to him and leaned on the railing. "We saw it at a distance, at first. We couldn't make it out until we got closer…"

Before them was a sea of driftwood—ship fragments left behind after a battle. Smoldering parts floated on the water, and Pate scanned for the bodies inevitably left behind after such a skirmish—and the creatures that would come to feed.

"Drop sails. We'll prowl the wreckage for survivors," Pate instructed.

"Why we lookin' for survivors, then? We's pirates, are we not?" a female pirate asked.

Pate recalled that she was Judith, the one Crimp had been fussing over a few days prior, his sister. She certainly looked the part with a long coat, a large bicorn hat that shaded her head, a pistol tucked in the sash on her hip, and a sword on the adjacent hip.

"Because, Ms. Judith, if we do not discover how it is these poor souls ended up here, we may yet end up in a similar predicament," he stated matter-of-factly. He had not the time nor the energy to grandstand with the crew, so he let the issue drop.

He pulled out his spyglass and sighted a cluster of debris further into the field of wreckage. He thought he saw—

"Bring her round to starboard so her port is facing that heap, over there." Pate pointed until Crimp, who was at the wheel, angled in that direction.

They trolled closer to the wreckage heap, and Pate saw that he was, indeed, correct. A man climbed over the side of the wreckage and flagged them down, waving a torn white flag.

"We've got a survivor. Bring him aboard," Pate instructed.

"But sir, it's an *El'wa*," Judith said with derision.

Pate pinched the bridge of his nose; that was it. He was stomping this out, now.

"I don't care if it's a damn goblin with nymph powder leaking out its nostrils and a thigh bone in its hand. If I tell ye to do somethin', ye do it—no arguments, no gripes, no complaints. Are we clear?" Pate said sternly, staring Judith down.

She was a hard, spirited woman, Pate could tell. You had to be to survive in this life. But you also had to know when that spirit was warranted and when it needed to sit dormant.

She's certainly got more spine than Henry 'n her brother, though, that's for damned sure.

But that would have to wait.

"…Aye, Cap'n," she relented, then quickly focused her gaze on the El'wa male, clinging to the wreckage as they approached.

Pate ran a hand through his beard pensively as Oculeth whispered in his ear, "There's fire in that one."

"Aye, I wonder if any other want-to-be pirate on this ship is so spirited?" he whispered back.

The debris field was too dense for the ship to safely get any closer to the lone survivor. They were still a good fifty meters away from him, too much space to swim on the open water. Not now.

"Throw down a raft and sail toward him. I want men manning the railing with rifles, pistols, a slingshot—whatever the fuck you have on hand. I want ten men in that boat, and all of ye had better be armed. Just because we can't see anythin', doesn't mean something isn't lurkin' about."

Ten men loaded up into the raft, and Pate watched as Judith climbed in as well. He nodded to them as they were lowered into the water, then surveyed the men manning the railing. He could tell they weren't seasoned with their rifles. Their aiming was off, and many of them had trembling hands. He noticed that Crimp had a rifle of his own, different from the flintlocks the others were wielding. It was an old, matchlock rifle.

Hr'll be lucky if it even fires.

He'd used matchlocks before. They were notoriously unreliable, and liable to jam or misfire.

"Check your sights. Check your shots. And watch out for any sudden or strange movement in the water," he instructed slowly. The last thing they needed was dead crewmen because these fisher folk never fired a gun before.

Oculeth walked over to Pate and whispered once more.

"I could use my Alyria. It may yet save a few of them from being shot by their own crewmates."

Pate shook his head. "These people are just as superstitious as me, if not more. Ye show them ye can throw fire balls and make shit float in the air 'n they may just mutiny."

Oculeth groaned. Pate was right.

"Then let's hope they know how to shoot."

"If they don't, let's hope whatever they miss isn't particularly hungry."

*****

Why the hell did ye go 'n get on the boat, Judith?

She kicked herself internally.

Maybe it was because she'd heard her brother Crimp say that she was too weak to do it. Maybe it was because she agreed with him. Maybe it was because she's never been one to back down from a challenge. As the boat touched down into the debris-filled water, she realized it really didn't matter, now. She checked her rifle. It was a flintlock that her and Crimp's father had given her.

"Why'd ye go 'n give to her?" Crimp had asked their father.

"Because she's the better shot," he'd said.

He'd been right. Crimp never could hit the broadside of a barn with a hand grenade. She looked up at him sitting on the firing line, his matchlock rifle hanging over the railing.

"…Ye see the Third Mate, up there?" she asked the man in the boat across from her.

He looked up at Crimp, then back at her in confusion.

"Aye, I do," he said.

"He's a terrible shot. Try to avoid finding out firsthand," she said, without further elaboration.

The men collectively shifted in their seats uncomfortably. Judith wondered if she'd have been better off daring *him* to come down here.

Back on the ship, Pate took notice of Crimp on the firing line. He watched his hands shake and watched him constantly reposition and readjust to look down the iron sights.

"Mr. Crimp," he said.

Crimp jolted in place and dropped his rifle before picking it back up. Pate pinched the bridge of his nose.

"How many times have you actually shot that rifle and hit a target with it?" Pate asked.

"…Not many, sir…" Crimp admitted, realizing that whatever story he cocked up, Pate would easily see through it.

"Right answer. Give it to me and go man the wheel with Mr. Henry," Pate instructed.

"But sir, I—"

"That's an order. Stars, you, and your sister both clearly didn't listen to your parents much as children," Pate said. "Give me your shot, powder, and matches before ye go."

Crimp solemnly handed over the requested items and went to the steering deck with Henry. Pate checked the rifle, lit his half-spent cigarette, and got into position.

Show time…

*****

"What's he sayin'?" Judith asked as they approached the El'wa. The man was shouting in his native tongue, and so the pirates, none of which spoke a single word of el'wish, were at a loss.

"Dunno, he might just be spooked is all. Whatever battle took place out here must've been a right nightmare," the rower said.

Judith wasn't so sure.

The man was waving his arms frantically and pointing to the wreckage around them. Judith followed his finger. The water was filled with stacked piles of driftwood and whole sections of ships that had broken off from the main body during their destruction. He was pointing at them repeatedly and shouting.

The dots began to connect in her mind. She focused on a pile of timbers floating on the water and noticed something shifting within them. She tried to discern what but then noticed similar movement from another pile, and another, and another…

Her flintlock rifle had a telescopic sight on it to help her see long-range. She aimed her rifle at one of the islands of wood and looked down the sight. Then she saw it.

Or rather, she saw them.

Clinging to the wood and hiding in its crevices were small, dully colored creatures. As she got a better look at one, she realized they were some kind of fish with eyes set high on their head as an alligator or crocodile might have. One of the creatures shifted on the upturned raft it was sitting upon and trained its gaze at the moving boat. It made a noise, but it was too far off and indistinct for her to make out what.

"Oh shit…" She murmured.

The others were beginning to take notice as well. She now understood what it was the El'wa was shouting about.

They were surrounded.

"We've got trouble," Judith announced.

"Trouble?" the man on the oars asked. "What do ye mean?"

They were nearly upon the El'wa. Judith realized there was a chance the men might turn around and abandon the poor knife-ear were they to learn just how much danger they were *potentially* in.

"Let's just grab 'em 'n go. We shouldn't stay out in the water for too long," Judith said vaguely, averting her gaze to the El'wa as they knocked against the clump of debris he'd been living on.

"Vash'a q'atra! Thank you!" he said hurriedly as he climbed aboard. "But we must leave immediately before they set upon us!"

The pirates were alarmed now and began pulling out their weapons. "Before what's upon us?" one asked.

The man at the oars looked at Judith. "What did ye see? Tell it true."

Before she could respond, their attention was drawn to the sound of something splashing into the water. This was followed by several more splashes. Judith looked at the El'wa and they shared a concerned gaze.

"Scavengers. Flying Gnaws—all around us, in the wreckage! They've been scouring for food, but they haven't had much success…" the El'wa explained.

Judith studied the lines on his face. He was a young-looking man, though that didn't mean much when you spoke of the El'wa. He had minute tattoos on the contours of his face, resembling vines. He might've been handsome were his face not scrunched in fear and exhaustion. And then there was that nasty looking slice across the left side of his face. His skin was bleached from days adrift at sea, and his lips were chapped from lack of water.

They collected him, then pushed off toward the Duchess.

The minutes crawled by in tense silence. Then, something knocked against the underside of the boat.

"What was that?" a man asked, looking over the side of the boat with his sword raised.

"Naq! Do not look!" the El'wa warned.

Something shot up from the water and latched onto the man's face, encompassing it in its mouth. The man screamed as the creature bit down onto his head, then neck. Everyone scrambled in shock as the man stumbled, clawing at the creature on his head. Judith pulled out her knife to try and stab the creature, but as soon as she rose to her feet, the El'wa man pulled her back down as the man tumbled over the side.

"Why'd ye stop me?!" she fussed, shoving the El'wa El'wa off her.

He didn't have time to respond before she found out why. The water exploded as dozens of shapes leapt out high into the air and dove at them. One of them slammed into a standing man's chest, knocking him overboard. The man with the oars struggled as something grabbed onto an oar, and he tried to shake it loose. He shouted as he raised the oar out of the water to see one of the creatures had bitten into it. It quickly released the oar and dove for him. He narrowly got out of the way as it landed in the boat. Now, they all got a good look at what was attacking them.

The creature was a fish, to be sure. But it had long, sail-like fins on its back and sides, extending the length of its body. It flapped its jaws and made a gulping sound, showing its fangs and snapping them open and shut.

Judith stabbed the creature as it attempted to crawl up the oar man's leg. The creature released a screech of agony as it launched itself off him and attempted to go for her face.

"Shit! Get it off me!" she shouted as more of the creatures attacked the boat.

"Stay still!" the El'wa instructed as he grabbed the creature by its spine sail and wrenched it off her. He'd pulled out his own long, ornate dagger, and gutted it immediately before tossing it back into the sea. A swarm of the creatures attacked the corpse of their fallen as soon as it hit the water.

Gunshots rang out as the men on the ship came to their defense.

"Keep moving! We'll cover ye!" Pate shouted at the top of his lungs before he shot one of the creatures as it sailed into the air behind the El'wa, ready to attack.

Judith pulled the El'wa to the deck now as another of the creatures sailed through the air at him. "Stay down, right?"

The El'wa nodded; she'd saved him.

The boat closed in on the ship as the creatures continued their frenzy, dive-bombing the boat to knock its occupants out. As the gunfire rained upon them, however, they aborted their attack, preferring to maul the bodies of their dead.

The remaining members of the rescue party were raised back onto the ship. All told, four of their party of ten had been taken by the flying gnaws. As Judith stumbled back onto the deck of the Duchess, her heart hammered inside her chest. She had faced death today. And the Stars, in their infinite wisdom and mercy, had spared her life. Four of her brethren could not say the same.

Pate stood by the boat, checking each man as they disembarked. When he got to her, he nodded.

"So how was your first taste of the pirate's life?" he asked.

Judith took off her hat and wiped some guts off her coat. "A bit fishier than I expected. I never liked them."

Pate chuckled. "Well, ye've still got your wit—so that's a good sign." He turned to face the El'wa. "You. I want to know exactly what the fuck happened out here and where the other survivors from your fleet went."

The El'wa shook his head as he caught his breath. "They're all gone."

Pate looked at Oculeth. They shared a concerned gaze.

"Gone? Gone where?" Oculeth asked.

The El'wa sighed, fresh sweat beading on his brow. "I need water, food, and rest. Give me these things, and I will tell you everything I know."

Pate nodded. "Done."

*****

Several hours had passed, and Pate stood on the foredeck smoking another cigarette. He seized his wrist to stop it from shaking. Shortly thereafter, Judith approached.

"Enjoyin' the breeze, cap'n?" she asked, startling him. His eyes were wide for the briefest moment, then narrowed back to normal as he turned to look at her.

"Ms. Judith…you should really announce yourself when ye approach people," Pate replied.

"Didn't know ye were people, cap'n. Ye strike me as the type to hear someone comin' from a mile away, though," she noted.

"Aye, ordinarily, that'd be the case. Today, however…well, I find myself on edge," Pate admitted.

"Why's that?" she asked.

Pate looked at her a moment, weighing how much information was prudent to give. Judith, from what he'd seen, was one of the smarter, ballsier crew members aboard this vessel. She was resolute, intelligent, and observant.

I really should've made her Second Mate.

He thought again. Except that would cause tension between her, her brother, and the rest of the crew. The last thing they could afford right now was a scandal. Still, she was much more water-tight than the others, and so he weighed that she was a safe person to vent to.

I hope.

"Our heading. Ye know it, yes? I'd assume everyone does, now."

"Who doesn't? It's the fucking Storm Tide—a place straight out of pirate folklore!" she gushed, unable to contain her excitement. She watched his eyes and saw something troubling in them. "…That's not the real heading, though, is it?"

"It is," Pate said, killing her fears and eliciting a sigh of relief from her. "But I neglected to explain the real reason why."

"Why?" she repeated.

"Why, indeed. The men were so eager to become pirate legends, none of them bothered to question why it is a pirate, hailing from the Storm Tide, would need a bunch of scraps from the bottom of the fishermen's barrel to serve as his crew."

She looked at him. He was right. "Why *do* ye need us to take ye there? Surely a man such as yourself has your own crew. If you're really who you say you are."

"I am, make no mistake. I *had* my own crew, my own ships—a fleet of them in fact—and was in the middle of securing a prize when fate reared its ugly head and stole it all away from me."

"What happened? How did ye lose your entire crew and fleet of ships?" Judith asked.

"Well, to make a long and painful story short, I ran up against the Dread Captain himself and came out the weaker man."

"The Dread Captain? Ha!" Judith laughed enough to bring a tear to her eyes. "Ye tryin' to make a fool out of me, cap'n? The bastard's dead. Has been for generations, now. Fucker's just a ghost story!"

Pate's expression was severe. "Do I look like I'm makin' a joke, Ms. Judith?"

She stopped laughing; he wasn't joking.

"…The Dread Captain? Alive? For real?"

"On me mother's grave and on the Stars' names."

"…How? That would mean all those sailor's tales, the blood moon, the shipwrecks, it—"

"All true. Real as the man yer lookin' at before you."

The gears in Judith's mind began to turn as she absorbed this revelation. "So, he's the reason your goin' back to the Storm Tide, then? To tell them about the Dread Captain?"

"Aye, I knew ye were a sharp one."

Judith looked out at the sea. They had left the shipwrecks behind, but she knew now why her captain was so adamant about finding a survivor.

"What did the knife-ear—I mean the El'wa. What did he say?" Judith finally asked.

Pate was silent a moment, taking puffs from his cigarette and slowly burning it up. He finished the first one, and he pulled out another one as it took effect. He held the hemestra cigarette for her and she took it. Then, he pulled out a lighter to ignite it. He noticed that his hand had finally stopped shaking. The hemestra had done its job.

"Ye may want to smoke somethin' for this one, lass. It ain't good."

XXVII

What's Done In the Dark

"There is a man that I wish for you to track for me. He wears an amulet like mine, but blue. A pirate captain. Upon his ship is what we seek. Find him, and you will find it. Bring him and it to me. Do you understand?"

Beneath the pale moonlight, two figures walked along the beach, away from the upturned Azura. They walked silently so as not to attract the attention of the other pirates.

"Keep moving, and keep your arms up," Osiris instructed as Yager slowed his pace and attempted to lower his arms.

"The shit's painful. I'm unarmed anyway," Yager protested as he lifted his arms back up, shakily.

"Unarmed or not, I want your hands where I can see them, turncoat," Osiris instructed icily.

"Ye that afraid of me, 'Siris? I'd thought you a stronger man than that," Yager said.

"I fear no man. But I'm not so foolish as to think no man can catch me unawares," Osiris replied. "Now shut up 'n keep movin'. Just a bit further, now."

"Where're ye takin' me, anyway?"

"Far enough away to turn ye loose away from the men, 'n give ye a head start," Osiris explained.

"A head start? Head start from what?"

"When I get back, the captain will have told the crew that we found evidence of your little treachery. After that, they'll explain that when I went to collect ye, ye bolted. Given that news, the men may react in one of two ways, I figure. They may take it sittin' down 'n leave ye to whatever dangers await in the jungle.

"Or, they may decide they don't want to leave it to fate, and they'll come huntin' for ye. This is to give ye the best chance you've got at feelin' the breeze before they come houndin' for ya. After that? Whatever they decide to do to ye is out of our hands."

Osiris stopped walking, and so did Yager. They stared each other down in silence for several long, tense moments.

I could kill you right now, and no one would care.

A darker part of Osiris' mind argued.

I told them I'd turn you loose. I keep my word.

A lighter side advocated.

"So," Yager gulped, "this the part where ye kill me, then?"

Osiris blinked. Was he really that easily read?

"I should. I want to—believe me. You've always been trash to me, Yager. I told them to keelhaul ye for what you'd done, but the captain 'n Stone stood against it. They saved your life," Osiris revealed bitterly.

Yager couldn't help but shake at the mention of keelhauling. It was perhaps one of the most horrific things a pirate could do to another. He was thankful that he wouldn't suffer that fate.

"Unlike you, however, I don't go back on a promise I make to my brothers. That's what separates us."

Yager laughed and wiped tears from his eyes. "Oh, laddie. There's far less separates us than that. We're pirates. We rob, kill, and steal from others to make our fortune. To hope for honor among thieves is to hope for a cold day in hell."

Osiris scowled. "Get gone, before I decide to follow that sentiment."

Yager nodded, then walked away.

Osiris watched him, then pulled out his pistol, cocked it and aimed it. "Yager!"

Daniel Yager turned around and froze as he saw the gun aimed at him. He couldn't find his voice.

Osiris smirked, enjoying the fear he saw in the turncoat's eyes. The fear his brethren who died at the hands of the Bluecoats felt, when they hung from a noose. The fear all wicked men feel in the pit of their bellies when they realize that their judgement is fast at hand.

"You deserve this. Remember that."

Osiris holstered his gun, spat at the sand in Yager's direction, and walked back toward the Azura. He could feel Yager's frightful eyes focused on him. And if he were looking, he would have seen the moonlight reflect off the singular tear that dribbled down Daniel Yager's face.

Yager exhaled a breath he didn't even know he'd been holding. He felt light-headed and tired, like he was high above the ground and the air was too thin to breathe.

So, this is what true fear feels like.

He realized. If only he knew how very wrong he was.

Yager walked, contemplating his next course of action. The purse the imperials had paid him with had a hundred and fifty gold kurtz within. Measured properly, he would easily be able to secure passage back to the mainland and begin anew. But first, he would have to survive the jungle, which would be no easy feat. All manner of predators could be lurking within, and he didn't know the lay of the land well enough to know where to avoid. He counted the amount of shots he had, knowing that in all likelihood he would only have the time to fire one if something were to attack him.

Assumin' I see the bastard comin', that is.

After the jungle, he would need to navigate the port town of Port De Morta. It was a small town, as far as he overheard, which meant that strangers would not go unnoticed. He would need to be very careful.

His stomach grumbled; he needed to find food and water. Without them, he would die in this humid heat when the sun came up, long before he could reach town. Yager contemplated how best it would be to find passage off the isle. If he could steal into the harbor, he could perhaps bribe the dock master for passage on the next outbound vessel. Yes, that would work perfectly.

He sat down at the water's edge and took off his boots, letting the water wash over his feet. He looked out over the sea. It looked serene, here, at the precipice. The ocean, and all its horrors seemed so distant, here. He was safe, here. He recalled the first day he and Reece were at sea, they'd watched a man get crushed by a crate in an accident as they were loading supplies onto the ship. The man's lower half had been taken, but he still lived, as the pressure held everything together. At first, the man was in shock, then he was in agony.

When they raised the crate up off him, his entrails released, and he died shortly thereafter. Looking back, that was the least of the horrors he'd seen. Yager stretched and began working his way into the jungle.

"...they may decide they don't want to leave it to fate, and they'll come huntin' for ye..."

Soon, his former brothers would be hot on his trail. Soon, one way or another, it would all be over.

*****

As Osiris entered the camp, he saw Stone looking at him, and walked over. "How did it go?" Stone asked immediately.

"I didn't kill him, if you're wondering," Osiris said. "I promised not to. I keep my promises."

Stone nodded. He had a bottle of rum in his hand as the men had been celebrating. They'd managed to clean the Azura's entire belly in the span of one day, record time. He took a swig, then offered the bottle to Osiris. Osiris looked at it a moment, then shrugged and took it.

"One question keeps poppin' into me mind, though. It won't go away. Why did he do it?" Stone asked.

The two sat on a log by one of the many fires lighting up the camp this evening. This one was, mercifully, all but deserted. They sat quietly for several minutes, drinking and staring into the fire before Osiris finally responded.

"Men's hearts are dictated by many things, but primarily a need for power. We seek power in many forms. Mostly for us, in gold. When a man has no power his entire life but beholds it in front of him, is it a surprise that he'd want it?" Osiris asked.

"The mutiny, I understand. Pirates mutiny all the time. But to betray us to the empire? Were a few gold coins worth all that?"

Osiris shrugged again. "When he made that decision, he did so after being all but ostracized by the crew, by me…everyone but you, really. He didn't see it as betraying his brothers, then. He saw it as betraying the betrayers." He sipped from the rum bottle again, then passed it to Stone, who finished it.

They sat there by the fire, watching it in silence and listening to the sounds of the men cheering and reveling. After awhile they heard a gunshot, and everyone grew quiet. They looked at one another.

It was time.

Osiris sighed and braced himself. "Let's get away from the light, first. Then choose a cheek and let fly."

"Aye," Stone responded, cracking his knuckles.

*****

Morgan stood at the center of the crowd of pirates. They were merry making, drinking, and smoking, rolling dice. He didn't want to tell them, but he knew he had to. Several men had already gotten into a brawl this evening, accusing one another of being the turncoat. This needed to end.

Yager, you traitorous bastard, look what you've done to us. I hope you ran fast and far, because I can't control what happens next.

Morgan cleared his throat as the men watched him and talked hush amongst themselves.

"First, I would like to congratulate you, gentlemen, for a job well done. You have accomplished in one day what men twice your number couldn't in two. We will be back at sea before long. Your freedom is close at hand.

"I have dour news to deliver as well, however. News for which I know I have no control over how you may respond. It is to one man among us that we owe our current predicament. One man who sold his brothers out to our enemies, and one man who is responsible for the deaths of those we lost aboard the Empress' Bounty. Until now, we have torn ourselves apart, searching for this…turncoat. Brother against brother. Those who we have fought with, killed with, broke bread with, and made merry with. We have been a house divided—but no more. We have in our custody the cause of our woes, the reason we have been so apart these past months. Daniel Yager."

The men went in uproar, shouting profanities and threats. Some shouted that they'd known him to be the culprit. Others noted that they should have killed him after the failed mutiny attempt half a year ago. All of them, however, wanted blood. Blood for their suffering. Blood for their dead brethren. Blood to sate their rage and to avenge their loss.

Morgan stood, watching the men whip themselves into a frenzy.

"Look at the savages slather at the prospect of murdering their own, once more. It would seem that Bill Louis was not sacrifice enough," Abbal mocked.

"You know nothing of our justice, spirit. You watch from a place removed from our strife, so you may not speak on our ways," Morgan said in a low voice, but he knew that Abbal could hear.

"I have watched savagery for longer than your kind have existed. I have partaken of it, drank it, and grown weary of it. An endless cycle of pain, death, murder, and misfortune. As primitive and futile now as it was then."

"If they need blood to sate them, then blood they will have—whether I will it or not," Morgan responded.

Osiris broke through the crowd and stood at the center in front of Morgan. "He's gone! Yager's escaped into the jungle!"

His lip was busted open, and he'd taken a mean blow to one of his cheeks, clear signs of a struggle.

Good. They'll believe it, then.

"We can't let 'em escape! The bastard has to pay!" A pirate shouted.

"Chase 'em down, scour the island for 'em! He's a dead man!" Another growled.

"You have till morning! After that, we must depart! Daniel Yager or not, we must save our own hides and secure our bounty," Morgan instructed. "I know ye want blood. I cannot deny you that, and I cannot stop you from meeting out your own justice. Be quick, brothers."

Bastard almost sounds like he meant it.

Osiris noted.

"Let us cut out his heart and eat it!" Steven Cage belted at the top of his lungs, an axe in his hand.

The men scattered, grabbing their weapons and running in all directions to find him, breaking into bands to cover more ground. Osiris, Stone, Flint, Cutter, and Huasca gathered by the bonfire.

"How far away is he?" Cutter asked.

"About two miles down the beach, headed east. He should be long gone, by now," Osiris said.

"And why are we lettin' the bastard go when I coulda just blew off his kneecaps?" Cutter scowled.

They all looked at Morgan.

"Because Mr. Stone felt sentimental, and I'd rather not be in charge of the execution of another of our crew so shortly after the last one," Morgan explained. "I'm growing too old to be judge, jury, and executioner. This way, the men have their chance at vengeance, and I can keep my hands clean of Yager's blood."

"Should've merc'd 'em anyway," Flint huffed.

"My thoughts exactly," Osiris grunted.

"It is too late to debate, now. The men have been set loose. What will come, will come," Huasca said.

They all turned as someone new entered the firelight—Armen Hanover.

"Shit—the kid heard us!" Cutter cursed.

"At ease, the boy is no threat—and his lips are sealed. Aren't they, young Hanover?" Morgan emphasized.

Hanover looked at Osiris, his anger with him not quite abated yet, and nodded. "My lips are sealed. Besides, them going after Yager means that everyone will quit accusing me."

As he sat in the fire's glow, Osiris took note of a bruise on Hanover's cheek, as well as cuts on his face.

"The fuck happened to ye, boy?" he asked.

"Nothing," Hanover said quickly. He carried his guitar with him, and he began playing it to fill the silence.

Osiris kept his mouth shut, but he looked over Hanover suspiciously, trying to discern who'd given him his new shiners.

Flint maybe, or Cutter?

But neither of the men seemed particularly guilty, and Hanover hadn't frozen up when he saw them, either.

One of the others, then. Hell, maybe a whole gang of them.

The pirate's life was hard when you were a grown man coming into it. Doubly so when you were a young man, or a child, as Hanover was. The others, many old enough to be Hanover's father themselves, would treat him harshly. Almost as harsh as they would a woman, in fact. Azura's pirates were all-male. Osiris hadn't thought to ask about it until he'd seen intersex, and even all-female pirate crews when they were in the Storm Tide. Morgan said it was easier to control a group of men when their attention wasn't split between him and a woman.

"The woman always wins," Morgan had said.

The pirates sat, talking amongst themselves, drinking, and listening to Hanover's guitar tunes for some time. Eventually Flint, Cutter, and Stone had opted to go and search as well.

"We have to make it seem like we don't know what's become of 'em," Stone explained.

Eventually, Claude Humris made an appearance, inquiring where everyone had gone.

"Gone hunting," was Morgan's only response. His expression and tone seemed to have been all Claude needed, as he asked no further questions. Moary came as well and immediately took notice of Hanover's wounds. He pestered the boy, trying to get the truth from him, but to no avail.

It was a few hours before sunrise when they began to filter in. Flint, Cutter, and Stone returned with a party of men, carrying something.

"Did you find him?" Morgan asked.

They stood wordlessly by the bonfire, their eyes wide in shock.

"Aye, we found 'em…what's left of 'em," Stone said. He strained to keep his voice even.

*****

As the ship departed, the mood was uncertain. The pirates, it seemed, had their revenge on Daniel Yager for betrayal. Not, however, in the manner they expected. As Azura departed Isle De Morta, her officers convened in the operation room, and beheld what strange fruit had fallen before them.

"What…did this to him?" Ryker asked, at a loss for words.

"Somethin' foul, to be sure. Beneath the mountains, me father'd spoke of strange beasts that hid deep within the tunnels 'n caverns. Pales, they called them, on account of their pale, translucent skin. The creatures liked to dress out their prey, like this. Feed on the innards…" Moary said, folding his thick arms and holding in a gag.

Sarkad reached over to close the eyes, but Ryker stopped him. "Don't touch this cursed thing, brother," Ryker warned.

"Oh, quit your blubberin'—it's a corpse, brother. Like any…any…" Sarkad started, then wretched in disgust. "Gods, that's awful."

Osiris leaned against the wall, watching from a distance as Claude Humris broke through the crowd and inspected the corpse.

And what a corpse it was to inspect.

Daniel Yager was almost unrecognizable, aside from the few sparse patches of reddish blonde hair left atop his mangled scalp. His jaw had been broken, left handing by its tendons, only. His tongue had been ripped out, perhaps even eaten. His throat was split open vertically, exposing where his larynx once would've been. It was gone, too. From there, however, things got much stranger. His ribcage had been broken open, the sternum completely removed, and the ribs bent outward, some of which had snapped from the force. His heart was, of course, gone. As were his kidneys, liver, and most of his intestines. His stomach remained intact.

"I guess it didn't want his leftovers, ay?" Flint said darkly. No one laughed but him.

281

Cutter, Stone, Huasca, and Cage stood silently around the body, looking it over and taking in its morbidity.

"They took his heart. I wanted that," Cage grunted disappointedly.

"...For what?" Cutter asked, knowing he'd regret the answer.

"Þessi hálfviti—why do you think? There is an old battle brew de elder crones would make from the hearts of dead enemies. It gives you strength and endurance, and you feel no pain for hours after you've consumed it!" Cage spat, as though this knowledge was commonplace.

"...Are we sure Cage didn't kill him?" Cutter asked, genuinely concerned that the man who did this might be in the same room with him right now, arguing with him.

"These wounds were not inflicted with an axe, or any blade for that matter. The gouge marks point to claws. Non, an animal, or at least something with long, sharp claws, did this to him," Claude announced.

"I wasn't aware something this dangerous even existed on such a small, out of the way island. What could have done this? No panther, or crab, or bear could have done this. It's too precise," Morgan noted.

Yager's face had the cheeks peeled off it, as well as the eyelids, but his eyes remained intact and uneaten, which would be completely unrealistic if he was being feasted upon by a wild animal. No, this was no simple animal that killed him. Morgan was sure of it.

"He's right. Animals don't meticulously dress out and dissect their prey, they just kill you and start eating," Osiris said.

Stone spoke up, "So if it isn't an animal, and it isn't a man, what the fuck killed Yager?"

Everyone looked at Claude, who inspected the corpse a few minutes longer before throwing up his hands and shaking his head. "I haven't the faintest clue. But, whatever killed him, it was powerful and meticulous. It sliced his throat open precisely enough to remove his vocal chords without damaging the surrounding tissue. It broke his arms, his legs, almost every bone in his limbs, and only ate specific portions of his internals. This is by far, the most bizarre killing I have ever seen in my life."

Morgan looked into Yager's open, terrified eyes.

"Mr. Huasca, would you be able to do anything with these?" he asked, pointing at Yager's eyes. "Perhaps a ritual to reveal what they last saw?"

Huasca, having been silent throughout the conversation stepped forward and looked closely at Yager's destroyed face. "It is possible, yes. If he saw what killed him, which I think he did, considering there was signs of a struggle where they found him, then I may be able to pry those last visions from them."

"Good, do it. I want to know who or what killed this man, if only to put us all at ease," Morgan explained.

Huasca looked at Claude. "Are you finished, doctor?" he asked politely.

"Oui, be my guest, Mr. Huasca," Claude said.

Huasca ripped the eyes from their sockets, nerves and all. The pirates had to look away in disgust. He pocketed the eyes, then left the room. Everyone else, save for Claude, followed soon after.

Claude looked over the destroyed body once more before throwing a sheet over it.

"No man can escape his sins. Au revoir, Monsieur Yager."

XXVIII

TRAINING GROUNDS

"Ahhh, ah, faster! Faster!" she begged breathlessly.

He pinned her hands to the bed as he thrust into her. She tried futilely to meet his pace, but instead opted to wrap her legs around his hips.

"How does it feel, my dear?" he asked, whispering into her ear.

"I love it! I love you, Lavvy, so much! So—Aaaahn!" Her voice reached a crescendo as she seized around him. He kept the same pace, then slowed down as he knew she liked it. His thrusting petered off, and then he laid beside her as she embraced him, running a hand dotingly over his chest. They laid there, holding one another as shafts of light filtered in from behind the curtains.

"After all these years, you still manage to surprise me, Lavernus."

Varryn smiled. Alessa was the only person in the world who he allowed to call him by his middle name. It was *her* name, reserved for only her lips. "I aim to please, Iolanthe," he said, running his hand through her golden hair.

"Well, if you're in a pleasing mood, perhaps you could spar with Gundyr and Ser Corinth in the yard, today?" she pleaded.

His breath hitched. "My dear, Gundyr would sooner drive his sword through my neck than spar with me."

"Now, dear, that is not true. Gundyr loves you dearly, his blood just runs hotter than most. He reminds me of someone else I know," she said suggestively.

Varryn chuckled. "I like to think my temper's cooled over the years."

"Well, dear, that all depends on who's affecting it and why. You could stand to have a lighter touch," Alessa admitted carefully.

"A lighter touch…" Varryn repeated. He thought back to his decision to suspend his small council. When Lord Farandus pleaded for him to reconsider, he also asked for him to have a 'lighter touch'. Perhaps he'd been right.

"Perhaps, my dear. Perhaps…"

*****

Adjacent to the imperial palace, in the western courtyard, was a training ground fitted with a myriad of sparring gear, practice dummies, wooden and metal training weapons, and spectator seating. Here, on these grounds, two sparrers fought.

"Too slow. If you swing on a competent enemy like that, you'll be dead in an instant!" Ser Corinth warned as he deflected another slow swipe from his opponent.

"I've been out here for four hours, already, ser. My arms feel like gelatin…" Gundyr groaned. He could barely feel his limbs now, as they refused to react to his urgings. It was like trying to move through water.

"Four hours or four minutes—it doesn't matter, my prince. An enemy will not care if you're tired or weary when he strikes. In fact, he'll be hoping for it. An impaired enemy means that his chances of dying to you just got drastically reduced," Corinth explained.

Gundyr marveled at the paladin's grace and strength in combat. Even without his armor he cut an intimidating figure. His reddish-blonde hair waved loosely in the wind, and his short beard gave the impression of a man wise beyond his years and in his physical prime. His hazel brown eyes were wise and caring, and they filled Gundyr with calm. Gundyr wanted to be like that man, so very badly. This was perhaps the first man he'd ever seen in his life that he admired.

A man of morals, unafraid to stand against evil.

That was all Gundyr wanted to be. A man who could stand up to the corruption he saw all around him, a man who could fight against it. A paladin.

"Think fast!" Corinth barked before charging Gundyr and knocking his training sword from his hand and pressing the dull wood of his own against the side of the prince's neck.

Gundyr blinked, shocked by the speed of the attack.

"This is the moment that you must avoid at all costs—the moment where you are at the mercy of your opponent," Corinth said, holding Gundyr's gaze. "As you are a prince, you are considered a high-value target on a battlefield. The enemy will not hesitate to capture you for ransom and interrogate you for information. The upside of this is that while you may be injured, you are more valuable to the enemy alive than dead, so they will do their utmost to keep you. The downside is that they will expend great resources to acquire you, and will likely kill your allies than keep them."

Corinth lowered his sword and Gundyr released a breath he hadn't known he was holding.

"You are your father's firstborn son. There is no end to the resources he would expend to save you. But that also means a lot of goodmen will be put in grave danger, and potentially critical resources or information could be jeopardized as a consequence of your capture."

Gundyr fumed, then began swinging at a practice dummy. "Better to let me die, then, if the loss is so great."

"Were you to be killed even greater tragedies would occur. Your father would have the whole countryside razed if that were to happen."

"My father would raze a countryside if its lord didn't address him by his titles—for which he has many," Gundyr said.

As if on cue, Varryn and four of his imperial guards, including Ser Roderick and Captain Davis, appeared at the entrance to the training grounds from the palace and walked down the stairs. Gundyr and Corinth stopped and watched their approach. The guards broke away in formation, revealing Varryn in his training gear. He wore a purple leather doublet, similar to the brown one that Gundyr wore.

"Gentlemen, I've come to see if all this training is finally paying off," Varryn greeted.

Corinth opened his mouth to speak, to tell the Emperor that his son had already been out here training for four hours and was ready to collapse, but he didn't get the chance. Gundyr grabbed a training sword and tossed it at his father, who caught it.

"Come on then, father. Let me show you what I've learned." Gundyr gripped his sword firmly and tensed his muscles.

A moment ago this boy was ready to keel over and die. Now, he looks like he's ready to take on a giant. Is he that eager to impress his father?

Corinth wondered and stepped out of the arena circle, watching keenly as the young prince and the Emperor sized each other up.

"You've put on a modicum of muscle, my son. Here I feared you'd remain a string bean for your entire adolescence." Varryn jabbed with a chuckle.

"This is me after only a month and a half of training. Imagine what a year would do," Gundyr retorted, flexing his fledgling muscles.

Varryn had the mental image of his son, taller and stronger than he, dominating him in a duel. It frightened him, a bit, but it also filled him with pride. Perhaps a year under the tutelage of a paladin would also teach him some respect for his father.

One can dream...

Varryn was broken from his thoughts as his son raised his sword and pointed it at him in a challenge.

"Are you going to fight me, or keep gawking in awe, father?" Gundyr prodded. "I'll die from the boredom!"

Varryn gripped his sword in both hands, and as soon as he did Gundyr charged him. Corinth was astounded that anyone in the world could be so bold as to charge at the Emperor of Kurza, even in a sparring match.

This child knows no bounds.

He marveled.

Gundyr clashed with Varryn, and the two sparred frenetically. The older Kurza went blow for blow with his son. Corinth had wondered how the Emperor had managed to maintain his physique, now he knew the man must have been training on his own.

"You call that a feint, boy? I saw it coming a mile away—do better!" Varryn spat, knocking away his son's strikes. He took the flat of his wooden sword and deflected a horizontal swing from Gundyr, quickly knocking the sword from his hands. Gundyr lunged for his weapon.

Can't give up! Can't be disarmed!

Gundyr panicked.

But Varryn kicked him away from his sword and pressed the tip of his own beneath the boy's chin. Varryn panted. In the span of no more than a minute, he'd beaten his son.

Kill him.

An errant thought suggested in the recesses of his mind.

What?

He asked back, startled by his own thoughts. But it dissipated, and he lowered his weapon before offering his son a hand. Gundyr, having been humiliated by his father in front of his mentor, declined. He rolled to his knees and stood on his own. Varryn sighed.

You've made it worse, you fool.

He chided himself. How did he think it would play out? He'd beat his son in a duel and suddenly all would be made well? No. He'd just reminded him of how superior he was and thrown a larger wedge between them.

"That was a good fight, son. I'm proud of you," Varryn said, genuinely.

Gundyr turned his back to him. "A good fight? You laid me down in less than a minute. If it were a real duel, I'd be dead!"

"You are a novice, My Prince," Corinth interjected. "You cannot be so harsh on yourself. You performed admirably for one so new to the swordcraft. You faced a man who has had decades of training and experience over you. Why would a cub begrudge itself for losing to a full-grown bear?"

Gundyr looked at Corinth and knew his words to be true.

"Yes…yes, you are right, master," Gundyr admitted. "I will best father, yet." He looked his father in the eyes. "Soon, father. Soon…" He promised.

"Yes, my son," Varryn said with a nod. "Soon."

His heart hurt a bit. His own praise truly meant nothing to his son, it was only because the paladin came to his defense that the boy did not walk away hating him more than before.

He wants to replace you…

Another niggling thought put forth.

That one stung.

"You performed well, your excellency. I had no idea you were such a swordsman," Corinth congratulated.

Varryn fought himself not to take offense. "Yes…well, a man must keep his secrets until such a time that they must reveal themselves."

Corinth quirked a brow but brushed the comment off. He got the notion that the Emperor was insinuating something but knew better than to suggest such a thing. Their relationship was far too fickle as is.

"Yes, of course, My King," Corinth replied finally.

"See to it that the boy is trained not only in swordcraft, but also in tactics. It has been some months since his studies have been postponed and I worry his mind may dull with time. He must know how to command a force, when the time arrives," Varryn instructed.

"When the time arrives, My King?" Corinth asked before he could stop himself.

Varryn had already started walking away, imperial guardsmen in toe. "See to it, paladin."

When the time arrives. What does he mean by that?

Corinth pondered.

After Varryn departed, Corinth turned to address Gundyr, only to see that the prince had fallen asleep on the ground, passed out from exhaustion.

He reminds me of myself at his age.

Corinth thought, then laughed. He remembered Grand Marshall Ludus, then only Chapter Master, dragging him by his shirt collar to his cot, passed out from exhaustion in the training square.

"Next time, I'll leave you to the buzzards," the Grand Marshall had promised. Thankfully, he never did.

He leaned over the boy and attempted to rouse him, and upon realizing he was too far gone to be awoken, he resolved to carry the boy up the stairs of the palace toward his chambers. And so, he made the trek from the outer courtyard, through the palace complex, into the inner courtyard, and then to the castle. He got questioning looks from the imperial guards, but none deigned to speak to him. He was a paladin, after all. He was, perhaps, the least likely person to do harm to a member of the imperial family other than Viceroy himself.

Viceroy…

Corinth groaned.

The man had been as much an obstacle as he was an aid. The pair barely spoke, save for the brief occurrences where they were both in their office quarters or when they did muster. At this morning's muster, Corinth had his first run-in with Yates and his 23rd Guard Regiment since the incident at the docks…

*****

Viceroy and Corinth stood atop the platform overlooking the gathered guardsmen, already amid their drills, as there were no pressing announcements this day. Corinth looked through a list of all the absentee guardsmen, for which there were several. This was normal in a city of this size, however. Over two-thousand men were in the city guard, and so it was inevitable that some of them would be missing on any given day, due to illness or due to other scheduling issues. Guards had to constantly patrol and watch the streets, so only about half of the men were present for muster on any given day. They'd rotate out with each muster, however.

His check finished, Corinth stepped down from the platform and walked the courtyard, glancing over the men as they trained and occasionally fixing a guardsman's poor form or improper execution of a drill.

"Have you forgotten how to do a push-up, guardsmen? Your chest should be touching the ground, then rise, keeping your core and back rigid!" Corinth admonished the men. He got to the ground next to the struggling guardsmen. "Follow my exact motion."

He proceeded to do a perfect push-up, keeping rigid, activating his chest, shoulders, and triceps. He did this several times, watching and pointing out flaws when a man would get dodgy with his form. After several minutes, though they were going slower, and doing less repetitions, their form was much improved.

Good.

He moved on to another group, which was of no less than fifty men, practicing their sword fighting. He watched them for several minutes, dissecting their maneuvers, when he noticed a familiar figure amongst them—Captain Yates. Corinth eyed the men around them and realized that all of them bore the 23 insignia, indicative of their regiment number. This was his 23rd. The paladin watched for several more minutes, reading Yates' lips as he spoke to several of his men, laughing, then going to pick up a sword to practice. Corinth focused in.

The Captain took several test swings with the weapon before going to a dummy to warm up. Yates' swings were rigid, his wrists locked too tight, and his posture was off. A slow smile spread across Corinth's face as he saw his opportunity to grill the captain.

"Captain Yates," Corinth said as he strode over.

Yates immediately froze as he heard the familiar voice, and his expression dropped. His men shared a similar response.

"Ser Corinth," Yates said tersely as he continued to swing, a bit more harshly, at the practice dummy.

"Your form—tell me, who taught you to stand as though you have a rod up your ass when you swing?" Corinth asked.

Yates scowled and paused his swings. "Do you have issue with my posture, Ser?"

"I have issue with the precedent it may set for the men watching you, yes. As for yourself…" Corinth let the words drop, watching Yates' eyes beam at him.

He opened his gloved palm in a silent order, and Yates briskly handed the hilt of the weapon to him.

"Watch closely," Corinth said.

He struck the dummy one-handed first, then two-handed, minding his posture and keeping an upright but loose form. It was important to stay limber, as an overly tense body was less agile. It didn't matter how strong your muscles were, a blade would slice through them all the same if you were unable to dodge it. His blows were quick and powerful. He repeated his motions several times, then handed the blade back to Yates.

"Repeat," he ordered.

He did.

"Good, again," Corinth ordered.

Yates looked at him, shrugged, then did the motion again, almost perfectly.

"Excellent, again."

This time Yates looked more severely at him. "Pardon?" he asked.

"Again," Corinth ordered uncompromisingly.

He repeated the maneuver, but this time his men were muttering amongst themselves. Yates was beginning to sweat.

"Again."

"Ser, please, I—"

"That was not a request, captain. While you are in my training grounds, you are at my mercy. Now do the maneuver again," Corinth instructed.

They carried on like this for over fifteen minutes in the mid-morning sun. By the end, Yates was heaving.

"Good," Corinth said casually with a nod. "When I return, I expect your men to do the same maneuver with just as much proficiency. Are we understood?"

Yates gave Corinth a look that could freeze a bonfire. "Yes…ser," he said sharply.

Corinth smiled, folded his arms behind his back, and strolled away toward another group of guardsmen. Before he left, however, he caught a glance of a tattoo on the captain's neck. It was, unmistakably, an octopus. As Corinth walked the courtyard, he pondered this. He couldn't recall ever seeing it before…

*****

Corinth laid the slumbering Gundyr on his bed and stepped out the room. Waiting for him outside were several guardsmen. He looked at their shoulders and saw that they were all 23rd Guard Regiment men. "How may I help you, guardsmen?" he asked.

The men looked at one another and laughed before addressing Ser Corinth. "Paladin Immanel Corinth. Or should we call ye Drill Master Corinth, as you've so made yourself out to be?" the one in charge asked.

Corinth folded his arms. "Are you boys still upset about this morning? Hah! You should be thanking me," he chuckled. "That was probably the most efficient workout you boys have had since you joined the guard."

"Ye made our captain look right stupid, Drill Master. A slight we cannot let slide," the man said.

Corinth looked at him severely, now. "Do not make such idle threats, guardsman. I will not take them lightly."

"Is it a threat when I'm about to do exactly as I say? I'd call it a promise, then."

The men closed ranks, pulling out their swords as Corinth stood watching them.

I have to dissuade them from making a grave mistake.

"I am a sanctified knight of the Church of the Stars and have been trained as such. With or without my armor, I am a deadly weapon of righteousness, and I pray to Idallon daily to ensure his blessings and teachings never leave me."

The guardsmen looked at one another, confused.

"I say this not to brag or boast, but to warn you that threatening me is threatening a soldier of the Stars, and in so doing, you invite more than my wrath—but the wrath of the Stars themselves," Corinth explained, raising his thumb to point warily at the ceiling.

"Sister, look at me," Corinth said, singling out one from the crowd. It was a female guardsman.

The woman in question looked uneasily at Corinth and slowly pulled her hand away from the hilt of her sword. She addressed him silently with a nod.

"I know not what the men who put you up to this told you, but I can assure you I am not your enemy. Do not throw your life away for a trifle."

The leader cracked his neck, and Corinth once again caught a glimpse of an octopus tattoo. He then noticed that all of them had them, beneath their collars.

What is this?

"You're right, paladin. You ain't our enemy, yet. Keep steppin' on the wrong toes, though, and all your warnings and pleas won't save you from the hammer that's hanging over you," the leader warned. "Come on, boys, let's go. We're done here."

The men walked away, and Corinth blinked at the surrealism of it all. These men were bold enough to approach him outside the prince's chambers. What if a fight had broken out? Surely, they didn't believe they could escape the imperial guard.

But they would have had to pass the guard to get into the castle…

He didn't like that implication. He resolved to return to his study immediately and dig deep into the records of the 23rd Guard Regiment. Whether those guards had meant for it or not, they had put a new lens on their operations. Immanel Corinth was far from ready to give up the ghost.

*****

A storm had begun outside, and water began to gutter down the high steeples of the imperial family castle. Water rushed down the sheer sides of the tower just outside the window to the Emperor's study, making sharp splashing and plinking noises when the water inevitably struck the glass or the sides of the building. Varryn lit a candle and sat down in the chair of his study.

"When did this arrive?" he asked.

"Less than an hour ago, my liege," Vexyn responded as he took his own seat across from Varryn. "Axios brought it to me."

"Have you read any of it yourself?" Varryn asked as he opened the unsealed envelope and flipped open the pages within.

"Nay, your grace. I have not."

The letters had droplets of blood on them, though not in large enough quantities to smear the ink. Varryn shuddered at the thought of what Ebonheart had done to the poor fool to retrieve this information. He knew it had to be the Dyonian, as he'd given express instructions not to cause any lasting physical harm to the Ballandry scion. Ebonheart, unlike Axios, took his orders *severely* and to the letter.

"I see." He took in a deep breath and sighed as he read the letter. "Let us see what Master Ebonheart has discovered."

He read the letter aloud.

"1st of Brunnda, 2995 A.S.

"Disclaimer: As I have been informed that he has been needing training, I brought Interrogator Axios as an observer to this interrogation. I am told my pupil has forgotten, once again, the imperative of our work: to elicit a confession from the subject.

"The subject is a Dyonian male, perhaps thirty years of age. His name is Wufei of the Jai-Nyng. He offered no last name, though I am aware that in their culture, it is uncommon for an individual of low-birth to carry a family name, as all members of a clan are considered to be of one large, multi-branched family.The subject was quite resilient to interrogation, and even under pain of torture was not forthcoming. Only after several days of meticulous and thorough inquiry was the subject willing to give prescient information. This is the transcription of the relevant portion of the interrogation. I have enclosed within the envelope the other, superfluous conversations and inquiries, but I suspect this is the most pressing. Read on, your grace.

Varryn flipped to the next page.

"Interrogator: I will ask again: Why did you come to Emperor's Rest, Wufei, and how did you arrive?

Subject: We came here in a hidden compartment aboard a vessel that anchored in the pier.

Interrogator: Finally, we make progress. How many of you were within this compartment?

Subject: Fifteen operatives.

Interrogator: Are all the other operatives still active in the city?

Subject: Only four.

Interrogator: What became of the other ten operatives?

Subject: They were... (subject muttered in what is presumed to be Dyonian).

Interrogator: Repeat your answer in Kurzan, Wufei. We have discussed this. I will not ask again.

Subject: They were killed by Uragirimono...the traitors.

Interrogator: You have mentioned these traitors before. Who are they?

Subject: They are Bōmei-sha. The Exiled. They were brought with us on this mission to ensure its success.

Interrogator: How would these Bōmei-sha have succeeded on their own, if they just killed two-thirds of their allies? That's working backwards, is it not?

Subject: The Bōmei-sha do not need numbers...

(The subject spoke frantically in Dyonian for several minutes. Needles were used to silence him.)

Interrogator: Why were you sent here? What reason did you have to steal away on a ship to this land?

Subject: We were sent to retrieve an artifact of great importance, stolen from us by your people.

Interrogator: What artifact?

(Subject began yelling in Dyonian. I threatened him with a hammer. He did not heed the threat. Subject's knee was fractured with the hammer.)

A blood stain streaked the parchment here, and Varryn winced.

Subject: The Eye of Atla. Empress Kagura knows. She knows that you Kurzans stole it from her. She has sent Bōmei-sha as her revenge. They will not stop until they have completed their task.

Interrogator: Why are the Bōmei-sha here? What is their objective? To retrieve this 'Eye of Atla'?

(Subject became inconsolable for several moments as delirium from the torture set in. Water was thrown on him after several moments)

Interrogator: Why are the Bōmei-sha here? What do they want?

Subject: They are Tad'Vong. They are evil. They will be the death of this land. Zetsubō! Zetsubō! Zetsubō!

(Subject fainted. Pronounced dead at 0545 Hours on the morning of the 1ˢᵗ of Brunnda)

"Final Notes: In his ramblings, Wufei mentioned 'The Exiled' several times, as well as the Tad'Vong. The good news is, if the subject is to be believed, that there are only four remaining insurgents in the city. The bad news is—again, if the subject is to be belived—that these remaining insurgents are worth a thousand soldiers, each. I will do more research on these Tad'Vong and report to you my findings, my liege. I must admit deep concern, however, at the implications of these attacks. The Empress has turned her ire directly to the seat of the empire. Only, instead of starting a war, she has sowed the seeds of chaos in our fair city. I do not what this 'Eye of Atla' is. I trust that such knowledge is above me. But I will leave you with this warning, My King. Wufei was a ninja, a trained assassin and saboteur. He cared not for his own life and was highly resilient to the tortures that I put him through. Yet even he feared the Tad'Vong. Who are they? What are their motives? Are they among us? Be vigilant, My King.

Sincerely,

Imperial Master Interrogator, Tarryn Ebonheart"

Varryn folded the letters closed and sat them on his desk. He massaged his temples.

"She found out rather quickly," Vexyn noted.

"Send for Master Erebus. Morgan Sarron has run out of time," Varryn instructed hastily.

Vexyn raised an eyebrow. "He has over a month left, sire."

"I care not. Send for him," Varryn said.

Vexyn held his tongue and nodded. "It will be done, your grace," he said as he left the study.

Varryn looked out the window as thunder peeled outside, rattling the shingles of the tower peak. He stood in front of the windowpane, running a hand over the ring on his right finger.

"And so, it begins …"

XXIX

THE FIRST WAVE

Cutter subtly shifted the wheel of the Azura, making sure to stay their course due west. As he did, he began to hum a tune to himself. He often sang shanties with the men to keep their spirits up when he was at the wheel. This day would be no different. His humming formed into a familiar melody, and he sang it aloud for the men above deck to hear.

"She's a fine three master, swift like a bird!" he belted.

"Heave ho! Star Serenta!" The men said after several moments, trying to recall exactly what shanty he sang.

"We have sailed through the storm. Now we'll find our way home!" Cutter sang.

"As we sail away through the Amaranthine!" The men sang their part.

"Oh batten down the hatches, pray to the wind! Heave ho! Star Serenta! Xallha's mercy, or we're all dead men. As we sail through the Amaranthine!" They all sang in a broken chorus.

They carried on singing, attracting Osiris from below deck, a chicken wing in his hand.

"You lot sound like drunken whores when ye sing! Hah!" he shouted with a chuckle.

"That's no way to speak about yer own mother, Siris," Cutter said before continuing the shanty.

The men exchanged hearty laughs and continued their song. Osiris noticed Hanover, listening to the shanty and clapping, but silent. They made eye contact and his expression dropped. He turned away and feigned being busy as Osiris approached.

"You've been in your feelings for the past two weeks. You really goin' to sulk all the way back to Oceanus?" Osiris asked nonchalantly as he finished off the chicken wing and threw the bone overboard.

"I am not sulking, sir. I am merely keeping busy until the time arises," Hanover said as he began varnishing a railing.

"Until the time arises?" Osiris asked.

"Yes, or have you so readily forgotten my declaration?" Hanover asked sarcastically.

Osiris hadn't forgotten, though he'd hoped the boy would have lost his stomach for it by now.

"You really do mean to go through with this, don't you, Hanover," Osiris resigned.

Hanover looked him in the eyes, and in that moment his soft, light green eyes looked a bit darker—and uncomfortably familiar, Osiris thought.

He's got the look in his eyes.

A look he knew all-too-well: the look of a killer.

As he opened his mouth to protest, the alarm bell rang, and Flint shouted from above.

"Ship sighted off the stern! We've got company, boys!"

Osiris ran to the steering deck and looked over the stern of the ship. Cutter, Hanover, and Steven Cage followed him.

"Hand me a spyglass," Cage requested, holding out his hand. Osiris and Stone looked at one another before Osiris pulled out a spyglass and handed it to Cage.

"Oh, Dark Mother, your blessings are untold," he said eagerly, handing it back to Osiris.

"What did ye see?" Stone asked, alarmed.

"Deathwatch ships. Two of them, gaining on us," Cage reported.

"Deathwatch? And here I'd hoped this voyage would round off smoothly," Morgan said as he and Huasca stepped onto the deck.

"What the fuck are Valkar doing out here?!" Cutter asked, grabbing the spyglass from Osiris so he could see for himself.

Morgan looked with his own spyglass. "They must be the ones who left that derelict. Everybody to their stations, get the men ready, and tell Moary to get the cannons up! We're going to try and lose them."

Morgan could tell the Valkar ships were slower than his, even if they were smaller. Azura's enchantments made her unnaturally fast for her size, and after she'd been cleaned, she'd be even faster.

"We could try and lure them to a favorable terrain—perhaps to an island?" Huasca suggested.

"We're off schedule, if we deviate further and engage in a protracted battle, I fear we may be delayed. Deathwatch are not simple Bluecoats or even pirates—they're savage raiders. We could lose a lot of good men, if we make the mistake of engaging them head-on," Morgan warned. "Better to outrun them."

"Valkar do not give up on a target, captain. They will chase us unto the ends of Hera, if they feel so inclined," Cage said.

"Splendid, then we'll outrun them," Morgan declared.

"About that," Osiris said, pointing west past the nose of the ship.

Ordinarily, the sea is constantly waving. Sending crests of blue and white-capped water in its eternal churn. Moved by the wind and its own, mysterious wiles. Before them, however, were calm waters. The waves were barely present, and those that were, small and inconsequential. The air began to die down, and their sails followed suit.

"Still waters up ahead! I think we're approaching a doldrum, cap'n!" Flint announced from the crow's nest.

"Oh, Stars above, no…" Morgan said as his stomach dropped. They all ran to the nose of the ship.

"And so it was that fate had turned against the will of the proud Immortal Pirate. And she took with her the winds so that he may sit becalmed," Abbal mocked.

"Is it our fate to die against savages?" Morgan asked in a low, sarcastic voice.

"There is a break in the water, but what it entails, only the Gods know…" Abbal replied.

"Stow the sails. We'll be getting no wind here," Morgan instructed.

"Sir, the Deathwatch ships are closing. They'll be locked in these doldrums with us!" Cutter warned.

"Then it would seem fate has decided we must fight them. Where's Mr. Moary?"

"Aye, I'm here, cap'n. Had to see it for meself. I couldn't believe what they were sayin'," Moary said as he looked behind them at the ships trailing them. "Deathwatch. When's the last time we ran into somethin' like them?"

"Not long enough for me to forget. This couldn't have occurred at a worse time," Morgan said.

The last run-in they had with the Valkar was years ago, and it was ugly. They were tenacious and merciless. Morgan had made the mistake of assuming a boarding skirmish with them would be wise.

That mistake cost him two-thirds of his crew.

He had brought forth a motion in the Brethren Court to go to war with them, but it was quickly shot down by the other lords. Put bluntly, a war with the Valkar meant they'd be opening themselves up to a fruitless conflict with an enemy that had more to gain than to lose. While they were not hugely organized, or even capable of fielding huge fleets of ships, they had potent Alyria on their side, as theirs is a society run by cultists, necromancers, and, if the stories were to be believed, other, darker beings. He had seen some of those beings.

He'd rather he hadn't.

No, going toe-to-toe with the Valkar was not the maneuver. But it looked as though his hand would soon be forced, as within the doldrums, it was only a matter of time before their enemy would close in, and they would be forced to do battle.

"Mr. Cage, what is your recommendation?" Morgan asked. He was reluctant to get council from perhaps the most suicidal member of his crew, but he was the only member who knew Valkar society and tactics as well as, if not better than himself.

Cage smiled like a giddy child. "We must face them, of course! The Dark Mother cares not from whom the blood flows, merely that it flows into her chalice!"

"If we fight those bastards head on, cap'n, it's going to be an ugly, dirty battle. We may lose a lot of good men in the fight, and we may find ourselves unable to fully-man the ship as a result," Stone warned.

Morgan nodded; he was correct.

"Mr. Huasca? You've been remarkably quiet. What do you suggest?" Morgan asked.

"These Valkar are said to have Alyrians, yes?" Huasca asked, looking at Cage.

"Every clan does, yes. The Deathwatch will likely have a corpse skald with them," Cage said.

"Then perhaps I can use my Alyria to hamper them," Huasca said.

"Hamper them?" Morgan asked.

"Yes, captain. If I can tap into my powers, I may be able to sense any Alyrians aboard their ship. We could use their own power against them," Huasca said.

"Can I do that?" Osiris asked, stepping forward.

"Not quite," Huasca said hastily. ""This is a skill I learned through the years. It is not something that could be taught in the timeframe we would require it."

Osiris felt like a child. He knew next to nothing about his own abilities, or how any of this Alyria business worked. Huasca had said that these things came naturally to an Alyrian. Why couldn't he do it, then?

"Aye…"

"We need to move quick, sir. It's only a matter of time before the Deathwatch launch their first attack," Cutter warned.

Cutter handed Morgan the spyglass, and he saw that already the Deathwatch were loading men onto boats in preparation to sail toward their target.

Damn.

If the winds were favorable, they'd be able to turn the ship to face its broadside at the approaching boats and deter them. Without the wind, however, they were dead in the water with their stern facing the enemy. The stern chasers weren't strong or numerous enough to reach the enemy before too many of their boats got within boarding range.

Unless…

A risky idea popped into Morgan's head.

"*I have need of your skills, amulet,*" Morgan said.

"*You mean to maneuver the ship without the wind, don't you?*" Abbal replied, having already read into Morgan's thoughts.

"*Precisely.*"

"*You know that these maneuvers are very taxing on us, now. We may not be able to maneuver her again for some time,*" Abbal warned.

"*I know,*" Morgan sighed.

Using the power of the amulet was draining on him, and in his advancing age it had become harder and harder to harness. And each time he did, a cost was exacted from him.

"*Do it,*" Morgan said.

The amulet glowed brightly as energy surged into it, attracting the gaze of everyone around him.

"Everyone, grab onto something, quickly. I'm going to move the ship!" Morgan shouted.

"Move the ship? But how, we're dead in the water!" Cutter said.

"He's going to use the amulet," Stone said, knowing it was the only way, now.

"The amulet? That glowing thing 'round his neck? I'd thought it was just a dead relic, now," Cutter said.

"Not quite, it's still got some spark left in it," Stone said as he followed Morgan, who was marching toward the steering deck. "Grab hold, men! We're about to make a sharp maneuver!"

Everyone scrambled and did as they were commanded, though they were visibly confused. There was no wind, no storm, no waves—why were they grabbing onto something?

"Mr. Moary, when I move her, I want your boys to load up the cannons and prepare to rolling fire on my mark, understood?" Morgan called.

"Aye, cap'n!" Moary said as he rushed below deck.

"Grab onto something and wait. When the ship moves to a firing position, go below deck and grab a cutlass and a pistol, understand?" Osiris instructed Hanover.

"A sword and a…yes, sir!" Hanover said.

"Flint, get down from the crow's nest! We're about to make an evasive maneuver!" Cutter shouted at the top of his lungs.

"An evasive maneuver? We ain't got a breeze to piss in, fuck are we gonna maneuver?" Flint asked as he began climbing down.

"Just do it, ye fuckin' idiot!" Cutter said.

Morgan grabbed onto the steering wheel and Stone did as well. "Get ready, this is going to be jarring to say the least."

"Aye," Stone said, bracing himself.

Morgan's eyes and body glowed bright blue. He grabbed onto the steering wheel, and Stone gasped as the entire ship was quickly covered in that same glow. It had been quite some time since he'd last witnessed Alyria in action. The hairs on his arms stood on end.

"Brace yourselves! Coming about to starboard, ninety-degrees!" Morgan announced at the top of his lungs—then turned.

The ship groaned loudly from the strain, and everything that wasn't tethered down shifted violently as the ship moved. Stone felt the air rushing past his face as the ship moved at a speed much faster than even a ship at top-knot could hope to. The ship settled as quickly as it moved, jostling back and forth in the water for half a minute. Men shouted in alarm as barrels and other odds and ends were thrown from the momentum, nearly wounding them in the process.

Morgan released the steering wheel and bent over, gasping. He felt as though he'd sprinted a mile. The blue light disappeared, and he felt the energy welling inside him quickly disperse.

"You're getting old, Morgan," Abbal said.

"And you're getting weak, amulet," Morgan responded.

"I think you surprised them," Stone noted, pointing to starboard at their enemy.

"Good, a scared enemy makes mistakes," Morgan said. He knew that the chances of them giving up that easily, especially now that they were trapped in the doldrums, was slim to none. "Tell Moary to fire the guns."

"Aye, cap'n," Stone said and turned to leave. "Before I go, I need to ask. The questions been burnin' in me for several days, now."

Morgan turned, already knowing the question. "No, Reece. I didn't have him killed."

Stone searched his eyes and knew his words were true. "Then who did?"

Morgan shook his head. "I don't know. But we have more pressing concerns, right now."

*****

Hanover opened the door to the armory and marveled at the selection of weaponry before him. He'd never been allowed in here before. What Morgan lacked in ships, he made up for in weaponry. Rifles, explosives, axes, daggers, swords, and spears. There was a weapon for everything here.

"...go below deck and grab a cutlass and a pistol, understand?"

That was what Siris had said. Oh, how he wanted to grab so much more, but he knew that if he did, Osiris would just force him to bring it back.

No, a cutlass and a pistol is all I'll need.

It wasn't about flashiness; it was about results. A rifle would be useless on a deck fight, it'd be too big and too long to reload, even more so than a flintlock. From what training Osiris had given him, he knew that the most important thing in a fight at sea was often who struck first. Ships were large, crowded, and hard to maneuver in the heat of battle. If you wounded your opponent, then chances were high that they wouldn't be able to get far.

He grabbed a leather-handled cutlass and gave it a few deft swings before finding a belt loop and scabbard for it. He checked the knife that he kept with him at all times and opted to swap it out for a longer, newer one from the armory. Osiris was unlikely to care about that. Finally, he grabbed a flintlock pistol, powder, and shot for it. He holstered his weapons and felt their weight heavy upon his hips.

Today, I'm going to kill a man.

The word 'kill' echoed in his head, but he let it ring out without further thought. He'd learned enough from Osiris not to give it pause. He couldn't help that it made his stomach unsettled, however.

He gave himself a once over to see that he'd gotten all he needed and left, but not before taking one last longing look at the armory. Soon, he would use every implement in this armory. Soon, he would earn their respect. Soon, he would be a full-blooded pirate.

*****

"On my order, begin fire, from left to right, here me?" Moary ordered as he walked the deck. It was imperative that they take out as many of the Deathwatch as possible. If they managed to make it onto the ship somehow, they'd have far more problems than the wind to deal with.

The men readied their cannons and Moary folded his arms behind his back. Stone raced down the stairs to the bottom step and the two locked eyes. Stone nodded. Moary gave the order.

"Fire!" Moary shouted at the top of his lungs.

The first crew lit the fuse of their cannon, then three seconds later another lit their fuse, following down the line. By time the third crew lit their cannon, the first cannon fired. The cannons launched their iron payloads in a wave, shooting balls of death into the air. There was a viewing window close to the stairs that Stone had come down from, and Moary used it to view the carnage being unleashed by his cannons.

The first few shots unsurprisingly found no mark. Even without much wind resistance, the act of firing a cannon, especially a kurzan cannon, was a guessing game. The cannonball would knock around a bit in the barrel on its exit, causing variance in its trajectory. It might strike more to the left, or it might strike more to the right, it might even overshoot a couple meters. The next several did find targets, however, and they did so with devastating effect. One of the death spheres skidded across the water, sending up waves before crashing through a boat and destroying it, injuring its occupants and likely spelling their doom. Another three punched into the water, sending up geysers of water with their momentum and flipping over boats that were too close to their landing point.

"There's the ticket," Moary grinned.

There were twenty-eight cannons on the starboard broadside, which meant it had twenty-eight attempts to rain hell down on its targets. At least a dozen of the cannon balls found boats, destroying them and undoubtedly killing their sailors.

"Reload and fire another volley. Repeat two times, for good measure, then reload and wait further instruction!" Moary ordered after several moments as the din of cannon fire and the ringing in his dulled ears died down.

"Sir, yes sir!" The cannon crewmen shouted.

Moary went above deck to view the carnage. He carried a rifle with him.

*****

Osiris found it odd.

Usually, during and after a cannonade the air would be filled with the screams of the dying, and the pleas of the living. After that barrage, however, there was nothing. He saw clear as day that the cannonballs had killed many men. Dozens, in fact, and injured just as many, if not more.

But they did not scream.

They did not plead. They did not flounder about in the water in a panic. No, all they did was swim.

Towards Azura.

"Are you fucking kidding me?" he asked aloud, unable to believe what he was seeing.

"Believe it, lad. That's what the Valkar do. They're an incorrigible lot who seldom retreat from a target," Moary explained as he shouldered his rifle and took aim before firing, punching a hole through the bobbing head of one of the Valkar swimming toward the ship.

"I want every man not firing a cannon to take aim and fire on these damn Valkar swimming toward us!" Morgan called down from above as he fired at them himself.

Osiris listened to the distinct, sharp reports of Morgan's enchanted flintlock, Bullet Rose. It sounded like a metallic wolf barking angrily. Each shot, he knew, was finding a mark and ending their life. His pistol could hold several shots in a revolving chamber that loaded into the barrel. He'd asked the old man how he could get a piece so magnificent, and Morgan told him that he'd have to find an Alyrian Duwa gunsmith and have him engineer one for him. He also said it would likely cost him a ship or two's worth in gold.

"I got the weapons, sir," Hanover said as he came beside him.

"Good. Put that pistol to work and aim for their heads," Osiris instructed.

Hanover blinked, gulped, then nodded to Osiris. "Aye, sir."

He took aim, cocked the pistol, and fired.

He missed.

He reloaded, taking over a minute to do so, earning Osiris' beratement, then fired again. He missed again.

He missed over a dozen times, in fact, using up all his shot before being forced to stand and watch as Osiris and the others fired at the enemy.

"Ye want to be a pirate but ye can't even hit an enemy that's moving slow as sap toward you in the water. Pitiful," Osiris shamed him.

Hanover could say nothing. He had never been the best shot, but he certainly never missed fourteen shots in a row, before, no matter the target. Today, however, his hands failed him. They trembled and shook, throwing his aim off. The gun itself felt uncertain in his hand. He was ashamed. Was he really so weak?

You want to be like them, but all wolves must slaughter, so why can't you take the first bite?

Hanover chastised himself.

The other pirates looked at him like he was a fool. He caught Flint gazing at him between shots as he reloaded his rifle. The bald, cold-eyed pirate merely shook his head and smirked.

"I knew I was right about you," Flint said.

Or so Hanover imagined he did. His mind was racing, and the sounds of gun and cannon fire became an indescribable drone in his head. Had it always been this loud?

"Hold fire!" Morgan finally shouted after several minutes. All the boats headed for Azura had either turned around or been destroyed, and the sea was red with the blood of the slain. Fish swarmed the corpses left in the water as the deafening roar of the guns died down.

They had survived the first wave.

*****

The day gave way to sunset, and the three ships, still gridlocked in dead waters, drifted. Stone stood watch, ever vigilant of their enemy as the sun dipped lower and lower to the west. The Valkar ships had drifted away from one another in the calm water. They were too far out at sea to weigh anchor. Evidently, they didn't have a sea anchor or storm drogue either. Just as well, he thought. The further apart they drifted, the harder it would be for them to communicate and coordinate with one another without letting on their plans to Azura.

If they move apart far enough, we may even be able to send boats to board one under cover of darkness.

He mused. It was a fruitless thought, he knew. Even under the best of circumstances, the Valkar were at their most dangerous in a close-quarters fight. They needed range to defeat them. No, the best course of action now would be to wait and see if a ship would drift close enough for a cannonade, the way he saw it.

Why are they wrapping their sails?

He wondered. He could see the enemy moving on one of the ships, but he couldn't make out what they were doing, other than furling up their sails.

"What're they doin', besides fucking goats and praying to their dark gods?" Moary asked, startling Stone.

He hadn't even noticed the Half-Duwa had climbed the ladder until he was cresting its top.

"Moary, ye bloomin' fool—ye nearly scared the piss 'n shite outta me! Don't ye know there's Valkar lurkin' about?!" Stone said.

"Well, I called ye a few times, brother, but yer ears must be filled with wax or siren's songs, cuz ye ne'er responded to it," Moary shrugged as he leaned on the railing.

"Aye, sorry, 'bout that. I been starin' at these damn Valkar ships for hours 'n have just about lost me mind," Stone said. It was partially true, though most of his thoughts had been preoccupied with something far more final than the uncertainty of their clash with the Valkar.

"Oh, piss on it, bhràthair. We both know what's really muddyin' your mind," Moary said frankly.

Stone was silent a moment, then looked Moary in his deep-set, reddish-brown eyes. "Aye…"

Moary placed a large, calloused hand on the man's back and patted it. "Still thinkin' about Yager, ay?"

The two men had briefly discussed the situation after he'd spoken to Morgan, Huasca, and Osiris about it, but they hadn't found the time to talk in private in several days.

"I just…I know he got what's comin' to 'em, Frederick. But damn, I didn't want to see it for true. I put all the remainin' good graces I had on the line, pleadin' on his behalf, that he may live to see another day. And for what? For him to get butchered 'n gutted like a pig?" Stone complained.

"Yer wonderin' if one of us did it, ay?" Moary asked.

"I asked the cap'n. He said he didn't put a man to it. 'N I don't see anyone rightfully crossin' 'em. Only man who I could think of to be so bold is Siris, 'n I don't think it was him, neither. So now I'm, just sittin' here thinkin' to meself: Who done it?"

Moary shrugged. "Could be one 'o these here Valkar did it. Ancestors know how long these bastards have been tailin' us. Hells, maybe they was doin' it since we found that derelict."

"I thought about that. I don't see it bein' possible." Stone pointed out at one of the drifting ships. "These bastards are so dense, they tailed us into a doldrum and sent their own men to die, trying to board us. Assassins, they are not. They'd have killed him 'n paraded his corpse up to our camp to do us the same—no— whoever killed me ald treacherous brother 'n black weren't a Valkar. But I don't think it was one of us, neither."

Moary nodded his agreement. He knew like any other these savages weren't capable of any higher thinking or planning above killing their enemies and looting their corpses. They didn't like waiting or planning, they moved like a shiver of sharks, swimming through the water, looking for the scent of fresh blood to frenzy and feed.

Still, the question remained.

"Then who killed Daniel Yager?" Moary asked the question they were both pondering.

Stone opened his mouth—and a crack like thunder killed his words. The men turned in the noises direction to see the flash of cannons firing from one of the ships. Both men made for the ladder and hurriedly climbed down, their hearts racing in their chests. They didn't hear where the cannonballs struck, but there were enough of them that they would have had to hit *something*. But as they hit the base of the ladder, and men began funneling out onto the deck, they quickly realized nothing had been hit.

"…What the fuck are those mush-brained barbarians doing—" Moary's question was cut off.

A cannonball plummeted from the sky and struck a man standing right next to Moary. Bits of him were sprayed all over the deck, and a sizeable hole was left in the deck where he'd just been. Moary gasped, a spray of the gore had struck him square in his open mouth—and he spat it out.

"Take cover! Cannonballs are raining from the sky!" Stone shouted at the top of his lungs, dragging the stunned Moary toward a door as another cannonball struck where they'd been only a few seconds prior. This stunned him to action, and he quickly pivoted around and began running for the door. He barreled forth, pushing several men through the door and into an officer's cabin. They huddled on the floor, still processing what was happening as they heard the hammer of cannonballs slamming into the ship from above, and their panic was renewed as one of the cannonballs came through the ceiling of the room and punched a hole through the torso of a man on its descent.

Several men gasped in shocked horror as the man lay dead on the floor. Moary approached after several seconds and flipped the body over, concerned that the cannonball may have penetrated deep into the ship to the powder room that sat several floors below them. It was a slim chance, but if the cannonball caused enough friction, or even a slight spark on its descent, then it could potentially have explosive consequences. He heard the cannonball rolling around on the floor below, and sighed in relief. The man may have been dead, but the integrity of the ship was safe. He only prayed that no other cannonball was able to do such damage.

After several more tense moments of waiting, they left the cabin through the open doorway, back out onto the main deck where crowds of panicked men had gathered.

"Mr. Moary, status report! What the bloody hell is happening?" Morgan shouted from his balcony above them.

"Sir, the Valkar fired a cannonade into the air, and several of the cannonballs landed on the ship!" Moary answered.

"Fuck!" Morgan swore. "Mr. Huasca is in the middle of a ritual to try and attack their Alyrians. We need to find a way to distract them until his ritual is complete!"

"We can't, cap'n! The bombardment has made it impossible for us to counterattack while we're dead in the water like this! Our cannons will take too long to move above deck, and by time they're set up and aimed, everyone to man them will be dead!" Moary warned.

"He's correct. These savages that you so dismiss have found a way to attack you from a distance and cripple you. Without unorthodox measures, this ship may be doomed," Abbal confirmed.

"Then we'll shield her. We can at least manage that," Morgan replied.

His body was still recovering from the last use of the amulet. Each time he used it, it sapped the energy from his body. When he was young, this was of no real consequence, he had seemingly boundless energy, and a good night's rest would ensure he had more to spare. Now, however, he was older and weary. Each use drained him immensely, and before too long he feared either he'd be incapable of harnessing its power or be undone by it.

"You play a dangerous game, Morgan," Abbal warned.

"I've no choice but to play it," Morgan said.

Morgan pushed through the panicked men and falling cannonballs to the ship's mainmast. He pressed a hand against it.

"Aeradin give me strength and Goffanyn give me wisdom," he prayed to the star gods of bravery and wisdom, respectively. He hoped, just this once, that they would listen to him.

He pressed his head against the mainmast as men screamed in their death throes and cannonballs rained upon them, splintering wood and spraying water. "Do it," he said, squeezing the amulet tight in his hand and channeling what Alyria lingered in his old bones to power it.

"As you wish," Abbal said aloud.

The blue glow enshrouded the ship once more, becoming a transparent shield around it. The cannonballs continued to rain, but now instead of splintering wood and killing men, they merely slammed against the shield, shattering on impact or bouncing back out into the sea. Morgan mumbled a prayer to himself to maintain focus as everyone calmed down and the chaos subsided.

"What…what just happened?" one of the confused, startled men asked.

"The captain just saved our lives, that's what! Hahaha!" Moary said with a hearty laugh, hugging the surprised sailor as everyone began to laugh as well, still shaken from their run-in with death.

As everyone laughed and cheered, Stone approached Morgan and placed a hand on his shoulder. The man was still as a statue, taking shallow, measured breaths.

"Cap'n?" he asked.

"I'm fine, just," Morgan stammered, trying to maintain his breathing and focus. "Just check on Huasca, tell him he must hurry! I do not know how much longer I can hold out."

"Yessir!" Stone said, running toward the navigation room.

As Stone left, Osiris came over, as did Cutter and Flint.

"What can we do, cap'n?" Osiris asked.

Morgan tried to form his thoughts into words while maintaining his breathing and concentration.

"Mr. Flint…" Morgan finally managed in a strained voice.

"Cap'n?" Flint replied, putting a hand on the old pirate's shoulder.

"…The black powder rifles, how many are there?" Morgan asked, an idea forming in his mind.

"Only three, sir," Flint answered.

"That's all we'll need. You, Cutter, and Osiris grab them, head to the foredeck, and take aim at one of the ships. When the barrier fails, start shooting at their cannoneers…"

"Sir, we only have enough ammo for—"

"It doesn't matter. Use it now or we'll be too dead to use it later," Morgan finished. "Go!"

The men nodded and made for the armory.

"Mr. Moary! Put all the men below deck. We're hedging our bets on our riflemen and Mr. Huasca. We need as little casualties as possible. Send one of the Tannis brothers to gather Claude, he'll likely still be holed in his study, waiting for the wounded to surge in."

"It'll be done, cap'n!" Moary responded, heading back to the gun deck. "Everyone clear out!"

Morgan nodded, pressing his head against the wood. It was a longshot. The officers might be unable to hamper their cannonade. Huasca might be unable to use his powers, but it was all they had right now.

The second wave had begun.

XXX

The Second Wave

How long has it been since last I came here?

Before him was an alien landscape. He was standing at the shore of a vast, moonlit beach. The waters were clear and pristine as mirrored glass. The sand was silvery blue, like the color of the moon overhead, but without the lustrous glow. The grass past the shoreline was a deep turquoise, and the trees were varying shades of turquoise, black, and other cool hues.

In the distance, he beheld a single, towering fern past the forest of trees. As tall as a mountain and almost as wide as one: Bawon Samedi's home. The monolithic tree emitted an ephemeral glow, the same color as his and Osiris' eyes when they glowed. The glow connected to the sky in vibrant swatches, clashing with the blues, blacks, and purples of the starry, eternal night.

"Beautiful..." He said. A firefly landed on his outstretched palm. It twinkled, then took flight.

"A livin' mortal? Here? My, my. It has been sometime since we had company in de Ghostlands. My masta, Bawon Samedi, did not inform me of guests, however," a feminine voice called. She came into view and paused, smiling as she beheld the visitor. "...Yaman, my mudiwo? You return to de Ghostlands?" A sibilant, feminine voice called to him.

The figure called him by his first name. A name that few in this world, excluding his Captain, his tribe, and Osiris called him by. She came into view, thick hips rolling with her stride, her eyes alight with that same piercing turquoise fire as his own. "And to what do we owe dis pleasure?"

"Yanzamu. You look as beautiful in death as you did in life. Did I ever tell you that? Why are you strolling through the fog alone, ah? Did you come to greet me?" Yaman Huasca chuckled, letting his Bagwham Xalli dialect come out as the dead woman strolled up to him. In the moonlight, he could make out her corpsid features.

Yanzamu was a dead beauty with a curvaceous frame. The only discernibly telling traits about her undeath was her pale, ash-colored skin, which had once been lustrous ebony brown, and the painting of a tree upon her face. Her nails, modest in length and trimmed to razor tips, gripped Huasca's hand in her cold, pallid ones. "You still have that silva tongue, I see. You want for me to cut it out, mmm? Maybe put it to betta use." She said in a coquettish tone.

"Nah, woman. I did not come here to play. I come to speak to de lord, I have need of his aid…" He turned, looking to the light in the distance.

"The masta? He has not been too happy of late, Yaman. He has been… brooding…" she warned.

A soul cried out in the distance, and the light emanating from the monolithic tree in the distance flared momentarily.

"What has angered our lord?" he asked.

"I do not know. But you know how dangerous Bawon Samedi can be when he not pleased…"

"All too well… but we have a bargain to uphold. And he will want to hear what I have to say," Huasca said, steeling himself and walking forward. Yanzamu shrugged, then followed.

*****

"Have you been to the homeland of late, Yaman?" Yanzamu asked as they neared the massive tree, towering hundreds of feet above them. She watched his face crease, knowing his answer before he uttered it.

"It has been quite some time since I last laid eyes on Bagwham. But you know this already, mmm?" he responded, looking her in the eyes now.

"Of course, I know, Yaman. You have always been a poor liar," she quipped smugly, grasping his arm a little firmer.

"I am a good liar, Yanzamu. But even the good ones need an honest ear from time to time," he responded equally smug, causing her to frown.

"So, you are saying you could lie to me, ah?" she asked.

"I am saying that if I did, my Mudiwa, how would you know?"

"I have my ways, Yaman." She said, confident.

"And I bet I know every way around them, when the time comes."

"Oh? We shall see about that, my Mudiwo," she chuckled.

They walked and talked for some time. Perhaps minutes, perhaps hours. Time was relative, here, in the Ghostlands. What to one man may seem a week, could be minutes in reality. This was true for the inverse, as well. Eventually, they reached the base of the tree. It had many large, spidering roots, thick as oak trees at their bases, digging into the earth and casting long shadows as they approached, going into a cave-like opening at the bottom of the tree. Eventually, they reached a doorway the size of a castle's archway. It was cast from the same ebony black wood that the tree itself was made from. From beneath its cracks, the turquoise ghost fire light leaked out, and Huasca placed a hand upon the wood. He closed his eyes and focused, and the door seemed to respond. It slowly creaked open, making noises like snapping tree trunks as it creaked. Within was a blinding portal of ghost firelight.

"Are you ready?" Yanzamu asked, almost nervously.

"I am always ready, mudiwa…" Huasca responded. He knew that he had to do it.

They walked through.

As though they had teleported, they found themselves at the top of the tree, high above the clouds, overlooking the Ghostlands. If he had looked, Huasca would have been able to see a myriad of environments within the domain of Bawon Samedi. But for now, his focus was placed squarely on the rows of prostrate spirits all kneeling in rows, facing towards the throne a short distance away. Upon the throne sat an intimidating giant of a man.

He wore armor made of bone and blackened wood, with a ribcage-like chest piece, and a large harness of horns, forming an X-shape on his back. It would have been spine-breaking on a normal man, but this was not a normal man. He was two to three feet taller than the tallest man Huasca had ever seen, and he wore a skull mask with dark eye sockets. His eyes were two glowing turquoise orbs, and his skin was black as night. His gauntlets ended in vicious claws with blades extending from the back of the hand. His shoulder armor pieces were the skulls of some terrible lizard, resembling saurians. He had long, silver dreadlocks, tied up in a bun, and he wore armored leg guards, fitted with claw-toed greaves. To top it off, he wore a large belt with a grinning human skull, its sockets glowing brightly with ghost flame. Almost all his armor comprised bone, leather, bits of fur, and black wood. He was a terrifying giant to behold.

He was Bawon Samedi.

"Bawon Samedi… my lord." Huasca greeted, falling to a knee, Yanzamu following suit after a formal bow.

"Yaman Huasca. What are you doing here in my shadow?" The voice of Bawon Samedi asked. It was deep timbre, one that rumbled in the earth. "Have you come to give me tribute?" he asked, displeased.

"I bring him before you, M'lord, not for tribute. He has a request to ask of thee," Yanzamu introduced.

"My lord, I come to you as a humble disciple of the Lord of The Fall. Lord of the leaves that wither and rot on the forest floor. Lord of the funeral pyre for which my ancestors have adjourned. Lord of the proper rest of all men, after this long and frought life on Hera…" Huasca intoned. He felt the heavy presence of his lord before him.

Bawon Samedi folded his arms. "I do not care to hear your airs, Yaman Huasca. I ask you again, why are you here before me? Is he in trouble?"

Huasca took a knee. ""My lord, it has been many years since I was stripped of my powers. I told you then, that I would only come to you if great need arose, and I have kept my word. But now, the need has come, and we face certain doom, should we not prevail. I ask that you lend me a small fraction of your power, once more, so that I may protect the boy."

Bawon Samedi leaned back in his chair, pondering Huasca's words. "What threat is so great that you would ask this of me?"

Huasca held back a smile. If Bawon Samedi was willing to listen, then his chances of success increased dramatically. "We are beset by the Deathwatch, Valkar raiders that worship the Forbidden Prophetess, Axodia."

Bawon Samedi laughed. "Ha! You come to me, cowering in fear of corpse-defiling savages? The old Yaman, without his powers, bested far greater threats than that. Have you grown so weak in your old age that you cannot fight off a few Valkar?"

Yaman frowned. Bawon Samedi was right, he had fended off much greater threats than them, before. But he was getting older, his body was less capable, now. Soon, the boy would have to defend himself. Soon, it would be time for Yaman to fade into the sunset.

"There is another threat, my lord. One that I cannot fully parse. I sense a foul darkness in the air, something that hides out of sight, but plots in the shadows. It has the mark of undeath upon it, and I cannot hope to beat it in my current state. The boy is no match for this threat," Huasca revealed.

He had told no one of the eerie feeling he got aboard the Azura, ever since they departed from Isle De Morta. He did not want to cause a panic, as they had already just escaped from tearing each other apart from fear. But whatever it was, it reeked of black Alyria, befouled by profane undeath. It was outside of the natural order.

Bawon Samedi huffed and leaned forward in his seat. "Undead? I will not tolerate such a profanity. I will give you a small sliver of power, Yaman Huasca, but be sure to mask it well. Should the Consortium scent you and the boy out, then I fear I will not be able to save you from them."

Huasca stood and bowed graciously. "Thank you, my lord. I will use the power you give me conservatively. We are too close to the promised time to fail, now."

Bawon Samedi nodded slightly, and raised a powerful hand, motioning for Huasca to come forth. He obeyed. Bawon Samedi's hand glowed turquoise and a sliver of energy fell upon Huasca's head, suffusing his body. Though he had been given but the barest crumbs of the vast bounty of a god's power, he felt revivified. Huasca gasped and panted, as though he had just breached from a deep dive into the ocean.

"Now go, child. Protect my vessel and cast this undead back to the grave it crawled from, so that it may never defile the natural order again," Bawon Samedi commanded.

"It will be done, Master."

*****

Osiris inspected the black powder rifle. Were a kingdom Duwa to be on the ship and discover that the humans had possession of these rifles, they would be killed on the spot.

Good thing Moary's only a Half-Duwa.

Black powder rifles got their name from the powder they utilized: Duwa black powder. It was, by order of magnitude, twice again as strong as human-made black powder. As a result, it propelled projectiles twice as fast, which meant they hit twice as hard. In a battle, this could be a game-changer. It meant that a heavily armored target, whose armor might've been made thick enough to repel an ordinary bullet from a human rifle, would be over-penetrated by the Duwa's black powder rifle.

It was also considered a taboo for them to be sold to other races. The Azura pirates themselves had only procured the weapons because one of the pirate lords, a Duwa himself, saw fit to gift them to Morgan. Otherwise, even Duwa pirates refused to share their people's technologies with outsiders. This made Duwa black powder rifles exceedingly rare for use in battles that didn't have Duwa using them.

Which means they won't expect us to have them.

Osiris thought, which bode well for them.

He loaded his rifle, then looked at his companions and nodded. Flint and Cutter nodded back.

They were ready.

"We'll fire from left to right. The goal is to take out an entire cannon crew before moving on. One fully disabled cannon is better than several partially disabled ones, so be thorough. Communicate who you're shooting, so the next man doesn't shoot at the same mark, we clear?" Flint instructed, being the best sharpshooter on the ship, he was the de facto leader of any marksmen group.

"Clear," Osiris said, checking that his gun was cocked and that he'd loaded it properly.

"We've done this before, Flint. I think we all know how to shoot," Cutter said, jumping at the opportunity to dig at him.

"Ye say that, but you still can't shoot past twenty meters for shit, so I think until ye manage to hit the broadside of a barn, you'll be needin' these refreshers," Flint said without missing a beat, or looking up from his rifle scope.

Cutter paused a moment, trying to come up with a good response. "Piss off," he flubbed. It was the best he could muster.

"Ouch. I don't know what hurts more, the fact that you took that long to say, 'piss off' or the fact you thought it was a good answer," Flint said, smirking as he got a bead on his first target.

"Cutter's always had a rock for a brain—I guess that's why he's friends with you, ay?" Osiris said.

Suddenly, the barrier dropped, and the men became serious. They described their targets, lined up their sights, and took their shots.

*****

Huasca came to, momentarily disoriented. He looked around and saw that Steven Cage had been posted at the door to guard him. At his stirring, the Valkar pirate turned and nodded at him. "Shaman, how went your ritual?" he asked eagerly. "Are you ready to kill the Deathwatch?"

"It went favorably," Huasca relayed. "Does it not bother you, Mr. Cage, that we will be killing your own?"

Cage laughed. "Does it bother you when you kill other Xallans, Mr. Huasca?"

Huasca pondered his answer. Framed like that, it seemed like a dumb question.

"I'll take that as a no, then," Cage answered him. "I am Valkar, but I am not of the Deathwatch. Rival factions kill each other—hells, rival clans and families kill each other—for sport, for honor, because they don't like each other. Were I back in my motherland, I would be doing much the same as I have since I was twelve years old—fighting and killing for the glory of the Dark Mother," he shrugged.

"Is there no loyalty among Valkar?" Huasca asked, genuinely shocked.

"Loyalty is like a sandcastle. It may hold for a day, a week, a year, or a generation. Eventually, however, the tide comes and swipes it away, and the sea takes what men so foolishly try to build," Cage said.

I didn't know Steven Cage was a philosopher.

Huasca thought. He heard cannon fire and stood upright. "What's happening? Are we being attacked?"

Cage nodded. "My kin must have a competent leader coordinating their ships. They tried an attack I've never seen them do before. They brought their cannons to their main deck and fired them skyward, raining death upon us."

"That's remarkably ingenious," Huasca admitted. He looked out the window at one of the ships. He could just barely see the specks of people moving aboard the ship, likely loading the cannons. "This captain of theirs is proving to be a real threat, even in such strange circumstances."

He looked at his arms and noticed his Alyria scars glowed brightly, even without the use of his potions. He remembered the task at hand and closed his eyes once more. He focused on the Alyria in the air and was surprised by its stagnancy. He tried to search for any large blooms of Alyria in their area, aside from his own and Osiris'. But there was nothing. No bloom of energy, no signs of an Alyrian anywhere near them. Just stagnant air, and that odd energy he felt, pervading the ship. He tried to focus on it, but he couldn't pinpoint it either, as though it was a fish in water, slipping out of his fingers as he attempted to grasp it.

Then I will be forced to try another attack.

He had hoped that he'd have an Alyrian to grab onto. A skald, perhaps. He planned to attack their mind and spirit and attempt to gain control over them for a time. Instead, he would use a member of one of their cannon crews and have him sabotage their cannons. He focused his mind, picturing himself flying over the sea like a fast-moving bird, then landed upon the Deathwatch ship. Even in this invisible, ethereal projection, he could feel the weight of their enemy. Each of the raiders before him were mountains of muscles and scars, wearing leather armor adorned with animal skulls and furs. He watched them load their crude, primitive cannons as they fired them skyward.

Walking the deck was a man with a goat-horned helmet, who Huasca assumed was their leader. He watched them load their cannons before barking a powerful, short order in Borran.

"Eldur!" he shouted, thrusting his axe toward the sky.

And they fired, sending another hail of ironclad death into the sky to rain down upon Azura.

You will be the instrument of your own undoing.

Huasca promised as he launched his projection into the leader. The man fought spiritedly, and Huasca was surprised to find that the Valkar was pushing him out of his body.

He should not even be able to sense that I've taken control—how is he fighting back?!

He couldn't ponder it. Instead, Huasca grit his teeth and forced himself into the Valkar, seizing control of the man's body as he leaned against a crate, growling and punching his own helmeted head. The Valkar looked at Huasca, confused. Thankfully, they were immediately distracted by one of their men falling dead to the floor. They shouted, "Leyniskytta!" and scrambled to locate the killer as another man fell to the deck.

As the Valkar scrambled to defend themselves, Huasca took the opportunity to grab a nearby powder horn and shovel it full of powder from an open keg. He chose a random cannon to overflow and nearly dropped the horn when a bullet whizzed past his head.

We are on the same side, you fools!

Huasca thought, but realized there would be no way for the others to know he'd taken control of one of their enemies. He dumped the horn into an upturned cannon and lit the fuse just as one of the crew noticed what he was doing.

"Hvað ertu að gera? Þú munt drepa okkur öll!" The man shouted, tackling Huasca—but it was too late.

Huasca departed from his unwilling host just as the cannon's wick burned down. It exploded, taking the confused Valkar officer and the crewman who tackled him with it. It set off a catastrophic chain reaction, damaging several of the cannons, setting them off, and causing a fire.

With just a horn of powder and a fuse, Huasca had managed to devastate the Valkar's attack.

*****

Huasca came to as an explosion echoed from the ship, and Steven Cage whistled in appreciation.

"Impressive, shaman. Remind me to never underestimate your galdur again!" Cage complimented.

Huasca stood just as Morgan opened the door and came inside, a pleased expression on his face. "Shall I presume the light show aboard that Valkar ship was your doing, Mr. Huasca?"

Huasca smirked. "It is a shame what a misplaced match and a faulty cannon can do."

"Save our lives, evidently. Men were dropping like flies, and that next barrage may have taken out many more, had you not come through."

The three men celebrated their victory, but as soon as the mood shifted for the better, Stone burst into the room.

"Cap'n! The Valkar launched a surprise attack while we focused on destroying their cannons! They've taken Siris, Flint, Cutter, Ryker, and Claude hostage!"

The men looked at one another in horror. The shock had silenced them.

"We have until sunrise. After that? We'll be rescuing corpses," Steven Cage said matter-of-factly.

Morgan kicked over a chair as the realization dawned on him; the cannonade was a ploy. Its goal was never to level the ship (even with all the damage it took, most of it was superficial). No, the goal was to distract them, capture key crew members, and use them as a lure to draw them into a deck battle.

That doesn't bode well.

If the Deathwatch were eager to engage them in a man-to-man battle, it meant they were certain of their ability to defeat them.

If we abandon all those officers, though, we'll be crippled. And the men won't stand for it.

"We need to launch a rescue. Subterfuge won't work. They're expecting us."

"If we launch a rescue, the rescue party will either need rescuing or burying," Stone said.

"If we do nothing, our sawbones, our boatswain, our second mate, and two of our enforcers will be dead. When the crew finds out, they'll want blood regardless. A deck battle is inevitable," Morgan said.

Stone sighed; he was right.

"I'll go, then. Send fifty men with me, and we'll see it done."

That's a fourth of our forces, all for one ship, no bigger than a barque. On paper, that should be more than enough men to wipe the ship and save our boys. In reality…

"Take twenty. Too many men and the whole ship'll be packed to the gills and the Valkar will have more bodies to butcher."

Morgan thought back to the report Osiris had given him after they escaped the derelict. What they'd done to those bodies…

"Besides, you need room to maneuver and get our men back. Show up with a whole ship's worth of men and they'll kill them on the spot. And one more thing," Morgan said, grabbing a bottle off Huasca's desk. "I'm coming with you."

"I will as well," Cage declared.

"You sure? Last I heard, Valkar don't treat those who turn away from their lifestyle very well," Stone warned.

"Turned? I have never turned from my roots, quartermaster. I merely sought a different route to give grace to my goddess. Besides, Deathwatch are no kin of mine. We would be enemies, whether I was with my own or not."

Morgan nodded as he pocketed the potion. "Then it's decided. And grab the boy, Hanover. It's time he learned our ways."

XXXI

THE THIRD WAVE

Osiris shook his head as he looked around the room, attempting to wipe the grime from his face, he was again reminded that he was shackled.

"Fuck."

He looked around and saw Flint and Cutter were in much the same shape. Cutter laid slumped in a corner, and Flint sat in the middle of the room, looking up at the grate in the floor above them. Moonlight beamed down, and he blinked before looking at Osiris.

"We're in the lion's den, now," Flint said frankly. "And we're not alone." He cocked his head in the direction of their remaining cellmates.

"Claude, Ryker, they got you too?" Osiris whispered.

Claude turned his head and nodded, propping up Ryker's head. "Oui, but they've injured Mr. Ryker in our capture. He attempted to protect me."

Osiris looked at Ryker and saw an ugly, bloody welt on his temple where they'd struck him, likely with the hilt of an axe or sword. "How is he?"

"Stable, but it is too soon to tell for how long," Claude answered. "Is anyone else injured?"

Osiris looked at Flint, who shook his head, but then nodded to Cutter. Osiris inched over to Cutter and listened, realizing the man was lightly snoring.

Is this fuckwit actually sleeping?

He kicked Cutter sharply in the shin. "Wake up ye fuckin' idiot—we've been captured!"

Cutter awoke with a start, flubbing around a moment before coming to. "Wuzzat? Siris…" he said groggily. "Fuck did ye do that for, eh?"

"The Valkar got us, you twit. We're in danger and they've knocked Ryker out cold."

Cutter sat upright in surprise and looked around. "Oh shit…" he said, as the reality set in. "What the fuck happened? We was just shootin' at one of their ships a minute ago."

"Ye mean to tell me you stayed out the entire time they dragged us to their boat?" Osiris asked in disbelief.

"I mean yeah, why wouldn't I?" Cutter answered.

Osiris looked at Flint in disbelief.

"I told ye he was brain-damaged," Flint shrugged.

Suddenly, the door opened, and the men turned to face their jailer.

"Did you sleep well, pirates? I hope so!" The man laughed as though he'd told the funniest joke in the world. "When we're through with you, I doubt you'll be sleeping quite the same ever again."

The man standing before them was tall, as most of the Valkar were. He wore little armor, from what Osiris could see, just a vest, exposing his bulky, muscular frame, and shoulder guards. Most striking was his helmet, however. It was a ponderous thing with a rack of some beast's horns on its sides, swooping upward menacingly. It had a face mask like a beast of some sort.

Osiris flexed his arms against the shackles, fruitlessly. "And what do ye mean by that, mate?"

The jailer leered at him. "You, that one, and him over there." He pointed to Osiris, Flint, and Cutter. "You three were the snipers that shot at our sister ship," the jailer accused. "Ordinarily, for every man that was killed, we would kill one in turn. I wonder if we pulled their charred corpses from the water, how many of them would have bullet holes in them?"

The men were silent.

"Yes, we know it was you." The jailer motioned to some men outside the doorway. ""Take them."

Osiris thought of putting up a fight. He supposed he could overpower one of the guards.

That jailer, though…

The man gave him pause. Most people didn't, so the fact that he did was enough to concern him. Before he could formulate another plan, however, the guards had already grabbed them and quickly hustled them out of the room. Claude looked at them one last time as they were taken away.

He said a prayer for them in Atarran, then quickly turned back to the unconscious Ryker as he tried again to rouse him from his slumber.

*****

The first thing that struck him was the stench.

Osiris gagged as the acrid, sickly-sweet smell of death filled his nostrils. He took a look around the dimly lit room cabin, and immediately understood where the stench had come from.

These were the ones that made that derelict, no doubt.

Bodies were nailed to the walls and left in mangled heaps around the room. A lone table sat in the middle, lit by a lantern at its center, and the men were sat down around it. An entourage of about ten men accompanied them and stood around the room. Osiris directed his attention to an altar on the far side of the cabin that the jailor knelt before. It was a corpse, sitting on a throne.

The jailor spoke in Borran, but Osiris could tell that he was praying to the corpse on the throne. It looked ancient. Its skin was extremely shriveled, taught to its withered bones. Its eyes were shriveled up raisins deep in the pits of its sockets. It had long, wispy silver hair. From his vantage point, Osiris could tell the body was dressed in furs, chains, and other ceremonial garbs.

Who is that corpse that they worship it so?

He knew very little of the Valkar, even more so of their different cults, such as the Deathwatch. He knew, given their name, that they obviously had something to do with death. Now, however, he saw that they worshipped it. He looked at Flint and Cutter, and both men silently watched the jailor pray to the corpse altar. This was bad.

He looked at the corpses nailed to the walls, floor and the various body parts sitting around the room. He didn't know what these monsters had planned, but he knew that it would end terribly for them if they didn't get out soon.

"I will ask this only once, mœgr. Where is the Eye of Atla?" the jailor finally asked as he stood up and faced the men.

How do they know about the Eye?

Osiris swallowed, and the trio exchanged blank glances. If these Valkar got the Eye, then they would die, surely. And if, by some miracle, they survived the Valkar, the Emperor's wrath would be upon them, and they would die all the same in due time.

"We don't know what the fuck you're talkin' about mate—" Cutter began.

"You lie!" The jailor spat, slamming the table. "Cut off his hand!"

Cutter's eyes went wide, as did Osiris' and Flint's. "No, wait no, don't—" but he was cut off again as a large man with an axe approached and two men grabbed him by the shoulders.

Osiris and Flint bolted up to his defense, but both were immediately knocked back down to their seats with swift blows to the backs of their heads. Osiris' head spun. He looked at Flint, sitting next to him, and saw that his eyes had dilated. Eventually, they regained focus, and he leaned back up, but both of them now had men holding them down.

"If you lie, you will be punished!" the jailor said.

Cutter kept spewing pleas as his shackled arms were pinned to the table. They watched in disbelief as the axe man brought his weapon down swiftly on Cutter's hand and dug it into the wood with a sharp crack.

Cutter stared at first.

Then he wailed.

Osiris grabbed at his ears as Cutter let loose a noise unlike any he'd ever heard from the man.

"Brother!" Flint cried out, trying to reach out to his friend. The jailor pinned Flint's hand to the table and grabbed him by the neck.

"Tell me where it is, or I will take your eye next, pirate! The last thing it will ever see is your brother-in-arms' screaming face!" The jailor demanded.

He dug Flint's wrist into the table, and Flint hissed.

"Fuck you, you mangy whore's sop! I'll kill you, and everyone you've ever loved—you hear me?! You fucking hear me?!"

The jailor looked at him, and though only his eyes could be seen behind the faceplate, Flint saw a twinkle in them. "I hear you, møgr. I see you, as well." He turned to the axe man. "Grab the gouger. I want this one's eye."

The axe man picked up Cutter's hand and held it in front of his face as he sobbed. Cutter looked at the severed limb, then at the stabbing, burning pain that was the stump where it used to be moments before, and he began screaming all over again.

Osiris seethed as the Valkar laughed at his brother in black's pain. The axe man dropped the limb on the floor, stepped on it, then walked away to grab the next tool of destruction.

*****

The axe man returned with the implement and handed it to the jailor, who slammed it on the table in front of Flint and Osiris. Cutter was hunched over on the floor. He'd vomited.

"I will ask you one more time, bald one. If you do not give me what I seek, I will take *your* eye. Where. Is. The Eye. Of Atla?" he pressured.

Flint looked at the gouger. It was some sort of scooping device, but it looked poorly suited to the task. He supposed that was the point. He was scared, but then he looked at Cutter, reeling on the ground like a wounded dog, and he felt nothing but anger. If he gave up the location of the eye, then they would be dead regardless. He knew that no matter how this played out, his brethren would be going to battle with these savages.

For all I've lost. What's one eye?

He shot a quick glance at Osiris. Osiris returned it just as quickly. The jailor saw this and grabbed Flint by the back of the neck. "Do it," he challenged. "Fight back."

With pleasure, you bastard.

Flint bolted out of his seat, this time balling his shackled fists and slamming them hard into the jailor's helmet. He cursed. The helmet was sturdy, and his hands shook in pain from the blow. Osiris did the same, getting out of his seat and grabbing the key he'd been eyeing from the belt loop of the axe man. He tried to grab his pistol too, but he'd only managed to knock it out of its holster.

The other Valkar stepped forward, but the jailor quickly shooed them away.

"This one is mine. Subdue the Xallan!"

Ten men were upon Osiris in an instant, and time seemed to slow as he concentrated. He could feel the Alyria welling within him, and his vision tinged blue green. He let loose a growl that made them halt their attack, opting to circle around him. The axe man lunged at him, and he plunged the key into the man's neck when he missed the swing. The axe man spasmed, dropping his weapon reflexively and clutching at the punctured artery in his neck. Osiris snatched his axe mid-fall and brought it around in a powerful swing as another attacker lunged at him. His motion was so quick the man barely had time to register it before the axe dug into his unguarded head.

The others fell back, surprised by the deadly attack. He jerked the man forward, ripping the axe from his head and spinning around for another swing. This time, his opponent dodged the swing and swung his sword at him. Osiris barely dodged the attack but was slammed from behind, dropping his axe, and was pressed against a wall next to one of the bodies nailed to it. This close to the source, Osiris wretched at the awful stench of rotting meat and felt his stomach turn. He looked at one of the long, thick nails used to pin the body and felt around as his attacker began punching him repeatedly in the back.

He took a deep breath and heaved with all his might, prying a nail from the flesh of the dead and stumbling backward into his attacker. He drove the nail backward, and it dug into the man's hip, causing him to cry out. Osiris twisted around the man whip-fast and held him hostage as the others formed a half-circle around them. He pressed his back against the wall.

Shit, they've got me cornered.

He tightened the chain of his wrist shackles around the man's neck, stopping him from breathing and fighting his grapple.

"You are finished, pirate," one of them said.

Osiris looked around and saw that Cutter, who had been incapacitated on the floor, had risen to his feet.

"Look out!" The jailor shouted as Cutter took aim at the men. He'd grabbed the axe man's pistol.

They all turned to face him, and Osiris took the opportunity to make his next move. He grabbed the pistol from his captive's side and kicked his knee out from behind, forcing him to kneel momentarily. Before he could react, Osiris slammed the side of his head with his fist.

The men turned again, this time to face Osiris, and engaged him again. Cutter fired the gun, striking one of them in the throat and making them scramble.

Three down, seven to go.

Osiris counted mentally. He shot the first man to swing on him in the chest, then sidestepped him as he fell. He threw the gun at one of the men, then picked up the sword of the man he'd just shot. His target knocked the projectile away, but Osiris closed the gap and swung his arms, digging the sword into the man's shoulder. He screamed, and another man came from his left to attack him. Osiris absorbed the blow with his manacle but nearly released the sword from the pain. He swung his head and connected it with his attacker's chin, then ripped the sword from the injured man's shoulder before following through with another swing. It connected with the man's arm before Osiris was tackled to the floor and his head was slammed into it several times.

"That's enough," he heard the jailor say from the other side of the room.

The men paused their bloody fight, and Osiris looked at the jailor, who held Flint face down against the table with the bloodied 'gouger' in his other hand.

There was an eye attached. Nerve and all.

"I will take the other one's and then his life if you do not sit down in that chair right now," the jailor promised.

Osiris looked at Cutter, who was pinned against a wall, looking worse for wear. The color was draining from his face.

He's got me beat...

Osiris swore, "Fuck!" and threw down his bloody sword before marching over to the chair and flopping down into it.

The jailor let go of Flint, and he dropped back into his own seat as Cutter was dragged to his as well. The three men looked at each other, and each looked like they'd been through hell. Cutter's skin was ashen, and he was still very clearly in shock about his lost hand. Flint's eye socket was bleeding, and he covered it with his fists. Osiris had splinters of wood in his face from where he'd been slammed into the floor a moment prior, and he was certain that his nose had been broken.

We can't die here.

This he knew.

He would hold onto this bitter resolve until it saw them through the night.

"That was fun! Now let's get back to business," the jailer said, this time sitting down at the table as well, across from Flint. He looked at Osiris, now.

"I do not have to tell you the consequences of not answering this question. There will be no more fighting, no more leniency. I will nail you to the wall like these bodies here. You will die slowly, in agony. Flies will buzz and crawl over your skin, your eyes, your ears. They will lay maggots, and you will be powerless to stop them as they feed on your flesh and burrow in deep. It will be a sad, miserable end," the jailor said, mirthlessly.

He slammed the table, once, and leaned into Osiris' face until he was but a foot away, and their eyes locked.

"Where. Is. The. Eye?"

Osiris looked at the pale Cutter, and the one-eyed Flint.

I'll kill him, for this. I'll kill all of them.

"All in due time." A voice unfamiliar to him said in his mind.

He blinked, not wanting to show the confusion on his face. It was time to speak. But soon, it would be time to act.

*****

They were waiting for them.

The Valkar stood at the starboard of their ship, watching as the pirates approached. They fired no cannons nor bullets.

I was right about the parlay.

Morgan realized as they approached. He had a hunch he knew what they wanted.

The Valkar threw down ladders and let the men board. What followed was a tense stand-off, and Morgan could see that his men were unnerved. Before them were monsters of men. Many of them stood taller and broader than the Azura's tallest man, and all of them were decorated with tattoos, battle scars, and skulls, and an air of menace. The Deathwatch Valkar regarded the pirates silently. They did not leer or intimidate. In fact, to Morgan's disturbance, they seemed unnaturally calm, considering they'd just lost a ship in their last attack.

"I can sense the rot of death, and the foulness of the Dark Ones upon them," Abbal hissed. *"They are abhorrent, tainted by the touch of darkness."*

"And they've got us in their jaws," Morgan noted.

He could only hope the beast didn't chew.

The main deck of the Valkar ship had a large, rectangular, grated opening overlooking the deck below. They were led there, and Morgan took in their surroundings. The morning sun beamed bright, illuminating much, but there were still shadows cast by the grates and beams. In the shadows, the Valkar stood, and Morgan's men crowded into the room, clearing out a space in the center as Morgan took a seat at the table that sat there. He felt again for the potion in his pocket and was reassured it was there.

A powerfully built Valkar stepped forward, and the crowd that formed around the pirates broke to allow his passage. Following him were his enforcers, no doubt, with the shackled officers in tow. Osiris gave Morgan an alarmed glare as they stood them to the side and the Valkar sat down across from him. The man's weight shook the chair as he sat down, and his scarred and tattooed musculature shook subtly. He wore a fur-lined, padded vest, with shoulder guards, and a large necklace of animal teeth. He also wore a severe-looking helmet with a face mask. It resembled some snarling, hellish beast. He looked at

Morgan silently for several long moments before removing it and sitting it next to him on the table.

Out of the corner of his eye, Morgan saw Osiris spit in the man's direction.

He smiled, revealing a wolfish grin and sharpened teeth.

"That flag on your ship. The skull with the stars on it. I have heard of it. It is the flag of the Immortal Pirate, Morgan Sarron. Is that you?"

Morgan nodded. "That I am."

The leader of the Deathwatch, for Morgan was certain that was who sat before him now, proclaimed something eagerly in Borran. He heard his name, however.

"*What is he saying?*" he asked Abbal.

"*He is telling them who you are,*" Abbal replied.

"So, a pirate of myth sits before me. I am honored, møgr. It is rare that one gets the opportunity to speak to a legend," the leader said, his smile broadening. "It is even rarer that two legends meet one another in these treacherous waters."

Morgan furrowed his brows, but before he could ask the question on his lips, Steven Cage stepped forward and spoke up, "The man you see before you, captain, is Ardvald Holvensonn. Or, as he is commonly known outside of Borra, Ardvald the Mangler."

The gears in Morgan's head clicked.

Ardvald the Mangler was a prolific Valkar raider. Prolific enough that the Brethren Court wanted his head, as well as the Warden of the North, Jotunn Wightsbane, and even the Emperor himself. He got his name from his preferred calling card, corpse mangling. Every town, every city, every port and every ship that he raided, he left a trail of mangled bodies in his wake. It was even rumored at one point that he may have been an avatar of his dark goddess, but sitting before him now, Morgan could tell he wasn't. He wondered what the odds were that he'd run into Ardvald himself.

"You know my name?" Ardvald looked at Steven Cage now. He sniffed the air. "You are Valkar."

Cage addressed Ardvald with folded arms and a mirthless grin, "I am."

"Hvaða clan ertu með?" Ardvald asked in Borran.

"Ég er heimskur," Cage replied.

Ardvald stood up immediately. "You are a World Reaver? What are you doing amongst these møgr?"

"Seeing the world, learning what secrets it holds, serving the Dark Mother the souls of my enemies."

"Meindýr, scheming, as your kind always does," Ardvald said bitterly.

"You call it scheming. But in your eyes the world is not complete until it is dead and gone. We know better," Cutter said.

"Begone, meindýr. I would speak with your leader, not some snake in the grass," Ardvald dismissed. "Your men tell me that you have something I seek, *Immortal Pirate*. I would suggest you give it to me."

Morgan looked at his captured men. Claude Humris and Ryker looked unharmed, but Osiris, and especially Flint and Cutter, were looking much, much worse for wear. Cutter was pale, and Morgan saw that a bloody rag covered his right hand. Flint was holding a rag over his right eye.

"You should be proud of your men, captain. They put up a fight. Killed several of my men on top of the ones they slew when they sunk my other ship. I punished them, of course, but I ensured they were still intact. Mostly."

"You came all this way for a useless artifact? Curious," Morgan said, stroking his beard. "I did not take Ardvald the Mangler as a collector."

Ardvald leaned back in his chair. "Were it up to me, no, I would not have come all this way for such a useless thing. The head of a legendary pirate, however," Ardvald's wolf grin returned. "That is a worthy prize."

Morgan stood, recognizing the challenge. "You wish to have my head, Valkar? Then you know what you must do to get it."

Ardvald stood as well and brandished his sword. "I would not accept it any other way."

Morgan motioned to Stone, who'd stood silently with his hand on his guns for the past several moments, and he backed away. As did Cage, who eagerly displayed the spear he wielded. Ardvald made a noise, and his men fell back as well, clearing out a large space in the center of the open-roofed compartment for them to duel. Morgan removed his coat, exposing his white, long-sleeve shirt underneath.

Ardvald stripped off his shoulder guards, then his vest, leaving his bare, tattooed chest and arms. Morgan assumed a dueler's pose with one arm behind his back, but Ardvald merely cracked his neck and charged.

Morgan parried the first several blows, testing the strength of his enemy's swings. Ardvald swung hard and fast, and he had the advantage of youth and woeful disregard for his own life. Ardvald upped the pressure, throwing a mix-up into one of his swings that nearly took Morgan's head from his shoulders.

"You are slow, old man. It would seem the Immortal Pirate isn't as immortal as everyone thinks," Ardvald goaded as they clashed blades.

"This wolf is old, but he's much more bite to give," Morgan said, breaking the clash and pressing the offensive.

Ardvald deflected his swings, growing more spirited and frenzied with each blow, as though instead of tiring him out, he was being energized by the attack. "Harder! Faster!" he shouted, as though they were playing a game, rather than mortal combat.

Morgan wasn't surprised. He saw much the same attitude in Steven Cage when he fought, as well as other Valkar he'd come across in the past.

"You're tiring," Abbal said.

"And he's getting carried away," Morgan replied.

Ardvald once again began pressing the attack as his Valkar cheered him on. They chanted at him, "Dreptu hann! Dreptu hann! Dreptu hann!"

"What are they saying?" Morgan asked.

"Kill him. They're telling him to kill you," Abbal answered.

Just then, Ardvald charged at him, and leapt for an overhead strike. Morgan tried to block the blow, but it knocked Blade Rose from his hands, and he fell back onto the deck. Ardvald pressed the tip of his blade against Morgan's neck. He'd been beaten.

"This is your last chance, *Immortal Pirate.* Give me the Eye of Atla, or I will parade your head around on a pike after I slaughter your men and take your ship for my own."

Morgan grit his teeth as the chanting reached a crescendo and his men booed and jeered at Ardvald and the Valkar. He could not give the eye to Ardvald. Not because it was owed to the Emperor, although that most certainly was an issue. Not because he cared even to spare his own life, for he did not. No, Ardvald couldn't have the Eye because conceding to him would mean the symbolic and literal death of his crew and his ship. He knew not for what ends this Valkar wanted the Eye, but he knew well enough that once he got it, not only would he have its power at his disposal, but he would unleash it on Azura regardless.

"Never," Morgan whispered.

He took aim with Bullet Rose, which he'd fumbled for as Ardvald grandstanded over him and fired.

Ardvald gasped as the bullet tore through his side. He clutched at the wound, then looked at Morgan in blank surprise as he stumbled backward. His enforcers immediately came to his aid, catching him.

"Vertu svo, huglaus," Ardvald muttered.

He dropped something on the deck that rolled toward Morgan, stopping at his boot. Morgan stood and picked it up, confused. Just then, the Valkar hastily retreated. Ardvald's enforcers carried him away.

"Why did they retreat? Unless…" Abbal said.

"Shit! Everybody take cover!" Morgan shouted as the skull, no bigger than an apple, began to glow bright green.

He chucked it high into the air, through the grates of the enclosure they stood in and up to the main deck.

It detonated in a burst of bright green light, then smoke, and it enveloped the deck in smoke.

Morgan coughed as Stone and Hanover took him by the shoulders, stabilizing him. "Here, sir," Hanover said, handing him Blade Rose.

Osiris, Flint, Cutter, Ryker, and Claude all rushed toward them as everyone funneled up the stairs and back to the main deck. Already, the Valkar were preparing to attack.

"I've stirred the hornets' nest. Make ready for battle!"

XXXII

DECK WAR

"Kill the mogr! Kill them all!" A Valkar woman shouted as they charged at Morgan and his pirates.

Morgan braced himself for the attack as Steven Cage cut in front of him and attacked the woman with his spear, catching her off-guard. She attempted to redirect his attack with her axe, but his spear pierced her forearm, and she yowled in pain, grabbing the shaft of his weapon to prevent him from ripping it out and striking again.

"Sly World Reaver scum!" she spat.

"The Dark Goddesses care not for the proud, only the strong and clever survive," he said.

She opened her mouth to rebut, but he kicked her in the gut, dislodging the spear and eliciting a shriek from her. She scrambled to her feet in vain as he thrust the spear through her neck. A male Valkar cried out in rage at her death, and Cage growled at him.

"She was weak! Are you?!"

Cage charged at the man, who came at him with a two-handed axe. Cage dodged a hefty swing before impaling the man through the knee and whipping out a knife. He plunged it upward into his chin, sending him to the maw of Irkalla with his beloved.

"Come, Watchers! Face this Reaver in combat and prove to your goddess that you are not as weak as you look!" Cage challenged.

A horde of them charged at him in response, and he smiled like a bear, feasting on a moose carcass.

*****

Osiris cracked open the cabin door and ushered Flint and Cutter inside. "Stay here. We'll get you when the fighting's done."

"I want to fight…" Cutter said weakly.

"You're in no position to fight, ye fool," Flint said. "And neither am I. We'd just get in the way…"

Claude grabbed Osiris' shirt. "We need bandages to staunch the blood flow. Mr. Cutter is fading."

"My shirt will have to suffice," Osiris said, stripping it off and handing it to him. It wasn't like it'd offer much protection from a sword or axe, anyway.

"Mr. Ryker, here," Osiris said, handing him a pistol he'd grabbed in the chaos. "Guard them."

Ryker nodded, still a bit sluggish from the unnaturally long slumber he'd just had.

"…Stay here. I'll be back," Osiris bid and shut the door.

He turned to see the carnage unfolding on the deck and prayed no one from the other side had noticed him hiding them. He'd only given Ryker one bullet, and Claude was useless in a fight.

He caught a glimpse of Hanover in the crowd, and he ran in immediately. He ducked past multiple fighters as he zeroed in on the boy, focusing on his unkempt, light brown hair. He saw the boy dip down, however, and lost sight of him.

What the fuck is he doing on this ship?!

He broke through and found to his dismay that Hanover was engaged in a fight with one of the Valkar—and he was losing. The large man had pinned him to the floor and was about to deliver a fatal blow with his mace.

Osiris struck immediately, leaping on the man's back and putting him in a chokehold. At the same time, he dug his fingers into the man's eyes—and pulled.

"Agh! Get off me! Get off! Get off! Get off!" The man howled, flailing fruitlessly, trying to pry Osiris off.

But Osiris showed no mercy.

He tightened the chokehold, completely cutting off the man's circulation, and gouged out the man's eyes with his fingers. The Valkar howled in pain and dropped his mace. Osiris released him, knowing that choking him would take far too long, and would leave him open to attack by his allies. Already more of them were taking notice of their screaming crewmate's struggle and were circling around.

"Fight or die, boy!" Osiris shouted.

I can't save him anymore. If he's so determined to be a pirate, he'll either become one today, or be buried at sea tomorrow.

Osiris grabbed the blinded man's mace and assumed a fighting stance just as one of the others set upon him. He didn't have time to take in who they were, or what they looked like. He simply eyed their weapon and dodged, escaping the swing of a sword before bringing the mace down on his attacker's shoulder. He felt and heard a crack, and he knew his enemy was done for.

Osiris spun around as another came for him, and he hissed as a curved sword sliced through his arm. The attacker smirked at his pain, and he swung his mace like a bat at their torso. The Valkar attempted to block, but his sword was knocked from his hands, and he earned a harsh blow to the chest from the mace. Osiris felt the man's ribs crack, and the man cried out, confirming the damage.

"Siris!" Hanover called out, and he turned just in time to see the two Valkar charging at him.

He tightened his grip on his mace and tried to calculate which one to go for first as a shot rang out and one of them dropped, his head was blown clean off. The other, visibly startled, had a large, scorching hole blown through their torso as the attacker approached from behind.

Reece Stone stepped over the bodies of the two dead Valkar and nodded to Osiris. The two pirates wordlessly stood back-to-back, watching around them as the battle raged. The Azurans were holding their own, but their hold was slipping. The Valkar were wild fighters who would only grow wilder as their numbers dwindled. They saw death in battle as a blessing, while the Azuran pirates saw death in battle only as an unfortunate inevitability.

"Where's their leader?" Osiris asked over his shoulder, keeping an eye on Hanover, who was leaning against a mast, hyperventilating.

"I don't know. I know he's not dead, and so long as that's the case the jury's still open," Stone replied.

"Ye think he'll make another appearance?" Osiris asked.

"I'd put money on it. The cap'n fought dirty 'n got 'em right pissed. He'll be back with a vengeance."

"He was shot in his side by Bullet Rose, mate. Ain't many can come back from that," Osiris said.

"You ain't fought many Valkar, then. The bastards are hardier 'n they've any right to be, 'n they don't scare easy," Stone said. "Where're Flint 'n the others?"

"I hid them in a cabin over yonder, told Ryker to guard them. Gave him a pistol, but that's it."

Stone nodded once. "Better hope no one comes lookin', then."

"What's the plan?" Osiris asked.

Stone focused in on several Valkar approaching them. They were covered in blood. "Survive. We've got company!"

Stone holstered his dragons and pulled out a longsword. Osiris turned around and picked up a discarded axe, dual wielding it with his mace. He counted five Valkar. Three men, two women.

"Hanover!" he shouted.

Hanover, who was lost in a frantic daze and was trying to level his breathing, looked up at him.

"Shake a leg already! You're up!" Osiris said.

One of the women went for Hanover, two short swords in her hands. Hanover froze a moment, perhaps surprised that a woman was attacking him, perhaps terrified because she was covered and blood and was a fair bit taller and bulkier than him.

"You hesitate, you die!" Osiris said, taking his eyes off his two attackers. He nearly got his axe knocked from his hand for that mistake. He weaved between their uncoordinated swings and noticed a wounded sword arm on one of them, likely from their last scrap.

Osiris leaned into his blow, knocking it away and causing him to falter. He tore a deep gash across from the man's throat to his chest and turned to his remaining attacker. Enraged by the death of his brethren, the remaining Valkar let out a battle cry and charged him, axe raised high into the air. He feinted to the right, baiting the swing before dodging to the left as the man dug the axe into the deck. He tried to pull it free, but he never had the opportunity. Osiris threw his own axe at the man and embedded into his side. He ended him with a mace to the top of the head, caving it in.

He looked over and saw Stone had dispatched one of his attackers but was trading blows with the remaining woman. By the looks of it, Stone was winning. He refocused on Hanover.

It didn't look good.

*****

"Time to die, strákur," she said as she squeezed his windpipe shut.

He saw stars. He clawed at her arm, trying to pry it loose, to get a gasp of air as his body burned. He thrashed back and forth, unable to free himself. He saw Osiris, looking at him from afar momentarily.

It's kill or be killed...

That's what he'd told him. Hanover wasn't ready to die yet. His vision darkened, and he thought of all the choices he'd made that led to this moment. Poverty. The life of a street urchin. His *brother*. Stowing away on the Azura and being found out. He remembered Moary pulled the men off him to stop them from beating him. He'd taken him under his wing and taught him all he knew about being a powder boy. And then there was Osiris, who'd taught him how to swing a sword and fire a pistol. They'd accepted him and gave him a fighting chance.

Now, his vision was fading. His body was cooking from the inside. He looked around one last time and scrambled for a splinter of wood hanging up from the deck. He pulled the jagged piece up from the floor and stabbed it into his attacker's face.

The woman relinquished her grip and shrieked in pain, clutching the cheek he'd stabbed the splinter into. He shoved her off him and picked up her discarded sword. He gasped, taking in lungfuls of cooling air.

Kill or be killed.

He would not be killed.

She growled and lunged at him after ripping the splinter from her face. He kicked her in the head, knocking her back onto the floor, then thrust the sword down into her belly, impaling her on the floor. She kicked and screamed in agony and shock as blood leaked from her onto the floorboards. He stumbled back, hyperventilating, staring at the woman who moments before was about to strangle the life from his body.

"Finish her," he heard a voice say right beside him. He looked and saw that it was Osiris, eyeing the woman pinned on the ground. He put a dagger in his hand.

"I-I-can't! I—" Hanover blubbered, tears streaming down his cheeks.

Osiris cut him off. "You already did. She's dead whether you slit her throat or not."

Hanover looked wide-eyed at the Valkar woman. Blood was sputtering from her lips as she muttered unintelligible words. Her eyes looked at him with naked hatred.

"If the roles were reversed, you'd already be dead. At least have the balls to finish what you started and end her suffering rather than leave her to drown in her own blood," Osiris said. "Finish it."

Hanover stumbled forward. His hands trembled, and he knelt as the woman gritted her teeth and spat blood at his face. She hated him. She wanted him dead. She was going to wring the life out of him. She would have given him no mercy, no quarter, no pity, no—

"Do it!" Osiris yelled.

Hanover lifted her chin with one hand and stabbed the dagger up into her chin with the other. She struggled violently, then went still. Her blue eyes looked at him reproachfully, then stared blankly at the sky. Her hair, a long halo of blood-streaked gold, fanned out around her in her death throes.

"Good. Now quit sulkin' 'n get up. There's more where that came from," Osiris said before walking away.

There would be time for tears later.

*****

Morgan fired another round, punching holes through several Valkar at a time as they rushed him. It was almost comical how they charged to their deaths, but for every five of their men he killed, two of his were ended, and they hadn't the numbers to lose. He watched as yet another of his men were cutdown viciously, and looked around to see who was left to fight. He couldn't see where Osiris or Stone were, though he knew without a doubt that Osiris was fighting.

"He could have hidden away. He was already injured from the outset," Abbal said.

"You'd have to kill that man to stop him from fighting, and he was still very much alive last I saw," Morgan replied proudly.

Osiris was worth a dozen men, easily.

He did worry about the Hanover boy, however. The Valkar were a formidable lot for a seasoned pirate to face, never mind one as young as he. And then there was the matter of Flint, Cutter, Ryker, and Claude. Claude was useless in a fight, hence why he typically hid when the fighting started and utilized his skills when the smoke settled. Ryker was generally too important to send into the fray. Like Claude, he and Sarkad were simply too important to lose. Without them, the ship would be limping along if trouble were to strike. Sarkad had fought Morgan to join the group to rescue his brother, but Morgan managed to talk him out of it, arguing his older brother would want him to take care of their pride and joy, Azura, first.

He hoped he was right.

And then there was Flint and Cutter. He'd seen that they were injured, and Ardvald had confirmed as much. He didn't need to know much about the man to know he'd go to great pains to get what he wanted—especially if it was inflicted on others.

"Great pains? And what of the pain you inflicted upon those Dyonians you took the Eye from? It would seem you've only gotten your just desserts," Abbal said.

"My duty is to my men. I did what was best for them, and damned be the rest," Morgan answered defiantly.

Another opponent came before him. This one wore armor adorned with furs and human skulls. Morgan paused as he recognized the helmet of Ardvald the Mangler.

"You shot me, mogr. You will pay for that, dearly," he said in his Borran-accented Kurzan. He brandished a sword that Morgan hadn't seen him wielding before. When he looked at it, it looked *wrong*. It put his hairs on end.

"That blade is blessed with a dark enchantment of some sort," Abbal confirmed.

"The kind that kills me or the kind that kills him?" Morgan asked rhetorically.

Two of his men charged at Ardvald blindly, and before he could even warn them, the armored Valkar cut them down. Morgan watched as the blade sliced one man in two, disintegrating his body immediately after. The second man, seeing what happened to his comrade, attempted to run. Ardvald swung the sword at the man and a crescent of darkness shot through the air and cleaved the man apart, disintegrating him as well. Morgan sidestepped just in time to avoid a similar fate. The dark energy dissipated a few feet past where he'd just stood.

"Does that answer your question?" Abbal asked.

Morgan pulled the potion from his pocket and downed its contents. It was now or never. He shook his head an electric chill ran through his body, and he felt awash with energy.

"An Alyria potion? Clever."

"Perhaps if you wore armor like that the first round, you'd be without a bullet hole in your side," Morgan said.

"You jest! Hahahaha!" Ardvald laughed, holding his sword in both hands. "When I behead you, I'll be sure to reanimate it, so that you can tell your wonderful jokes to all of Borra as I parade around it with your rotting skull!"

Ardvald charged Morgan, and Morgan focused as he channeled the energy from Abbal into himself. He would need all the help he could get in this fight.

He dodged just in time to evade a thrust from Ardvald, then brought Blade Rose down on his back. The blade bounced and he saw a blue spark fly off the armor, leaving it completely unscathed.

"What in blazes…" Morgan said, dumbfounded.

"It is swaddled in Alyria, pirate. Your blade will not even nick it," Ardvald said triumphantly.

Enchanted armor? How in Sheolhenna did this bastard get hold of that?

"Their Dark Goddesses gift their champions with weapons and armor coated with their foulness. I suppose this brute is one such champion," Abbal said.

I need more power, then. Blade Rose isn't even nicking that damned armor, normally she'd cut clean through plate mail.

"It will be done."

Blade Rose began to glow a faint blue, just as Ardvald went to slice at Morgan. He deflected the blow, and the blades clashed together with a metallic shriek. He could see through the eye slits that Ardvald was surprised.

"Unexpected. Most blades break against the might of Black Frost," Ardvald admitted.

"Blade Rose isn't like other blades," Morgan answered, running a hand appreciatively over its edge and drawing blood from his finger. Every cut reminded him of her. Of Rose.

"I guess we shall see whose blade is stronger, then!" Ardvald said, attacking with an overhead slash.

Morgan saw an opening and sidestepped the swing, then pulled out his pistol for the counterattack. He fired Bullet Rose, and the bullet ripped through Ardvald's armor, puncturing his sword arm and causing it to go limp.

"Gah! But how?!" Ardvald gasped, clutching his dead arm and releasing his hold of the sword.

"You aren't the only one using enchanted weaponry, Valkar. Say goodbye!"

Ardvald grunted, gripping the sword in his left hand and wielding it one-handed. "Never!" he growled.

He swung the sword and unleashed a frenzied barrage of swings, trying his hardest to catch the old pirate off-guard.

He's getting sloppy again.

Morgan smirked, knowing that the angrier the Valkar got, the more mistakes he would make. He didn't have time to load more ammo into Bullet Rose, but he knew that if he could make one more fatal flaw, leave one more opening, he'd finish him with a sure strike from Blade Rose.

"It would seem your goddess has forsaken you, Valkar. You said her armor was supposed to protect you, but it couldn't even withstand one of my bullets. Perhaps she's displeased that you've allowed an old man to best you in combat," Morgan goaded.

"Axodia would never forsake her children, mœgr. Unlike your dead, forgotten gods, ours are alive and well—and eager to kill!" Ardvald snarled.

"Your gods are as dead as you will soon be, I assure you," Abbal said aloud, catching Ardvald by surprise.

"What trickery—" Ardvald said, breaking his focus.

Morgan wasted no time, he swung his cutlass down hard and sliced clean through Ardvald's left arm with a mighty screech of metal and a spark of blue light. The Mangler howled in pain as blood gushed from the wound, and he tried in vain to clutch at it with his deadened right arm. He was finished.

The Valkar despaired, crying out for the loss of their leader, but the battle would be over soon. Without Ardvald, their coordination would crumble, and they would be picked off, perhaps even forced to flee.

Morgan smiled and prepared to behead the Valkar with a swing.

"Wait! He may yet prove useful!" Abbal intervened.

Morgan froze, less than a foot from Ardvald's neck. He realized that the amulet was right. They needed to find out who had sent the Valkar after them.

"You will yet live, Valkar. Count your blessings," Morgan said, panting.

"No, I am dead already, Immortal Pirate, as you soon will be," Ardvald muttered before slumping over. He would be dead soon if they didn't staunch the blood flow.

XXXIII

A Cold Wind Blows

The Deathwatch did not take well to Ardvald's capture. They fought viciously to save him, and many of the boarding party were killed in the process. When they managed to escape, almost all the men they'd brought with them in the rescue operation had died. All told, twenty men from the rescue party had been killed. There were only twenty-three men in the party, to begin with.

When they returned, all hell broke loose. The Azura pirates wanted their pound of flesh from Ardvald for the death of their brethren. Morgan could barely convince them not to keelhaul him then and there, but by the grace of the Stars he did.

Now, they sat in the cargo hold, and Ardvald sat tied to a chair, unconscious. He was in bad shape, and would likely be dead before too long, as not even Claude Humris could do much of anything to stop the bleeding and infection now. Morgan looked at the battered Valkar for several long, contemplative moments before he spoke.

"Wake him," he instructed.

Flint, who was adamant that he be part of the interrogation, obliged. He grabbed a bucket filled with bilge water and dumped the foul-smelling swill on Ardvald's face.

"Drink up, cocksucker," Flint said.

Ardvald slowly came to, blinking, before looking at the stump where his left forearm used to be. He laughed mirthlessly. "Þetta kemur allt með kalda vatninu…how the tables have turned."

Flint glared balefully at Ardvald.

"Cutter wanted to be here, but he's passed out in the infirmary. Ryker's fine, thankfully, even though your boys knocked him out cold for the better part of a half-hour," Flint said venomously. "I told them I'd get their payback."

Ardvald yawned and looked at Morgan. "This one whines like a bitch. Does he not know that cold winds blow on mountaintops?"

Morgan looked at him, uncertain as to what he meant. Flint was also confused, though he was still staring daggers at Ardvald and fiercely thumbing the one on his hip.

"You are sjóræningja—pirates. Killing, maiming, violence. You do these things upon your enemies and your victims. Do not be so surprised, then, when it is done upon you," Ardvald said, looking disinterestedly at Flint. "And do not bitch about it. How many men have you done such harm to? You are as deserving of that new eyepatch on your face as I am of my new arm stump," Ardvald raised the bandaged, red stump where his armor had been cleaved clean through.

"Enough of the moral lessons. Who sent you?" Morgan asked, already tiring of Ardvald's antics.

The Valkar looked at him, then. His expression was all business; the mirth had left him.

"And why would I give you that information, møgr? I am a dead man anyway," Ardvald shrugged.

"Because giving me that information will dictate whether we give you back to your people or not," Morgan said.

Ardvald frowned. "And why would I care about that?"

"Because if we kill you and cast your body into the sea, and your crew are unable to find your remains, then your goddess will not be able to resurrect you as one of her champions," Cage said, walking out of the shadows.

"Skemmtilegur, meindýrasvikari við myrku gyðjurnar!" Ardvald hissed venomously. "He lies!"

"Oh? Because what I just saw turned my skepticism into certainty. You may not fear death, Valkar, but you certainly fear being lost to your precious goddess. The sea is a vast, cold place. I doubt they'll find one shred of your corpse once the fish and the crabs get to it."

Ardvald was silent for several moments. They'd called his bluff. Osiris stepped forward to chime in, "We could always do this my way and bust his kneecaps till he squeals."

"Something tells me our friend here has no desire to prolong his suffering any longer," Morgan said as he leaned forward. ""Who is it? Because I very much doubt the Emperor sent you to fetch us, or the Dyonians, for that matter."

Ardvald shrugged before cracking that same cocksure grin. "Whether I tell you or not makes no difference. Your fate is sealed, even now. The one who's coming for you, Immortal Pirate, is far worse than anything I could hope to muster. No, *your* fate is much more terrible, hahahahahaha!"

The pirates stood, perplexed for several moments as Ardvald laughed himself into a bloody coughing fit.

"You have quite the story, Captain Morgan. A story so fantastic that even I found it hard to believe. I wouldn't believe it, even now, were it not that I ran across someone from your past," Ardvald began as he composed himself.

"From my past? Hah, you'll have to be more specific than that. There are hundreds of people in my past," Morgan said.

Ardvald nodded. "Yes, but only one of them is as illustrious—or infamous—as you. Some would argue they're the reason the world even knows who you are, in fact. The Immortal Captain Morgan Sarron, savior of King's Rest, champion of the Free Folk of the Chained Lands. You know, you may very well be the reason these bastard Kurzans run the empire like it's their own. But without him, I'd dare say you'd be just another footnote of a pirate, left in the forgotten, unwritten passages of history."

The cogs in Morgan's mind once again turned as Ardvald's words took shape. He felt a cold chill run through his veins as the truth dawned on him.

"It can't be, he's…" Morgan began.

He thought back to the flash he'd had when he'd touched the Eye of Atla. It felt like he was right back there, in that collapsing cave, with *him*.

"Don't leave me here, please! Not here!"

"Please! PLEAAASE!!!"

The memory screamed at him.

"Could it be? It couldn't be…I would know, wouldn't I?" Abbal said, talking to himself.

But how? How could it be? I killed him. I watched him die! It's impossible, he—

"Cap'n?" Osiris asked, placing a hand on his shoulder.

Morgan was startled, looking around wildly before seeing Osiris. "What?"

"You were…mumbling, sir…"

"We followed the scent of death across the rolling sea, until we found the source. We beheld a man, a revenant of death and dread. He bid us to find you, to bring him an object—this *Eye of Atla* in your possession. He told me to bring it, and you, to him. He is coming for you." Ardvald warned somberly.

"You can bury your demons, Morgan Sarron, but you can never kill them. A shadow will always follow you, and the past will find its way back to you. As sure as the sun rises in the east and sets in the west," Ardvald said. His skin had grown incredibly pale, and it caused him visible strain to speak.

"Do not play games with me, Valkar. TELL ME WHO SENT YOU! TELL ME!" Morgan snarled, grabbing hold of Ardvald by the necklace.

"I tell no lies…pirate…and I have no more news to give. That Eye of yours…it marks you. Worser powers than I want for it. You, and your men, are at the center of something…something…" Ardvald began to nod off, and sleepily blinked. His skin was a sickly pale, now. "Take me back to my men."

BOOM! BOOM! BOOM! BOOM! BOOM!

Several cannons discharged from above them and shook the ship ever so slightly. Morgan pulled out his watch and checked the time before closing it with a dark smile.

"What…what was that?" Ardvald asked slowly as he faded more and more. It was hard for him to keep his eyes open.

Morgan scowled and looked Ardvald in the eyes. "That? That was the sound of what was left of your crew being damned to a watery grave."

As the stark reality sank in, Ardvald lifted himself from his chair with the last of his strength and stood before Morgan, who stood up in turn. Though the man was taller, broader, and by all accounts stronger than the old pirate, he looked small and weak. Morgan towered over the dying Valkar, and he folded his arms behind his back as he looked at him.

"You made a grave and terrible mistake attacking us, Ardvald Holvensonn. You say you know my legend. If that be so, then you know I cannot allow anyone who would dare attack us to live. That includes you, and your wayward crew. You dared to challenge Azura, so you will pay the price for your insolence," Morgan eulogized.

Ardvald fell to his knees. Both his arms were too damaged to hold him up, so he crumpled to the floor and used what little core strength he had left in him to lift upright and look into Morgan's eyes. How had he been bested by this old man? He had him and his men in the palm of his hand. How could someone as mighty as he, a champion of Axodia, Goddess of Corpses, Queen of the Dead, be brought down by a mere old pirate? He felt the grasp of death tighten upon him, and his eyes grew heavy.

"Oh, Goddess Axodia, Mother of the Dead and the Lost…I have failed you…I have…forgive…me…" He fell back and landed headfirst on the seat of his chair, knocking it over as he spilled to the floor.

Where he went, he saw only darkness before him…

*****

Morgan sat in his quarters, looking out the window to the aft of the ship. Though they had survived the Valkar, they were still in the doldrums. How long they would remain, it was impossible to tell. They could be stuck for a few more hours, days, or even weeks. Without wind, they would be forced to float, and soon they would have other problems, far more pressing than a lack of wind or a missed deadline. After going through the stores with Stone, Ryker, and Sarkad, they'd calculated they had about two and a half weeks' worth of food and water, if rationed properly. The Valkar ship had been too dangerous and contaminated with death to risk taking provisions. Steven Cage had warned them that the Deathwatch would often poison their food, as they were immune to its effects, but it would ensure that any stowaways, or looters, would die should they take from them.

Burn the crops and salt the earth. Spiteful bastards.

And there was still the matter of what their leader, Ardvald, had said.

"…We beheld a man, a revenant of death and dread. He bid us to find you, to bring him an object—this Eye of Atla in your possession. He told me to bring it, and you, to him. He is coming for you…"

While they were rare, the undead did roam the world, much as the Church of the Stars and the empire liked to act as though they didn't. But the odds that an undead—a revenant, no less—would be looking for *him* of all people was exceedingly rare.

"Can you feel him?" Morgan asked.

"Feel whom? The ghost that the mad Valkar proclaims lives yet? No," Abbal dismissed.

"Could he live?"

"In this world, anything is possible. But revenants…are rare. What would make him so important that an outside force would resurrect him after all this time?"

Morgan sat in thought for some time.

"...A shadow will always follow you, and the past will find its way back to you. As sure as the sun rises in the east and sets in the west..." Ardvald's words repeated in his mind.

A shadow.

My shadow...

*****

The mood on the deck was somber and bleak, Osiris noted. He knew exactly why. Twenty of their men were killed, and two were horribly maimed in their encounter. The Valkar had left their mark, even in death. The late afternoon sun was beating down on them in a white screen, and the dead air left the heat beating down on them with no reprieve. He walked the deck, spying the various crew members and listening into snippets of conversations. He greeted many men as he walked, many of them asking him what he'd experienced, in the clutches of the Valkar. He didn't know what to say.

Flint and Cutter lost an eye and a hand, respectively. Claude Humris said that Ryker would likely suffer wracking shivers because of the amount of time he'd been knocked out, though it was hard to call it, now.

I've got both me arms, both me eyes, and a broken nose. I got off easy.

He'd wished he had an opportunity to fight Ardvald himself, to pay him back personally for what he'd done to his brethren, but alas, he couldn't. In the end, Captain Morgan had killed him. He would have to satisfy his thirst for vengeance with the memory of Ardvald's broken, pitiful end, and the knowledge that inevitably, he would face more Valkar one day. Hopefully then, he would have full control of his powers, and if he did, he would make sure to give them a taste of the punishment their kin had dealt upon his crew.

"Anyone seen Hanover of late?" Osiris asked aloud.

"Ye mean Blondie? Last I seen 'em he was down in the galley, drinkin' himself to oblivion," a pirate said. "I've half a mind to join 'em."

Osiris raised a brow.

Blondie?

"Aye," he said, then made for the galley.

He opened the door and as he descended he noticed that no one was down there, save for Hanover evidently, as no sound was heard from below. As he reached the bottom of the stairway he looked around the dimly-lit dining room and saw Hanover sitting at a table in the middle of the room. He didn't even look in Osiris' direction, though he knew he'd had to have heard his footsteps echo as he came down the stairs.

"Hanover?" he called out, stopping himself from saying 'Boy'.

Hanover looked over his shoulder at him momentarily, before sipping his tankard and slamming it down onto the table. Osiris approached and saw that he had a tall bottle of alcohol with him. It was crystal-clear, a strong brand of plant absinthe.

"I don't think I've ever seen you drink anything stronger than beer, save for Moary givin' you those moon spirits," Osiris said.

He sat down across from Hanover and was taken aback by how much older he looked, now. It had been hours since he'd last seen him, but in that time his face had become drawn and heavy, like an old sailor, and his eyes were distant, staring far past and beyond them. Hanover said nothing, merely pouring more of the greenish liquid into his cup before downing several drags of it with a hack and a cough.

Osiris again took note of his wrist tattoo, which the boy had scratched pink.

"Strong stuff, ay?" Osiris asked, filling the silence.

Hanover said nothing. His face was wet, his hair hung in messy coils in front of his face. He lifted the cup to his lips again, but Osiris stopped him with a hand, forcing him to lower it back to the table.

"No more drink. What's got your tongue?" Osiris asked, grabbing the bottle of crystal-clear and sitting it next to him.

Hanover focused on him, now. His green eyes looked changed, but he couldn't be certain in the low light that the table's covered lantern provided. Those distant eyes dilated as they focused on Osiris, as though noticing him for the first time.

"P-p-pardon?" Hanover asked, stumbling over the word. Even his voice sounded changed, somehow meeker, but also older.

"What's wrong with you?" Osiris asked, rephrasing his question. The concern was plain on his face now.

"Oh, nothing sir. Right as rain!" Hanover said cheerily with a drunken chuckle. "Right as rain," he repeated, laughing at his own words. "Like rain clouds…"

Osiris folded his arms. He didn't believe him.

"You know, they say that the rain is the tears of the gods, come to wash away the sins of the world. But when I was in the streets the rain killed more of us than starvation and abuse ever did," Hanover said, gripping his cup with both hands and drinking.

Osiris didn't stop him, this time. He leaned back in his chair and listened.

"The rain. The cold. Freezing, shivering children in the streets, too cold to beg, too cold to move. When the rain came, it brought death with it, not absolution. I called out for my brother, then. He never came. Now, I get to thinking…maybe the rain *was* washing away our sins. The sins we were yet to commit. Stopping boys like me from becoming…" he froze, and both looked at Hanover's shaking hands.

Osiris was puzzled. He hadn't known Hanover had a brother. He leaned forward and placed a hand over Hanover's, ceasing their shaking. "Breathe, boy…"

"I can't…can't…" Hanover stammered, shaking his head before dropping the cup and covering his head with his hands. "Can't breathe, can't sleep; I can't dream. All I hear, all I see, all I feel is her screams!" he shouted at the top of his lungs.

Hanover dug his nails into his scalp as he began to whimper like a child. "All my fault…it's all my fault. It's all my—"

"Enough!" Osiris slammed his hands on the table, and Hanover sat bolt upright. "You wanted this life? Well congratulations, boy, you're in it, now! You've taken a life! And nothing, nothing you can ever say or do will take that back…"

They sat in silence for several tense moments.

"Does it ever stop?" Hanover asked soberly.

"…No…and I still hear them, sometimes…" Osiris said.

Hanover hung his head. His sobbing had ceased, but the vacancy had returned. He let out a long, drawn-out sigh. He had been shown their ways. He had taken a life. Now, he had to make peace with his own.

"She's goin' to get me…" He heard Hanover mutter under his breath.

"She's dead, boy. She ain't gettin' shit but maggots 'n gulls," Osiris assured him.

"Not her. The old woman, she…" Hanover muttered before covering his mouth.

Osiris cocked an eyebrow at him. "Old woman?"

Hanover shook his head; he would say no more.

*****

Huasca dipped his hands in the basin and plunged Yager's eyes into the water, releasing a reddish cloud into it. He splashed water on his face. He'd been out for some time, the ritual to possess the Valkar drained his energy, and he was just now coming to terms with the fact that, like Morgan, he was getting old. He wondered if he'd even be able to survive Bawon Samedi giving him his old powers back.

It would probably kill me.

Huasca hated to admit.

When he sacrificed the bulk of his powers to avoid being tracked by the magisters, he had been a young man. That was a quarter-century ago, now. He was getting older, and his body simply couldn't handle the strain such energies had on it, anymore.

He wiped the water from his face with a cloth and looked at his reflection.

"It is almost time," his reflection said, morphing into the image of Bawon Samedi.

Huasca gazed into the water at the face of his patron god. He knew this moment would come. "He is not ready."

"He will never be ready if he is not tested. He has been kept in the dark for far too long," Bawon Samedi said.

"A bit longer, my lord—please! I beg of you!" Huasca said hastily.

Bawon Samedi paused and stared at Huasca for several long moments. "You've become too attached. He is a child no longer."

Huasca bit his tongue, stopping the words from leaving his lips. "When this voyage ends, when the Eye of Atla is delivered, I will deliver him to you."

Bawon Samedi said nothing. His immense presence weighed on the cabin like a ten-ton brick.

"Time is running out, Yaman Huasca…"

He disappeared, his voice echoed through the room, even in his absence. Huasca closed his eyes and eased his breathing.

Time…

He plunged his hand into the basin and pulled out the eyes. It was time to see what killed Daniel Yager.

*****

Moary entered the empty galley and observed the lone Hanover, sitting silently by lamplight.

"Siris tells me you've come down with pint fever, laddie. Your first kill turned you to a drunkard?" Moary asked as he walked over to the table and climbed onto the seat, his considerable mass creaking its frame.

"I'm not a drunkard, Mr. Moary, sir. I just…" Hanover said. "The drink, it keeps the…voices…away."

"Voices, ay?" Moary said, taking the bottle from Hanover and chugging an eye-opening amount himself. Almost all human-made alcohols felt weak and lacking to him. Even the crystal-clear was only mildly intoxicating for him. The curse of being Half-Duwa. "Let me tell ye somethin', ay? A story. Might be it helps you come to terms. Might be it doesn't, but we'll try all the same."

Hanover ran his hands through his hair, not looking at Moary but not objecting either.

"When I was a young lad, about fifty odd years ago, now, I was a homeless bastard. Me father was human, and he'd left me 'n me mother to starve amongst the ghunbeann. Duwa who was cast out from beneath the mountains. So, I signed up to join the navy, in hopes of makin' some coin to get me mother out of poverty. Wanted to join the Bluecoats, but they figured a half-breed like meself wasn't welcome in their ranks. Abhorrent, they called me. So, I turned to the black. Shacked up with some pirates who came to port, lookin' for recruits. They saw a young, strong, naive youth to take advantage of, and I saw food on the table for mum.

"She cried and begged somethin' fierce for me to stay. In a different life, I like to imagine I listened to 'er. In this one, well, we all know which way the coin flipped. Our first voyage we ran afoul of slavers, 'n they opened fire on us, for fear that we'd take their human cargo. We chased them down, 'n we got into a boarding skirmish with 'em. I was one of the first across, and I was in the thick of the fightin'. My first kill was a young lad, no older than your age, I'd wager. At first, I felt strange about killin' someone young as meself…that was until he tried to stab me. Got me across the cheek, here." Moary ran a finger across the scar on his left cheek.

Hanover had always wondered where that scar had come from.

"I ran 'em through. Killed 'em where he stood, 'n felt right terrible for it. It was an ugly death. He blubbered 'n screamed 'n begged for his life. I left 'em there to die, couldn't even bear to put 'em out his misery. In spite of the fact that he was a slaver, 'n had partook in the bondage of his fellow man, I still felt terrible for killin' 'em." Moary took another swig from the absinthe bottle and slammed it down on the table.

Hanover could smell it on his breath as he belched and ran a hand through his beard. "Thing is, son, if I hadn't killed 'em he'd have killed me, whether he wanted to or not made no difference. We were pirates boardin' his ship, 'n he was a slaver, protecting his masters' unwilling investments."

Hanover leaned his head down, lost in his own thoughts again. Moary reached over with one of his massive hands and placed the calloused mitt on the young man's shoulder.

"I'm not here to tell ye not to mourn. You've done somethin' that can never be undone. But I need ye to understand that in this life we live. There aren't heroes 'n villains, just the living 'n the dead…" Moary said. He hopped out of the chair and set the nearly gone bottle of crystal-clear on the table. "You're a pirate, now, laddie—but you've got a soul to save. Be good, son."

Moary walked off, leaving Hanover to his thoughts. He picked up the bottle as the deathly gasps returned to his ears, and his hands began to shake. He went to pour the absinthe into his mug but instead drank directly from the bottle. He drank until the clear-green liquid was gone. And with it went the sounds of his victim, and the whispers nipping at his ears. Now, in the thrall of the absinthe, he could rest.

*****

Moary stepped out the doorway at the top of the stairs and breathed in the open air, he heard gulls cawing melodically on the wind, and admired, for a brief moment, the beauty of nature. It was easy to forget how the world isn't all bad, when you're faced with danger, day in and day out, and you've seen some of the terrors that the sea can dish out. But moments where it was bright and sunny, and the water was calm, and the birds chirped and cawed and floated on the breeze reminded Moary that life went on outside of the trials he and his brethren were facing. Then he looked at the sails and was once again reminded of their current predicament. How long would they be trapped in these doldrums?

I wonder how mom's doin?

He pondered as he leaned against the railing. He lit a cigar, comically huge in the hands of a regular human, but for a Half-Duwa like himself it was right at home. The last time he'd seen her was two years ago, now. They'd had a nasty falling out; she never made peace with him becoming a pirate.

"You're killing me, Freddy," she cried.

"I'm doin' this for ye, Mom," he'd said as he handed her a pouchful of gold coins.

"I don't want gold; I want my son," she shouted, smacking them from his hand, sending them skittering out on the floorboards of her cottage.

He blinked the memory away as he became aware of someone calling his name. "Pardon?" he asked, realizing it was Osiris.

"I asked if ye got through to him?" he asked again.

Moary scratched his face and breathed smoke. "I dunno. Boy's deep in his cup 'n deeper in his thoughts. He's real shaken up over his first kill."

Osiris leaned against the railing next to him, looking out at several gulls riding the breeze. "He didn't wanna do it. I made him do it."

Moary shook his head like a disapproving father and offered him the cigar. Osiris took it. "Shouldn't 'ave done that, Siris. It had to be his choice—ye know that sure as I."

Osiris puffed the cigar, an awkward—ponderous thing in his human-sized hand—and exhaled. "I didn't tell 'em he had to. He insisted he wanted to. When the time came, however, I guess his mark wasn't the one he was hopin' for."

"Ye said it was a woman, ay? Terrible business, that. I've had to kill a few meself." Moary shrugged. "I don't think that ever gets easy."

"I have as well, and all of them wanted me dead," Osiris dismissed as he handed the cigar back to Moary. "I'm not sayin' it ain't hard, but I'm sayin' it's part of this life."

"This life?" Moary mused. "This life is for those with no other recourse to make a livin'. This life is for those society turned its back on so that they can curl up 'n die in a gutter somewhere. This life ain't for wee boys tryin' to take the piss 'n prove thar manhood, say," Moary said, beginning to bleed Duwa in his accent. "The boy is still a boy, findin' 'imself. I dunno if it was wise to take 'em on, but he didn't have much in the way 'o options. Now he's here, 'n he's got blood on his hands. I weep for 'em, cuz his soul will never be the same. But it's too late now…"

"Would you rather I babied him forever, then? Cap'n was on my side—he had to learn our ways," Osiris said.

"Well, now he has then, hasn't he?" Moary said. He took a deep inhale of the cigar. "And now he's lost his way in the dark. Let's hope he finds it again."

"He'll find his way when he accepts what he's done. He wants to be a pirate? Well, it's time he's learned the cost of it," Osiris dismissed. "Can't be a pirate without gettin' your hands bloody."

"Ye were but a wee babe when ye came into this life, lad. Ye were raised by pirates. Ya saw firsthand how cruel folk could be from when ya were barely walkin'. But ya don't know what it's like to have lived clean yer whole life 'n wake up with blood on your hands for the first time. Ya don't know what it's like ta tell yer mother, her baby boy is a killer. She never forgave me for livin' this life, 'n I think she never will. That's a hard drink to swallow," Moary said.

"Gertrude didn't understand that her son was doin' the best he could with the cards he was dealt. That's tough, but a man's gotta do what a man's gotta do. I would hope an orphan boy off the streets of Spirus would understand that. If not? Then maybe he really isn't cut out for this life," Osiris answered.

"Ya never knew the warmth of yer mother's love, did ya laddie? It shows. You're a cold soul, Osiris…" Moary sighed in defeat, took one last puff of his cigar, then handed it to Osiris and walked away. "Enjoy the air."

Osiris stood there in the near-breezeless midday sun and took one last drag from Moary's half-gone cigar before ashing it and stuffing it in his pocket. "It's a cold world, Moary…"

*****

"Where is it?" Flint asked.

"Down in the bilge, now. I had some men come and carry it down, shortly after the battle. I was glad to be rid of it," Claude admitted.

"Better to be rid of it. Be rid of *him*," Flint said.

He hissed as Claude pulled back the eyepatch and checked the fresh stitches he'd put in over the eyehole.

"How bad is it?" Flint asked.

"Well, Mr. Flint, if you were hoping to ever see again, I believe I have bad news for you. You won't, not out of this gash, not without some powerful Alyria at play."

"Perhaps I'll luck up 'n find something to replace it," Flint joked, "a magick gem to replace my lost eye, ha!"

Claude chuckled. "Here's to hoping. Stranger things have happened, I suppose."

"Aye," Flint agreed. "Aye…"

Their laughter quieted down as Claude worked. He grabbed a syringe and a vial and drew the brownish lesser anathema fluid from it. "This will numb the pain, some."

Flint nodded and braced himself, then grit his teeth as he felt the thick needle pierce his arm. "Ye know—ack!" he felt the burn as the fluid entered. "I feel like I got off easy. I mean, I lost an eye, but Cutter lost a damn hand. How can ye work without a hand?"

"It is curieux…Mr. Cutter said similar words, when I was inspecting him earlier," Claude said as he depressed the needle's plunger and forced its contents into Flint's body.

"The fool. He's in worse shape than I am, 'n he's worried about me?" Flint said.

"In all my years as a surgeon I have never seen two pirates share a friendship as strong as yours, mona mi."

"That's because most pirates ain't been through the shit we been through. We'd each be dead a dozen times over without the other. The bastard's had my back since we was kids. Closest thing to a brother I ever had," Flint praised.

"Cherish that. All my friends are dead and gone, and most of them died on this operating table while I tried to save their lives…" Claude said remorsefully.

"Claude…" Flint began.

"Vous avez terminé—you are done, and may leave now, Monsieur Flint," Claude cut him off.

Flint nodded and hopped off the table. Already he could feel the lesser anathema taking hold and killing the sharp, burning pain where his right eye used to be. "Ye can't save 'em all, mate," he said. "You're a good man. Ye did the best ye could."

Claude fixed his spectacles and picked up a bloody rag, dipping it in a basin. "Au revoir, Mr. Flint."

Flint nodded, went to the door, and left.

Claude soaked the rag until it went from red to pink and wrung it out. Cutter's hand stump had been in rough shape. Whatever blade the Valkar used to chop it was impure, and caused an infection to set in. Claude had been forced to give the man the last of his white star syrup to sedate him so that he could cut another several inches of flesh and bone from his wrist. The procedure had gone well, but he would have to check the wound again in a few hours. He opened a drawer and pulled out a clear, unmarked bottle before he uncorked it and took a strong whiff of its contents.

Almost all of my syrup…

White star syrup, while it was a powerful painkiller and sedative, also had mildly hallucinogenic properties. Ingested in small, controlled doses, it could put the user in a mild state of euphoria, giving them a very mild high. In very high doses, however, it could cause heart failure. Fortunately for Claude, he knew exactly how much to take. He grabbed a spoon and drizzled some of the clear sap onto it before ingesting it.

Just a little to sleep.

That was what he told himself. And it *did* help him sleep. It also helped him to not feel so bad about the men they'd lost today, and the men he'd lost many other days on his operating table. He heard something knock over onto the floor behind him and instinctively turned to address the noise. He walked over to see that some of his instruments had fallen to the floor, likely because he'd left them hanging on the edge of the desk. He looked in the mirror attached to the desk, finished sucking the syrup off the spoon, which he held in his mouth, and bent over to grab the fallen tools. He sat the tools—a saw and a pair of scissors—back on the table. He caught a whiff of something sickly sweet smelling as he leaned back down to check for any other tools that might've fallen, then lifted himself back up slowly as the syrup took hold.

He took another look in the mirror.

Daniel Yager's broken-jawed face glared into the mirror at him over his shoulder, inches behind.

Claude screamed.

A hand came over his mouth, muffling him and shoving the spoon violently into the back of his mouth, with his other hand, Yager stabbed the scissors through Claude's palm on the desk, pinning it. Daniel Yager gave him a broken-jawed smile as he grabbed the saw and dragged Claude toward the operating table. His hand was split open as he was dragged away.

Claude tried to scream again, but between the effects of the white syrup, the spoon piercing into the top of his throat, and the hand covering his mouth and nose, he could not.

XXXIV

A MESSAGE

"Must we wait forever, My Lady?" Ardvald asked, folding his arms as the officers sat, waiting patiently in the water. They had been doing this for the past several days, sitting idle in the water, waiting for a sign.

"We will wait until the source comes. The Corpse Mother bids it," the woman said. She was a formidable woman, standing at eye-level with Ardvald, though her frame wasn't quite as robust. Her eyes were like shards of ice. They glowed, even in the moon's light, with a fierce light. All the Valkar revered her, and Ardvald bowed his head in her presence.

"Yes, My Lady, as you say," he quickly responded.

There were a dozen ships in the Valkar fleet. The one her officers stood on was at the head of it and was by far the largest and most well-armed. They called it the White Shark, and with it, her captain, Helya Jottunsdottr, planned to conquer the entire eastern seaboard of the empire. But first, the Corpse Mother told her that she must wait for a sign. And so here she waited, day and night, for the providential sign from the goddess. The crew talked amongst themselves, but her and her officers stood silent. Waiting.

And so, it came.

The moon turned from a cool blue to a fearsome, blood red, and a bank of fog materialized just past the horizon and rolled in toward them. Ardvald looked at Helya, uncertain. She looked straight ahead, a hand on the shaft of the spear fastened to her back. The crew stopped bantering and faced the incoming fog in silence. The wall stopped about a quarter mile away from the White Shark, and the shadow of a lone ship appeared in the fog.

And then another.

And another.

Before long, the silhouette of at least double the Valkar fleet's ships appeared in the fog, but only one broke through. It was at least galleon size, if not larger. It flew a red banner and a black one. As Helya gazed at it through her spyglass, she saw that the black banner was a jolly roger, a flag commonly used by pirates. The red flag, however, was unfamiliar. It had a black skull with gold teeth on it, its jaws wide open as though it was silently screaming.

"Do we fire, My Lady?" Ardvald asked.

Ordinarily, the men would have already run to their battle stations. In the presence of this ship, however, they were unsure.

"No. I think this may be it," Helya said.

The ship approached slowly, alone, though the other ships still sat waiting in the fog wall. Helya couldn't make out any occupants in the darkness. Eventually, the ship came close and sidled up next to White Shark, much to Helya and her men's surprise. The ship maneuvered as though it wasn't beholden to the wind, and it came about with impossible maneuverability and precision.

"Greetings, Valkar. I had a feeling I would come across you this night," a man called out from the ship. He spoke Kurzan.

"Who goes there?" Helya called out, asking in broken Kurzan. It was not a language she spoke often, though she had been taught some of it, so that she may better read and understand the words of her prey. Her Valkar were becoming anxious.

As she got a good look at the ship, she saw that it was opulently furnished with gold trimmings and statues all over. The figurehead mounted beneath the ship's nose was a gold bust of a woman bound in chains and blindfolded. As Helya got a better look at the ship, she saw that it was covered in gold chains, serving as the shrouds and hoist lines. If she had to estimate, the ship by itself would have been worth enough to buy an army's supply of arms, armor, and provisions enough to last a year or more.

As if on cue, gold chains snaked out from the ship, fixing themselves to the side of the White Shark to anchor the two boats together. The Valkar nervously raised their weapons, as did Helya.

"Do not fret, dear. If I wanted you dead, I'd have done it by now," the voice said, and finally, a figure approached.

A gangplank dropped down from the ship, bridging between the two, and several figures emerged from the gloom. Helya tightened her grip on her spear, and Ardvald cursed as they saw them. Four figures took the lead, and one of them was nearly twice the height of a man, and broader than any man she'd ever seen. His footsteps shook the planks beneath him, and he carried with him a bloodthirsty menace that oozed from his every pore. Three of them, including the giant, flanked around the one Helya supposed was their leader. This was confirmed when he approached her directly.

"Who are you?" she asked.

"I will answer all your questions in just a moment, dear. But first, I would recommend you order your men to stand down for their own sake," the man warned.

As if on cue, a swarm of figures descended the gangplank and climbed over the ship's sides from the sea. The Valkar were—in an instant—surrounded on their own ship. Helya, Ardvald, and even some of her officers gasped in shock.

The figures that surrounded them were not men but a strange form of undead. Their skin was ashen, some even had entirely black or blue skin. It was also covered in jewelry. Some of them didn't even have eyes, but instead, glittering gems set into the sockets. Their teeth were gold, ruby, emerald, or other colorful, precious stones and metals. Their clothes were equally bespoke, covered in rope chains of silver, gold, diamond, and everything in between. It was positively excessive, but the look of pure murder on their faces killed all thoughts of taking any part of their treasured bodies and clothes.

One of the creatures, standing behind her with a sword resting on her shoulder, looked deep into her eyes. His eyes were like gold orbs that blazed with hellfire. His skin was black as a charred corpse. He pulled back his thin lips and sneered at her, revealing perfect golden teeth.

"Shall I devour her, cap'n?" The Damned croaked.

"Nay, Mr. Smith. We have need of her. Indeed, we have need of all of them," the man instructed. "If you please, madam," he said calmly.

"Stand down!" Helya snarled in her native tongue.

The Valkar quickly lowered their weapons, and the man nodded for his undead to do the same.

"Very good. Now, we make the proper introductions. I am Felix Helregal, Captain of the Flagship of Sheolhenna, Anathane's Pain. It is a pleasure to make your acquaintance, I have been told much about you," the man, Felix Helregal said with a regal bow.

He is not a man; he is something else...

Helya observed. His eyes were an unnatural, glowing red. His ashen skin gave away the fact that he, too, was undead. That gold mask…Felix Helregal, the undead pirate captain. How very strange…

"I am Helya Jottunsdottr, daughter of Jotunn Wightsbane, Warden of the North," she said. She could not hide the venom in her words at the mention of her father's name.

"The daughter of the Warden is a Valkar? How curious…" an unfamiliar voice chimed. It sounded very close, and she realized it was coming from the pulsing, glowing red amulet around Helregal's neck.

She recoiled when she realized it had a face and *eyes* that were looking right at her, smiling. Helregal palmed the amulet and smirked as well. "Do not fear him, child. He is a *friend* of mine, and any friend of mine is a friend of yours, I think you'll find."

"The Corpse Mother tells me to come here, tells me to wait. I suspect that the one I am waiting for…is *you*," Helya said, already knowing that he knew why she had come.

"Astute observation, Helya Jottunsdottr. You are correct. We abiders of death have a common cause, I believe. You wish to make the empire crumble, and I wish to kill its ruler. Aid me, and I will aid you. United, we stand stronger than ever," Helregal propositioned.

She closed her eyes and listened to the whispers of the Corpse Mother. He spoke true.

"For what reason did you call me here, Felix Helregal?"

Helregal pulled an envelope wrapped in twine from his pocket. It was sealed with a purple wax octopus insignia. "I have a message that I need you to deliver to your matriarch, Vrykul Dojadottr. In it is instructions for a plan. I need her in it. Deliver this to her personally, and your part in this will be played. It is of the utmost importance that you get this message to her in a timely manner, understand?"

Helregal held out the envelope, and she inspected it in his palm a moment before taking it. "Very good, child. You have great things in store for your future; I can sense it."

She paid it no heed and looked at his companions warily. Up close, the giant she had seen was all the more menacing. More so than even the undead that held a sword to her neck, threatening to eat her. She knew this being was no human, or El'wa, or Duwa. It was something else, and it exuded murderous intent like a cold glass on a warm afternoon.

The giant, realizing she was staring at him, smiled. His thin lips peeled back to reveal rows of serrated teeth, like some bestial, twisted mockery of a man, with slits for nostrils. The giant laughed, and his deep grumbling quaked in her chest.

"Do I scare you, little human? Have you never seen a Drakkari before?" The giant asked mockingly.

"Dra…kari?" she said, sounding the word out loud. She had never heard that one before. She was surprised the creature could even speak. The giant again laugh ed at her confusion but didn't elaborate further.

The other two figures accompanying Helregal, a short woman with a black hood and electric green eyes and tattoos, and a figure that looked little more than a pair of blackened bones shrouded in shadows, were equally ominous, but her focus kept returning to the white-skinned giant with the demonick black skull tattooed over his face.

These undead are more powerful than any that I have seen in all my years. Corpse Mother, where did you find such champions?

She received no answer. She knew it was beyond her understanding.

"I will deliver this message," Helya said flatly.

"Oh yes, child, I *know* you will," Helregal said. His words sent a chill down her spine. "There is one more task I have for you and yours, Helya Jottunsdottr. There is…a man. One who has proven a thorn in my side for quite some time. I would like for you to send a few of your ships after him. He is a formidable pirate captain—a worthy opponent for any of your finest men, I assure you. He has in his possession a relic of great power—and great importance—to our plan. Send your best officer after him and retrieve this relic for me."

"A relic? What relic?" Helya asked, confused at his request. Why did this relic matter? What was so important about it that she needed to send one of her best after it?

"An orb known as the Eye of Atla. It has immense power within it. Power that will serve us well in the coming days. Retrieve it." Helregal insisted.

Helya nodded to Ardvald, who nodded in return and stepped forth. "I will hunt this pirate captain. What is his name?" Ardvald asked in muddled Kurzan.

Helregal looked at him. "The captain's name is Morgan Sarron, the Immortal Captain. Find his ship, Azura, and you will find him. Locate him, secure the Eye of Atla, and kill him. Bring me his head," Helregal said.

Ardvald looked to Helya, who nodded once more. "It will be done, then. I will take two ships with me," he answered.

"Only two?" Helya asked.

"That is all I will need, My Lady," Ardvald assured her.

He turned to leave, and Helya placed a hand on his shoulder. He froze, then turned to look at her.

"Be safe, My Champion. The Corpse Mother is not done with you yet, and neither am I," Helya squeezed.

"Of course, My Lady," Ardvald nodded, momentarily placing his hand over hers before walking away.

"Young love. How tragic," Helregal chuckled.

Helya scowled. "Are we finished here, Captain Helregal?"

Helregal nodded. "Until we meet again, Lady Helya."

As quickly as the Damned came, they left, crawling back into the darkness of the fog and receding back out into the sea. Eventually, the fog receded as well, and with it went the blood moon, which returned to its ordinary pale blue. Helya clenched the envelope as she watched Ardvald and his ships sail off and pondered what grand scheme she now found herself in.

XXXV

THE HYDRA

He awoke with a burning pain in his shoulder as the tattoo emitted a fierce cyan light, illuminating his cabin. Pate gasped and gritted his teeth, clutching at the burning mark. He recoiled his hand, however, as it stung from his touch. He grabbed a nearby bottle of alcohol and drank it to kill the pain. After several hair-splitting minutes, it subsided, and he could think again. He got up and put his clothes and tricorn hat on, sighing at every ache and pain. He felt old.

He checked the time and saw that it was one minute to three, and felt his skin turn to goose flesh. He heard a tapping sound coming from somewhere in his cabin, but he opted to ignore it. Instead, he stepped out onto the balcony and watched the crew patrol the deck. He watched and noticed several gaps in the patrols, noting that they didn't overlap at the nose or the sides of the main deck. Left unchecked, that would leave them open, should a ship happen upon them in the dead of night, or worse, should some creature capable of crawling up the sides of the ship use that as an opportunity to sneak aboard.

It needed to be corrected.

He sighed and came down the stairs to stop them, but just as he opened his mouth, he heard Judith call out.

"Oi, pissheads—ye want to get us all killed if we get ambushed? I told you cockups earlier to close the gaps in your patrols! A damn whale could fit through the spaces you lot leave! Cap'n will have your hides, he will!" she shouted in annoyance.

The men paused and one of them dug a finger into his ear. "Quit your banshee screamin', bitch! We told ye, ye ain't the officer in charge, so ye ain't got say in how we do our rounds!"

Just then, Pate made himself known, startling all of them. "Cap'n, w-w-we was just—" the man fumbled on his words.

"Just what? Half-assin' the job, like it seems a good third of you lot are want to do? That it, McDunham? Jarvis? Louis?" he called the men out by name.

They were quiet.

"Seems like Miss Judith here is the only one who actually wants to *live* to see the Storm Tide. Maybe you lot should follow *her* lead. In fact, I think that's just what you'll do from now on. Because Miss Judith here is going to be our new quartermaster," Pate decided.

McDunham's jaw dropped, and the other two looked stunned. "S-sir—"

"That wasn't a suggestion. When I give you an order, the only thing I want to hear from your lips is 'Sir, yes sir'. Understand?" Pate said, getting up-close to McDunham's face.

The man stumbled back and nodded his head silently. The other two fell in line.

"Good. Miss Judith." Pate nodded. "Carry on."

Judith's mouth hung open. "Yes sir, right away…"

She turned to face the three lazy patrolmen with a smirk. They looked back at her in defeat.

*****

"Interesting choice, making her an officer. A bold one," Oculeth said, having watched from the steering deck railing.

"I'd been meanin' to for some time. She's more qualified than the others, that's for sure," Pate said, fully aware that Third Mate Crimp, Judith's brother, was right behind them at the wheel.

"There's sure to be a shake-up because of it. I can't imagine a female officer on a predominantly male ship is going to go over well," Oculeth said skeptically.

"Well, we've got an El'wa on the ship, 'n most folk from the empire ain't too keen on them, either. And ordinarily, you'd be right. It's why I keep most of my crew male, but we couldn't afford to be choosy so we took what men—and women—that we could. There's women pirate captains in the Storm Tide, El'wa too, and they're tougher than some of the men, in fact. If they want to be part of this, then they need to understand how this world works. Strength of mind is just as important as strength of body, here. And at sea, whether your crewman is a man, a woman, an El'wa, a Duwa, or a fuckin' Wuhlven—doesn't matter. So long as they've got your back." Pate said.

He turned and looked at Crimp, who was silently at the wheel. "Your sister is our new quartermaster, Mr. Crimp. What say ye?" Pate asked.

Crimp was unable to hide his displeasure at the news. His eyes went wide, then he frowned slightly. "Just as well, sir. She's a good sailor, come to find. She deserves it…" he said.

Pate nodded. He could read through his disguise.

"Very good sir, carry on," Pate said and nodded to Oculeth to follow him. He waited till they got out of ear shot before speaking, "He's hiding somethi— Ah!"

Pate gasped and clutched at his right arm. He leaned against the railing, trying to stave off the pain. It felt as though the sun was bearing down on his arm, cooking it. He gritted his teeth and groaned as his head swam and dozens of indecipherable whispers assaulted his ears.

He felt as though he was going mad.

"Damn it all!" he cursed.

"You've felt it too, then," Oculeth said, clutching his own arm.

"Felt it? It's been driving me mad," Pate said beneath his breath, trying to keep his voice low and resist the urge to cry out.

"It's the Call of Nyalotha, beckoning us into its embrace…" Oculeth revealed as his vision danced.

"It's done more than beckon. It's damn near scared me to death! The things I've seen, Oculeth, it's beyond the pale—"

"I've uncovered something, something that may help us break the thread— to escape the Nyalothans!" Oculeth said hurriedly. "There is an island, a place in the Southern Amaranthine in the Maaug Haunt, known as The Isle of Myths. I believe that there is a book there that can save us!"

Pate was silent for several moments, composing himself. "That's all well 'n good, Mr. Oculeth, but our destination is the Storm Tide. We'll need all the aid we can muster to take on the Dread Captain."

"Captain, if we do not do *something* about these marks, about the Nyalothans, then we may not live to face the Dread Captain!" Oculeth said.

Pate blinked away a tear as the pain subsided. He held Oculeth's gaze and saw his own fear reflected in it. "That is a risk, Mr. Oculeth, that I am willing to take. The Storm Tide takes all precedence. Every night that monster goes uncontested, countless lives are being destroyed."

"What does it matter if those lives are being destroyed? You're a pirate! You kill people for treasure!" Oculeth spat.

Pate grabbed Oculeth by his shirt and snarled at him, "You listen to me, and you listen to me good, Alyrian! Everything I do, everything I have become I did to further my cause! The people I kill, the people I rob? They've been doing the same, in a different measure, for generations! These merchants goods are bought and paid for in blood, sweat, and the labor of those less fortunate than them!"

He saw his rage-filled reflection in Oculeth's spectacles and felt the man trembling in his grip. He sighed and released him, then lifted his hat and ran a hand through his sweat-streaked hair. "I don't expect ye to understand my logic, Mr. Oculeth. If it so moves ye, I'll chart ye a boat to take you to this island. But good luck convincing them to go into the Maaug Haunt. Even I'm not mad enough to go into the territory of a Dead Sea God…"

Oculeth said nothing. He was still recovering from the pure, unfiltered rage he'd just seen in his companion's eyes.

"Goodnight, Mr. Oculeth," Pate said, then returned to his cabin.

Oculeth winced as his mark began to flare again and returned to his own quarters.

We'll never be free.

*****

With the cloudy morning came the final leg of the Duchess' journey, and her crew beheld the Storm Tide's namesake. It shook them to their core.

"We're to sail into…into *that*?" Second Mate Henry asked, quivering. "It's a damn sea tirade! It'll tear the ship apart 'n us with it!"

"It's our only way to the Storm Tide. How do you think it got its name?" Pate said.

"Cap'n, this is suicide! There's no way we can sail into that and survive!" Third Mate Crimp protested. The crew echoed his sentiments.

"He's leading us to our deaths!" Someone shouted, and the crew began to panic.

Pate let them carry on shouting and jeering for several moments as he collected his thoughts. If they didn't learn to trust his judgment, then they would never survive, not here, and certainly not in the months to come.

"If the cap'n says we can do it, then we can do it!" Judith shouted over the crowd. Several others agreed with her, including the other female crew members.

Oculeth sidled next to Pate. "Why are you letting them fight like this? Surely you have a plan to make it through the storm wall, do you not? Make it known to them!" he whispered.

Pate leaned over and whispered in his ear, "I'm seeing which way the wind blows, and sorting out who are my allies, and who is yet to be converted."

Henry, Crimp, and many the male crew were arguing against sailing into the storm. Judith, most of the female crew (who were outnumbered by the men almost three to one) and several others, including McDunham, Jarvis, Louis, and to everyone's surprise, even the El'wa, were advocating for him. It wasn't many, but it was a start.

Pate lit a cigarette, took a hit, then pulled out his pistol and fired skyward. Everybody froze and looked at him.

"...I realize you all have your concerns about what lies before us. What I ask of ye is no small leap of faith—but it is one ye must take if we are to ever survive the coming days. Ye want your fame 'n fortune? Ye gotta have faith in your cap'n 'n crew. Hesitation 'n division will undo us all, mark my words," Pate said.

"In the Sha'nav, we must follow our leaders' orders to the letter, or have our ears cut off. Do they not have such rules among you humans?" The El'wa, who they'd come to learn was named Daveth, asked.

"Depends on the crew," Pate answered. "Some are more severe than others. I like to rule through respect rather than fear."

Pate had heard of how the Imperium's navy was ran. The Imperials were strict, but fair. In the Imperium, however, a man had to follow his captain's orders to the letter, every time, or face dishonorable discharge, exile, or worse.

He pulled out a gold coin from his pocket and held it for all to see. Though they could likely not see it from a distance, it had a skull and crossbones engraved on one side.

"This coin will open the way for our traversal. It is a coin given to all captains of the Storm Tide. With it, I will part the wall so we can sail through to the island proper," Pate revealed.

Everyone collectively sighed in relief.

"See? Cap'n Pate knows what he's doin," Judith said.

Henry and Crimp looked at her begrudgingly.

"Faith, gentleman. Without it, we are nothing," Pate stated.

Just then, the ship shook as something passed under it. The man in the crow's nest shouted in alarm and rang the bell.

"Somethin' passed under the ship! Somethin' big!" the watcher shouted.

Oculeth looked at Pate. "Another test?"

Pate shook his head. "No, something worse…"

The water to the right of the ship exploded as something large breached the water. Everyone turned to face it, and several of them began to pray as a large, serpentine head rose to gaze at them.

"It's a hydra…Hermalla's mercy…" Pate said.

The creature regarded the ship as another head broke the surface.

And then another.

And another.

And another.

All told, seven heads surfaced, all near-identical in appearance, all towering high enough to reach the main deck and gaze down at its occupants. The creatures regarded the men with porthole-sized, slitted eyes that blinked away rivulets of water streaming down from the massive heads. Each of the serpent heads were easily the length and size of a horse-drawn carriage. The lead head, sitting a few feet higher than the others, flicked out its serpentine, forked tongue, and scented the air. A large dorsal fin, running from the tip of its snout down its back, flexed and fanned open. This made the already large and intimidating creature appear even larger and made several men jump.

"Daveth, get below deck into the stern of the ship and stay there until we summon ye," Pate whispered into the El'wa's ear.

"Sir, I would rather fight than—" Daveth protested.

"If ye die here then your story dies with ye, and our chances of avenging yer comrades dwindles," Pate stated.

Daveth, biting his tongue, nodded. "Yes, sir." He slowly crept toward the stairs leading down into the lower compartments.

The other hydra heads sat stationary, fins folded, flicking their tongues, and blinking occasionally but remaining otherwise stock-still. The men were beside themselves, shivering with fear, and many of them were mumbling prayers out loud. The finned hydra's head appraised them, blinking slowly and flicking its tongue. The creature easily kept pace with the ship. This thought terrified Pate, as he knew that it was likely much faster.

"What do we do?" Oculeth asked worriedly.

He'd read of hydras before, but hoped he'd never meet one in person. The giant sea serpents were theorized to be relatives of dragons, and looking at one in the flesh, he could see how. Its heads resembled dragons, albeit more serpentine in appearance and mannerisms. It also had vibrant, brightly colored aquamarine scales. He also caught a glimpse of the indigo underside of its body. The fact that the creature hadn't attacked yet gave him hope that a fight could be averted. He'd read enough to know that they were ill-equipped to combat such a beast, now. The cannons weren't numerous or strong enough to destroy it, and pirate ships didn't come equipped with the armaments that the Mygredo's ships had.

The main head began to hiss at the men, swaying its body side to side, head sitting perfectly in place.

"Oh no..." Pate gasped. "Ready the cannons," he ordered, keeping his voice even.

"Sir?" Oculeth asked, confused.

"That's a threat display telling us to leave its territory. If we don't turn around in the next few seconds, it's going to attack!" Pate said. "Ready the damn cannons!"

The men moved to their attack positions, and the finned head fixed them with a glare and a grumble. Its nostrils flared, and everyone watched in confusion as it took in a deep breath.

No, no, no, no,no!

"Get out the way, it's about to—"

It opened its jaws wide, flashing its arm-length, hooked teeth. It depressed its tongue, and an opening at the top of the throat winked at them before spewing a geyser of steaming water at the ship. The crew in its path didn't even have time to react before the spray washed over them, blasting them to the deck, into crates, and for some, over the side of the ship. After about five seconds, the spray ceased, leaving a cloud of steam and screaming bodies. One of the unlucky crewmen stumbled out of the steam cloud.

Pate held back the urge to vomit while a woman let out a high-pitched scream.

"It's Jarvis...dear gods..." Oculeth gasped.

The man had been boiled alive, his clothes were absolutely sodden and destroyed. His exposed skin was the color of a boiled lobster. His eyes, milky and blind, stared from a wrinkled, partially caved-in head as he opened his mouth. "AAAAAAAAAAAHHHHHHH!!!!" Jarvis screeched, blood and water dribbled from his lips as he clutched at himself with melted fingers.

In a flash, the finned hydra head launched forward and snapped the man up in its jaws.

"FUCKING SHOOT IT!" Pate shouted at the top of his lungs.

The cannons fired at the hydra.

*****

"Take cover!" Pate shouted.

Judith scrambled behind the main mast as another wash of geyser-hot water sprayed across the deck. She hissed as the steam cloud licked her, and covered her face and hands in her coat, making herself as small as possible. When the spray stopped, she took off running from her cover, stepping over writhing, boiled bodies as she made for below deck and the armory.

The din of the cannon fire was deafening, but it was preferable to the sound of the hydra breathing boiling-hot death on her comrades. She could smell the boiled flesh and could hear the screams of the dying, even from down here.

"What's the situation above deck?" Henry asked, having taken control of the gun crews.

"It's a fucking massacre! Get to the armory and arm yourselves!" she shouted, charging past everyone to the armory door. She shoved open the door and fumbled for the first weapon she saw. A spear. She grabbed it, then braced herself as something slammed into the side of the ship, shaking it. She grabbed a flintlock pistol, a knife, and then a short sword, then holstered all of it before fumbling to load a shot into the flintlock.

A mighty roar echoed through the walls, and she paused as another bombardment of cannon fire went off. Finished loading the pistol, she ran back out the armory room just as the others began filing in at the door.

"Move it!" she shouted, shoving everyone out the way as she made her way to the stairs. "Send men up above to fight the creature. People are getting slaughtered up there!" she instructed Henry.

"Fight the hydra? Are you mad?! The cannons are barely working against it! What's a spear and a few pistol bullets going to do other than piss it off?!"

"Fuck if I know, but I gotta try! You really gonna let your brethren get eaten because you're too yellow to fight for them?" she goaded.

"I ain't yellow, I just don't wanna die!" Henry shouted frantically.

"Ye think I do, mate?! I watched my friends get boiled alive 'n eaten! Think I'm not pissin' me knickers right now? The fuck I am, but I don't wanna die so I gotta do what needs doin', otherwise we'll all be hydra shit in a few hours!" she said, then bolted up the stairs. She took a deep breath, tried to calm herself down, then went back out into the fray.

"Crazy bitch…" Henry shook his head. He turned to his men and nodded. "Well, boys… it's time to work."

*****

Pate dodged out the way as one of the heads made a go at him. He stabbed it with his cutlass and let it drag along the blade. A gout of purple blood sprayed him and the deck as the head retracted, and the hydra hissed in pain. He watched as several more heads launched and grabbed people, cutting them in half or swallowing them whole.

It's toying with us…

At any moment, the creature could close the gap and grab onto the side of the ship. Its sheer bulk would be enough to flip everybody above deck over the side and into its killing grounds. Instead, the main head sat back, and the others lunged at the ship, biting at crewmen and slamming into the ship.

There isn't a damn thing I can do about it, either.

The cannons were largely missing the creature, and the ones that hit didn't seem to be phasing it, even as blood spurted from cannonball-sized puncture wounds. Their weapons were too small and weak to cause it any real harm. It had happened upon the perfect target. Why was it just camped outside the storm wall? Wasn't it afraid of the sea tirade? Or had it realized that if it simply lingered in the area for long enough it would happen upon a ship that couldn't overpower it. Were these creatures smart enough to do that? To plan?

"Look out, cap'n!" Judith called out.

He turned to see that one of the heads had taken aim at him again—and was about spew boiling water at him. Judith grabbed him and flung them both down the stairs. They tumbled, slamming into steps and ballister slats as they fell. When he opened his eyes he saw that he was pressed down on top of her, and the two locked eyes a moment as he got up and helped her up.

"My thanks," he said quickly before turning to watch the creature's movements.

"Your welcome, cap'n," she replied, pulling out her spear as another of the heads made a go at them.

They both sidestepped the creature's lunge, and Judith speared it. It recoiled with a hiss and took the spear with it.

"Damn, it took my fuckin' spear," she said.

The pair watched in fascination as the finned head carefully removed the spear with its teeth, ripping it out the neck of the other head. Pate was chilled by its intelligence. The finned head turned to face them, fixed them with an unreadable stare, flicked its tongue, then shot forward in tandem with three other heads.

"Shit!" Judith shouted.

"Get out the way!" Pate said, this time he was the one to grab her, and pulled her into cover behind the stairs they'd fallen down. The creatures narrowly missed them, but nabbed several unlucky crewmen before spraying several more gouts of boiling water across the ship. They watched helplessly as the men screamed for help, and then were summarily torn to pieces by the hydra heads.

"We can't beat it…it's goin' to tear us all limb from limb," Judith said in dispair as she watched the many-headed creature play with its food.

Pate said nothing. They were nearing the storm wall, though, and with it they had hope. If he could get to the nose of the ship and flash his coin without getting eaten, the storm wall would open, and they could escape the creature within. That was over a hundred feet away, across a clustered and treacherous deck, however.

"I need to get across the deck," Pate said. "If I can reach the nose of the ship, I can open the storm wall and we can pass through it."

"How the hells are ye gonna do that? This thing wants our blood, its chompin' folk left 'n right," Judith said.

Pate pulled out his double barrel pistol and a grenade.

"If I can get it to eat this, then I can blow it and use that as a distraction to get across the deck," he offered.

"How the fuck are ye gonna get it to eat a fuckin' grenade without eatin' you too?"

She was right.

The grenade was too small for the creature to pay any mind, and he'd need it to grab it in its jaws in order to detonate it. He scanned around, looking for something big enough and appetizing enough to get it to take the bait

A crate? No, it was wooden, and from what he'd seen the creature wasn't dumb enough to go for that, not by itself. No, he needed something organic to entice it. The livestock below deck could do the trick, but he'd still have to cross the deck to get to the livestock hold.

Think, think, think…

The creature would obviously go for him, but that would be suicide, as it would be for anyone.

Wait.

He spied a body on the deck a few meters away from them. One of the men had been sprayed by the boiling water and was succumbing to his wounds on the deck. Pate had a dark thought.

I can't. It'd be immoral—just let him die in peace.

But if he didn't, then they would all die. The others still had a chance to live, but anyone who'd been scolded by the hydra's breath was doomed to a slow and agonizing death. No, he had to do it.

"I've got it…" Pate said quietly as the hydra let out another spray, and more people screamed in horror as they were scolded.

"What are you—" Judith began, seeing him gazing at the dying man.

He gave her no time to ask. He sprinted, then dove at him. He gazed into his blind eyes as he mumbled to himself.

"Mommy…mommy…please make it stop, i-it…it hurts, Mom, it…" He babbled. A tear streaked down his cheek, and it sizzled on his skin, joining the cloud of steam emanating from his body.

"I'm sorry, son…" Pate said as he pulled out the grenade and looked over at the hydra. The finned head locked eyes with him and pulled back its lips, baring its fangs as the sail fin flexed. It was about to lunge.

No time to waste.

He lit the fuse and put it in the mumbling man's hands.

"Cap'n? Is that you…" he said, semi-coherent.

Pate looked closer and realized it was Henry.

"Oh, Xalhanna…forgive me…" Pate muttered as he placed the lit grenade in the man's hand.

"What is…what are you doin', sir?" Henry asked as Pate lifted him to his feet.

Pate bit back the tears he felt coming on and raised the man, whimpering and wailing to his feet. He could hear his bones snapping and his flesh sloughing off. The smell was nauseating. "What needs to be done," he said finally, choking back his emotions.

"It hurts! It hurts, please! Make it stop!" Henry whimpered pitifully.

"Gonna make it go away, Henry, gonna make it—"

The maw of the hydra-head opened wide and closed in, and Pate stared directly into the jaws of death.

"I'm sorry, Mr. Henry…" Pate whispered as he thrust the body into the maw of the hydra—and barely got out the way.

The jaws clamped shut, leaving only Henry's clenched fist exposed. And the grenade with it. As the creature pulled back out to the water, Pate took aim as a tear fought through and slid down his cheek at what he'd done.

"I hope this hurts," he growled.

He fired both barrels and struck the grenade.

It detonated with immediate effect.

The heads of the hydra cried out in pain as the main head was blown open by the explosion. The bottom jaw, hanging by a few loose tendons to the base of the neck, flapped. Most of the skull had been blown apart, leaving a wet, purple-blooded mess that flopped back and forth before falling into the water. As the creature reeled from the painful blow, Pate made it to the nose of the ship and pulled out his coin.

As if on command, the clouds in the sky parted, and a shaft of sunlight struck the skull face of the coin. It emitted a loud, reverberating ring, and after several tense moments, the storm wall began to part.

"It worked! Stars above, it worked!" One of the men rejoiced. "We're gonna live!"

"I wouldn't get so excited just yet, look over there," Judith shouted, pointing at the hydra.

Pate turned slowly to see all the hydra heads screaming in unison as the stump of the finned hydra head split open to reveal two new, identical heads forming within. In seconds, the bloody stump of the old head fell away, and the two fresh ones, covered in a milky blue film, opened their eyes and mouths, tearing free. They raised their dorsal fins and roared in unison with the other heads.

The hydra charged at the ship.

*****

They were quickly overtaken. In less than ten seconds, the hydra closed the gap and raised its front legs onto the back of the Duchess, grabbing hold of her and shaking people to the floor as it dug its claws into the wood. The heads surged forward in a frenzy, winding around the ship and into the shrouds, biting and tearing at sails, snapping ropes, and ripping men in half.

"We're all dead! We're all—" A sailor screamed but was promptly silenced in the jaws of the hydra's heads.

Pate pulled out his cutlass once more.

They wouldn't make it into the Storm Tide. Not with this creature holding onto them.

So be it.

Pate stepped down the stairs of the forecastle calmly and picked up a discarded axe, making his way toward the hydra's heads. As men screamed and were devoured, he was calm, and strode toward his fate. As the two finned hydra heads lunged at him, he sprinted forward, ready to fight—and die.

A blast of blue light stopped him dead in his tracks, and when its blinding light ceased, he saw that the hydra heads had been destroyed, leaving boiling stumps.

"What…"

He saw another spear of strange blue light and saw Oculeth launch it at the hydra's heads, obliterating another one.

"What good is hiding my powers if we're going to be eaten anyway?!" Oculeth shouted as he launched another spear of energy. He threw them with both hands, one after the other, as his eyes blazed with Alyria and his tattoos glowed, shining through his clothes.

The hydra was taken by surprise, and the heads scattered, some of them still trying to attack the crew while others lunged away, not wishing to be destroyed. He smote them all, and a mass of boiling, bloody stumps were all that remained of them as he formed a blade of pure energy and slashed at one of the

378

hydra's claws, causing it to release the ship as the creature fell back into the water with a gigantic splash, rocking the ship and releasing it.

The men cheered once more, and some even grabbed Oculeth, raising him into the air as they sailed to safety through the storm. Pate and Judith went to the back of the ship and stared over the railing where the hydra had sank back into the water.

"That kill it?" Judith asked.

"Nay, all that did was piss it off. Those heads will all grow back with twice as many to count, and the next ship that runs into it is goin' to have a hell of a time puttin' it down," Pate sighed.

"What the fuck do ye have to do to kill one of those things, then?" Judith asked.

"Destroy their body. Whatever strange power hydras use to regenerate their heads resides there," Pate said. "I'll tell the Brethren Court they've a hydra problem."

He started walking away.

"Cap'n," Judith said, stopping him.

He turned. "Quartermaster?"

Judith locked eyes with him. They both were drenched in the blood of the hydra, and both were shaken by what they'd just seen. "I trust your judgment."

Pate regarded her a moment, wiped the blood from his face, and looked up at the cloudy sky. "Aye…"

XXXVI

ARRIVAL IN LIVERA

A tropical paradise was before their eyes, but the crew of the Duchess couldn't see beyond the haze of their grief.

They had only been at sea for six weeks.

Until this moment, many of the sailors had never seen the true dangers of the open ocean. Sailor's tales and second-hand accounts simply didn't do it justice.

"That thing...devoured our brethren like candy," Crimp said, barely keeping his composure as he threw a sheet over yet another body. He couldn't even tell who it was, their face had been so badly scalded by the hydra that it was unrecognizable.

"How many dead?" Judith asked.

"Thirty, that we can tell," Crimp said.

"We need to reach the port town, Livera. We can take stock of our dead and regroup once we've made it there," Pate said, looking out at the coastline.

Crimp gave him a scornful look from behind and turned back to the corpse in front of him. He couldn't even tell who it was. "We've got men missing as well."

"Missing? How many?" Judith asked. There was a sinking feeling in her gut now.

"Twelve. Can't find them, and nobody's seen them since..." Crimp trailed off.

"If they're unaccounted for they're dead. The hydra likely swallowed them or knocked them into the sea. Either way, they won't be coming back," Pate declared.

"We can't be sure!" Crimp spat. Several men stood up in agreement with him.

"Can't we?" Pate said, turning to face him now. "And how do you figure they survived? This ship is big, but not so big that a man can't be found. So clearly, they aren't on board. Best case scenario they fell into the sea, either trying to evade the hydra or trying to escape altogether."

"We could still save them if we turn back, then! We could—"

"Are we going to cut open the hydra and fish them out? Because that's what became of them, I assure you."

"We killed it—First Mate Oculeth killed it!" Crimp shouted. The men agreed.

"No, First Mate Oculeth incapacitated it by cutting all its heads off. That didn't kill it," Pate said.

He could see the shock on their faces. Judith, already knowing the answer, leaned back against the railing, staring at the fallen.

"What we just faced was a sea hydra. Hydras regrow not one but two heads when one is cut off or damaged. We faced seven heads, then I destroyed one, and two more grew in its place. Mr. Oculeth cut off nine heads. That means that the same hydra now has *eighteen* heads. It will be angry, it will be hungry, and it will have immediately devoured any men left in the water, as well as any creature it could get its claws on afterward. They're dead and half-digested by now."

Everyone was silent; seagulls cawed in the distance.

Pate pulled a half-finished cigarette from his pocket and lit it. He needed to calm his nerves.

"That, gentlemen, is but one of the legions of creatures lurking out there in the open ocean. They are numerous, they are unpredictable, and they are *lethal*. They see us, and everyone like us as food. If we are to survive threats like *that*, as well as our own, then we must band together. You must listen to me and listen well. Otherwise? The next time a hydra or any other monster strikes, it will devour us all," Pate stated flatly.

He grabbed a sheet and threw it over the body Crimp had been staring at. He looked briefly at the man's boots and recalled who it was. "This was Mr. Louis," Pate said.

Crimp covered his face with his hands. Judith placed a consoling hand on her brother's shoulder, but he shrugged it off. She sighed in defeat.

"Everyone, make ready to port. There'll be pirates and cutthroats much tougher than any of you in Livera, and you'll need to look the part if you want to avoid them taking advantage," Pate said.

The crew begrudgingly returned to their work.

"We'll mourn and bury our dead once we've made safe harbor. They deserve a better send-off than a few white sheets and a toss into the drink," he added.

"Cap'n, I think I found one of the missing…" Judith said in a low voice.

Pate looked up, following her gaze, and gasped. The faceless man sat tangled in the ropes above, looking down at him. He blinked, and it was replaced with the face of a crewman.

But I could've swore…

He thought back on what Oculeth had said about the Isle of Myths and wondered if he'd made the correct call.

✳✳✳✳✳

Oculeth sat at his chair, panting as though he'd ran five miles at top speed. He felt as though he did. His lungs burned, his vision was blurring, and he tasted copper on his tongue.

And then the pain flared.

He gasped. He felt the mark on his shoulder burst to life. He stripped his jacket, then his shirt and undershirt off, feeling as though he was cooking in his clothes. When he was done, his Alyria tattoos and the mark of eternal return glowed a bright aquamarine. The whispers echoed in his head like the gong of a church bell and he was deafened by their cries.

"Come to us!"

"You are mine!"

"Your soul is claimed!"

"Cry out Her Name!"

Different voices, some male, some female, all shouted at him, deafening him. He could feel them clawing at him from the inside, like phantom fingers dancing along flesh, or spider's legs.

"Enough!" he shouted, swiping his arms out before himself and silencing the voices as he panted.

Begrudgingly, they fell silent.

He knew they would return, however. They always did, and soon they would come, not just with words and knocks but with shadows and violence. He ran a hand over the mark of eternal return. Two black and white serpents circled around each other with four lines coming out of the corners. The serpents represented life and death. What the rest of the symbol meant, however, was lost to him. The mark was hot to the touch, hotter than the rest of his burning body. He felt ill. He just wanted to be free; that was all he ever wanted. Free to live as he wanted, free to study Alyria, and its beautiful magicks. Free to find love…

But he knew that to be Alyrian was to be hounded for your own nature. By the Consortium, by frightened banals, and by those that coveted their power.

Freedom…that's all I've ever wanted…

For now, the crew was thankful for his powers, but soon their gratefulness would turn to thanklessness, and they would turn on him in fear. His only hope was that the pirates of Livera were more accepting of one with his gifts than Pate and his men had been.

It doesn't matter. All that matters is that I charter a ship for the Maaug Haunt and find this tome.

He flipped through one of the books sitting on his table, titled "Gods of the Old World". He hoped and prayed that its words were true, and that the island was real. If it wasn't, if he couldn't find the tome with the purple begonia flower, then…

Someone knocked on his door.

"First Mate Oculeth, sir? We're nearing port. The captain requests your presence," he heard Crimp say from the other side.

"Yes, Mr. Crimp. Right away," Oculeth answered.

He grabbed a fresh shirt and put it on, rolling up the sleeves and leaving the top buttons undone to give himself some breathing room. He flipped the book closed, tied back his hair, and stepped back out into the midday sun.

*****

"Fly the jolly roger. Everyone remain calm and avoid sudden movements and *do not* reach for anything in yer pockets.," Pate said sharply.

"Sir?" Crimp asked, confused.

Pate pointed toward a large fort atop a cliff overlooking the coastline. "Over there? That's Fort Freedom. It's packing more cannons than ye can count 'n they've got the poundage to turn a man 'o war into poxed cheese. If we don't raise that jolly and play nice, they'll unload the fort on us and we'll be shark chum."

"All the way over there?" Crimp said. "They can barely even see us, let alone shoot—"

A geyser of water shot up next to the ship as something large and fast narrowly missed them.

"That was a warning shot! Do it now!" Pate ordered.

The men followed suit, hoisting the flag, and keeping an eye in the direction of the fort. Thankfully, it didn't fire any more shots on their approach, though Pate could see through his spyglass that someone in the fort was watching them. He wondered if they recognized him. It'd been over a year and a half since he'd last made an appearance here, and he had six ships with him at the time.

But now...

The memory of Brunt shot through his mind like a shooting star, and he felt fresh determination and rage fill him.

"Listen up!" he shouted at the top of his lungs, startling the crew.

"When we get to port, I want all of you wax-eared children to listen to me and listen well. I've said more times than I can count that to make it as pirates you'll have to listen to me. Well, consider this your last warning. When we reach that port a horde of pirates is going to be waiting to sniff us out and figure out who we are and what we're about. If you fold, if you show weakness, and if you are not keeping your eyes peeled at all times, you *will* be killed. Understand?"

Some of them nodded, many simply stared at him. He could tell that they were frightened by all they'd been through. They probably resented him for inadvertently leading them into the hydra attack, but none of that mattered now. The Storm Tide was not a place for the weak, the meek, or the stupid. The pirates here were some of the most ruthless, efficient, and dangerous that this world had to offer.

Pate folded his arms behind his back and walked the deck. "You've made it this far, so you have some grit in you. Well, so does every pirate on this island. They've all killed people with it. There is no law here, only loyalty and respect will keep you alive in Livera. And I am your only shot at getting through your first night alive. I am proud of what you've done so far. Ye survived an ordeal that most men would be broken by. But that is just one of many trials to come. Follow me and ye will be rich beyond your wildest dreams and become pirates of legend. But first ye must *learn to survive.*"

After a brief pause, Judith stepped up. "Aye aye, cap'n."

Seeing his sister take the lead, Crimp stepped up as well. "Aye aye, cap'n!"

Oculeth stepped forward, nodding to Pate. "Yes, captain."

Soon, every man and woman on the deck stepped forward and voiced their agreement. Pate didn't show it, but a wave of pride and relief went through him. Perhaps they would live, after all. Now, they needed to make port.

*****

"Remember, El'wa, you're a pirate, just like us. Got it?" Pate asked.

"Pirate? I am a proud Sha'nav officer! To lower myself to such drudgery would be—" Daveth gasped.

"If ye tell them who you really are they'll have all of us strung up in the square by sunset. So, before I let you off this ship, I need to know you won't be a problem. Otherwise, I'm going to have to hogtie you and throw you back into the brig." Pate said.

"A pirate—yes of course!" Daveth said.

"Good," Pate said. "I only want about twenty men or so going into town with us for now. If we don't keep people on the ship at all times, we won't have a ship—mark my words."

They anchored the ship amongst the hundreds docked at the port. The docks stretched for miles in each direction, and more than once the crew of the Duchess gasped in awe at the ships they'd passed. Some were bigger, others smaller, but they all came in different shapes and sizes and with heraldry and decorations that ranged from regal to daunting. Xallan ships, Dyonian ships, Brovan, Atarran, El'wa, Duwa, and even Wuhlven ships were moored here.

"I haven't seen so many ships in one place in my entire life…" Crimp said in awe, pointing at a ship with a wolf's head on the flag. "Those men, they're carrying crates single-handed—how?!"

Pate looked over as they readied to disembark. He saw several humans, standing around and talking to one another, occasionally glancing in their direction. There were men and women, and several of them were, in fact, holding barrels and crates, slinging them over their shoulders, or holding them in their arms as they spoke. He caught a glimpse of one of the females' eyes when she glanced in their direction, and Pate knew exactly who they were.

"That's because they're Wuhlven," he said.

The crew were mesmerized. It was doubtful any of them had ever laid eyes on a Wuhlven in their entire lives. Crimp opened his mouth to speak, but a group of men approached them as they made their way down the dock, and Pate motioned for them to pause.

"Can we help ye, mate?" Pate asked.

The head of the group, a smiling man with a few missing teeth and breath that reeked of alcohol looked the group over before responding. "Brought a few lost lambs to the Storm Tide, ay? Gotta pay a fee for that, 'n we're here to collect," the man said with a smirk. "And what's this? Fuck is an El'wa doin' with you lot?"

Everyone turned to look at Daveth, and Pate placed a finger to his lips, motioning for him to keep quiet.

"Ah, yes, well, I come from a long line of sailo—pirates! My family is all pirates, actually! Ha, it's our family trade, you see!" Daveth stammered, nearly outing himself.

"Family trade, ay? What's your last name, then?" The lead pirate asked, scratching his chin.

"Ah, you wouldn't know of us, friend, we weren't a very notorious lot, you see. Small timers, really," Daveth said.

The pirate looked skeptically at his comrades.

"Small timers…aye. So why ain't you with them, then? 'Case ye weren't aware, knife-ear, these is all humans," he said.

"Indeed, they are! Well, you see, my old crew had a bit of a misfortune. A kraken attack, you see—killed all of us, would've killed me too if I hadn't been smart enough to hide myself in a barrel! Ha!" Daveth said, laughing loudly and clapping Judith on the back, who looked at him like he had two heads.

"…So ye got saved by these n's here, and decided to shack up with them? Odd, never known El'wa to take much stock in humans, 'less they're fuckin' them, that is. All a part of their *grand* plan to expand the Imperium across the world, they say. That your plan, knife-ear? You fuckin' one of these n's?" The pirate pressed.

Daveth began to laugh again, squeezing Judith's arm for support. "Help me," he whispered.

"Aye, uh…yeah. He's uh…he's fuckin' some of the girls, yeah," Judith said, making sure not to make eye contact with any of them.

"That so?" The pirate asked, unable to hide his surprise. "Hear that, lads? This knife-ears gotten himself a wee harem of whores to fuck at sea!"

The other pirates laughed, and Pate palmed his face. He could tell the pirates weren't buying the story; they were just having a laugh at their expense.

"If you're done flapping your jaws, we've business to attend," Pate interrupted.

The lead pirate looked at Pate and the smile fell from his face. "What's your story, then? Ye look a might familiar, mate. Ye've been here before, ain't ye? Had to be. You're the only one out of these cockwits who look like they'd have a coin on them. That'd make you a cap'n, then," the lead pirate sniffed.

"What I am 'n who I am ain't really none of your business, mate. I'm here, so obviously I've got the right to be here, or we'd have never made it past the storm. Now piss off," Pate dismissed. He pushed past the man but was barred by his entourage.

"On to the matter of the toll, then," the lead pirate echoed from behind him.

It was Pate's turn to smirk, now. "Funny that, because when I was here a year and a half ago with my fleet, I ain't see you here, then, and I sure as fuck don't remember any tax for new arrivals on the isle. Does Captain Marcellus know about this, then?" Pate challenged, looking the man in the eyes. The man was tall, close to six and a half feet, but Pate stood in front of him, unconcerned.

"Ye know Cap'n Marcellus, do ye? Well, I don't recall him tellin' me anythin' about a mouthy lubber like you—"

"Captain Marcellus knows my name well enough not to tarnish it by saying it to whoresons like you, that's for damn sure. Now piss off, before I show you what happens to pirates who try to slight me," Pate cut him off, waving his hand dismissively before walking away. "With me."

They pushed past the flustered pirates and carried on. Pate could feel the pirate's eyes burning holes through the back of his head. "And tell whatever fool captain you're under to get a new racket. We're pirates, for stars' sake. Leave the tolls to bandits 'n highwaymen."

Oculeth, Judith, Daveth and Crimp looked at the disrespected pirate with wide eyes as they walked past, and the man who'd tried to tax them spit at their feet in anger, grumbling to himself. Several other pirates fell in around the man, whispering among themselves and eyeing Pate.

A decorated-looking pirate with scars crisscrossing over his face and a large tricorn hat approached the Duchess crew, locking eyes with Pate and smiling warmly at the man, welcoming him with open arms.

"Well if it ain't the saltiest seadog above the waves, Captain Edward Patron, as I live 'n breathe!" The man cackled, embracing Captain Pate, who embraced him in turn.

"Marcellus Teach, as I live 'n breathe. Still ugly as a seahag's ass, I see," Pate grinned.

"Still as fire-tongued as a dragon. It's nice to see that some things never change," Captain Marcellus replied.

"Some things, but not all, it would seem," Pate sighed, looking around and nodding to Captain Marcellus. "Shall we have a chat, old friend?"

Pate motioned to a tavern further down the way. It had pirates pushing in and out its doorways, and mounted on its front face was a large wooden sign with the words 'Storm Brew' painted on it.

"Aye, I believe it's time to parlay."

*****

The tavern was abuzz with life. Pirates, big and small, were dancing, drinking, and chatting at the bar. Humans and Duwa sat, playing drinking games with one another. El'wa talked amongst themselves, some laughing at the humans and Duwa drinking, others talking about matters completely removed. Wuhlven conversed with one another over full mugs of beer, playing dice, cards, and other activities of leisure. Barmaids and bartenders bustled about, taking orders, conversing with customers, and talking to one another as well. The front door opened as the crew of the Duchess filtered into the tavern.

"Eat, drink, mingle, whatever. I'll gather you lot later. And mind your company. These ain't De Morta folk. First Mate Oculeth, Third Mate Crimp, Quartermaster Judith keep an eye on the crew. If anything should go awry it's on your heads. If someone tries to give you trouble, tell them that Edward Patron will see them shortly," Pate said, nodding to his officers before following Marcellus.

Captain Marcellus walked over to the bar and a freckle-faced barmaid wearing a bandana over her head regarded him with a nod and wink. "Captain Marcellus, to what do we owe the pleasure? And is that Edward Patron that I see?" The woman asked in her naturally husky voice. "It's been too long, dearie."

"Tilly," Pate said with a smile and a tip of his tricorn hat, "nice to see you haven't lost your looks, dearie."

"The sea may churn and time may turn, dear, but so long as potions exist and this tavern is open for business, I'll not stop turning heads," she joked proudly.

"Tilly, dear, Edward 'n I are goin' in the back. See to it that we aren't disturbed, savvy?" Marcellus asked.

"Aye, Cap'n. No one will disturb you so long as Boris is here." She pointed to a stocky, tall gorilla of a man standing near the hearth at the back of the tavern. The gorilla of a man nodded to them reassuringly, winking and then placing a hand on the cutlass on his hip.

"That man could scare the piss out of a tiger," Pate chuckled. "What I wouldn't do to have a couple Boris' on my ship."

"Last I saw, you had more than a few men meaner lookin' than Boris in your fleet," Marcellus pointed out.

"Aye, that… let's go into the back."

The men went into the back room behind the bar. Pate scanned the room a moment, observing that Tilly still used it for storage, as it was filled with boxes, crates, a table, two shelves on opposing sides of the room, and a mirror to one side, across from the window. Marcellus pulled out two chairs and set them up by the table. Pate sat down and Marcellus went over to a nearby cabinet. "Let me see if it's still here…" he paused for several seconds as he rummaged through, looking for something. "Ah, here we are!" he pulled out a box and blew the dust off it, then sat it on the table.

"This old thing's still here? I'd figured Tilly'd have used it all up by herself by now," Pate admitted.

"You 'n me both, mate."

Marcellus opened the plain brown wooden box to reveal several pouches of a strong-smelling substance and rolls of paper.

"Still smoke hemestra, Eddy? Or d'ya get soft with time?"

"Sheolhenna'll freeze over before I go soft," Pate said.

"Aye. Ye might be the one bloke I actually believe when they say that," Marcellus said, pulling out a lighter and flicking it on before lighting the cigar he'd just rolled.

"When'd ya get that fancy piece, there?" Pate asked, a bit jealous. He always wanted a gold-plated lighter.

"Fleeced it from some merchant we raided a year or so back, shortly after you lot sailed off," he replied, taking a puff of his cigar before handing the lighter to Pate, who'd rolled his cigar, but was now attentively playing with the lighter, flipping it open and shut, and pressing down the little clip that ignited the flame. He watched it spark in and out of existence with the flick of his finger, then picked up the cigar to watch it ignite, inhaling the scent of the burning herb. He sucked in its earthy fragrance and exhaled a gout of white smoke into the room, joining the clouds that his friend made.

"Lucky find, that." Pate sighed, content now.

"So, Eddy. I seen that tub you sailed in on. Tell me what happened to the Hail Mary," Marcellus deadpanned, taking on a concerned tone.

Pate grew silent, smoking his cigar for a moment as he tried to formulate an answer. He'd been trying to figure out how he was going to say it to the Brethren Court. How could he explain that his whole fleet had been wiped out by the undead?

"There's a hydra that's taken roost just outside the storm wall. We managed to injure it, but not kill it. We didn't have the weaponry for it," Pate began.

"Must've been a straggler from the southern migration. Probably saw a ship and thought it'd be easy pickings, then opted to stay when it proved true," Teach said. "We've had a few ships go missing of late, now we know what got to them. I'll alert the brethren court. I'm surprised that dingy ye came here on was able to survive a beast like that. You're an exceptional cap'n, Eddy."

Pate waved his hand. "Can't take all the credit. Me crew came through, and an Alyrian in our ranks did most of the work of downing the beast."

"An Alyrian? Fortune favors ye, brother, that could be a game changer for your new crew," Teach said.

Pate thought back to the visions of the faceless man, and the man-eating livestock in his fever dream—and that talking corpse.

"Or a nightmare. Time will tell…" Pate trailed.

"Aye, I know too well. I've had an Alyrian or two in me crew before. They're deadly in a fight, but they're just as dangerous outside one, as well…"

"Aye," Pate agreed, taking another hit from the cigar before passing it to Teach. "…There's been an incident."

"An incident? What kind of incident?"

"…I…" Pate sighed in frustration.

"Come on, mate, we've been like brothers for years, we've sailed together. You can tell me, ye know that," Marcellus pressed, putting a hand on Pate's.

Pate's hands were cold and clammy to the touch. "Your hands are cold as a corpse, mate."

Cold as a corpse.

"If I told you, Marcellus, you'd think me mad… but I am not, and I must," Pate said, taking a thoughtful pull on his cigar. "Tell me. What do you know of ghost ships?"

"Ghost ships?" Marcellus repeated, confused. "Eh, the same as any pirate, I suppose. There's the Hulk of Shan-Zin, the Ghost Slavers of the Chain Lands, the Barquentine of Baghwam, and other such stories."

"Stories, ay? Well, what if I told you I'd ran across one from the stories. And it wasn't nearly as hyperbolic as Captain Ursaal had led us to believe?" Pate asked.

Marcellus laughed. "You mean to tell me a ghost ship sunk your whole fleet, Eddy? C'mon, now. Be serious with me—"

"I'm serious as the hangman's noose. No navy fleet could get the drop on us. You know my methods. I keep scouts watching every horizon, twenty-four hours a day at sea. You'd need a naval fleet to sink me, and a fleet's too damned large to sneak up on Hail Mary."

"So, a ghost killed Brunt 'n them? A fucking ghost, Edward? Do you know how mad that sounds?!" Marcellus asked.

"Mad as a hatter, I'd imagine. But true all the same, I promise you on my life."

Marcellus looked at Pate with scrutiny, searching his face for a hint of the joke.

But there was none.

"A ghost ship… by the Stars, Edward… you're serious, aren't you?" Marcellus asked, the sincerity of his words sinking in. "How do you know it was a ghost? You could be mistaken, it could be a rogue, it could be—"

"Red sails with a black, gold-toothed skull. Gold chains behind it, like the crossbones of a jolly roger. You remember that flag, brother? You remember whose it was?" Pate asked, reciting the description from memory.

Teach was silent, his skin going pale.

"Let me finish, then. A ship, nearly the size of a man 'o war, with gold chains for shrouds. They say that it only appears after dark and that it's heralded by a blood moon. Her captain is neither dead nor alive, cursed to wander the seas until the end of days. They say he once ruled Kurza as a king, and held the world in a vice. Sound familiar?"

Teach leaned forward in his chair. "Edward, you can't mean to tell me—The Dread Captain? He's dead and gone, has been for a century—he's just a—"

"A ghost story? Yeah, I thought the same damn thing, Marcellus. Then I saw him. We was out hunting a Duwa trade caravan, and he appeared in the middle of our battle. I saw him with me own two eyes, and barely escaped with me life. Were it not for Brunt 'n that damn Alyrian, I'd have died that night, fighting that 'ghost story' to the bitter end." Pate spat.

"Hells. I wish I had…"

Pate thought of all the good men he'd lost that night. Andrews, Smith, Jackson, and Franklin. All good lieutenants, all great sailors. He'd worked with those men for years, and wasn't even there to see their final moments…

"If what ye say is true, Eddy, then we're in for a world of trouble. The Brethren Court has to be warned," Teach said.

"Aye, that's what I aim to do. I aim to warn them 'n gather as many men as I can to hunt the bastard down," Pate said, slamming his fist on the table.

"They'll need proof, Eddy. They won't just take ye at your word, no matter your reputation. Sayin' that a ghost pirate sank your fleet simply isn't goin' to fly."

"That's why I brought the El'wa with me. Bastard lost his whole fuckin' fleet to 'em. I figure he's as good a witness as any, at least enough to get their consideration," Pate said.

"I hope so." Teach sighed, taking the cigar from Pate and dragging from it. "because if what ye say is true, dark days are truly upon us…"

XXXVII

Close Call

"Lass has anyone ever told you that you have the body of a goddess." Crimp fawned over the waitress that handed him his drink, shouting a compliment at her over the din of rowdy pirates.

Oculeth and Judith cringed at his compliment.

"Among other things, I have been told, and I quote, that I have 'an ass that could hold a library', 'a rack that could mount trophies', 'a face that could melt ice', and, of course, my all-time favorite, one bloke said that I 'have a figure like an hourglass and I want to stick my cock up your ass'. Real charmer, that one. Rest assured, you won't be going any further than he did," the barmaid responded curtly. She was of a light caramel complexion, with warm, reddish-brown eyes and long black tresses of hair.

You are positively breathtaking.

Oculeth admitted to only himself.

"But I don't think men hit on me just to make me feel good about myself," she continued.

"Sweetheart, I can make you feel good *inside* yourself," Crimp continued, earning a disgusted glare from his sister.

The barmaid rolled her eyes. "Somehow, you managed to say something to make you even less appealing. Congratulations," she said bemusedly, pouring ale into Judith's cup.

"Apologies for my *whoreson* of a brother's manners." She punched Crimp in the shoulder. ""He was dropped a lot as child. Probably because of his potty mouth," Judith said.

"Fuckin' hell! That hurt, Judy!" Crimp complained, rubbing his bruised arm.

"Good, ye fuckwit," Judith said, relishing his pain.

"It's quite alright, dear. On an island full of pirates, the real shocker is when they don't make filthy comments at you," the barmaid said. She placed a sympathetic hand on Judith's shoulder. "My condolences for your brother."

The pair shared a laugh at his expense before she moved onto Oculeth's cup. She made eye contact with him. "You've been awfully quiet, specs. Do ye have a vulgar comment to make like your friend, here?"

Oculeth fixed his glasses, offered a curt smile, and shook his head. "No, Ma'am. Some things need no words to be admired."

The barmaid froze momentarily as she leaned over to grab his cup. "Well, that's a new one. I've never heard that before," she said, pleased. "And here I thought chivalry was dead."

Judith gave Oculeth an approving nod, patting him softly on the shoulder. Oculeth chuckled. "I don't believe in chivalry. I believe in honesty and decency. If we all treated each other decent, and were honest with our intentions, I rather think the world would be a kinder place." He let out a drawn-out sigh. ""Unfortunately, having lived in this world all my life, I believe that may just be a naïve dream of a long-gone child's last hopes for civility."

The barmaid laughed, having finished pouring his ale. "And a philosopher? A cute, young one, too? Oh you don't belong here, specs. They'll eat you alive."

Crimp butted in, throwing an arm around Oculeth's shoulder. "They should be more scared of 'im! Bastard felled a hydra by himself! He's a damn Alyria—"

Judith clapped a hand over Crimp's mouth. "Excuse my brother, he's a knack for the dramatic, y'see. And talking out his ass."

"Oh, bless his heart," the barmaid said. "What's your name, specs? I'd hate to keep calling you by your glasses."

Oculeth sipped his ale. "Oculeth. Taren Oculeth at your service, ma'am," he said, offering a palm to her. She took it, and then he kissed the back of her palm.

"A proper flirt, a philosopher, and a gentleman. Oh, aren't you rare as star diamonds," the barmaid beamed. "My name is Tellarya, Tellarya Aberdeen. Pleased to meet you, Taren Oculeth," she said, squeezing his hand.

"And what's yours, dear?" Tellarya asked, looking at Judith.

"Judith Shaw. I'm the quartermaster of the Duchess. Oculeth here is the First Mate, 'n my brother over there is the Third," Judith explained.

Crimp bolted out of his seat and extended a hand. "Name's Crimley Shaw, but ye can call me Crimp, gorgeous."

She crinkled her nose at the hand, then at Crimp. "Charmed. The First, the Quartermaster, 'n the Third. Where's your Second?" Tellarya asked.

They went quiet a moment. "…Our Second, he…the hydra got 'em," Judith said, trying to push the mental image of Henry's half-melted body getting thrown into the maw of the hydra by Pate, before being blown to bits.

"Sailors have been comin' in, talkin' about that creature for weeks, now. Thought it'd move on by now, gone with the rest of the southern migration, but I guess not," Tellarya said. She saw someone raise their mug out the corner of her eye. "My condolences, dears. I've got more mugs to fill."

Tellarya looked at Oculeth. "Hope to see you here again soon, Taren. Be careful. Livera is full of cutthroats, killers, marauders, and all manner of folk who'd love to get their hands on someone like you. Men *and* women." She winked, then walked off.

The trio sat and drank awhile longer, with Crimp fuming over Tellarya's dismissal of him. After a while, however, Oculeth took to his feet and stretched.

"Where you off to?" Judith asked, tired of her brother's whining. She was looking for any excuse to escape him.

"I'm off to explore a bit and enjoy the night air," Oculeth said.

"I'll join ye then," Judith said, rising to her feet before Oculeth put a hand on her shoulder.

"I'd advise against it. We need someone responsible watching the crew, and I worry your brother will be too deep in his drink to notice soon," Oculeth said.

"Hogwash, I'd rather explore. They're all grown men. They can handle themselves!" Judith protested.

"There is also the matter of our El'wa friend." Oculeth pointed to Daveth, who was currently at a table full of other El'wa, laughing and playing cards with them.

"He's fine." Judith shrugged.

"Except if things get heated, and he ends up spilling the proverbial beans on his origins. Then, the laughter may very well turn to bloodshed, and then we'll all be in danger," Oculeth said.

Judith sucked her teeth. "Dammit all. Fine, but get back soon, we can't be dawdlin' on our lonely 'round here!"

Oculeth nodded smugly. "I'm an Alyrian, Miss Judith. I believe I can handle a few swarthy fools trying to give me trouble."

He took in a breath of the night air and tried to ignore the hints of pig swill, tobacco, and alcohol that pervaded the air. He looked around, making mental note of where the Storm Brew was located. He took a left turn from the front doors and began walking along the sandy, unpaved street. There were shops and people crowded all around on either side of him.

"Well, aren't you fancy, love? Care to take a swing with me?" a woman, scantily dressed, beckoned him from a nearby three-story building. He saw a mural of a naked woman and man, mid-coitus, painted on the wall behind her and knew for certain it was a brothel.

"Apologies, madam, but I've neither the coin nor the stamina for one such as you this evening," he said with an apologetic smile.

He kept walking before she could solicit him further.

Oculeth had never been to the Storm Tide before. He had joined Captain Pate's crew only a half-year prior, so he'd only heard of it from his crewmates. It certainly lived up to their descriptions, no more—and no less.

Prostitutes were on every corner, chatting amongst themselves as they advertised their bodies for johns and janes. Groups of scruffy, unwashed, and booze-breathed men hung about in alleyways, in front of stores, and in the middle of the street, unbothered about whether they were barring someone else's path. He maneuvered around all of them, keeping his head low and keeping his hands in his pockets lest someone try to pick them. He noticed, to his surprise, that there were even children running about. Occasionally he would see one of them run up to one of the pirates, grabbing at them or calling them by name.

It had never occurred to him that families could live here, in this place. In such a lawless environment, how could one safeguard what they held most dear? He pondered this as he turned a corner and found it to be a dead end, leading to a shop flanked by jungle brush on either side. He looked around, saw that he was alone.

He leaned against a palm tree, then pulled out his notebook. He began writing in it when he first noticed the men blocking the street behind him. He groaned, then turned to face them. He squinted, recognizing one of the men. The one grinning at him with a half-toothless smile.

"Well, well, well, what have we here? A fish separated from its pack. Pity, that," the man said.

"Fish live in schools, not packs," Oculeth corrected.

He folded one arm behind his back as he raised the other, bracing in front of himself. "Let's not do anything foolish."

"Foolish? Hah! Get a load of this posh bastard. He's the one surrounded, without nary a gun or a blade to be seen, 'n he's worried about *us* bein' the fools!" The tall pirate with the missing teeth laughed.

Oculeth knew for certain now that it was the same one from earlier. Which meant there was almost certainly no peaceful way of dealing with this.

Damn, I didn't want to draw attention to myself.

If he used his magick on these fools, now, it would make a scene and mark him for it. Everyone would know he was an Alyrian, and on the off-chance that a magister somehow found their way to this starsforsaken place, he would be apprehended and hauled off to the Consortium.

"Yer cap'n made me look right yellow, earlier, four-eyes. Bet you lot had a real good laugh in the Storm Brew about it, didn't ye?" The pirate said, pulling out a knife.

This isn't good. I'll be forced to blow my cover entire.

"Well, now my crew's laughin' at me. My reputation's been dragged through the mud because of it, see. I gotta break bad, now. Protect me honor. Now, I was goin' ta pop a squat until ol' Cap'n Loudmouth came swaggerin' out of the tavern. But then I seen you pop out the Storm Brew, Specs. Ma boys been watchin' ye, they tell me yer his First Mate. Ye may not know this, mate, but that's a pretty important role round here. Hard to replace.

"See, I want to send a message to yer Cap'n. Pate's his name, innit? I wantem' to know that the Storm Tide's not the same as when he last came round, 'n his jib just ain't cut for it. Put it blank. There's consequences for yer actions. 'N someone's gotta pay. Now, I could go rag a whore round, rustle me jimmies, air out me bag. Or… I could get revenge. Whores are only good for so much. But vengeance? That's a gift that keeps on givin'," the pirate said, looking to Oculeth's right as a man burst from the brush.

Oculeth thrust the hand that he'd held behind his back at the man, and as he felt the Alyria surge through his palm, he screamed in agony as it backfired, and the brand on his arm ignited his nerves. His Alyria tattoos glowed bright purple, and he seized up. The man clotheslined him, laying him out on the sandy ground as the others fell in around him and his body refused to cooperate. The pirates closed in around him as he rose to his knees. He counted five of them in all.

"Why's his body glowin'? He a fuckin' Alyrian?!" One of the men asked, backing up.

"Don't know; doesn't matter. Looks like his little spells backfired on 'em, damn devil-blood," the lead pirate said.

"Don't…do this. We can talk it over," Oculeth panted.

The disgraced pirate kicked him in gut, knocking the wind out of him again and making him see stars.

"We discussed it, alright. We even reached a verdict. You're dead as a fucking door nail, freak." The man said as he and his crewmates kicked, punched, and spit on Oculeth.

The world was a blast of pain and dirt, sand got in his hair, his eyes, and his mouth as he was battered into submission. Every breath sent a shock of pain through his ribs and his gut. He curled into a ball, hiding his belly and his head from the assault, but they kicked his sides, his head, and his buttocks. The pirates spewed insults as they assaulted him.

"Fucking die, boy!" The disgraced pirate growled. He gave several harsh, heavy kicks to Oculeth's head.

Oculeth felt himself fading out, their hateful words became dulled and watery as he slipped from consciousness. They flipped him over on his back, kicking and punching him a few more times before the lead pirate brandished that knife again. Oculeth sputtered blood and sand from his airways as he tried to talk.

"S…stop…" He gurgled, he felt bile rise in his throat and he vomited in his mouth. His vision swam, his throat burned, and he felt himself passing out.

He was also starting to suffocate.

"Say goodnight, mate. This is the end for y—" The disgraced pirate was cut off as a gunshot rang out. It shot clean through his chest.

"W…what?" he gasped, confused, turning to look. He saw Captain Pate standing behind them, his pistol aimed at him.

One of the barrels was smoking.

The lead pirate fell to his knees, then collapsed.

"Kill em!" Another pirate shouted, but he was shot in the throat the moment he raised his sword.

The others were shocked, not expecting a fight, and fumbled to grab their weapons. Pate closed the gap before they could. He wordlessly picked them off, punctuating the scene with slashes of his cutlass. He cut down the fourth man as the last one attempted to make a run for it. He didn't give chase, he simply watched him cower as he fell to the ground and crawled away before getting back to his feet and running, cursing and panicking all the while.

Pate shot him in the leg for his trouble, forcing him to hobble away.

"Hmph. Tell your friends I have more waiting for them, boy," Pate shouted at the man as he fled. "I'm ready! Come at me!" he challenged as others congregated around the scene, drawn by the sound of screaming and gunfire. He stood menacingly, his pistol and his sword held out at his sides, waiting for someone to challenge him.

There was a mad look in his eyes, and a faint purple glow emanated from them.

No one came forward.

Oculeth looked at his savior through blurry eyes, blood and sand caked to his face. He vomited onto the ground next to him, heaving the contents of his gut onto the sand. "T…thank you… Captain…" he managed weakly.

"Let's get you cleaned up, Mr. Oculeth," Pate replied, lifting the wounded man and supporting him with a shoulder as they walked back towards the tavern. "Anyone asks who killed these scum, tell'em' that Cap'n Pate did it." He shouted over his shoulder as he carried Oculeth to safety.

*****

Pate pushed open the tavern door and carried Oculeth behind the counter. He'd passed out on the way back to the tavern, and so Pate was forced to half-carry, half-drag him. Tilly immediately opened the door to the backroom and Pate nodded to her. "Thank ye, Tilly," he said, shutting the door behind him. He picked up the cigar box he and Marcellus had been using and tossed it onto a shelf before dropping Oculeth on the table. Judith and Crimp burst through the door, guns at the ready.

"We heard what happened. Who did it?!" Judith asked.

"Hermalla's tits, they fucked him up *bad*," Crimp observed, looking at Oculeth's unconscious form.

"That fool from earlier who tried to extort us at the port decided to try and take revenge. Instead of attackin' me, however, he and his crew happened upon

Mr. Oculeth here. Beat 'em within an inch of his life, too," Pate explained, running a hand through his hair. "We need a doctor, and those are a precious rarity around here."

The men stood over Oculeth and looked at the damage that had been done. Pate observed that his eyes were swollen shut, his glasses were broken, and he was covered in blood and sand. He also reeked of vomit.

Not good. Not good at all.

Pate racked his brain, trying to think of what they could do to help him. He was no doctor.

"He needs whitestar syrup, or some form of painkiller. His body could potentially make a full recovery, assuming there isn't any internal damage," Pate said.

"And if there is?" Judith asked, taking the broken spectacles off of Oculeth's face.

"Then we could be burying our First Mate. But let's not jump into the deep end just yet, there may be a way that we can—"

"I can help him, with the right tools, that is," a newcomer said as he pushed open the door.

"Oh great, it's the razor-tongue bar whore." Crimp moaned, still hurt from earlier. Judith smacked him in the back of the head.

"Your First Mate is dying and you'd rather hurl insults over your wounded pride? Boy, did I dodge a bullet with you." She crinkled her nose in disgust, looking Oculeth over more closely. She quickly unbuttoned his shirt and opened it, exposing his chest. There were bruises all over it. She pressed her head to his breast, listening to his heartbeat as well as his breathing. His breath was faint, but it was there. His heartbeat was irregular, however.

"Ask Tilly for my medical tools from the cellar and bring them to me," she instructed, pointing to Judith and Crimp.

"Aye." The two nodded and exited the room.

"Captain, I need you to keep watch. I'd rather not have those pirates come back to finish their business with Taren, here."

"Aye, Miss Tellarya," Captain Pate replied. He walked over to Oculeth and nodded to him. "Keep fightin', mate."

Tellarya watched him leave, then went to the door, listening to them talk on the other side. Judith and Crimp were descending into the cellar through the floor hatch, by the sound of their boots hitting the ladder rungs. Captain Pate was talking to Tilloula, describing the men who'd battered Oculeth.

"Should've used your magick, Taren. I told you people were dangerous around here." She sighed, pulling out a book from her pocket, emblazoned with an embellished silver star-symbol. The words 'Book of the Stars: Canticles' was written upon the leather cover in raised letters. She flitted to a page and murmured the words to herself before shutting the book and nodding. "Let us begin."

Judith and Crimp opened the door, as if on cue, and she grabbed the bag from Judith.

"We got the—" she began.

"Yes, yes, wonderful, now get out, I have work to do!" she shooed them, pushing them back out the door as she rifled through her bag. She pulled out a syringe, then opened a bottle of clear-brownish liquid, dipping the needle in. It sucked in the liquid, filling the syringe and she held it up to a candle, squeezing out some of the liquid. Satisfied with the amount she'd extracted, she stuck it into his arm, injecting the liquid after wiping away some of the grime from his face. He murmured to himself then sighed heavily, souring her nose with the stench of blood and bile.

"Yeesh. Your breath could kill. Not to worry though, I'm going to fix you right up," she whispered, satisfied that he was sufficiently under.

She removed his dirtied jacket, vest, and then his undershirt. She appraised his slim, toned physique for a moment before lifting an arm to inspect his ribs. She ran her hands along his ribcage. She pressed on each and listened to his breath. His gasped, and his face grimaced; she'd found the broken rib. This wasn't something that could be fixed with medicine.

Time to use something else, then.

She recited the verse she'd been reading and focused on the incantation.

Verse, then purpose.

She repeated, remembering her training. She recited the verse in her head, then the purpose for which she was reciting it. She closed her eyes and imagined a bright light, a warm light that healed the body; she could feel her hands warming up and knew that the spell was working. She opened her eyes and saw a small, bright light floating between her palms. She pressed it against Oculeth's side, and he released a long sigh. She saw the light suffusing through his body and knew that it was healing him. She pressed her head to his chest once more, feeling his chest rise and fall and hearing his heartbeat return to a normal rhythm. She could hear the bones in his chest shifting.

The miracle worked.

After several minutes, there was a knock at the door. "Miss Tellarya, how fairs Mr. Oculeth?" Captain Pate asked.

"He is well, Captain. I believe I've fixed his injuries," she called back.

The door opened, and the pirates re-entered. Captain Pate immediately approached Oculeth.

"My, he even looks better, like the color returned to his face," Pate noted. "Thank you, Miss Tellarya. Your medical skills are exceptional. Why not open a clinic?"

"Pfft. A clinic? On an isle full of pirates? Certainly profitable, but hardly practical. Folk 'round here hate paying their beer tabs, let alone a medical bill. Truth be told if it weren't for me sis, Tilly, I'd have left this place long ago. But here she remains, and here I shall stay. Someone's gotta look out for her," she replied. "Besides, I didn't save 'em because he needed savin'. I saved 'em because he seems like a decent sort."

"I can't fault that. Pirates aren't exactly the most appreciative folk, 'n there are plenty around here that I suspect would sooner sell you as a slave and make a profit than keep you as a sawbones when they have their own at their disposal. Even if slaving is outlawed 'round here," Pate sighed.

"Precisely. So tell cud for brains over there to keep his mouth shut about how the apostate got healed, or my last act on this isle will be to make Tilly cut off your hemestra supply as well as your alcohol," she half-joked.

Pate laughed, then fixed Crimp with a frown. "Open your yapper about our First Mate's miraculous recovery, 'n you'll be sleeping with worms and dung beetles, savvy?"

Crimp went wide-eyed. "Aye sir!"

"Good. I knew ye'd catch on," Pate answered. "On to business then. When should Mr. Oculeth be waking from his slumber?"

"A few hours, at most. His body's still recovering. He should be alright by the morn'," Tellarya said.

"Good. That means I have a few hours to do what comes next without him getting in the way," Pate said, his tone turning dark.

Tellarya looked at him, confused. "What comes next…what do you—"

Pate began loading his double-barrel pistol. "Mr. Crimp, Ms. Judith—are your guns loaded?" he asked absentmindedly as he checked the barrels.

"Yessir!" Judith said immediately, posing with her rifle against her chest, facing the sealing.

"Aye, cap'n." Crimp nodded, holding his matchlock rifle one-handed.

Pate finished loading the pistol before cocking it and putting it in his holster. "Very good. We're going to gather some men and get after that last straggler. I saw his face, and he was bleeding when he ran. Trail shouldn't be too hard to pick up."

Tellarya protested, "Captain, if you do that then—"

"Then it'll mean war with their crew, aye. I'm countin' on it, actually. Your sister still got that armory stash down under? I've need of it." Pate finished as he made his way to the door and cocked his head, motioning for Judith and Crimp to follow him.

Before she could say another word, the pirates filed out of the room. "Watch him, please. And thank ye again, Miss Tellarya," Pate said, shutting the door behind him.

Tellarya sighed; she knew better than to try and dissuade pirates from vengeance. Still, the look in Pate's eye was pure murder. Enough to make Brahmund smile with envy. He was about to do something awful to those pirates. She almost felt sorry for them. Almost.

"Nothing to it," she said to no one. She sighed, grabbed a cloth, wet it, and began to clean the dirt and blood from Oculeth's sleeping body.

*****

Oculeth felt wet cloth on his face, he opened his eyes to see a dark, candle-lit room, and a familiar, beautiful face standing over him as she concentratedly scrubbed dirt off of his face.

"Miss Tellarya?" he asked, finding his voice.

"He yet lives. Welcome back to the world of the living, Mr. Taren," she smiled, helping him sit up.

"I didn't think I would, in truth."

"Considering the beating you took? No, you probably shouldn't be waking up. Those pirates did a real number on you, they broke a rib and beat you bloody. For a minute, your heartbeat had become erratic. You were almost lost. *Almost.*"

"And you saved me? Without Alyria? Quite the feat, Miss Tellarya," Oculeth observed.

A cheeky smile began to form. "Now, where did you hear me say that I didn't use Alyria, Mr. Oculeth?"

Oculeth's eyes twinkled. "I thought I could sense an Alyrian here, I'd sensed them as soon we broke through the storm. Why are you here?"

"I studied healing miracles in a clerical monastery. I probably would've stayed there, had things gone different. But they didn't, and so I left, met up with my sister, and here we are."

"What made you leave?"

"Fate and the cruelty of men, preying upon those who're defenseless," she responded, sounding defensive and tense.

"I see—I'm… I'm sorry to ask, Miss Tellarya," Oculeth responded, looking away.

"Don't it's… I'm sorry, it's not your fault. You had nothing to do with what happened."

"May I ask?"

"Perhaps. But first, I'd like to know what the purpose of that mark on your shoulder is," she reflected, pointing to his unclothed arm. He rubbed the mark reflexively, then looked in the mirror sitting at the far wall of the small room. With concern, he realized that the eternal return symbol had changed over time. The serpent heads had distorted, growing a third eye on their heads. The four lines shooting out from the corners now curved, like hooks. The mark had also grown larger, originally no wider than an egg, now nearing the size of his palm. "A tattoo, much like any other," he lied. "I've had it for years, now."

"Interesting design, I'll give you that. I've never seen someone tattoo the symbol of eternal return on their arm before. It's beautiful, in a way. It glows, like an Alyria tattoo." Tellarya complimented.

Oculeth looked at the mark a moment, wondering why it had changed over time. Is that why it was flaring so much? Because it was changing? He ran a hand over it and bit his lip, even a light touch caused it to burn.

"You know of the symbol for eternal return? I'd thought it only taught in Consortium schools."

"The church teaches of its significance as well. All clerics and paladins are taught of it."

"Interesting…" Oculeth said, surprised. "Yes, well. It was done back when I was in the Consortium. As a means of reminding us of the fundamentals," he lied.

"Well, I love it. The artist is very good with a needle," she smiled, running a hand over the mark.

He gritted his teeth and smiled. It burned like hell.

"About your departure from the monastery," he pressed, trying to ignore the pain.

"Hmm…" she paused, looking deeply in his eyes for a moment. She seemed pleased with what she saw and responded, "I told you that I was trained at a monastery. In truth, I grew up there."

"You grew up in a monastery? Astounding, what was it like?"

"For the most part? Dull. For years, a disciple will study the word of the Book of the Stars, learning its verses, studying its scripture. It wasn't until my teen years that we began to learn the basics of casting healing spells, or miracles as many know them. It's all the same, really. Verses, ciphers, scriptures and finally spells. I'd left shortly after learning my first incantation. A healing spell… the one I used to save you."

"Well, thank you for staying a cleric long enough to save my life from being ended by angry pirates," Oculeth complimented as he sat up fully. He was surprised that he felt no pain, he could even twist his core without feeling a stabbing in his ribs. "My, healing miracles do wonders!" he beamed as he stood, flexing his muscles and stretching.

"I'm glad. I've only used it a handful of times, so I wasn't sure if I'd made a mistake in the execution," she admitted.

"I'm surprised you haven't done it more. There can't be a lack of potential patients in a place as rough as this."

"Your Captain said something to that tune earlier, but I don't have any interest in saving these people—if I'm being frank. Pirates are violent, rash, and incorrigible. If it breathes, they either want to kill it and eat it, kill it and rob it, or sell it. The women here are almost always as bad as the men, sometimes even worse. The whores lie, steal, deceive, and occasionally murder as well, all the while being raped, accosted, or intimidated by the larger pirate crews. The only reason I manage to get by without turning to such banality is because of Tilly owning the most profitable tavern on the isle and Boris being a vicious bear of a man with a love of bludgeoning or shooting any riffraff that enter those front doors. Otherwise? I'd either be a pirate or a whore. This world makes monsters of us all, in the end."

"Monsters, yes..." Oculeth thought of the things he saw in his dreams, and the day he lost his mentor and began down this wretched path. "I'm sorry that you live in such a hell. To be a kind soul, surrounded by violence, savagery, and thievery. I guess the goodness and decency of kith is truly dead," he said solemnly, watching as she put her things back into her bag.

"It isn't your fault that folk are awful, Oculeth. Men, El'wa, Duwa, Wuhlven... all kith have evil in them. That's the nature of humanity, of having a soul. Unfortunately, that evil can take many forms," she appraised him once more, grabbing him by the chin as she twisted his head side to side, checking to make sure there wasn't any other injury to him that her weak spell may have missed. "But you seem quite well. So, I'll leave you to get your bearings. Captain Pate will be back soon enough, he..."

Tellarya was at a loss for words. She knew that telling him about what Pate was going to, or likely was in the process of doing, would likely result in him trying to stop him. Likely getting hurt again in the process.

"He?" he said, looking into her eyes.

She put on a smile. "He went... with Captain Teach... to go and prepare for your... meeting with the Brethren Court!" she stumbled, finding the words as she spoke.

"Ah, yes, the Brethren Court," Oculeth groaned. The reason they came here in the first place, and the reason so many of their crew was now hydra food. He thought back to the chilling story that Daveth had told them, and his stomach churned. If what the El'wa said was true, then they were in for a rude awakening...

XXXVIII

THE WRONG PIRATE

Everett hobbled his way toward the ship, and nearly collapsed when his brethren caught sight of him.

"Everett? Where's Royce 'n the others that went with ye?" one of his rescuers, Hauser, asked.

Everett panted, "Dead…all dead. That Pate bastard cutdown every one of 'em…"

"Bloody bastard'll pay for this," Haanz, another of his crew said. "Gotta tell the cap'n bout this."

Everett nodded weakly as they carried him aboard the ship. The rest of the crew above deck stood watch as they carried him below deck. Upon reaching the galley, Everett was greeted with the crew of the Cutthroat in the midst of dinner. He spied Captain Farce, sitting at the head of the long table, chatting and eating with his officers. Upon seeing him, he motioned for them to quiet down, and stood up.

"Mr. Everett? Where is Royce, Shawn, Benweth, 'n Mills?" The man asked.

"That fucker, Pate, killed them, sir. He got the drop on us when we had his Alyrian cornered," Everett reported as he sat in a chair, unable to stand any longer. The bullet wound Pate had given him had been leaking blood the whole way back.

"I thought ye were goin' after Pate himself? Fuck did ye tangle with an Alyrian for?!" Farce yelled. "Ye know those demon-blooded bastards are more trouble 'n they're worth!"

"We ain't know he was an apostate, sir! We thought he was just a regular officer, 'n he was weakened anyway, couldn't cast a spell or anythin'! We had 'em surrounded before his cap'n fell upon us."

"One man bested all five of you? Pathetic! Now we'll have to go 'n kill the bastard before he raises a stink about it," Farce cursed, slamming the table. "I told Royce he should've left it alone at the damn port, told 'em he keeps runnin' that scam with the port toll, he was askin' for trouble. Did the bastard listen? No. Now he's dead, 'n now we've got a pirate cap'n 'n crew to deal with. This'll get real messy now, cause of that dead bastard."

"We thought we had 'em, cap'n!" Everett pleaded. "It's just one man', we thought. 'How hard can it be, we've killed dozens of 'em?' But the fucker's a thing possessed. He put a bullet through Royce's chest before we even saw 'em. By time I blinked, Shawn 'n Mills were on the ground, 'n Benweth was getting a blade through his gut!" Everett shouted hysterically. "That…that *freak* just kept comin'!"

Everett was shaking, now. He could still see the mad look in his eyes, those strange, purple eyes.

"Pitiful," Farce shook his head. "Hauser, Haanz. Gather up a posse, we've got work to do—"

Something fell down the stairs to the galley and rolled toward the long table.

"No…" Everett coughed.

It was a grenade.

Its wick burnt down, and it detonated, releasing a cloud of gas and smoke into the cabin. The men scrambled.

"Clear out!" Someone shouted.

Everyone made for the stairs, gasping, coughing. The ship exploded in screams as people were trampled, funneling up the stairs to get out of the gas. Farce made his way up in the middle of the pack, but Everett was abandoned in the galley. His cries for help were drowned out in the stampede.

As they emptied out onto the deck, it erupted in gunfire as they were met with a firing squad of men, emptying guns on them as they filtered out. Soon, the men were screaming and tripping over bodies as they tried to get their bearings.

"Cease fire!" A man barked, and the firing stopped.

The Cutthroat pirates, disoriented and ambushed, stood with their hands up as Farce made his way to the front and stood before the dozen plus pirates, aiming at them with smoking guns. Breaking through the firing line and smoke, two men stepped forward. He recognized them immediately.

"Captain Teach…and you must be Edward Patron," Farce coughed.

"Guilty as charged," Pate said, pulling the cigar from his mouth breathing smoke in Farce's direction. "And who would you be?"

"This, is Captain Harold Farce. Captain of the Cutthroat, and leader of those men who nearly killed your First Mate a few hours ago, Edward," Marcellus explained.

"We ain't do nothin' to nobody! Ye attacked us out of the blue 'n killed my men! The Brethren Court'll hear of this!" Captain Farce said indignantly.

"Oh really?" Pate said, looking at the bloodstained floorboards, then following the trail with his gaze out to the docks. "That blood trail leads from where my man got ambushed, all the way back here. And the survivor from that ambush is on this ship. Probably half-dead down in that gassed out galley, actually."

Farce wiped sweat from his brow. "I…I don't know what you're—"

"Cut the bullshit. Your men meant to ambush me, fucked up 'n went after one of my men, then paid the price for it. I know it was you, Marcellus here knows it was your men what did it, 'n I mean to settle this right here, right now, tonight. I challenge ye to a black duel on the beach, just you 'n me. No more men need to die over this bad business," Pate said casually.

"Bad business?! You *raided* my ship 'n killed my men! To Sheolhenna with your fuckin' duel!" Farce spat.

Pate shrugged. "Then I'll be killin' all your men 'n takin' your ship for myself, here, tonight."

He raised his hand, and a dozen guns took aim at the Cutthroats again.

"M-Marcellus! Ye can't just let this fool kill us like this! It's against the code!" Farce reached, grasping at whatever straws he could.

"Actually, he can. 'If a man should be wronged, and he should find his wrongdoer, then he should act thusly according to his judgement of the severity of the slight.' That's what the code says. And with everything that's transpired, the blood trail, and the fact that the man in your galley almost certainly has a bullet hole in his leg of the same size as the bullets fired from Captain Pate's gun, the Court would rule that he had enough right and evidence to act," Marcellus answered.

The color drained from Farce's face.

"Duel me or condemn all your men to death. The choice is yours, Farce. You too yellow to fight another man in a fair scrap? Or are the Cutthroat pirates too cowardly to face their opponent head on?" Pate challenged, looking over Farce's men.

Feeling slighted, the men began goading their captain to action. "He's right. The code dictates ye gotta accept the duel," Haanz said.

"To hell with the code!" Farce outburst, regretting his words immediately. His men turned on him.

"You too cowardly for the code?" Hauser asked.

"The code is law! The code is law! The code is law!" The Cutthroat pirates, as well as Pate and Marcellus' men chanted.

Farce looked around and growled. He'd been caught. "Fine! Meet me on the beach a knot north of Livera at midnight. We'll see who the better man is, there."

Pate nodded slowly and puffed his cigar. "Aye. That we will." He lowered his hand and walked away after finishing the cigar and stomping it into the floorboards. "See you at midnight, Farce. I'll be waiting."

Pate and Teach left, as did their men, leaving the Cutthroat pirates to gather themselves, and deal with their dead.

*****

A HALF-HOUR PRIOR…

Pate looked through his spyglass, watching as the wounded attacker limped to his crew's ship, trailing a thin stream of blood behind him as he went.

"Found 'em," he said, crouching against a tree overlooking the port. "Ready the guns."

"Ye plan to kill 'em all? It'll be a bloodbath, Eddy. Good men'll be wasted just because a of a few shysters' folly," Marcellus Teach warned.

Pate rolled the idea over in his head. He saw at least ten men standing on the ship's main deck, and it was large enough that it would likely have at least a hundred and twenty men onboard. With the element of surprise, they'd be able to lockdown the ship's exit points and trap the men within. From that point it'd be like shooting fish in a barrel.

That is a lot of good men dead, however.

Men that may have had nothing to do with the attempted murder of his First Mate. He knew all too well that in a pirate crew, men seldom worked in unison, except in the midst of a hunt. Even now, some of the men were likely plotting a mutiny against their captain. What were the odds some of them were running a racket behind their crew's back, skimming coin on the side?

"What do ye suggest, then?" Pate asked. His mind was focused on murder, and nothing more.

"Cut off their head and they'll crumble. Challenge their cap'n to an honor duel 'n beat 'em in front of everybody. It'll send a message and stop a lot of good pirates from sleeping with the fishes by sunrise," Marcellus suggested.

Pate nodded. It was a fine plan. One that, were he not currently dealing with a burning pain in his shoulder from the mark that Oculeth had tattooed into his skin, as well as an intense rage at the audacity of these men to try and ambush him, he might have considered. "Very well. We'll give 'em a chance to avoid slaughter. Judith, Crimp, take some men and the grenade thrower. If things get hairy, I want ye to send their ship to kingdom come. Clear?"

Judith nodded, the grenade thrower in question propped on her shoulder. "Aye cap'n."

Marcellus handed Pate a lit cigar. "Calm your nerves, some," he said.

Pate took it and rose from his crouched position as they took the man below deck, likely to meet their captain.

"Time to move."

*****

"They're here," one of Teach's men announced as the party sat around a fire, playing cards.

Pate stood and stretched, grabbing his sword and buckling the holster about his hips. He strolled down the beach, Teach and twenty men in toe. They stopped about forty paces from Farce and his men, and the two locked eyes. Pate could tell they were angry, but not just at him. Then, they dropped a familiar, wounded man on the ground in front of Farce, and he pointed to Pate.

"This man is the last of those responsible for the ambush of your First Mate. Take 'em and bury the hatchet," Farce said, kicking the man, who was tied up and wheezing.

Pate looked down his nose at him and raised an eyebrow. He nodded to one of his men, McDunham, who grabbed the whimpering Everett and dragged him in front of Pate.

"P-p-please, don't kill me, please…" Everett pleaded.

111

"Quit your whining," McDunham said, dropping him in front of Pate before retaking his position to his right.

Pate knelt down and looked at Everett, who was looking worse for wear. He'd been beaten, and the gas had left welts on his skin from the irritation. The two locked eyes, and Everett began to shiver, unable to hold Pate's gaze.

His eyes took on a faint purple hue again, and he grunted slightly as his mark began to flare up again, casting a visible cyan glow at the top of his collar. He avoided the urge to grab at it, knowing it would do him no good.

"Edward?" Marcellus began.

"It's nothing. We'll discuss it later," he responded through gritted teeth. He took aim with his pistol.

"No!" Everett shouted.

Pate fired, hitting him in the chest and throat.

Everett gurgled and twitched for several moments before going limp, and everyone was silent. Farce let out a sigh of relief and turned around to walk away.

"We're not finished here, Farce. I know a snake in the grass when I see one. If I let you go tonight, you'll be back tomorrow night with fifty men, ambushing me and mine when our guard is down. No, this only ends one way. You're still responsible for your men ambushing my First Mate, and I challenged ye to a black duel, so turn 'n fight, coward," Pate challenged.

Farce paused as his men blocked his path. He knew then there was no getting out of this without a fight. He clenched his fists. Why hadn't he stopped Royce's racket when he first caught on? He knew the bastard would fleece the wrong pirate and pay the price for it. And he had, but unfortunately, he'd gone after *this* pirate.

Edward Patron.

He'd heard about him, before. He was one of the few dozen pirate captains on this isle that wasn't a pirate lord that had a fleet of ships. He was a big fish, here, hence why Marcellus Teach shacked up with him as soon as he'd shown up. If Royce hadn't been a blowhard idiot, he might have taken note of that and backed off. But now, here they were. Pate may not have his fleet anymore, for whatever reason, but he was still a surly fire drake of a man with a take-no-shit demeanor, and he was a principled sort to boot.

Just my fucking luck.

Farce cursed, then slowly turned around.

"...Aye, I figured ye'd say that. Well, there's no helpin' it then." Farce sighed. He knew his men wouldn't be backing him up. He'd been de-escalating a mutiny when Everett burst into the galley. Now, the mutineers had a perfect opportunity to rid themselves of him. "Let's get it over with, then."

Farce dropped his coat, checked his pockets, and pulled out his sabre sword.

Pate cracked his neck and handed his coat to Teach. His short-sleeve shirt glowed on the arm where the mark of eternal return was branded, and he noticed it had begun to travel down his upper arm.

What the...

"You an Alyrian too?" Farce asked, eyeing the glowing tattoo on Pate's arm. Everyone else was looking at it as well, as it lit up the moonlit beach in a small area around him.

"I'm no spark. I've been cursed by one, however," Pate said truthfully. Even now, he could hear faint whispering at the edge of his perception. He had to focus, or it would lose him the duel.

Pate pulled out his cutlass and gave it several test swings through the air. He made a mental note that he hadn't reloaded his double-barrel pistol, so the only one he had left was the flintlock tucked behind his back. He knew his opponent wouldn't be above trickery, even if it was dishonorable.

The two men approached one another slowly, weapons drawn, sizing each other up. Pate knew he was almost certainly a better sword-fighter than Farce. He asked Marcellus about him on their way to the beach, and he'd told him that Captain Harold Farce wasn't much of a duelist, conveniently enough. He preferred gunfights, and he wasn't known for fighting clean, either. That meant his sword fighting skills would be lacking, and he'd look to find a way to get an edge over Pate. He flicked his eyes at the man's gun, making note that it was on his left side, so he'd be drawing from the right.

"Dance!" Farce shouted, charging, and swinging at Pate suddenly.

Pate dodged the swing, and Farce followed up with several sloppier swings in rapid succession. Pate waited for an opening to strike—and took it. In three swings he'd disarmed Farce and cut his sword arm open. The man howled in pain and fell back on the ground. Without thinking, he closed the gap—and was blinded when Farce pulled something out his pocket and sprayed it in Pate's face.

"Gah!" Pate gasped, rubbing the burning powder, which could only be smelling salts, from his eyes.

"Cheater!" McDunham shouted, pulling his gun out, ready to fire at the treacherous Farce. Men on both sides drew their weapons, and Farce pressed the advantage, swinging at Pate, forcing him to dodge blindly as he tried to wipe the salt from his eyes.

Marcellus lowered McDunham's arm. "Let it go. This fight is between Harold Farce and Edward Patron! Any and all attempts to intervene will be seen as an act of treachery against Piracy and be met with death!"

"The bastard's cheating! He threw somethin' in the cap'n's eyes!" McDunham protested.

"And Pate will have to fend for himself, unfortunately," Teach sighed.

Pate barely managed to clear the salt from his eyes when Farce slashed his arm, disarming him. Pate hissed, then dove for his sword, narrowly evading Farce's downward slash. As Farce's sword buried in the sand, he struggled to free it—and Pate struck. He swung his sword, slashing Farce's other arm and making the man reel backward, releasing his sword. Pate wasted no time, bolting to his feet and charging into the man, who pulled out his pistol, but was unable to cock it and aim it in time.

On the ground, now, Pate wailed on Farce, punching him repeatedly in the head again and again. Farce attempted to shoot him, but missed as the gun misfired in his hand, exploding. Pate grunted in pain as shrapnel grazed him, and Farce screamed bloody murder as his hand was mangled by the exploding gun, and he got shrapnel in his face. Pate continued battering the man, fighting through the pain from his brand, the voices in his head, and the burning sensation in his cheek left in the wake of the pistol's misfire. He saw red, and punched Farce until his fists were bloody and useless. Then, and only then, did he grab his sword.

Farce, beaten to a pulp, couldn't even form words to protest as Pate raised his sword. "Finished!" he roared as he buried the cutlass to the hilt in Farce's face. He stood, caked in blood and sand, panting. Every nerve in his body was aflame. He pointed at Hauser and Haanz. "Get lost. 'N find a better captain."

The Cutthroat pirates, disgusted with the cowardly loss of their leader, looked at one another. Haanz and Hauser stepped forward and stood before Pate.

“You hard of hearing?” Pate asked, wiping blood from his face, and gritting his teeth as he irritated a bit of shrapnel stuck in the side of his head.

“You killed our captain in a fair duel, and he was dishonorable against the code. We’d like to elect you as our new captain, sir,” Hauser said, taking a knee in front of him. Haanz did the same, and the other Cutthroat pirates followed suit.

Pate looked around, leaning on McDunham and Teach, who’d come to his side. He took in their request a moment. He needed more men, needed a new ship to begin regrowing his fleet. This was as good a start that he could hope for.

“Very well, then. Clean this yellow bastard’s corpse off the beach ‘n dump ‘em somewhere,” Pate ordered. “I need a drink ‘n some stitches.”

XXXIX

SEEKERS

Overlooking Emperor's Rest, perched on a bluff, lies a silver spire. Its tip stretching nearly to the clouds. This spire, looming over the capital of the Kurzan Empire, easily visible from every corner and every building, stands as a stark reminder to all who observe it of the might of the empire, and the Emperor that commands it.

They call it the Seeker Spire.

And here, on a bright and sunny morning, several organized rows of its occupants stood in the outside courtyard, preparing for a mission that would spell certain doom for their unlucky targets.

"Seeker Clive, step forward," a robed man, wearing gold chains with a dangling, S-shaped emblem woven into the robe, commanded.

A pale-skinned young man with short, shaved, brown hair and fiery brown eyes stepped forward. He was clad in plate armor. He planted his sheathed great sword into the soil before him as he stood proudly at his summons.

"Seeker Tora, step forward," the robed man ordered as he nodded to Seeker Clive. A bronze-skinned young woman clad in plate armor, with short, black hair and a trident stepped forward, and saluted the robed man. Her eyes were a striking emerald green. He nodded to her as well.

"Seeker Sedrick, step forward," the robed man called. A young man with a short mohawk and dark blue eyes stepped forward, this time wearing mail armor, reinforced with plate at the shoulders, chest, and legs. He wielded a long, rune-covered rifle. Its barrel was long as a normal man was tall. It was slung over his shoulder, and he saluted the robed man, who nodded to him in return.

"Seeker Frond, you may step forward as well," the robed man said. A tall, helmeted man in thicker plate armor, more reinforced than Clive's, stepped forward. He was a giant of a man, easily six and a half feet in height, and he wielded a longsword and a round, metal heater shield with a red dragon, the national heraldry of Kurza, engraved on it. He braced his shield in front of him and pressed the flat of his sword against his breast, pointing toward the sky. The robed man nodded.

"And finally, Seeker Ephala, step forward. You will be the leader for this mission," the robed man declared.

A pale skinned young woman with long black hair, tied into a bun and piercing ice-blue eyes stepped forward. She wore sleeker armor than her companions. Hers was intricately woven metal scale mail, only her shoulder pauldrons, boots, and leg armor were plate. She wore two long dirk daggers on her sides, and she stepped forward, brandishing them in a cross-armed salute to the robed man.

Each of them, including the rows of Seekers behind them, bore a tattoo of a heavily stylized S upon their foreheads.

"Master Erebus, we are at you and the Emperor's command," she said, bowing her head.

"Very good. Follow me, Seekers. Your duty awaits," the robed man, Master Erebus, said.

They broke away from the rows of armored Seekers, who saluted them, many looking on with envy and pride as five of their most promising were called to action.

*****

"The task before you is one of great importance, and as such requires equally great discretion. An artifact of immense power lies in the hands of privateers, hired by the crown, to retrieve it," Vexyn explained as he stood in front of the throne.

Tora raised her hand. "Privateers, sir?"

"Pirates," Varryn corrected, his head leaned forward, resting on his left palm.

Ephala raised her hand, and Vexyn motioned for her to speak. "If I may, your excellency, and Lord Advisor…why were…pirates…used to retrieve this artifact?"

"That is of no consequence, Seeker Ephala. All that matters is that you must retrieve it, and silence these pirates when you do," Vexyn explained.

Both women nodded in agreement. "Yes, Lord Advisor, sir," they said unison.

Sedrick raised his hand, now.

Vexyn nodded for him to speak.

"How will we track them? We have never seen these men before, and so have not had the chance to imprint a tracking sigil upon their person," Sedrick asked.

"I am so very glad you asked. These pirates were given an envelope filled with letters of marque. Each of these marques are imprinted with a small, trace amount of Alyria to allow us to track their location," Vexyn said. He pulled out a rolled-up map. "This map will allow you to track each and every marque. In the event that the pirates chose to cut and run, they will be required to carry these marques to evade capture and execution for piracy, which means they will be traceable."

Clive raised an eyebrow and looked at Frond and Sedrick, Sedrick gave him a bewildered look, and Frond slowly turned his head forward. He raised his hand.

Vexyn pinched the bridge of his nose. "Yes, Seeker Clive?"

"So…what if all of the pirates split up, sir?" he asked. "We could be searching for months…years, even."

"Then you'd better hop to it, then. Last we checked, all of the marques were in the same location. I would suggest you find them before that is no longer the case," Vexyn answered.

The Seekers saluted. They were ready to begin.

"At the ready, sir!" Seeker Ephala announced.

"The artifact you will be hunting is a bright, turquoise colored orb, about the size of a clenched fist, called the Eye of Atla. It will likely be stored in a chest, so should the pirates not give you the artifact outright, look for a black chest. A lot of people have died for this artifact, and we have reason to believe a lot of people covet it. So, expect resistance from more than just the pirates.

"You will be given a ship-of-the-line to hunt your quarry. She is large, but she is fast for her size. You will be given a crew of six-hundred plus Bluecoats mariners to man the ship and its three gun decks. Master Erebus will introduce you to your officers and crew at the port. All the mariners are seasoned pirate killers, and they will follow your every beck and call. We are entrusting you with enough firepower to level a fleet of ships, Seekers. Do not fail us," Vexyn said, turning to Varryn.

Varryn sat upright and addressed them. "This mission is of the utmost importance. The future of our empire lies in the balance, and this artifact lies at the heart of it. Failure is not an option. Go with my blessings, and may the Stars guide you, Seekers. You are dismissed."

*****

They rode through the city, and as they went they, everyone who saw them would turn and run, hiding in buildings and alleys to escape their gaze.

"Seekers."

The word was whispered on every corner, and in ever shop. Ephala avoided their gazes as they traveled. Here, they were referred to with the same fear and disgust as apostates. Seekers were reviled, seen as little more than living weapons, ready to destroy at a moment's notice. She let their gazes, their revulsion, their fear wash over her and slide away like rain on a windowpane. They knew not the sacrifice she and people like her made for their safety. They knew not that she was going to save their way of life! They knew not that she stood as the shield of protection from the dangers of the wild, untamed world outside the city walls! Where goblins, trolls, demons, fae, and all manner of ravenous, man-eating monsters prowled, waiting for them to venture into their domain!

"We're near the port," Erebus said as they made their way into the dock district.

On their way, they passed by a man clad in golden armor, carrying a great sword on his back. He stood in prayer with a group of nuns, and Ephala locked eyes with him briefly. He gave her a blank stare, unburdened by hatred or fear, but indifferent all the same. He continued praying.

As they dismounted, they were greeted with the sight of a ship larger than any they had ever seen. It towered above them so much so that they were forced to look up at its decks. They stood at the aft and could clearly see the large bay windows of its officers cabins and captain's quarters. They could see the gunports lining the three-gun ducks like square, wooden tiles, perfectly uniform. Mariners in blue uniforms saluted them as they approached, and several decorated officers came to greet them.

"These are your officers: Seekers Ephala, Tora, Sedrick, Clive, and Frond.," Erebus introduced. "They will be your eyes and ears on this voyage."

419

All of the officers bowed. "It is a pleasure to be in your presence Seekers, and especially you, Master Erebus. Your reputation far precedes you, sir," one of the officers, a middle-aged looking man with a standard military haircut said. He was clean cut man with a salt and pepper beard, and several badges woven into his coat. His hat identified him as a captain. "I am Captain James Avery, of the Imperial Naval 57th Fleet, at your service, Seekers. My compatriots and I will be your acting lieutenants upon this voyage. We would ask that you use us as such."

Ephala stepped forward. "A pleasure to meet you, Captain Avery, I am Seeker Ephala Farandus, I am captain of the Seeker squadron you see before you. This is Seeker Sedrick, our sharpshooter, Seeker Tora, our metamorph, Seeker Clive, our swordsman, and Seeker Frond, our guardian."

Each of them stepped forward as their names were called and nodded to the naval officers.

"I am Ensign Cambridge Golde, I will be the acting Gunner aboard the Black Bess, ma'am," a young officer said, stepping forward and saluting. He had a fair complexion, blonde hair, was clean shaven and young in the face, and of a proper demeanor.

Another officer stepped forward, this one was closer to middle-age in appearance, like Captain Avery, and was a bit portlier in size. "I am Lieutenant Commander Jukel Staunton. I will be acting Quartermaster aboard our fair Black Bess, at your service, ma'am." He saluted.

Finally, the fourth officer stepped forward and saluted. This one was a tall, muscular man a full beard and bald head. "Lieutenant Commander Ambrose Castell, at your service, ma'am! I will be your acting Deck Commander aboard the Black Bess," he said in a powerful baritone.

All of the officers were decorated, save for the ensign, who appeared to be much greener than the other officers, at least in terms of career. Ephala was curious as to whether he could truly be expected to command the gun crews of the ship. She imagined Ambrose, or even Jukel to be better fitted for the role. There was a sharp intelligence in the young man's eyes, however, and she knew all of them would have been properly vetted for their roles beforehand.

"I am pleased and honored to have all of you decorated officers aboard for our voyage. Our mission is of the utmost importance, as I am sure you are all aware. How much longer until we can get underway?" Ephala asked.

"We'll be ready to depart by first light, ma'am," Captain Avery responded.

"First light?" Ephala asked, looking past the officers at the men loading cargo onto the ship. There was no more freight on the dock around the ship, either. "From where I'm standing, it seems we'll be ready no later than this evening."

Captain Avery quickly responded, "Ah, yes ma'am, but it is customary for a ship to depart in the morning for a maiden voyage. Idallon's blessing is bestowed at first light, you see—and so it is best to—"

"With all due respect, captain. Idallon can be beseeched at all hours, and we do not have the time to have a priest come and bless the Black Bess before we can depart. Our quarry will not be waiting for us to receive blessings to come and hunt them. Every minute wasted is a minute further jeopardizing our cause," Ephala explained, her eyes piercing through Captain Avery's.

"Yes, ma'am. As you say," Avery relented, recognizing immediately that his words would hold no sway here. The Seekers were considered second to royalty, and so they held authority over all of them.

Better not to agitate the Alyrian lap dogs.

He told himself. Avery had seen first-hand what danger Alyrians posed, and he had no interest in seeing what an empire-sanctioned one could do with free reign.

"I agree with our Fair Lady. Pirates are flotsam creatures. They will disperse to the cardinal winds if we allow them time. Who knows what havoc their scum will wreak, then?" Ensign Golde said.

"If we're to get underway immediately, then I would do a provision check first. I would hate to get underway only to discover we're out a cow, or flock of chickens," Ambrose said.

"And I will muster the men to greet you, Seekers," Jukel said.

"Very good. Let us proceed then," Ephala said, arms folded behind her.

The officers boarded the ship, and Ephala turned to face Master Erebus and the other Seekers. Erebus gave her an approving nod. "You did well, Seeker Ephala. I see that your lessons in leadership have borne fruit."

Seeker Ephala flashed a reserved smile. "Yes, Master, under your careful tutelage, I've learned much. I will command these men to your exacting expectations."

Erebus turned. "See it done and return victorious, Seekers."

The Seekers watched Erebus stride away, mount his horse, and bid the other horses follow him as he rode away.

"Our first royal mission. I must confess, I didn't think we'd be chosen," Sedrick said. "Tomund, Uldrin, and Farnesse must be eating their own hearts out, now," he chuckled.

"Of course, we were chosen! Top of our class, we are. Also doesn't hurt that Ephala, here, is the daughter of high nobility. The name Farandus means something, here, in the heartland," Clive said, nudging Ephala.

"My family name has nothing to do with why we're here. We arrived by our own merits, as is the way of our order. Nothing more, nothing less," Ephala snubbed.

"That true? If that's the case, then why the hell isn't Tomund here? He's the most capable leader in all our graduating class, and you know that as well as I, love," Tora pointed out.

"And tell me, is that because of his skill or because of your infatuation with him, Tora?" Ephala lashed back.

"Struck a nerve, did she? You always were jealous of ol' Tom, weren't you, Ephala?" Sedrick jabbed with a smirk.

"Why would I be jealous of someone that I'm better than?" she replied.

"Better? No. Cockier? Most certainly," Tora said with a wry smile. "Besides, I only have eyes for one Seeker." She looked at Frond, who folded his arms smugly.

"Then why am I the leader of this mission, then? Do you really believe Master Erebus would allow favoritism to trump pragmatism?" Ephala asked, looking directly at Tora and Sedrick.

"Our Master is too shrewd and calculative of a man to allow Ephala's noble birth to cloud his judgment. If anything, I'd argue it probably was a strike against her," Clive said.

Tora and Sedrick looked at each other skeptically.

"What do *you* think, Frond?" Tora asked, placing a hand on the shoulder of the towering warrior.

Frond looked at her, then the others, who were all watching his response. Even Ephala was giving him an inquisitive glance. "Whether she was most qualified or wasn't, it matters not. She is here, she is our squad leader, and she will see us to victory. We have more important matters to attend, and we must seem unified in front of these men."

"Aye, I'm all tens there," Sedrick nodded.

"Right then, it's settled. From this moment forth we're a unit, we move as one, we think as one, we decide as one. And we carry our decisions forth with the crew," Ephala said.

"Aye," said Sedrick.

"Aye," said Clive.

"Agreed," said Tora.

"Yes, ma'am," answered Frond with a salute.

"Let's move out then," Ephala said.

And so their mission began.

*****

There were six-hundred and thirty-two men and women aboard the Black Bess. The Seekers were introduced to every squadron of them, which numbered fifty. They were introduced to the squadron leaders, of course, as well as the officers that worked under each of her lieutenants. There were so many of them, Ephala had given up trying to remember them all after the twelfth squad leader. Sedrick tried to joke with a few of them to break the monotony, but judging by their reactions, you'd have thought he threatened their lives.

As time went on, she realized they had. They stared at her. All of them did. Most specifically, they stared at the *S* on her forehead. It marked her as different, and not in a good way. Even here, amongst the military, she was feared.

I'm on your side. Can't you see that?

She leaned back into the leather of her captain's chair. Though Avery was the ship's captain, he had opted to stay in the cabin below hers. And she had opted to share her cabin with Tora, so that the boys would have their own. They would have to share storage, but somehow, she doubted that would be a harder compromise for her than Sedrick, Clive, and Frond.

Sedrick and Clive were snorers. This she knew from sleeping in the same bunk hall with them. They were also used to sleeping in beds rather than hammocks.

"You seem troubled, Seeker-Sister," Tora noted, sitting on the edge of her hammock, removing her armor. "Is it the stares?"

Ephala looked squarely at her.

How did you know?

"What gave it away? Hahah," Ephala asked, trying to sound nonchalant.

"Because they were staring at me, too. I could feel their gaze everywhere I went," Tora admitted. "They're scared of us."

The two women sat in silence a moment. Tora disarming herself, and Ephala leaning in her chair, hands in a pyramid of contemplation, trying to puzzle out everything that had happened that day.

"This mission, I get that it's important, but...why would they put us in charge of an entire ship-of-the-line? We've no naval command experience, and we've barely been on ships before. Wouldn't it have been better to just attach us to the crew as a special detachment and send us out that way, rather than having us command it?" Tora asked.

"Ah, yes, that. I've been pondering that same question..." Ephala admitted. "I figure there must be something deadly special about this artifact for His Majesty to have put such significance upon it. I'm thinking he anticipated we'll be needing significant force to take down these pirates. He also wants to ensure that we are in control of the operation to ensure that this artifact takes precedence over everything—even our lives."

"What artifact could be worth a ship-of-the-line, several high-ranking officers, and a squadron of Seekers?" Tora pondered.

"This *Eye of Atla*, evidently. I've never heard of it. Apparently, the sailors have, though," Ephala said. "I overheard the officers talking about it. It's strange. The Lord Advisor did not say what precisely this object does, merely its importance."

"Perhaps they don't even know what it does," Tora said.

"But they could describe what it looks like? Down to the chest we would find it in? Unlikely," Ephala ran a hand through her hair. "No, they know. They don't want us to know, however."

"It matters not. We are the Emperor's blades. If he so demands it be retrieved, then we shall retrieve it," Tora said, putting away her armor in the wardrobe. Her Alyria tattoos, intricate lines weaved into her flesh on her arms and chest, were on display, though they were inactive.

"As you say, Seeker-Sister."

*****

"Alright then, let's handle this like civilized lads," Clive said as Sedrick and Frond stared each other down.

"I'm not sharin' a chest with either one of you louts. Specially not you, Darwin," Sedrick stated, looking up into Frond's small, brown eyes.

Darwin Frond had removed his helmet, finally, as well as his armor. He stood shoeless, in a sleeveless aketon shirt and padded pants. His Alyria tattoos, which had been meticulously carved into his flesh by the Spire's flesh scrivener, were on full display on his arms, neck, and the bits of his chest that poked out his shirt. Without his armor he was still an intimidating giant of a man. Even though he was only nineteen years old.

"Fine by me, pip squeak," Frond said, glowering down at Sedrick, who stood more than half a foot shorter than him.

"I don't need my rifle to floor you, ape man," Sedrick shot back.

Clive ran a hand through his hair as he watched his Seeker-Brothers argue over storage. How exactly did Ephala think they were going to sort this out? There was one chest that needed to fit the armor of three men. Otherwise, the pieces would be knocking around the room at all hours of the night, causing a racket and waking them.

"I won't even need my Alyria to squash you," Frond said, his eyes already taking on an unnatural hue.

"Then why you chargin' up, then?" Sedrick asked, his own tattoos beginning to glow.

"Because I know you'll cheat," Frond said, knowing Sedrick's tactics all-too-well.

"You're damn right I will! I'm not getting crushed by you!" Sedrick shouted.

"Enough!" Clive said, silencing them.

They both turned their heads in his direction, having forgotten he was there.

"We'll take two chests from the crew. They won't be happy about it, but they'll just have to deal so we can store our armor." Clive stated. He was confounded they hadn't even considered that before arguing over the one chest.

Frond opened the chest and dropped his armor pieces, which were tied together with rope, into the chest. He glared at the irritated Sedrick the whole time.

"Sedrick, go down to Quartermaster Staunton and request two storage chests," Clive ordered.

"But I—" Sedrick began.

"Shut up!" Clive shouted. "Stars above, it's like dealing with children!"

Sedrick grumbled loudly and walked out of the room. Frond, on the other hand, had already settled into his hammock like a victorious bear.

"Children. I'm surrounded by children," Clive muttered, dragging a hand down his face.

To Damian Clive, they were children. He was twenty-three years old and was eldest of the squad. In his mind, he should have been the leader. Ephala was two years younger than he, and he definitely had better leadership chops.

The Master knows best.

He told himself. It was not his duty, nor his right to question the decisions of the Master, and evidently he decided that Ephala was better than him in that regard. Perhaps he was right, or perhaps not. Only time would tell. For now, he contented himself with sleep. It had been a long day, and there would be many more before they set eyes on their quarry.

Have to be ready. Have to be prepared.

He told himself. Perhaps he would spar with these mariners. They were said to all be trained pirate killers. He wondered how they'd fair against someone like him. Moreover, he wondered what was so dangerous about these pirates that the Emperor felt it necessary to send someone like him after them.

XL

SHAPESHIFTER

Cutter pushed open the door and fell out onto the sunbaked deck, vomiting. "Oh, Gods…what the fuck?! What the FUCK?!!" he screamed. Flint, Ryker and Sarkad were right behind him.

"Hermalla's mercy…it got him too," Ryker gasped.

"Claude…" Sarkad sighed, cupping his hand over his eyes.

Morgan walked out of the room next, followed by Osiris, Huasca, Cage and Stone, who solemnly marched out onto the deck, haunted by what they'd seen. Morgan leaned over the railing, looking out into the sea as he tried to process the ruin he'd just laid eyes on.

He cleared his throat, and in a shakey voice he said, "Mr. Stone, gather the um…" his voice left him. "Gather the men and notify Moary. We're going to have to tell them what happened," he finished. He felt like a heavy boulder had settled in his chest.

His face…dear Stars, his face…

"Aye, cap'n…I'll see it done," Stone said, his own voice small and troubled.

"A grave danger lurks this ship; something unholy. We need to find it and slay it before it is our undoing," Abbal declared aloud.

"A grave danger, eh? Well tell us where *the fuck* it is, then!" Cutter screamed, pointing at Morgan and the amulet.

"I can ascertain no more. Its presence is hidden from me," Abbal answered calmly.

"Hidden, eh? Mighty fuckin' convenient. That magickal rock around your neck has been useful for fuck all since before we set sail and now it wants to speak to the choir after our surgeon gets cut up?!"

"Cutter…" Flint began, placing a hand on his shoulder.

"Fuck off!" Cutter lashed out, knocking his hand away. "Nah, it needs sayin! We're in deep fucking shit! First the widow crab, then the Dyonians offing themselves! This whole *fucking* voyage has been cursed from the start! And ever since that damn artifact got on this ship? It's gotten *worse*! Bill Louis flew the fucking coup, all right, maybe it was a one-off. But then Yager's mutilated body turns up! And soon as we get back under way, we're chased into doldrums by Valkar—who chopped my *fucking* hand off! That relic—that Eye of Atla is a beacon for all our misfortune, I fuckin' know it!" Cutter said. "And *you* know it too, cap'n. That fucking amulet knows more than he's lettin' on. He's havin' a laugh at our expense, mark my fuckin' words."

Cutter stormed off, and the other officers stood in silence.

"Cap'n..." Ryker began. His head began to twitch and shake, and Sarkad grabbed hold of him, supporting him as he placed a hand on his head, trying to stop the involuntary motion. The 'wracking shivers' that Claude had told him he would suffer from were spot on. He got them periodically, ever since he'd woken up. They were debilitating. "What's happenin' to us?"

Ryker looked Morgan in the eyes, a man he'd known for well over a decade, now. And for the first time for as long as he could remember, Ryker saw genuine fear in the eyes of his captain.

Morgan opened his mouth to speak but couldn't find the words. "I don't know. I don't know, but you, me, and everyone here must stand firm because when those men get word of this, they are going to need us to direct their anger, their fear, and their grief. I am sorry, all of you, for what has been wrought upon us. But the only way out of this hell is through," Morgan said, placing a hand on Ryker's convulsing shoulder.

Ryker nodded once, between bouts of shaking, and he squeezed his fists together and concentrated on stopping the spasms. He thought of his dearly departed friend, and all they'd been through, and he calmed down as his brother gripped his shoulder. "I'm ready."

Morgan nodded and looked to the others. He could see their hearts weren't in it.

Just hold it together a little longer.

They turned, hearing the men grumbling and talking amongst themselves as they filtered onto the deck. Morgan looked back at the door to Claude's cabin, and shut it, and the horror inside, away. He and his officers wordlessly ascended to the top of the foredeck, so that they would be standing over the crew, and he cleared his throat as he looked over Azura.

"Men...there has been an incident..."

"What do we know?" Morgan asked as he settled into his chair. Most of the officers were present. Ryker and Sarkad sat in chairs across from him with Huasca sitting on the edge of the desk beside him. Flint and Cutter glowered from a corner. Steven Cage was sitting in a chair sharpening a knife with a whetstone. Osiris simply stood, looking out the windows behind Morgan.

Huasca was the first to speak. "I performed a ritual on Daniel Yager's eyes…"

They all looked at him with bated breath, waiting to hear what he had to say next. He kept them waiting for several long moments as he mumbled to himself.

"…I do not know how to describe what I saw. The thing that killed Daniel Yager resembled a mermaid of some sort, but…wrong."

"Wrong? What do you mean wrong?" Morgan asked.

"It did not look like any mermaid I have ever seen. Moreover, the creature dragged itself onto the beach…and grew legs. I have never known a mermaid, of any sort, to do that."

"Perhaps it was an Alyrian mermaid? Alyrians can do all manner of freakish shite with their magick," Stone said with vitriol. Osiris looked at him over his shoulder. "No offense, mate. You 'n Huasca ain't like any other Alyrians I came across." Stone addended.

"Perhaps. But why would an Alyrian mermaid attack Daniel Yager, of all people? And to maul him in such a vicious fashion…that is not how merfolk conduct themselves. What attacked him did so like a savage animal," Huasca shuddered.

"Maybe they were a savage? Outcasted from their people?" Flint suggested. "It's not like we know much about merfolk. Maybe they fear Alyrians as much as we do?"

"That *thing* was not a true mermaid, I don't think. Its shape was…odd." Huasca said.

"Odd?" Morgan asked.

"I do not know. It is…difficult to describe. It killed Yager very quickly, so his eyes were not active for long. The last thing I saw was it baring down on him," Huasca explained.

"How did it get aboard the ship without our knowing?" Osiris asked. "I find it hard to believe that a half-fish, half-man monster would be able to slip under our noses."

"He raises a fair point, aye," Ryker spoke up. "Me 'n Sarkad 'ave looked over the ship a half dozen times already, inspecting it as we do, after every battle. We saw no sign of anything other than all of us living on this ship."

"Well, that is puzzling. Even the creatures known to climb aboard ships at sea end up belying their presence. Droppings, half-eaten meals—things of that nature," Morgan said. "Hell, we have livestock on the ship."

"Aye, and I'd have sniffed them out," Osiris pointed out. He routinely walked the ship as part of his duties to ensure nothing and no one was stowing away unauthorized. He'd killed a fair number of unwanted creatures—and a few people—that way. "This thing, whatever it is, isn't a dumb animal."

Everyone turned to face Osiris, keen to hear his opinion.

"What are your thoughts?" Morgan asked, leaning back in his chair.

"Way I see it, Yager was a fluke. I dunno what brought it to us, but it killed him for reasons unknown, maybe just because it could. In hindsight it was an omen of what was to come. Claude Humris, though, that was no fluke. It killed him with precision 'n strategy. Mr. Flint, ye were the last to see Claude alive. Did ye notice anythin' strange? Anythin' out of place?" Osiris probed.

Flint shook his head. "Nay, not a peep. Everything was normal, we was talkin', he was checkin' out me stitches 'n gave me painkillers for it." He absentmindedly ran a hand over his eyepatch. "We joked about my eye. Then the subject turned to Cutter, and Claude reminisced about the old days, all the people that died on his operatin' table."

"Blimey. We found him on the operating table…" Stone said.

"When was this?" Osiris asked.

"Maybe eight hours ago, around midnight," Flint said.

"We found 'em an hour ago. So, between midnight last night and seven in the morning, Claude Humris was butchered in his room. Nobody heard anything, nobody saw anything, and the killer managed to slip out without a trace…" Osiris listed off. "And to top it all off, we're trapped in doldrums, for Stars know how long…"

"Which means we're trapped with whatever killed Yager and Claude, with no hope of escape. Well played," Morgan said thoughtfully.

"Do ye think it's a coincidence? Maybe the Valkar were behind this all along," Stone suggested.

"Ardvald the Mangler was not a man of subtlety or guile. I do not see him being so clever as to orchestrate this," Cage said, shooting down Stone's suggestion.

"Hells, maybe ye were in league with 'em. Playin' the long con!" Cutter growled. "Did ye know that bastard was goin' to take my fuckin' hand?!"

"Mr. Cutter, simmer down!" Morgan ordered, pointing at him with a calloused finger. "I gave you leave with your outburst earlier. This is no time for it now."

Before Cutter could open his mouth again, the door to the captain's cabin opened and Moary slid in solemnly, clicking the door shut behind him.

"Sorry for the wait, gents. The men are beside themselves," Moary said, announcing his presence without his usual jovial zest.

"Has anyone mentioned anything? Maybe they saw something or heard something in the night?" Morgan asked him.

Moary shook his head. "Nay, cap'n. I spoke to all my gunners, 'n I asked all the men on watch 'n in the galley—nobody, not one bloody soul saw anythin' or heard anythin' near Claude's cabin. It's the damndest thing…"

Morgan exhaled an exasperated breath. They were out of leads. Something had killed two of his men and managed to slip away without a trace, and he hadn't the first clue what it was, save for Huasca's description of a mermaid-like monster.

Unless…

"Mr. Huasca, could you perform the ritual you used on Yager's eyes, on Claude's?" Morgan asked.

Huasca face lit up, as though he'd just heard the most obvious thing in the world. "Of course. All I need is his eyes, and then I will be able to see what he saw in his final moments before he died!"

"Excellent. Extract his eyes and tell me what you find," Morgan said.

"Immediately, captain," Huasca obliged, standing up to act and knocking over a bottle of alcohol sitting on the edge of Morgan's desk in the process. It rolled, and Moary picked it up in his massive hand.

"Brovan Almond Liquor, Vintage 2945 AS…this shite is old as I am," Moary noted. "Ye holdin' out the good shite on us again, cap'n? I think we lads could use a hard drink. Stars know the boys outside are deep in their cups, today."

The men looked at Morgan, now. He could see the desire in their eyes for something to help them momentarily forget the hell they found themselves in.

"Baah, just a nod—all of you! We need to keep our wits until we figure out where our unwelcome guest is hiding," Morgan relented.

"Aye, sir. Just somethin' to take the edge off. We've all been pulling out hairs since the Valkar attacked," Moary said, popping the cork. He took a sip of the dark liquor and handed the bottle off to Huasca, who drank and handed the bottle to Stone.

"Seems like yesterday we were all sittin' in this room, laughin' 'n celebratin' victories past. Now, we're down a man 'n we're beset by adversity. How times change, ay?" Moary reminisced.

Morgan thought back on the day they had won the El'wa prize, back at the beginning of the year. Things seemed so very hopeful, then. They were laughing and joking. They'd also lost fifty-seven men that day. When they investigated the derelict, the widow crab killed nine. When they took the Empress' Bounty, they lost twenty-four men. And finally they lost another twenty in their skirmish with the Deathwatch. This didn't include Bill Louis, who walked the plank for attempted murder of an officer and was summarily eaten by a shark in front of the whole crew. Nor did it include Daniel Yager and Claude Humris, one a traitor, the other their beloved sawbones, killed by some new, unknown force.

All told, one-hundred and thirteen men had been lost in less than six months. The majority of which had died in the past month and a half. Morgan couldn't think of a time he'd lost that many men, that quickly.

We're dropping like flies. Soon, this ship will be manned by a skeleton crew.

Azura held over two-hundred and fifty men at max capacity. She was nearly down to half that number. After Osiris took a swig from the nearly empty bottle of almond liquor, Morgan downed the rest. It had a sweet burn to it, counteracting the bitterness he felt inside.

They need this moment; let them have it.

"All of you in this room have sailed with me for over a decade each. Altogether, nearly a century of comradery stands in this room. We are in dark times the likes of which we have never seen. But I tell you, as one who has been through such darkness before, that the light will come again. We are the strong, the proud, and cunning hunters of these seas. We are the Azura Pirates, feared and renown across Hera. And I am proud of all of you. We will survive these trials yet," Morgan said with a nod. He thought to open his drawer and pull out more bottles, to let his officers mourn the loss of one of their own, and steel themselves for what was to come.

"We cannot afford to languish. This threat must be eradicated. I can sense its darkness, even now," Abbal warned.

Moary stood, nodded, and turned for the door. "If we're done, sir, the men need me."

Morgan nodded. "You may go, Mr. Moary. And should you find him, send Armen Hanover to me."

Moary nodded, bid farewell to his fellow officers, and marched out the room.

"Now that we're down a sawbones, we are in even more dire straits. We have no one who has practiced amputations, so should a man have an infected limb, we will be forced to perform the deed ourselves," Morgan said, returning to the matters at hand.

All of the men collectively winced.

"Fuck. They'd be better off dead, then," Flint said.

"Aye. I got one good arm, I'm no good for choppin' limbs, now," Cutter said. "Shit, I'm not good for anythin', now."

"That's not true. You're good for a laugh," Sarkad chuckled. "You used to be all left, but now you're all right."

Everyone lightened up, and some even smiled at the poor joke.

"Don't worry, mate, I only need one good hand to fuck your Mum, and that's just to steer," Cutter shot back.

"Our Mum wasn't partial to cripples; she preferred her men to use both hands," Ryker said.

Cutter raised an eyebrow. "I know you've got damage now, but I'd think your brain would've been sharp enough to realize how bad that comeback was, Shakes."

Flint, Ryker, Sarkad, and Cage laughed.

"I dunno why you're laughin', Cage. Don't they fuck goats as well as family where you come from?" Cutter asked.

"I've never fucked a goat in my life. But even a goat would be a better lay than a man who lost the hand he wipes his ass with," Cage replied, waving a hand over his nose like he smelled a skunk. "Or is that just your natural stink, brother?"

This made even Huasca and Osiris laugh. Morgan cracked a smile and shook his head.

"I'll have you know Claude gave me a rag for that, isn't that right Clau—" Cutter began, then paused.

The laughter died.

"He will be missed," Morgan said.

They all agreed.

Suddenly, Moary opened the door and returned. He looked around the room casually, then stopped on Osiris with a questioning look.

"Mr. Moary, back so soon?" Morgan asked. "Where is Armen Hanover?" He looked him over, puzzled.

Did Moary change clothes?

"Hanover? But Osiris over there just told me he was goin' to get 'em," Moary said, confused.

The officers all looked at each other, equally confused.

"That is not possible, Mr. Moary. Osiris has been here, the whole time," Huasca said. "You just left the room to go and tend to your men…" Huasca explained.

"Moary, ye were just here a moment ago—did the cannon blasts finally scramble that peanut-sized brain of yours?" Cutter asked.

"Nae, I wasn't. I was with the men down in the galley. They've been drinkin' in honor of the boys we lost to the Valkar, 'n poor Claude," Moary explained, scratching his head. "But ye say ye seen me here a moment ago? And I just saw Siris, comin' down the stairs. Said he was goin' to fetch Hanover…"

The rest of the room caught on.

Huasca bolted upright. "Bawon Samedi, ndichengetei! De killer! He was here!" he shouted.

Everyone bolted for the door and scrambled down the stairs to the main deck.

"Fan out! Find him!" Morgan ordered as he pulled out Bullet Rose.

The others pulled out their weapons as well.

"Stick together!" Stone warned. "The bastard slipped right out under our noses, 'n we don't know what else he's got under his sleeve!"

They broke off into groups of two. Huasca and Osiris went toward the officers' cabins, as did Flint and Cutter. Ryker and Sarkad went below, into the lower compartments. Moary and Cage went down into the galley. Morgan and Stone broke off for the spare compartment leading down into the bilge.

"Meet back in this spot in fifteen minutes!" Morgan shouted before they broke away.

*****

Moary and Cage legged it down into the galley. "I was here but a minute ago with some of the men, Armen should be down here as well. If anyone came down, someone must've seen them!"

"I'll gut them like a fish as soon as I get my hands on them for what they did to the sawbones," Cage promised.

"We can't alert the men yet. I know ye aren't the sort, Steven, but I need ya tae stay calm, and be covert!" Moary pleaded just as they made it to the bottom of the stairwell.

Cage scowled in a murderous anger, but nodded. "I will be as calm as a dead winter night."

"Good," Moary said, and they went into the galley.

Men mingled and drank, but the mood was more somber than usual. Several men nodded and greeted Moary, and he spied Hanover leaning against the bar counter a few yards away, through the throngs of men.

"Did ya lads see anyone come down here since I been gone?" Moary asked with a smile, accepting a tankard from one of the men.

"Nay, Gunner, we ain't seen anyone come down since ye left. Why do ye ask, sir?" One of the men, a man named Khruschev, asked.

Moary shook his head quickly. "No reason, lad. Been a bit out of sorts since the sawbones passed, is all. Could use some strapping lads like yerselves to send him off, though. If ya'd be interested?" he asked, tossing the lead.

Khruschev nodded. "Aye, sir. We'd love to help send Mr. Claude off proper, isn't that right boys?"

The other two men with Khruschev. Anatoli and Borus, nodded. Satisfied, Moary turned his focus back to Hanover, and saw that Cage was sitting next to him, now, talking to him. He approached and caught the end of their discussion.

"...killed a hundred men, at least. Do you think that I give them any consideration, boy? I don't. They were weak, and I am strong, and my Goddess put them in my path to be cut down. Had they been stronger, I would be dead; the same goes for you."

Hanover, deep in his cup, shook his head. "Of course, you'd think that, aye Mr. Cage? You don't feel remorse anymore for anything. This was my first, and it was…it was…" Hanover swiped his cup off the table in frustration. "It was a woman! I stabbed her through her chin and killed her!"

Cage gave a blank grin and shrugged. "You think I haven't killed women before, boy? Anybody who can hold a blade in their hands can be killed with one. I've killed men, women, monsters, and everything in between! Boys young as yourself took up the sword as I lit fire to their homes and I cut them down sure as I cut down their fathers and mothers."

Hanover's jaw hung open in horror at what Cage had just confessed. "How…how do you sleep at night?"

Cage placed his hands on the side of his face, mimicking a pillow. "Like a wee babe."

Moary cleared his throat, and the two looked at him. "Ay, lad. How're ye holdin' up?"

Hanover shrugged and turned back to his cup. "I'm trying new flavors of alcohol. Last night it was rum, today it's whisky. I preferred the rum, to be honest."

"Still descendin' into alcoholism, I see. Careful, lad, that's a dark path to go down, take it from someone who knows," Moary warned.

"Better the drinking than the gasping," Hanover shrugged, taking another sip of whiskey, and coughing.

Moary looked at Cage and shook his head. Their quarry wasn't here. Cage nodded his agreement, and they got up to leave.

"Make peace with it, son. There are worse monsters in this world than you, trust me," Moary said.

"I don't have to live with *them*," Hanover said back.

Moary said nothing, and they walked off.

*****

"He looked like Moary, sir…" Stone gasped. "Stars above…we drank from the same bottle as him!"

"Stay calm, we don't know what we're dealing with, so all we can do act upon what we *do* know," Morgan said.

They checked the spare cabin, then unlocked the door to the stairway leading down to the bilge, Morgan unhooked the caged lantern next to the doorway and lit it. Then, he looked down into the yawning, stinking darkness below and took a deep breath. He placed his foot on the first step, and Stone stopped him.

"...That's where Yager's body was tossed," Stone whispered low into his ear.

Morgan knew. He was the one who authorized it. They wrapped his body in an oil-skin tarp and plopped him down in the bilge. He wanted to toss the body, but Claude had insisted he needed to keep it for further examination.

"Non, capitaine. I need him, still," Claude had said.

"Why? That corpse has cast an even blacker pall over this ship than the one already shrouding us," Morgan had responded.

"I need to know what killed him. For all our sakes. He may still provide us with answers," Claude rationalized.

How wrong you were.

Morgan blinked. He wondered if it was possible that Yager's corpse...wasn't quite a corpse? He cocked Bullet Rose.

"We'll put a bullet in the body, just in case," he said.

If it was undead, Yager's body would go up like kindling the moment a bullet from Morgan's flintlock struck him.

"The enchanted pistol, ay? I feel better already," Stone said leerily, pulling out his own, unenchanted gun. They descended.

The smell of low tide, and something spoiled grew stronger as they descended. The bilge was already the worst smelling place on the ship, and now it would smell even worse with a corpse stewing in it, even if it was wrapped up in a water-proof tarp.

"The bilge needs to be pumped," Morgan said with disgust. The water was already deep enough to reach his shins.

"I'll have men get right on it," Stone said.

Assuming we don't get mauled by a corpse.

Stone thought.

They waded to the alcove where Yager's body was stored and paused as they looked at the black-wrapped shape sitting there. Morgan wasted no time and aimed his pistol.

"Wait," Stone said.

Morgan raised an eyebrow at him.

"If ye shoot him, the bullet hole will leak even more water in here and it'll have to be patched with oakum. Better to just stab 'em," Stone pointed out.

Morgan nodded after a moment's consideration; he was right. He pulled out Blade Rose and plunged her tip into the tarp, expecting the corpse to start writhing in its binding and burst into flames. Morgan had the mental image of the zombie, realizing it had been found, springing to action, ablaze and angry, grasping at him. Stone kept a white-knuckled hand on his longsword.

But nothing happened.

"Well…" Stone said, releasing a breath. "That answers that."

"Hang on," Morgan said. Something wasn't right. He pulled back the tarp to reveal the face of the corpse.

"Oh, shit…"

Wrapped in the black tarp was the body of a crewman, but it was *not* Daniel Yager.

"Hang on, this is—"

"Borus Arlov," Morgan said.

"But where's Yager?! Where the fuck did he go?!" Stone asked, panicking.

"I don't know. But we need to warn the others," Morgan said, and they retreated up the stairs, leaving the body to float in the water.

*****

Cutter opened the drawer next to his hammock in the officers' cabin and pulled out a clear bottle of whitestar syrup, he unscrewed the lid and sat it on the top of the dresser with a shaking, clammy hand. His phantom pain had come back with a vengeance, and he knew he needed the syrup to numb it. He'd nicked the last of Claude's supply from his cabin, and he carefully drew the liquid into the needle, trying to quell his shaking hand. He hated needles, but he knew the most effective way to kill the pain now would be to take this needle and plunge it into his arm.

"Breathe, mate," Flint said, sitting on the hammock across from him.

"I'm fuckin' tryin'. It burns so damn much I can't focus!" he snapped, dropping the syringe on the floor and cursing as it rolled under Flint's hammock. Flint bent over and grabbed it, took the bottle into one hand and sucked up the syrup into the needle with the other, straining as the thick, viscous liquid slowly drew into the needle. Claude normally heated it before injecting it into their body, to loosen the fluid and make it easier to absorb. They didn't have a flame source on hand.

"Only a little, ay? Claude only ever injects a small dose of the shit. I'd hate to think what happens when you do too much," Flint warned.

Cutter snatched the needle from him with a shaky hand, took a deep breath, and stabbed it into his left arm. He cried out as he injected the liquid.

Just a bit.

He injected a small dose of it, and pulled the needle out, causing a pearl of blood to pool on his skin. He handed the needle to Flint, who took it calmly and injected himself in the arm to kill the shooting pain in his head. After several long moments, the pain, which had once been sharp and blinding, dulled and faded.

"How do ye feel, brother?" Flint asked.

Cutter took several deep breaths and nodded.

"What are we gonna do when this shit runs out?" he asked.

Flint looked away. "I dunno. Guess we'll deal with that storm when we come to it. Let's go check below. Ryker 'n Sarkad can't cover all that area by themselves."

Cutter nodded and handed the bottle back to Flint, who pocketed it.

*****

Osiris and Huasca silently scoured the room.

"What are the odds the bastard actually came in here again?" Osiris asked.

"Sometimes, the killer will return to the scene of the crime to gloat over their kill," Huasca said as he checked around Claude's hammock. Light streamed in from outside, illuminating the operating room, but still, it was quiet and dark.

"I've never gloated over someone I've killed before," Osiris said. He rifled through the cabinets, throwing the doors open and aiming his pistol inside should someone try to jump out at him.

"I'm not talking about pirates. I'm talking about murderers, people who hunt other people not out of necessity but for sport," Huasca said.

"For sport? Ye mean people like Cage, then," Osiris said.

"Correct," Huasca said as he stood up and put his hands on his hips, stumped. There was no one there save the corpse of Claude Humris, lying motionless on the table. He stared at the covered body for several long moments and took notice that the sheet was untucked in a corner, near his head. They'd taken care to tuck all around the body earlier. It was a small detail, but it nagged at him. He walked over to the body as Osiris looked at him confused.

"Old man, don't—"

Huasca held up a finger, silencing him. He took a deep breath and pulled back the sheet. He gasped. Claude Humris' butchered corpse grinned at him with the smile his murderer had cut into his face, and he gazed blindly back at him. He was missing his eyes.

"Chikara icho—they took his eyes!" Huasca announced.

Osiris peered at the corpse. "Shit. He heard you talking about using his eyes for your ritual—to see what he looks like. He must've taken them so that we couldn't figure it out."

Huasca cursed, then slung the sheet back over Claude's ruined face. First they killed him, then they took his eyes so that he couldn't show them what his killer looked like. "It makes sense, now. It is a shapeshifter…"

*****

"Clear!" Sarkad called out as he checked the corner of the storage room. Ryker had gone to check the livestock pen, on the off chance that someone had taken to shacking it up with the pigs. He heard them squealing in the background in protest of his intrusion, but he didn't hear Ryker call back to him.

"Ryker? You okay brother?"

The pigs squealed, but Ryker didn't answer. Concerned, Sarkad made his way over to where he'd seen him last. He moved slowly and quietly. He heard a rapid knocking sound, so he pulled out his pistol as he rounded the corner. He nearly stumbled over Ryker laying in the doorway to the pig pen, foaming at the mouth, convulsing. His head was knocking against the floorboards.

"Brother!" Sarkad cried out, leaning down to support his head. He thought back on the last conversation he'd had with Claude Humris about his brother's new condition.

"I am…sorry, Sarkad. There is nothing I can do to help your brother. The head trauma he sustained from being knocked unconscious for so long is beyond my ability to help," Claude had said sorrowfully.

"There must be something to be done for my brother, Claude! He can't live like this!" Sarkad had pleaded.

"I cannot, his issues are beyond what modern medicine can mend. But Alyria…when we make landfall next, search for a cleric of the Stars. They can

perform healing miracles, and perhaps they may even be able to fix your brother's condition. Until then, you will have to watch him like a hawk. He could flare up at any moment, and in the wrong circumstances it could be fatal," Claude had warned.

"What can I do? He just starts shakin' n…there's nothing I can do to stop it!"

"Hold his head, prop it up on a pillow, or something soft, and let it pass. Put a rag in his mouth to stop him from biting his tongue off. That is all we can do, for now. Mitigate the symptoms…"

Sarkad focused back on the situation at hand.

"I've got you, brother!" he promised, pulling out a rag from his pocket and stuffing it into Ryker's mouth as he propped his head up on his leg. "Hang on. It'll pass."

Ryker, unable to speak, simply grunted and convulsed, his eyes going wild in their sockets. They focused on a shadow, creeping up behind Sarkad, and he tried vainly to warn him. He made urgent grunts, flicking his eyes back and forth.

"What's wrong brother?" Sarkad asked.

The pigs squealed even louder, looking wide-eyed in their direction and backing into a corner. Sarkad heard a floorboard creak behind him. He whipped his head around, aiming his pistol. "Show yourself fucker!"

He caught the briefest glimpse of a head poking back around a corner, and the shadow disappeared quick as it came.

*****

Six Hours Later…

"We send your body, brother in black, to the fate that all sailors face, in the end," Morgan said, holding a bible in his hand.

The afternoon service for Claude Humris had begun, bitter and solemn. The Azura had lost one of its most vital members in a truly horrific way, and every man aboard her knew it. And so, as Osiris, Moary, Khruschev, and Anatoli carried Claude to the edge of the steering deck, the crew watched on.

"To the bosom of the sea, where our bodies will one day be. Go with peace and know that you are not alone. For your brothers and sisters passed, await you in your new home. May Xalhanna weigh the scales of judgement and find your soul light as a feather. May you fly high like a midnight dove, far from this world and its bitter storms. We mourn you…" Morgan paused.

Osiris led the motion, and the men threw Claude Humris overboard into the sea below. He landed with a splash, and his white-wrapped body sank slow into the aquamarine, still blue waters. Osiris wiped his brow. The day was hot and unforgiving without the caress of the wind.

"Go in peace, brother. Until we meet again…"

The men said their goodbyes; some cried. Osiris saw Flint wipe away a tear from his good eye, and Cutter walked off as soon as the body was tossed over. Most stood solemn, however. Stone's face was unreadable, as was Steven Cage's. As they dispersed, Osiris leaned against the railing, watching as Claude's body faded into the water. Already he could see shapes moving from down in the deep, ready to partake of the bounty given unto them.

"How did he go?" Khruschev asked, leaning next to Osiris.

Osiris looked at Khruschev, studying him. The captain had told him about the body of Boris, though no one else had been notified yet. He wondered if the Khruschev standing before him was the real Khruschev, or an imposter? Boris had not been seen since earlier in the day. Could it be because the shapeshifter had taken on a *new* face? Perhaps the face of the man standing before him. In the bleached white light of the sun, Khruschev looked calm and genuinely curious.

"Ye know he was slain, ay?" Osiris asked.

Khruschev nodded. "That's all I was told, I'm afraid."

Osiris nodded slowly. It made sense that he wouldn't know. Only the officers knew the true details of Claude's death. That the person that killed him wasn't a regular crewman, but something else—a shapeshifter.

"He was felled upon last night. Cut up something fierce by his killer," Osiris elaborated.

"Stars…so that's why his face was," Khruschev began, and shivered. "I'd thought it was some sort of freak accident."

"It was freak, alright. But it was no accident. He was slain," Osiris revealed.

"Hermalla's mercy, sir. Who would do that?"

Osiris shook his head as he walked away. "A monster. Watch yourself, Mr. Khruschev. He could be anyone."

He left Khruschev standing in confusion, and spied Hanover standing apart from the crowd, arms folded, leaning against the railing. Hanover made eye contact with him, and he was surprised to see the boy maintaining it. He walked over and leaned next to him. "You're surprisingly calm."

Hanover shrugged. "I guess I'm sort of beside myself. I can't believe someone would do that to another person. And that was just from what I saw of the face. It's awful; the worst thing I've ever seen, in fact."

If you only saw the rest of him…

Osiris thought darkly.

Claude Humris' face was mutilated. He had a scalpel taken to it, cutting apart chunks of his skin and exposing raw, bloody flesh. A smile had been cut into it, from ear to ear, nearly severing the jaws in the process. Before his eyes were taken out, they were wide in the most abject horror Osiris had ever seen a person's face convey. His nose was broken and leaning sharply to one side.

His body was even worse.

It looked as though whomever killed him had bitten pieces of flesh from his body, and had peeled off the skin from his belly, exposing the fat and muscles beneath, which had been partially eaten. His intestines were hanging out, and they were forced to wrap the lengthy tubes of flesh around his body when they wrapped him in cloth. He was also missing fingers from each hand, as well as several toes from one foot. Some of them had been found in bloody pools around the room. Others had simply vanished, likely eaten by his killer. It was a scene from a butcher's shed, and it smelled like one as well. If he thought too long, Osiris could smell it, even now—piss, shit, and blood.

Claude Humris had been tortured, mauled, and eaten by his killer. And if the bloody smears all over the room were any indicator, he'd been alive for a good amount of that time, struggling.

"Yeah…it might just be the worst thing I've ever seen, too," Osiris said, breaking from his trance. He placed a hand on Hanover's shoulder, and the teen looked at him, concerned.

"Sir?" he asked.

Osiris took a deep breath, unsure of what to say. "We ain't exactly been on the best of terms as of late, b—" he stopped himself. "Hanover. And I want to apologize."

Hanover was visibly surprised. "…Think nothing of it, sir, I was being a—"

"A teen. That's what ye are. You're trying your best to adapt to this life, and I know well as anyone how trying that can be. You've been through a lot these past months. Lesser men than you would have died or quit by now. For that, ye deserve my respect."

Hanover was dumbfounded, and he stood there in shock for several long moments, jaw hanging open. "Thank you, sir. That means…that means a lot to me, truly."

Osiris removed his hand and folded his arms. "Good. Back to business then. We're in the doldrums and its hot as an Infernal's balls without the wind. I need you to stay sharp at all hours while you're performing your duties, understand? There's a killer aboard this ship, and we don't know who they are or who they'll attack next."

Hanover nodded his head rapidly. Moary had told him some of what was going on, about the killer on the loose, but when he asked who the Half-Duwa suspected might be the culprit, he said something that perplexed him.

"Everyone." Moary had said. *"Suspect everyone."*

"Do you have any idea who it could be, sir?" Hanover asked, hoping Osiris would give him more insight.

"No. I wish I did." He leaned in close. "Suspect everyone. Anyone actin' strange, anyone tryin' to pull you away from the pack. Don't follow anyone into any dark corners, or any secluded compartments, especially after dark—understand?"

Hanover nodded. "Aye, sir. I'll keep my eyes peeled."

"Keep your eyes peeled, keep your ears pricked, and keep your finger on the trigger. It might be the only thing saving you, should the time come," Osiris warned. "Lest ye end up like poor Claude."

He could smell it again.

*****

From a crack in the spare cabin door, she watched. She had fun with him. What was his name? Claude? Or was it Daniel? Or Boris? It didn't matter. Their names didn't matter. All they were was food and temporary entertainment. Their cries for help, their muted screams of pain. The realization on their faces when they realized that it was too late, that no one would come for them, and that they were hers, now and forever. Their fear…

She looked around, plotting her next move. They were trapped in dead waters. They had no idea what they were up against, who to trust, or what to do. They were all dead; they just didn't know it yet. Soon it would be time for her to make her next move. Walking amongst them in the daylight drained her, but it was necessary to uphold the façade. She would need to feed again soon. She watched them disperse. She was learning their routines, their vulnerabilities. She could sense an Alyrian among them, however, though she couldn't pinpoint who. She suspected the bald Xallan man. She knew that the amulet of saviors around Morgan Sarron's neck would eventually detect her. She had been playing it close; she was certain he would know when she grabbed the bottle of alcohol off the floor. Evidently, it wasn't as powerful as the Dread Captain had made it seem.

Regardless, she came here for a specific purpose. She could not afford to linger. So, she sighted her next target, waited for everyone to turn their backs, and made her way out across the deck. She passed by the other Xallan, the young man with the tattoos on his arms. She thought, momentarily, that *he* might be the Alyrian. She couldn't be sure until she saw a tell. Besides, she would eat him later. Either before or during their massacre at the hands of her master.

For now, she would content herself with a small fish.

But soon, it would be time to shake the barrel.

XLI

WATCHERS

Immanel Corinthian strode into the Grand Cathedral, passing under the archways made with two angels holding hands, as well as the elaborate ceiling fresco that depicted angelick and demonick forces warring with one another in graphic fashion. The stained-glass windows, themselves artistic depictions of the faces of various robed figures, cast a rainbow of colors onto the long rows of pews leading up to the altar. He passed dozens of church-goers who stood and marveled at the paladin as he made his way to the altar of Xalhanna, the patron goddess of the Grand Cathedral of Emperor's Rest. To attend this church, one had to be flush with coin, and it showed in every silken gloved wave of a noblesse, trying to court his interest. Noblemen, eager to break bread with an honest-to-stars paladin, beckoned him as he marched.

He ignored them all.

He prostrated himself in front of the altar as the Star Goddess of Balance and Order stood over him, holding a long stave with scales on either end, perfectly balanced in her stone arms. Xalhanna was one of the fiercest of the Star Gods, and the mason who carved this statue of her wanted to embody that with her piercing, judgemental gaze. He knelt before her and placed his scabbarded great sword on the altar in prayer. He felt the warmth of the Stars flow through him, and bright yellow light surged behind his closed eyes. His body glowed with a sheen of that light.

A throng of people formed a half circle several yards behind him, mystified by what they were seeing. Several of the women fell out on the floor, or into other onlookers' arms, overtaken by excitement. Corinth ignored them still. This was not for their pleasure; this was for the worship of Xalhanna.

"It is always a spectacle to see an ordained knight of the church in worship of the Gods. It is as though we're watching a scene out of the very Book of the Stars itself," narrated a man with an elderly, orotund voice. The crowd of people broke, and many bowed their heads in reverence of the speaker as he came forth. "Marvel, my children, at a guardian of the flock: Immanel Corinthian, Paladin of the Stars."

At the saying of his name, Immanel rose and turned to greet the speaker. "Archbishop Kalen, how are you this fine day?"

The archbishop gave a fatherly grin and motioned to the nearby pews. Corinth obliged and sat. "Begone, children. Church matters are at hand."

The onlookers, noblemen and women, many of which were likely the members of some of the most powerful families in the city, fled like school children at the request of Kalen. Such was his power. After the doors shut and they were certain they were alone, the archbishop cleared his throat to speak.

"To answer your question, I am well, paladin. Though I could do without the early summer heat. I swear the capital feels as though it's kissing the surface of the sun, this time of year. No thanks to recent events, of course," Kalen said peacefully. The elderly man, the indulgences of high-living evident in his plush frame, waved a fan ineffectually at his liver-spotted face.

"Ah, yes," Corinth sighed, leaning forward in his seat, and resting his elbows on his knees as he looked at the statue of Xalhanna, gazing down at him. "The bombings."

"Can you believe that these saboteurs would be so bold as to target a church on Sundus, during mass?" Kalen sighed like a tired, grieving grandfather. "Those poor souls."

Three days prior, another bombing had occurred at a small parish on Bree Street, in the lowtown district. The attackers set a bomb in the bell tower of the church, as well as incendiaries on the exits. The bell tolled at midday, during mass, as is custom. Then the bell tower detonated, dropping the bell, easily the height of man and a dozen times the weight, down into the church, along with the ceiling rafters and cobbles. Those who weren't killed by the falling bell and ceiling were trapped and immolated by the burning exits. It was a quick, calculated, and lethal attack. By time the guardsmen came, the horrified onlookers were staring at the burning ruins of the church.

There were no survivors.

Corinth himself had seen the carnage. Whatever explosives were used were much higher grade than anything he had ever seen military use. The flames cooked people where they stood, reducing them to ash. The twisted, charred, fused remains of hands sticking out of the rubble would forever mar his memory.

"Poor indeed, father," Corinth said, reliving the horror in his mind. "The workers arrested at the docks, were you able to convince the Emperor to release them?"

Archbishop Kalen's doughy face creased in deep remorse. "He will not listen to me, child. He says that they will go free when the arsonists have been found, and not a moment before. He is positively incorrigible, now."

"For what reason? The bombings persist—clearly, those men have no hand in this!" Corinth protested, then bowed his head. "Apologies, Archbishop, I...I just..."

"You care deeply for the people, Paladin Corinthian. It is admirable. Do not apologize for concern for the innocent. Mercy and kindness are pillars of our Lords," the archbishop said.

"Thank you for your understanding, archbishop."

"Now, onto the matter I summoned you for. I need you to accompany me to the ruins of the church on Bree Street. It is unlikely that its destroyers will return to the scene of the crime. But I would feel that much safer, paladin, if you were to accompany me," Archbishop Kalen said.

"Of course. It would be my honor," Corinth said. "When do we depart?"

The archbishop gave a wry smirk. "Well, I am due for the speech in an hour—so now is most preferable."

Corinth chuckled. "You planned this all along, then?"

"Surely not. In my age, I have grown a bit forgetful, child. Forgive an old man his absentmindedness, will you?" Archbishop Kalen pleaded, trying to sound as weak and feeble as possible.

The two shared a laugh, and Corinth helped the archbishop to his feet. He grabbed his great sword from its perch on the altar and pulled it a sliver from its scabbard. It glittered with holy light. "I shall fetch the carriage."

*****

The carriage trundled swiftly through the city streets, with people stopping and waving as its white, polished wooden frame with golden trim passed by. Stallion horses drew it, and the carriage driver himself was finely dressed as well. In the carriage cabin, the archbishop and Corinth sat across from one another, occasionally glancing out the window.

"Our guard is startlingly light, Holy Father," Corinth noted. They often travelled with at least a detachment of imperial guardsmen. Today, all they had was themselves and a small wagon full of men tailing behind them.

"Not many would dare to accost one of my station in broad daylight, Ser Corinth. Even less so with a paladin at my side, I fear not. Only the forces of the Infernals would be so bold as to make such a move, and theirs is a pithy lot, these days," Archbishop Kalen dismissed.

He was right. In the five years Corinth had been a sanctified paladin, he had only come across *one* demon, and that one had been during an exorcism. It was small, weak, and easily dispatched. He was told that at one point in time, they scoured the land in the tens of thousands, sieging cities and terrorizing mankind to no end. Now, however, all was quiet on that front.

"Tell me, young paladin, have you ever laid eyes on a demon before?" the archbishop asked, his face shifting to a pensive expression.

Corinth nodded. "Once, Your Holiness. During an exorcism."

"I see. What kind of demon was it?"

Corinth shook his head. "An impling. It was weak and small, malformed, even."

"I see. So, you have never faced a true demon, then?" Archbishop Kalen pressed.

"A *true* demon, father?"

Archbishop Kalen nodded, his expression darkening. "The forces of chaos and disorder. Imps, cambions, devils; creatures borne of Sheolhenna, come to Hera to accost, seduce, and destroy all mankind…"

Corinth leaned forward, seeing the severity in Archbishop Kalen's eyes. "No, archbishop. I have only read of them in stories and texts."

"Hah! I can assure you, child, those books do not do them any justice. I have seen them with my own eyes, and I have seen the devastation they can cause. Did the grand marshall ever tell you of his time on the frontlines, fighting the Red Legion?"

Corinth's face darkened, now. The Red Legion was an army of demons and cultists that raged across the inner empire for five years, sieging several major cities, as well as citadels of the Church. Grand Marshall Ludus had fought on the eastern front.

"He mentioned it briefly, though he was often reluctant to speak at length about it," Corinth admitted.

"I can understand why. At one point in time, he saved me from the Red Legion, during the siege on Halmar Citadel," Kalen revealed.

"You were at Halmar, Holy Father?" Corinth asked, fascinated.

"I was. I was there when the brahmak, Kralkotoric, and his army of hellguards sieged the citadel. His wings, black as obsidian, each wide enough to shadow a tavern. He cut through a hundred men in less than so many seconds, and his grave flyers plucked men from the earth, carrying them away to their dooms. His eyes…" Kalen began, his voice low and keening. "Like gazing into the fires of Sheolhenna."

The archbishop had a haunted look in his eyes. He shook it away. "Stars be willing, such black days are behind us forever. I need you to be prepared, should that not be the case, however. There may yet come days where your blade and your faith are your only weapons against insurmountable odds. You must be ready and willing to face them, no matter the time nor circumstance, Immanel Corinthian."

Ser Corinth placed a gauntleted hand on the left side of his breastplate. "I am ready, always, Holy Father."

Archbishop Kalen searched his face for a moment, and having found what he wanted, he smiled warmly, and nodded.

"We're nearly there."

The carriage stopped, and Ser Corinth stepped out onto the street cobbles, cupping a hand over his eyes to ward off the glare of the sun. Already, a crowd was growing at the steps of the ruined chapel. Many were mourners, crying and grieving openly at the steps, placing flowers and wooden crosses to memorialize their fallen. Behind him, the imperial guardsmen were piling out of their wagon. They wore no helmets, so he could see the familiar faces of various men he'd been training out on the yard.

"Captain Rumford, good to see you on the detail. I need you to have men scour the perimeter. I don't want any unwanted surprises while the archbishop speaks," Ser Corinth said.

Rumford nodded to his men. "Canarsy, Henry, Atula, cover the alleyways. The rest of you fan out into the crowd."

The guardsmen followed Rumford's orders promptly. He was a good captain, one of the few that Corinth genuinely liked. He was no-nonsense, hard-working, and straightlaced. Where other guard captains tried actively to fight him over trivial matters, Rumford, his cousin Crawly, as well as Tabetha and McHenry were the ones that aided him during the drills.

"Do you suspect trouble, Ser Corinth?" Rumford asked as they watched the carriage driver, as well as another guardsman help Archbishop Kalen out of the carriage. It creaked from his shifting weight, and he walked unsteadily toward the steps of the ruined church.

"Nay, but I would rather not leave it to chance. There are those other than the terrorists that I am wary of," Corinth whispered into Rumford's ear.

"The Loyals, I presume?" Rumford whispered back, looking as one of them came into view, having been in the crowd.

The Loyals were a small sect that had been growing in popularity in the city over the past several years, from what information Corinth had gathered. What once was just a small band of rowdy, impassioned men and women had become something altogether more concerning, however. He saw them, often shacking up with the guardsmen at posts, in taverns, and even out and about on the streets. Even now, the one he was gazing at was conversing with one of his men.

Rumford didn't trust them, not one bit. He also didn't like that the Emperor seemed to turn a sympathetic eye upon them, and Viceroy simply looked the other way. The paladin seemed to be the only one who took him seriously, other than Crawley, when he made mention of their danger.

"They circle like crows to a carcass," Corinth said.

The men strode after the archbishop, who was nearly at the steps of the destroyed church. Even now, it smelled of burnt timbers and…

And burnt flesh.

Corinth shook the thought from his mind.

When he strode past the Loyal talking to the guardsman, Corinth noted the purple octopus tattoo upon the man's neck. It matched the bright, vibrant purple and white tunic he wore, denoting the heraldry of Kurza Proper, or the kingdom of Kurza.

In the empire, it was well-known that those born in the kingdom considered themselves better than others, oftentimes. This wouldn't be noteworthy, as the Atarrans, Brovans, and of course the Lordalans, all thought themselves to be better than the other kingdoms within the empire.

Kurzans, however, were a different sort. Corinth had been in the Paladincy his whole life, almost, so he identified himself as a member of the church first and an imperial citizen second. He wasn't even sure what kingdom he hailed from if he was honest. Neither Grand Marshall Ludus, or any of his instructors seemed keen on telling him either.

Why are you here?

Corinth wondered. They seemed always to hover when he was around, and it made him feel watched in an insidious way. He couldn't prove it, however. The Loyals, up until now, had been careful to keep their distance from him. The Loyal noticed his gaze and stopped talking to the guardsman. He winked at Corinth and gave him a genial smile.

Like a crocodile smiling at its prey.

Archbishop Kalen cleared his throat as the people died down, their faces peering at him with rapt attention and somber hope.

"Children of the empire; sons and daughters of our Holy Stars. I come to you today with a heavy heart. Behind me was once a place of worship, now turned into a tomb for the unfortunate souls who attended mass here. Faithful servants of our Holy Stars, cutdown in a senseless act of terror and hate. In Advent 21:6, Aeon said to their disciples, who would become the Holy Stars, 'I am the beginning, and I am the end. Those who walk with me shall live forevermore and be merry in the presence of their Creator.'

"Because their word is the gospel truth, we know that our fallen brothers and sisters are not truly gone, but in the presence of the Stars, waiting for us in Rapture," Archbishop Kalen said.

"Praise the Stars! Gods of all!" An onlooker cried.

"May the Holy Father bless them in death!" Another shouted.

"Hermalla's Mercy and Idallon's Guidance will carry them to Rapture!" A woman said, waving an arm in the air and chanting to herself.

The archbishop raised his hands up and closed his eyes. "Let us pray, children. Let us pray for the departed."

They said the Stars' Prayer; a prayer Corinth that just about everyone who lived in the southern empire knew by heart.

"Shine bright in the twilight, souls of a feather. Like birds in migration, we flock together. No matter the hour, no matter the weather. We will carry the fire; our vigil is forever. Until the end of days, until the last tomorrow. We will not break, not even in sorrow…" they chanted, heads bowed.

"Praise Be…" the archbishop finished. He lowered his arms as sweat dripped down his brow, and he let loose a tired sigh, as though he had just laid down the burden of the world from his shoulders.

The people dispersed, slowly. Some were sobbing, still. Others left their flowers and hugged each other as they walked away. Corinth and Rumford watched as the Loyal that was talking to the guard surveyed them for a moment, then began to walk away, showing his back. A bright, bluish-purple octopus was embroidered on the back of his shirt, and as he turned, they saw a dozen others flash their backs at them.

"They were hiding in the crowd, and we didn't even see them…" Rumford whispered.

"Yes," Corinth said. "They're like wolves hiding in a throng of sheep."

His gaze scanned over the street, but something pulled his gaze upward. At first, he was confused as to what.

But then he saw it again.

Something *shimmered* atop a building across from him. As Corinth watched, he realized that whatever it was, it had shape to it, rather than just heatwaves shimmering atop the sunbaked thatching of the roof. No, whatever was in front of him was a *being*. As if to confirm his suspicion, the shape made a slight shift, loosing some thatching on the roof and causing it to slide down the side, then drop onto the street. He could, just faintly, make out the outline of a crouching figure.

He put a hand on his great sword's hilt.

Rumford noticed and put a hand on his longsword, looking at Corinth, then following his gaze. He squinted, unable to make out whatever it was that had him alarmed.

"Sir?" Rumford asked.

"Over there, on that roof…" Corinth said in a low voice, casually raising his hand and pointing.

Rumford looked again but saw nothing. "I don't—"

Something moved, and another piece of roofing slid and fell off the roof. That time, Rumford saw something.

"I saw it," he said.

Corinth looked around, and he slowly began to identify several more transparent silhouettes on the roofs. He leaned into Rumford. "They're all around us…"

"How many?" Rumford said, not wanting to alarm the archbishop, who had stepped down to speak to several commoners who'd remained after the crowd dispersed.

"I count…four…"

Surrounding them, the four transparent shapes inched closer, watching them silently. And no one, save for Corinth and Rumford, seemed to notice.

They stood there tensely for several long moments. Corinth with his hand on his great sword, Rumford with his hand on the hilt of his longsword, and the figures, perched almost perfectly still, watching them like hawks. They wouldn't be able to warn the others quick enough for them to muster a defense. How could you explain to someone that several nearly invisible figures were standing on *roofs* watching them?

"What do we do, sir?" Rumford asked, warily.

"Nothing…they aren't doing anything, so we won't, either," Corinth said. They didn't know what these ghost-like figures were capable of, and he didn't want to provoke them, putting the archbishop in danger, to find out.

So, they waited.

And eventually, the figures disappeared, just as quickly—and quietly—as they came…

XLII

DESPERATE MEASURES

"And you say they were there the whole time?" Viceroy quizzed, leaning over his desk at Corinth.

"So it would seem. I only just noticed them when we were readying to depart from the church grounds," Corinth said.

Viceroy slammed his armored hands on the desk, shaking it and the floor beneath it as he grumbled over to the window. "Dammit all! Clever bastards are using some form of Alyria to conceal themselves. That would explain how they've managed to get to and from the destruction sites unnoticed."

"There is still the matter of the Loyals, sir. We cannot disqualify them from potentially having a hand in this," Rumford put forth.

"The Loyals? To Sheolhenna with the bloody Loyals! We need to focus on these damned invisible figures running around, blowing up buildings—and people, all over the city!" Viceroy shouted.

"Rumford is right, Knight-Commander, the Loyals were present at the church grounds during the archbishop's speech—we cannot disregard the possibility that they had something to do with those invisible figures, or the bombings!" Corinth agreed.

"Pfeh, of course you would agree, Ser Corinth, your loathing for these Loyals has persisted since the day you stepped into the city. My decision is final, we need to focus on finding a way to capture one of these invisible figures. Perhaps they are these Tad'Vong that the Imperial Advisor has spoken of," Viceroy stated.

"Tad'Vong? What is that?" Rumford asked as though he had just been told of some strange, exotic food he'd never heard of.

"From what I've been told, they are an elite clan of stealth fighters and assassins, hailing from Dyona. We have no evidence, but it seems plausible that they're the ones perpetrating these attacks. The imperial interrogator managed to pry that information from that spy you found, Ser Corinth," Viceroy answered.

Corinth had nearly forgotten about the spy. The man had been completely out of it when he'd found him and that nobleman. "What of the nobleman, has he been questioned yet?"

Viceroy folded his arms, mulling something over. "Rumford, leave us."

Ser Corinth raised an eyebrow, but Rumford simply saluted and walked out of the chamber, closing the door behind him. "For what reason did you send the captain away?"

"Because what I am about to say next he needn't hear of," Viceroy said, turning back to face the window and looking out over the hightown district from above. "The noble boy you found unconscious in the wharf district was Donivus Ballandry, of the Ballandry royal family of Atarra."

Corinth stumbled backward. "An Atarran royal? Here? On what business?"

"Clandestine, it would appear. Master Ebonheart is having a tiff trying to interrogate him. Can't maim the bugger like he can other twats, instead he has to keep the gloves on," Viceroy revealed.

"Has the Emperor reached out to his house? Surely they would be forthcoming, were they to learn that one of their scions is in the custody of the imperial crown for suspected espionage," Corinth asked.

Viceroy shook his head. "No, nobody, save for you, me, and a small circle of confidants knows that an Atarran royal is being imprisoned here. The Emperor wants to extract as much information from the boy as possible, before we turn him over to his house."

"Do we not run the risk of earning their ire, holding onto one of their members in such conditions?" Corinth asked.

"Most certainly. But the Emperor knows best, and he supersedes all royalty from all kingdoms," Viceroy said.

Corinth didn't know if he agreed with that sentiment.

"How was the archbishop's speech? Rousing as usual?" Viceroy asked, changing the subject.

"He offered them comfort and prayed with them. The mood was still somber, but I could tell that the people were buoyed by his presence," Corinth said.

Viceroy nodded his head slowly. "Good. Did he seem to be…slowing down at all?"

Corinth reflected on the implications of Viceroy's question. "He is growing older, now. His age, plus his weight is…well, it's not helping things. He was quite winded, even after just a few minutes of speech."

Viceroy nodded once more, whatever he had been looking for seemed to have been confirmed. "The archbishop is a good man. And he is also one of the few who seems to be able to get through to the Emperor when his mind is clouded."

"Evidently he hasn't enough sway to free a few innocent dock workers, however," Corinth said. "Instead, the Emperor is determined to keep them incarcerated."

Viceroy moaned in annoyance, pinching the bridge of his nose. "Why must you prattle and fret about those men? What are they to you?"

"They are innocent men, imprisoned for doing the right thing—for helping. I would not be much of a paladin if I overlooked such things. If it is dangerous even to be a good soul, then I worry what that says about the state of this city."

Viceroy turned to face him again. "I told you before that you would learn that in Emperor's Rest, things that ought to be often aren't, and the things that shouldn't be, are. Did you think I was speaking in riddles?"

Corinth sighed and sat at his own desk. "I had hoped it was just more of your overwhelming hospitality bleeding through."

"What hospitality?" Viceroy asked.

"Precisely," Corinth said.

"Yes, well, I've matters to attend. So, while I do enjoy our ear-grating conversations, I must away," Viceroy said, dripping derision.

The feeling is mutual.

Corinth wanted to say.

Viceroy went to the door and opened it before pausing. "Oh, and…good work at the morning musters. You've been whipping these boys into shape. Commendable work, really," he said before shutting the door behind him, not giving Corinth enough time to respond.

Corinth, feeling just a little bit more upbeat at the unlikely compliment, stood up. He had a mind to visit Sister Minerva's parish in the midtown district, now. Perhaps praying to Idallon, his patron god, would help clear his mind. And then, perhaps he would go and pray with the dock master, Hedrick Norton, and the other falsely imprisoned dock workers.

As he got up to leave the chamber, he thought back to those shimmering, half-invisible figures watching them from above. Were they these Tad'Vong that Viceroy had mentioned? Or were they some new trick orchestrated by the Loyals?

*****

"He is being quite difficult, your grace," Ebonheart said in his icy voice. "He knows that I cannot touch him as I would like."

The master interrogator, normally only seen in the dark confines of his interrogation chambers, looked like a fish out of water, standing in the Emperor's throne room. His black and brown leather attire looked like it belonged in the shadows, rather than out in the light of day. And he still wore his skin-tight mask with the small nasal slits and eye holes. Vexyn never could understand why all the Emperors allowed him to wear it. It made his face almost impossible to read.

And it looks dreadful.

Vexyn thought.

"Vexyn?" He heard Varryn say his name, and he snapped from his stupor.

"Your grace." He responded.

"Master Ebonheart was explaining that we may have to use unorthodox methods to pry information from the Ballandry boy," Varryn reiterated.

"Unorthodox?" Vexyn asked. "In what manner, sire?"

Varryn pointed a limp finger at Ebonheart.

"I propose that we do a mock execution to loosen his lips," Ebonheart said.

"Execution, sire? On a royal?" Vexyn gasped.

"A *mock* execution, Vexyn. There is no real threat of death, merely the illusion of it. Up until now, the boy has stood firm with the knowledge that his royal blood made him untouchable. Destroy that assurance, and I believe that we will see a marked change in his tune," Varryn smirked slightly. "And I do so love getting under the skin of those troublesome Atarrans."

Vexyn opened his mouth to speak, but resigned himself, knowing that Varryn would not see the danger in this stunt. "Where will the mock-execution be held?"

"Out at the city center," Varryn answered.

"The city center?! Sire, that is in plain view of the entire populace! The Atarrans will be sending an army by the end of the next month!" Vexyn said, unable to stop himself.

Varryn waved a hand dismissively. "They will do no such thing. The boy will wet his pants and give in long before the guillotine swings."

"My lord, we have no way of guaranteeing that! If we misstep here, then we could be plunging the empire into a diplomatic crisis!" Vexyn pleaded.

"Beyond those front gates, deadly saboteurs rampage unmolested, blowing up buildings and killing our people, *my* people. If this boy can give us any information about that, then I think it is worth the risk. No physical harm will come to him, and we will send him back to Atarra, shaken but whole. They will not risk war with the empire over this boy—they will not!" Varryn snapped back, irritated.

Ebonheart stood silently, observing the both of them. Varryn noticed he was still standing, arms folded politely in front of him. "You are dismissed, Master Ebonheart," he sighed in exasperation.

"Your grace, Lord Advisor, I take my leave." He bowed, then walked out of the throne room, leaving the two to their argument.

"Leave us," Varryn ordered the guards, who stood at the door. They stamped their halberds on the floor in compliance, turned, then marched out of the room, shutting the doors behind them.

They sat in uncomfortable silence for several minutes, Varryn rubbing his temples and groaning in annoyance, and Vexyn curtly scowling, arms folded in front of him, clasping his text log. Neither wanted to make eye contact with the other.

"…Why must you sound the alarm at every opportunity?" Varryn finally asked, still looking forward.

"Because if I do not tell you what *may* happen as a result of your actions, your grace, I fear that no one will…" Vexyn said, chancing a look at the most powerful man in the empire.

The man who could have me killed with a snap of his fingers. My family…my children…

"This is not the first time in these past few months that we have come to disputes," Varryn noted. "First the missives, then the Loyals, and now this. Speak your peace, I tire of this beating around the bush."

"You have become fixed, my lord. Fixed on an uncertainty, a notion put forth in your head by Stars know who, that a relic of a dead era *may perhaps* help you ensure your sovereignty. You have sent spies, then pirates, and now *Seekers* after a dream, and may have potentially started a conflict with Dyona, all over this…Eye of Atla? You have dismissed the judges; you have even dismissed your own small council. You have ignored missives from the people that *need* you, that you *swore* to protect. And now? Now you flirt with civil war over a boy who may not even have the information we seek. You walk on a razor's edge, Varryn…and I do not know which way you will fall," Vexyn said candidly.

He could only hope, now, that those words would not be his final ones.

Varryn sat, silently contemplating the words Vexyn had spoken. His face was an unreadable mask. He sat like that for several more uncomfortable minutes. "Leave me to my thoughts, please…"

Vexyn sighed, nodded, and walked away.

"As you wish, my lord."

He looked to his left and was thankful that Alessa was busy meeting with the noble women in the council hall. He knew that she would have sided with Vexyn.

He contemplated for the briefest of moments whether he truly had taken things too far. But then his mind turned to the dangers, to the things he risked by not pursuing this course to its end. He was in too deep now. The Dyonians, whether he had the Eye of Atla or not, were on his trail, now. And then there was the matter of the spies in his own city. Who was feeding that Ballandry boy intelligence, and for how long? The Eye, he knew, would reveal all of that to him. It would make clear what course to take next and show him what plots his enemies were forging against him. Yes, he was far too close.

Soon, he would have the Eye.

Soon, it would all be made clear.

"Soon…"

A dull voice said in the back of his mind.

Soon.

XLIII

THE BRETHREN COURT

Atop the highest mountain peak on Storm Tide Isle sits a parthenon, known as Storm Peak. Storm Peak sits directly in the shadow of a colossal statue of a pirate standing vigil, trident in hand, over the island. Large pillars, thick as oak trees, hold up a hulking stone slab ceiling for the Storm Peak. Within the parthenon were rows of elevated steps made to seat hundreds of onlookers, fashioned in a semi-circle. On the dais sat the seven chairs of the pirate lords of the Brethren Court. In each seat sat a pirate of wildly different appearances and attire. Though all of them were divergent in appearance, they all gave off an air of intensity and prestige. All of them were lords, and all of them commanded the attention of those who looked upon them. In front of the lords, going beneath the stands was a hallway that connected to the steps that led up the mountainside. From the direction of the hallway, left to right, were the Pirate Lords Vale Kryta, Vadim Zakum, Krait'Malai, Xin-Jun, Grindalf Firebeard, and Valentino Goldfang. The seventh chair, sitting in the middle and above the other six, was vacant.

The left most pirate, Vale Kryta, was a Kurzan woman, pale of skin and beautiful of countenance. Her hair hung down from beneath her bicorn hat in blonde curls and tresses. Her eyes were a vibrant aquamarine, hooded with indifferent lids and a coldness to her expression. Upon her right cheek was a tattoo of an anchor. Her garb was decorated with naval patches, sewn into the fabric on the arms and front of the coat. One hand's long, black-painted nails clicked impatiently on her armrest, while the other held the neck of a long pipe to her lips.

To her left was a dark-skinned Xallan man, wearing vastly different clothing. His coat was decorated with beads, feathers, and around his neck was a necklace of teeth from various fanged animals. His tricorn hat was also decorated, with feathers and beads. He sat with a peculiar staff, adorned with more beads, feathers, and a goat skull at the tip laying over his lap as he leaned back in his seat in a meditative state. This was Vadim Zakum.

To his left was Krait'Malai. The El'wa Pirate Lord was a statuesque beauty, with long, moon-colored limbs, and an organic coat made of green plant fibers interweaved with living flowers and leaves. She sat cross-legged, arms folded in her lap, her tricorn hat sitting comfortably upon her head, decorated just like her coat.

To the left of her sat an older Dyonian man, wearing an impressive kimono robe, armored at the shoulders and neck. The neck guard obscured the bottom of his face, though it was scowling all the same. His long black hair was tied in a clean bun. In front of him was a large, golden sword, resembling a large, long, curved katana blade. He ran a whetstone over it, causing glittering sparks to jump from the blade and glow, even in the light that drenched the parthenon. His almond eyes were focused on sharpening his blade, seemingly oblivious to the other pirates sitting around him. This was Xin-Jun of the Lotus Forest.

To his left was a stout, fiery looking Duwa man with a red beard. He wore a heavily embellished bicorn hat, upturned in the front, and embroidered with the symbol his pirate clan, The Flame Hammers. His beard was long and immaculately clean and braided. His hard gaze was currently trained on a bottle of Duwa stout beer. He took heavy swigs from the tall, full bottle, and groaned impatiently as he waited for whatever reason it was they were summoned. He leaned forward onto the stone desk in front of him, stretching, before turning to look at the man to his left.

"Fancy a bottle, wolf-man?" he asked soberly to the man sitting next to him.

The final Pirate Lord was a handsome, brown-skinned man, with curly black, shoulder length hair hanging from beneath a strikingly designed tricorn hat, with sharp edges. It was trimmed with gold. He wore a similarly posh pirate coat, and a bandana around his neck. Nothing peculiar stood out about him, other than his charming features and flashy, gold-covered captain's clothes, save for his eyes. They were a fierce, piercing golden-yellow, that glowed. They burned with an unnatural intensity, and full eyelashes, making them look all the more outstanding. The man grunted, a deep, grumbling baritone.

"I have no want for drink, Firebeard. What I want is for this meeting to begin—so that it may end," he grumbled impatiently, his arms folded.

"Aye, you 'n me both, laddie. I got plunder to sort through, 'n business to attend to."

"Business? You mean whores, don't you?" Kryta asked skeptically.

"Whores and plunder are my business, Kryta." Firebeard laughed with a growl, belching loudly.

Kryta scrunched her nose, as did Krait'Malai.

"How anyone could find a boorish, drunken pig like you attractive never ceases to amaze me, Firebeard," Kryta stated disdainfully.

"How any man could ever shag a frigid bitch like either of you is a right mystery ta me as well, Krait," Firebeard shot back at both women.

Krait'Malai smiled coldly. "I've been told I'm quite warm. Just not around ugly little goblins like you, Grindalf." Krait'Malai added.

"Is it lonely up there, lassie? On your high horse?" Grindalf asked.

"Better to be lonely than to have you for company, I assure you," Krait responded.

"I'd rather have sex with an inbred troll, before I even considered looking in that ape's direction," Kryta chimed with derision.

"Ye know, Kryta, I sometimes have ta remind maself that yar more useful to me alive than ya are dead—fer now, that is," Grindalf said through slitted eyes.

"Try it, Duwa. Better—and taller—men than you have tried. Now I have their gold and their heads. I always win."

"Until ye don't, that is," Grindalf said, draining the last of his bottle as his cheeks grew hot and rosy, before turning away from them and dismissively tossing the bottle over his shoulder at them.

The bottle arched high, then landed on Xin-Jun's head—or it would have, had he not caught it.

Kryta and Krait'Malai both looked at Xin-Jun, then Firebeard.

Goldfang merely watched and chuckled.

"What are ye laughin' at, wolf?" he scrunched his red face.

"You nearly struck the Lotus King," Goldfang replied with a grim smirk.

Grindalf slowly turned to look at Xin-Jun, who was holding the bottle, having stopped sharpening his blade. He looked at it, then looked at Grindalf.

"Watch where you throw your trash, Duwa Lord. Most talk before they act. I do not give that courtesy," he stated, simply. He tossed the bottle back to the Duwa and continued sharpening his blade.

"I may not even have to do you in myself, Grindalf. I can just let your stupidity catch up with you," Kryta smiled, looking at Xin-Jun.

Xin-Jun quietly scraped away at his blade, already disinterested in the conversation. He sharpened the blade for several more moments before pausing and tapping the edge with his finger. He ran it along the edge for the briefest of moments, then lifted his calloused finger to see that the edge had cut through, drawing blood. "Vadim, how long must we wait for this meeting to bear fruit? We all have other matters to attend," he finally said, looking to the Xallan Pirate Lord.

Lord Zakum shifted in his seat, his ears pricking up at the sound of his name. He pulled out a pocket watch and checked the time. "...Now," he responded, just as the men began walking down the hallway in front of them, into the room they occupied.

Captain Pate, Captain Marcellus, First Mate Oculeth, Quartermaster Judith, Third Mate Crimp, and Daveth all entered the parthenon, shielding their eyes from the light of the sun, having just ascended a gloomy stairwell up the side of a mountain.

"Lords of the Brethren Court of the Storm Tide, it is on this most auspicious of days that I present to ye a familiar face on this isle, Captain Edward Patron of the Hail Mary pirate fleet," Captain Marcellus said, removing his hat and bowing to the men and women before him, then turning to Pate. "It's your show, now, Eddie." Marcellus patted him on the shoulder as he stood to the side, his part having been played.

Captain Pate stepped forward, removed his hat, then bowed to the Pirate Lords. His face was bandaged from where he'd been healed by Tellarya's magick. He could see that none of them were particularly interested in being there.

Tread carefully, Edward.

He warned himself before beginning. He cleared his throat. "Lords of the Brethren Court, Kith of the Sea, Exalted and Feared Kings and Queens of Piracy... I come before ye today with no small amount of ceremony...but I bring dour news all the same," he began.

"Well, out with it. What news do ye bring, Captain Pate?" Lord Kryta asked impatiently. "Or have ye lost the wit to explain to us as to why it is that ye waste our precious time, summonin' us here to this damned mountaintop?"

Oh, wonderful, she's in a good mood.

Pate sighed internally. This would be a difficult conversation.

"Ye may remember, yer Lordships, that I command a small fleet of my own. The Hail Mary fleet. For half a decade, now, I have had the honor of commanding a budding fleet. Five ships. Three barracks, a barque, and a galleon for the flagship. All of my ships were fully rigged, fully manned, and heavily-armed with no less than sixteen-pounders on all but the flagship. Hail Mary had twenty-pound cannons on her decks."

"Aye, Cap'n. I remember yer maiden voyage party well! I got besotted that night, heh," Firebeard shouted jovially, shaking the new bottle in his hand.

"Aye, Lord Firebeard. I remember you drinking my vintage rum. 2955 Baghwam Sugarcane. I'll never have rum that old again." Pate scowled.

"Damn shame, that, laddie. It was good un'," Lord Firebeard announced unapologetically.

"I'm sure—"

"Back to the task at hand, please?" Lord Krait'Malai chimed, clicking her nails on her table.

Captain Pate trained his eyes on her now. He knew very little about Lord Krait, save that she was an El'wa. He was always wary of them.

"Yes, M'lord. Several of you here today either know me, personally." He nodded to Lord Firebeard, who tipped his hat to him. "or have heard of me, in some way, shape or form through the years. I've been a pirate for a decade and a half. I've taken part in more raids, hunts, and battles than most pirates on this isle—and lived to tell the tale, thank the Stars. When I sail into battle, I do not relent until the sorry bastards who challenged me are either dead or dying. I say that, not to brag of my successes, M'lords, but to underscore what has happened in no uncertain context. My fleet, my flagship…and my crew have been sunk to the bottom of the Amaranthine by an unnatural force!" Captain Pate announced, wracked with emotion.

"Your whole… fleet?!" Lord Goldfang finally spoke up, leaning forward in his seat now.

"Mwari… how did dis happen?" Lord Zakum asked.

"By ma bastard ancestors, what happened to yar fleet, Patron?! Five ships of that grade don't just go quietly into the night! Surely ye jest with meh, boy." Lord Firebeard spit the beer out of his mouth.

"What I speak is cold and ugly truth. My fleet has been destroyed by the Dread Captain, Felix Helregal. I came here to ask for your aid in goin' after 'em, in the hopes of stoppin' him before he can do to others what he's done to me. I have a survivor from another of his attacks to back my claims. Come forth, El'wa." Pate waved Daveth over.

Daveth took several steps forward. Before him were some of the most wanted men and women in the world. Were his commanders here, they would order him to plunge a knife through each of their hearts, cut them out, and offer them to the admiralty. He lifted the sleeve of his shirt to reveal his naval tattoo.

Goldfang growled monstrously upon seeing it on his arm. "Filthy Sha'nav, here, in our court? I ought to have this boy keelhauled for even setting foot on this island!" he roared.

The Sha'nav were the El'wa's naval forces, and to the pirate lords of the Brethren Court, they were even more hated than the Imperial Navy. The Sha'nav had a reputation for not only torturing and hanging pirates but enslaving them as well. They also had strong relations with the Alyrian Consortium and employed sanctioned Alyrians in their crews, often to devastating effect.

"Rufu kune vezvikepe! Death to the navy scum," Lord Zakum threatened, clutching his staff. The skull on its animated, its eye sockets glowing with the same ghostly light as Zakum's.

"At ease, gentlemen, I am sure that Captain Patron has good reason to bring a Sha'nav to our haven. As I am also sure that he is aware of the consequences that could be incurred, should we deem that this slight was unwarranted?" Lord Krait fixed Pate with a hard, scrutinous gaze.

"Make it damn good, Captain. I'm liable to shoot the lot of ya where ya stand, if not," Lord Kryta warned, one hand already reaching for her hip.

Lord Xin-Jun merely watched silently, his arms crossed.

"M'lords, I have brought this Sha'nav here as an unbiased witness. Know that he has no reason to speak in my favor, merely to tell the truth as he knows it." Captain Pate looked at the ensign, now. "And may he be well-aware the cost of lies in this court."

Daveth stumbled forward after getting a shove from Crimp. He measured his steps, trying not to make eye contact. He cast his gaze to the floor and nodded to the Pirate Lords. "M-m-my Lords. A pleasure..." he stuttered.

"Bow down, navy scum. Pray to the Stars that your next words are not your last," Goldfang ordered, his fingers digging into the stone of his table.

"Ma blunderbuss hasn't blasted any Sha'nav in months, boy. It tears through armor like paper... I wonder what it'll do to your head?" Firebeard sat the weapon in question on his table, running a thick-skinned mitt over it. "Talk."

"Tell 'em about your fleet, boy. Tell them what happened," Captain Pate instructed.

Daveth looked at the pirate lords. He was not afraid; he had seen enough horror to know that there were fates worse than death. He was not a particularly brave man, but he knew that avenging his fallen was more important than his own life, now. He looked at Pate, who implored him with his eyes to tell his story. And he thought of the Dread Captain, who had stolen the lives of his comrades.

This is for you, my kin.

"Zamsk…" Daveth swore in reluctance, "…it was a dark and foggy night."

XLIV

THE DRIFTER

Daveth lit a cigarette and leaned against the table in the galley.

"Where do you keep finding smokes? Lach'dan won't give me a stick, swears up and down he's not storing away any tobacco—I know he's lying!" Gosrin complained. He reached for Daveth's pocket, to which Daveth responded by slapping his hand away.

"I had to beg Lysander for this stick. I'll not be sharing it with you, Gosrin!" Daveth hissed, taking a deep inhale of the tobacco as Gosrin glowered at him from several feet away.

"When we get back to port, I'll be sure to remember this when you need money for the pleasure house, kin," Gosrin complained.

"When we get back to port, I'll have other things to worry about than courtesans." Daveth shrugged.

"Still clinging to that notion of running your father's alchemy. Would Daveth-Un-Sorrel truly be satisfied with such a dreary life?" Gosrin asked.

"Better to live a dreary life, earning mundane coin, than fighting with pirates, the sea, and whatever ugly beast it chooses to throw at us on a given day. And with talks of another expedition to the southern sea on the horizon? I'd sooner take my chances with business than in those waters," Daveth said quickly.

Gosrin smirked. "Where's your sense of adventure, fro'kal? Do you not wish to have your name written down in history?"

"History? Hah! Hahahaha!" Daveth couldn't help but laugh, earning a withering gaze from Gosrin. "Do you really think either one of us will be written down in a history book for taking part in an expedition to the Southern Ocean? We are neither of notable birth nor deed. More likely we will be stuck under the thumb of some pompous upstart noble with a point to prove and lives to waste. I'll not become a footnote in some fool lord's glory tale."

Gosrin shrugged. "Nothing ventured, nothing gained. I *will* make my name, fal'ren, and no lord will stop me."

Daveth clapped his hands mockingly. "Bravo, Gosrin, with an attitude like that, you'll make a fine footnote!"

Gosrin scowled and stood from the table, stretching. "You've grown meek, old friend. How disappointing."

"Meek? No, I am far from the coward—but I am no fool, either," Daveth said as he stood and stretched. "Come, we've a watch to keep, and the officers will wear our hides if we dither any longer."

Gosrin voiced his agreement, and the two went above deck to continue their patrol. The main deck of the Lamellar, their stationed ship, was a long and spacious thing. Stretching over three-hundred feet from bow to stern. As they came up and walked the starboard side of the ship, they noticed, in the full moon's light, a small boat approaching the ship. Daveth raised his arm to signal Gosrin.

"See that? A raft approaches," Daveth said.

"I do. What is a raft doing floating through our fleet formation?" Gosrin asked.

Daveth wasn't sure either. He pulled out a scope and looked at the boat. "There's someone in the boat. They look to be in distress…"

He could make out a prone shape in the boat but not much else. They were wearing a black cloak, or robe of some sort, and so they almost blended in with the shadows of the boat, were it not for their arm hanging on the side, exposing a pale hand.

"Sound the alarm for a man overboard," Daveth instructed as he went to grab a rope ladder. "I'm going to inspect them."

"Be careful, kin. We know not their origin, or their aims," Gosrin warned.

"If their aims are to attack a Sha'nav fleet, then they'd need to do better than sending one man in a boat. Now signal the others," Daveth said.

Gosrin grumbled and went to ring the alarm as Daveth grabbed a rope ladder and fastened it to the railing before unfurling it. The boat was drifting closer to their ship. Whomever it was, they were fortunate the fleet was adrift for the evening, as there'd be no way their rowboat would have caught up otherwise.

"State your name and your business, stranger," Daveth called out. The figure didn't move, as he'd suspected they wouldn't. He got the feeling they were unconscious. He pulled out the lantern attached to his hip and lit it, before fastening it back and climbing down. The boat tapped against the side of the ship, and Daveth dropped down into it before tying the mooring rope sat in the boat to the rope ladder, ensuring it wouldn't drift away from the ship.

He heard the alarm ring and knew backup was only a few seconds away. He flipped over the figure to see a pale woman passed out in the boat. It was a human. "Are you alive, human?" he asked, shaking her. She stirred slightly.

He cupped her chin and raised her head, inspecting the strange black markings he saw snaking down her neck, disappearing into her robes. She wore black lipstick, which he found odd, figuring it would be smeared off by now, were she long at sea.

"Do they live?" The captain, Val'Roy, called from above.

"They live, but they are unconscious. It is a human," Daveth reported.

"A human? Here?" Val'Roy puzzled. "Bring them aboard."

"As you say, sul'ren," Daveth responded, then grabbed hold of the woman, throwing her over one shoulder as he mounted the ladder.

*****

Daveth eyed her keenly from across the table, uncertain what to make of this strange human on their ship. They were in El'wa waters, and so finding a human here, floating alone in a boat, was a peculiarity.

What are you doing here, human?

She did not appear to be a slave or a convert. Though it was too early to tell, he did not imagine her to be a Wuhlven either. Their kind had an unforgettable stink of Alyria around them. No, this was an ordinary human, from what he could tell.

She roused, and he stood upright to call for Val'Roy as she got her bearings. "She wakes," he said through the slit in the cabin door.

"I will inform him," the officer by the door said.

The woman blinked and looked around. Her dull green eyes scanned the room, then fell on Daveth. They locked eyes.

"...Where am I?" she asked dreamily.

"You are aboard the Sai'Haluud Imperium vessel, Lamellar. I am Sha'nav Seaman Daveth-Un-Sorrel. You are in our brig, awaiting further questioning by the captain."

The woman did a slow blink. "Do you have any food?"

Daveth opened his mouth to speak, but Captain Val'Roy opened the door and relieved him. "I will take it from here, da'nem."

Daveth gave her one last perplexed look, then stood. "As you say, sul'ren." He bowed, then left.

He could feel the young woman's eyes on his back as he left, and even when he shut the door, her gaze seemed to sear over his skin.

What an odd woman.

He thought but gave it no more and left.

*****

Several hours later, Daveth found himself again before the door to the woman's cell, this time holding two bowls of food.

"A drifter washes up on our deck and you feed her like a queen, kin? I'm almost envious," Gosrin joked. "I can barely get a cigarette out of you."

"How's this? I'll share my last stick with you when I'm done feeding the human. Will that get you off my ass, kin?" Daveth offered, tired of hearing Gosrin's complaining.

"For now. I've other duties to attend. The captain wants the livestock pen cleaned," Gosrin groaned. "Like it wasn't bad enough smelling their swill, now I've to clean it as well."

"Complaining won't make the duty easier, Gosrin. I assure you," Daveth dismissed. "Now begone."

Gosrin chuckled and walked away. "Fair enough. Enjoy your human, fal'ren."

Daveth ignored him and called out to the person on the other side. "It's Daveth. I bring food for the prisoner."

The captain had pried a name from her, and Daveth now knew her to be Byzarra. A bizarre name, indeed.

The guards let him in, and Byzarra's eyes fell on him again, wide with anticipation as he placed the two bowls of food on the table before her. Her hood was down, now, and he could see her long, black hair tied up in a messy bun. She looked quite beautiful, all considered. Even if she did give off the air of an uncivilized animal.

He handed her a spoon, and she quickly began shoveling the oatmeal down her throat. He watched in fascination as she tucked the oatmeal away in less than a minute before moving on to the bowl of stew next to it. She scooped the diced cubes of meat and vegetables in the broth into her mouth, finishing the stew just as quickly as the oatmeal. She paused then, taking deep breaths. Daveth and the men stared at her, stunned as she leaned back in her chair and belched before reaching for the bottle he'd brought with him.

She has the manners of a pig.

He thought and handed her the bottle of weak wine. She doused the entire bottle in seconds.

"Stars, child. Have you no manners?" One of the guards couldn't help but ask. "You behave like a tribal."

She leaned back in her chair, her belly bloated with food and drink. She let out another belch, yawned, then leaned forward in her seat. She took a deep, long breath, then fixed Daveth with a warm smile. "I was positively starving, little El'wa. Thank you. I think I shall spare you," Byzarra said nonchalantly.

"Spare me?" Daveth asked as the two guards behind him, an El'wa man and woman, looked at one another amusedly. They shared a laugh, unable to contain themselves. "Spare me from what?"

Byzarra put on an insidious, almost insane grin. "Why, this of course!"

As if on cue, her eyes lit up, going from a dull green to a glowing, charged electric green color that Daveth had never seen before. She raised her arms, causing the sleeves to fall and reveal the tattoos on her arms glowing the same.

Oh no.

She was an Alyrian. How she had managed to suppress her energy from the ship's magister, he didn't know. But now, she was charged with energy, and was poised to attack.

"Get down!" Daveth shouted, throwing himself to the floor as Byzarra cackled and the two guards froze in place. "What are you doing?!"

Their eyes rolled into their heads, and their jaws dropped open, stretching to the point of popping as they let out the most ear-splitting screams he'd ever heard. Their veins, now visible beneath their skin, blackened, as did their lips. Their chins creased toward their necks, and Daveth watched as they began hugging their own bodies, shaking violently in convulsions. Soon, a red froth bubbled from their lips, and they fell dead at his feet as he hid under the table. He stared into the dead face of one of the guards as Byzarra walked past. He held his breath as she paused and bent over to look him in his eyes.

"I would advise you to flee, little El'wa. You'll not like what comes next," she warned. Daveth hitched his breath as she reached out with one pale, black-nailed finger and tapped it upon his cheek. He felt icy cold, like the grave. She walked out the door, leaving him with the corpses as more footsteps approached, likely drawn from the commotion.

What have I just done?

Daveth crawled out from under the table and grabbed the weapons of one of the dead guards. He knew that against an Alyrian this was a gamble at best. But he had to try. He popped open the Alyria pistol from the dead guard and reloaded it with a shot, then holstered the sword on his way out the door.

✶✶✶✶✶

"Detain her!" An officer shouted.

Daveth came above deck just in time to watch Byzarra tear apart a wave of crewmen charging at her. She waved her arm at them, and a peculiar green wave passed over the charging attackers. They began convulsing and vomiting, and some of them were clutching at their throats. They all fell to the deck, spasming in their death throes.

"She's a witch! Magister Siwan, detain her!" The officer shouted just as Byzarra lobbed a sickly green ball of energy at him. It struck him dead on, and Daveth looked away as the man began rotting away in front of them.

"Sibilas!" The Magister shouted, uttering an incantation.

Byzarra grunted, as though she'd been punched, but then smirked at the magister, waggling a finger at him.

"A silencing spell? Did you think that such a weak incantation would work on me, magister?" Byzarra tutted. "Allow me to demonstrate proper Alyria! Master, lend me your power!"

Her eyes changed from green to red briefly, and she pointed an open palm at the magister. "Rise!" She said, her voice sounding masculine. The magister ducked out of the way, expecting another ball of green energy. He was confused, then, when the bodies of the dead crewman instead rose and charged at him. Their skin was splitting open, sprouting nuggets of gold and emerald.

She's not a witch; she's a necromancer!

Daveth took cover and realized that his weapons would be of no use against Byzarra. She was, evidently, a very skilled and powerful Alyrian. All his pistol and sword would do was anger her. He peered from behind the mast he'd hid behind to see the magister frantically throwing bolts of electricity at the shambling undead. Byzarra stood, arms folded, watching the scene unfold with a low chuckle.

"Can you really destroy your own crew, magister? How heartless!" she mocked.

"Be silent, necromancer! Your foul, apostate Alyria is tainted with the filth of the Infernals! I will cut you down where you stand!" Siwan pledged as he formed a glowing yellow sword from his own energy and used it to cut the undead down. Then, he raised his arm and focused a beam of energy at Byzarra.

Daveth's hair stood on end as the air was saturated with Alyria. He could taste the peculiar flavor of it in the air, almost like the smell of electrical discharge. He watched as Byzarra launched her own beam of energy, colliding with the magister's and sending out a burst of light and energy, bright enough to alert the whole fleet.

Daveth smiled; she'd doomed herself. Soon, the might of the fleet and the other magisters within it would descend upon her, and she would be destroyed. The burst sent Siwan falling backward, but Byzarra merely planted her feet and weathered the wave.

"Now die, magister dog," Byzarra spat with venom.

She raised both her hands, and Siwan was enveloped in the sickly-green glow, flailing and groaning in pain as she lifted him in the air. She was muttering hushed phrases under her breath in a staccato tone, and Daveth realized she was chanting a curse. And if any of her other magick was an indication, it would be the end of Siwan.

And it was.

As the moon shined high in the sky, bleeding from blue to red, Byzarra cackled madly as Siwan began to *melt* before their eyes. Daveth wretched as the smell of fouling flesh reached his nose and combined with the scent of Alyria on the air, it made him vomit. Siwan let out a long, low, keening groan that bled into a croak, then silence as the flesh and hair fell away from his skull. His body, little more than a yellow robe and decrepit looking bones, fell into a heap on the deck as more crew encircled her on the deck. Gosrin came from below and placed a hand on his shoulder, leaning out from behind the mast they hid behind.

"What in the hells is going on, Daveth?!" Gosrin asked, looking in shock at the bodies piled on the deck.

"That damned drifter was no ordinary human—she was a necromancer!" Daveth shivered. "And she's been killing our crew left and right. She just slew Magister Siwan."

Gosrin looked and saw as the captain came into the fray from the other side of the deck, flanked by officers with rifles pointed at Byzarra.

"Enough of your heresy, necromancer. Your end is nye; your judgment imminent!" Captain Val'Roy declared, pointing his sword at her.

Byzarra cocked her head. "Is it? I do believe we've only just begun…" she raised her hands in the air, and as if it were on cue, the sea erupted as dozens of ships surged up from the depths at the front of the fleet formation. From their vantage point near the front, they could hear and see as the ships emerged. They flew many banners, but all of them had a red flag flying above them. And they all looked waterlogged, gutters of it running off them back into the sea.

"What witchcraft is this?" Captain Val'Roy asked, utterly stunned by the impossibility he'd just witnessed.

"Witchcraft? No, I do believe this is an ambush. And this?" Byzarra said.

Just then, a horde of black bodies emerged from the sea and climbed onto the deck. Daveth could scarcely believe what he saw before his eyes. People—or what used to be people—some thin as skeletons, covered in gold and waterlogged jewel-covered clothing. One of them climbed over the railing and hissed at him and Gosrin, flashing glittering ruby teeth at them.

"Is your doom."

The undead, for Daveth knew that was what they were, charged at them— and all hell broke loose.

*****

Daveth clashed blades with the undead that charged at him as Gosrin engaged another coming from behind them. Up close, the thing was even more hideous to behold. The eyes were gone, and only a dull yellow glow emanated from the vacant sockets as the creature tried to sink its teeth into him. He shoved it away, barely escaping its ruby jaws. The things, though mostly thin of body, were surprisingly strong. He struggled to get the rail-thin creature away from him, and as it grabbed hold of his arm, he felt his shoulder and neck pop when it jerked.

"Get off me, un'ghol!" Daveth growled, aiming the pistol he'd taken from the guard at the creature's head.

He fired, and a blue burst eviscerated the undead's skull as the Alyria-laced bullet discharged at point-blank range. The creature stumbled backward and fell overboard, the stump where its head once was leaving a trail of blue smoke.

"Daveth! Help!" Gosrin shouted from behind him. Daveth spun around to see his friend pressed to the ground, the undead attacking him gnashing its teeth as it inched closer and closer to his face. Its blackened body almost blended with the darkness, were it not for the glittering jewelry reflecting the moonlight.

"Gosrin! I'm coming!" he shouted just as gunfire ripped past him and he hit the floor.

He heard laughing to his right as Byzarra taunted her attackers. "I told you before, your bullets are useless!" she shouted.

He scrambled across the deck, thanking the Stars above that none of the bullets had torn into him. The same could not be said for Gosrin and the undead on top of him, however. Gosrin cried out in pain as Daveth scrambled toward him. He could see a glowing blue bullet hole in his side, and knew his friend was in dire straits, now. He closed the gap just in time to tackle the undead off him, and Gosrin groaned as Daveth fought the bullet-riddled undead. It seemed not to care that it had been run through with enough bullets to fell a horse. Instead it hissed and snapped at him.

"Flesh!" The creature hissed in the driest, coldest voice Daveth had ever heard.

These monsters can speak?!

He was startled, and the monster used the opportunity to throw him off. He fumbled to pull his sword from the sheath and angled it upward as the undead fell on top of him, now. It screeched, burning from the Alyria-infused blade's edge. Blue smoke billowed from its gut. Its arms swung, and slashed Daveth across the face as he used all the strength he could muster to throw the creature off him, blade still impaled within it. It slammed into a door, and Daveth rose to his feet as it scrambled to its own. He was disarmed and had nothing to strike it with now.

"Daveth!" Gosrin coughed, dropping his own weapon, an ordinary rapier, onto the deck. Daveth looked at it and dove immediately. He grabbed the blade just in time as the undead lunged for him again, and this time he impaled it through the mouth and threw it off him. He stabbed it multiple times with the rapier, but the weapon did nothing to stop it, merely emitting more screeches as it tried to get at him. He looked around and saw that the creature had dropped its own sword on the deck when it was knocked off Gosrin, and so he grabbed it. He felt a strange sensation rush through him as he picked up the weapon, and he felt the immediate urge to drop it and never touch it again.

He ignored the sensation and brandished both weapons. The undead lunged at him again as the guard's sword, having burnt a sizable hole into its belly, fell away. The creature stumbled over the blade, losing its footing momentarily and Daveth took the opportunity to swipe its head from its shoulders—using its own blade. The head soared through the air as golden fluid sprayed all over from the stump, and Daveth, already ill from earlier, wretched as some of the foul fluid got in his mouth. He spat and saw himself covered in gold as the undead clutched at its head stump. He dropped the rapier and held the creature's sword in both hands as he ran at it, hacking off its arms, then a leg.

He stood, panting as the torso flailed on the ground, oozing gold for several moments. The head rolled nearby, and he was disturbed to see it still looking at him, gnashing its gem-encrusted teeth at him. He grabbed it by the thin shocks of hair on its head and tossed it overboard into the sea. After several more moments of thrashing, the body ceased. He gasped, wiping golden liquid and his own blood from his lips as he stumbled towards the moaning Gosrin. The bullet wound had stopped burning, which was a good sign. That meant the bullet had exited his body, and he wouldn't be poisoned or burned further by its volatility. The internal damage, however, was likely far greater.

Gosrin looked at him with red-tinged eyes, taking shallow, pained breaths as Daveth lifted him to a sitting position.

"How are you feeling, fal'ren?" Daveth asked, holding Gosrin up.

"Considering…I just…got shot…and nearly…got…eaten?" he gasped with great effort. "I'm…just…peachy…"

Daveth's heart broke at the strain Gosrin was showing just to speak. He smiled and laughed, holding back his alarm. "I see you haven't lost your wit. We'll get you fixed up in no time," he promised.

Gosrin shook his head and placed a hand on Daveth's, then swallowed blood. "Organs…were ruptured…by the bullet…" he coughed, touching his side gingerly. "We're… in the… middle of…an… ugly… surprise battle… with undead. Face it…I am a dead man."

Daveth shook his head immediately. "Over my father's grave! You will cleave to *life*, Gosrin, do you hear me?!"

Gosrin smirked, and Daveth saw blood in his teeth and lips. "…It may not…be some… great expedition…kin, but I… rather think… I *will* go… down… in our history…now…"

"To the hells with history, Gosrin! What we need to worry about now is survival!" Daveth protested.

"No, kin." He said quickly, trying to get his words out. "What *you* need to worry about is survival. Me? I'm going to be singing psalms with Herma'Morra, soon," Gosrin said, invoking the El'wish name of the Star-Goddess of Peace, Love, and Serenity.

Daveth shed a tear. He'd been sailing with Gosrin for over ten years. It wasn't long, not when you could live a thousand years or more. But at sea? That was a long time. He'd seen good men die in that time frame. More than he could count. Now, it would seem, he was about to watch another go. Remembering his promise, he lifted Gosrin to his feet, eliciting a hitched breath and a hiss from the dying El'wa. He helped him into through the door, smeared with the golden blood of the undead he'd slain, and sat Gosrin up against a crate.

"Well, at least I'll die away from the noise," Gosrin mused with a labored laugh and a wince. He was leaking blood, now, and it had gotten all over Daveth as he carried him.

"And you're less likely to catch another stray. I'd hate for that necromancer to send a spell our way," Daveth said. He tried to push the memory of the magister melting in front of him from his mind. He could not. Instead, he lit his last cigarette, took a hit, and held it to Gosrin's lips.

"You… really… do treat… me nice, kin," Gosrin said with a weak smirk as he took a shallow puff from the cigarette.

Before, Gosrin could burn through a third of the cigarette in one breath. Now? He barely even burned off the end. He released a thin wisp of smoke from his lips and coughed. Daveth took the cigarette and saw that there was blood on the end. He smoked it anyway as he heard the cannons begin to fire, shaking the ship.

"What…what a way…to…" Gosrin said began but broke into a coughing fit that turned into wheezing.

Daveth held his friend upright with one arm as he brought his shaking hand to his lips for another pull of the cigarette. "Easy, kin. Take it easy…"

He sighed smoke and offered the end to Gosrin, who happily took one more hit. This one was a long, drawn-out inhale. As Daveth went to congratulate him on the long toke, Gosrin leaned his head back, then slumped over, releasing his last breath in a plume of smoke.

"Gosrin, eld fal'ren?" Daveth asked softly, shaking him once. There was no response. He put a finger to Gosrin's throat. There was no pulse. Daveth felt one more stubborn tear drip down his face as he finished the bloody cigarette and stared out the nearby window into the red moon. "Yaren el'kali, eld fal'ren. Rest well…"

Daveth kissed Gosrin's body on the forehead and departed.

*****

The deck was a bloodbath.

Bodies, half-eaten, still being feasted upon by these strange, glittering undead, were strewn across the deck. He saw Byzarra standing in the midst of it all, chanting. She was levitating a few feet off the ground, her eyes and tattoos glowing bright, and a faint aura emanating from her, like a transparent, ghostly-green flame. Beneath her was Captain Val'Roy, dead on the ground, leaning against his sword. Daveth said a silent prayer and looked around for a way out. The ship had stopped firing its cannons, which told him that the gun crews were either dead, or engaged with the undead. In which case, they would die shortly. He watched as ships passed them by, forging into battle and breaking the formation. He could see that the other ships were boarded by the undead as well.

He watched as a large, glittering, gold-trimmed galleon with a golden statue mounted beneath its bowsprit approached their lead ship. A sunderer-class ship, called the Sun Spear. The two ships opened fire, and he was shocked to see that the gold-covered ship all but ignored the harrowing blasts of Alyria that the Sun Spear put out. Its own shots struck home, however, and he watched from afar as the mightiest ship in their fleet was lit ablaze by this mysterious flagship. He could hear the men screaming, even from here.

"Isn't it beautiful?" he heard someone whisper from just by his ear, he jolted to see Byzarra standing right behind him, her eyes completely shrouded in electric green energy. Having her this close made his hair stand taught at the ends, as though they were trying to pluck themselves from his skin.

He had half a mind to try and slay her, but he knew it would do him no good. She had slaughtered his whole crew, with men and women far better trained and equipped than he. Instead, he just gave her a frightened, reproachful look.

"Watching my people die? No, it is the very opposite, in fact," he responded tersely.

"Darling, they were destined to die, one way or another. At least now, they'll serve a greater purpose," Byzarra chuckled.

"And what purpose is that?" Daveth asked, not particularly keen on hearing her answer.

"As food and bodies, of course. For my master's Armada of the Damned," she answered proudly.

"Armada of the Damned?" Daveth repeated, uncertain why those words sounded familiar. "Surely you don't mean to—

"Raise them? But of course. The ones that aren't eaten, at any rate. They will be resurrected temporarily, and given a choice: join us, or be condemned to oblivion. You would be surprised just how many comply, especially after seeing their friends getting mauled to death—again, and again, and again…"

He shivered as he felt her icy, evil hands upon his shoulders. "I told you I'd spare you, little El'wa. I would encourage you to leave. My master may decide not to be so charitable. There is nothing left for you here, after all. My suggestion is to find a boat and start rowing or find a barrel and start hiding," she warned, and then walked away.

Daveth gazed long at the burning hulk of the Sun Spear, watching as the small figures of burning men leapt overboard into the water to be devoured by the black shapes, lingering there, waiting.

Just then, he heard a monstrous, bone-rattling roar in the distance and turned to see a large figure attacking the men of another one of the ships, a few hundred yards away. He couldn't make out distinct characteristics, but he could tell the figure was huge in size, dwarfing even the tallest men around him by at least two or three feet. The roaring figure tore through the attacking sailors, and Daveth was horrified to hear it let loose another, triumphant roar. Whatever that monster was, he knew it had something to do with the drifter, and he prayed he never had to face the thing himself.

He weighed his options. Were he to sail, he ran the risk of being discovered, swarmed, and devoured. Were he to go below deck, he would be trapped, and should the ship go down, he'd drown. Instead, he took Byzarra's second piece of advice and grabbed a barrel. There was one rolling about the deck nearby, and so he grabbed the empty barrel, as well as its lid, and dropped it into the rowboat Byzarra had come in. He saw that at the moment, none of the undead were encircling the ship he was on, perhaps sensing that almost all its occupants were already dead. He acted quickly, making his way down the ladder.

Just then, a loud series of explosions rocked the boat, and he was flung into the sea. He surfaced, and thanked the stars above that the barrel was still sitting in the boat, uncompromised by the water. He climbed aboard and opened it before climbing in himself and shutting the lid. Another explosion flipped the boat over and tossed him and the barrel into the sea. Thankfully, the seal around it was watertight, and so he was safe from drowning within it.

And there he waited, surviving, just as Gosrin had bid him. He heard the explosions. He heard his kin's muffled screams. He heard the roar of that monstrous figure, and the guttural howls of the undead, but somehow, through it all, he survived…

XLV

JUDITH

Daveth absentmindedly ran a hand down the scar on his face from where the undead had tried to get at him.

"After everything had gone quiet, I opened the lid and saw that I was alone. Many of the ships were destroyed, but several remained as wreckage. When the good captain here found me, I had been sitting on that driftwood for the better part of a week, surviving off rainwater and some of those man-eating fish sifting through the wreck…" Daveth finished. His face was stone, and he folded his arms behind his back, watching the faces of the pirate lords.

Lord Krait'Malai leaned forward and addressed him, "…These undead, kin. You tell me that they were covered in gold and jewelry?"

"Yes, all of them were. Some had gems encrusted in their skin, in their eyes, on their teeth…it was as though someone had taken a treasure trove and made mockeries of men from it."

The pirate lords muttered amongst themselves worriedly. Then Kryta addressed him, "What banner were they flying? Ye get a good look at it?"

Daveth nodded; he had. "A red flag with a black skull. It looked as though there might have been gold teeth on the skull, as well as gold chains in the fashion of crossbones behind it."

Lord Zakum frowned. "Intriguing. Do you have any other witnesses, Captain Patron?"

Pate shook his head. "Only myself and the Alyrian. We had my First Mate, Mr. Brunt, but…"

"He succumbed to his wounds," Oculeth finished.

"Our condolences, captain," Zakum said solemnly.

Pate nodded. Did they believe him? Was it enough?

They deliberated for several minutes, and in that time, Judith sidled up next to Daveth and punched him playfully in the arm. "Ye did good, Daveth. I think your story got through to them," she congratulated.

He gave her a sideways glance, his face still stoney. "It was no story. It was the most painful experience I have ever known."

Judith froze, realizing how she'd come off. "I—"

Lord Zakum slammed his gavel down. "We have deliberated, and come to a verdict…"

Pate stepped forward, waiting to hear what they had to say. "Yes, my lords?"

Lord Zakum sighed apologetically. "Without physical proof, Captain Patron, we are left only with the words of a decorated pirate without a crew, and a Sha'nav, whose words, while compelling, are not to be trusted."

Daveth growled, "Not to be trusted?! Who are you to throw stones in glass houses, pirates?!"

Pate grabbed him and kicked out the back of a knee, forcing him down and whispering, "Do ye want to die, you fool? Control yourself!"

"Control your little Sha'nav, Pate, or I'll be forced to blow his brain matter out the back of his skull," Firebeard said with a steely expression.

"Of course, Lord Firebeard. He is beside himself, is all," Pate said. "Isn't that right Mr. Daveth?"

Daveth stared harshly at the pirate lords. "Yes."

"As I was saying," Zakum continued. "We do not have enough evidence to move off your claims, I am sorry. We need *evidence* of the Dread Captain's presence before we ask a large force of our pirates to mobilize after something that isn't a promised return on investment."

"Surely if Captain Morgan were here, he would vouch that you should look into this matter. Felix Helregal is the single greatest threat the Brethren Court has ever faced. Why then would you not jump at any hint of his return?" Pate argued.

"You are correct, captain. If Lord Morgan was here, he would almost certainly speak in your favor. But the good captain has been gone for over five years, and has sent neither word of his whereabouts, nor have we heard of him. So, his vote is rendered mute, at present," Lord Kryta said.

Pate was wounded, but he nodded. "Aye…"

He'd failed them. Failed Brunt. Failed Smith and Andrews; Jackson and Franklin. And the five-hundred men at his command. He failed them all…

"Be that as it may, captain, you are a man of some renown, here. And, we are told, you have already been making moves to regrow your fleet. Is that correct?" Lord Krait asked.

Pate nodded, remembering that he'd just acquired the deceased Farce's crew. He rubbed the bandaged patch on his face. "Aye…"

"Then, if you are so moved, perhaps you could do us a favor, perhaps even helping to solidify your position here, and garner more men to your cause. Like, say, slaying the hydra roosting outside our gates?" Lord Krait suggested.

Pate raised a brow, then nodded. "You wish to have one of our own handle it, rather than using an outside force like the Mygredo."

"Saves on cost and may just help you get back some of what you've lost," Lord Krait said. "I will even supply you with a ship that has the necessary armaments to combat the creature."

Pate thought to ask why she didn't send her men to kill the creature, then, but thought better of it. If he could bring down the hydra and parade its corpse through Livera, he stood a fair chance of recruiting more crews. Pirates respected power, just like any other, and attaching themselves to a captain who was a bonified monster-slayer made those involved look all the more powerful by association.

Pate nodded. It didn't fix all his problems, but it gave him something to do, and an avenue to make use of his time here, until he could figure out what to do next. "It will be done."

Lord Krait clapped. "Very good. I will show you your new ship on the 'morrow."

*****

The dejected officers of the Duchess, and Daveth, all sat in the backroom of the Storm Brew, licking their wounds and drinking from their rejection.

"Not enough evidence? How the fuck are ye supposed to get evidence that a fucking revenant killed all your men? A disembodied arm?" Judith griped.

Oculeth shrugged. "Perhaps I should have tried to take one of those Damned creatures heads with us. Might've lent more credence to our tale?"

Pate shook his head as he sipped his drink. "Wouldn't have mattered," he said. "They're afraid of him and have every right to be. Perhaps they think it

484

better to ignore his existence and hope he'll go away, than face him head on and gain his ire."

Crimp leaned forward out his chair. "What could be so fuckin' scary that the Pirate Lords of the Storm Tide are afeared of it?"

Oculeth gave him a sideways glance. "If you'd seen what the Dread Captain was capable of, I rather think you'd be scared of him as well."

Judith shook her head disappointedly. "You daft, brother? You forgotten the stories? The bastard is a nightmare what had damn near the whole world in his grip for a spell."

"Mind yourself, sister. I'm still the Third Mate," Crimp said, attempting to leverage his position over her.

Oculeth looked at Pate, who shrugged and leaned back in his chair. "You do realize that the Quartermaster position is something of special class on a ship, correct?"

Crimp slowly turned his head to look from Judith, who was smirking at him, to Oculeth, who was sitting, one leg over the other in his chair with a book in one hand. "'Scuse me?"

Oculeth sighed and ran a hand down his face. "Tell me, Mr. Crimp, what does a quartermaster do?"

Crimp shrugged. "Guard the treasure 'n hand out shares."

"And?" Oculeth probed.

Crimp sat in uncomfortable silence for several long moments, clearly trying to figure out the right answer.

"Well go on then, what else?" Pate finally chimed in, impatiently.

Crimp scratched at his chin and let out a sigh of defeat. "And…what else, then?"

Oculeth continued, "A quartermaster is also in charge of disciplinary actions, boarding maneuvers, and often times general management of the ship in absence of the captain, such as, say, when he's sleeping, or ashore."

Recognition dawned on Crimp's face.

"With all of those important duties, the quartermaster equates to nearly the captain in terms of importance. Even higher than First Mate, actually," Oculeth informed him. "I say all of that to say—"

"She outranks you, mush-for-brains," Pate said impatiently.

Crimp, visibly irritated, stood up from his seat. "We've been at sea for no more than a month and a half, and she outranks me? She wasn't even an officer when we came on!"

"When you came on, we were low on manpower, experience, and a bevy of other things a pirate crew needs. I needed bodies to man the ship, and I needed them yesterday. Where it stands, almost none of you have the experience needed to make it in this life, and it was a *miracle* that we made it past the hydra," Pate said, standing up as well.

Judith hung her head, as did Crimp. Oculeth closed his book, fixed his glasses, and listened.

"Miss Judith, here, is the most competent person on this ship, aside from myself, and at times Mr. Oculeth. What she lacks in sailing experience, she makes up for in drive, intuition, and gumption. I pirate needs that in an officer, direly. So yes, Mr. Crimp, your sister outranks you. And I suspect that was the case a *long* time ago," Pate finished.

"To wit. What is our next course?" Oculeth asked.

"I'm going to charter you a boat to the Maaug Haunt. If your cure is there, then you'd best be on your way to get it," Pate answered. "As for us? I'm going to see about this ship Lord Krait has for us, and I'm going to get the Cutthroat crew to man it, if possible."

"Why not have our boys do it?" Judith chimed.

"Because our boys can barely handle a soft-toothed, repurposed merchant galleon, let alone an El'wa beast killer," Pate answered, finishing his drink before grabbing his coat and heading for the door. He froze at the entrance and clutched his arm a moment, trying to play it off like it was an itch. "I'm goin' to have them train with some of the Cutthroats, see if they can't show them a thing or two about piracy. Hopefully they're more useful than their former leader."

"Captain…" Judith said as Pate went to open the door.

He paused, then turned his head to look at her. "Quartermaster?"

"About that fight on the beach. Your arm…what was that?" she asked. He could see Crimp was curious as well.

"Let's just say that when Mr. Oculeth and I escaped the Dread Captain we had to take drastic measures. It cost us," he answered, then exited.

Judith and Crimp looked at Oculeth, then. He gave an awkward smile and leaned back in his chair.

"Right…"

McDunham grunted as he swung his sword again. The man he was training with, Hauser, parried his swing, shoved him to the sand, and pressed the flat of his sword against his shoulder as McDunham tried to scramble to his feet. He'd been defeated again.

"That's six times in a row," Hauser said. "At this rate I'd be better off fighting a hangover. At least that'd put up a fight."

McDunham swore, kicking the sand. "You laid me on my ass more times than a bar whore."

"Ye've disappointed me more times than a bar whore's father. How many times have I told ye to watch your footing?" Hauser lectured.

"You keep saying that—but what the fuck does that mean?!" McDunham asked.

Hauser demonstrated, "One foot forward, the other back. Always. Never stand with both feet next to each other. It ruins your stability and all but guarantees that if your opponent presses on ye, ye'll fall over. Ye do that in a real fight? Gasp to fishes, you're a dead man."

Just then, Haanz approached. He'd been overseeing the training of the other Duchess pirates. Or rather, he'd been watching his men wail on them and crack wise while doing so. "How many more times you gonna beat the poor sod before he cries uncle?"

Haanz was a lean-built man with tattoos blacking out his arms and neck. Probably much more, but McDunham couldn't see much more. He was a swarthy bastard, to be sure. He didn't joke much, he was almost always business-like, and he had a gaze that could curdle milk. He and Hauser reminded him of the navy boys that would sometimes come back after years at war. Hardened, unfriendly, and of few redeeming qualities other than their ability to drink, brood, and keep you on edge.

Hauser offered him a calloused hand and yanked him sharply to his feet, making him feel like he was almost flying for a moment. Hauser was equally tattooed, a fair bit more muscular, and had a raised scar running down the bottom of his chin from the right side. He had an equally steely expression, but he had seen him smile once or twice.

McDunham was surprised to find the man had all his teeth, considering a fair amount of the pirates he'd met were missing some—or even all, replacing them with wood, or sometimes metal dentures or caps.

"As many times as it takes," Hauser said. "These wet-eared bastards need to learn to fight and learn fast if they want to have a piss and a prayer to last in a real fight."

Haanz shrugged. "Or we could use them for fodder."

"We do that, Cap'n Pate will have our hides. He told us to train them, not waste them," Hauser rebuked.

Just then a fight broke out across the beach, and everyone stopped sparring to watch. Hauser, Haanz, and McDunham looked at each other before running toward the brawl.

*****

"Keep your hands off her, you fucking ape!" Judith screamed as she elbowed the man in the nose, causing him to stumble back sharply and clutch at it.

"Stupid bitch!" The man cursed. He was easily six and a half feet tall and built very much like the gorilla Judith called him as. He'd been grabbing on Linda, one of the Duchess' girls when Judith caught him. Linda was struggling with him.

"Touch one of my girls again, and I'll wear your guts for garters—understand?" Judith warned, a sword in her hand.

"I was just tryna teach the little whore how to break a hold," the man said.

"Break a hold? By feeling on her tits and lady bits, ay?" Judith said skeptically and looked at Linda, who shook her head.

"Smelly bastard was looking for a reason to put hands on me all mornin' 'n saw a right opportunity for it. Said he wanted to spar. He ain't wantin' to swing with a sword, Judy," Linda said.

Judith gave a slow nod and looked back at the man. She couldn't remember his name, but he was one of the men she'd known would be trouble. She never liked the way he looked at her, or any of her other girls. Now, she wondered why she hadn't just told Cap'n Pate about it.

Haanz and Hauser broke through the crowd and looked first at Judith and Linda, then at their man to the left.

"Fuck is all this?" Haanz asked.

"He was tryin' to rape me on the beach in front of everybody, is what it is!" Linda accused.

Hauser folded his arms and gave an incredulous smirk. "That true, Mr. Gregory?"

The big man, Mr. Gregory quickly shook his head, hand still covering his busted, leaking nose. "Ain't do shit, Hauser—bitch is crazy!"

Hauser appraised him for a long moment, staring him in the eyes. Then his smirk turned to a scowl and he shook his head. "You lied to me, mate. You was tryin' to crack a kettle."

Gregory shook his head again. "No, Haus, I ain't do no such fing—I swear!" the big man pleaded, looking at Linda and Judith. "Tell 'em!"

Hauser walked in front of him, shaking his head. "Didn't I tell all of you what for the other day? You touch any 'o these boys 'n *especially* the girls, there'd be hell ta pay?"

The men were quiet; everyone was.

Gregory shook his head again. "I didn't, sir. I didn't—"

"I know you, Greg. I know your ways," Hauser said as he closed in on him. Gregory was stuck in place, shivering.

"Wait!" Judith said, stepping forward.

Hauser paused and turned his head to look at her. He had a knife in his hand.

"Let me do it. Right here," she said. "Fight me."

Hauser raised a brow, and looked at Gregory, then back at her. "You mad, ma'am? Gregory's got 10 stones on you, easy. He'll clobber you."

Judith fixed an icy stare at Hauser. "I can take him."

Hauser put his hands up in surrender. "Be my guest." He looked at Gregory, who was clutching his sword with a cock-sure grin, now. He nodded, and the big man charged at her.

Judith waited for him to get close, then quickly dodged to the left, out of his sword arm's reach. She swung her sword backward and Gregory howled as he was slashed across the back. He fell from the pain, grabbing at the wound and pulling his hand away bloody.

The crowd whooped and roared, utterly stricken with surprise at the upset. Judith stood at the ready as he got back up, knowing the same tactic was unlikely to work again.

"That hurt, wench. That fucking *hurt!*" Gregory groaned as he readied for another strike.

"I told you I'd wear your guts for garters. Fess up, and you'll live," she instructed.

"Piss off!" Gregory said as he made another go at her.

This time he did a wide sweep with the sword, forcing her back. McDunham watched her feet as she stepped backward with each of his swings.

"One foot forward, the other back."

That was what Hauser had told him. Judith was doing just that. She parried two of his swings before she realized that doing that would spell her defeat. Gregory was slow, but he had a lot of power, and if she tried to parry many more of them he would break her guard and cleave her open. She ducked under one of his swings and feinted again to the left. He punched her in the gut. She gasped as the wind was knocked out of her, and he immediately put her in a head lock, lifting her off the ground with one arm.

"You fucked up…wench," Gregory growled into her ears as his muscles closed her windpipe. Judith gasped, the last of the air leaving her and her tongue poking out as she began to suffocate.

He's only using one arm.

She realized the opportunity and grabbed her knife from her hip, then as he attempted to restrain her further, dropping his sword. She stabbed the knife into his gut. Gregory gasped, then began to howl in pain as she stuck him—again and again. She stabbed him at least a half dozen times, and her vision began to fade, but Gregory let go and she landed on her feet, clutching her throat as she breathed. She turned slowly to see Gregory still howling, clutching his bleeding gut.

"Stuck me—she stuck me!" Gregory blubbered, bending over to grab his discarded sword. Judith let loose a war cry as she fell upon him, mounting his back and stabbing him in the shoulder over and over. Gregory flailed, attempting to pull her off him and failing, earning burning stab after burning stab for his trouble. "Help me!" he pleaded, looking at Haanz and Hauser.

Haanz stood there with a pensive expression, and Hauser merely shook his head. "Shouldn't have tried to rape her, Greg. You're a dead walrus, now."

Judith dismounted Gregory as the big man fell back to his knees, heaving for air as blood sprayed from his neck. The cheering had died down, and everyone watched as Gregory breathed his last before falling face first into the sand.

Judith stood, bloody and triumphant over Gregory as the crowd cheered and Pate ran through them, followed by Oculeth. Everyone fell silent as he looked around and appraised the dead pirate, hunched over, bleeding out on the sand. He looked at Judith, then at Linda, who was standing meekly to the side, and then at Hauser and Haanz.

"Well, well, well. What in blazes happened here?"

XLVI

Delilah

Osiris, Huasca, Stone, and Morgan stood in the hallway that led to the small compartment storing the Eye of Atla. Outside of the doorway were two dead guards, devoid of eyes, and enough blood to ruin someone's evening scrubbing it off the floorboards and walls. Huasca sighed and pushed open the door, already knowing what he'd find.

"It is gone..." Huasca said.

Everyone's heart sank.

Morgan leaned against a wall and then punched it in frustration. "Dammit!"

"I wonder how long they've been dead," Stone pondered. "When was the last guard shift?"

"No more than two hours ago," Osiris answered. "I oversaw it."

"Did you?" Stone asked suspiciously.

"Aye, I did," Osiris answered, his eyes locked with Stone's.

"It could not have been Osiris. He was with me for the better part of the last two hours since the guard rotation, and regardless, there would almost certainly be blood on his clothes. He would have had to change them," Huasca pointed out.

Stone, unable to argue with the logic, relented.

"They have the Eye. For all we know, they could be a hundred miles away, now, and we're still dead in the water..." Morgan sighed.

"I still sense their presence aboard this vessel," Abbal answered, allaying that concern.

"Then where in Sheolhenna are they?" Morgan asked, irritated.

"Before, I thought that the reason I couldn't pinpoint the source of this dark energy was because I had grown too weak to do so. Now, I suspect that they are using a spell of some sort to suppress their energy, so that they cannot be sensed by another Alyrian," Abbal suggested.

"A spell? So, this creature truly *is* an Alyrian," Stone sighed. "Great."

"Yes, and a powerful one. We know that they are a shapeshifter, but it is rare to encounter a shapeshifter who can transform into people, almost perfectly mimicking them," Abbal said. "Mr. Huasca has some thoughts on this."

They all looked at Huasca. "This man-imitating shapeshifter, we have legends of them in Bagwham—munchinja, or man-changer, in Kurzan. They are dark druids, practitioners of forbidden rituals that allow them to mold their body into that of another man."

"I see. How do we find them?" Morgan asked.

"A munchinja is not an exact copy of the person they are imitating. They have some of the memories of the person they imitate, but they cannot replicate them perfectly. Small differences, mannerisms, clothing and the like, the munchinja will not be able to faithfully replicate it. It is like a man picking up a sword, trying to imitate a master. He can swing the sword, but he will not have the finesse that a master would," Huasca said.

An idea began to formulate in Osiris' mind.

"Would it be possible to dispel whatever magick this shapeshifter is using?" Osiris asked.

Huasca pondered his answer. "Perhaps. I do not know any spells to nullify whatever Alyria our unwelcome guest is using, but I believe that I can modify an Alyria sapper to work on objects—and people. The downside of this is that it will nullify our abilities as well," he said, looking at Osiris.

Osiris didn't like the sound of that. Though he had poor control of it, his Alyria was the thing that gave him an edge over most opponents, big or small. Without it, he had just his swordsmanship and wits, which likely wouldn't help against whatever enemy they were facing. Which meant…

"Do whatever you can. If the bastard is still here, he's here for a reason other than the Eye. We'll find him," Osiris said and walked away quickly.

"What happens if your amulet is wrong, and the bastard's already given us the slip?" Stone asked impishly.

Morgan looked at him, genuine worry creased the aging roadmap of his face. "Then, Mr. Stone, we are in for a world of trouble beyond reckoning. Not only will none of you lot be getting a letter of marque, we will never know peace again in this life. Varryn Kurza will come down upon us with the wrath of God, and he will send every man that is able to erase us, the Storm Tide, and everyone we've ever known and loved from the face of Hera…"

Stone was at a loss for words. He thought of all the people back home that could be in genuine danger because of him. Would the Emperor be so cruel as to raze a little village in the moors of Sarx just to find a nothing like him?

Huasca stood, contemplating what needed to be done to find the munchinja was using—for all their sakes.

Osiris stumbled back into the hallway. "Cap'n!"

They all looked at him, surprised.

"Siris?" Morgan replied.

"You'll want to see this…"

*****

Moary stepped down the stairs into the galley, followed by Anatoli and Khruschev. "Siris? Ye fixin' ta become a drunk like Hanover, now?"

Osiris shook his head with a smirk. "I like alcohol, but I don't believe anythin' is good in excess, save for gold 'n women, perhaps. Care to play a game, brothers?"

The men looked at one another, shrugged, and sat down. Osiris pulled out a deck of cards and grabbed several more bottles of alcohol and dried pork jerky from the galley counter. The men chewed the jerky and sat as he divvied up the cards.

"Up for a game of Delilah?" he asked.

"Haven't played in months, might be rusty," Moary warned.

Osiris laughed as he began shuffling cards. "You? Rusty? Like an eel's belly. You're one of the best card players on this boat."

Khruschev chimed in, "Aye, ye beat me 'n Anatoli's ass maybe a fortnight ago, or d'ya forget?"

Moary laughed. "Caught me, did ya? I was hopin' ya'd forgotten."

Osiris handed everyone, including himself, a king and a queen card, then reshuffled the deck and handed each of them four random cards, face down. Then, he set aside the two remaining king cards, face up, on the side of the table, before setting down a face card. He pulled out Moary's half-spent cigar, then lit it.

"That's a five. Need fifteen to make twenty, mates," Osiris said. They all knew the score, so they nodded.

Osiris looked through his cards and appraised his hand. He had his king, which was worth ten, his queen, which was worth eight, a two, a five, a seven, and a dead eye. He looked at the others, who looked at each other in turn. Each of them was trying to guess the hand of the others. He'd seen a slight smirk on Khruschev's face. Anatoli was looking neutral, while Moary looked right puzzled.

He placed three cards, all face down. "Five, Seven, and two. That's fourteen."

Anatoli placed two cards, face down. "Eight and seven. Fifteen. I win."

"How d'ya figure? Still two more lads what didn't play there hands, brother," Khruschev chuckled, placing three cards face down. "Three fives. I win as well."

Osiris gauged both, looking them over before looking at Moary, who hadn't placed his bid yet. "Mr. Moary, ye gonna play your hand, or do ye need me to pick 'em for ya?"

Moary chuckled. "And have you learn my hand? Bugger that," he said as he placed four cards, face down. "Four fives. That's twenty, I win!" he declared confidently.

The others laughed. "Win? According to you, ye broke five over—ye didn't win shit," Anatoli said. "I think ol' Moary's gettin' a bit soft in the head." He nudged Khruschev and Osiris.

"Maybe that, ay? Any calls?" Osiris asked.

The men looked at one another, but no one called the other's bluff. "Alright then. Anatoli, Khruschev, ye both get two. Congratulations," Osiris said joylessly.

He took a breath from the cigar and reshuffled the face card back into the pile. "Onto the next. Moary, you forget how to play or somethin'? I figured you'd call Khruschev's bluff."

"Didn't bluff shit, sir. 'N even if I did, the rounds over, ha!" Khruschev said triumphantly as he added two cards to his deck from the pile, as did Anatoli.

"Fair enough," Osiris smirked.

He placed another face card, face down. This time it was a dead eye. Since he dealt, he called the value of the card. "The dead eye is an eight. Need twelve to break twenty."

The men nodded and looked at their hands.

Osiris placed two cards, face down, immediately. "A king and a two. I win," he said confidently.

Khruschev made a click of disapproval.

Anatoli placed his three faced down cards with a grin. "An eight and two two's," he declared.

Khruschev groaned and placed two faces down cards. "Fucking whoreson—a king and a dead eye. I win, dammit. It fucking cost me, though."

Moary, still looking a bit perplexed, placed one of his remaining cards face down before him. "I place a queen," he said, uncertain.

Osiris smoked his cigar. "Any calls?"

Khruschev looked Osiris in the eyes a moment, then nodded. "I do; First Mate Osiris, I call your bid."

Osiris chuckled. "Do ye, now? Any other callers?"

Moary looked at Khruschev, then Osiris, then Anatoli. "Mr. Anatoli, I call your bid, sir."

Anatoli groaned. Osiris flipped his cards over, as did Anatoli.

Khruschev cursed and pushed away from the table. "Dammit all!"

Osiris had revealed his cards. A king and a two, just as he'd said. "Better luck next time, mate. Thanks for the four extra cards." He smirked.

Anatoli's hand was false; he'd placed three threes.

"Looks like you're out, mate," Osiris said.

Anatoli grumbled and handed over his three remaining cards to Moary, who took them after a moment's pause.

Osiris put the cards he'd bid back in his hand, then drew eight more from the pile. "And then there were three."

Khruschev fumed. He'd lost cards, and now he'd just supplied one of his opponents with more.

Osiris took another puff from the cigar and began to shuffle the cards again. "How's your mother, Gwen, Mr. Moary? I saw ye wrote some letters to her, in the cabin."

Moary shrugged. "She's alright I suppose. She never seems to want to write me back, however, ha!" he laughed, hiding his pain.

Osiris nodded. "I know the feeling. Me 'n mine aren't on speaking terms, neither," he admitted as he chopped the cards. "I guess I'm better off than some, though. Hanover bein' an orphan and all, I feel it ain't right to complain about it, ay? He still drinkin' himself into a stupor over that Valkar woman he slew?"

Moary tried to hold back a laugh but failed. "Is he? Boy's all peaky-eyed in his hammock right now, he is. Right shame, really."

"Yeah, he's a bit of a soft blanket, that one," Osiris placed a face card on the table. It was a jester. "Well look at that."

Khruschev looked at the card and grumbled, "Fuckin' great. I miss a round now, too?"

"That's what the card says, yeah," Osiris said, looking at Moary. "Just me 'n you, Duwa."

"*Half-Duwa*," Moary corrected. "'N don't ye forget it, boy."

"*Half-Duwa*," Osiris emphasized as he took another hit from the cigar and offered it to Khruschev, who took it with a frown.

"Since a jester was played, the card value is 5. Gotta get fifteen again," Osiris said, going through his own cards. "Mr. Moary, ye never grabbed your four cards from the pile."

Moary paused a moment, realizing he hadn't, then grabbed the cards. Khruschev passed the cigar to Anatoli and whispered something into his ear. Anatoli gave him a raised brow as he smoked from the cigar.

Osiris picked the cards he wanted to play from his hand. Everyone already knew he had a king and a two. What they didn't know is that he picked up an extra queen and another dead eye from the pile, along with a jester and five number cards. This was points round, and with his cards, he could end the game right now, assuming Moary didn't have more points than him, that is.

"I think you're growing soft yourself, Mr. Moary," Osiris goaded as he laid out his bid of three faced down cards with a slight twitch of the corner of his lip. "Ye've been stumblin' around like a blind man this whole game."

Moary, took a swig from his bottle and laid out his own bid of five cards. "Mayhap I'm just tryin' to play the fool, brother."

"Perhaps. I put up a queen, a five, and a two. That's fifteen. Or is it?" Osiris asked.

"Maybe it is? Or maybe it isn't. I bid a king, and four ones," Moary said with a cocksure grin.

Osiris laughed. "Nay, I think you're full of shit and you're a damned liar, Frederick Moary. If you knew the rules of the game, you'd know this acts as a final round. There are no bids, just points."

Osiris looked Moary dead in the eyes as he laid out his hand, flipping over all his cards. "Show your hand."

Moary, his eyes hard and unreadable, placed his own cards on the table, then flipped them all.

Khruschev and Anatoli whistled while Moary scowled deeply.

Osiris had eleven cards: a king, a queen, two dead eyes, a jester, a three, three sixes, a seven, and an eight. That brought his total point value to seventy-five.

Moary had nine cards: a king, a queen, a jester, four fours, and two sixes. Bringing his points to fifty-one.

"I win, and *you* lose," Osiris said, meeting Moary's dead faced scowl with his own.

Anatoli passed the cigar back to Osiris. It was nearly gone, just a two-inch stub, now. He took a small puff before offering it to Moary. Moary shook his head, declining it. Osiris grinned, showing his teeth as he finished off the cigar.

"Let's go down the list, shall we? It's been an interesting game, I'd say. First off, Mr. Moary, I find it odd that ye forgot to how to play a game that, as Khruschev and Anatoli kindly pointed out, ye wiped the floor with 'em at just a fortnight past. Forgot the rules of it too, ay?" Osiris asked.

Moary was silent.

"Then, there's this cigar, here. You gave it to me, remember? In fact, I don't recall a time you've ever turned down a smoke. Funny, that," Osiris continued.

Moary gave a bemused shrug. "I'm tryin' to kick the habit while we stew in the doldrums, is that a crime?"

Osiris shook his head. "No, it ain't. Except, here's the kicker." He leaned in, his eyes beginning to glow. "Ye forgot the name of your own mother. It ain't Gwen…it's Gertrude."

Moary said nothing. His expression dropped like a hammer on an anvil and became blank and indifferent.

"Just what I thought…oh, and me mother? She's dead as a fucking door nail—just like you." Osiris whipped his hand out and aimed his pistol at Moary's head, then fired faster than anybody could react.

"Gotcha, ye fucker."

*****

The officers of the Azura stormed into the room, drawn by the sound of gunfire. At the top of the stairs were a small cluster of pirates, also drawn by the noise. Morgan and his entourage pushed through them, coming down the stairs into the galley.

"How d'ye know it's the fake?" Khruschev asked, skeptically.

"Because the real Moary is dead above deck…" Osiris said soberly.

Even knowing it was a fake, the men were taken aback by seeing the dead face of Frederick Moary with a smoking bullet hole splitting it open. "Is he dead?" Stone asked.

Osiris stooped over the corpse and pressed a hand to its neck. "No pulse."

"I know we found the real him, but…" Cutter began, uncertain how to state his thoughts.

"I know, doesn't sit right with me neither," Osiris admitted.

"Where is the Eye of Atla?" Morgan asked concernedly. "Is it on his person?"

"Something is wrong…" Abbal whispered.

Khruschev bent over the corpse and rifled through its pockets before pulling a rather large and glowing cyan-blue orb out of its breast. "I found it, sir!"

Morgan breathed a sigh of relief. "Good. Perhaps all isn't lost. Give it to me, please."

Khruschev stepped over the body of Moary and walked toward Morgan.

Cutter gasped, "Holy Stars above…"

"It still lives…" Abbal shuddered.

Khruschev looked over his shoulder and froze, as did everyone else. The body of the shapeshifter stood up, and it began to change—violently. To the horror of every man in the galley, the being let loose an unsettling roar, prolonged and loud enough to make their ears ring. In that roar was the familiar screams of all their missing crewmen, taken by it, and the sound of countless inhuman creatures. Cutter tried to clap his hands over his ears, but remembered that he was missing one, once again, and resigned himself to curling into a ball on the floor, covering his ears with his arms. Flint and Stone fell over a table, backing away from the thing. Anatoli ran and hid behind the bar, while Ryker, Sarkad, Huasca, Osiris, Cage, and Morgan stood in an uneasy circle around the howling creature. It shot out an arm and grabbed hold of Khruschev, pulling him in in an instant.

It changed, and in its transformation, they saw a menagerie of ugly shapes. Faces twisted in agony or glaring hatefully. Animal heads, complete with gnashing jaws or mandibles, and the arms and legs of different creatures juxtaposed to a heaving, shimmering mass of flesh.

To their despair, Khruschev was savaged by the changing creature as a dozen claws and jaws tore him apart before their eyes. The creature's howl blocked out most of his screams, but they could still see him struggling in its clutches.

The standing officers aimed their guns at the being as it settled into its final shape, much less horrific than its previous ones, but no less unexpected. The tall shape of a woman stood before them, one wrapped in white bandages and wearing pieces of golden armor, and a gold mask. She regarded them with a slow turn of her head as she held the mangled head of Khruschev in her embrace. His body was eviscerated, left a raw, bloody mass of bone and gristle on the floor. It was all that remained of him. She cocked her head and swung his head around in a graceful gesture before dropping it on the ground. In her other hand was the Eye of Atla.

Broken from their stupor, the five men opened fire on the shapeshifter, and she let loose a high-pitched shriek as bullets tore through her. Just then, Armen Hanover and a half dozen other men stormed down the stairs into the galley, confused by what they saw. The shapeshifter looked at them, then immediately transformed into a large, leopard-like humanoid creature that lunged at them. Hanover shouted, fired, then dove to the side as the creature launched into the crowd and began tearing men limb from limb.

"Shoot it! Stab it! Fuck—do something and kill it!" Morgan ordered as he kept firing at the creature.

The leopard-monster yowled from the gunfire and pounced behind the counter for cover.

"No, no, no—AAAAH!!!AAAAAAAHHH!" Anatoli shouted, then screamed bloody murder as the creature savaged him behind the cover. He grabbed onto the counter, attempting to climb over, but was immediately pulled back down by the leopard-monster. The men formed a firing line and hurriedly began to reload their guns, many of them fumbling and dropping their bullets, powder, or guns, in fear. Anatoli's mangled head raised up from behind the counter, and the men recoiled. The creature threw it over the counter, causing several men to waste their shots firing at it.

"Hold fire, ye fools!" Stone shouted as he pulled out his pistol. Everyone still alive in the galley stood in the firing formation, aimed at the galley counter.

There were multiple cabinets full of alcohol by the counter, and they were all loathe to fire at it. Should one of them catch a spark from a bullet, a conflagration could spark.

Morgan stood in the front of the line. "We have you surrounded, monster. Come out now, or we'll load you with so many bullets you'll be shitting lead."

All was silent for several heartbeats as everyone kept their eyes on the galley counter. Then suddenly, an object was hurled from behind it and the men scattered, some firing, others simply breaking and running to the corners of the room. As the smoke cleared, they saw that it was Anatoli's body that they'd shot.

Just then, something large and black surged from behind the counter and skittered across the ceiling. The men cursed and scrambled as a black spider, the size of a man with long, hairy legs, crawled toward the stairwell.

"It is escaping! Shoot it!" Huasca yelled, firing at the creature. His bullet missed, and in the gun smoke filling the compartment, the creature made its escape.

Everyone coughed and called out to one another, getting a headcount of who was still alive. Morgan ordered them all back out onto the main deck, and everyone made for the stairs. Cries of alarm echoed down from above as Morgan pushed the door open to the main deck. Two men laid dying on the deck.

"What happened?" Morgan exclaimed.

"It came so fast—it was the most horrible thing I ever saw!" A man exclaimed. "Spider, big as a man came tearin' through. Killed Kyle and Miller before they even had time to react," he said, pointing out the two dying men on the deck. One appeared to have his neck torn open, and the other was nearly cut in half at the gut. Both men would be dead in minutes.

Morgan punched a mast in frustration and grief. In less than five minutes, he'd lost nearly a dozen men. And perhaps just as terrible—

"It has the Eye," Abbal said.

*****

There were three Alyrians.

Volldah knew that, now.

The being that lived in the amulet around the captain's neck, the old Xallan, and the young one. How had he seen through her disguise? Had she truly been so careless in hiding the body? Perhaps she had grown too bold. These pirates, while they were formidable by human standards, were of no real consequence to her. They did not understand her greatest weakness, after all. She had shown them just a sliver of what she was capable of, and it was enough to chill them to the bone.

"Remember our bargain, dear."

The voice in the Eye said. Volldah had to be conscious of her thoughts and actions, with this strange artifact around. She listened to what the pirates said about it and scavenged the occasional errant thought from the minds of those she'd slain. If memories were to be believed, this 'Eye of Atla' was a thing of cursed myth to pirates. And it had a special history with this 'Captain Morgan' that her master wanted her to bring to him. She wondered what made it so coveted. She felt no more powerful with it on her person. She didn't feel as though she could tame the seas, or summon Alyria storms, or conjure the power of a god.

The young Xallan man had discovered a chink in her armor. She could not remember everything that her prey knew. She grabbed memories and thoughts that seemed prescient but could not hope to contain it all. Now, she would have to be careful. While he would not be able to sniff out all her disguises, he would be able to notice obvious lapses in knowledge.

Osiris. That was his name, wasn't it?

He was clever, that one. His constitution was stronger than his peers, and she got the inkling that he would prove a much more difficult mark than the others. His eyes…they glowed with Alyria. She wondered if he could see through her imitations with those eyes. She resolved to pluck those eyes before she was finished with him. Ordinarily she would let them keep their eyes, so that they could see what devastation she had inflicted upon their flesh. But then the shaman had gone digging into the last sight of her prey, potentially compromising her disguises.

So now, she ate their eyes.

As she would do Osiris' when she dealt with him.

"Soon, dear. Soon. The doldrums are almost done. We wouldn't want to spoil the surprise, would we?" The Eye of Atla spoke to her in a honeyed, motherly voice.

Volldah was ever so aware of the faint hint of Alyria behind those seductive words. She was eager to be rid of it.

XLVII

DIVERGENT PATHS

Pate sat in his cabin aboard the Cutthroat.

He liked the one in the Duchess. It was spacious and whoever captained her before his arrival definitely liked their hammock and their amenities plush. But there was something to be said for the hard rope of a pirate's hammock. In his heart of hearts he knew he would always be a man prone to hardness. He had to be in order to survive this life. He had taken lives many times to spare his own, some of which were kin in black.

And so, it was of no real surprise to him that he sat at his desk looking at Judith, soaked in the blood of some handsy, foolish bastard from the Cutthroats named Gregory. He was a big man, but Pate knew just from watching him that he had a giant's complex. Which meant he'd forgotten, with his goodly size, that a sword, a knife, or a bullet, was just as deadly in the hands of a woman a hundred and fifty pounds lighter, and a foot and a half shorter than him, as it was in his own hands.

That mistake cost him his life.

"Good riddance, ay?" Pate said, having sat there mulling her over for the better part of five minutes. He ran a hand over the bandages covering his bloody knuckles.

Judith released a breath she hadn't known she'd been holding and gave an almost impish smile to him in return. She didn't really know what to say, in truth. Were it any other man, she would be all piss and vinegar, glaring daggers at him and daring him to try and argue why she was in the wrong for killing Gregory. But with Cap'n Pate it was different. Not only was he just as fiery in temperament as her, but he was someone who she'd grown to respect.

Even though he used one of his own men as bait.

She corrected, still recalling the unflattering end of Mr. Henry. Officially he'd died in the chaos of the hydra attack, just like the twenty-nine other men who were killed. Technically, it was the truth.

But the twenty-nine other men hadn't been thrown directly into the maw of the beast, like Mr. Henry had. But she couldn't fault him. By sacrificing an already dying man, Cap'n Pate had saved the crew. He did what had to be done, just as she had when she killed that pig, Gregory.

"Aye…good riddance," she responded.

He opened his jacket slightly, revealing the familiar dark green of a bottle. "A drink with your cap'n. How's about it?"

Judith gave it mock consideration. Right about now, she could use a stiff drink.

"That's a funny way of punishin' an officer what killed one of your men in cold blood, innit?" she half-joked, half-truthed.

"Well, that's because I'm not punishin' ye for what ye did, Ms. Judith," Pate explained as he pulled out two clouded slug glasses. They looked like a dozen pairs of unwashed lips had kissed them. "Ye did somethin' that's quite rare 'round these parts, far as I can recall."

"'N what's that?" she asked as she accepted the slug he offered her.

"Ye protected one of your crewmates, 'n ye meted out justice. For a man, that's quite ordinary, but for a woman, against a man twice her size and with far more combat experience? That's decidedly extraordinary. Most others in your shoes in that situation would've shut up 'n kept pushin', for fear of death. That takes bullocks, Judith. That takes courage that I can personally attest that a lot of folk don't have. Ye stood up for what's right, 'n I know in this life that can be real grey water to tread," Pate said.

He drank his slug, hummed, then poured another. Judith drank hers without much fanfare. He offered her another shot, and she took it.

"To keep it plain, sir, I…" Judith pondered. Did she trust him enough to be honest?

Pate's eyes, a deep green like emeralds, appraised hers with a respectful gaze. She believed she could.

"I was scared out of my damn wits. That Gregory bloke was the size of a damn small ogre, 'n he had the temper of one, too. But I knew that if I let it go, he'd do it again, 'n the others would too. Pretty soon, the girls would start turnin' up disheveled, ghost-eyed and beaten down. Most of us came on because we wanted to get away from the troubles back home. Linda got beat on by her father, so she grabbed her shit 'n left with us. Girl can't be no older than eighteen, maybe? She ain't sign on to be raped. So, I had to set an example, scared or not…"

She felt vulnerable, so she drank the slug and grabbed the bottle to pour another. Whatever was in the bottle was powerful, but it was a mix of different alcohols. Some form of alcosav—strong alcosav at that. She needed it.

"I understand. People can be right terrible, 'n pirates, well—we sure as shit ain't different, I'll tell ye that much. We need people like you to set the example. So I'm not gonna penalize ye for offin' Gregory," Pate said.

"…But?" Judith asked, knowing there was more to it.

"No buts. Watch your ass, stay your path, and keep working. Ye may yet find yourself a cap'n yourself, one day," Pate said proudly.

"A cap'n? Ha!" Judith chuffed. "When the sky is red and the moon is purple, maybe."

Pate shrugged. "Stranger shit's happened—trust me."

"True. I once saw a dragon sleepin' on the shoreline when I was a babe. No one believes me till this day," Judith said.

"A dragon? I figured your isle to be too small for one to roost there. You'd all be dead within its first ranging season," Pate said.

Dragons needed large tracts of land to hunt when they awoke. Many of them would go on rampages, called 'ranges' when they awoke from a long slumber. It wasn't uncommon for them to scour an entire countryside and burn several villages to the ground in the process, either. Plus, most of them tended not to fair too well at sea.

"See? Just like the rest of 'em," Judith jested.

"If ye say ye saw it, well," Pate gave her an appraising look. "I believe ye." He poured them both one last shot, feeling himself slipping past tipsy and into the murky depths of drunkenness. "To red skies, purple moons, and dragons!"

Judith raised her slug. "Cheers!"

They clinked their glasses and knocked them back.

*****

He found himself in a room. He wasn't quite sure how, or when he'd gotten here. Maybe he'd always been here, or maybe he'd only been here a few minutes. He couldn't really tell. His mind felt like it was covered in mud, slow and plodding. He rubbed a hand across a wall of strange, dull purple stone. It was polished like marble to a reflective shine, and to his utter astonishment it began to glow with a scrawl of strange patterns and symbols.

No...

No, they were quite familiar.

He couldn't remember where, precisely, but he knew he'd seen them before. It became a glowing cube of the purple scrawl, as though fingers with long nails had etched into the polished purple stone. His mind tried to sound out words—incantations—decrypted from the writing on the walls. It became a storm in his mind. Too many words, too many phrases.

The truth is a lie. The lie is a truth. In the Isle of Myths, Ignorance is bliss.

"What does that mean?" he asked aloud.

"Have you forgotten so quickly, Taren?" A voice said, no more than an inch from his ear.

He jumped back, and for a moment he saw a familiar, beautiful face. But just as quickly as it came, it was gone. Instead, a faceless sentinel stood before him. It sashayed toward him, reaching a taloned hand forward as its hips swayed enticingly. He backed away as the thing grabbed for him, and he stumbled backward onto a balcony. He gasped, looking out over a starry expanse with a dark, bruised purple sky and a twinkling of enchanting stars. He knew now that he could not be on Hera.

The figure closed in, running a hand across its modest breast while cupping his face with the other. Its skin, purply pink and perfectly smooth and featureless, inched closer to his own, and he felt the overwhelming urge to scream as a dozen small black pours opened in the face. He let loose an alarmed cry.

And then he awoke.

*****

Oculeth gasped into the waking world, his glasses had fallen away from his face and his hair had turned into wet, coiling serpents on his head and shoulders. He was lying in a bed, a priceless commodity in this arc of his life. Too many nights spent swaying in a tight, cushion-less hammock had turned his back into knots, which the feather-stuffed mattress of the tavern room had begun to work out.

I'll have to thank Tellarya personally for this room.

The woman had insisted he stay in the room for free, which was something none of his crewmates could say. Most of them slept in their hammocks aboard the Duchess. He wanted to enjoy what time he had away from that for as long as he could. He knew that soon, he would be returning to the sea, and all the vagaries and horrors that brought with it. He lit the covered candle by his bedside and sat up, placing his feet on the cool wooden floor. He'd had another nightmare of that place.

He didn't know what it all entailed, but he knew that he had to find out, and find out soon. The mark of eternal return he'd tattooed onto he and Edward Patron's arms, once a ward to protect them from the evil that haunted them, was growing. It swallowed a good portion of his arm, now, and glowed faintly at all times, a low, dull blue color. He worried what would happen if it kept growing. Would it consume him? So that when it flared in agonizing reminder of his predicament, it would drown him in pain? He didn't want to find out what would happen then.

He heard a knocking at his door and combined with the dull whispers in the back of his mind, constantly, he was put on edge. He formed a small blue flame in his palm, and clenched it, ready to attack whatever was on the other side of his bedroom door.

He heard the knocking again and saw a shadow shifting beneath the door. He took a deep breath and drew near. When the knock came again, he flung the door open a quarter, arm hidden just out of sight, ready to ignite whatever thing was trying to lure him.

It was Tellarya. She made an "O of surprise with her mouth, flicking first to his eyes, then to his chest.

He remembered he was shirtless.

"Oh dear—Miss Tellarya, I apologize! Is something the matter?" he asked, concernedly.

She composed herself, her eyes lingering just a fraction too long and gave him a nervous smile. "Apologies, dearie. Cap'n Pate told me to hand you this note."

She handed it to his outstretched hand and curled the fingers closed with her own. He stared at it for a moment and realized his hand was trembling.

"Are you alright, Mr. Oculeth? Your hand is clammy as a wet dog and trembling like one, too," Tellarya pointed out.

Oculeth hitched his breath, then offered the most convincing smile he could muster. "I'm—I'm fine, Ma'am. Had a bit of an…a nightmare, is all."

"Oh? Did I startle you? I'm sorry, I should've waited until the morning—"

"It's quite alright. Knowing the good captain, it's probably urgent."

"Yes, well…" she fixed him with a heartwarming smile, her hazel eyes lingering on his. "I guess I'll let you get your rest."

He thought to invite her in. In fact, it was the thing he wanted more than anything at that moment. But then his arm began to burn, and he was reminded of his plight.

She doesn't deserve to be entangled in this.

"Yes…goodnight, Miss Tellarya. And thank you," he said before quickly closing the door.

He pressed his back against it, cursing his damnable luck and biting his lip as the pain began to flair, and his arm began to flare brightly. It felt like he was being held closer and closer to a low flame. He flipped open the note and read it by candlelight.

"Dock nineteen. 0400 Hours, Tordus. Come alone."

Oculeth sighed and checked the time on his pocket watch. It was midnight. He resolved to enjoy his last few hours in bed and laid back down.

*****

Oculeth was amazed that the storm that surrounded the island seemed to all but disappear once you made it to the shoreline. He hadn't given it much thought before. On this cloudless night, however, the moon cast a beautiful blue ray across the sea, and everything looked serene and peaceful. He wondered what powerful Alyria must have been at work to have that effect. He hadn't come across any Alyrians here, save for Tellarya. But she had told them they *were* here, amidst the crews and the like, though they tended to keep their own company.

He had seen an alchemy shop on his way through town. Under ordinary circumstances an alchemist would only be able to sell simple potions to civilians. Tonics and tinctures to heal the humors or remove warts. The strong stuff was reserved for magisters, specialist imperial agents, and the Mygredorians, though their kind seldom used it. He wondered what they sold here.

"You're late," Pate admonished him.

"I had to make sure all my things were in order, and then got lost on my way here," Oculeth said, truthfully.

"Got lost? What'd ye go sight-seein'?" Pate asked.

"I'm on an isle with a sea tirade constantly storming around it, with a sprawling town full of pirates. There's nothing but sights to see here. Fantasies are written on places like this," Oculeth said.

"And men die for wandering, in places like this," Pate reminded him. "Or did ye so quickly forget your run in with the Cutthroats?"

How could I?

It had nearly cost him his life, and when he'd discovered Pate had recruited them after killing their captain, he was perplexed to say the least.

Under ordinary circumstances, when his Alyria wasn't working against him, he'd have been able to fight them easily, though it would almost certainly have killed them. Though considering Pate wound up killing all of them anyway, he supposed it would have made no real difference.

"Come. I've chartered a boat for ye, to the Maaug Haunt…" Pate said, though Oculeth could tell he had reservations.

"So soon? I'd figured it would take some time."

"Nay, I figured ye'd want to get ghost as soon as possible, so I moved to make sure ye could do that."

I'm not trying to run away. I'm trying to save our lives, Captain…

He wanted to tell him that, badly. But he knew it would be futile. In Edward Patron's eyes, Oculeth was running from responsibility, even if it meant both their salvations.

The pair walked down the dock, and Oculeth saw a small, two-masted brigantine. Several men were standing aboard it, talking amongst themselves, smoking, or otherwise being idle. They were approaching a man standing near the gangplank at the side of the ship, and Pate waved him over.

It's now or never, I suppose…

"Captain, I…"

"Mr. Dufrain, this is Mr. Oculeth, your passenger," Pate said, cutting him off.

Mr. Dufrain, an old and swarthy-looking pirate, looked at Oculeth through a heavy, squinting brow and scrunched his pinched lips at him. He was holding a torch, and so Oculeth had a clear profile of his face. The man was at least seventy. And he looked fit to keel over at a moment's notice.

By the Stars, Edward Patron has found an old, beaten down nag in a sailor's cap to sail me to the Isle of Myths.

"We're going to die," Oculeth whispered under his breath.

"Pardon?" The old sailor asked.

"I want to say hi! How are you, sir? This is a fine ship you have," Oculeth said with his best smile as he pointed at the ship.

Pate gave a half smirk as they walked, having heard Oculeth's quip. "Cap'n Dufrain is an old hand at sailing. Man was born with a steering wheel in his hands and saltwater in his veins, isn't that right Dufrain?"

"Oi, 'n me charad was a sturgeon, it was," Dufrain responded with mock enthusiasm. "Bah, make no mistake, laddie, I not be a senile grape, raisinin' in the sun. I'll get yer to the Maaug Haunt. But we'll need a blessin' from th'sea first, or we'll be sailin' to 'er graves."

The man spoke with a strong Sarxian accent. That bode well, in Oculeth's mind. Most Sarx were natural born seafolk.

"A blessing?" Oculeth questioned.

"He means you'll need a tide priest to ward the ship from the beasts of the Maaug Haunt, lest ye run afoul of somethin' foul. Or even fouler, Maaug herself," Pate said, lowering his voice at the mention of the Dead Sea God.

Oculeth had read about Maaug. She was alleged to be a gigantic orathid. She resided in a stretch of the Southern Amaranthine between Kurza, Xalla, and Dyona. And she'd been terrorizing it for as long as kith have been recording history on Hera. Not much else was known for certain about her. But sailors were known for their tall tales, and even more so when they were scared out of their minds by a near death experience.

He'd read stories that the creature had tentacles covered in teeth and eyes, and that a swarm of devil squid constantly surrounded it. He didn't know how true any of that was, however. He'd personally seen many creatures in his travels. He'd rode a griffon, crossed paths with a wandering red dragon, and nearly been murdered by fae in the untamed wilds of Lordalus. These Dead Sea Gods, however, were things alleged to be far more dangerous than anything he'd ever faced before.

"How would we go about getting the blessings of a tide priest?" Oculeth asked.

"On the southern shore of the isle is an enclave of 'em. Keep to 'emselves, mostly. 'Casionally they'll send some 'o their own into town to trade for goods 'n services. We'll be needin' to go to 'em if we're wantin their blessin', however," Dufrain said.

"Is it necessary?" Oculeth asked before he could stop himself.

Both pirates looked at him and he knew he'd asked the dumbest question in the world at that moment.

"Necessary?" Pate repeated. "Necessary is taking a deep breath before you dive into the water. Necessary is sharpening your sword before a battle. No, this isn't necessary. It's absolutely paramount. Ye go into Maaug's Haunt without the blessings of the sea god? You'll be dead long before you reach that 'Isle of Myths' you pine after."

Oculeth nodded quickly. "Understood, sir."

Dufrain shook his head, still disapproving of his impetuous question. He had a tobacco pipe hanging from his lips and it quivered as he worked his jaw and walked back toward the gangplank. It reminded Oculeth of an old, hunched over bird, walking toward its roost.

"Lovely man, Captain Dufrain. I think we'll get along swimmingly," Oculeth said sarcastically. He'd make better friends with a puffer fish.

Pate gave him a mirthless smirk. "Thick as thieves, I'm sure." He looked down the dock at the ship.

They both knew this was the end of their journey together, for now. Oculeth wondered if they would ever meet again. If he would return in time to save Captain Pate from the curse. He searched his own feelings. He wasn't sure.

"So, this is it, then?" Oculeth said, breaking the silence.

Pate nodded once. "It would appear so."

They stood there, looking at one another. Oculeth could see some resentment in those eyes but hidden in his anger was a small twinkle of longing. Edward Patron would miss him, in his own way.

"I will mourn them, just as you have. And though you cannot see it now, in this moment, captain, I am doing my part to avenge them. Smith, Jackson, Andrews, Franklin—all the men that were lost that terrible night…and William Brunt…" Oculeth said, remembering his solemn burial on that hill outside the Ford farm.

Pate wiped his nose, tipped his hat and nodded again. "…We mourn them in our own ways, Mr. Oculeth. You in yours, and me in mine. May you find whatever it is ye seek. And may we both be the better for it."

Oculeth saw in the moonlight, a single twinkling tear track trickled down from Pate's stony emerald eyes. The men clasped hands, and Pate shook it before patting him on the back.

"Stars guide you, Taren Oculeth," Pate said.

"And may they guide you as well, Edward Patron. To victory," Oculeth said.

He looked one last time at Livera and thanked the gods that he got to see it once in his life, even though he'd nearly been killed by it. He was thankful to have met Tellarya, though he wished he'd gotten to spend just one night with her. He prayed that he would get the opportunity again. He rubbed his arm, grabbed his bag of supplies off the dock, and walked toward the awaiting ship, leaving Edward Patron and his old life behind, once more.

XLVIII

The Hydra, Part II

On a sunny morning, they set out. Seventy men and women, both human and El'wa, aboard a hunter-class ship. Lord Krait had called it Sunsetter. It was rigged like all El'wa ships seemed to be with sails shaped like fins, mounted fore to aft. The ship was armed to the gills, not for ship-hunting, but monster-hunting. And now, Pate was about to discover if it could be used to kill the hydra haunting the outer storm wall.

"I will watch this hunt with great interest, captain," Lord Krait said. The icy El'wa pirate lord with piercing, glowing blue eyes and long, knife-like ears had opted to come on the hunt. Why, Pate couldn't fathom. All she'd done was watch him and his men work and consult with her officers. But he couldn't begrudge her. This *was* one of her ships, after all. He'd taken note of a large bow on her back, engraved with strange, El'wa symbols and wrapped in green vines. Did she plan to use *that* against a hydra?

"Of that I'm assured, Lord Krait'Malai. And I thank ye for use of your ship, once more," Pate said, trying to be as polite as possible. If it were Firebeard or Goldfang, he would probably be able to get away with speaking more aggressively. With this El'wa, however, he was none too sure. He needed her to at least like him.

"How polite. Are you this amiable with all the pirates you meet?" she asked, cutting through his veneer.

He hadn't expected that, not so soon.

"I…no, Ma'am. To be quite frank, I ain't particularly kind. I find it to be a liability when dealin' with cutthroat folk," he admitted. All cards were on the table, now.

She smiled. Hers was a pretty but unreadable one, and Pate didn't know if it was the smile of a predator about to pounce, or a genuine one. "I find that being polite only gets you so far. I didn't reach this station with kindness. Nor did you yours."

With that, he agreed.

He nodded, tipping his hat. "Touche."

A few minutes later they reached their hunting grounds, and Pate became all business once more. "Drop the probes. We'll force it out," Pate ordered.

His men took to the task immediately. The El'wa looked first at him, then at Lord Krait. She looked them over and stated simply, "His orders are my orders."

They nodded and carried it out. The probes, as Pate called them, were long chains with metal balls at the end. The ball had glowing, flat-tipped spikes that thrummed with Alyria. After several moments, the probes activated, and the whole ship vibrated with enough force to rattle Pate's teeth. The deck filled with teeth-chattering as the probes did their work. He looked at Judith, who stood next to him and saw her biting the sleeve of her coat to avoid biting her tongue. Lord Krait stood calmly, evidently quite used to the sensation.

After about a minute, the vibrations stopped.

"Did we get it?" Judith asked him.

He raised a finger, listening to the sea a moment. As if on cue, something surged up at the starboard of the Sunsetter, and Pate sprung into action. "Fire the harpoons!"

The crew, already at their stations, fired. A dozen serrated harpoons, anchored to the ship by chains were fired at the breaching creature and struck their target, and as the smoke cleared Pate beheld their quarry.

"Shit…"

"Congratulations, captain. You've felled a whale!" Lord Krait said with a regal laugh. The other El'wa laughed as well. The humans, however, were not so amused.

"Bloody thing must've came up to escape the probes. Got speared for its troubles," Hauser said.

"Where's our real quarry, then?" Judith pondered.

"Bastard must've gone to a different quadrant of the storm wall. Probably figured this area would be too hot," Pate sighed.

Which means we could be searching for the monster for days, maybe even weeks.

He kicked himself. He didn't figure a hydra to be a particularly keen planner or thinker. He wondered if the damn thing didn't just abandon the area entirely after having all its heads cut off.

"Reel in the harpoons. We're going to sail northward, see if the beast might have gone there," Pate said, trying to hide the doubt in his voice.

Hydras, like most sea monsters, were mostly a mystery. He had no real idea where it might roost, what its activity patterns were, and he most certainly didn't know whether they were smart enough to change location after being attacked. All that was known for certain was that in the summer months they went south to spawn and feed in the warm waters around Xalla, and in the cooler months they would travel north, to hjbernate in the cold waters.

"Are you so sure that it remains here? Perhaps it has moved on to clearer waters," Lord Krait suggested.

If it has, then this whole endeavor was for naught.

Pate thought.

"When last we saw the creature it had the fire in it to grab onto our ship to try and prevent our escape. It had a tenacity about it. I'm inclined to believe that wasn't a random act, but a telling of its nature," Pate responded.

"Indeed? Perhaps that is why the beast was able to harass so many ships these past few months. It has a temperament that refuses to be bested," Krait mused.

"Indeed, it does. Perhaps we share that in common," Pate said as he gave a sweep over the horizon, checking for more movement.

"Turn her northward!" he ordered.

*****

Judith approached Linda, seeing the women struggle to reel the harpoon in from the whale's hide. She offered a hand, grabbing the crank and using all her strength to help release it. The harpoon ripped free, and left a bloody rent in the whale's hide, gushing blood. "That's going to attract predators," Judith warned.

"Aye," Linda agreed.

"How are you, sister? You've been quiet these past few days," Judith pointed out.

Linda shrugged. "I've been fine, I suppose. The bruises are goin' away, now."

"No one's been givin' ye trouble, have they?" Judith said, adding a bit of edge to her voice.

"Trouble? No. In fact, just the opposite. Everyone seems to steer clear of me, now," Linda admitted.

"That so?" Judith asked. "That's a surprise."

"I think they fear getting cut up by ye, now. Since Cap'n Pate gave ye the all-clear," Linda said, casting a wary gaze his way. She wasn't the only one giving him fearful looks, these days. Most of the Duchess pirates were fearful of him, now. Pate was an ambitious and fearless man, but he had little use for the simple fisher folk of Isle De Morta. He had killed a pirate captain in full view of his crew and taken control of it. He had shown that he was willing to kill anyone who got in his way. And while the Cutthroats praised him as a good leader, the crew of the Duchess were scared.

Judith's gaze crossed with Pate's, and he nodded to her reassuringly. She did the same.

"Aye…"

As the ship came around and began its course northward, it shook violently and stopped dead in its tracks.

"What was that?!" Linda asked.

Judith listened and heard something scraping along the bottom of the ship.

"Trouble."

*****

The water around the Sunsetter exploded like a geyser as the heads of the hydra burst up from below. Eighteen heads surrounded the ship, and Pate was dismayed to see the familiar finned heads of the original hydra head he'd blown to bits. They raised their fins in agitation and hissed. They remembered him.

"Fire!" Pate shouted at the top of his lungs.

The harpoon gunners let loose, and though many of the harpoons missed their evasive targets, several of them struck true, spearing the heads through their necks and anchoring them in place. The creature flailed in pain and anger, and the four, finned heads took in deep breaths to spray the ship long-ways with their boiling breath.

"They're about to spray! Take cover!" Pate warned.

He looked to Lord Krait, who'd taken a knee and knocked back three arrows between her fingers as she took aim with her bow.

"Lord Krait! Get down!" he warned.

She ignored him, whispered something beneath her breath, and fired the arrows as they took on a bright green glow. Pate watched in disbelief as the arrows weaved through the rigging of the ship and shot across toward the hydra heads.

What in the...

She smiled satisfactorily as the arrows struck three of the four heads—and exploded. The creature let loose a howl that shook Pate's bones, and the remaining head released its steam breath. Folk who couldn't take cover were scalded, and their screams mingled with the sound of shivering timbers, splashing water, and hissing serpents. The heads swarmed, attacking the deck and snatching people up left and right.

Pate heard Judith scream as a head attacked her and Linda. He rushed to their aid unerringly.

The creature had taken hold of Linda's leg in its jaws, and Judith wrapped her leg around her as she held onto the railing.

"It's going to sever her leg if we don't hurry!" Krait warned and fired an arrow at the creature's eye, making it cry out in pain and release Linda's leg. Pate grabbed hold of Judith and jerked both women back onto the deck, using pure adrenaline to complete the feat. The serpent head opened its jaws wide, determined to claim them. He pulled out his sword and felt the voices dancing at the edge of his hearing as his left arm burned. He used the pain to fuel his swings as he hacked furiously at the carriage-sized head with his sword. The blows left ugly bleeding cuts on its jaws, like splashes of paint. The creature roared—and lunged. Pate roared—and charged. He fired his pistol at the creature's good eye, and exploded the boulder-sized orb in a spray of blue lens and purple blood. It bit him, grabbing hold of his left arm and lifting him high into the air.

"Pate!" Krait shouted.

"Cap'n!" Judith and Linda shouted at the top of their lungs.

Hauser, seeing the commotion, charged over and pulled out the blunderbuss he'd been stowing, blasting at the head of the might beast as it held Pate in its jaws less than a dozen feet above his head. The creature made a gurgling noise and released Pate, who landed in a heap and howled in pain. Two more heads approached, and this time Krait fired her glowing-green arrows, blowing it open and deterring the others from joining the frenzy. Judith and

Hauser grabbed hold of Linda while Krait slung Pate over her shoulder effortlessly and carried him to safety.

"I'm fine," Pate said as Krait carried him.

"Fine? You nearly had your arm torn off by a hydra! You are far from fine!" Krait protested.

"I'm fine!" he shot back with fire and forced her to put him on his feet. "Take Miss Linda to safety," he said, looking at Judith and Hauser. They nodded. "Firing crews! Get those Alyria cannons out NOW! We need to blow its heads off while it's still pinned!"

Pate's voice carried with such ferocity that even the El'wa hopped to his command. Lord Krait stood by, taken aback. While his coat was tattered, Pate's arm seemed almost entirely intact, though bloody. "Lord Krait. I know ye have somethin' in mind to finish this beastie off. What is it?"

She blinked. "See that windlass over there? Next to the one for lowering the probes? It has a device called a depth shocker attach to it. Lower it, and it will release a shockwave in the immediate vicinity of the ship."

Pate nodded. "And the shockwave will fry the bastard, stopping its heart and whatever beastly Alyria allows it to regenerate so."

Krait nodded; he was correct.

Just then, the Sunsetter shook as the giant arms of the hydra rose up and dug into the deck. It shook the ship. Pate was thrown from his feet, and he had to grab onto a railing at the last moment to avoid being tossed into the sea. He caught Krait with his spare arm, saving her from the same fate. He watched as men and women were thrown from the ship, either into the sea below, or into the waiting jaws of the hydra's many heads. Pate turned and saw one of his crewmen get thrown to the edge of the ship and grab the ledge. As he attempted to hold on, he was slammed by a crate and sent flailing into the maw of the beast. He watched powerlessly as the creature's jaws closed around him.

Just then, the gunports slid open as the Alyria cannons on his side of the ship poked out. He strained his arm and looked at Krait, who held on for dear life.

"Fire!" They both roared in unison.

After several tense moments, the cannons fired and a deep blue glow blinded them a moment as the cannon just beneath them went off, blowing apart the head of the hydra that was closing in on them from below.

The mighty beast had almost all of its heads destroyed, now, and only the one remaining head with its fins fanned out, as well as a few stragglers, remained intact. It let out another defiant howl of fury and pain as it was brought to the brink of death by its implacable quarry. The arms released, and the harpoons still dug into the monster's intact heads ripped free as its weight fell back down into the depths.

"It's retreating! Release the depth shocker and finish it off!" Pate said as he heaved Krait and himself back onto the deck. He stumbled and gasped for air, his body aflame with pain and soreness as he tried to recover.

Thankfully, some of the surviving crew turned the windlass for the depth shocker, and Pate heard the sound of something heavy and metallic dropping deep into the water.

"How…how long?" he asked Krait, trying to catch his breath.

"A few more seconds…" She said, leaning against him for support.

And a few seconds later, just as the ship settled and things had gone quiet again, Pate tasted something electric in the air, and felt his hair stand on end before a sound like a muffled thunderclap sounded from below and he heard arching electricity surging far beneath his feet. He looked over the railing and saw that the water beneath the ship had become a tempest of electricity. He saw fish, frying from the lightning, bubbling to the surface. And far below, he saw the unmistakable shape of a near-headless hydra twisting and turning, mid-electrocution.

He relished its pain, thinking of all the good men and women he'd lost to its hunger. "I hope it hurts, you serpentine bastard…"

✶✶✶✶✶

It took several minutes for the body to resurface. It nearly tipped over the ship as it did, and when the boat settled once more, the crew of the Sunsetter beheld their dead quarry. The hydra had but four remaining heads, and all of them were quite cooked—and quite dead. Pate stared triumphantly into the vacant eyes of the last finned hydra head, and he felt his pain subside, replaced by euphoria as he finally tasted victory at the end of his long road of defeats.

"Excellent. Kin! Extract the pearl!" Lord Krait ordered, placing a hand on Pate's shoulder in approval.

"Pearl?" he asked.

"Ah, yes. When a hydra dies by electrocution, the organ that controls its regenerative properties transforms into something called a hydra pearl. It has powerful Alyrial properties and…fetches quite a nice price on the market," Krait said with an avaricious smile.

"Ah, so that's why ye came, then? To see if I could collect your payday for ye?" Pate said, half-offended, half-admiring of her cunning.

"That, and I wanted to make sure that you didn't turn my ship into driftwood trying to hunt it down," Krait admitted.

"Well. I'll be expecting my cut in gold, then. Kurtz, Xallan coins, Dyons—makes no difference, really," he said. He was demanding, not asking.

Lord Krait chuffed, "You would make demands of me, captain? The nerve!"

"Considering I saved your life, saved ye manpower, 'n saved ye from losin' a ship? I think my men and I have more then earned our share. In fact, I know we have," Pate said.

Krait's people fell in around him, weapons drawn. Krait held an icy frown for a moment before turning it into a pleased grin. "I do so like your bravery and brazenness, captain. Do see that it doesn't get you killed."

She motioned for her people to back off, and so they did.

"It'll take a lot more than this to kill me in the end, M'lord. Stars as me witness," he replied with the tip of his hat. Pate lit a cigarette and went to check on his injured mate.

XLIX

At the Brink

Osiris snapped his fingers in front of Hanover's eyes.

The young man didn't respond, he was in the fetal position, rocking back and forth.

"Ay! Hanover! Snap out of it, for Goffanyn's sake!"

He didn't acknowledge him, all he did was rock and mutter to himself, "She's coming, she's coming, gonna get me—get me…get me…"

"Who's coming, dammit? The monster? That what's got ye crackin' up?!" Osiris asked, snapping his fingers over and over again. "We're gonna kill it. It's goin' to be fine, I promise."

But Hanover wouldn't respond. Osiris began to wonder if all the trauma and stress had finally gotten to him, and he'd been rendered dumb by fear.

"Let me try…" Flint said, kneeling in front of the boy and snapping his fingers, training his remaining eye on him intently. When he got no response, he slapped him sharply across the face, knocking Hanover on his side.

Hanover, miraculously, came to.

"Aeradin's Spear—that hurt," Hanover mumbled, rubbing his cheek.

Osiris nodded approvingly. "How'd ye know it'd work?"

Flint gave a half-hearted smirk. "I didn't."

Morgan came back down into the galley. "Who's living and who isn't?"

Stone shook his head. "Got about five corpses here. All we got left of Anatoli is a severed arm, looks like. And that stain over there," he said, pointing at a grizzly, pulpy splotch in the center of the floor, which Steven Cage was staring at pensively, "is all that's left of Khruschev, if ye can believe it."

Morgan gasped and wretched, as did Huasca. "That thing tore through us like a scythe through a wheat field."

"And it took the Eye of Atla with it," Huasca added. "If that creature escapes with it, it will be lost to us. And with it, our lives will be forfeit."

"Where in the blazes did it go?" Cutter asked, still shaken up from what he'd just seen.

"Below deck, probably. Have to scour the whole ship to find it," Osiris answered with a sigh.

"Scour the ship? That creature is a menace. It can take on anyone's form, and when she's cornered she turns into a thing plucked from the depths of Sheolhenna—we can't fight that!" Ryker said. His body began to shake. Whether it was in fear or from his head trauma, no one could tell.

"We have to! She has the Eye of Atla, and with it our salvation! We've come this far, we can't stop now—" Morgan protested.

"And look what it's gotten us!" Cutter began again. "I ain't got a fuckin' hand, cap'n! Flint's missin' an eye—two of our officers are dead!"

Morgan held his tongue.

"That creature…it ate our bullets like they were nothing, captain. Even yours seemed to only piss it off—and yours is an enchanted weapon," Steven Cage noted aloud as he stared at the stain that once was Khruschev. "A creature like that…only the Dead Three could conjure something so repulsive into this world."

He reminisced on some of the rituals he'd seen in Borra. The things he'd seen the Pestilence Skalds birth from their putrid flesh pits…he felt a chill rattle his bones.

"Is the Northman afraid? Hell, is that even possible?!" Cutter gasped in surprise.

"I fear nothing, cripple. But I know first-hand that beings of such Alyria can only be undone with Alyria," Cage asserted.

"Alyria…wonderful." Stone turned his nose in disgust. "All we need is more magick to fix what it began."

"Mr. Huasca, could your shamanic rituals offer us a way to combat this foe?" Cage asked politely.

Huasca turned, looked at him, looked over the bloodbath that the galley had been turned into, and shook his head. "Nothing that I have access to, can aid us against such strange power. This…being…is much stronger than anything I have seen in *years* of practice. It's Alyria is…"

"Unholy. Dark as the night and dripping with the taint of the Infernals…" Abbal finished.

"Can you locate it?" Morgan asked. "Can you tell us where it is? If it's escaped?"

The amulet glowed in a slow thrum of blue light. "I sense it here, still. Its presence has not waned. I wager, it is not finished with us. It remains, for what purpose, I do not know—"

"Of course it doesn't. That's just the rub, innit? Ye lead us here with yer vague warnin's, 'n yer convenient impotence. Ain't that just the perfect coincidence? Get wise, cap'n. That little magickal necklace of yers is havin' us for fools. It knows shite that it ain't too keen to reveal," Stone said, tired of dancing around.

Morgan looked at him. Was he right?

"Tell 'em, Abbal. Tell 'em what we already know. This was yer plan all along, wasn't it? Ta get us here." Stone stepped forward, staring at the amulet. "What's yer angle, spirit? Or whatever the hells it is ye are."

All eyes were on Morgan, and in turn, Abbal. Morgan removed the amulet, and he felt his energy drain as he did. Though it caused him strain, he held it aloft and looked at it.

"Answer him," Morgan said, his own anger growing.

The amulet's glow intensified, and a pair of clear white eyes and a scowling face looked at Morgan.

"The fate of Morgan Sarron, and in turn the fate of Azura, is inextricably linked to the fate of this world. The Gods, in their infinite wisdom, have destined him a part in their grand designs. For a century, it has been my duty to safeguard him from death, so that when the time arose for him to play his part, he would yet live to see it done.

"I do not know what that purpose is, truly. I have not been told what the future holds. But I know that you all were chosen by fate to be here, and to embark on this voyage. The Eye of Atla is but a singular piece in a much bigger picture. But we are all too *small* to see its significance…" Abbal said that with an almost resentful tone.

"I am sorry that your fellow pirates have been killed. But their fates were destined to end, here. As it may be the fate of us all. Morgan Sarron is right. You are in *far* too deep. Whomever sent Ardvald the Mangler and his Deathwatch has their eye on you. I doubt that they will let any one of you live, even if you were to renounce this mission and hide in the shadows for the rest of your days…"

The men stood there, hearing what some part of them already knew. They were damned. They were destined to be here. Destined to die here. And they were powerless to stop it.

Armen Hanover stood up. "So that's it? We die. We get killed by that monster, or whatever bastard sent it prowling after us? We're the Azura Pirates, dammit! I spent my life hearing stories of how mighty and feared pirates were! Most of all the Immortal Captain and his cutthroat crew! A man who's bested death a hundred times! Who slew a villain, hellbent on conquering the empire! A man of legend! Legends are made by their feats! What is this, if not another test?! We're locked in, aren't we? Fated, as that amulet says, to be here—to die, here!"

Hanover stood tall, and in that moment, Morgan did not see him as a boy, but as a man. Standing defiant in the face of adversity.

"Pirates don't yield! They fight and rage and kick against their enemy, leaving them dirty and bloody. They fight till their last bullet's spent, and their sword is dull, and their rum is gone! Those are the stories I was raised off of! That's what I came here for! To be a legend! If we let ourselves go quietly now, we will die all the same, right? But we'll die in obscurity. The legend of Azura will die like a flame flickering in the wind! Is that what you want?! To yield?"

"Ye know nothing about what ye speak, boy—" Flint began.

"I know that I killed a woman. A *woman*, to be a pirate! I know that good men died in this voyage! Good men who had hopes and dreams, stolen from them by an indifferent sea and the men who sail it! I know that if we give up now, they all died for *nothing*!" Hanover spat back.

He looked at Osiris. "This isn't a game. We can't just bow out when the hand looks bad. This is real life. Look, I'm scared as shit, just like everyone else. I'm eighteen years old and I don't wanna die a virgin who got killed by a shapeshifting monster from hell on an errand for the fucking Emperor! But this is the hand we're given. I may not have learned all I needed to, these past few months, but I learned that this life is fucking *hard* and that's just how it is. I'm not ready to let this be my final chapter. Are any of you?"

They looked amongst themselves. Cutter clutched at the stump where his hand used to be, and desperately craved the painkillers Claude Humris had been giving him. Flint rubbed his eyepatch, reminiscing on the days where he saw with two eyes. Ryker longed for a time when he could drink water without spilling half of it and seizing up in his sleep, as did Sarkad. All of them wanted something better than what they had now.

And none of them wanted to die here.

Morgan clapped his hands, having put the amulet back on. The others, slowly, followed suit. He wrapped a hand around Hanover's trembling shoulders and embraced him like a proud father might.

"The youngest of us, in our darkest hour, has become the wisest and most fearless. Idallon said that the meek would inherit Hera. Perhaps he was right. Because this boy looked more like a man just now than all of us, combined," Morgan admitted, then frowned.

"Brothers, we are in the belly of the beast. We have lost too many good men, and we stand to lose all of them, if we don't stand our ground. We know our enemy, now. Ugly as it is, we know what it's capable of. It has the Eye of Atla. We cannot let it escape. I don't deserve your loyalty, not after all I've wrought upon you. But those men out there *do*. If we fold our hands now, we forfeit ourselves, and we forfeit *them*. Do not do this for me. Do this for them. Do this for Azura…do this for piracy. I ask you this now, and I cannot begrudge you for declining. Will you stand with me, one last time?" Morgan asked.

Osiris stepped forward and nodded, hanging his head. "I will."

Steven Cage looked away from the smear on the floor and nodded his head. "I will."

Cutter clutched his stump and bit his lip. "I…I will."

Flint did much the same. "I will stand with ye, cap'n."

Ryker and Sarkad stepped forward in unison and bowed their heads. "We stand with ye, cap'n."

Huasca bowed his head. "I will stand with you."

Stone folded his arms, looked over the rag-tag band of officers he was proud to call himself a member of, and nodded. "Aye, cap'n. Till the end."

And finally, Morgan turned his gaze on Armen Hanover. He looked at him differently, now. He had seen the spark of rebellion in him, now. "Mr. Hanover, how do you rule, sir?"

Hanover's breast swelled with pride and anxiety. He stopped himself from rubbing the tattoo on his wrist.

"It is my honor, sir. I will stand with you."

✶✶✶✶✶

The hold of Azura was a large compartment split in two by a narrow hallway, spanning the entire deck level, just below the gun deck, and just above the waterline.

Osiris and Hanover checked the hold thoroughly. They opened crates, overturned barrels, took a more than passing look through of the treasures they'd stolen from the Empress' Bounty, and agitated the remaining chickens enough that one of them was presently trying to get out of its cage and likely peck one of Osiris' eyes out.

"Well, I think we can safely say she's not hiding, here," Hanover said as he closed the last crate of goods. He'd pulled out a piece of jerky and begun gnawing on it.

"I knew she wasn't, actually," Osiris admitted.

Hanover gave him a perplexed look. "How do you figure?"

Osiris shrugged. "This shapeshifter did everything in *her* power to hide amongst the crew. A ship is a big place, but a small one at the same time. She probably knew we would all go looking for her, so she's probably taken on a new form. She's already someone else, looking through the ship, like everyone else…"

Hanover nodded slowly. That tracked very well with how she had moved, actually. She was never just sitting somewhere, undisguised. She was always maneuvering, always hiding in plain sight, always taking on a new form to get the drop on her unsuspecting prey…he cast a nervous glance at the angry chicken in the cage. "…Do you think…"

"No, Hanover, she is not disguised as an irate chicken in a cage trying to pluck our eyes out," Osiris answered immediately.

Hanover wasn't so sure and kept an eye trained on the chickens as Osiris spoke.

"I brought ye here to speak in private, like. I wanted to congratulate you, 'n tell ye that I'm proud of you," Osiris admitted as he sat down.

"Proud of me? For what?" Hanover asked.

"I dunno how ye did it, but you went from a shaken mess to a rallying crier back there, and ye saved us," Osiris said.

"Saved us?" Hanover repeated. "Saved us from what?"

"From ourselves. From giving up. I was pretty damn close after watching that freak kill Khruschev and Anatoli…and after I found Frederick's body…"

Hanover choked on the jerky he was eating and coughed it out. His eyes watered. "Frederick…Frederick Moary? It got him?!"

Of course, he doesn't know. We haven't told anyone, yet…

Osiris sighed. "Aye. You didn't see it, but the thing attacked after it took on the form of Frederick Moary and I beat it in a game of Delilah. I got it to slip up and reveal itself when it couldn't play the game properly and couldn't remember Moary's mother's name. So, I called its bluff, and I shot it. Then…all hell broke loose…"

Hanover's eyes continued to water. "Mr. Moary…he…"

He wiped away his tears and composed himself. "He was a good man. I'll make that thing pay for killing him."

Osiris nodded. "That he was. And that we will…"

Hanover sighed. "Can I be frank with you?"

Osiris shrugged. "Always, brother."

Hanover paused at that, and his lips spread in a warm smile. "I meant it when I said it. I'm fucking terrified. All of it, everything, this whole fucking voyage has been nightmare after nightmare. The sea wants to kill us, other men want to kill us, and I can't sleep right ever since I killed that woman. Drinking doesn't help 'cause all it does is make me fall asleep drunk, then I dream of shit even worse than the shit I'm seeing in my waking life. When I was talking to you lot, I was talking to myself. I was reminding myself that…that I'm still here…"

Osiris nodded. He understood that all too well.

"Does that make me weak, sir?" Hanover asked.

"No, Hanover. That makes ye human. No man can stand what we experience and be unafraid of it. A storm in the dead of night, a monster coming up from the depths to swallow you, and men at every turn looking to avenge the ones you've killed to survive…we're in a warzone, Hanover. A warzone that we can never escape from, not fully. Because even when you leave the battlefield, the scars and the memories will haunt you for all time…" Osiris admitted, putting a sympathetic hand on the young man's shoulder.

Hanover sighed, the smile faltering just a bit. "I really do wish sometimes that things had been different. That me 'n my brother weren't separated. That I wasn't an orphan on the streets. That I had a chance to be something *else*, but…"

He began to rub his tattoo again.

"Armen…who is the woman you keep talking about when you're sleeping?"

Hanover looked up at him, his eyes wide. "She…"

Just then, a man came to the doorway, behind Osiris, and turned to look at them. The hallway was pitch black, the man would have needed a lantern to traverse the corridors in the dark. His eyes glowed a bright and unearthly red.

"Behind you!" Hanover shouted.

Osiris acted immediately and spun around to see the figure stalking towards them. The man's face was a blank stare, and Osiris knew immediately who it was. He pulled out his dual spadroon swords and stood in front of Hanover, whom the man seemed fixed on. The man regarded Osiris a moment, cocking his head to the side.

"Move, little pirate. Begone!" he said in a voice that was not in keeping with his face. It was raspy but sounded distinctly female. It had a second, doubling voice beneath it. The second voice was much, much deeper and masculine sounding. It said the word *begone*, as though two different entities were speaking at once from the same mouth.

"If you want him, you'll have to go through—" Osiris said, but paused mid-sentence to dodge out of the way as the man's arm transformed into a whip-like tentacle and lashed at him.

The attack was incredibly quick, and he barely had enough time to dodge before a second blow came and threw him back against the wall with a crash. Hanover gasped and fumbled for his pistol, but the tentacle was already upon him, wrapping around his hands, binding them, and yanking him toward the creature, who grabbed him by the chin and forced him to stare deep into its eyes.

Hanover's jaw dropped open as he saw old, unmentionable horrors in the creature's eyes. The eyes of something who had stolen a thousand shapes, and countless more lives. Its victims' last, terrified looks, and their pleas for mercy before destruction. He was frozen by fear, then fainted.

Osiris struggled to his feet. The wind was knocked out of him.

The shapeshifter cast one last glance at him, revealing its true, masked face.

"Catch me, if you can!" The shapeshifter cackled before taking off, Hanover slung over its shoulder.

Osiris stumbled after them, swords out and ready to fight. "Get back here!"

*****

Morgan and Huasca followed the sounds of shouting men to the nose of the ship. Morgan noted a strong breeze was pushing the sails as they ran. They saw Osiris standing, swords in a fighter's stance, facing a man with a tentacle for an arm, holding Hanover, slung over his shoulder like a sack of grain.

"It is the munchinja!" Huasca declared, pulling out his pistol.

Morgan quickly forced his arm down. "You'll shoot the boy!"

Dozens of armed men stood, guns aimed, staring down the shapeshifter, using Hanover as a shield.

"Shoot me (shoot) and the boy will die (do it). Follow me, and the boy, and the Eye, will be yours (follow me)," the shapeshifter said, jarring them all with its strange, doubling voice.

"Why not kill him?" Morgan asked, taking a tentative step forward. "You spared no such mercy for Frederick Moary, or Claude Humris, or any of our other brethren that you butchered."

The shapeshifter smiled, stretching the face of the man it was imitating to disturbing limits. "Does it hurt, knowing that you were powerless to save them (powerless)? That they died (devoured) because of you (your sins)?

Morgan scowled harshly. "They died because you killed them, monster! That was your choice!"

"They died because you set them on this path (this path). They died because you lied to them, Morgan (your path). Let us see if you can save this one (lost lamb)."

Without waiting for a response, the shapeshifter tossed Hanover high into the air over the sea and leapt into the water. Immediately after, a large, shark-like creature leapt into the air and swallowed him whole before falling back into the water, and swimming away.

"Hanover! No!" Osiris shouted, running to the railing.

"Man the wheel! We have wind!" Morgan ordered, pointing to Ryker and Sarkad.

"Aye, cap'n!" The two men said, almost in unison, and made for the steering deck.

"Abbal! Track that creature, I do not care how much energy it takes, do it!" Morgan growled, clutching the amulet.

"It will be done," Abbal said.

Azura unfurled her sails, and they took after the beast, who torpedoed away with Armen Hanover and the Eye of Atla in toe.

L

THE CALM BEFORE THE STORM

"Come on, big boy. Give me all you've got!" The sailor grunted as he braced himself.

Frond gripped the man's hand and placed his elbow on the table. This was the biggest, and perhaps the strongest sailor he'd arm wrestled, today. But Frond knew he would go down like any other. Even without the use of his Alyria, he was much stronger than any of these men were liable to be.

"On my count!" Sedrick cheered, serving as the referee between the two as the sailors cheered, hedging their bets on who would win.

"I've got ten silver kurtz that says that Frond plows his arm down in the first ten seconds!" One man said confidently.

"Kennarsy's beat every sailor he's ever fought, he has. Seeker or no, the boy's got no chance!" Another sailor countered, laying his own coins on the table. "I put fifteen down sayin' Kennarsy floors 'em. Any takers?"

Several men cackled and put their coins on the table. One of them, a big, stitched scar running across his neck gladly dropped ten gold kurtz on the table, sparking awe amongst all the men, who began throwing down their own bets in earnest.

"That boy's barely human. Wouldn't surprise me to find out he's got Duwa or somethin' in 'em. He'll mop the floor with Kennarsy, Jory—anybody. My gold's on *him*," the man declared, pointing a thick, calloused finger at Frond.

After several more minutes, the commotion died down, and Sedrick quickly began to deliberate again.

"As I was saying: on my count. Three..."

Frond tightened his grip, as did Kennarsy.

"Two..."

Kennarsy wiped a bead of sweat from his heavy brow and gave a broken-toothed smile to the fresh-faced Frond.

"One…"

Frond gave him a passive gaze with his small, reddish-brown eyes. He resolved that he would crush him.

"Go!"

The two men flexed their arms. Frond had to give it to this Kennarsy fellow; he was strong. Most of the men on this tub had poor form, but Kennarsy knew all the tricks. He fought to try and get Frond to reposition his elbow and throw off his leverage. He didn't budge, but neither did Kennarsy. For his part, Frond was implacable. His gaze was unwavering and not even a bead of sweat dripping down from his brow.

Kennarsy, on the other hand, was sweating bullets. Frond guessed the sailor to be at least thirty-five years old, almost double his own nineteen years. He knew the older man would tire sooner than him. He had been trained to hold a one-armed ledge hold for more than five minutes. That was his entire body weight, hinged on one arm, for five minutes. This was nothing.

They reached the one-minute mark, and everyone sat with bated breath, wondering when a victor would be decided. Frond had been holding that same position the whole time. He began to falter, however, and Kennarsy started pressing his arm down, with great strain.

"I've got ye, you big fucker," Kennarsy said with confidence as Frond inched closer to being beaten.

Frond said nothing. He knit his brow, pursed his lips, then flexed his arm sharply. Kennarsy gasped as Frond brought his arm down in less than five seconds, and he was powerless to stop him.

"I win," Frond said simply.

He stood, he stretched, and then he went looking for food. He left an equally booing and cheering crowd in his wake, and a flabbergasted Kennarsy.

"Thank *you*, Frond," Sedrick said with a snicker as he collected his winnings and split them with the man with the scar on his neck. Nearly everyone had bet that Kennarsy would win, so the two had a large pool to pull from. The sailors grumbled away, their pride wounded.

"Pleasure doin' business with ya, mate," the man, Creyton, said.

"And you as well, Creyton," Sedrick said.

Creyton was a clever old rogue of a sailor. Born and bred in the heartland of Kurza Proper, Sedrick found a kindred soul in him. The man had pride in his kingdom, pride in his people—and he also had an eye for a good score. So when

Creyton saw Frond easily toss one of the sailors in an arm wrestle earlier in the day, he immediately approached Sedrick, who'd been betting on him, about a bigger score.

"And I thought this ship'd be boring," Sedrick laughed as he pocketed his gold.

"The Black Bess? Bah, she's full of seasoned mariners with full pockets and fuller egos. Everyone here thinks themselves the queen's garters 'n are eager to prove it at their leisure," Creyton explained as he counted his coins put them in his pouch. "And now they're a few coins lighter in their purses."

The two exchanged pleasantries but paused as someone came running. "It's Clive! He's beating the britches off these boys on the middeck."

The two looked at one another, puzzled. Creyton shrugged and walked off, "Not my business," he said.

Sedrick followed the man.

*****

Clive stood with his practice sword at his side, panting eagerly as he stood over his opponents. Four mariners laid sprawled on the deck, bleeding and unconscious from the beatings he'd given them. Just then, the remaining Seekers, as well as the deck officers arrived.

Ephala looked at Clive, then looked around at what he'd done. Her face turned red with anger. "Clive, you fucking moron! What have you done?!"

Clive calmed down and looked at her and the others. "I trained with them, of course. The mariners said they could take me in a sparring match. Things got a bit heated and, well, I proved them wrong."

Golde stepped forward and whistled as he looked over the barely conscious men. "Is this what you call heated, Seeker? My, I would so hate to see what happens when things get *hot*."

Castell knelt over one of the men and held a finger in front of his eyes to check if he could focus. He could not. "This man has a concussion. He'll be lucky if he only has the occasional shiver. If he isn't…" Castell stood and looked dead at Clive. "Then you may have just ended his naval career."

Clive looked at the man unapologetically. "They said they could handle it."

Castell stepped forward, forcing Clive to look up at him as he stood face-to-face with him. "Indeed, they would have, were you an ordinary man. But you are not. Your body is hardier than theirs, and you have Alyria to back that. They posed no real threat to you, Seeker. But you knew that…didn't you?"

Clive scoffed and looked away. "Watch yourself, Lieutenant Commander. Last I checked, you're still beneath me."

Jukel Staunton got down on one knee and helped a woman to her feet. "Are you alright, ma'am?"

She blinked slowly. There was blood leaking from her nose. "I think…it's broken…"

"The nose? Yes, mariner, it's definitely broken," Jukel answered bemusedly. "Off to the infirmary with you. The doctor will have you ship-shape in no time!"

The fatherly man helped the others to their feet as well, checking them as he did.

"What were you thinking, Clive? Did you forget these are our allies?!" Ephala growled, her eyes taking on a faint blue glow.

Clive shrugged. "They wanted to spar, so we sparred. It isn't my fault their bodies are fragile!"

Ephala stood in front of him, looked up into his scowling face—and slapped him. Clive recoiled, clutching his cheek. She heard him start to curse, then bite his tongue.

"*I* am the leader of this team. *I* am the commander of this ship! You will not touch a single hair on *anyone's* head unless I tell you too—are we clear?!" Ephala asked.

Clive looked at her, then the others, and nodded. She'd made his lip bleed. "Yes, ma'am."

"Good. Frond, escort him to his quarters."

Frond said nothing and wordlessly grabbed hold of Clive's arm in a vice grip. Clive said nothing, and the pair walked off, but not before Clive cast an ugly glare at Ambrose Castell. Castell returned his gaze, unphased and unconcerned.

"Are we to expect more of this savagery? I was not informed that my men would be subjected to beatings by your Seekers, Lady Farandus," Captain Avery said with a frown.

"No, Captain Avery, that is *not* our intent. Clive is a…bit of a hot header, even in the walls of the Spire. I should have known better than to leave him at leisure," Ephala apologized.

"A hot header, ma'am? This young man is barely coherent! He may very well be disabled because of his antics!" Jukel chimed in furiously. The overweight officer's face had turned beet red as he wagged his finger. "We are supposed to be hunting pirates! Not hurting each other!"

At that, Cambridge saw fit to chime in. "Now that, I do agree. One of those poor sods was part of my gun crews. Now, a cannon may not be able to be fired, when the time comes," he said, mildly irritated. "Every man and woman aboard this ship is a necessary member to ensure our success."

"It will not happen again, I assure you," Ephala said.

"Won't it? My apologies, Lady Farandus, but Seeker Clive did not appear particularly apologetic for his actions. Only…inconvenienced," Avery said sagely.

"Clive has a difficult time understanding mundane folk, captain. He doesn't understand that you all are…fragile," Tora chimed, trying to watch her words.

"I assure you, Seeker Lady, we are far from fragile," Ambrose stated. "But we need to work together, and respect one another, or when the time comes, these pirates will tear us apart."

Ephala was silent. She had heard stories about the Azura and its pirates. They were a fearsome lot. Each man aboard her was wanted for murder, thievery, and far worse. Each of them had killed naval men, as well. Her captain, Morgan Sarron, was said to be all but immortal, having been around since before the unification of the six kingdoms and the formation of the Kurzan Empire. That put him over a century in age. Young for an El'wa, perhaps. That was much older than any human she knew, however. Even the richest of men tended to die before they reached seventy years.

"We will keep Clive in line. He will *not* have an outburst like that again, I promise you." Ephala nodded. "Dismissed."

Ambrose, Jukel, and Cambridge all looked at Avery, who nodded as well. "As you say, My Lady," Avery bowed. The others followed suit, and they all dispersed back to their duties.

Ephala let loose a breath she wasn't aware she'd been holding and looked at her comrades. The trio shared a concerned glance.

*****

"What was he thinking?" Ephala gasped as she sat at the captain's desk.

"It's Clive. Thinking isn't something he does when his pride's on the line," Sedrick said.

"And to Clive, his pride's on the line anytime someone speaks out of turn, looks at him the wrong way, or stars forbid that he feels like he has something to prove," Tora groaned.

"What in blazes does he have to prove? How much of a fucking idiot he is for nearly killing four people?!" Ephala asked.

"Perhaps. He always felt as though he was destined for more," Tora admitted. "Perhaps he hoped to prove his mettle."

"Well, all he's done is prove that we can't be trusted. And if we keep this up we may well have a mutiny before we reach these pirates," Sedrick said. "How far, Seeker Sister?"

Ephala pulled out the map and laid it bare for the others to see. Two points upon it glowed brightly, and the Seekers looked it over intently. "We are here. About three days out from Oceanus. They were instructed to deliver the Eye of Atla to the envoy back at Oceanus. Their current course seems to be taking them down the coastline. We'll intercept them here." Ephala pointed to a small, seaside town called Spirus. "We should make contact within the next two to three days, if the wind keeps up."

Clive nodded. "That means we have two to three days to get all hands onboard to fight these pirates."

*****

Frond stood, looking out over the moonlit sea from the forecastle. This had been the longest he'd ever been at sea. And, though he could do without the deck beneath his feet constantly shifting with the waves, and the bed-less, cramped living conditions—or the constant smell of unwashed men and sea water, he loved it. In a different life, perhaps, he had been a sailor. If such things happened. His ears pricked up as he heard someone approaching stealthily from behind.

"State your name and purpose, quickly," Frond said simply.

He turned his head to look over his shoulder at a sight that, under ordinary circumstances, would have perplexed and probably terrified a normal man. A black panther, its fur sheening in the moonlight, appraised him with a playful swish of its tail.

"Even in this form, you still manage to hear me coming," the panther said in a familiar, feminine voice.

"I didn't graduate with top honors for lack of hearing, Tora," the giant man said.

The panther padded over to him and put its front paws onto the railing, looking out at the sea next to him. It morphed suddenly into Tora, who leaned an elbow against the much taller Frond. "How are you liking the sights. Big Boy?" she asked, using her pet name for him.

Frond shrugged. "Better than other sights I've seen, I suppose."

Tora stood, soaking in the sea air and the rolling blue expanse. In all the years she'd known Frond, since childhood, in fact, he had never been a man of many words. He carried himself like someone much older than his nineteen years, though it was easy to mistake it for ignorance when he kept to himself and kept quiet. Even when their clothes were off, and all the airs of the outside world were thrown away, he still seemed so removed.

"And here I was hoping this beautiful evening air would inspire you to sing me a soliloquy," Tora said with a chuckle.

"Me? Sing? When the Stars return and ignite the sky at the end of days, perhaps. Till then, I think I'll content myself with the songs of nature..." Frond said, simply.

And so, they did. They listened to the waves, and the gulls, and the occasional conversation of patrollers walking the deck. They took in the scent of salty, sea air, and the cigarette smoke from the mariners. She ran a bare hand over his as he stood, still as a statue. The joints in his neck popped as he looked at it, clasped it in his own hand, which eclipsed hers, and kissed it quietly. They stood there a while longer in silence, enjoying the warm breeze and lost in their own thoughts.

"Did Clive give you trouble?" Tora asked.

Frond shook his head. "He was silent. I don't think he really cares, to be frank."

"Why would he? He knows we need him for this mission to succeed. He is immune to recourse until we make landfall again, and we'll all be much too preoccupied to worry about him, then," Tora admitted.

"He's clever."

"He's short-sighted," Tora corrected. "And stubborn. Mr. Jukel was positively livid when he brought that poor mariner girl to the infirmary."

"He's a kind-hearted man. One wonders how he managed to make it this far in the ranks," Frond noted. "Good men seldom prosper in the ranks of the admiralty."

"Good men are needed, everywhere; Jukel Staunton is needed in the navy."

Frond nodded his agreement, then froze in place, searching around them with his eyes. Tora waved a hand in front of him. "What is it?"

"Can you feel it?" Frond asked, breaking the quiet.

"Feel it?" Tora asked, looking at him. "Feel what?"

Frond looked at the horizon. "Something's coming…"

"Should I alert the crew?" Tora asked, alarmed.

He shook his head calmly. "No point. It's too far away, now. But it's coming."

"How can you tell?"

Frond took a slow, meditative breath. "Because the air, and the sea…is frightened."

"Frightened? Of what?"

Frond shook his head slowly. "Not sure. Not yet."

He squeezed her hand. "We need to be ready when it reveals itself."

Tora squeezed back. The young Seekers stood awhile longer, watching the horizon and enjoying the calm.

In his mind, Frond saw visions of a bloody battle beneath the moonlight. He saw a looming shadow with piercing yellow eyes and a hellish roar. His hand trembled, slightly.

"Something wicked this way comes."

LI

Prelude to Chaos

A black ship, glittering with gold sailed through the night. Fish swam away from its wake, and the air turned cold when touching it. Beneath the waves, trailing behind it was a fleet of large shapes, cutting through the water. It was crewed by men and women covered in lavish jewelry, fit for royalty. But their hearts and bodies were hollow and empty. They meandered in half-sleep dormancy, automatically going about their tasks, almost in a trance.

Anathane's Pain.

Byzarra walked the deck casually, flipping through a notebook of hers and scribbling down an incantation fragment as she walked. The glittering gold that furnished every railing, every chain, and every grate of the ship cast its own reflective glow in the moonlight, though her eyes didn't need it. She was often in awe of the sheer opulent majesty of the Pain. For all the horror it wreaked, you would likely never know it at first glance. Figureheads made of gold and silver, tastefully inlaid with jewelry. The sails were made of dazzling red and black silks. The shrouds were the only ones that she had ever seen made of chains, and the chains were golden. It looked as though she was walking upon a floating castle.

The crew was dressed in attire made from the finest silks, even though they were often tattered and covered in gems, growing out of the skin of their wearer. The entire ship gave off resplendent air, but it was ever tainted with the scent of blood. For the crew were not men and women, but undying, half-aware corpses. And as she walked, the ones that surrounded her broke and bent away from her path. She stopped, however, as she was confronted by a zombie unlike the others.

This one was a familiar sight—a rail-thin corpse, just skin and bone, but black as the night, wearing equally dark attire. He stood, gazing at her with vacant, implacable eyes.

Like dead, white lights in his skull.

"Shade, you really must stop staring like that. I would hate to pluck those little white raisins you call eyes from your decrepit skull," Byzarra stated acidly.

Shade stretched a slow, crackling smile over his face. "I would welcome the attempt, necromancer. The Dread Captain requests your presence in his lower chambers."

Byzarra regarded the vaporous shadow of a corpse a moment longer before shrugging and sidestepping him before walking away. She could feel his gaze on her, briefly, as she left.

"Human," Shade said, stopping her.

"What is it, wraith?" she asked.

Shade opened a bony palm and handed her a peculiar looking object. A small, obsidian rock.

"A present, for me? I didn't think you the giving sort, I must admit. In fact, I kind of assumed you were incapable of thinking of anything other than killing people and looking ugly," Byzarra admitted.

Shade seemed completely unfazed by her rude remarks. "Should you find yourself in need of my skills, whisper my name into that stone. I will hear it, and I will come, so long as there is a shadow for me to emerge from."

Byzarra laughed. "Me? Need your help? It will be a hot day in the Grave before then."

She took it and stuffed it into a pocket before walking off.

*****

In the lowest compartment of Anathane's Pain, where the bilge would collect on an ordinary ship, there was instead a vast atrium, spanning the entire bottom of the three-hundred-foot-long ship. Rows of candles, paintings, and other finery lined the walls of the spacious compartment, and there was a massive portrait on the far end of a man and woman posing together. The woman bore a striking resemblance to the golden statue mounted at the fore of the ship.

An elaborate system of sound-funneling tubes lined the roof of the compartment, connecting to every other compartment on the ship. And beneath the portrait was a throne, nailed to the floor, befitting royalty. In it, the Dread Captain sat, holding a cello and bow. He drew the golden hair of the bow across the cello strings, playing a sorrowful chorus with his fingers, as though he were in a deep trance. He played the song from memory, line for line, note for note. And he did so for hours.

Were there a living soul aboard the ship, save for Byzarra, they would perhaps be stricken by the cello music's mournful beauty. But only the Damned and the dead roamed her decks, and a moldering necromancer who preferred the chorus of flies over music. He played the song, his eyes closed, his face ever hidden behind the golden skull mask that shielded it, and he travelled to a faraway time.

He saw her face, there. Still young, radiant, and hopeful. He saw her smile, heard her voice, and felt his heart surge at the memory of the only soul in this cold, uncaring world that ever truly loved him. As his bow plucks became more frantic, he saw her wither before him. Saw the scars from the torture, the burns, the cuts, bruises, and…

"My master…"

Helregal growled, "No!"

He saw her body, broken and beaten on the night that they came for them. The night she died. He seethed. He saw hell fire and heard broken screams as he returned to the present. She was gone, but in her place was Byzarra. His pupil.

The necromancer, normally impassive in her demeanor, looked genuinely concerned at the revenant in the chair. His hands clenched the bow of the cello fiercely, and he realized that he'd thrown the instrument to the floor.

"Yes…child?" he asked as he regained his composure.

"You summoned me?" Byzarra asked, trying to hide her unnerve.

"Yes," Helregal said, composing himself and standing. "We are burning the midnight oil, now. I can feel them, close at hand."

Byzarra nodded; she felt it too. "Yes, master. It won't be much longer, now."

"You have learned much in these past months. You have grown in power. Soon, it will be time to test it. I have shown you how I turn the dead. That same power resides within you. Soon, it will be time to use it fully."

Byzarra smiled. She'd watched him turn the Hail Mary pirates, the Duwa, an El'wa fleet, and a dozen others, now. Long had she sought the power to animate the dead. She had spelunked ruins and browsed forgotten tomes, but the art had escaped her. She had wondered if perhaps she was not strong enough to do that most unholy of acts that only the strongest, most devout of necromancers could perform. But then, Death spoke to her, and bid her to answer the Dread Captain's call.

Yes, he had taught her much. And soon, she would unleash her terrible power upon all those who had hurt her…

He placed a cold hand on her shoulder, and she blinked, having been lost in her own thoughts. "You have taught me well, master. I will not fail you," she promised.

"I know, child. He has told me so."

The red glare of Caine materialized in the black orb around Helregal's neck and glowed bright red. Byzarra always felt so very small and afraid beneath that gaze.

"Child of Death, you have been brought here as a pupil to His Chosen Son. You have sailed with him and learned from him. In the battles to come, you will fight for him. Do you accept the gift that is given?" Caine asked, his voice a reedy, ugly hiss.

"Yes, Dark One. I accept."

Caine smiled, revealing shark-like teeth. "Good. The Father will bless you with a black harvest, child. Mark my words."

She couldn't wait.

*****

Byzarra approached the beast, standing tall and imposing over the Damned milling about the deck. When one faltered, he would bark an order at them in Graven, the language of the dead. She was often left in awe of the Drakkari. She had never seen such an imposing creature in the flesh. She had read of their kind, but books seldom did justice to reality. He was at least three meters tall, and his chalk white skin was calloused over with thick skin reminiscent of a lizard's hide. His face, though not quite human, was similar in layout, but had a mouth much wider than any man's, complete with a short, blunt snout. His eyes were piercing, belying the predatory cunning hidden behind the black skull painted around them, as well as the knife-like fangs he bore when he belted his orders.

He never said his name. The Dread Captain never asked it of him. So instead, they called him Black. Black like death itself. Like the skull tattooed on his monstrous face. And like the heart that no longer beat in his burgeoning

541

chest. He looked at her, and she felt the weight of an untamed beast's gaze upon her.

"Fair Lady. Why do you gaze upon me?" he asked, his voice was a low, deep, heavy baritone that rattled in her bones. He towered over her, forcing her to look up into the large, piercing yellow torches that served as his eyes.

"The Master says to prepare for the coming battle. The cannons are to be fully loaded, and the dread fleet is to be given their standing orders," Byzarra instructed.

Officer Black nodded. "So it begins. I will send for them."

She walked away as Black let loose a loud, piercing roar that made all the Damned freeze and look at him. They seemed to come alive at that moment. The moment they were told that battle was coming. That they would be able to kill. She watched the sea in the wake of Anathane's Pain as ships broke through the water. The Dread Captain's song ended, and she knew that soon he would come forth to convene with his dread lieutenants. She opened up her notebook once more, and appraised the diagram she had made for her latest creation she was working on. Soon, she would raise the dead on her own, without the help of her master.

Soon, she would begin her beautiful work in earnest.

LII

Into the Storm

It had taken three weeks of slow drifting through the doldrums of the Mid-Amaranthine for Azura to find stable wind again. But it took only three minutes for them to set off after the shapeshifter. Azura sailed after it, unerringly, for three days straight.

"She's toying with us, I'm certain of it, now," Morgan said as he watched the large fin of the beast that swallowed both the Eye of Atla and Armen Hanover *whole*, pause and circle around in the water, waiting.

The creature was too large and nimble in the water for them to have any hope of catching it outright. If it wanted to run, it would have.

"Toying or not, we have to capture it!" Osiris fumed, the fire still burning in his veins as he flashed back to that moment, over and over again. It grabbed him like he was a toy and carried him away. Osiris had been powerless to stop it. Now, Armen Hanover was likely dead, rotting away in the belly of that horrible monster.

"He's lost, son," Ryker said, placing a consoling hand on his shoulder. "I know it's hard. But he could not survive in the belly of that creature, not for three days."

Osiris shrugged the hand off. "Don't care. Dead or alive, I'll find him. And I'll make that monster pay. Mark my damn words."

*****

Cutter fiddled around with his new toy. A dagger blade, attached to a metal prosthetic that fit securely around his arm and the stump where his hand once was. Flint and Cage had made it for him, using various odds and ends lying around the ship, and in Claude Humris' belongings.

Even now, the old sawbones is lookin' out for me.

"How does it handle. Is the harness secure?" Cage asked, watching as Cutter tested out the new tool.

"It's a bit pinching at the stump, and a little too tight at the elbow, but it works like a charm," Cutter complimented. "I didn't figure you for an engineer, Northman."

Cage folded his arms and leaned against a wall. "I am no engineer. Most of the concept came from Mr. Flint over there." He nodded to Flint, who was himself polishing a pistol. "I just handled the assembly."

Flint nodded to Cutter. "I always knew ye were good for somethin', brother. Never figured it'd be somethin' useful."

"Half of my uses are savin' your ass, so I'd say in your case, I'm plenty useful," Flint pointed out. He lifted his eyepatch to scratch at his stitches. They were less pronounced now, though the pirate was loathe to remove the eyepatch for long.

"Do ye figure there's any chance that he's alive, somehow?" Cutter asked.

Steven Cage shook his head regretfully. "Not a chance. Even if he wasn't chewed up or digested, I doubt there is any breathable air in the gullet of a fish underwater. He probably drowned or suffocated."

Cutter looked at Flint, already knowing his answer.

Flint didn't look up. He'd turned to sharpening his sword, now. "We'll see."

That wasn't the response he'd expected.

"That's a surprise. I figured ye'd be happy as a fly on shit the poor boy's become fish food," Cutter admitted.

Flint gave him a stiff look. "The boy stopped us from going off the plank when he had no reason to. He's fucked up—a lot. But he don't deserve that fate."

Cutter was surprised. He didn't think it'd be possible for Flint to do anything other than hate the boy. "Well, let's hope he survives, then."

*****

THREE DAYS PRIOR…

Hanover awoke. Cold, wet, and cramped. He felt like his body was squeezed into the tightest crawlspace on Hera, and his head was foggy. It smelled like brine and vomit. He vaguely remembered that he'd been grabbed by someone. He couldn't recall by whom, however. He remembered he'd been dreaming. Someone had been calling his name in the dream, far off in the distance.

"Armen…" a female voice called.

He gasped, startled by the voice so close to his ear. When it spoke, a bright turquoise light illuminated his surroundings, but none of it made sense. The walls were pink, and they seemed to pulse around him. He could hear rushing water outside, and every so often he would be thrown around by sudden movement outside.

"Who…who are you?" he called back after catching his breath. "*Where* are you?"

"I'm right next to you. By your head," the voice said, and this time he could see it clearly for a moment.

That's impossible. Is it really—

"Are you…are you the Eye of Atla?"

"How very astute. But yes, I am, child," the glowing orb said, again illuminating their surroundings.

"Why are you talking to me? And where on Hera are we?"

The orb pulsed rhythmically with light. "Well, you may want to sit down for this one," it chuckled. "You're in the belly of a rather large shark."

"What?!" Hanover shouted, trying to lift his head and bouncing it off the springy, wet flesh above him. "The belly of a—how?! Why?! Am I dead?!"

"Well no, not yet. This is no ordinary beast that's swallowed you up, you see. This is the…I believe you all call her the shapeshifter, yes?"

The shapeshifter.

It all came crashing down on him. The monster they'd seen in the galley, the one that Osiris said killed Frederick Moary. It attacked him and Osiris and captured him, somehow.

"Why am I still alive?"

"As I mentioned before, child, this is no ordinary beast. For some reason, she has opted not to turn your body into mush and absorb it. It would seem she has another use for you," the Eye explained.

"This is all your fault!" he accused. "This monster only came onto this ship because it wanted *you*! Now I'm stewing in its guts because of *you*!"

"Now, now. That is very hurtful to hear. I never wanted any of this. All I wanted was to be set free from this prison. I've been here for millennia."

"Millennia? What's that?" Hanover asked. He'd never heard that word before.

"A *very* long time indeed, dear."

"Why were you trapped in there?" Hanover asked, genuinely curious.

"Well, that is a rather long story," the Eye said. "But I suspect you've nothing but time on your hands. In fact, we'll be here for awhile yet."

Hanover rolled over, attempting to get somewhat comfortable—as comfortable as one could get in the tight confines of a shark's belly. "I'm all ears, I suppose."

*****

"It was on a day, much like any other. Nazara, my homeland, was in full summer bloom. Flowers of every color you could imagine fluttered in the breeze, and Alyria pervaded the air, fountaining up from the World Well. I sat upon my dais, addressing my people's grievances, as always. I remember a farmer was complaining of the taxes I had recently placed on foreign exports. We wanted to be self-sufficient, once more, as tensions between Uldaman and Sai'Haluud mounted. We did not want to be absorbed into their coming war. So, we isolated.

"But then, a quaking came that shook my homeland to its very foundation. The days were filled with tremors and frightful quakes beneath our feet. Mountains blew their tops, and the sea began to recede. We thought that the end had come. How wrong we were. The tremors tore the ground beneath our feet, casting great fissures across Nazara. After a day, the sea water returned from miles out, and with it came a tidal wave of apocalyptic size. I, and my sages, used all the Alyria our bodies could muster to form a barrier around our island, channeling the power of the World Well. I plead to the Gods to save us from this terrible fate.

"But the waters could not be contained, and we sank beneath the waves. Our barrier broke, and the sea surged in around us, swallowing us all. And as the end came for me, I received my answer in the form of a strange, talking octopus. It offered us salvation, but it would come at a terrible price—our servitude. I refused. 'I am a queen, and I will serve no one' I said.

"Then you and your people will drown, and you will walk the bottom of the sea until it boils away at the coming of apocalypse', it said. I saw visions of my people's lost souls, wandering the bottom of the sea, drowning eternally. I had no choice. I accepted.

"Our new pact changed our bodies. Where once we were drowning, we breathed again. Where once we were sinking, we swam like fish. We did not look like ourselves, however. Some had extra eyes, others extra arms. Some did not have faces much at all, but fish-like snouts. We were transformed and we were horrified. My people had been saved from death, but some fates are worse, still…"

Hanover blinked. As the Eye spoke, he saw fevered visions of some far-off place that must have once been her homeland. "How did you come to be trapped in this…orb, then?"

"Ah, you mean my Eye…" she said somberly. "My people were not happy with their new lot in life. Never again could they breathe fresh air or walk on two legs. Never again would they till the soil. They turned on me, in their fear, confusion…and rage.

"They turned on me. Even my sages followed suit. And in my desperation, I talked to that dark power once again, begging for salvation. My body was saved, but my soul was trapped in one of my eyes, plucked out and turned to stone. And there I remained, for two millennia."

Hanover couldn't believe what he'd just been shown. He had few interactions with El'wa, or even Duwa for that matter. Seeing one of their ancient cities, like from the story books, was breathtaking. "But why does the Emperor want you so badly? What use could anyone have for an ancient El'wa queen trapped in a magickal rock?"

Atla paused a moment, perhaps considering her answer. "In life, I was quite the sorceress. I used my powers to save my people from many threats and gained renown for it. One power of mine is soothsaying. I can read people's minds. It helped me more times than I could count. So, I offered my services to others, in hopes of securing my freedom. Promises were made, but never kept. I would be used, my powers abused—then I would be discarded. Cast away! Like a pawn to be sacrificed!"

Atla raged, her voice raised in pitch and the shapeshifter twisted about momentarily, jostling them around. But the beast settled into its pace once again.

"Now, I am once again a pawn to be sacrificed. They promise me freedom…but I will never have it," she sighed. "To them, I am a thing to be used.

A tool. A weapon. I am a queen no longer. And now? I am not even a person. 'Until the coming of the apocalypse' indeed."

Hanover pondered her words. It wasn't right that she be used so. To be treated not even as a living being…he knew that all too well. He thought again on those cold, rainy nights, when he pined for his brother to save him. And warmth.

"How do I free you?" he finally as the silence grew overlong.

"Free me? Child, you do not—"

"If you can get me out of here…I'll free you."

Atla was quiet again, though her eye pulsed light at a heartbeat pace. "…Do you promise?"

Hanover whiffed the acrid stench of the shapeshifter's gullet and became ever more aware of the claustrophobic squeeze of its confines. It was either this, or whatever terrible fate the monster had in store for them.

"Yes, I promise."

"Very well…lay your hand upon me."

*****

PRESENT DAY…

The sun dipped low on the horizon as the day gave way to sunset. Morgan looked through his spyglass for their quarry but saw nothing. "It's disappeared beneath the waves. We've lost it…" he said aloud. He ran a hand over his amulet. "Can you sense them still?"

"They are close, still. It has not gone far…" Abbal answered.

"So what's our next move? Do we wait until the end of the world, then?" Stone asked.

Morgan shook his head. "It led us here for a reason. I wager if we wait long enough, we'll find out just what it is we were led here for."

And so, they did.

*****

"We're almost there…" Ephala said with finality.

She looked at her Seeker sister and brothers. They were ready. Tora was anxiously gripping her trident with one hand, and Frond's hand with the other, while Sedrick meticulously loaded his rifle. Frond held his helmet in his free

548

hand and looked at it fixedly. Clive sat distantly on a chair to her right side, running a whetstone over his great sword. The air was positively electric.

Outside, she could hear Captain Avery giving a spirited speech to the mariners, and she knew that Ensign Golde and the two Lieutenant Commanders weren't far behind. In a few minutes, their quarry would be on the horizon. Their approach would, fortuitously, be covered by the setting sun. The eve of battle was upon them, and though Ephala doubted that even the strongest of the Azura pirates had a prayer in hell against her Seekers, she couldn't hope but feel a pit of anxiety growing in her belly.

Earlier that day, Frond had taken her aside and warned her that there was something dark on the horizon.

"Something's coming, and it isn't the pirates."

She couldn't feel it then, but she felt it now. She looked at her brethren and they at her, reading the unspoken thoughts and words that fast friends had.

"I..."

A knock came at the door, and they all looked at it.

"Enter," Ephala said.

Captain Avery, Ensign Golde, and Lieutenant Commanders Jukel and Castell all entered the captain's cabin.

"The mariners are ready, Lady Seeker. How soon will we be upon our quarry?" Captain Avery asked. There was an eager gleam in his eye.

"A half-hour at most. We should be covered by the setting sun," Ephala said.

"Very good. I shall have the cannons ready for the attack. With luck, Seekers, we may be able to scare them from battle," Ensign Golde suggested confidently.

The chances of the Immortal Captain backing down from a fight with Bluecoats is slim to none.

Ephala said to herself.

The man was renowned for surmounting impossible odds. She recalled a story she'd heard when she was young of him facing off against a Dead Sea God—Bane, no less—and surviving. That alone made him a rare breed. He would not go quietly, and this would *not* be an easy fight. If it was, then the Seekers would not have been sent.

"I'd mind your ego, ensign. The Seekers are not sent out on simple errands, and Morgan Sarron has killed a hundred men with the same overconfidence as yourself," Captain Avery warned.

Golde seemed taken aback by his suggestion but kept his composure. "Yes, captain. My apologies, I did not mean to overstate my skill."

Ephala was surprised by his response. Until now, though he'd kept it under wraps, Cambridge Golde had seemed like a woefully overconfident young man. Smart and skilled, but cocky.

"I will have my men load chain shot, in case they should attempt to escape capture. We will not load regular shot or carcasses until after the artifact has been retrieved and orders have been handed down. This, I vow," Cambridge said sharply.

Perhaps there's a reason he earned his rank.

Ephala nodded.

"I will have our best shooters at your disposal shortly, Seeker Sedrick, as you requested," Jukel reported.

Sedrick nodded his approval. "My thanks, quartermaster. The shooters and I will provide cover for the boarding party."

"What is the morale of the crew, Lieutenant Commander?" Ephala asked.

Jukel gave a flex of his puffy jowls. "They are...anxious, to be honest, Lady Seeker. On the one hand, they are eager to hunt pirates as notorious as the Azurans. On the other...well."

Ephala looked at her companions, then back at Jukel. "They fear us still."

Jukel cast a reproachful gaze at Clive. "Due to the outburst of Seeker Clive, many of the mariners feel as though they cannot count on your aid during the battle. They feel as though they are being thrown into a meatgrinder."

"Yes, I've heard much the same sentiment," Castell admitted. He too was looking at Clive, who was, in turn, glaring back at him.

"Do you have issue with me, Lieutenant Commander?" Clive asked rhetorically. "I thought we were fast friends."

"Friends don't beat friends to a pulp and leave one blind in one eye," Castell said icily. "Hopefully you'll attack our enemies with the aplomb you've shown battering your allies."

Clive shrugged. "I suppose we'll find out, won't we?"

Ephala shot him a look. "Seeker Clive will be boarding with me, on the frontline when the fighting commences."

And where I can see you.

She added silently.

"Moving back to the subject at hand, please…" Golde added, trying to move things along.

"Yes, Lieutenant Commander Castell, give your report, please," Captain Avery instructed.

Ambrose Castell held Sedrick's gaze a moment longer before breaking away and addressing the others. "Lieutenant Commander Jukel and I, have armed every mariner above and below deck with standard-issue cavalry swords, flintlock pistols, and breech-loader rifles.

Breech-loaders? Those are new.

"How effective are the breech-loaders?" she asked.

This time, Clive piped up, "A measure weaker than my rifle, but faster loading. In a pinch, it can be a lifesaver when you can't be bothered to reload mid-battle."

Castell nodded. "The admiralty wanted to use this as a test run to see if they might become our new standard issue. If successful, it could become the new rifleman's gun for the regular military, as well."

Ephala was again in awe at just how much resources had been expended to send them after this Eye of Atla. Was it really worth all this?

The map flared up and made a loud chiming noise, startling them. Ephala approached it, took a glance at it then, walked out of the cabin to check the eastern horizon. Barely, just barely, she could make out the shape of a ship.

It's time…

That feeling in her gut did not go away.

*****

Osiris leaned against the railing, eyes set in the last direction he'd seen the creature swimming. His ears pricked up as he heard Morgan's familiar footsteps approach him. "Cap'n?"

"You've been up for three days straight, Siris. I haven't seen you this intent since Huasca and I taught you the way of the sword years ago, now," Morgan said.

Osiris thought back to over a decade prior, when the two older pirates had beaten him to a pulp with wooden swords until he finally learned how to combat them. He could still feel the bruises. He felt a smile spread across his face. "That long, ay? Some days I swear I still feel the bruises."

"Funny, isn't it? How old wounds can crop back up like a phantom limb to haunt us. I like to think they serve to remind us how far we've come," Morgan said.

"Is this the part of the story where you sit and give me something thought provoking to mull over while I wait to carve up our enemies again?" Osiris asked bluntly.

Morgan chuckled. "I don't think that's quite what I had in mind, my friend. I use words to motivate the men, but really the motivation comes from within. All I'm doing is striking a nerve to see if it yet feels. It's up to them to decide whether that sensation is pain, pleasure, excitement…or nothing at all."

"And how am I meant to feel now? Am I meant to feel rallied to the cause? Ready to cut down a hundred men? Or perhaps to fight a horrible shapeshifting monster that killed my friends and swallowed the closest thing I had to a little brother?" Osiris asked.

"I figured you two were close. Never knew whether the feeling was mutual, however. I heard you two got into a row after that business aboard the Bounty," Morgan said.

"A row, ay? I wouldn't call it that."

"Well, what would you call it?" Morgan asked.

Osiris rapped his knuckles against the wood as he gathered his thoughts.

"I've spent my whole life as a pirate, boy! I didn't get to choose! So why the fuck are you wasting yours?!"

His words from that night echoed in his mind.

"A disagreement of sorts," he finally answered.

"About?"

"I…when Hanover came onto our ship, he was a lost child looking for a hot meal and companionship. Then, as he learned his way around the ship, he got it into his head that he wanted to be like us. I had hoped the first battle he saw would change that, but it didn't. He kept pushing for it. I taught him how to swing a sword, beat his ass when I did it, too. Didn't change a damn thing. I wanted him to understand that…" Osiris sighed.

"Siris?" Morgan pressed.

"That this life? It ain't for everyone. I didn't choose it, it chose me. He had a chance to be different. To keep his hands clean, to save himself from carryin' this burden on his shoulders for the rest of his days…"

"You wanted him to take the chance you never had to be an ordinary man," Morgan guessed.

"I wanted him to be different. Instead, he chose to fall into the same black trap we all did. Cap'n, I will be a pirate till the day I die, and proud of it. But if I ever have a child…I will keep them as far away from this as I possibly can."

Morgan nodded slowly. "I understand, son. I understand better than most. I had a family, once. I thought that I could keep the black and still keep them safe. But I was wrong. My sins came back to haunt me and took them from me as payment. We can't control the choices others make, Siris. We can only make peace with them. Armen Hanover chose this life, he took a life to be inducted into it, and it's time you accepted the choice he's made. Otherwise, if he yet lives, he will die an ugly and senseless death like so many of our fallen brothers. But unlike theirs, you'll have played a part in his. It's up to you to guide him, Siris. You're one of the best damn pirates I've ever seen and you're five years junior to your closest peer."

"He should've chose different, cap'n. This life…it only ends one way, we both know that. He's sealed his fate."

"Aye, he has. His chances are slim, and the odds are long. But I've never known you to be one to care about the odds, Siris. You've defied them for so long, they're but a suggestion for you. Who better to teach the boy how to *survive* than you? Or do you want him to go as so many of our brothers have?"

Osiris looked at Morgan, then said, "Not so long as I live."

Morgan smiled. "Then when the time comes, teach him. Teach him to be a pirate and teach him what it takes to make it in this life."

"Ye think he's still alive, then? Truly?" Osiris asked.

"I've seen the impossible happen time and again, Siris. Anything is possible. And something tells me that boy, wherever he is, is still breathing, waiting for his brothers in black to save him. Will you answer that call?"

"For my brothers in black, I'll go to hell and back, sir."

LIII

THE BATTLE BEGINS

Morgan had seen the ship-of-the-line first as a small dark smudge on the horizon. He had given it no real credence, then. A half hour later, however, and it was very clearly a ship that was approaching them. A large one. Too large, and coming too fast, to be able to outrun. The coastline was another fifty miles away, and by time they made it there, they would be at the mercy of a ship that was made for breaking blockades and sinking man 'o wars. Azura would not survive its cannons.

"There are Alyrians aboard that vessel," Abbal had informed him.

He knew for certain then, that their time had run out. They were flagged down and boarded.

"The Immortal Captain, Morgan Sarron. Do you know who I am?" The armored, black-haired woman before him asked. Her question came with no less than forty rifles pointed at him, and his men.

Yes, he knew exactly who she was.

"Well, judging by that interesting little mark on your forehead, ma'am, I would presume you to be an Imperial Seeker. Am I correct?" Morgan guessed, cordially.

"I am. I presume you know why I am here?" Ephala asked.

Morgan appraised the young woman. She could be no older than Osiris' age, likely younger. Was this child meant to slay him? He was almost insulted by the Emperor's brazenness. "You are here for the Eye of Atla. Nearly a month early, by my estimation."

Ephala blanked; she was unaware that the pirates had been told of their coming. Why had the Emperor and the imperial advisor not mentioned this?

"The Emperor has grown impatient," she answered simply. "Pirates are want to neglect the duties given to them, like rats are want to eat cheese."

"Rats will eat anything. Even people, if given the opportunity," Morgan said with a wan smirk.

"Are you threatening me, captain?" Ephala asked.

"Threatening? No. Merely correcting the metaphor. The Eye is this way. I presume you'll want to inspect it?" Morgan asked, motioning to the door.

"Indeed, I will. I hope you won't mind if my compliment follows us?" Ephala asked rhetorically, then began walking.

The pirates eyed her, as well as her entourage. Reece Stone stood overlooking them from the steering deck, watching silently. Yaman Huasca stood beside him, whispering. His eyes glowed a bright, ghostly turquoise. The Tannis brothers, Ryker and Sarkad, sat on the bottom of the steps leading from the steering deck, one chewing on jerky and the other smoking a cigarette, casually observing the Bluecoats aiming rifles at them. The main deck of the Black Bess sat easily five feet above the main deck of Azura, so the Bluecoats that remained aboard looked down at them from their vantage point, many of which were aiming at the pirates.

As they passed by, Clive bumped into Steven Cage, who stood imposingly at the doorway. The two men locked eyes, and Cage gave the Seeker a wide, toothy smile and breathed foul, rum-scented breath into his face. Clive placed a hand over his nose and the other on the sword on his back. Cage gave him a taunting look.

"Northman! Over here, ye twit," Sarkad called out, getting his attention.

Cage shrugged, then walked away as Clive and the other Bluecoats, clearly unnerved by his brazenness, followed Ephala and Morgan down into the hold.

*****

"He's a bold one, isn't he?" Tora noted, nodding to Steven Cage, who stood next to Frond, overlooking the Azura. "And by the sound of it, he's a Valkar. What are one of theirs doing here?"

"Valkar and pirates are birds of a feather. Perhaps they finally realized," Frond offered.

"Stars, I hope not," Tora rebuked. "I don't want to imagine what'll happen if the two of them work together."

Frond shrugged. "Wholesale slaughter of their ranks, for one. The navy is growing, has been since the formation of the empire. They need to be able to complete with the Mercantile to the south, and the Dynasty to the east. Pirates, even an organized collective of them, are no match for us. And the Valkar will need to go through the Warden of the North before they can launch a proper assault down here."

"Don't forget the Imperium. They've been making more trades with the Duwa kingdoms. I don't think they've quite forgiven us for the last war. And the Wuhlven…"

Frond started at their mention.

Many of the Wuhlven were once humans, casualties of the War of the Empires. Humanity had been cruel to their former brethren, exiling many of them to Blackrock, a region in the distant Sai'Haluud Imperium of the El'wa. Now, the wolf-like beasts had a grudge against their former kin. The empire feared a reprisal from them, and the idea of going to battle against half-wolf, half-man hybrids didn't sit well with him.

"The empire will take on all comers and prevail," Frond said assuredly. "Pirate, or otherwise…"

Tora reached out and he squeezed her hand.

"Yes, Seeker-Brother," Tora said, reassured.

Captain Avery approached the pair, keeping an eye on the pirates the whole while. "Seeker Sedrick and his riflemen are perched in the crow's nest, awaiting the signal to begin firing. When the battle begins, the ensign will order an opening broadside on the ship. The lieutenant commanders stand ready to board the ship afterward."

Tora nodded. "As you were, captain."

*****

"Your ship is quite spacious within, captain. I must confess, I was under the impression most pirate ships were places of squalor," Ephala said. "This place almost looks like a proper sailing ship."

Morgan spoke, "There are many kinds of pirates, Seeker. Not all of us are ragged beggars on boats."

"Beggars or not. You're still bandits, at heart. Bandits set on pilfering what isn't theirs," Clive spat.

"Thievery is a matter of perspective. What do you call it when slavers come and round up slaves for the market, shipping them across the empire? Or when a local lord finds gold in one of his peasants' lands, and summarily seizes it for mining, offering them a pittance, or the headman's block as reward?" Morgan asked.

Clive was silent. He looked at Ephala for a rebuttal, but the Seeker was wholly focused on watching the captain's movements. They reached a door at the end of the hallway they'd tread, and Morgan produced a key as two guardsmen, armed with blunderbusses, looked wide-eyed at the two Seekers and their Bluecoats entourage, who aimed their own rifles at them.

"At ease, gentlemen. Our friends, here, have come to collect their prize." Morgan waived.

The men dropped their aim and nodded, moving aside. "Yes, cap'n," one of them said.

Morgan opened the door and ushered in Ephala to the small compartment, barely large enough for the chest and one man to stand with it. She looked at him warily, then stepped inside as Morgan squeezed past her to open the chest. He searched his person for the chest key.

"Tell me, Seeker. Did the Emperor or his advisor make mention of *why* he sent us to retrieve the Eye of Atla for them?" he asked.

"No, we were assured such information was irrelevant," she dismissed.

"Irrelevant? Is it irrelevant that Idallon himself spoke to the Emperor, declaring that I should be given this task? Is it irrelevant that the Stars seem to have aligned themselves for this event?" Morgan probed, still searching his pockets.

He sniffed the air as one of his men outside the door lit a smoke and offered it to Clive, who grunted his refusal.

"The Stars aligned at the Emperor's birth to bequeath him the mantle of Emperor, as ordained by his father and the Church of the Stars," Ephala answered dogmatically.

Morgan shook his head as he produced the key. "So, the rumors are true. You lot really are the Emperor's lap dogs…" He didn't give her time to answer as he unlocked the ornate, black chest that the Eye sat in. He took a deep breath.

"Ready?" Morgan asked.

"Ready." Abbal answered.

He undid the lock of the chest, making an audible click and metallic pop. Though Ephala could not see it, Morgan's eyes glowed blue, as did his amulet beneath his coat. As he completed the motion, opening the chest to reveal it empty, Osiris opened a door further down the hallway and took aim.

The two guards, seeing Osiris, dropped down to the floor just as the Bluecoats turned to face him, and were met with the spray of the blunderbuss in his hands.

BANG!

The discharge deafened everyone in the hallway, and alerted the men above deck, who began their own coordinated attack.

Clive grunted as the shrapnel bounced off him in sparks of blue. He was shaken, but mostly unphased by the blast that had cut down the half dozen men that were with him.

"What the—" Osiris gasped, confused.

Clive charged at him just as the other two pirates unloaded their blunderbusses at him, he took the blasts fully to his back and roared in frustration as the magick barrier that protected him broke from the force of the twin blasts. Pellets dug into his armor, some of them even piercing him as he grunted in pain and stumbled forward.

"Clive!" Ephala shouted and ran straight for him as Morgan raised his pistol behind her.

He fired, and a bright burst of energy flooded the compartment as his gun broke through her barrier and a wave past through the cramped hallway, causing everyone's ears to pop, and momentarily stunning Osiris, who'd been moving in to finish off the weakened Clive.

Ephala, realizing the danger they were in, grabbed hold of Clive's shoulder and closed her eyes, focusing on a point aboard the Black Bess and blinking out of existence with a whoosh of air and a spark. Before she disappeared, she threw a bolt of energy at Morgan, who dodged it.

"Starsdammit all—we almost had them!" Morgan cursed. That had been their best chance to eliminate their leader and thwart their attack before it began. He helped Osiris to his feet as they regarded the scorched remains of the two pirate guards, who'd been killed by Ephala's parting gift for Morgan.

Now, the battle had begun.

*****

Hearing the signal shot, Ryker wasted no time lunging at the Bluecoats aiming his rifle at him and ripping it out his hands. The weapon discharged, striking a nearby pirate and killing him as Sarkad went to aid his older brother, pulling out a knife whip-fast and plunging it into the chest of the second

Bluecoats, who'd taken aim at Ryker. Ryker cracked his attacker in the head with the rifle stock before pulling his brother down into cover. The fighting had gotten underway and several of the Bluecoats aiming at Azura opened fire, killing more pirates in the volley.

*****

Across the deck from Ryker and Sarkad, toward the nose of the midship, a barrel top popped open to reveal Flint, holding a lit grenade in his hand. He squinted, picking out a target as he sat unnoticed. He eyed a cluster of Bluecoats, firing down at the pirates a few dozen yards away, perhaps. He tried to judge the distance between him and his target, but with his one good eye he overshot the throw and cursed as he was spotted.

"Grenade!" he heard the men shout as he closed the top of his barrel and began rolling it away.

He prayed that none of their shots landed, or he knew that the barrel would be his tomb. He couldn't hear much as he rolled away, disoriented, but he did hear the concussive boom of the grenade detonating, followed by screams. He may not have hit his intended targets, but someone aboard that damned ship-of-the-line just had a bad, bad day.

*****

Flint's grenade sailed over the heads of its targets, but instead, it bounced between the rope lines of one of the running rigging mechanisms holding the main sails in place. When its wick burnt out, it detonated several feet in the air, sending out a spray of white-hot shrapnel, killing three unfortunate Bluecoats, injuring several others, and damaging the rigging mechanism. This released the rope lines it was holding. In turn, this release unfurled a portion of the main sail, sending its canvas blanketing Seeker Sedrick's sniper team's view of the battlefield immediately after Sedrick fired his first shot.

"Fuck!" Sedrick cursed. "We have to reposition, there's no clear line of sight here."

The Bluecoats snipers and their Seeker squad leader then began laboriously climbing down from their perch.

Though Flint didn't know it, he had just saved his fellow officers above deck from certain death. All, save for one.

*****

"Charge!" Steven Cage howled at the top of his lungs, rushing across one of the gangplanks, flanked by a dozen Azura pirates.

Across from him, charging from the Black Bess' side of the same gangplank, was Jukel Staunton and a crush of Bluecoats mariners. The overweight, but well-seasoned Staunton thrust his officer's sabre at the bare-chested, tattooed Cage in challenge.

"Valkar filth! We will have your head!" Jukel shouted, charging at Cage as several Bluecoats ran past him to meet the pirates attempting to board them.

"Foolish pig. I will roast your corpse on a spit! Hahahaha!" Cage cackled as he charged toward Jukel, slicing open one unfortunate Bluecoats with the sword in his left hand before braining another with the mace in his right.

The two forces engaged, as did several others across the gangplanks connecting the ships together. Cage locked eyes with Jukel, and the two clashed blades as the fighting raged around them. The gangplank was wide enough for several men to stand shoulder to shoulder, but the pirates and Bluecoats pulled back to give the two duelists room to maneuver. Staunton had the high ground, but Cage had two melee weapons instead of one.

"Throw your mace aside, savage. Fight me as a duelist!" Jukel demanded.

Cage shrugged and charged the lieutenant commander, ignoring his request. Staunton attempted to sidestep the blow, narrowly parrying it with his sword.

Jukel took several measured steps, avoiding the edges of the gangplank. He sidestepped as Cage attempted to knock him off, and the Valkar teetered on the edge before throwing himself away from it. The two men went at each other again and again, with either side cheering their respective fighter on. Jukel was losing, however. He was forced back by the unrelenting blows of Cage, who had no real concern for his own well-being. Jukel landed a glancing blow on Cage's arm, but the Valkar pirate didn't even seem to register the injury, let alone recoil from it.

Cage pushed Staunton and his men back onto the deck of the Black Bess, knocking away his blows and swiping at him, trying to slice open the lieutenant commander.

"Stop squirming, pig! I will stick you soon enough!" Cage rasped as he thrust his sword at Staunton with all his might.

Jukel sidestepped the blow and smirked as he went to counter—but as he went to attack Cage's back, the Valkar ducked, seeming to sense the impending blow, and spun around to bring his mace down on the outside of Jukel's knee. Staunton grit his teeth and let out a muffled groan of pain as his knee buckled. He faltered, and Cage wasted no time in capitalizing. The Bluecoats' cheers turned to jeers, then silence as Cage swiftly ended the honorable mariner with a swipe of his sword… and a roll of Jukel Staunton's head.

Cage let out a war cry as blood spurted from the corpse of the slain lieutenant commander, and the Azura pirates surged around him to attack the Bluecoats before they could react.

*****

Tora watched in disbelief as Jukel Staunton fell. "He killed Lieutenant Commander Staunton!"

Frond nodded, pulling out his sword and shield. "And many more men will die yet, this evening. Sedrick is repositioning to get a better view of the battlefield. We need to clear the deck so that his men aren't swarmed by this pirate filth and don't join Staunton in the grave. I'll handle the Valkar."

Tora put her hand on his shoulder. "No. He's mine." Before he could react, she took off across the deck as her body morphed rapidly into that of a black panther, charging at her target.

Frond turned his attention to another of the gangplanks in which the pirates were pushing across and made his way into the fray.

*****

"Is that a—AAAHHH!" Someone screamed.

Cage turned toward the sound, having just slain another Bluecoats with his now blood-spattered weapons. "What the…" he barely had time to process what he was seeing as a large, black panther charged at him from across the deck, rending several in its wake as it yowled and beelined for him.

"This is for Staunton!" The creature spoke.

Cage leaped out of the way but was caught by the creature's paw and laid out on the deck. It began clawing at him violently, and he hissed in pain as it cut at his arms. "What manner of beast is this?! A druid?" he gasped as he fought desperately through the searing pain as it tore at him.

"Die, Valkar! Die as you have lived!" Tora screeched, her voice strange and guttural, coming from the vocal cords of an animal not suited for speech.

561

"I will not die this day, druid! I will *not!*" he spat as he threw the beast off him with all his might.

Tora landed deftly on her paws, and went in for another attack, but was harassed by pirates, defending Cage. She yowled and leapt back as blades and axes came swinging at her. She maneuvered quickly, bouncing off a mast and a crate before leaping back at the pirates and knocking one to the ground, sinking her fangs into his neck and tearing it out, cutting off his death wail. Another slashed at her side with his sword. Her barrier deflected it and she hissed before knocking the weapon from his hand and swiping him across the face. Her last attacker attempted to stab her from behind, but she kicked back with her hindlegs, knocking him back several feet before tackling him to the deck, cutting him apart with a flurry of angry swipes.

"Now for—" She turned to see another pirate coming to the defense of the Valkar. This one was a lean, fair-skinned Xallan man with an afro. He had dark brown eyes that were glowing faintly, and a reproachful gaze.

"What the fuck is this thing? A talking cat? Is it the shapeshifter?!" Osiris asked as he helped Cage to his feet.

"No, it is not. This one is a druid of some sort, one of the Seekers, no doubt," Cage said.

"Druid, shapeshifter—makes no difference. You're dead all the same!" Osiris grunted. His eyes went fully aglow with turquoise light, and his tattoos glowed as well.

"An apostate? Here?" Tora pulled back her lips, bearing her fangs. "The magisters won't even have enough of you left to put in a cigar box when I'm done with you!"

She leapt at him and was immediately taken aback when he deftly rolled under her and slashed at her belly, mid-leap. Were it not for her barrier, he would have disemboweled her. She let out an involuntary hiss and flopped onto the deck, losing her footing. Cage, seeing an opportunity, came upon her and swung his axes, nearly embedding them into her exposed belly. Her barrier again stopped the blow, however.

Tora let out a howl of surprise as the axes attempted to dig into her. She twisted beneath him, transforming before their eyes into a much smaller, black-feathered shape. She took flight in the form of a raven, escaping the losing fight.

"That thing just turned into a bird, and we couldn't land a single blow on it," Osiris gasped.

"We'll get her later. We need to capture their captain!" Cage shouted above the carnage. "Behind you!"

Osiris spun around to see a Bluecoats taking aim at him with a rifle. He leapt into the air, dodging the gunshot and landing on the surprised Bluecoats, running him through with his spadroons. "Too slow, blue boy!"

LIV

Brothers Lost

"Brother! Speak to me, brother!" Sarkad cried as he held Ryker's convulsing body in his hands. His older brother had taken a bullet in the left side of his chest and was releasing a red foam from his lips. His eyes blinked constantly and rolled into the back of his head. "Claude! Claude help…" Sarkad cried out, then stopped when he remembered that their sawbones was long gone, now.

"What happened?!" Flint shouted as he scrambled across the deck toward them. "Cover me!" he said as several Bluecoats charged toward them, seeing an opening. Thankfully, several more crewmen stepped in and intercepted the charging attackers, and a scuffle broke out several meters behind them.

"He…he got hit! He got hit!" Sarkad gasped, holding his brother's clenching hand while he supported his head. "Starsdamn it—he got hit! He needs help!"

Flint took a brief moment to look over Ryker and knew that there was nothing he could do to help him. Not even Claude's medical skills would save him, now. And in a few more minutes, not even a priest of the Stars would be able to bring him back. "He's goin' out, brother…he's…"

"Shut up!" Sarkad lashed out, hyperventilating. "He's gonna make it, he's gonna—"

Flint put a hand on his brother in black's shoulder and shook his head sorrowfully. "No, brother…" he remembered the bottle of whitestar syrup in his pocket.

"*…I'd hate to think what happens when ye do too much…*" Flint had said.

Flint pulled the bottle out and took off its top before placing a hand over Ryker's and Sarkad's. Sarkad looked at his hand, then at him, then at the bottle in his other, shaking hand.

"What is…" Sarkad asked.

"It'll put 'em at rest…" Flint answered, solemnly.

Sarkad opened his mouth to speak but lost his voice. He looked at his brother, unclasped his hand from the other two, and ran it down his wrinkled cheek, creased in an open-mouthed frown as his seizure continued. "Do it…"

Flint raised the small bottle to Ryker's lips and tipped it, holding his sweaty, bloody, quivering neck as the thick syrup slowly went down. At first, he began choking on it, but Flint ran a finger down the bottom of his chin to his Adam's apple, over and over, until he swallowed the syrup.

Then, very quickly, Ryker's convulsions began to slow, and his eyes fluttered slower and slower, until they winked shut. Ryker stopped seizing, and Sarkad felt his wrist for a pulse. It was slow and fading. "Brother…"

Sarkad whimpered like a child, running a hand down his cheek one last time. Flint placed a hand on his shoulder and nodded. Sarkad laid his brother down and stood up, panting with rage. He looked around for the sniper who'd shot at his kin, and saw the man take aim and fire at another pirate. "I'll avenge you…" he promised.

He tore off running, grabbing a discarded breech-loader rifle from one of the Bluecoats his comrades had slain, before taking off toward a gangplank to board the Black Bess. A bullet rang out, missing him narrowly as he roared across the plank and into the fray.

Flint cursed, "Hermalla's fucking mercy."

He begrudgingly chased after Sarkad, knowing that the last Tannis brother would get himself killed if he didn't help. His part of the plan had been played, regardless. Captain Morgan had ordered him to cause a distraction aboard the Black Bess when the signal was given and kill as many of their sharpshooters as he could to minimize casualties. He had done that best he could from Azura. Now, he would help with the fighting aboard the Black Bess. He knew that Cutter would be on their gun deck, now. He would help Sarkad settle his score, then head below, if the fighting hadn't already ended. He grabbed one of the fallen Bluecoats' breech-loader rifles on his way.

Or we don't all get killed.

A fearful voice said in the back of his head. He silenced that voice and took after Sarkad.

*****

"Ha! Got another one!" Sedrick laughed as he put another pirate in his sights and shot him. He'd saved another of their boys from being killed by their filth. He loaded another round into his rifle, lined up another shot, and fired, this time killing one of the Azura's own marksmen. "Better luck next life, ay bugger?" he chuffed before cursing as a bullet pierced the head of the man next to him. "Shit! Man down!"

He looked around for the shooter and realized the shot had come from behind them. He spun around just in time to see the blast of a muzzle, and he cursed as a bullet ricocheted off him, sending out sparks of blue as his barrier protected him from the kill shot. "We've got company!"

Two pirates stood behind them, one with an eyepatch and a bald head, another with shoulder-length, reddish brown hair. That one had both his eyes, and they were glaring daggers at him. They had them dead to rights.

"How'd you lot get up here?" Sedrick asked.

Sarkad spat on the deck. "You killed my brother…"

Sedrick scratched his chin. "Gotta be more specific, mate. I've killed a lot of people's brothers, today."

Sarkad, unamused, let off another shot at one of Sedrick's men. Sedrick scowled as the man stumbled backward and fell overboard, clutching his shoulder. "Well, that wasn't very—"

Flint let loose several shots in rapid succession, firing at another sharpshooter, then another, then another. One of them drew on him, he whipped out his pistol and fired it from the hip, nailing the man in the clavicle and causing the gunshot to miss its target, sailing harmlessly through the air. He said nothing as he automatically reloaded his weapons, never taking his eye off the stunned Bluecoats, and the Seeker. He'd picked up on how to use the breech-loader rifles intuitively and was using it to deadly effect.

Sedrick whistled. "Deadeye aim on you, pirate. You must have been deadly, back when you had two of them, ay?"

Flint gave him an unsettling smirk. "Still am, boy."

"So, I killed your brother, eh? And why does that matter? I'm sure your murderous brother killed plenty of men in his day," Sedrick said.

Sarkad nodded. "He did. We all have, it's part of the trade. I'm here to settle accounts."

Sedrick laughed while his men stood uneasily, arms raised. He could survive whatever they had in their chambers; his men could not. "Let's all just calm down, and—"

"Die, fucker!" Sarkad roared, shooting at Sedrick's head again. And again, the bullet bounced off with a blue spark.

This time he'd seen it with his own two eyes, as did Flint. "What the…"

"Neat trick, innit? We Seekers are taught to maintain a barrier of Alyria around us at all times. Comes in handy in the heat of battle. A stay bullet, arrow, or bolt, or spell would do a normal man in for sure. Us, though? You'll be lucky if it even hits me, hehehehe," Sedrick chuckled.

"Fucking spark," Flint cursed.

"I don't care what it takes! You're dead!" Sarkad growled and charged at Sedrick, his rage clouding his judgement.

"Sarkad, no!" Flint called out.

"That's the spirit! Let's dance, pirate!" Sedrick challenged. He held his rifle like a club and swung it at Sarkad, who ducked it and swung his sword at him. The blade bounced off Sedrick's barrier and left the irate pirate wide open. Sedrick capitalized immediately and brought his rifle butt down on Sarkad's head, cracking him with it and sending him to his knees.

Meanwhile, the remaining two sharpshooters took aim at Flint, who dispatched one of them with a rifle shot from the hip, then the other with a spare pistol shot before they could get their shots off. He would need to reload his pistols before he could use them again. He focused back on Sarkad and Sedrick just in time to see the thing he dreaded.

"Brother…" Sarkad gasped as Sedrick smashed the butt of his rifle down on his face, breaking his nose. "I'll…"

Sedrick swung the butt again, this time striking his mouth. There was an audible cracking sound.

"Av…enge…" He sputtered through broken teeth and a busted jaw.

"Fuck it," Sedrick grunted and spun the barrel around, preparing to fire.

"No!" Flint gasped. "Fucking hell!" he whipped his own gun around and fired it at Sedrick, who grunted as the bullet bounced off him.

Sedrick looked at him. Flint grabbed another rifle off the deck. "Pirate," he began.

Flint fired another shot at Sedrick's head. It bounced off; Sedrick scowled. He grabbed another rifle and fired again, this time he saw a faint blue crack in the air, a few inches off Sedrick's skin.

"That's—"

Another shot, this one caused Sedrick to recoil. The crack widened. Flint grabbed another rifle.

"Enough!" Sedrick growled.

Flint fired one last time and this time the barrier shattered, sending out a concussive wave and knocking him off his feet.

"You broke it? How the fuck did you—" Sedrick gasped, then dodged out the way as Flint fired at him again, panting.

"Everything breaks, eventually, boy." Flint panted as he rose to his feet. "Let's see how tough you are without that barrier to protect you."

Flint held two service pistols he'd snatched from his quarry in his hands; Sedrick took aim. Flint dodged immediately to the left as Sedrick fired. The bullet whizzed past him, grazing Flint's side and making his heart jump into his throat. Just then, several pirates charged up the stairs and attacked Sedrick, who spun around to fire at them. Flint capitalized, firing both pistols just as Sedrick pierced a hole through two men with one round. Sedrick stumbled, opening him up for a blow from one of the remaining three pirates in front of him. The man swung and grazed Sedrick's shoulder, who gasped and grabbed the man by the throat, lifting him briefly in the air before chucking him overboard. Sedrick's body glowed dull blue.

"No more games!" He spat.

The other two pirates came at him, and he pulled out the sword on his hip, gutting one and blocking the other's attack with the body of his rifle. He shoved the man back and turned just in time to see Flint charge him with a cutlass in his hand. The two locked swords, and Sedrick shoved him off as the last pirate came yelling at him. He turned, swung his sword, and embedded it in the man's throat. As he pulled the weapon free, he gasped as he felt a sharp blow to the back of his head and stumbled forward.

"What the…" he turned to see Flint standing, empty-handed.

"Keep your eyes on the prize," Flint said with a wolfish grin. "Shouldn't have gotten cocky."

Sedrick felt the back of his head and ran his gauntleted finger over the blade of the sword embedded in his head. "Fucking…pira…"

Flint ran forward and kicked him in the chest with the bottom of his boot, sending the Seeker over a railing to the main deck. He walked over to Sarkad. The man had his face all but ruined by the rifle butt blows. His jaw was pushed back, what teeth Flint could see from his agape mouth looked shattered, and his nose was smooshed to one side of his face. His eyes were vacant. Flint crouched down and heard a weak, reedy breath come from the man's throat.

"Stars, why…" He stood up and looked at the ruined, barely alive face of Sarkad. He wasn't going to survive this, not in the middle of a battle, and not without Claude Humris to mend him. He'd used the last of the whitestar syrup to put Ryker out of his misery. But now, his brother…it may have been more merciful to have let the Seeker shoot him.

"I avenged him, Sarkad." Flint sighed. "I avenged *you*."

If Sarkad could hear him, his face wasn't able to register it. Flint shook away a forming tear and loaded the service pistol with a round from one of the dead mariners. He pointed it at Sarkad's head. "Stars guide you, brother."

And he fired.

*****

Ephala pushed open the door to the captain's cabin and carried the barely conscious Clive to her hammock before dropping him there.

"I'm…fine…" Clive protested, struggling to form words.

"No you're bloody not, you fucking big idiot! Now sit here and recover! I expect you back out there, killing these pirates in ten minutes tops, do you understand?!" Ephala spat.

Clive offered a weak nod. "Yes…Ma'am…"

"Good!" she said as she stomped toward the door trying to collect her thoughts. How had she not seen the ambush coming?

Of course, the bloody fucking pirates didn't give up the Eye willingly! Why the fuck did I actually think they would? The bastards had a full hour to plan while we closed on them. They knew we were coming, eventually.

Now, Clive had nearly died, the pirates were storming their ship, and they couldn't even blow theirs to smithereens because the Eye of Atla was still on it.

We had them dead to rights. But that cagey old bastard was never going to go out easy, was he? He outsmarted me.

She opened the door to see Frond on the other side. The large Seeker was covered in blood and was holding Sedrick in his arms. Sedrick had a sword sticking out of the back of his head.

"…What…" She asked, her jaw hanging slack.

"I said one of the pirates nearly killed Sedrick. He needs to heal, and they're giving the mariners hell below," Frond repeated. "Tora's down there, trying to beat them back."

How is this happening?

Ephala stepped out of the cabin past Frond and ran her hands down her face as she looked at the setting sun in the west. It would be dark in a few minutes. They had thought that the pirates would be easy to dispatch, and so they launched their attack at sunset. Soon, the pirates would be crawling all over them like termites in the dark. Which meant it would be that much harder to find the Eye of Atla, which meant that it would take that much longer for them to—

A series of concussive booms rocked the ship.

"What…was…" Ephala gasped.

"Seeker Lady! The Azurans have opened fire on our hull!" Ambrose Castell shouted as he stormed up the stairs.

"What are the confirmed casualties, so far?" Ephala asked, trying to maintain her composure.

Ambrose shook his head. "I cannot begin to fathom, My Lady. The entire lower compartment section beneath our gun deck was in the line of fire, the starboard crew quarters…"

"Hermalla's Mercy…" Ephala couldn't help but gasp. "Frond, you and Lieutenant Commander Ambrose lead the charge across to the pirates' ship. We must find that Eye at all costs! Tear the whole bloody tub apart if you must and kill any and every bastard that isn't wearing our uniforms while you're at it!"

Frond nodded. "As you wish."

"Yes, My Lady." Ambrose bowed.

Frond dropped the unconscious Sedrick on Tora's hammock and took off with Ambrose. Ephala turned her baleful gaze toward Azura once more, looking through the bay windows of her cabin. The ship was swarmed by her men, but even from here, she could tell that the mariners were losing. The pirates seemed to be fearless in the face of overwhelming odds, and their leader and his officers were vicious and effective in their maneuvers. They'd started off the battle with a reverse ambush, and now they were seeking to disable the Black Bess in the chaos.

She locked eyes with Morgan, who stood atop the Azura's steering deck, far opposite her across the battlefield below. She made out his tricorn hat and the bald head of that other Xallan she'd seen earlier. A wash of anger and indignation came over her. Even when they won the battle, the casualties would be unacceptable, now, because of his little stunt.

I'm going to tear the location of the Eye of Atla out of him, then I'm going to parade his head across Emperor's Rest on a pike!

She focused on her target location, pulled out her dirk daggers, and closed her eyes to channel her Alyria. It was time to get her hands dirty. She zipped from existence with a quick flash of light and a spark of energy.

*****

Tora slammed against the wall, narrowly escaping the hail of gunfire that ran down the compartment hallway and sprayed down several of her comrades. Across from her on the other side of the narrow hall was Ensign Cambridge Golde, who nodded to her as cocked his officer's pistol, a dainty silver-trimmed piece that looked custom-made. She nodded back, and channeled her energy into her trident, ready to attack.

"Come on out, lads. We just wanna chat, is all," Cutter called from down the hall.

"Chat? You blew a bloody hole the size of a bell tower into our ship, killing dozens and injuring far more. You slew my gun crews and ruined several of my cannons. I must say, pirate, if this is how you chat, I do so wonder how you fight," Cambridge answered, his anger palpable.

"Let's just say this isn't the most bodies I've stacked in a scrap, boy. And considering it's an all-or-nothing game? I don't see why I should stop, here," Cutter laughed. "My boys have broomsticks ready to paint your carcasses on the walls of this hallway, soon as you come out of hiding, that is. And judgin' by the fact that ye haven't turned tail yet, I'm bankin' that there's a whole lotta nowhere to run down there. Now, I'm ordinarily a patient man, see? But I gotta say, I'm in a bit of a time crunch. See, when my brothers over there ready up for another volley, they're gonna gut your ship's starboard. I don't wanna be here for that.

"But I also don't like the idea of lettin' one of you Seekers go unaccounted for. So how's about you come on out, missy, 'n we go for a walk? I'll let your friends live if ye come with me. Otherwise? Well."

Cutter knocked a grenade against the wall. "I've got a little present that should smoke ye out real nice like. It'll be the last present that boy commander ever gets, though."

Tora looked alarmedly at Cambridge, who gulped, a leisurely smile on his face.

"Now, now, there, pirate. Let's not spoil an opportunity for parlay, shall we? I'm worth much more to you alive than dead, surely you must know that."

Cutter laughed coldly, as did the pirates with him, aiming blunderbusses down the hallway, waiting for their targets to show themselves. "I do, actually. I thought it a little odd to see a wee lad in officer's britches. Real nice ones, at that. Must've cost your family a pretty penny to grease palms 'n cocks for you to get here, boy. I'd hate to paint your prissy ass all over this hallway, but I will if it means I smoke out your lady friend.

"So how's about both of ye come out, hands raised, 'n we go take a walk on over to Azura to parlay?"

Tora spoke up, "Why do you want me so bad? I'm more dangerous than all your men combined, blunderbusses or not!"

She half-truthed. She was deadly, but against a dozen blunderbuss blasts, in a narrow hallway like this. Her shield would burst, and she'd burst with it, like a ripe melon filled with dynamite.

"Seeker or no, I haven't met an Alyrian yet who can survive what we're packing. Not all at once. We'd make short work of you, I reckon. But I'd rather not waste the ammo. Cap'n wants ye alive, so I'd rather give ye over still breathin'," Cutter explained. "Time's up. Ye've got fifteen seconds or I'm throwing this grenade down the hall and knocking out your deadlights."

Tora looked at Cambridge, who sighed and uncocked his pistol. They were dead to rights. She sheathed her trident over her shoulder, and the two walked out from behind the corners, arms raised. She glanced briefly at the mangled corpses on the floor before focusing down the hall. The man Sedrick had been running bets with, Creyton's mangled, bullet-riddled corpse was amongst them. Before them were at least a dozen pirates, wielding blunderbusses aimed straight at them, and standing in front of them was a one-handed man with sandy-blonde hair and angry, reddish-brown eyes. Where his left hand should have been, there was instead a dagger blade. She had seen a mug shot of this man's face, before.

"You are Volld Cutter, the Mad Sea Dog," Tora declared.

Cutter smirked wolfishly. "Haven't heard that title in *years*. No one calls me that anymore. Everyone on Azura is a killer, see? That name don't mean shit. It's just Cutter, now."

Cutter motioned for them to leave, and the pirates marched them above deck.

LV

A Momentary Truce

Morgan sensed her before she even struck. He spun around and deflected her strikes. "Surprised?"

She disappeared again.

"Look out!" Morgan shouted.

Huasca dodged too late, suffering a slice across his back as Ephala materialized behind him and swung at him. He turned around and inhaled deeply before spewing a gout of turquoise flames from his lips and enveloping her in them. The Seeker shouted in alarm and patted at the flames, but her barrier protected her from most of the damage. "Another Alyrian?!" she gawked.

"You are out of your depth, child. You have already been outmaneuvered," Huasca warned.

"Clearly you have no idea who you're dealing with, old man. I have yet to reveal my true hand!" Ephala's daggers began to glow with energy. "Now, which one of you should I kill first?"

"You will kill no one, human! We do not have time to continue this pointless slaughter any longer!" Abbal shouted.

Ephala froze in place as Morgan clenched at his amulet.

"W…what magick is this?!" Ephala asked.

Her body was paralyzed; she felt as though she'd been constricted by a serpent.

Morgan wiped a bead of sweat from his brow. "We need to talk, Seeker. Mr. Huasca?"

Huasca nodded and raised an arm, pointing it at Ephala. Suddenly, she was enveloped in dull turquoise light and began to levitate. "I will keep her bound, for now."

"Thank you, old friend." Morgan nodded.

"We need to conserve our energy," Abbal warned.

"I know. Let's get on with it," Morgan said.

*****

"Kill the Bluecoats! The captain wants the Seekers a—" The pirate's words were cut off as a shield, tossed from several yards away, crashed into his face, and left him in a heap on the deck. His killer, a tall and well-armored knight, almost comically out of place against the backdrop of leather and cloth-wearing fighters, cracked his neck as he surveyed the deck through his visor slit.

"Search below deck. I'll make my way toward their captain. I believe I saw him on the steering deck," Frond instructed.

"As you say, Seeker," Ambrose said, breaking off toward a stairway leading down into the ship.

"And where do you lot think you're going?" Someone called out, grabbing both Ambrose and Frond's attention.

The Bluecoats faltered. Frond lowered his shield and holstered his sword.

"They have Captain Avery!" Ambrose shouted, stepping towards the two pirates and their captive. Frond stopped him.

Osiris stood, a pistol pressed to the side of Avery's head, with Cage standing beside him, bloodied, bruised, and grinning.

"That we do. Old bastard put up quite the fight. Got the jump on Cage in his cabin," Osiris said.

Cage spat at the floorboards in front of Avery, who looked impassively at his men. The distinguished sailor's attire was ruffled and bloodied from the scuffle he'd had with the two pirates, and one of his eyes was swollen shut.

"I think this goes without saying, but if you take one more step towards us, I'm going to spray your captain's brains all over these floorboards. Though, considering how much blood's been shed already, I reckon it wouldn't make much difference," Osiris mused.

The deck was covered in several dozen bodies, now. It was going to be hell to clean this all up.

If we make it to the sunrise, that is.

"And we wouldn't want that, now, would we?" Morgan said as he came to the railing of the steering deck. By now, the fighting had died down as everyone realized that the pirates had captured the captain of Black Bess. Morgan pointed at Cutter and his entourage, who escorted Tora and Cambridge. Cutter nodded to his captain and then had Tora and Cambridge lined up next to Avery.

"Delivered as promised, sir."

The sun had set.

"Excellent, Mr. Cutter. Now." Morgan turned and looked at Ephala, who strained her bonds. "You came here looking for the Eye of Atla? It isn't here. We had it until a series of unfortunate events saw it taken from us."

"Taken?" Ephala looked at Morgan, straining from her magickal bonds. "Taken by whom?"

"By *him…*" Abbal said with a tremble. "We are too late."

Morgan looked over the side of the ship to see the moon rapidly cresting on the eastern horizon. It was blood red, and with it came a wall of fog. It was a thick, reddish haze. To Morgan's eyes, it looked as though the moon was weeping, and the fog was leaking out from under it like a mist of tears.

"No…"

"Cap'n? What is it?" Osiris called out, still pressing a pistol to Avery's head.

"Let him go…" Morgan said in a low voice.

"Cap'n?" Osiris asked, uncertain as to what he'd heard.

"Let them go! The Seekers, the officers—let them go! He's here! Stars above, he's here!" Morgan shouted.

Osiris, confused, lowered the barrel from Avery's head, who looked at him just as confused. The captain stood and rubbed his head, looking at his men. They were waiting for his signal. Cage walked to the eastern side of the ship and gazed at the horizon. Osiris looked at Morgan, who was staring, transfixed, to the east. He saw Reece Stone come up from the deck below, dragon guns in his hands, looking just as befuddled as him. The two walked over next to Cage and looked at the horizon. A dark shape sat on the horizon. A ship. As it silently drew near, the shadow of four more ships appeared, flanking the first.

"This is bad, mon. Real bad…"

That voice in his head said, sounding genuinely worried.

Worried about what?

The voice didn't answer.

Seeker Frond sidled next to him, and Osiris rested his hand on his sword, fighting the urge to attack the armored knight.

"Something wicked has come…" Frond said, echoing his own words.

"What is it, Frond?" Tora called out, having been begrudgingly released by Cutter, who still aimed guns at her and Cambridge.

"A dark energy unlike anything I've ever felt before. It has come for us. It has been waiting…" Frond said.

"Fuck is he on about, cap'n?" Cutter asked.

"You were right, Abbal. Starsdamn you…you were right," Morgan cursed. "Azura! Get to your battle stations! This fight has only just begun! Seekers, Bluecoats, I'd recommend you get your asses back on your ship and get ready for the fight of a lifetime. You want the Eye of Atla? It's aboard that flagship on the horizon. And hell is coming with it."

The mariners, having just been engaged in a bloody battle for their lives, looked at Captain Avery and Ephala for guidance. Huasca carefully set Ephala on the main deck and released his hold on her.

"Those ships…what are they?" Ephala asked.

"They're the fleet of the Damned. And they're coming to wipe us out," Morgan said. "At their helm is Felix Helregal, the Dread Captain. I believe he's coming for me," he said. "You can stay and fight us. We'll be forced to fight back, of course. If we're lucky, we might kill each other in the few minutes we have before they're upon us. If we're not, they'll descend upon us in the heat of the battle and pick at us like vultures over a carcass."

Ephala looked again at the horizon; she could feel that evil coming, too. Something far worse than these cutthroat, thieving, murderous pirates. "Frond? What say you?"

Frond was lost for a moment. The vision of the battle beneath the moonlight returned. He was certain, now, that the battle in his vision was about to begin, here. He looked directly at her. "The evil has come. We can kill the pirates after."

"To Sheolhenna with that! These murderous bastards have killed scores of our men already!" Ambrose Castell shouted, then looked at Captain Avery. "They killed Jukel. That filthy Valkar over there beheaded him!"

Avery had seen Jukel's head when he was dragged across the deck by his two captors and an entourage of their brethren. The look of shock on Jukel Staunton's face was inked into the back of his eyelids. "I know. And they will pay in due time. For now? All hands to their stations. It would seem we have a new threat to contend with."

Ambrose growled, "Seeker Lady, please! These pirates are our enemies! The crown demands that we kill them!"

Ephala looked at Avery and nodded. "And we will, Lieutenant Commander. As soon as we deal with this new threat, we will exact his wrath upon them."

Just then, Flint stepped forth from the crowd and stood in front of Avery and Ephala, looking up at Morgan above them. "They killed Ryker 'n Sarkad, cap'n…" He kept his voice even. "We gonna let 'em go after that?"

Morgan broke his gaze from the ships and looked at Flint. "We will avenge our fallen brothers—all of them—when we survive the night."

If we survive the night.

Morgan thought.

Flint looked all around him at the Bluecoats, still standing about, talking amongst themselves, processing what was happening. "Get off our fucking ship, or I swear, Aeradin and Goffanyn as my witnesses, that I will put a bullet in each and every one of you…"

Ambrose sneered and again looked at Avery. "Sir…please…"

"That's an order! Get to your battle stations, now!" Avery shouted, finding his voice. He marched toward them.

"Seekers! Back to the Black Bess!" Ephala instructed, following suit.

The pirates stared, partially in disbelief, but mostly with naked hatred for their retreating enemies.

"Good riddance!" One shouted.

"We'll deal with you lot later!" Another promised.

"Should've gutted 'em and tossed 'em into the sea," one of them muttered.

Ambrose Castell walked toward the gangplank after most his men had departed. He paused, his foot on the edge of the gangplank, and looked severely at Steven Cage. "Pray that whatever happens tonight, Valkar, I don't survive it. Because I'll be coming back for you. The Black Bess needs her hull scrubbed. And I plan to use you as the sponge…"

Cage chuckled. "I have fought monsters, demons, and champions of the Dark Goddesses. You, little man? You are not even a roach to crush under my boot."

*****

The fog came before the ships did.

This made their silent approach all the more unnerving. They didn't make noise, they didn't change flags, or even try to hide their identity. They approached like a shiver of sharks, prowling the sea at the scent of spilled blood. The Azurans didn't even have time to mourn their dead. The crew busied themselves tossing corpses overboard and preparing for battle, while the remaining officers convened in Morgan's study.

"You can bury your demons, Morgan Sarron, but you can never kill them. A shadow will always follow you, and the past will find its way back to you. As sure as the sun rises in the east and sets in the west…"

Ardvald's words echoed in Morgan's mind, again and again. Like the tolling of church bells. Now, on the eve of his reckoning, he thought back on the part he'd played in bringing them to this moment. Killing Felix, all those years ago. Sailing the seas, pirating, and amassing wealth, cultivating a brotherhood of pirates the likes of which the world had never seen. He wondered if he would ever see his beloved Storm Tide again.

"Cap'n, ye can't really mean that the Damned are here?" Cutter spoke up. "They're just a…a bloody legend!"

Morgan looked across his desk at him. "And so am I, to those who've never seen me in the flesh. Yet here I am. Do not believe in fairytales and allegories. Not in this world. Because nightmares are real, the fairytales are history lessons, and what's dead doesn't always stay buried."

The officers looked at one another, concerned. None of them had ever faced such monsters before, save for Huasca, who stood impassively next to Morgan.

"If the undead come, then it is my duty as a disciple of Bawon Samedi to rid this world of them," he said plainly.

Stone chimed in, "Mr. Huasca, surely you can't believe that—"

"That shapeshifter that stalked our ship was not a living being. I could sense the Alyria of death. The Valkar, Ardvald the Mangler, said that a dark entity was coming for us. I believe that shapeshifter was sent by it to lure us here," Huasca theorized.

"Why? They've got the bloody eye, isn't that what they wanted?" Cutter spat.

"Nay…they want ye cap'n, don't they?" Stone said, recalling what Flint had told him of the Mangler's interrogation.

All eyes were on Morgan.

"A bad moon rising', that's what you called it, right?" Osiris asked. "Is this what ye were talking about? Did you know that the Dread Captain was coming for us all along?!"

Morgan shook his head. "I didn't, Siris. You asked me then what we had brought aboard our ship. I suppose now, I should be frank with you all about it."

"Ah, the liar speaks truth at last…" Abbal said.

"You're not off the hook either, spirit, or amulet, or whatever the fuck you are!" Cutter said, not forgetting his argument with Abbal for an instant. "We lost good men and I know for damn sure you played a part in it!"

"Volld Cutter, for years I have watched you and your kind aboard this ship, providing council to your captain in secret. Though you are a deplorable dreg of your species' existence, I hold no ill will toward you, as even a cockroach has its purpose in the wheel of fate," Abbal dismissed.

Cutter blinked. "…Did you just call me a cockroach?"

"Shut up, Cutter. Cap'n, I think it's time ye explained to us all what in Sheolhenna is happenin', before we're all too dead to listen," Stone said, folding his arms.

Steven Cage sat down in a chair nearby, looking out a window in the direction of the approaching ships. "We do not have long…"

*****

"A century gone, now. I was a young pirate, plying my trade in the Amaranthine. Those were treacherous times. Piracy ran rampant and unchecked for generations as the kingdoms of men warred with one another, with demons, the undead, and all manner of other calamities. Most kingdoms, save for Sarx and Borra, didn't even have their own navy to speak of. So, a pirate could rob from the east to the west without fear of anyone or anything but their fellow pirate.

"But that all changed when the continental navy came about. Lordalus, Sarx, Brova, Borra, Atarra, and even Kurza, came together to try and put an end to the pirate raids across the coastline, and the Valkar raids bleeding out of Borra, to the north. Suddenly, we found ourselves hunted. So, we were forced to unite. In so doing, we consorted with merfolk to seize the power of the Eye of Atla, a relic of great power, said to allow a man to see into the eyes of others, hoping that we could use it to undo our enemies. It worked spectacularly, and we brought the navy to its end. But it cost us dearly.

"As I said before, I was there when the Eye was lost to the sea. I lost a good friend of mine, Thunderbolt Colt, in the process. He used the Eye's power to predict and lure the bulk of the continental navy's main fleet into a head-on battle. It cost him his crew, his life, and the Eye of Atla, which disappeared back into the sea. I had thought it gone, then."

"What about the Dread Captain? Is it true that you slew him at Emperor's Rest?" Osiris asked.

Morgan sighed like an old man with the weight of the world on his shoulders. "Felix Helregal…we don't have much time, so I'll spare you the details. All you need to know is that he's real. And if he has returned, the *world* is in grave danger. The Damned will be with him. This is going to be the fight of our lives, gentlemen. I don't know how or why he's here, but I doubt it's pure coincidence that it happened shortly after we retrieved the Eye."

"Varryn Kurza said that Idallon spoke to him, telling him that he must retrieve the artifact. I cannot help but ponder why the Star God of Hope and Rebirth would choose such a path…" Abbal said.

"And then there's *you*," Cutter said.

Osiris silenced him with a hand. "How much do you know, truly? What is your part in all this? No lies. No vague statements. Truth."

The amulet blinked slowly before responding. "I was sent here, many, many years ago, to safeguard the life of Morgan Sarron. I was told that he had a part to play in the coming war. I was not told, however, what part he would play. Savior or destroyer? I know not. All I can do is offer counsel and play upon his better demons."

"Did you know that the Eye of Atla would bring back the Dread Captain?" Osiris probed.

"…I did not know that the Eye would be the vector of his return, or at least it appears to be. But I warned your captain decades ago that he would return, one day."

Stone spoke up, now, "Ye said before that we was destined to be here? What crock of shite was that from?"

"All of you have travelled many years, whether you realized it or not, to come to this moment. You have each survived death many times. You were *destined* to be here, through some act of fate."

"Do ye know that for true?" Stone asked.

"Nothing is certain; everything is fluid. But I find it hard to believe that you survived this long in such a dangerous business as piracy without a purpose. Better men than you have tried and died long before they made it this far. Morgan would know. He watched them," Abbal said.

Morgan had a distant look in his eyes.

"If that shapeshifter is aboard the Dread Captain's ship, then I'm going for her. Hanover may still be alive," Osiris said.

"Yer chasin' a corpse, boy," Stone warned.

"I'm chasing my brother in black. What about you?" Osiris shot back.

Steven Cage stood up, hands on his weapons. "We are out of time. They're here."

The pirates stood and looked at one another one last time. There were so few of them, now.

Morgan looked out the windows behind his desk to see the shadow of a ship blocking the moonlight. "Before you go…I have a plan."

LVI

The Shadow Has Come

"Well, well, well. What have we here? A yellow-bellied, craven, traitorous serpent that calls himself a captain. Morgan, old friend. It's been too long…" Helregal said, looking down at the pirates of Azura below him.

"Is that you, Abbal? Are you still holding out hope for this one?" Caine called out.

"Until his part is played, I will remain. That is all I have to say to you, demonick," Abbal said promptly.

"Felix. And here I'd thought you'd stay dead for good after you ruined my life and I took yours," Morgan said with a tired expression. "Shall I send you back home? The Dark Depths must miss you."

Helregal laughed mirthlessly. "Back? To the Depths? After I just clawed my way out of that abyss of drowning corpses and gnashing teeth? I'll sooner chuck myself into the fires of Sheolhenna itself before I set foot back in that darkness. No, old friend. I won't be going back again, but I will be sending you and your crew down in my stead. The Dead Sea Gods have been restless of late. I think your aged bones might be just the bit to satiate them a while longer."

"Send me into the Depths, will you? The last time we met, you had a crown on your head and an army of Damned behind you. Now you've got a mask and a few guns to point with. You've been off the account for a long time, Felix. I'm no longer the young man you fought an age ago."

Helregal leaned over the railing a bit, looking at him. "No, no you aren't, are you? You look like a hard cough might knock you down for good. Yee gads, Morgan, you've really aged like a raisin in the sun."

Helregal laughed at his own joke.

"Well, no matter. My new friends and my budding fleet are going to set you straight and stitch a smile on that dour face of yours before we send you on down."

As if on cue, several thin figures approached from behind Helregal and stood, overlooking Morgan and his crew. They were silent, and in the moonlight, they glittered like gemstones. And as Morgan watched, golden chains snaked out from Anathane's Pain and began wrapping around the timbers of Azura, locking them in place.

"Kill them."

The figures howled and descended upon them.

*****

"They're gaining on us. We won't have enough time to spin for a broadside!" Ambrose Castell shouted up at the steering deck as Captain Avery manned the wheel.

"Then prepare to fire on them as they close. If they try to board, we'll cut them down!" Avery commanded.

"The remaining cannons are ready, sir. Of the sixty-five we had, half are still operational," Ensign Golde called up from the stairs to the gun deck.

"Good. Between gunfire and cannon fire, we should have more than enough fire power to—" Avery went quiet.

A lone figure climbed over the side of the ship and looked at him. They were black as midnight, but their eyes shone like polished silver.

"Who goes there?!" Avery called out, pointing at the figure.

Ambrose turned and looked at the figure, who was only a few yards away from him and froze. He was close enough to make out the thing's face.

"Stars, give me strength…"

Its eyes were orbs of silver, devoid of pupils or irises. It pulled back the thin sheet of skin that served as its lips and bared its teeth, equally silver. Its body was draped in what once was probably an officer's clothes of some sort, now torn open and soaked from the sea, revealing gemstones growing out of the skin beneath. It was gaunt as a corpse, as well, and had thin, wispy strands of hair. It mumbled something in a guttural language he couldn't understand, then charged at him.

Ambrose pulled out his officer's pistol and fired at the thing, hitting it straight in the head. The bullet bounced off a gemstone crusted into its dome. It bit down on his forearm, and he cried out in pain as men swarmed him to get the creature off him. He pulled out his knife and drove it into the thing's throat.

It ignored the blow, simply gurgling and biting down harder into his forearm. "Get this damn thing off me!"

Several men grabbed hold of it and started yanking it away, but it held firm and he cursed from the pain as he felt it tearing off part of his arm. Thinking fast, Ambrose began sawing the Damned's head off with his knife. The thin flesh gave like jerky, but he frantically cut it before getting to the spine. Another man, realizing what he was doing, broke through the neckbone with his own knife, and the creature's body fell away, leaving the head chewing on Ambrose's forearm.

"Fucking hell—it's still biting!" Ambrose shouted.

He dug his fingers into the eye sockets and ripped it off his arm. It clicked its teeth together, turned red with his blood. He tossed it to the floorboards. Avery came down and inspected his arm in disbelief of what he'd just seen.

"That creature…it's an undead…" Avery gasped, making a nine-pointed star pattern on his chest.

"Unholy spawn! Smite it!" A mariner shouted, kicking the head across the deck.

As it rolled, several more Damned climbed over the side of the ship, bearing their weapons and roaring.

"There's more! Look out!" Ambrose warned.

It was too late, however, as the savage monsters attacked immediately.

"We're under attack! Sound the alarm!" Avery ordered.

The mariner who just moments before saved Ambrose Castell, ran and rang the alarm bell before being set upon by one of the attackers. His screams were muted by the bell's ring.

*****

"How are you feeling?" Ephala asked Clive, who was standing and stretching.

"Considering my armor's been compromised and that damned pirate with the glowing eyes nearly killed me? I feel fit as a fiddle. How did the battle go? Did we take him captive? I'd like to put hands on him," Clive asked nonchalantly.

"…The battle with the pirates has ceased at present," Tora answered, seeing Ephala's distress.

"Ceased? What do you mean 'ceased'?"

"We're facing a new threat," Ephala explained pointing out the windows at the back of the cabin. Outside, four ships approached Black Bess, and they were closing in.

"More pirates? Pfft, they brought friends, then? We'll cut them down as well," Clive shrugged, grabbing his great sword.

"Those aren't pirates. Or, at least they aren't any I've ever heard of," Sedrick noted. His head had fully healed, though he was groggy and light-headed. "They're all flying multiple flags." He pointed toward a close one. "That one there? It's flying El'wa Imperium Naval colors. The one to the east, over there, is flying the flag of Duwa merchant company, I do believe. Even the builds of the ships are different. They clearly aren't human."

The others approached and saw that he was correct.

"I've never known pirates to keep the colors of the ships they capture," Tora said.

"Neither have I…" Ephala confirmed.

"They aren't navy or merchants, any longer," Frond stated.

They all turned to face him, perplexed.

"Those ships are flying the banner of the screaming skull, The Dread Captain's colors," Frond recited from memory. He remembered the story of Felix Helregal well from his historical studies at the Spire. "He's turned them into his thralls."

"Thralls? Like a lich?" Ephala asked in a hushed voice.

"Yes," Frond answered. "And they're coming for us."

A racket outside the cabin drew their attention. Someone was rapidly beating on the door on the other side. They let out a scream before there was a slam against the door, and then a dragging sound.

"Correction: they're already here," Sedrick said as he cocked his rifle. "It's time for round two."

*****

They were walking, armored corpses, and they could regenerate everything but their head.

It cost them a dozen men before they realized that.

Osiris watched one of the Damned run into a crowd of scared men and tear into four of them before they managed to subdue it. It was only after Steven

Cage brought his mace down on its head that it stopped growing back golden limbs and stayed down for good.

"Destroy their heads!" Cage shouted as he brought his mace down on another Damned's kneecap. The undead buckled at the knee, and he partially severed its neck with an ugly slash of his sword.

"Watch out!" Osiris shouted, coming to Cage's aid as two more of the Damned approached from behind him in a sneak attack. In an instant, Alyria surged through him and he was upon the skulking zombies. He swung his swords in twin arcs away from his body and slashed the backs of the two Damned. They stumbled, and Cage turned to face them.

Osiris finished them quickly, digging his sword into the mouth of one and plunging it through the back of its head. The other lunged at him, and he swung his other sword, cutting its throat wide open and causing it to stumble around, grabbing for its head. He stood in horror, watching the Damned stomp around, gurgling and spurting gold-colored blood as it attempted to fix its head. He kicked it over the side of the ship.

"These creatures are terrorizing us," Cage observed.

"Aye. If this keeps up, the Bluecoats will be sifting through our corpses before the night's out," Osiris admitted.

"The Bluecoats? Ha! They're being attacked just as we are! If they could barely handle a few hundred pirates on a lone ship, I doubt they'll be able to deal with the Damned!"

Osiris looked over toward the direction of the Black Bess. It was nearly consumed by the fog, but he made out its shape, flanked by several other ships.

They're doomed.

He realized. There was no chance of them escaping these 'Damned' if they were attacking them in numbers like this.

"Damned or no, I'm going to board that ship," Osiris said.

"For what? Plan or not, Stone is right—he's dead, boy, you have to know that by now," Cage argued.

"Dead or not, I won't give up till his body is in my hands. He'd do the same for me, the plucky bastard."

Osiris gave him no time to answer as he charged toward the ship. There were several gangplanks laid down for their attackers to pour from, and he made his way toward one.

Cage watched him go and shook his head. "Ye going to let your brother die, then?" Stone asked, coming up behind him.

Cage looked at him and muttered something in Borran. Stone started toward Osiris. "Well, come on then."

*****

Ambrose Castell stood shoulder to shoulder with his men as they squared off against their attackers. The four ships had closed ranks with them, and the inhuman attackers leaped between the ships, unconcerned for their own safety.

"Stand strong, men! Pirates, undead, or whatever the hell these things are, it makes no difference! We are the empire's strongest and fiercest fighters! We will prevail!" he shouted as he led the charge.

The Damned cared not and met them with a ravenous zeal. Ambrose watched in horror as his men were broken by the undead monsters. He watched a sailor clash blades with one, only for it to lung forward as his blade dug into it and tear out his throat. He watched a woman get skewered in three different directions by the savage creatures. He locked eyes with her before she was savaged.

"Commander! Behind you!" Another woman shouted.

He spun around, and a Damned covered in rubies and emeralds tackled him and attempted to bite down into his throat. He struggled with it, attempting to push it away as it locked its fists around his arms and bore down, mouth agape. "Get off me, you freak!" he growled. His opponent was implacable. No matter how hard he shoved, it came bearing down on him, inch by inch. He thought of his wife and daughter back home. Would they even see his body? Would they ever know his fate?

"No!" Castell grunted, pushing with all his might.

"Get off 'em!" The woman ordered.

The Damned looked up and locked eyes with her. It hissed just as a gunshot blew half its face off. The creature released its hold on him, and he threw it off. Castell stumbled to his feet and looked at his savior.

Before him was a young officer woman with bandages over her nose bridge, wrapping around her head. He remembered her. She was one of the ones Clive injured sparring. "My thanks, mariner. What is your name?"

"Sergeant Hilda Swanson, at your command. Think nothing of it, sir!" she replied, saluting him before reloading her rifle. "We've got more coming!"

Ambrose turned to see a half dozen Damned approaching, having just finished off a squad of his men. Ambrose pulled out his sword, adrenaline pumping in his veins. "Come at us, hellspawn! We'll take all comers!"

Just then, a blast of blue light turned the six monsters into blue-tinged smoke and ashes. Ambrose looked at the pile of ashes, then at Hilda. They looked at each other in bewilderment before looking behind them to see Ephala standing with a palm glowing, and the other four Seekers flanking her.

"Stand back, Lieutenant Commander. We'll handle them," Ephala promised.

The two mariners moved to the side as the five Seekers stepped forward into the fray. Already the enemy had taken notice, and over a dozen more Damned began charging at them.

This time, Tora stepped forward. She ran at the horde, then fell onto all-fours as she morphed into a hulking, roaring dire bear. Ambrose grabbed the star rosary around his neck and kissed it as he watched the spectacle unfold.

Tora tore into the horde immediately. She slammed into them, knocking them out of the way before grabbing one in her jaws and savaging it until its limbs began to tear off. Another stabbed at her with a sword and she grunted. It's blow bounced off the barrier surrounding her. She spun around and swiped the thing's head clean off its shoulders. Four more leaped on her back, and she shook them loose before crushing two of them and seizing the head of one in her jaws. She chewed on it until its bejeweled skull cracked—then popped under pressure. It sprayed golden blood all over, and she spat it out. The last Damned charged at her recklessly, and she spun around and kicked it with her back legs. The thing became a blur as it was launched across the deck and crashed into a feeding horde of its kin, drawing their attention.

The Damned howled at Tora, and she roared back at them. Before she could rush them, however, Clive charged into them. His sword glowed blue as a full moon, and he cleaved into them, hacking limb from limb as the undead attempted to fight back. Their attacks were useless as his Alyria barrier blocked all their attacks, and he stood triumphant over their mangled corpses, but retched in disgust when he saw what they'd been feeding on.

"They're eating our men!" Clive reported.

The Seekers and the two mariners looked around in horror at the realization. Strewn across the deck, the Damned were downing the mariners and feeding upon them. Their screams permeated the air; they were being eaten alive.

"Destroy them! Destroy them all!" Ephala shouted at the top of her lungs.

They watched in horror as the mangled corpses of the Damned that still had their heads began to leak viscous gold that formed into new, shining limbs, and they rose again.

Tilda aimed her rifle at one of them and fired between its eyes, blowing out the back of its head. The creature fell, and its golden limbs disintegrated to liquid. "Their heads! Shoot their heads!"

"They can't reanimate if there's nothing left to regenerate." Sedrick aimed his rifle, and the barrel hummed with energy as the runes along its length lit up and he channeled his energy into them. He fired, shooting projectiles that detonated as soon as they struck. He blew up several packs of the Damned in rapid succession before reloading bullets into the chamber. Frond ran into the smoke left behind, charging further into the deck skirmish as Ephala and the others contended with the Damned already clambering up the sides of the ship to attack them.

"Tora! Cover Frond!" she shouted.

"On it!" Tora grunted. Her voice was a deep grumble in her chest in her new form. She galloped after him.

"We'll aid them," Ambrose said.

Ephala nodded. Ambrose Castell and Hilda Swanson went after Tora and Frond.

*****

Frond tore through the Damned on a warpath. His vision flashed, making it hard for him to separate what was real from what was imagined. Still, he fought. He cleaved heads from shoulders and arms from torsos. He sent his shield spinning through the horde, ricocheting between targets with enough force to crack their gem-covered bodies and leave them broken on the ground, twitching.

"Show yourself!" he demanded, standing amid the horde, bodies mounted at his feet. Around him were the screams and booms of battle, but all he could hear was the echo of the shadow's roar. His hair stood on end as he turned to face it, blade raised, but paused as he saw the ursine Tora trotting toward him.

"What is it, Frond?" Tora asked.

Frond looked around to and fro, but saw naught but the mariners and Damned, going at one another in pitched battle. What was this oppressive energy he felt in his bones?

"I can't see it, where is—" he looked at Tora again. "Behind you!" he sprinted toward her, reaching out.

"What? Where—"

A shadow fell over her, and her nose burned with the stench of death, and…fear…she could smell the pheromones leaking out her own body. She turned slowly and saw piercing yellow eyes glaring down at her, and the outline of an unnaturally pale figure.

"Fall to your knees and pray…" A voice like an earthquake said.

It took all her strength not to do just as it said. Even in her bear form, the figure towered over her, easily ten-plus feet tall. The figure was wide, and even its profile belied its immense strength. It stood there, arms at its sides, looming over her. She felt Frond grab her by her scruff and yank her back.

"Do not touch her, demon. I am your opponent," Frond declared. Though he stood taller than most men, in the shadow of this dark entity, he was dwarfed like a child.

The figure raised its head, and the blood moonlight reflected off it, revealing the side of a monstrous face. Its jaws were too wide and large for any man. It had long, sharp fangs, and its thin, blackened lips were pulled back in a grin of pure malice. It had a black skull tattooed across its face.

"Who are you?" Frond asked.

"I? I go by many names. But the one placed upon me now is 'Black'. Officer Black. And I am your executioner."

LVII

Enter, the Beast

"This way!" Osiris shouted as they stormed down the corridor, as soon as he rounded the corner, he met face-to-face with a Damned officer, who immediately lunged at him. The undead slammed him against a wall and went for his neck. In an instant, Osiris threw the creature off, slamming it into the opposite wall and bringing his spadroon down on its head, splitting it in two with a loud crack and tearing sound.

He ripped the blade free and was sprayed with a fresh gout of golden blood. He marched on unperturbed, he could *feel* that Hanover was close.

Or is it the shapeshifter I'm sensing?

He wasn't sure, and the voice in the back of his head wasn't telling him, either.

Stone and Cage followed immediately after him and marveled at the Damned he left crumpled on the floor.

"How'd ye manage to overpower it so damn fast? Ye finally get control of them powers 'o yours?" Stone asked.

Osiris shrugged, still following the trail. "Dunno. But I'll need all of it if we're to fight these fuckers off."

Cage watched the corner behind them and saw shadows on the wall, projected by a lantern at the end of the corridor. "We're being followed."

"Nay, we're bein' hemmed in," Stone said, already knowing what was to come. He'd reloaded both his dragon guns. He only hoped they were enough to make a difference.

Osiris stopped in front of a door.

"This is it," the voice said.

"Hanover, or the shapeshifter?"

Silence.

"Over here!" he said aloud.

He cracked open the door to see a small compartment, he scanned it over, his eyes well adapted to the low light. They fell on a figure, slumped against a wall in the far corner. Armen Hanover.

"He's here!" Osiris called out, crossing the room to shake Armen Hanover awake. "Armen! Armen can ye hear me, brother?!"

Armen Hanover was slow to come to. "…What…where…where am I?" his eyes focused on Osiris'.

"You're aboard Anathane's Pain, the Dread Captain's flagship," Osiris explained as he lifted Hanover to his feet.

"Dread Captain…like…from the stories?" Hanover asked dreamily as he stumbled forward a few steps, still finding his legs.

"Trust me, mate. This shit ain't no story," Osiris said.

"Siris…" Stone said in a low voice, looking up at the ceiling.

Cage was standing next to him, crouched down, weapons out. His eyes were wide and alarmed.

Osiris felt the hairs on the back of his neck raise. He slowly lifted his head up to see several pairs of red eyes gazing at him from the ceiling. As his eyes adjusted to what he was looking at, he ran for the door, pulling the groggy Hanover along with him. "Time to go!"

The thing dropped down from the ceiling and skittered after them. Stone slammed the door shut on it and the four pirates sprinted down the hallway.

"What is it? What are we running from?" Hanover asked.

"Something big and ugly," Osiris explained briefly. "And it don't look too friendly, neither."

*****

Stone was right about the ambush. They'd been waiting for them just around the corner. The four were so scared, however, that they pushed clean past the Damned and kept a breakneck pace toward the main deck, climbing the stairs like a demon was at their heels. They could hear the thing chasing them crash into the Damned, and the creatures made startled, guttural noises as whatever it was barreled past them.

"Keep moving! We need to get back to the Azura!" Stone shouted, leading the charge.

"We have more company!" Cage reported, seeing the Damned still aboard the Pain close off their escape route.

"She's still gaining on us!" Osiris said from the back. In the blood moonlight, he could see what it was that was chasing them properly. He wished he hadn't.

"Leaving so soon (soon)?" The creature said in a chittering, raspy voice that doubled over with a deep, demonic one. It resembled a spider, and perhaps in some realm of Sheolhenna, it would pass for one. But its eyes were too expressive and malicious to be those of any dumb animal.

Osiris, realizing that they were cornered, bore his spadroons. If he had to choose his opponent, he didn't want to turn his back on this hideous monstrosity.

The creature's mandibles clacked together, and its eyes locked with his. "They call you Osiris, yes (Osiris)? You tried to kill me. I shall return the favor two-fold."

The fact that it spoke made it all the more vile in his eyes. "They do. But I don't think you'll be the one doing the killing, tonight. Nay, I think I'm goin' to rid this world of you, once and for all, freak."

The creature metamorphosed back into the shape of a tall woman wrapped in bandages with gold armor. In her hands were two claw-like weapons, with long, bladed, hooked fingers. "Then let us dance, mortal (dance). I will make you sing me a symphony of agony, tonight (scream for me)."

As if on cue, the Damned closed in, and Stone emptied both his dragon guns, cutting a flaming swathe through them. Cage grabbed the still dazed Hanover by the arm and dragged him toward the gangplank. "Go, now, boy! Go find Huasca and the others!"

"But what of you?!" Hanover pleaded. "I'll fight with you!"

"Fight with us, boy? These things will *kill* you!" Stone said, pointing at Azura. "They're already killing us!"

Hanover watched as one of the men he'd been drinking with was cut down by one of the strange, gem-covered zombies. The man was still screaming when it started eating him. He couldn't believe what hell he'd awoken to. "Stars…"

"Find Huasca! He'll protect you! Leave the freak to us!" Osiris called over his shoulder, giving Hanover a sidelong gaze. "We'll talk soon, brother."

Hanover nodded. "Aye, sir," and took off down the gangplank.

Stone and Cage turned to face the enemy, and Cage charged with reckless abandon into their ranks. "Draugr, undead, Damned? Whatever they call you, I will put you to rest forever! And Irkalla will devour your souls!" Cage cackled as he jousted with two of the savage beasts.

Stone reloaded his dragons as the monsters were preoccupied with Cage, then he whistled to draw some of their attention. "I got some heat for ye. We'll see which burns hotter. Hell, or my dragon's breath? You let me know when I get down there." He raised the guns at the approaching enemy and pulled both triggers.

BOOM!

The dragon guns roared explosively and sprayed flames and metal on the Damned, shredding them to bits and scorching the pieces. He holstered the guns, then pulled out a sword.

Behind them, Osiris and Volldah faced off. One set on avenging his fallen comrades, and the other hellbent on tearing out his shining eyes…and devouring them.

*****

She moved like a dancer, pirouetting and spinning. Her blows came in wild, unpredictable jabs and swipes. He couldn't block them, for fear of being rent by her claws. One of the Damned attempted to interfere with their duel, and it was cut in two by a single swipe. He narrowly dodged the same fate and found himself taking cover to escape her attacks.

How do I fight her? She's more flexible than any man and she can attack from any angle.

"Use your power," the voice instructed.

"I don't know how!" he responded.

"Yes, you do. This monster killed your friends. It is up to you to avenge them. Fight like you want to live!" The voice commanded.

He dodged out of the way just in time to avoid being grabbed from behind. She dug deep tracks into the wood of the mast where he'd just been standing, then lurched forward.

"They begged, as you will (begged)!" Volldah hissed. "They begged for the pain to stop (cried)!"

Osiris faltered; she noticed.

"Did I strike a nerve, mortal (weakling)?"

He felt his blood run hot.

"Does it hurt, knowing that they died alone (alone)?"

"Stop it…" Osiris warned her. He was panting, now.

"That they died, begging for mercy?"

"I said stop it!" Osiris growled under his breath. The glow in his eyes intensified.

"Frederick Moary begged for his mother when I tore out his eyes (help me)—does that make you angry, boy?!" Volldah taunted, her voice changing with each word. "Mother! Mother, please! It—it—it hurts! I can't see and it *hurts!*"

She mimicked Moary's voice.

"Fire and glory, indeed. He died like a stray dog."

His vision clouded with turquoise light.

"I said SHUT THE FUCK UP!" Osiris roared.

His voice doubled, one tone was his own, and the other was deeper and unfamiliar. His eyes glowed blindingly bright, and his tattoos twisted across his skin like living, pulsing, turquoise veins.

Their weapons crossed again, but this time, Volldah was the one being pushed back.

*****

Chains. Chains everywhere.

Hanover crept across the deck in utter shock of what had become of Azura. Thick gold chains wrapped around her masts and tangled her yardarms and ropes, binding her to Anathane's Pain. Smaller chains crept lazily across the deck of their own accord, wrapping around half-eaten corpses and dragging them toward the Pain, where they disappeared. Though the battle still raged across her decks, the pirates were losing, and the Damned were feeding.

He paused.

Barring his path to the steering deck and the officer's cabins were several Damned, feasting on corpses. The bloodied horrors were oblivious to his presence, wholly focused on gorging on entrails. He watched one lift its head up, a thick chunk of flesh and sinew dangling from its over-wide jaws. It looked around lazily, and he hid behind a crate to avoid its gaze. It dug back into its meal, and he peered around the side of the crate. He felt the urge to vomit.

"Isn't it beautiful?" A female voice whispered.

He hitched his breath and slowly turned his head to see a woman in a black robe crouched next to him, observing the feeding zombies.

"B…beautiful?" he responded incredulously. "This is the most horrible, awful thing I've ever seen…they…they're eating my friends and comrades…"

"Your *friends* and *comrades* would have become maggot food one day, anyway, inevitably. Or food the gulls," she said flippantly. "Now, they get to die in spectacular fashion. Eaten by my master's thralls. A true honor if I am so bold as to say."

"Your *master*?" Hanover said with venom.

"Get away from him, necromancer!" Huasca called from the other side of the feeding Damned.

They reacted immediately, bolting upright to confront him. Huasca waved a glowing hand and the creatures were ignited in turquoise flames, dancing around futilely, trying to extinguish themselves.

Byzarra stood casually and fixed him with a mock smile. "I would do him no harm. He still has the Eye on his person, after all."

Hanover tapped his pocket and recalled that he *did* still have the Eye. Why hadn't they taken it from him as soon as they captured him? He was unconscious; he couldn't have put up a fight if he wanted to.

"Good. Now come with me, child." Huasca extended a hand.

Hanover looked at Byzarra, half expecting her to grab him then and there, but she did not. He walked past her and the torched corpses toward Huasca, who placed a reassuring hand on his shoulder.

"Our business is not concluded, shaman. I have heard tell of your kind's Alyria. I would see it for myself. But the boy will only get in the way. So, I'll give you a moment to hide him," she said toyingly. "Don't worry, dear, I'll be along to collect you soon after I deal with the shaman."

Her voice was ice, and it made Hanover shudder.

"Go, child. Wait for us in the captain's quarters," Huasca said.

Hanover nodded and ascended the stairs. "Be careful, sir. There's something…off, about her."

"Oh, I know," Huasca said, his eyes flaring with turquoise light. He smiled. "It has been a long time since I fought one of your kind, necromancer. Let us see who is stronger: your corpses, or my spirits?"

Byzarra smiled wolfishly, and her eyes changed to a glowing electric green. As she raised her hand, she revealed the glowing green tattoos covering her arm. The charred corpses of the Damned and the half-eaten men stood up and faced him. Their eyes glowed green as well. She no longer needed her master's power to raise them.

"Bring me his head," she instructed.

The corpses, hissing and moaning, shambled toward him.

*****

Frond's world became a blur of pain and whooshing air as he was slammed across the deck of the Black Bess. Several mariners and Damned were in his path as he flew, and each got flattened by his flight. He coughed blood and stood up from a pile of wood splinters, which was all that remained of the stairway he'd crashed into.

"Tora!" Frond called out.

The metamorph was in a heated fight with the giant, who was weathering the swipes of her claws as though they were kitten scratches. Ambrose and Tilda approached, and the two froze as they tried to make sense of the monster before them.

"What…what is that?" Tilda gasped.

Ambrose cocked his pistol, uncertain as to what damage it would do to something that big. "A monster."

Black slammed Tora against a crate, then turned to face the two with a bloodthirsty grin. "Little humans, run and hide. Your weapons can do me no harm."

Just then, several rifle rounds bounced off his back, and Black turned to face the mariners who'd shot at him. He raised one of his axes and threw it at them, and it embedded itself into the chest of one unfortunate sailor. He ran with startling speed toward them, and Ambrose watched in horror as he savaged a dozen of his sailors in seconds. The beast was sprayed in their blood, and it mingled with his own black fluid coating his body in swirls. He ripped his axe out of the body of the remaining mariner. The man gurgled and gasped in pain, and Black silenced him with a claw-toed sabaton to the head, crushing it.

"It's…it's a demon, it has to be…it…" Tilda stuttered.

"Get away! Protect the captain and warn the others! We will fight this creature!" Frond ordered.

Ambrose nodded and grabbed Tilda by the shoulder, shaking her from her stupor. "Come. We've other fish to fry."

With the Lieutenant Commander and the sergeant gone, Frond could focus squarely on their enemy. He watched as Officer Black belted a command at the Damned in some strange, guttural tongue as they tried to close around Tora, the undead reacted immediately, and backed away from her, going back to attacking the other crewmen.

He can command them.

"Say goodnight, metamorph," Black said as he raised an axe high.

Frond threw his shield, and it knocked the axe from Black's hand. The behemoth turned to face him.

"Still standing? And here I thought your ribs would be broken. Intriguing…" Black said. He spoke much more intelligently than his bestial appearance would suggest.

"You underestimate us, creature. We are the Emperor's chosen," Frond said as the shield returned to him. He strode toward Black.

"Chosen? The only thing you have been chosen for is to be the first of my victims," Black said as he met Frond's stride.

Black swung an axe, and it slid across the side of Frond's shield, scraping sparks that danced on the dark wood of the deck. The behemoth was on the offensive, and Frond danced the razor's edge on defense, trying to avoid another blow like the one that sent him crashing into the stairs. This was the strongest and most agile (for his size) opponent Frond had ever faced, and the implacable knight was beginning to sweat from the pressure.

"I can fight like this all night, Seeker. I do not tire, and I will not relent, hahahahaha!" Black laughed. It shook Frond's bones.

Black feinted on a swing and Frond fell for it. He gasped as Black brought his other axe to bear and smashed him across the helmet with the flat of it. Frond stumbled and raised his shield to cover himself. Black shouldered into him, breaking his guard, and sending him sprawling onto the floor. Black moved in for the kill.

"Get away from him!" Tora roared as she leapt onto his back and bit down into his thick, muscular neck. She bit into him, tearing his throat open and peeling away thick, white hide and flesh. His wounds gushed thick black ichor, and Tora fought back the urge to vomit from the foul taste on her tongue and in her nostrils.

Black grunted and dropped his axes to get a better hold of her thick fur in her ursine form.

"Get off me, whelp!" Black gurgled as he spat blood and dug in his thick claws, then slammed her to the deck. He struck her with such force that it splintered the wood and burst her Alyria barrier.

He raised a claw and slashed at her indiscriminately, cutting her snout, chest, and neck. Tora roared at him in bestial rage and pain, and he raised his claw again to strike her. A blur of bright blue shot through his arm, and Black looked at it confusedly. "What—"

Another shot rang out, this time striking him in the side of the head and blowing it clean off. The beast fell off her as blood sprayed from his wounds.

"Take that, freak," Sedrick eulogized. He held his smoking rifle as Ephala and Clive raced past him to aid their wounded brethren.

"Ambrose told us a monster was attacking you, but I didn't expect *this*," Ephala said as she grabbed hold of Tora's bulk, and Clive aided her.

Tora transformed back into her human form and stood on her own. "I'm fine. Worry about Frond, he—"

"Will live," Frond interjected as he rose to his feet, and cracked his neck. His helmet was dented on one side, so he removed it to reveal his bloodied, bruised face. "We need to beat back these attackers."

"I believe that will be of no worry," Ephala said assuredly. As soon as she spoke, the cannons of the Black Bess discharged, shaking the ship and blocking out all other sound for several moments.

The Seekers marveled as the smoke cleared, revealing the devastation Black Bess wrought upon the ships that attacked them. Two ships had flanked them on either side, and both were heavily damaged by the broadside attacks.

The deck was silent, now.

"Reload for another broadside, now!" Captain Avery shouted from the steering deck, finally audible above the battlefield. The man had the steering wheel in a stranglehold and had gold blood on his coat. Several Damned corpses sat around him. Ambrose and Tilda still flanked him, panting from the fighting.

"Now we just have to clear the deck and—" Clive started, looked behind Frond and grabbed the hilt of his great sword. "Move!"

Frond dove away just in time to evade the axe blade cleaving the air where he stood. Officer Black stood there, panting. His face was intact once more, and red steam wept from his skin.

"Did you think me defeated so easily?" Black asked. "I have only just begun."

"Seekers! Kill the beast!" Ephala ordered.

Clive charged at Black, jumping over Frond, who was getting his footing. His great sword glowed with Alyria and cleaved straight into the goliath's neck and stuck there. Clive's eyes went wide as he tried to pry his blade free, and Black swung his axe at him, breaking through his barrier with a concussive blast and digging it into his shoulder in the same motion.

"GAH! He broke my barrier, he—" Clive gasped, and Black silenced him with a swing of his other axe, beheading him in a spray of blood.

"Clive! The bastard killed Clive!" Sedrick shouted at the top of his lungs. His sightline clear, he took aim and fired at Black over and over, emptying round after glowing round into the approaching monster.

"Keep fighting," Black said.

A round shot through his left pectoral.

"Keep struggling," he continued.

Another round punched through his stomach.

"I'll always," Black said.

Sedrick panicked and fired blindly, missing the looming terror several times in succession before another round shot him in his open mouth.

"Keep coming!" Black roared as blood dribbled down his lips, then charged.

Sedrick fired one last desperate round, then did a backward flip several meters into the air to put distance between them as Ephala leapt at Black's back and stabbed him in the back repeatedly.

"Die! Why won't you die?!" Ephala snarled.

Black grunted from the repeated blows. Ephala's blades burned his flesh and cooked it, causing his blood to sizzle out from the wounds. He threw an elbow back and struck her in the chest, knocking her away. "Noisome gnat."

Just then, Tora leapt at him, transformed back into her jaguar form. The large cat dug her claws into his throat and shredded it open again. The damage was visceral, ugly, and under ordinary circumstances, more than fatal. These were not ordinary circumstance.

Black gurgled from his torn throat and dropped an axe before grabbing the great cat by her throat, squeezing it closed. His burning yellow eyes bore into hers, peering into her core. She swung her paw and slashed one of them closed. "Struggle! Fight!" he challenged, then squeezed tighter.

Tora let out a strangled yowl, and she felt the pressure in her head build to the point she feared her eyes may burst from their sockets.

Can't breathe! Can't move! Going to die! Going to—

Frond brought his sword down Black's arm—and severed it. His blade burned with fiery blue Alyria. Then, he swung his shield at Black's head, striking it with a resounding CRACK!

Tora spilled onto the deck and scrambled to her four feet, before transforming back into a human. She fell over again, the breath barely squeezing through her lungs, and she crawled away from her would-be killer as Frond stood in front of him.

Black looked at the burnt stump where his forearm had been moments before and gritted his teeth. "You, little Seeker knight, are stronger than your kin."

He flexed his muscles, repeatedly, as though he was trying to force something out of the stump. Frond cocked his head to the side, confused.

What is he doing?

"I had thought your kind all weak and pathetic. Not worth my attention. You, however…"

The charred, blackened stump split open, and a gush of black blood surged out of it as a shape grew out of it.

No. That's not possible…

Frond raised his guard.

Again, the red steam wept from Black's body as he flexed the digits of his new arm, spawned from the amputation.

"I'm going to *savor* you…after I kill your friends."

He picked up the axe he'd dropped to strangle Tora, and swung the blade, testing it. "I am the reaper, and I have come to harvest."

LVIII

A FRANTIC FIGHT

Morgan narrowly dodged Helregal's sword swipe. The strange blade had an air about it that made Morgan's skin crawl.

"Keep dodging, old man. You'll tire, eventually," Helregal taunted.

"And when you do, your crew will be damned," Caine said darkly.

The revenant was commanding the fight, his strikes wild but calculated, keeping Morgan on his toes. As soon as Morgan went to strike, Helregal would dodge out of the way, forcing him to step into strike range to attack. They continued this deadly dance for several moments before Morgan managed to find an opening. He fired Bullet Rose, and the gun blasted a hole straight through Helregal's chest.

"Well, blow me down…" Helregal said, staring at the hole in his chest. His heart dangled by an artery, visible inside the gaping hole. It didn't beat.

"Back to the Depths with you," Morgan said, swinging his sword and digging it into Helregal's head.

The Dread Captain glared at him. His red eyes clashed with the gold of his mask. "Were it so easy…"

Morgan ripped Blade Rose from Helregal's head and watched him drop to the deck before he sheathed it and turned away, setting his sights on the battle on his ship.

Or bloodbath.

He stepped onto the stairs, then turned as he heard a slithering, rattling sound coming from behind him.

"I told you, old friend. It wouldn't be so easy…"

Morgan attempted to evade as several golden chains rushed toward him and wrapped around his body, dragging him back toward Helregal, who now stood unharmed.

*****

Huasca murmured an incantation and channeled it through his hands, sending several wispy, turquoise orbs at the burned undead shambling toward him. The orbs struck them, phasing into their bodies before blowing them up from the inside, spewing viscera all around. Byzarra stood and tapped her foot on the floorboards. Guts had gotten in her hair, and she wiped it away with a scowl. "Lovely. Just lovely."

"Your corpses are too weak. They can barely put one foot in front of the other," Huasca chided her. "Pitiful."

Byzarra's smirk faltered a moment. "Well, those weren't really meant to attack you."

Huasca looked around. The deck was shaking. Byzarra's smile widened, and he looked behind her to see something horrible striding toward them from the direction of Anathane's Pain. It stood tall above all the others. "What is *that?*"

"Something I've been working on. When Volldah returned and told me that a Xallan Shaman was among your crew, well, I decided it was time to test out my prototype. I do hope you enjoy my work," Byzarra said flippantly.

Huasca blinked, realizing immediately that the deck was too narrow and crowded for him to fight this creature and the necromancer at the same time.

I need to separate her from the corpses. She'll only use them to her advantage. But how?

"Bring them here," Bawon Samedi said. *"Show them what de Ghostlands have in store for them."*

Huasca began another incantation as the abomination came within a dozen feet of them. It was tall, comprised of pink, sickly-looking flesh, and muscle. It had no face, only a barren, grimacing skull with raw musculature attached to it. Its eyes were bloodshot and vacant.

"Flesh…" the thing grunted in a wet, raspy voice.

"Yes, my pet." Byzarra toyed. "Eat up!"

She pointed to Huasca, and the abomination growled as it strode toward him, one arm reaching out to grasp him. The other of its arms had a blade made of bones and ribs.

"Repulsive. I think we shall fight on my terms, however," Huasca said, opening up a portal on the deck floor. Ghostly hands reached out and grabbed the abomination and necromancer.

"What in the grave is—" Byzarra gasped before she was pulled under.

Huasca heard Morgan cry out from the steering deck. He turned and saw the captain bound in golden chains. He balled a fist and threw a ball of turquoise flame at the chains, melting them and freeing Morgan, who landed on his feet and turned, nodding to him.

Good luck, old friend.

Huasca nodded back and leapt into the portal.

*****

Volldah morphed into a large, black serpent and attempted to slither away from Osiris. He dug a sword into her tail and dragged her back toward him. The serpent let out a hiss of pain and transformed back into the woman once more. She couldn't believe that she was being beaten by a mortal. She had thought, in her ages of undeath, that she had overcome such frailties. But he did not fear her, and without fear, she couldn't utilize her full potential.

"It's too late to run, shapeshifter. Your days are done." Osiris stabbed at her repeatedly with his spadroons, skewering her repeatedly. "How does it feel? Are you afraid? Are you in pain?!"

Volldah swung a claw arm at him and was surprised to see him knock the blow away. He severed the arm. She couldn't help but laugh. "Afraid? I have seen horrors far worse than anything you could do to me, little human," she said through gritted teeth. "Do what you will."

"Oh, I will," Osiris said as he stood over her, having cut off a leg to stop her from fleeing. He panted, his eyes glowing and wild with a rage he had never felt before. "I'll make sure there's nothing left of you to even fit in a tinder box."

Just then, he felt something strike him in the back and send him tumbling to the floorboards. He scrambled and clawed as he watched the shapeshifter contort her body and crawl away with one leg and one arm.

"Get back here! I'm not done with you!" he growled in that two-tone voice as his head was slammed into the deck. He realized he was being mauled on by the Damned.

"They're on him!" he heard Stone shout.

Suddenly the Damned were thrown off him as Steven Cage and Stone frantically hacked and beat them away. "Stars, how is he still intact?" Stone pondered.

Cage shrugged and helped Osiris to his feet.

"She's getting away!" Osiris shouted. He made to run after her, but Cage grabbed his shoulder and shook his head.

"Nei, brother. We have more important things to worry about," Cage said, pointing down at Azura from the railing.

The deck was a bloodbath. Few of the Azura pirates were left, and the golden chains were dragging off corpses and pulling them into the dark guts of the Pain. They were losing, severely, and those that remained were fighting frantically for survival.

"We need to help them," Stone said, stepping onto the gangplank. He didn't see Cutter or Flint, and that worried him.

Osiris turned and looked at the grate Volldah had crawled through. She had escaped. He shook his head and walked toward the gangplank.

"Her time will come," the voice in his head promised.

"It better," he responded.

*****

Cutter dug his prosthetic blade into the belly of the enemy and blew a hole through its head with his pistol, silencing it. He ripped the blade free and turned to see Flint finishing off another behind him. He wiped his blade off on its coat.

"These things ain't so bad when they don't have the numbers," Cutter said. "Just gotta avoid the teeth and the metal bits."

"And remember that they don't give a fuck about a missing arm or leg," Flint added. One of them was crawling towards him, missing both its legs. Already it was starting to reform them in gold.

"I've got it," Cutter said, walking over and stepping on its head, pinning it to the floor. The Damned reached for a sword laying on the floor nearby and he severed its hand for the attempt. The creature hissed as its golden blood spurted from the stump. "The bastards bleed gold, though. They can make limbs out of the stuff. I wonder if we could squeeze 'em dry 'n barter with it?"

Flint nodded his head. It was a valid question. Could the corpse of one of these creatures, covered in gemstones and jewelry, and dripping liquid gold be worth something? If not to a fence, then at least to a scholar of some sort?

"Cutter, old friend, ye might be onto somethin'," Flint said. "Could store one for later, after we behead it at any rate."

Cutter grinned at the thought of selling one of the monsters that were killing his brethren for a profit. This tragedy could potentially be a bounty in disguise. He cut off the Damned's other hand. All that was left was a legless, handless, hissing torso. "Oh, chin up, bones. It could be worse. You could be headless!" he said, releasing its head from under his boot.

The Damned grunted something in its guttural language, and Cutter frowned as it looked up at him, gnashing its teeth and glaring hungry, hateful daggers at him.

"Are you upset? Well just imagine how I feel! Ye killed me brothers, ye did!" Cutter said, motioning to the slaughterhouse all around them. They'd been hemmed into the gun deck, and the Damned had killed off all but a handful of their cannoneers.

A survivor walked over and stared at the pitiful, amputated zombie. He spat on the thing and kicked it.

"Killed all my friends, ye did," the man, a crewman named Christopher, hissed through his teeth. "Good men, all of 'em."

"We could take this one," Flint suggested.

"Nay. Want a whole one. This one's missing its head," Cutter said before bending over and sawing its head from its body. He held the head as it chewed futilely at the air.

Stone, Cage, and Osiris came down the stairs, and Cutter dug his prosthetic blade up into the Damned's brain, silencing it, then dropping it onto the blood-covered floor. "Brothers, ye live. Good to see it."

"Could say the same for you." Stone nodded to the corpses littering the floor. "Looks like our cannons are done for good."

"Cannons, boarding parties. Everyone, really. I heard screaming down below in the galley. I hate to imagine what happened to the men down there," Flint said.

"We're dropping like flies," Osiris said. "Soon there won't be anyone left to bury the dead."

"Bury the dead? We'll be lucky if we don't join 'em," Cutter said. He looked at the handful of men he still had left. "The plan's fallen through. We couldn't even load the cannons before we were swarmed. Now there isn't enough men to matter anyway. Did ye save the boy?"

"Hanover? Aye. We sent him off with Huasca. He should be safe in his cabin. For now, anyway," Osiris said.

"Ye really think Mr. Huasca can withstand that horde?" Flint asked skeptically.

"He's an Alyrian, and an experienced one at that. He'll be alright. He's with the third most dangerous man on this ship," Osiris said.

"Third?" Stone raised an eyebrow. "The cap'n's first. Who's second??"

Osiris smirked and made for the stairs. "There's still me to worry about."

*****

Tora stood, watching as Frond and Ephala went toe to toe with the monster. Out of their entire graduating class, Ephala and Frond were the two strongest fighters she'd known. She had watched Ephala floor three other Seekers, barehanded, during her final examination. Frond had nearly killed two of his opponents in the first thirty seconds of his bout. Against this creature they seemed like children, swinging their toy swords and daggers ineffectually, their target merely annoyed by their attempts.

She had thought to join them. To turn back into a bear or jaguar, or perhaps try and assume a new form to combat this indomitable threat. But she knew no animal could hope to beat it. No, she would have to employ her marshal skills. She brought her trident to bear and channeled her energy into it like she'd been taught. She imagined it like a conduit and an extension of her body. She closed her eyes and focused. With this weapon, she would fell Officer Black, and she would push back against their enemy, so that the Emperor's will would be done. With this weapon, she would met out penance for these unholy abominations' sins.

She opened her eyes, took aim at Black, and chucked her trident with all her might…

The trident struck him in between the shoulders and buried into his hide. He grabbed at it reflexively, trying to rip it free, but unable to reach it with his bulky arms.

"Stand clear!" Tora shouted.

Frond and Ephala cleared away from Black, who turned to look at her.

"What have you done, gnat?" he barked at her.

The trident burned a bright, incandescent white—and exploded. The light blinded everyone who gazed at it momentarily, and Tora was forced to cover her eyes to protect them. When the spots faded and she opened them, a wall of smoke covered where Black had once stood. Her Seeker-kin stood next to her, and they all stood with bated breath, waiting to see if their nightmare was over. Several tense moments passed, and Tora saw no movement in the smoke.

"Is it dead?" Sedrick asked, aiming his rifle at the smoke.

"One can hope…" Ephala panted.

"No. It isn't that easy," Frond said after a moment.

The ship shook.

"Clear out!" Frond shouted, and the Seekers leapt out the way, save for Sedrick.

As he propelled himself, a hand burst up through the floorboards and grabbed hold of the sharpshooter.

"Sedrick!" Tora cried out.

"No you don't!" Ephala said, rushing toward Black at top sprint. "I won't let you kill another one of my family!"

She went to stab him with her daggers but was knocked away when Black *swung* Sedrick like a club and swatted her. She coughed as all the air was knocked out of her, and Sedrick cried out in pain as both his and Ephala's barriers were shattered by the impact, sending out a shockwave.

Black dropped Sedrick just as Frond launched his shield at him. He caught the spinning shield with one hand and brought the edge of it down like a guillotine on Sedrick's screaming face.

"Sedrick no! NOOOOOOOO!" Tora screamed at the top of her lungs as Black slammed the edge of the shield down, over and over.

The monster grunted as he turned Sedrick's head into pulp. The others, stunned by the sheer brutality, watched in horror as another of their brethren were slain. Frond, unable to hide his anger, charged straight at his kin's killer.

"That's enough!" Frond growled, swinging his sword at Black. The blade dug into his arm, and he swung the shield, slamming into Frond and cracking his barrier. He went back at his adversary and slashed the arm holding his shield. He cut halfway through the limb before his blade got stuck and he was disarmed. Black punched him in the face, sending him flying backward and putting another crack in his barrier.

Even through the barrier, I can still feel it…

Frond noticed, wiping blood from his lip. His face hurt, he smelled nothing but blood, and his body was screaming in protest. "I won't let you kill anymore of my friends, beast."

Black ripped the sword, still glowing with Alyria, from his arm and tossed it at Frond's feet. He did the same with the shield. He pulled his axes from their sheathes and clashed them together, making red sparks. "Do you want to save them, little knight? Then kill me, right here, right now. Otherwise, I will rip off your arms and make you watch them die."

Frond looked at Tora, who was still gazing at Sedrick's headless body, then at Ephala, who was panting, trying to catch her breath as she held onto the weeping Tora. The two locked eyes and Ephala nodded.

Frond nodded back and took up his weapons. He closed his eyes and channeled all the energy he had left in him. His Alyria tattoos burned beneath his armor, and the joints and gaps glowed with their light, as did his eyes. He opened them and ran straight at Black, who stood with his axes resting on his shoulders. As soon as he was in striking range, Black brought the blades down with wicked speed. Frond deflected both of them, knocking them away and swiping at Black's core, slashing it open. He dodged away from a follow-up slash, and as Black dug it into the floor where he'd just stood, he brought his blade across the limb, making a new slice just above the other one.

Not deep enough.

He needed to sever Black's arms to stop him from attacking. If he didn't do that, then he was just one swing away from defeat.

Black brought his other axe down and Frond parried it, then riposted, digging his sword up into Black's chin and through the top of his head. Up close, the monster's head didn't look human at all. More like some horrible lizard creature with huge teeth and an uncanny face. Black roared at him, making his ears ring as he ripped his sword free and put distance between them. If the damage had any effect, he couldn't tell.

Black ripped his axe free from the floorboards and spat black blood on the deck before charging back at Frond. Frond dodged but was still clipped by Black's shoulder as he charged past. He spun and righted himself just in time to see Black crash into several men, pivot, then run straight for him. Frond saw Ambrose Castell and a dozen men approaching from behind Black and held up his shield, erecting a concentrated barrier in front of him and using it to absorb the shock as Black tackled him, carrying him along for several yards before throwing him into a cross beam of one of the sails. He slammed into the beam and fell to deck, gasping, but still alive.

"Take this, monster. Open fire!" Ambrose shouted.

Black turned to see a dozen men aiming at him with rifles and blunderbusses. He raised an arm to cover his face as the guns discharged in a flash of muzzles and gunpowder. The bullets hammered him repeatedly, and the blunderbuss shrapnel ripped at his thick hide. Black ate the blows until the firing ceased, then charged at them. Ambrose dodged out of the way, but didn't clear in time to avoid getting clipped by Black, who crashed into his men like a bowling ball.

"Aack! My leg!" Castell cried out. He knew his leg was broken as soon as Black slammed into it. He attempted to scramble for Hilda, who was lying motionless on the deck across from him. Black stopped him, however.

"I told you, your weapons are useless," Black said, grabbing Ambrose and lifting him in the air.

Ambrose Castell stared his impending doom in the face, pulled out his service pistol, and shot Black point-blank in the face with it. The bullet didn't even penetrate.

"Defiant to the end. Admirable," Black admitted.

Castell thought again of his wife and child, waiting for him back home in Angar Marsh.

"Lynda, Calleese, I am sorry, my beloveds. I'll be watching over you, this night."

Black flexed his massive fist and snapped Ambrose's neck, silencing him.

Just then, a hot blast of light struck him, momentarily blinding him and causing him to drop Ambrose's corpse. He opened his eyes to see Ephala standing off with him, both her hands glowing the same blindingly bright blue as whatever had just struck him. He realized that she was throwing pure Alyria energy at him. He ran at her but was stopped dead in his tracks by several more balls of energy slamming into him.

"Die! Die! Die you abhorrent freak DIE!" Ephala screamed as she threw ball after ball of energy at him. Her throws were frantic and wild. Several of the orbs flew past Black and struck objects and people behind him, ashing them where they stood. She swung her arms, her only goal was to throw as much Alyria at him as she could as fast as her body would allow her.

Tora joined in, channeling her Alyria into head-sized balls of pure energy and throwing them at Black's silhouette.

"This is for Clive and Sedrick!" she wailed, throwing all her pain and rage into her attacks.

The two Seeker-sisters unloaded, careless as to how much damage they caused, so long as they annihilated the monster that killed their brethren. After several chaotic moments their barrage ceased, both women exhausted.

"I…think…we…did it…" Ephala panted.

"I should…hope so…" Tora agreed, wiping sweat from her eyes.

A smoking blue crater was all that they could see where Black had been moments before. They were lucky they hadn't detonated any munitions with their attack or sent the whole ship crumbling around them.

Frond stumbled over to them, coming around the crater as the remaining mariners encircled the hole. The crew of Black Bess cheered as the smoke cleared, revealing nothing but burnt timbers. They had lost many this night, but at least they had slain the beast. Captain Avery placed his hands on the shoulders of the two Seeker women and nodded solemnly at the hole.

"Ambrose would be proud," he said.

"Is it gone?" Ephala asked Frond, who was clutching a head injury.

He shook his head. "I don't know, I can't…" he paused.

The blue smoke funneling from the crater in the deck turned purple. Then, it turned red.

"No…" Frond gasped.

"It can't be…" Ephala muttered.

"Stars, have mercy on our souls," Tora sobbed.

LIX

MOONLIGHT MASSACRE

Byzarra dragged herself onto land and coughed water from her lungs. She didn't really understand how it was she'd ended up in the ocean, but when she came through the portal, she found herself breathing water and sinking fast. She watched as her creation dragged itself awkwardly out of the water as well, its body not well-suited for swimming.

"Welcome, necromancer, to de Ghostlands," Huasca announced.

Byzarra turned to see the shaman standing before her. His tattoos glowed fiercely, and she could sense the power emanating from him. Whatever had happened, he had grown stronger. And that didn't bode well for her. "Where are we? What is this "Ghostland" you speak of?"

"It is the domain of my master, Bawon Samedi," Huasca said. "Lord of the Afterlife."

"Lord of the—ha! There is only one true lord of death, shaman, and his name is *not* "Bawon Samedi". Your master should know that well."

"Perhaps you will tell him yourself, after I take your soul before him for judgement," Huasca responded.

Byzarra smirked cockily and pointed at him. "Tear off his arms and legs. I may yet need him alive to take us back home."

The abomination grunted its approval and sprinted at Huasca, who held a staff in his hands now. He tapped it onto the off-white sand and glowing circle formed around him and expanded. Spectral figures appeared around him and ran at the abomination, intercepting it. The creature let loose a battle cry as it swung its blade arm at them, impaling one of the spirits on it and making it disappear in a puff of ephemeral mist as others grabbed at its arms and tried to hold it down. The creature flung one up into the air and punched another with its fist.

A ghostly warrior with feather-covered armor drove a spear into the beast, however. The weapon left no wound, but the abomination gasped in response, and turquoise vapor came out its mouth. The warrior ripped the spear out and a twisted mass of spirits were drawn out of the thing, attached to the spear. The spirits screamed, begging for release as the warrior drew them out of the abomination.

"Not so fast!" Byzarra shouted, shooting an arc of green electricity out of her hand, and striking the warrior, who shuddered from the current before turning to vapor.

The trapped spirits were slowly sucked back into the abomination, clawing, and screaming. Huasca watched in horror and disgust.

"Souls…you've been binding *souls* to this creature, to hold it together?!" he gasped.

"Indeed, I have. As you saw, my ability to animate the dead is still quite novice. But I discovered that binding spirits more than made up for my failings in keeping the construct animate and under my control," Byzarra said diagnostically.

"Those are *people*, you apostate witch! You are trapping *people* in that rotting mass of flesh!" Huasca shouted.

"People? Oh please, they're nothing but energy, now. Energy to be used and manipulated as is needed," she dismissed. "Now finish him off!"

The abomination ran at him again, knocking away more of the spirits that tried to stop it. Huasca twirled his staff, causing ghost trails of light to flash through the air before he aimed it at the charging foe. A web of threads spread out like a net in front of Huasca, and his opponent ran straight into it. The thing fought, trying to muscle its way out of the trap, but was unable to do more than tug on the threads wrapping around it, further covering itself with the glowing silk.

"A web? You covered my golem in web? Surely you didn't think that would stop it?" Byzarra asked, confused. Already, her creation was beginning to cut the silk with its blade arm.

"Stop it? No. The web was not meant to *stop* your monstrosity…" Huasca said, mimicking the tone she'd used earlier, he turned his head to the right, looking into the thick jungle backdropping their fight.

Something large was rustling the trees and bushes as it approached. More threads shot out from the jungle and ensnared the golem. It let out bestial cries as it kept cutting away the threads. It was nearly free, now.

"Oh no…" Byzarra said, realizing what it was.

"Say goodbye to your *construct*, witch."

A furry, light blue, black-spotted tarantula the size of a bear crawled out of the jungle and skittered straight for the abomination. When the creature laid eyes on its prey it spun around and sprayed more silk from its spinnerets before turning around and bolting at the trapped monster. The golem roared once more, struggling with all its might as the tarantula pounced on it. The beasts became a blur as they struggled. The tarantula pinned it to the sand with its legs and brought its powerful fangs down on the beast, stabbing it and injecting its venom.

"My pet!" Byzarra gasped.

"Is no more. Now face me on your own," Huasca interjected, assuming a fighting stance.

Byzarra watched in horror for several more moments as the tarantula wrapped her limp construct in more silk before dragging it toward the jungle. She shuddered to think what would become of it now. She shot Huasca a withering look of pure contempt and conjured her Alyria, arcing between her fingertips. "Very well, shaman. Let's see how you fair against my *other* abilities."

Byzarra pursed her lips, then opened them.

A swarm of black insects flew out of her mouth and clouded around Huasca, taking him off-guard. He swatted at them as the insects stung and bit at him, crawling under his clothes and attempting to crawl into his nose and mouth. Byzarra circled him, still seething with anger at her lost pet. She balled up a fist and sickly green light leaked from between her fingers.

"I'm going to make these last few moments of your miserable life a hellish nightmare of stings, blisters, and pain…" she promised. She muttered an incantation in the same guttural tongue the Damned used and opened her palm.

The sickly green light snaked toward Huasca like serpents made of smoke and surrounded him. He began chanting a new spell but was interrupted by the insects crawling in his mouth. He wretched and spat them out as they stung his throat.

"Enough!" he shouted, and a wave of energy shot out around him, blasting away the murderous insects and dispelling the curse she'd put upon him.

"How did you dispel my curse?!" Byzarra gasped. "You shouldn't have been able to think, let alone cast a spell!"

"I told you, child, this is my master's domain. My power here is greater than yours. You cannot win."

Huasca thrust a palm at her, and a volley of wisp-like energy sprayed at her, forcing her to flee. She narrowly escaped them, taking cover behind a tree as the orbs flew past her into the jungle.

That cursed shaman is going to kill me, here. I can't summon anymore of my constructs, and he can dispel my curses.

She tried to will the spirits flying through the air and trees all around her to bend to her will, but they rejected her influence. No, she needed freshly deceased, lost souls to control. Everything here had been dead longer than she'd been alive, and their spirits were firmly rooted in this strange place. She wondered what God owned this realm. Clearly it was a god of death, but those were many, each representing it in their own fashion. This one seemed to be some sort of nature deity, judging by the jungle foliage and almost serene, albeit strangely blue, environment. The Ghostlands? She'd never heard of this place.

No constructs, no spirits, and no curses. I'm at a severe disadvantage. If I cannot subdue the shaman, then I will be trapped in this strange place until he either catches me, his deity finds me, or another animal like the one that claimed my golem comes for me...

She ground her teeth; she hated to lose, and especially to flee. But her enemy had the upper hand, and she could not afford to die, not here.

Unless...

She remembered the item in her pocket, given to her by Shade aboard the Pain.

"Should you find yourself in need of my skills, whisper my name into that stone. I will hear it, and I will come, so long as there is a shadow for me to emerge from."

That was what he'd said, wasn't it?

Well, I guess the Grave is burning, then.

She heard scraping wood and struggled as vines emerged from the soil at her feet and around the tree she was hiding behind, binding her down. Thinking fast, she raised the stone to her lips just as it was wrapped in vines and immobilized.

"*There* you are, child. Did you think you could hide from me?" Huasca asked as he came into view. The shaman seemed much more dangerous to her, now. His eyes burned bright with that strange turquoise light that seemed to emanate from this place. He scowled at her.

"Shade—quickly, I—" Vines wrapped over her mouth and dug into her skin, drawing blood.

"Be silent. No more curses and spells from you," Huasca said with a victorious grin. "My master will want to see you, I think. He will interrogate you, before he tears your soul from your body, that is."

Her heart raced. She could *not* die here! Not here! Not when she had finally found a mentor and could begin enacting her plans! She struggled, but the vines held her firm. Her eyes looked around wildly as the vines entombed her. She saw movement in the shadows behind the shaman and saw dead white lights staring at her.

Thank you, Gravefather.

The last thing she saw was that skeletal wraith creeping up behind her captor, before the vines covered her completely, and she fell unconscious.

"Now, I have you, witch—" Huasca gasped as he felt ice cold pain stab him in the back.

"She's not yours to take…" Shade hissed into his ear.

He threw Huasca to the side.

The cold spread through Huasca's body and he lifted his head to watch the vines receding and a strange, shadowy skeleton in pirate clothes pick up the unconscious necromancer before fading back into the shadows. Then, he passed out.

*****

Ephala dragged herself across the deck toward her dirks. Around her, flames raged, and timbers fell as the Black Bess burned. The smell of blood and death was replaced with the scent of cooking flesh and burning wood. She heard the massive footsteps approach her, slowly, and she began to weep.

"Do not cry, little Seeker. Your fate was sealed long before this night came. You will be reunited with your beloved brethren soon…" Black said as he stood over her.

Across from her, she stared into the blank eyes of Tora, staring at her from across the deck. She was ripped in half.

"Burn in the fieriest pits of Sheolhenna, you demon!" she cursed him with every fiber of her being as she crawled towards her weapons, ignoring the shadow standing over her.

"Sheolhenna has no room for me. But I will send you there in my stead," he said as he reached for her neck.

Frond leaped over burning timbers and charged at Black. His armor was dented, and one arm was twisted at an unnatural angle as he thrust his sword and dug it into Black's hip.

"Get out of here, Ephala!" Frond said as he strained and pushed the blade deeper.

Black growled and spun around, punching Frond in the face and knocking him down close to the flames. "I am done with you, knight. It is time for you to die!"

Ephala grabbed hold of her weapons and sobbed over Tora, closing the dead woman's eyes, and pushing a strand of blood-matted hair from her face. She turned to see Black holding Frond aloft and punching him, repeatedly. The two Seekers locked eyes for a moment.

He was telling her to leave.

She turned away. She could not defeat this monster. She would have to abandon the ship. She saw Avery pinned under a piece of wood as the flames approached him. She lifted the wood away with ease and helped him to his feet.

"We have to go. Frond is distracting the monster."

"Go? Child, I am a naval captain, and this is my warship. I will die before I abandon her."

An explosion rocked the ship, and Avery placed a hand on her to stabilize himself. "My duty lies here. I will fight that monster as best I can and accept my fate."

"Are you mad? Did you not see Ambrose and his men get obliterated by him? He will kill you, he—"

"Has killed my men, has destroyed my ship, and has cost me my career," Avery cut in. "I know very well how this ends, Lady Ephala. But if I must choose between scrambling for my life in a losing battle or going out defiant like my officers before me? I choose defiance."

Just then, a figure limped toward them through the haze of smoke. Ephala raised her daggers. Cambridge Golde appeared from the smoke, stumbling and covered in blood, both human and Damned. He panted, looking at the two with bloodshot eyes.

"Ensign Golde? I had thought you perished," Avery said.

Cambridge looked over at Black, who was still bludgeoning Frond's limp body with one hand.

"Perhaps I should have. It's a bloodbath, down below. The lower decks were swarmed, we…I…" he stumbled over his words between pants. "They're all gone."

He had a haunted look in his eyes.

"The ship is lost. Frond is offering what distraction he can so that we can escape with our lives. The captain is staying behind. Will you join me, or will you die here?"

Golde looked at Avery with concern. "Captain, you—"

"Go, ensign. You have my leave. You are young, do not die an old fool's death like me," Avery said as he pulled out his service pistol, a thick, heavy-barreled flintlock. He also pulled out a strange-looking object from his pocket.

"Sir, is that…" Golde asked with wide eyes.

"Yes. My dead man's hand. This is as good an opportunity as ever. With luck, it may even stop it," Avery said.

Every captain in the Imperial Navy was given a dead man's hand at their maiden voyage. In the event that ship was overtaken by the enemy, they were expected to detonate it, blowing themselves up with a powerful explosive, and igniting the ship, guaranteeing that it would never be taken by the enemy. It was a final act of defiance in the face of defeat, ensuring that whatever foe took down the ship would die with it as well.

The old captain took off his hat, nodded to the two youths, and strode toward Black. The goliath turned to face him. Frond was motionless at his feet.

"The captain comes to face me, now? Your ship is lost," Black said dismissively.

"Yes. I have you and your unholy minions to thank for that," Avery said, motioning to the burning carnage around them.

Black picked up his axes and walked slowly toward Avery, looking past him at Ephala and Golde, who disappeared into thin air. "The Seeker flees, and you stand at the brink of destruction. Why?"

"Because I am a captain of the imperial navy. I have served her faithfully for thirty-three years and lived a long and prosperous life. I have never lost a ship, but if I am to lose one now, it is my duty to go down with it. That is my code of honor. A foreign concept to something like you, I'm sure," Avery said.

"Honor? Honor means nothing in this world. The weak are devoured by the strong. The strong need no honor, only might. And I will use mine to save my people, by any means necessary."

Avery gave him a puzzled look, not understanding what the monster was talking about. More timbers fell, and a wave of hot air made him cover his face. Black set his sights on Azura.

"I will leave you to your death. I have other lambs to slaughter." Black dismissed him, even going so far as to walk past him toward a rowboat.

"My death? This burial at sea is for the both of us," Avery said, pulling the dead man's hand out of his pocket and lighting it.

"My death? You cannot kill what is already dead, mortal."

Avery aimed his service gun at Black's head and cocked the hammer. "Then your destruction."

Black frowned and stood over the much smaller human. "If you wish me to end your suffering, then so be it." He brandished one of his large ebony axes and placed the blade on Avery's shoulder. "Say your eulogy."

Avery pressed the pistol barrel between Black's eyes.

"When I go before my makers, I will go with a clear conscience. Can you say the same?" Avery said calmly, locking eyes with his executioner.

"My mind is clear. I feel no fear. When I am gone, I will be revered," Black said. "Tell your gods what I've done."

Avery held the dead man's hand between them as the wick burnt out. He closed his eyes.

"Amen."

A bright flash winked in and out of existence as the Black Bess was blown in half.

*****

Armen Hanover sat in Huasca's armchair. He felt weak, as though a fever was wracking his body. His vision clouded, and voices too hushed to understand whispered in his ears. He felt drugged. He pulled the Eye of Atla from his pocket and looked at it. There was a gap in time that he couldn't account for. He recalled the belly of the shapeshifter, but after that his mind was fuzzy. When was he tossed into that cabin? Why didn't the shapeshifter take the Eye from him and kill him? He didn't know, and trying to remember made his head hurt.

The cabin door opened, and he raised his throbbing head to see Osiris, Stone, Flint, Cutter, Cage, and another pirate that he was struggling to remember the name of. He believed he was named Chris. And a Damned. They were carrying the corpse of a Damned. The back of its head was blown out, rendering it inert.

"Where's Huasca? He should've been guarding you!" Osiris asked, alarmed.

"He left…to fight the…necromancer…" Hanover mumbled, finding it hard to talk.

"Necromancer?" Osiris asked, looking at the others in confusion. "Fuck is that?"

"An Alyrian who manipulates the dead to do their bidding. There are many of their number amongst the Deathwatch," Steven Cage explained.

Osiris didn't notice her, though he was hard-pressed to sense *anyone's* energy, other than the oppressive taint of the Dread Captain. He wondered who or what else was skulking around the ship in the chaos, waiting to leap out at them. "Ye said he left? Left where?"

"Through…portal…" Hanover slumped over, and Osiris rushed over to him.

"Hanover! Hanover, wake up! Hanover!" he pressed a hand to his head. It was burning hot. "He has a fever or something. Must've caught something in the guts of that freak. Where the fuck is Huasca when ye need 'em?"

As if on cue, a circular portal opened up in the wall and Yaman Huasca stumbled out of it, gasping for air. The pirates, startled, aimed their weapons at him before realizing he was an ally.

"Troll tits—where the fuck did *you* just come from?!" Stone gasped.

"I…had an encounter with a—"

"Necromancer, we heard. Hanover's sick," Osiris cut in.

Huasca caught his breath and walked over to Hanover, pressing a hand to his forehead. He was near scalding to the touch, and unresponsive. "How long as he been like this?"

"A minute or two, no more," Osiris said, checking the door. "Do ye have something that could help him? I know medicine isn't your specialty, but without Claude, you're the best hope he has."

Huasca thought a moment. "I could create a poultice for him, to potentially bring the fever down. But anything further would require time we do not have. The necromancer escaped my grasp, and we have to assume she will be returning to the battlefield. There is a wraith with her, and he nearly poisoned me with a dagger."

"A fucking necromancer, a wraith, a revenant, and an army of gold-blooded undead who eat bullets like candy. Fucking terrific," Cutter groaned.

Huasca looked puzzledly at the corpse of an aforementioned gold-blooded undead lying on the floor, arms and legs chained. "Speaking of which…why are you carrying one with you?"

Cutter grinned as he pointed at it with his prosthetic. "Because the bastard has diamond eyes and diamond teeth—that's why! Imagine what we can sell 'em for!"

"We should grab another one," Christopher suggested giddily. "Bring it with us for a profit."

"We've got our hands full with one 'n we still need to figure out how we're gettin' out of here," Flint said grimly.

"He's right. The situation above deck is dire. There's only a few men left, now," Osiris said, looking through a crack in the door. They'd cut a path through the Damned on their way to the navigation cabin, but even that wasn't enough to turn the tide. He saw only a few dozen men still fighting. The remainder he had to assume were either down in the belly of the ship, likely getting torn apart like Flint and Cutter's group, or more likely they were already dead. He watched the golden chains grab more bodies and pull them aboard the Pain. Where they were taking them, he didn't know.

"We need to get the cap'n 'n get out of here," Stone said. "He's our best bet of escapin' this mess, now that we have Hanover 'n the Eye."

Osiris recalled the plan that Morgan had laid out for them before the battle with the Damned had begun. "Does he really mean to try 'n communicate with that thing?"

Huasca spoke up, "There is a sentient being living within it. Atla is still there, though she may not be more than a shadow of what she once was."

"Do we really want to trust a merqueen with our salvation? What if all those millennia trapped in there's made her bat shit insane?" Stone suggested.

Huasca gave a worried look. It was definitely a possibility. "Then we are doomed. Azura will not survive this fight, she has taken too much damage, and there aren't enough men still living to man her properly. We *need* the captain, and the Eye to escape this place."

"I say we leave 'em both 'n grab some rowboats, head west, toward land. We can't be more than a hundred miles from the coast, now," Cutter said.

"We do that 'n we'll be killed before we can ever reach land. Ye really think the Dread Cap'n'll just let us waltz on outta here, brother? He's a score to settle," Stone said.

"We stand with our own. The cap'n has things to answer for, yes. But right now we need to stand with 'em, so we can get out of here alive," Osiris said, putting an end to the discussion. "Let's go. Huasca, you watch Hanover and recover. We'll go and help the captain."

"Help 'em? He's fighting the fucking Dread Captain! How are we supposed to fight that?!" Cutter asked.

"Same as we have everything else—with steel, bullets, and an iron-will," Osiris answered.

LX

THE LAST STAND

Morgan panted and took a knee. He was tiring, and he'd sustained numerous injuries that should have been fatal from his opponent.

"We're losing. I cannot keep sustaining you like this, Morgan. A few more hits, and I will be unable to heal you. He will kill you," Abbal warned.

"We have to keep him distracted until they save the boy and get the Eye back. Without it, we're doomed anyway." Morgan said.

"You've gotten old, slow, and weak. Pathetic," Helregal grunted as he approached.

"I'd hardly consider it a fair fight. You've had a hundred years to rest and recover from our last fight. Meanwhile, I've been adventuring and building a pirate empire," Morgan said smugly.

"You mean the empire I helped start? The one you robbed me of, along with my dreams, ambitions…and my life," Helregal said resentfully.

Morgan rose to his feet. "I killed you because you were going off the deep end, and someone needed to stop you before you did the unthinkable. I was just the one who had the gumption to do it."

"Is that what you call it? Gumption? Leaving me to die in the cave after you shot me in the back. Looting the treasure while the ceiling came crashing down on me—is that what you call gumption?!" Helregal growled as he swung his sword.

Their blades clashed, and Morgan felt the weight of Helregal's hatred in the blade.

"Because I'd call that treachery!" Helregal shouted, swinging his blade again.

Morgan blocked his blows as Helregal sloppily swung at him. He measured his swings and parried the last before firing Bullet Rose at Helregal once more.

The bullet surged through him with sparks of Alyria, but Helregal didn't even flinch.

"Same old trick!" he aimed his pistol and fired it at Morgan. He narrowly dodged the bullet, but a wave of maroon-colored energy came with it and clipped him.

Morgan howled in pain as the energy burned away the clothes on one side of his body and burned the skin beneath. He clutched his gun arm and winced in pain as the skin began to heal. "Stars…"

"They can't hear you here, old dog. Yip and cry all you want. Nothing will save you from your fate!" Helregal said as he took aim at Morgan again.

Just then, Osiris came flying at the Dread Captain. He slashed at him, knocking his aim off and stopping him from firing the fatal bullet. "What in the—"

Osiris wasted no time, he buried his swords into Helregal's chest. Osiris pulled the blades out and kicked him, knocking him to the floor. "Too slow."

"Cap'n! We've got the boy and the amulet, we need to go," Stone said, whispering into Morgan's ear.

"If I try to leave the fight now, he'll tear this ship apart trying to get me. No, I have to stay and fight," Morgan said, keeping his eyes on Helregal, who lay sprawled out at the edge of the deck.

Osiris turned his back on Helregal, walking toward the group as Stone and Flint helped Morgan to his feet. He felt the hairs on the back of his neck stand on end again, and he spun around just in time to see the Dread Captain rising back to his feet, popping his shoulders back in place as a red mist enveloped his body and the necklace around his neck crackled with energy.

"This one has spunk! He will make a fine Damned, I think," Caine said as Helregal fully regenerated.

"Yes. After I teach him a lesson, that is," Helregal said. "Have you brought your men to die with you, Morgan? How thoughtful. You can all die together, one big, happy family."

"My men have nothing to do with our duel, Felix," Morgan dismissed as he dusted himself off. The left side of his body was burned from the blast, but all considered he was lucky Abbal had stopped it from blowing it clean off.

Helregal looked at the remaining Azura officers. Flint had lost an eye, and Cutter a hand. Stone and Cage were covered in blood and looked ready to collapse. Then there was Osiris, who had gashes and cuts all over him.

"You lot look like death warmed over. And as much as I'd like to kill each one of you, personally," Helregal paused and looked past them. His frown turned to a dark smirk as he watched the Black Bess detonate from midship and fracture in half. "…Something tells me Officer Black will handle that."

The pirates all turned to marvel at the crumbling Black Bess. Not too long ago, it had been the bane of their existence. Now, Morgan couldn't help but feel that its fate was a grim omen of things to come.

"It's gone…" Stone gasped in disbelief. "The whole bloody ship is up in smoke…"

"Yes, it is. And the thing that did it is on his way here to do the same to *you*," Helregal said, unable to contain his mirth. "Hahahahahaha! Morgan, I'd suggest we get this little duel over with quickly, or we'll be fighting on driftwood before long."

"Remember the plan," Morgan whispered to Stone over his shoulder.

Stone bit his lip and nodded. "Let's go, boys. We need to see what this 'Officer Black' is about."

Osiris opened his mouth to protest but closed it when Morgan nodded for him to leave. He looked over his shoulder at Helregal. "This ain't over."

Helregal and Caine laughed together. "Oh, boy, it's already said and done. You just haven't realized it yet."

*****

Black scaled the side of Azura with his claws, digging holes into the wood as he climbed. When he clambered over the railing, he found that the Damned, regretfully, had done most of the killing. The ship was a graveyard of corpses, and the Damned were feasting upon them. He had thought the battle over when the last holdouts of Azura came charging at him from across the main deck. One of them stood out, however. A bronze-skinned man with a wiry afro and glowing turquoise eyes. Where the other faces were masks of fear, uncertainty, and resignation, he alone stood defiant. His was one of resolve, fearlessness, and rebellion in the face of annihilation.

"Rage, rage against the dying of the light, mortals," Black said with a rictus grin. He bore his weapons and charged headfirst into the fray.

The Azurans' battle cries turned to screams of terror as he broke through their ranks. Like a shark tearing through a school of fish, he carved them apart.

"Come unto me and fall before the slaughter!"

"Not so fast, big boy. We've still got some fight left in us!" Stone shouted as he and Cutter stood side-by-side, aiming their guns at him.

Black stared down the barrel of a blunderbuss and two dragon guns and braced himself as the weapons roared at him.

"The bastard's still kicking!" Cutter shouted in surprise as the smoke cleared.

Osiris stood behind the firing line, watching in disbelief as Officer Black stood defiantly, having just survived enough firepower to cut down twenty men with ease. He looked around at the Damned, circling around them from all sides, ready to strike. He looked again at this 'Officer Black' creature, who looked less like an officer and more like a savage animal let loose upon the ship. They locked eyes.

"You lot…handle the Damned, rally everyone you can. Ye need to try and fend them off. I'll handle him," Osiris said.

"Handle 'em? The bastard just ate two dragon shots and a blunderbuss shot to the face! What the fuck can ye do that we haven't already?!" Stone gasped.

"I'll cut him limb from limb and toss his corpse into the sea, for starters. Don't worry about me—worry about the men we have left and getting rid of these undead!" Osiris commanded as he stepped forward.

"This one not like any of the others ye fought, boy. This one dangerous, real dangerous. Between him and the Dread Captain, I not know which one you stand a worse chance against," the voice in his head warned, finally speaking up again.

"Doesn't matter. I'm the only one who can stand a chance against the bastard, so I have to try. For my brothers' sake," Osiris answered.

"Mmm…be careful, boy. What happens next? Is on your head." the voice finished, then faded away again.

*****

Osiris stood across from Black. All around them the last stand of the Azura pirates against Helregal's Damned played out in desperate fashion as the pirates fought off the inevitable. The two combatants, one a sentinel, trying to save his comrades in their darkest hour. The other, a bloodthirsty beast, come to kill all that the sentinel held dear in this cold world.

"What is your name, human?" Black asked. He stood with his axes resting on his shoulders, observing the young mortal he towered over. In his eyes, Black did not see the fear and dread that consumed all the other little humans around him. He saw a fearless resolve. A strong man, come to test his mettle.

A warrior.

"You are not like the other mortals I've killed tonight."

Osiris stood with his spadroons in his hands, ready to strike. He regarded the much taller, much bigger adversary with impassivity. He was cut, bruised, and bleeding. He had been through much these last few months, and he got the distinct feeling that these trials were coming to their inevitable end. Before him was the monster that the hero was meant to slay at the end of the fairytales from his childhood. "My name is Assahj Osiris."

He couldn't remember the last time he'd said his full name to someone, much less an enemy. He normally killed them before they got to ask. "What is your name, creature? It can't be 'Officer Black', that's for damn sure."

Black's murderous smile widened a smidge, revealing his blade-like teeth. "I go by many names. Most of my enemies die before they ever hear one of them. To my victims this night, I am Officer Black. To *you*, human..." Black scrutinized him further. "I am Jar-El-Kalgrontild. I have told you my name. Now, it is time to die."

Black aimed an axe at Osiris in challenge. Osiris closed his eyes, took several deep breaths, and felt a surge of Alyria run through him as the pain in his body and the fears in his mind faded away. A turquoise aura emanated from him like a glow, and he knew then that he was as ready for this fight as he ever would be.

The two charged at one another, indifferent to the chaos of battle unfolding around them. When their blades clashed it was as though the world hushed a moment. Even Morgan and Helregal momentarily paused their duel to the death to look at the two fighters, before returning to their own fight.

Osiris pushed Black back before swinging at him with his spadroons, slashing at him and leaving bloody slits in his thick hide. He was surprised to see his opponent bled thick black ichor but did not ponder it as he continued his onslaught. He kept swinging, testing his enemy's reflexes. His opponent moved much faster than his size would suggest, blocking attacks that something of his size shouldn't have been able to.

Osiris faltered.

He overextended himself with one of his swings, and Black cracked him in the head with an elbow in retaliation. He stumbled. He heard his nose break.

Black swept at his legs with one axe, forcing him to jump over it before being clotheslined mid-air by his other arm.

He moves fast as a damned viper!

Osiris realized as he ate the blow and was sent flying several feet. He landed on his back, and he coughed as he tried desperately to get more air in his diaphragm. He rolled over just in time to avoid being cleaved in half and stumbled to his feet.

"Get down!" he heard Stone shout, and Osiris fell to the deck and curled into a ball as Stone unloaded another volley of dragon shots at Black.

Black stumbled from the attack, his focus zeroed on Osiris. Osiris sprung to his feet and used the opening to stab both his swords into Black. One in the gut, and the other angled up at his throat. He ripped the blades from his target immediately, cutting him open and leaving wounds that would have easily killed an ordinary foe. If the attacks registered, Black didn't show it. Osiris gasped as the hulking brute began swinging his axes wildly at him in a counterattack. The pirate backed off, evading the axes but bumping into a Damned fighting with Christopher.

The creature hissed, and Osiris immediately shoved it into the range of Black's attack. He cut it apart with two mighty swings, and the creature fell to pieces. Then he charged at Osiris. Osiris dodged, but Christopher was struck by the charge and sent flying off the side of the ship. Black went for him again, bringing his axes down vertically, and Osiris dodged before swinging both swords together and slashing the back of Black's leg. The metal leg guards sparked from the blades, and Osiris ate a kick to the head in response. Dazed, he stumbled away as Flint and Cutter came to his aid. Cutter fired his blunderbuss one-handed at Black, spraying him and everyone standing behind him with shrapnel.

Black roared just as Flint took aim with his rifle and shot him in the eye with a breech-loading rifle he'd stolen from the mariners. He emptied the gun on Black, aiming for his head with every shot. He's shot out an eye, as well as landed several shots in the beast's open mouth and face.

"That should've killed 'em…" Flint said, still unable to believe that Black was not only still standing, but actively coming toward him.

As Black closed in, Steven Cage jumped from atop a crate and buried his axes into the beast's shoulders, hanging on as Black tried to dislodge him.

"Meddlesome pirates! Stand aside or be crushed!" Black growled as he tried to grab Cage, who was just out of his reach.

The Northman laughed and pulled out a knife with one hand as he clung. He dug the blade into Black's throat before he was thrown off. Black didn't even bother to remove the knife before he turned on Cage. One of Cage's axes was still stuck in the giant's back, so he was left with just one to defend himself. "Your soul is black as night, creature! By Mgdogn's beard, I will carve it out of you!"

Black said nothing as he lunged at him, but Cage slipped just out of reach as a yardarm came crashing down from above, separating the two. Black turned his attention back to Osiris as something came rolling toward his feet from across the deck. He looked down to see a grenade burning down its wick at his feet. He covered his head as the bomb detonated, punching a hole in the floor where he stood and peppering him with its splintering payload. He fell into the lower compartment, and Osiris breathed a momentary sigh of relief.

*****

"He's going to tear the ship apart!" Abbal warned aloud as Morgan dodged another charged shot from Helregal's gun. One of his last shots had severed a yard arm and punched holes through the sails of the ship.

"Azura is already doomed," Morgan said solemnly as he shattered several chains that came snaking after him. "We're just trampling her corpse."

He hoped that he'd left enough time for his men to deal with 'Officer Black'. He hoped that they would forgive him for all he'd done.

Most of all, he hoped that his daughter would forgive him for abandoning the ship he named after her.

I'm sorry, my dear. I'm so very sorry.

He fired at Helregal, but all his shots were either deflected or went wide. He was tired. He panted as the fatigue caught up to him, and he looked around at the devastation that had befallen his beloved Azura. Her masts were splintering, her yardarms and shrouds were crumbling, and her sails were tattered. She would not sail again. Not after this.

"Have you finally stopped running, Morgan?" Helregal asked with a bored expression. "You've hardly put up a worthy fight. I suppose old age really has taken the fire out of you."

Morgan wiped the sweat from his brow and blood from his lip. "Time may have slowed me, Felix, but it has left you even less of a man than you were the day I dethroned you. You have become something so cold and dark and ugly that even a murderer and a thief such as I cannot help but turn away."

Helregal shook his head. "And who was I, before you betrayed me, Morgan? Nothing but a man looking to reclaim what was owed to him. You took that from me. You sent me down this path the day you shot me and left me to die in that cave. Now, the hens have come home to roost. Your sins have come back for your judgement day."

Helregal took aim once more, and this time the barrel of his gun burned with maroon-colored Alyria. Morgan had no more fight left in him, and he had nowhere left to go. He holstered his weapons and looked Helregal in his blood red eyes. Though his face was covered in the golden skull mask, he could still feel the anger in his gaze.

"Be done with it," Morgan sighed.

Helregal tilted his chin. "With pleasure."

His gun fired, unleashing a blast of energy that consumed Morgan as he shut his eyes and let it carry him away. When the flash died, all that remained were scorched ruins where Morgan had once stood.

Helregal holstered his gun and sword, then came over to the ruined splinters of the steering deck railing and looked down at what had become of Azura.

"Pathetic," Caine sighed.

"Time to deal with the boy and the Eye," Helregal said, still gazing at the black smudge where his old enemy used to be.

LXI

Desperate Times

Stone opened the door to Huasca's study and nodded to the shaman, who was watching over Hanover. The shaman put a hand on his weapon before easing up and nodding to them as they entered.

"I heard roaring out there. What was that?" Huasca asked as he bandaged the poultice onto Hanover's forehead.

"Something big, ugly, mean, and whatever gods be willing, dead. How is he?" Osiris asked.

"He is still unresponsive. The poultice should break his fever. Instead, he has grown hotter and more agitated." Huasca said.

Hanover fussed in his sleep. He was sweating profusely and muttering under his breath. Whatever he was dreaming of had him scared.

"We don't have much in the way of time. Get ready to move him. Those things will be bored with our dead brothers and turn on us in minutes," Osiris said.

Suddenly, there was a knock on the door. Osiris, Stone, Flint, Cutter, and Cage all bore their weapons, ready for the attack.

"We are out of time. The horde is upon us…" Cage said. He muttered a prayer in Borran as he waited for the inevitable.

"Not like this. I can't go out like this," Cutter groaned as he reloaded the blunderbuss. "Was supposed to be with two whores at me side 'n too much alcohol in me blood."

"Did you really think ye'd be that lucky?" Flint asked.

"No, but I'd always hoped," Cutter admitted.

"I hoped I'd get to watch ye idiots die at least a few years before I kicked the bucket. Damn shame," Stone sighed as he finished reloading the dragon guns. "Guess I'll be seein' Sheolhenna first-hand with you."

"Fuck you too, Stone," Cutter muttered.

Osiris walked over to the door, curious as to why it hadn't already been broken in. He looked at the others, took a deep breath, then cracked it open, half-expecting to see a Damned peeking through at him, followed by a blade's edge.

What he saw instead surprised him. "Cap'n?"

Morgan pushed the door open and shut it behind him. His clothes were burnt tatters and he looked like he'd just gone toe-to-toe with a bonfire and lost. "We haven't much time—where is the Eye?"

Huasca held the orb in his hand and offered it to Morgan as the others still drank in the fact that he was somehow still alive. Morgan took it. "What is wrong with the boy?"

"He ails. We do not know from what. If we do not get him help, however, I worry that he will…" Huasca sighed.

We have already lost too much.

Morgan frowned. "We will get him aid. I need time to complete this…ritual. Keep me safe until I return," Morgan said. He looked at Osiris. "I need my sentinel."

Osiris thumped his chest and nodded. "Nothing will get past me."

Morgan gave Osiris an honest smile; he believed him.

"I know they won't. Do it."

"We begin the communion," Abbal stated.

The Eye of Atla pulsed in steady, brilliant cyan thrums of light. In the relative quiet of the cabin, he could even hear a low hum coming from it. How long had it been doing that?

He gripped the Eye of Atla in both hands, and immediately Abbal reacted. He felt like his hands were holding onto a ball of lightning. The Amulet of Saviors glowed a brilliant, deep blue, so bright that it blinded all the men in the room and cast a glow throughout the cabin.

When the light faded, Morgan stood frozen in place, his eyes glowing and his feet hovering inches off the ground, a blue glow emitting from him.

As his sight returned, Osiris opened his mouth. "What was—"

A familiar, gut-turning roar howled from outside the cabin, and officers all looked at each other with alarm. That roar could have only come from one creature.

"He's back…" Flint said.

"I'll handle him. Stay here and guard them," Osiris instructed before slipping out the door.

"Osiris…" Huasca spoke up.

Osiris paused and looked at the shaman with an unamused expression. "Mr. Huasca?"

Huasca gritted his teeth. "Come back in one piece, boy."

"I'll try, old man. Farewell, brothers."

He slammed the door before they could respond.

"He's waiting for you," the voice said.

"Good," Osiris said. *"I won't keep him, then."*

*****

The Damned stood lined up in organized rows, they turned and looked at Osiris as he walked, but they made no move against him. He stepped over the entrails and bodies of men he'd known for years as he walked toward his opponent. He steeled himself with each step, playing over all that he'd been through since this voyage began. The laughs he'd had with his brothers in black, the arguments with Hanover, his conversation with Moary before he was slain.

"You're a cold soul, Osiris…" Moary had said.

He wondered if he'd see him again when this was all said and done? He wondered if he'd be proud of him. His thoughts turned to Frederick Moary's mutilated body, then Claude Humris', and then he thought of Yager.

"Oh, laddie. There's far less separates us than that. We're pirates. We rob, kill, and steal from others to make our fortune. To hope for honor among thieves is to hope for a cold day in hell."

"I hope you're wrong," Osiris said aloud as he stopped a few dozen paces from Officer Black.

Steven Cage's axe and knife were still stuck where he'd left them, which somehow made the beast look even more menacing. He let loose another monstrous roar as the red mist swirled around his body. He was howling at the moon. He reached around and ripped the axe from his back, and Osiris watched as the wound immediately closed itself. He turned, and they looked at each other face to face once more as he ripped the knife from his throat, and the wound sealed, leaking a small amount of black blood as it did.

"Are you surprised?" Black asked him, studying his enemy's face.

Osiris shook his head.

"Surprised? I'd be disappointed if a few stab wounds, a grenade, and a tumble through the floor was enough to kill you," he admitted. "You survived a ship exploding on top of you."

"Then you know how this battle is destined to end," Black said.

"I think so, yeah. I've made my peace with it. I've done a lot of rotten things in my life. I'd consider it fair play if this is how I die," Osiris admitted.

"Rare is the foe that knows his fate, and fights against it all the same," Black said. "There are few warriors like you left in this world, Assahj Osiris."

Osiris shook his head. "I'm no warrior. I'm a pirate. Nothin' more, nothin' less, ay?" he pulled out his spadroons and scraped the blades together in a vain attempt to remove some of the blood caked onto it. "Let's get this over with, then."

Black shrugged and wielded his own weapons, throwing out several test swings as he prepared himself. "So be it."

The beast and the sentinel went at one another once more. A final, deadly dance, in the throes of Azura's demise.

*****

"You come to me at last. As I knew you would, of course."

Morgan opened his eyes to see two figures standing in front of him, standing in pitch darkness. One was a glowing blue man, with wings like an angel. He stood, arms folded, appraising a glowing purple woman with his sheet-white eyes. The woman, a breathtakingly beautiful El'wa, gazed back at him with mischievous, brilliant amethyst-colored eyes. Her wings were bat-like, and she had long, flowing hair, a darker shade of purple than her glowing flesh. Her locks danced slowly in the air like they were floating underwater.

"What is your game, Atla? And why does this 'Dread Captain' covet you?" Abbal asked, point-blank.

"Why does anyone desire anything, I wonder? To fit one's aims, I would suppose," Atla chuckled.

"The Dread Captain desires me for his goals. You desire me for your own as well, do you not?" she asked.

"..." Abbal looked at Morgan. "This one wishes to broker a deal, spirit. A bargain."

Atla looked at Morgan, appraising him with unreadable eyes. After a brief moment, she smiled at him. "You? I remember you. You touched me once before. Just as he did."

"He? You mean Felix," Morgan responded, finding his voice.

"Felix Helregal, Dread Captain, Captain Helregal, Bringer of Pain... names, titles, nothing more. He is the one who has hunted you across the Amaranthine. He is the one who will bring about your end in very short order—should you not secure my aid, that is," she said. "Yes. He did touch me, just as you did. The same day, the same circumstance. But we could not speak, then. No. It wasn't time yet, though I do suppose it is time now, isn't it? After the mess you've made, you need Mother Atla to come and clean it up for you... don't you, Morgan Sarron?"

Morgan scowled. "Do not call me by that name ever again. I am Morgan, now and forever. Sarron died when I buried my wife and child. My parting gift to the lights of my life, snuffed out by a backstabbing, scheming old snake of a man I used to once call a friend."

"A friend? A friend," she repeated in a sing-song voice, playing with the tone of her words. "Friends turn to foes when the times turn to woes," she cocked a hip, resting her head in her palms. "Tell me, Captain Morgan, what is it that you request of me, precisely? To kill your old friend, or to free your new ones?"

Morgan stood in silence.

Abbal looked at him, his gaze hard. "If you walk this path, Morgan, you know what the outcome will be. Do you think that Rose and Azura want you to turn into the thing you hate? The thing that killed them?"

Morgan shook his head, regaining his focus.

"I want my men saved. I know that the Azura is lost... and I will lament that sad reality later. Right now, I want safe passage to the Storm Tide for my surviving crew and myself," Morgan said.

"A noble and reasonable request? Hmm, well that is a surprise. My cards showed a rather different outcome. How quaint." Atla hummed. Her whimsical smile turned flat and neutral, however. "And I can honor that request, Captain. It is quite handily within my purview. However, the question of remuneration still remains: What do I get in return for helping you? I have a pre-established agreement with our mutual friend. An arrangement to keep. To help you, I do suspect, would incur the wrath of my tenuous bedfellows. My neck, Captain, would be on the line."

Morgan and Abbal looked at one another. Neither of them had quite considered that. Morgan supposed, in hindsight, that was a pretty glaring issue with their plan. They had nothing to offer at the table. A thought occurred that made Morgan smile.

"You knew that I would be coming here, you said as much. So I would assume you also know that I haven't much in the way of leverage. What do you want, Atla?" Morgan asked.

"A sharp one, you are," she replied, her smile returning in devious fashion. "I knew that you would be in no position to argue, this is true. That card, it would seem, proved correct. Delicious…"

Something about her tone, the way she said that last word…

"What is it?" Morgan reiterated.

"Nothing too extravagant, really. If I am to take on the risk of aiding in your escape, I would request that you take me with you," Atla said.

Morgan made a confused expression, turning to Abbal again. Abbal's expression was as neutral as ever.

"You are in our hands already. Why is that your request?"

"Because your crewmates will almost certainly vote to throw me out to sea once you make landfall. I want to prevent that unfortunate little mistake. For both our sakes," she said, quite serious.

"Don't look a gift horse in the mouth, so they say," Morgan mused.

"This is no horse. It's a viper wearing the skin of a garden snake," Abbal cut in.

"We have no other choice. We must aid her if we are to escape," Morgan responded.

"But we do not know to what ends we are aiding her. She seems carefree, indifferent, near lackadaisical. She is not. She wants something, and I cannot discern what," Abbal warned.

"We have to accept that risk. Death is no alternative," Morgan said.

"There is a boy, he is sick and will die without aid. Save his life, and consider it done," Morgan spoke, this time aloud. He held out a hand to the glowing spirit-woman. Atla looked at it curiously for a moment, chuckled, and took his hand in hers.

"Young Armen Hanover? Easily done. Do we have an accord?" she asked.

He thought back to the chambers of the Emperor, shaking his hand.

What on Hera have I gotten us into?

"We do."

"Then it will be done."

Stars have mercy on our souls.

A deluge of purple light enveloped them.

✵✵✵✵✵

"You've reached your limit, boy," the voice said.

"I've only just begun!" Osiris answered.

"Your body cannot handle anymore Alyria. De Drakkari is too powerful for you to defeat in your current state," the voice explained.

"I don't care if I can beat it, all that matters is that my brothers escape this place!" Osiris said.

His body glowed with Alyria, but even in his heightened state he could tell the fatigue was setting in. First the Bluecoats, now the Damned. His body was reaching its limit.

"You're slowing down, human," Black said.

"Slow or fast, I'll beat you regardless," Osiris assured him. The two traded blows with each other, but neither could land the killing blow. Osiris leaped over a swing and landed behind Black. He slashed his back furiously before Black swung around, trying to elbow him. He leaped again, this time landing on a low-hanging wooden beam attached to one of the masts. Black looked around a moment before realizing where he'd gone.

"This fight is pointless. Bold as you are, you are not strong enough to beat me, human," Black said.

"I don't need to beat you. You killed the Seekers and sank a ship-of-the-line. I'd be better off fighting a titan. But I'll be a rat's ass if I let you kill the only family I have in this world while I still have breath in me."

Osiris dove at him. Black blocked the attack, and Osiris hit the deck.

One last trick. Here goes nothing...

He squeezed his eyes shut and cried out as he flexed all the muscles in his body, drawing in all the Alyria he could muster. As Black brought his axes down on his vulnerable target, Osiris blocked just in time, using all the strength he had left to throw Black off him. The Drakkari was launched backward through the air and slammed into the stairs leading to the forecastle.

Osiris was upon him instantly.

His blades glowed with his Alyria as he channeled the remaining energy into them. He burrowed both blades into both sides of his mighty foe's chest and smirked in satisfaction as Black gasped in pain. The blades burned into his chest, pumping the volatile energy into his body and making his mouth and nostrils glow turquoise.

"That was…a good attempt…pirate," Black gasped as Osiris pressed the blades deeper into his chest. He gripped his arms like a vice. "But not good enough!"

He ripped Osiris' hands from the blades and launched him backward, sending him tumbling across the deck as a peel of thunder cracked the sky, followed by a flash of lightning. Rain pelted down from above, looking almost like blood in the moonlight.

Osiris coughed and rolled over to see the Damned encircling him, growling and screeching as their leader approached and broke through their ranks. He tried to stand, but his legs gave out from under him.

He was defeated.

"I warned you, boy…" the voice said in a sad tone. *"Now, you gotta learn a hard, painful lesson."*

"I have beaten you," Black said as he stood over him.

"So you have!" A newcomer said cheerfully.

Osiris turned his head slowly to see the Damned making way for the Dread Captain as he approached. "But this one had the gall to try and kill me. So now, I want you to make him suffer in his final moments, Mr. Black."

The Dread Captain crouched down and grabbed Osiris' chin. "I won't lie to you, boy. What's about to happen next is hell. But the beautiful thing about tonight is that you'll never have to endure it again! I think you'll come 'round to my way of thinking after I've raised you up without a working bone in your body. You can let me know what you think after he's finished with you…"

He looked at Black. "When you're done with him, scour the ship and find the boy and the Eye. They're trapped here, so I'm not in any rush." Then, the Dread Captain let out a triumphant laugh as he walked away and the Damned closed in around them.

Black cracked his neck. "You fought well, warrior. A pity you won't die well."

As the rain came down, Osiris stood up one last time in defiance. "Bring it, freak."

Black cracked a murderous smile and punched Osiris in the jaw. The pirate fell, too weak to fight back. He gazed into the eyes of his executioner and saw hellfire in them.

"Now, I will break you…"

LXI

BRUTALITY

Black grabbed him by the throat and lifted him off the ground. Osiris couldn't stifle the groan of pain that escaped his lips.

"Save your breath. You'll need it for the screams to come." Black flashed him with a grin.

Osiris could feel the bloodlust emanating from him. Black's chalk-white skin seemed to glow red. He stared at Osiris like a butcher looking at a juicy section of meat, ripe for the cut. "Any last words, little pirate?"

"Fuck…you…"

Osiris hocked a bloody globule of spit into Black's face. It dribbled down his cheek. His smile deepened, like a toothy wound splitting open flesh.

"Good."

He grabbed hold of Osiris' arm—and broke it.

Osiris screamed. The last of his glow died as the pain shot through him like arcs of electricity. He was silenced by a rough punch to the gut. Blood spurted from his lips like water, spraying Black in the face and dribbling down Osiris' front.

Black tightened his grip on Osiris' throat.

"Now!"

He punched Osiris in the gut again.

"You!"

He punched him in the groin, this time.

"Will!"

He punched him in the kidney, sending him sprawling out onto the deck.

"Suffer!"

A horde of the Damned jeered at him, feasting on bits of the fallen Azura pirates as they cheered for his destruction.

Osiris released a weak moan of pain as he felt the vice grip of Black's hand seize his ankle. He was lifted into the air. Black swung him around, picking up speed. The joints in his body popped from the momentum, and he felt the bones and tendons in his ankle snap.

He was delirious with pain, now. He couldn't even hear himself screaming. Osiris couldn't make sense of what he was seeing. He was swinging around in a blur as Black thrashed him. He saw bits of the blood moon, flashes of the ruined ship, and fractions of the carnage around him. The twisted faces of the Damned juxtaposed with the savaged corpses of his brethren.

I'm in hell, already.

Black slammed him onto the deck, striking his head against the wood with a crack. He could hear the blood rushing in his ears. His broken arm dangled awkwardly. It hurt, still. But it was drowned out in the cacophony of other aches and pains that scalded him like boiling water.

The claws of the monster dug into him as he was lifted over Black's head. Black held him in the air over the crowd of cheering undead like a trophy. His vision was too blurry and broken to make sense of the scene around him, now.

"It's almost over, now. Everything you know. Everything you thought mattered in your miserable speck of existence in this vast and ugly world. You lived as a hunter, a fisher of men. Now, you will die as the hunted. Goodbye, little pirate."

Black knelt—and brought Osiris' back down against his knee. A resounding wet crack echoed briefly through the air.

Osiris went limp.

He stopped screaming.

Black dropped his body on the ground, stood over him, and howled a triumphant, bone-rattling roar at the sky. The Damned cheered at their champion's triumph as the rain washed away Osiris' blood.

*****

Huasca felt a hard lump rise in his throat as he heard that terrible roar again, followed by the deathly rattles of the Damned. He knew in his heart that something terrible had befallen Osiris.

"Come to me, immediately," Bawon Samedi said.

"Yes, my lord," Huasca said. *He knew better than to argue with a god.*

"I…I must go," Huasca said remorsefully as the men stood around, watching the door and Morgan, who was still hovering in the air.

"Go? Bloody where? We're surrounded on all sides!" Cutter said confusedly.

"I am called. I cannot explain it any further than that. I…I may not return. I want to tell you all that sailing with you has been some of the best years I've spent in this life. If I could take you with me, I would." Huasca said, holding in his own emotions.

"Ye abandonin' us brother? Here? Now?!" Stone asked, unable to hide the hurt in his voice.

"Abandon you? No, Reece Stone. I would never leave you to die in the storm. The captain will save you all, this I know for certain. No matter the cost. But I must save that boy out there…he…"

Stone nodded, placing a hand on Huasca's shoulder. "I understand, brother. I had one too. Go."

Flint and Cutter looked around, confused. Steven Cage folded his arms. "You have a calling to answer, shaman. Answer it. We all have our duties to attend."

Huasca was unable to hide the surprise on his face, but he nodded his thanks. "Thank you, Mr. Cage."

"You better be right about the cap'n, Mr. Huasca. I'd rather not find out how hot Sheolhenna is tonight," Cutter said.

"And I'd rather not die getting eaten alive by gold-covered corpses," Flint said.

"You will live. This much I know. But now, I must go," Huasca finished.

He blinked and his eyes turned turquoise. He clapped his hands together, then pressed them to the floorboards as a small portal formed beneath his feet, and he fell through it. It closed as quickly as it formed.

"Alyrians…" Stone sighed, running a hand down his face. "I liked it better when we were just using guns 'n swords."

Flint laughed. "Join the club."

*****

When he opened his eyes, he stood before Bawon Samedi's altar, and Yanzamu stood at his side. The god stood up from his seat and pointed to a pool of clear water. Within, Huasca saw a vision of the battlefield he had just left. He could see the sinking wreck of the Black Bess. He also saw that two of its occupants had miraculously survived. The young Seeker woman, Ephala, as well as the officer Cutter had captured earlier, Ensign Golde, hid behind a crate, watching as the Damned and a tall, monstrous humanoid stood chanting and roaring in triumph. The battle was lost, and now, they were preparing for…something.

"Where is he?" Huasca asked.

"Look closer, Yaman…and prepare yourself. It is… not pretty…" Bawon Samedi warned.

Huasca looked closer and saw a broken, bloodied body wheezing and coughing blood on the deck at the monster's feet.

"Oh, Zafuma…" Huasca gasped.

"He is fading," Bawon Samedi said. "Under ordinary circumstances, Yaman Huasca. Dis be the time that I would be reading the dying's last rites and drawing their soul here to be released into the Ghostlands. But this one…I still need this one. Go to him. Bring him here so that he may be mended. Before it is too late for even I to intervene."

Huasca wasted no time, he leaped into the pool.

*****

"Stars above…even a pirate deserves a better fate than that," Golde sighed.

The pair had watched the whole fight. They found themselves rooting for the pirate, considering him the lesser of two evils. They were disappointed to see him lose, but they were shocked to see just how badly the nigh-invincible Black had brutalized him.

"I'm surprised he's still breathing. He won't be for long, though," Ephala said.

On the one hand, she felt the pirate had gotten what he deserved. On the other, she didn't like the idea of that monster getting another brutal kill this night. He had taken everything from her already. Soon, this ship would be overrun, and either the Damned, the chains, the Dread Captain, or Black himself would come for them. She didn't like the alternatives. She had seen some truly horrible things this night.

"What are our odds?" Golde asked her.

She peered out of cover a moment longer, risking discovery. "Do you want the truth, or do you want something that will make it easier for you to sleep?"

"I won't be sleeping ever again. Whether we miraculously make it out of here alive or not," Golde answered honestly.

"The pirates are held up over there, in that cabin." She pointed to the navigator's cabin. "The odds of them welcoming us with open arms are non-existent, and even if they did, they'll be dead soon enough…just like us," she said, her voice hitching.

Golde gave a tired smile and nodded his head. "So it's curtains, then?"

"For us? Most assuredly. The lifeboats have been destroyed by these damnable chains, and the ship is in just as rough a shape as the Bess was. We're trapped, ensign. And it's only a matter of time before they find us," she answered truthfully.

"Well then. I guess we'll be going out like Captain Avery after all. Pity, I think the explosion would've been quicker," Golde admitted. "I regret that we never got to properly make friends, Seeker. I rather think we could've been fast ones. I guess I'll just have to satisfy myself with being the last friendly face you see before we meet our makers."

Ephala smiled; somehow, the young and snobbish-seeming Cambridge Golde had turned out to be just as steadfast as his superiors. She knew that, were he to survive tonight, he would have made a great addition to the admiralty.

Would have…

But he wouldn't survive tonight, and neither would she. She had to make peace with that if she was going to go through with it.

"To friendly faces, then." Ephala stood up, and immediately one of the Damned homed in on her, hissing and pointing. Cambridge stood up beside her, his silver pistol in one hand and a cutlass in the other.

"It's been a pleasure," he said.

They charged at the horde as Black looked over his shoulder at them and belted an order to his minions. "The last scraps off the table. Feast on their bones."

Across the deck from them, another combatant came screeching into the fray, belting words in what Ephala vaguely recalled as Borran.

"What in the six hells is he doing here?" she gasped.

*****

"Mørkets mor, hør min bønn. Gi meg styrke til å ofre for deg!" Cage shouted in his native tongue. He prayed to the mother for strength, so that he may die a glorious death, reaping the souls of the undead for her.

"You again? Haven't you—"

Cage threw an axe that embedded itself between Black's eyes, silencing him momentarily. "Silence, demon! The soul of my kin cries out for protection! It is not his time to go into the dark night! Now face me! Mgdogn has whispered his curses into my ear, and Irkalla has given me her blessing! Face me!"

Cage let loose a war cry, and his tattoos glowed an inky purple color as he charged at the Damned. He wielded but one axe, gripped in both hands, but with it he cleaved them in two. He hissed and howled like a wild animal, slashing limbs and crushing skulls with the flat of his axe. The Damned circled around him as Black approached, ripping the axe from his face with a gush of black blood. He laughed and tossed the axe over his shoulder as he approached, whipping out both of his bloodied, ebony axes.

"I sense darkness in you, human. Are you a Valkar? You smell like one," Black said, flaring his nostrils as he inhaled the air like a dog. "Who is your goddess?"

"The one true goddess to rule them all! De Dark Mother, Irkalla!" he proclaimed as he ducked around Black's swings with ease.

Ephala came up from behind, stepping over the dying Osiris. She threw a spear of blue light at his back. It pierced through the middle of Black's chest.

"You as well, little Seeker? Have you not learned your lesson?" Black asked, sounding irritated. "Very well. I tire of playing with you! It's time I put the little humans in their place!" he growled as he dug his axes into the floorboards and let loose a piercing roar that stunned all the combatants in the melee. Even Cambridge, who had been jousting with one of the Damned, was stunned by the noise.

Cage and Ephala watched with alarm as Black's skin turned red as the blood moon and glowing red mist wept off his skin like smoke from a mountaintop. His muscles bulged and striated from the strain and his veins pulsed. His mouth opened incredibly wide, easily enough for a man's head and shoulders to fit inside. He stomped the deck, splintering the wood and balling his hands into fists as whatever power he was conjuring took hold of him.

"What…is…he doing?!" Ephala shouted as she covered his ears. No one could hear her, however. Cage wrapped his arms over his ears, trying futilely to block out the deafening noise.

Suddenly, a portal opened up at Black's feet, and he ceased his screaming as he was grabbed by a massive hand and thrown high into the air before plummeting back down toward Anathane's Pain. The fighters stood in confusion as an ebony black arm the size of an elephant flexed and swatted away the Damned like insects, sending them flying into the ocean or across the deck before disappearing back into the portal. Yaman Huasca appeared next and looked around at the stunned fighters before focusing on Osiris. "There is no time. I must take the boy and leave."

Ephala and Cambridge stood stunned, still shocked by how quickly the thing that was probably about to kill them was dispatched by the shaman.

"Do it quickly, shaman. It is only a matter of time before the Dread Captain takes notice," Cage warned.

Huasca gave him a perplexed look, wondering why his tattoos were glowing. Had Steven Cage secretly been an Alyrian this whole time? It didn't matter, he didn't have time to ask. He scooped up Osiris' broken body. He could feel the broken bones shift as he lifted the dying man into his arms. "Mr. Cage. Thank you for coming to his aid."

Cage nodded simply. "He is kin. He would do the same for me."

Huasca looked at the Seeker and ensign. Though they were his enemies, and likely had not attacked the monster to aid Osiris, they had also played a part in making sure that he was safe. "Be well, and whatever happens next, may you find peace."

He didn't wait to hear their response. He stepped back into the portal, Osiris in his arms, and fell back into the Ghostlands…

"…I'm starting to think we were sent to slaughter against these pirates," Ephala said aloud, looking at Golde.

"You and I both. What do we do about him?" Golde asked, pointing to Cage, who was staring directly at them.

Ephala sighed and wielded her daggers again. "I guess there truly is no rest for the wicked. We're up against another Alyrian pirate."

Cage chuckled, then pointed behind them. "I believe it better if we focus on the undead that want to eat us than each other. For now."

The trio turned to face the remaining Damned. Bloodied, fatigued, drenched in rain, and facing long odds, they combated death once more.

LXII

THE SHAPE OF THINGS TO COME

The door to the navigation cabin burst open as the Damned surged inside, hellbent on slaughtering the last living pirates aboard the ship. Reece Stone rallied the men in front of Morgan, covering him until the very end. "Look alive boys! Meet yer makers with blood on yer blades and bodies at yer feet!" he shouted. He fired his dragon guns into the surging horde, cutting down a swathe of them with its fire.

Volld Cutter fired his blunderbuss, adding to the devastation and cutting down another wave of the Damned in the small compartment. Its boom deafened the men, but nobody cared to cover their ears. It would be over soon enough. He dropped the gun and swung his prosthetic blade, ready to meet the horde.

Callen Flint fired his breech-loading rifle into the crowd, punching holes through heads even with one good eye to aim with. When the bullets were spent, he dropped the weapon and pulled out his sword and waited for the horde to come at him.

The trio went blade to blade against the mob, and just as death was about to ensnare them in its maw a bright purple light enveloped them, and the Damned were left swinging at empty air.

The cabin was empty.

*****

The bright purple light enveloped the two ships. It disappeared almost as quickly as it appeared, and with it, the remaining Azura pirates were saved from an awful death. Standing atop the steering deck of Anathane's Pain, Felix Helregal watched as the light came and went. Realizing what had just transpired, the Dread Captain scowled behind his golden mask. "It would seem we have been betrayed…"

Caine lit up, and the amulet's normally malicious grin was instead a pensive sneer. "Disappointing."

The Dread Captain snapped his fingers. "Finish her."

Immediately, the gun ports of Anathane's Pain slid open, and a devastating volley of shots was fired into Azura as the chains that bound her receded. Already devastated by the rigors of the battle, the ship began to crumble and sink. Once the home of many a boisterous pirate, her halls were silent tombs drenched in blood, corpses, and feasting undead. Her windows shattered from the cannon fire and rising water pressure, gushing forth cold, black saltwater spray that filled her compartments. Once a legend of pirate lore, Azura was reduced once to a floating tomb and now a sinking mausoleum. Another casualty of the Dread Captain's wrath. The statue of the chained, blindfolded woman mounted beneath the mast of Anathane's Pain bore silent, blind witness to Azura's death.

*****

Helregal watched with wrathful indifference as Azura sank into the sea. His ships circled around her like vultures over carrion. He turned his focus to Officer Black as he came lumbering up the stairs to the steering deck. "Officer Black. My, my, you look like wet shit washed out of the brine."

The lumbering Drakkari gave him a blank look. The surprise attack by the Xallan shaman, as Byzarra had explained who he was, caused mostly superficial damage. He had sustained severe splinters from fracturing wood on his descent, though that mattered little to him, undead or not. He ripped several sharp chunks from his body and dropped them on the deck before resetting his hanging jaw and snapping them together. "I will survive."

"Well, I would certainly hope so. I've seen you survive much worse than that," Helregal said before turning to face the other officers that filed in behind him. He looked them over. Save for Shade, Byzarra, and Volldah both looked much worse for wear. "We underestimated the abilities of our enemies. They struck a bargain with Atla, it would seem. She let them escape," he said with disdain in his voice.

Black took the knee first, immediately followed by the others. Helregal stood in front of them. He could not blame them. He himself had underestimated his old enemy's resolve to live, as well as the skill of his officers.

He hadn't even deigned to use the full might of his armada, instead opting to send ships on to Spirus to begin the coastal assault.

"We have failed you, master. Such incompetence will not happen again. Not on my watch," Black said. Even when the beast apologized, he was too proud to grovel, even to a force strong enough to destroy him.

"What say the rest of you?" Helregal asked, folding his arms.

"I underestimated the shaman, master. Due to my incompetence, my golem was destroyed, and Shade was forced to rescue me," Byzarra explained, looking first at his boots, then peering up into the implacable gaze of her master.

"Do not fret, child. You will have many more opportunities to prove your power, as you did with that El'wa fleet," Helregal reassured her.

Volldah was missing an arm and a leg and had been forced to drag herself up the stairs on the regenerating stumps. The silent shapeshifter let out a guttural croak and whimper, pressing her masked face to Helregal's boot. "This one is sorry, master (a thousand apologies)" she hissed. Her voice doubled as usual, and even that sounded sorrowful. She trembled at his feet.

Helregal squatted down and ran a callous, cold hand over her helmet. He looked at Shade, and the inky black skeleton took off his hat and bowed his head low.

"We have failed this day, brothers, and sisters. But the Gravefather is not displeased. We have seen what lengths our enemy will go to in order to escape death. Now we know what to expect, when next they sit on our plate. Morgan Sarron and what remnants remain of his pirates will die in due time. For now, we have other business to attend," Helregal said as he turned his gaze toward the rattling chains that approached, carrying two limp bodies with them.

Ephala and Cambridge were deposited on the deck before them, and Helregal regarded them. "Officer Black tells me that you two have been quite an annoying little thorn in his side this evening. You even came to the aid of that mettlesome little Alyrian pirate that I had bid him torture. Now, instead of his corpse, I have you two before me. How disappointing…"

Ephala coughed and lifted her head to peer into the eyes of the Dread Captain for the first time. Those blood-red pools made her bones shiver. "That monster killed my friends, my crew, and my officers. To hell with the pirate, I had a score to settle."

"Now, now, Seeker. Manners," Cambridge warned as he looked around at their alarming new company. He kept a wary eye on the chains that had dragged them here, still dancing and slithering in the background like living metal serpents. "You kept us alive. Why?"

Helregal looked at him, then chuckled. "You can cease your performance, Calligulus. You have performed your role admirably."

"Calligulus? Who is…" Ephala looked at Cambridge as he rose to his feet, a grin spread across his face from ear to ear. He looked at her and knelt, running a hand down her cheek apologetically.

"Apologies, Lady Seeker. I have been untruthful as to my origins. You see, I am not Cambridge Golde. Though, we do bear a striking resemblance. We could be almost twins, you could say," the man, Calligulus, said, unable to hide his amusement.

"You…what have you done, and where is the real Ensign Cambridge Golde?!" Ephala demanded.

Calligulus pursed his lips and made a clucking sound. "Who could say? Perhaps he is dead, perhaps he is not. All that matters is that his persona got me here, right where the Gravefather meant for me to be…" he fanned his arms out in grandiose fashion. "Oh, and sorry about the gun crews. To their credit, if I hadn't sabotaged their equipment, they probably could have saved your ship. More's the pity, I suppose."

"You did what? You…" Ephala's face twisted with rage. "You sabotaged them?! You're the reason we were overwhelmed?! The reason we…"

Calligulus shrugged again and waved a hand dismissively. "I said probably. I suppose we'll never know, now, will we?"

"I am in need of a messenger to deliver to Emperor's Rest. Seeker Ephala, that is the reason you yet breathe. Acolyte Calligulus, you are to deliver the good word to your masters of my coming. Tell them that the Gravefather's plans have begun."

"As you say, my lord." Calligulus bowed.

Helregal handed him a sealed, black envelope.

"I would rather die than help you, monster," Ephala said through gritted teeth. The air was silent. So quiet that she could hear the wind billowing through the sails of Anathane's Pain. Helregal turned to face her now. His mask made his face unreadable, but she could tell he did not like her response even by his posture. He walked over to her slowly. Each of his steps seemed to echo in the silence before he stopped in front of her and slowly stooped down to become eye level with her.

"…Are you sure about that?" he asked her icily. "She would disagree, I think." He looked behind her.

She looked over her shoulder. "Tora…no…"

Before them was Tora, or what was left of her after Black was finished with her. He'd broken her neck, and it lulled from side to side as she moved in a hunched-over lurch. Her lower half had been reaffixed back to her body from where Black had ripped her in two, and an ugly gash where the skin and armor had been torn was plain to see.

She walked like she didn't know how to use her legs.

Suddenly, Tora was lifted into the air by coils of gold chains, covered in sharp spikes that dug into her flesh and coiled around her like serpents. Her armor was dented and damaged, and the chains seemed to twist it and bend it further where they moved. She looked like she was in agony. If her face was any indicator, she was. Her lips moved in a silent scream, and her eyes looked at Ephala with a mix of mute terror and pleading desperation.

"You should know by now, Seeker, that there are fates in this world a thousand times worse than death. Your Seeker-sister here can attest to that. She will serve as your reminder of that fact from here on out. A pair of eyes to watch you, and a grim omen of things to come, should you ever get it in your petulant little head to cross me. Understand?"

He crooked a finger under her chin and forced her to look into his eyes. The rain dripped down his mask in clear rivulets. Tears blurred her vision as she gazed into the cold, red eyes of pure evil.

"I understand."

"Good. Now, listen close. I have a task for you, Seeker Ephala…"

*****

The moonlit shore was calm and quiet. Seagulls lazily cawed and rode the waves and the wind as a coconut crab crept close to one positioned atop a palm tree. The crab clacked its claws together as it crept closer, digging the tips of its legs into the wood of the tree as it silently hoisted itself closer. The wind blew, rustling the tree fronds. The gull lazily flapped its wings to maintain its balance as it moved with the wind but remained perched in the tree. The crab made it into the canopy and began crawling down the long palm leaf the gull sat on. It quickly skittered near, closing the gap as its prey was nearly in its grasp.

Suddenly, the calm was broken as a blinding flash of purple light cracked the sky, shining bright like a second moon. It was followed by a thunderous noise that destroyed the calm of the beach and sent the palm trees shaking. The gull took flight, escaping the crab, who fell to the ground and crawled away as the bodies of several humans were deposited unceremoniously on the beach.

Cutter rolled over and sat up. "I know I've been askin' this a lot lately, but in fairness, shit's been gettin' even weirder than usual, ay?" Cutter began as he stood to his feet. "But WHAT THE FUCK JUST HAPPENED?! Are we dead?!"

"Cutter, I pray to the Stars above 'n the Infernals below that when I die, ye are somewhere far, far, *far* away from me," Stone groaned as he rubbed his head and wiped sand from his grey hair and face.

"Aye to that," Flint agreed as he rose to his feet and wiped sand out of his eyepatch and stitches. "Fucking sand gets everywhere." He blinked his good eye and froze in disbelief as he saw Steven Cage standing a few yards away, covered in blood and cuts and stumbling around on the moonlit beach like a lost child. "Cage? Is that you?!"

Cage squinted his eyes in disbelief and ran toward his brethren, who clapped their arms around him in greeting. "Surely this must be a trick from the gods! Ha!"

"If it were, I'd think they'd come up with somethin' a wee bit better 'n your ugly mugs, ay?" Stone laughed.

Morgan and Hanover were the last to rise. Morgan dusted himself off and wiped sand from his blood and sweat-caked beard. He took off his hat and wiped it off as well as he looked down at the stirring Hanover. "You alright, boy?" he asked.

Hanover stirred and opened his eyes.

Morgan blinked, for a brief moment, Hanover's eyes looked bright purple, but when he looked again, they were their ordinary light green color. The boy sat up, blinked his eyes dreamily and yawned.

"Where are we?" he asked.

Morgan looked around, then looked up at the mountaintop far in the distance, through the thick jungle covering. His heart swelled, and a smile spread across his face as he began to laugh. "Sink me low and tie my hands—we're home! Boys, look! We're home!" Morgan shouted, pointing to the mountaintop.

The other officers paused their conversation, looked where he was pointing, and began to laugh and cheer, unable to believe their eyes. They beheld the towering statue of a pirate captain holding a trident high above a mountain peak.

They *were* home.

✶✶✶✶✶

Pate stood at the nose of the Duchess, gazing far off into the wall of the storm that surrounded the island.

He couldn't sleep, not tonight. He felt that something was off. The wind and water were calm; still. That never bode well. He was lost in thought when he saw a bright purple flash out of the corner of his eye, originating from somewhere on the other side of the island.

"What the…" he froze and tensed his left arm. The mark was flaring up again and he grit his teeth. It felt like was being branded all over again, but much, much worse. The pain kept ramping up. It got hotter and hotter still. He cried out and fell to his knees, tearing his coat off to reveal the mark burning bright and changing from cyan to a deep purple color. The light was blinding, and so he squeezed his eyes shut as he cried out in pain.

Several crewmen gathered around him, reaching out as he warded them off. "Stay back!" Pate shouted, leaning against the railing and howling in pain. The men covered their eyes and ears as Pate's voice rose several octaves and the glow in his arm shone blindingly bright. To an onlooker, all they would see is a ball of screaming, purple light.

Eventually, the pain and light subsided. Pate slid down until he was plopped onto the deck as the men crowded him, murmuring to each other in between questions, asking if he was alright. McDunham and Crimp broke through, offering their hands to him.

"Are ye alright, Cap'n? Ye were screamin' loud enough to wake half the damn town!" McDunham asked.

"Ye look awful, sir. Just awful…" Crimp admitted with a worried gaze.

Pate was drenched in sweat, with deep, dark circles around his eyes. His skin was ashen white and looked wet and waxy at the same time. He looked like he was dying.

"I'm fine. Get back to your posts…" Pate said in a small, distant voice.

"But sir, you're—" Crimp began.

Pate found his fire, shouting this time, "I said get back to your posts!"

The men bolted to their tasks. McDunham and Crimp following shortly after. "Yes, sir…" Crimp walked off.

Pate sat, chin between his knees as his body came down from the harrowing ordeal he'd just went through. His ears pricked up; he heard distant, watery voices.

"She comes!" One said.

"The mistress!" Another said.

"She beckons!" A spirited, giddy voice said.

"A debt to pay!" A dark voice uttered.

"You will all pay!" An angry voice promised.

"Shekhinah!" A jubilant voice cried.

"Glory!" A final voice praised.

He looked around… but no one was there. He was alone.

Pate heaved himself to his feet and looked back into the storm wall in the distance. He could see vague, unnatural shapes shifting in the clouds. He squeezed his eyes shut… and vomited.

*****

The sea raged, and the rain turned torrential as white capped waves big enough to capsize ships rose and rolled all around them. Anathane's Pain rode the waves effortlessly, unable to be drowned by them. The moon peered through black clouds the size of cities, raging overhead with thunderheads dancing within them. The officers and crew watched on as the Dread Captain stood at the nose of the ship, Byzarra at his side watching in rapt fascination as he called forth bolts of red lightning and waterspouts. In the moonlight, it looked as though the water was blood.

Ships rose from the sea, five times as many as the four that came with them during the attack. They flew banners of all kinds, El'wa, Duwa, Kurzan, Xallan, Dyonian, and many more. But all of them flew the Dread banner as well—a red flag with a screaming, gold-toothed, black skull. A vortex formed in the water, and the remains of the Black Bess were dredged up from the deep. Her waterlogged crew reanimated themselves, standing at attention and turning to face Helregal as their ship righted itself.

"Down, down, down in the abyss. The light never shines. You pray for remit. Treading the sands of the lightless wake, gasping for a breath to take. And in those depths, at the gates of hell, are where all sailors' souls will dwell.

656

Damned to tread the treacherous waters. Never to see your sons and daughters. Where Dead Sea Gods lurk and wait. Prowling there, your soul to take…” Helregal sang, his voice carrying on the wind.

“You have seen what awaits you. I offer you an escape. Will you be conquered by your damnation, or will you conquer it? Sail with me as the undying kings and queens of the sea or drown forevermore. The choice is yours. Those who would take up the accord, speak it now,” Helregal said.

The newly risen dead looked at themselves and their brethren. Helregal saw the horror painting their faces and haunting their eyes. Theirs had seen what no mortal’s should. He knew they would take this accord, even if it meant that awaited them was a new hell.

Ambrose Castell, Jukel Staunton, and James Avery looked at their men, now resurrected just as they were. In life, they were strong, powerful, proud sailors, but in death…

“Will we bend the knee so easily, and court a pact with the devil?” Ambrose asked.

Jukel Staunton shivered as he held his head in his arms. “To be devoured by monsters at the bottom of the sea, or to serve the Dread Captain? If I must choose…then I think it obvious which one is preferable, Ambrose.”

“Avery? Will you bow to him, too?” Ambrose asked as he looked around and saw the answer on all their faces.

Avery was quiet. His body had been blown apart, and the damage was plain to see. His organs hung from him like fruit from a vine, and his face was unrecognizable. All that identified him was the star and stripes on the breast of his tattered jacket. He said nothing.

“An accord is made; a debt to be paid…” the former crew of Black Bess said in unison.

Helregal smiled behind his mask. Caine cackled maniacally.

Black Bess sat, fully reconstituted on the water. Her Imperial Navy banner, a blue flag with white wave caps, was tattered. Above it, she now flew the screaming skull banner.

“Excellent. We have work to do.”

*****

657

He was standing on the deck of Ruby's Prize again, staring at pale blue moon and listening to the waves crash against the side of the ship. He blinked and looked around, seeing Ricken to his left, giving him a queer expression.

"You alright, mate?" Ricken asked.

Baker let out a bated breath. "Aye...I uh. I had the weirdest dream, ay?"

Ricken pinched the bridge of his nose before laughing. "A dream? Did ye marry the Queen of Brova in that dream, brother?"

"Pfft, I fuckin' wish. Nay, my dream was dark as hell. I saw..." Baker paused, thinking he'd heard something rattle in the background. Had they been using chains to bind the cargo again?

"Saw what?" Ricken pressed him, annoyed.

"Bah, doesn't matter. We still on patrol?" Baker asked as he lit a cigarette and leaned on the railing. He heard that rattling again, but louder, now.

"The patrol never stops, brother," Ricken said.

Baker paused mid-puff. Ricken's voice sounded off. He looked over at him...and dropped the cigarette from his lips. "No..."

Ricken stood, bound in chains, neck snapped harshly to the side. His eyes were bloodshot and wide open, and his lips were cut, showing the bloodied teeth behind them. "It never stops..." He lurched toward Baker.

"No, no, no...it wasn't a nightmare, it wasn't..."

"A nightmare? Open your eyes, Baker. You're livin' in one, right now!" Ricken laughed. Blood and spit dribbled from his twisted lips. "Wake up, brother! Wake up!" he lurched closer and reached out with waterlogged, blackened hands...

Baker startled himself awake as his boat tapped up against the end of a dock platform. He blinked. An elegant looking spear tip was pointed inches from his face. In fact, there were several.

"Oh, shit..." Baker breathed.

"State your name and your business in the City of Leaves, ver'mak," one of the spear-pointers, a guardsman in green, vine-covered armor, asked.

"I-I-I come in peace!" Baker stammered, raising his hands a little too quickly for the guardsmen's liking.

"Make a sudden move again and I'll spear you through the head," the guardsman warned. "I'll ask again: Why. Are. You. Here?"

"I was-was told to deliver a-a-a...a message! Yes! I have it here—" Baker reached for his pocket.

He froze when the tip of a spear pressed into his chest, right where his heart was beating. He reached slowly and pulled the envelope out. The lead guardsman snatched it from him, and they pulled their spears back, still watching him.

The guard flipped the envelope over in his hand, inspecting the purple octopus seal. "You say this message is for who?" The lead guardsman asked.

Shit! What was his name? What was his bloody name?!

"Ah…ah…sell…semen? Sell semen! Yes!" Baker said with an overly wide smile. His heart was in his throat.

The guardsmen looked at one another, then at him, then back at one another. "Is this a joke to you, human?" The guardsman asked, running a hand down the side of his face.

Shit. Wrong name.

Baker laughed nervously as he tried his damndest to remember the name of the person he was meant to meet.

"Thaman! Sel'Thamman! He-he-he's…"

"The patriarch of the House of Umbra? Ha! You? A lowly ver'mak pirate, drifting along in a dingy, reeking of sweat and swill?" The lead guardsman chuckled unamused. The other guards chuckled as well. None of them were amused. "I think I'm going to kill you now, ver'mak. Thank you for the laugh, I'll be sure to tell my kin tonight."

"Wait please! On my mother and my grave I promise what I'm tellin' ye is true, mate! Honest! I was sent here by…"

The image of the Dread Captain's piercing gaze stopped him short.

"I was sent here by my cap'n to deliver this message *personally* to er, Mr. Sel'Thamman. It's for his eyes only, it is!" Baker said.

The lead guardsman narrowed his eyes. "You will refer to him as lord, and only lord, or your tongue will be taken. A human captain wishes to deliver a message to the Patriarch? Who is this captain you speak of?"

Baker could feel a cold lump settle in his gut. He felt that if he told them who sent him, he would either be slain by them, or slain by *him* for uttering his name.

"I cannot say, sir. Not here. I must speak with Lord Sel'Thamman immediately. I can say no more," Baker said, trying to keep his composure.

The lead guardsman shrugged. "Very well, ver'mak. I suppose it really makes no difference to me. Lord Sel'Thamman will deal with you himself, should you prove a waste of his time. Follow me."

He was grabbed out of the boat and walked down the docks, and they made their way into the city proper. Baker couldn't help but gasp in wonder at what he saw. He had never been to an El'wa city before. Indeed, all he had ever heard of them was what he'd grabbed from random travelers and the stories of his youth. They didn't do it justice.

The city was bright, even in the night. It was abuzz with the chirp of crickets and night animals, as well as the drip of water. He saw hanging gardens attached to almost every building he walked past, and realized that the lights he saw were not torches, but blue and green and pink glowing fungus. They were attached to street posts, to the banners of buildings and archways, and of course were growing organically on trees and rocks. It was positively dazzling. As they walked, they went past what appeared to be some sort of park or garden, and several flying eel-like creatures, luxills, he remembered they were called, flew above their heads.

He gasped as one stopped in front of his face and gazed at him with a blackened pupil. It's skin was like that of a jellyfish—all blue and purple and shimmering. It appraised him a moment, then bore off to the left, rejoining its pack and flying through the air toward the water, nabbing insects in the air as they went. He wished Ricken could see this. It was the most fascinating place he'd ever seen.

Eventually, they reached a large estate, complete with a gate and walkway. The lead guard spoke to the men at the gate and they were allowed through, though not before laughing amongst themselves and speaking ill of the pirate in their midst in el'wish. They continued onto the main house of the estate, and the lead guardsman knocked at the door. Baker, meanwhile, stood gap-mouthed, marveling at the pillars that held up the porch overhand and the white marble stone the building was carved from.

A woman opened the door. She had dazzling, dusky blue colored skin, sharp red eyes, angular, symmetrical features, and snow-white hair. She, too, was beautiful, but in a much more sensual way than the city he had been walking through. She gave him a questioning look.

"Sohathin mel'dus, da'nem. For what reason does the city guard stand at our doorstep in the middle of the night?" The woman asked. Her voice was as dusky as her skin.

"Apologies, la'ren. This…ver'mak…seeks to speak with Lord Sel'Thamman. He says he has an urgent message for him," the guardsman said, unable to hide his skepticism.

The woman appraised Baker closer, cocking her head slightly to the side. "Is that so? Well. This evening has certainly become interesting. What do you have for my lord, human?"

Baker cleared his throat. "A message, m'lady. For his eyes only, I'm afraid."

She chuckled in the back of her throat. "I see. Very well, follow me. I will take you to him. Samak'nalem, guardsmen."

The guardsmen all bowed to the woman, and she shut the door behind him before silently walking past and urging him to follow her. The inside of the house, though it was more like a mansion, if ever Baker had seen one in his life, was also lined sparsely with glowing fungus. He could also see vines wrapped throughout as she led him through the main hall. It was wide enough for several men to walk, shoulder to shoulder.

They did not speak when they walked. He could sense that she had no interest in conversation. Were he to see her at a bar or tavern, he would probably have been so bold as to strike up a conversation with her. Here, however, he knew better than to potentially insult or irritate a stranger that knew his environment much better than he.

"This way," she said, stopping at a large doorway and twisting the metal nob open.

"Wait. What is your name, ma'am?" Baker asked. He regretted saying the word ma'am immediately, as she visibly frowned at it.

"I am *Lady* Vellarra Duskrunner. Follow me, and be silent until spoken to," she said, reiterating her command.

He nodded and followed her through the doorway.

They stood at a balcony overlooking a large chamber with a glass dome built into it, filtering in moonlight from above to what looked like some sort of workshop or study setup in the middle of the room. Vine-wrapped pillars, covered in flowers, held up the massive slab of ceiling above them, and Baker was once again taken aback by the pristine and organic beauty of this place and its architecture. Water streamed into the area around the study, forming a small, easily traversable moat around it.

And standing in the center, writing in a thick tome, was a tall and imposing El'wa man with skin like Vellarra's, and fiery red hair. His features were sharp and beauteous like hers, though much more masculine. He stroked a perfectly groomed moustache and goatee as he wrote, then turned his bright, glowing yellow eyes on them as they stood overhead. He wore fine, white-colored robes with red trim. The man had a confident, refined stance.

"Sohathin mel'dus, ch'tara. Why is this stranger in my house, this night?" The man, presumedly Lord Sel'Thamman, asked. His gaze was a heavy weight on Baker's shoulders, and he bowed reflexively.

"I-I-I bring a message, M'lord…from…" Baker stammered.

Vellarra stepped down the stairs toward Lord Sel'Thamman. A small stone walkway a few meters from the base of the stairway allowed her to cross over to Sel'Thamman without stepping into the water. She handed him the envelope, and Baker patted his pockets, not even realizing she'd taken it.

Lord Sel'Thamman took it gingerly. "Basham varel, ch'tara," he thanked her with a slight smile. "Let us see why this human stands before us."

Sel'Thamman opened the envelope with a letter-opener after running a thumb over the purple seal and pulled out several vellum notes within. He read through them carefully and quietly before looking once more at Baker and nodding.

"Ah…so it begins. Well…Vellarra, make our *guest* at home. I must make preparations. Sa toren vallo viscien." Sel'Thamman said briefly, evoking a relaxed nod and smile from Vellarra.

She ushered Baker out of the room.

Lord Sel'Thamman regarded them one last time. "Human? Thank you for delivering this to me. I am sure that you have been through much to reach this place." He said, knowingly. He nodded, and waved them goodbye, his glowing deep yellow eyes glancing back over the contents of the message once more as Vellarra led him away.

LXIII

Epilogue

The sun beat down harshly on Emperor's Rest. Vultures took shelter under the eaves of rooftops to hide from the summer heat, and every animal that didn't walk on two legs did the same. A crowd gathered in the city's center. Folk had been gathering for hours, now. The center was perhaps the oldest part of the city, from back before it was even a city at all. It had been renovated time and again, and the shops and guilds that existed here were the oldest in the city. Thatched roofs overlooked the cobbled streets and sidewalks. Buildings that had seen the sacking of the city at least a half dozen times from a half dozen different would-be conquerors. Corinth had heard that when the Dread Captain took the city a hundred years ago, he had all the nobles who didn't kneel to him hung, right in this square.

Oh, how history rhymes and riddles.

Vendors were offering fresh fruit to eat and water or ale to drink, and selling off their spoiled stock for people to throw when the spectacle began. It had been many years since the last public execution was held in the city center. Not since the days of Vagran the Fifth had a man been executed here. And that was twenty odd years ago, now. Nobles and guildsmen turned up their noses as the rabble from the lowtown made their way into the district as well. Many of them made snide remarks about the 'stench of poverty' or 'the intrusion of the commoners'.

It made Corinth's blood boil.

He had tried to reason with the Emperor. Or rather, he tried to reason with Ser Roderick, who had been fortuitously placed outside the gates when he asked to have an audience with the Emperor.

"He is currently preoccupied with imperial affairs. He is not holding court today," Roderick had said with an impish grin.

Now, all he could do was stand in the crowd like everyone else and wait. Mock execution or no, the people had been promised a show. For many of them, this was the only entertainment they would have for a fortnight or better.

"Care for a rotten apple, sir?" A street vendor offered him as he passed by. The man had a little stall, likely wheeled in from another district, with baskets of apples on either side. In an open box sitting beside him on his countertop were browned and molding apples. A cloud of gnats had descended upon the rotting fruit. Corinth wasn't wearing his plate armor, so perhaps that was why the vendor thought it wise to ask him.

"A rotten apple? Why in Aethera would I want that?" he asked, knowing the answer.

"Why, for the show of course! If you're lucky, sir, ye might even strike gold 'n nick the bastard in the head with it before it rolls, hahaha!" The street vendor responded giddily.

Corinth couldn't help but scowl. For all these people knew, a man really was about to be beheaded today. Was this really how they intended to treat him on his day of judgement?

"You would throw rotten fruit at a condemned man about to hang? Why?" Corinth asked.

The vendor looked at him, surprised by the question. He looked him up and down, sizing him up. "What's it to you?"

Corinth's frown deepened. "I am a Paladin of the Stars. It is my duty to see that my fellow man is treated justly, even on the day of their execution."

The man shrank behind his stall. "Ahaha! Apologies, Ser Paladin! I didn't realize I was soliciting one of the Stars' chosen, today!"

"Indeed," Corinth said. He placed a gold coin on the table and slid it to the vendor, who snatched it up immediately like a rodent pining for cheese. "Go down to the orphanage and give the rest of your fresh stock to the children, there. They need it more than these people, I assure you."

The vendor gave him a perplexed look, then shrugged and pocketed the coin. "As ye say, Ser Paladin."

Corinth turned his attention to the center of the crowd as people began gasp in awe. The scaffolding was fully assembled, now. The two executioners, likely the two imperial executioners, Ebonheart and Axios, stood ready as a carriage rolled up to it. A wave of imperial guardsmen pushed the crowd back as the imperial family filed out of the carriage. Corinth watched from afar as the

Emperor, then Empress Alessa, carrying Prince Andryn, then Princess Odessa, then Prince Gundyr stepped out onto the cobbles and approached a platform made to seat them.

He saw Viceroy coordinating the guards from the side, as well as Rumford leading his platoon, and Captain Yates. Ser Roderick also passed his field of vision, talking to several guardsmen as he walked to his position. He pushed through the crowd and made his way through the guards as he approached, clearly surprising Viceroy and the others to see him out in public without his armor. He approached the Emperor immediately. The guards gave him a wary gaze at first, but upon realizing who he was, they lowered their guard.

"Paladin Corinthian. To what do I owe the pleasure? Varryn asked as he mounted the stairs to the viewing platform.

"Your grace, I know that this is only a mock spectacle, but I must warn you that these people are expecting *real* blood when that boy comes out and mounts the guillotine," Corinth said. He could feel Gundyr's eyes on his back, but he didn't have the time to exchange pleasantries with his pupil.

"The people will be blockaded by a hundred-plus armed guards and knights. I would hardly worry that they will put hands on the boy," Varryn dismissed.

"I am not worried about the crowd putting hands on him. I am worried about the message you are sending them by even doing this at all. These people see death as a spectacle, a form of entertainment. It is awful enough that the boy would be humiliated so in public. But now you're toying with his life in front of them. You're telling them that this is a game, that you can and will bring men to the razor's edge just to prove a point. Does that not seem…tyrannical…your grace?"

Varryn sat down and gave Corinth a frigid look. "A tyrant? Is that what you think of me, Ser Corinthian? You think of me as a tyrant?"

Corinth paused, choosing his next words very carefully. "I do not see you as anything other than our just ruler, your grace. But I feel it is my duty to warn you of the potential consequences of your actions in the eyes of your people. They watch you. They watch every action you take, every choice you make. Right now, these people see your word as being ironclad. Unshakable, but fair. After this? They will see it as a thing tarnished, like rusted metal. Then, someday, even that will erode…"

Varryn laughed. "All that doom and gloom over a staged execution? Pfft, surely you jest, paladin? You speak like a prophetic doomsayer, not a man of faith and reason. Donivus Ballandry will be fine. The people will keep their composure, and the day will trudge on much like any other. Now, either take a seat by the boy or step down and return to your prayers, it matters not."

He laughed, but Corinth could see the irritation and anger in Varryn's face. Only his pride was speaking, now.

Corinth sighed. "Try as I may…as you say, your grace."

He made his way over to Gundyr, greeting the rest of the imperial family as he went, then sat down. They were a few seats away from Varryn, close to the steps.

"You tried to speak reason to father, I presume?" Gundyr asked in a low tone, mindful of their company.

"Tried…and failed," Corinth sighed.

"Do not despair, Ser Corinth. I fail to get through his iron-thick skull all the time," Gundyr said.

The two chuckled, then went silent as the carriage holding the star of the show opened, and Donivus Ballandry marched toward the scaffolding, a black hood over his head. The crowd cheered and jeered, screaming profanities and clamoring for blood. It sent a chill down Corinth's spine.

Donivus was shoved to the scaffolding and made to ascend it. From his vantage point, Corinth could hear the young man muttering as he climbed. Corinth realized he was saying a prayer in Atarran. He leaned over the railing to get a better view.

People had already begun throwing rotten fruit. A tomato, or some other red fruit had struck Donivus in the leg and he gasped in surprise as he was stood in front of the guillotine.

"Order! The next person who throws something is going up there with him!" Viceroy shouted as he stood in front of the scaffold.

The crowd booed, but they stopped throwing fruit. Moments like these made Corinth realize just how little power most men had against an angry or unruly mob. He saw thousands of people packed tight in the street. It wouldn't take much for them to push passed the guards, and then Donivus would be…

"Donivus Ballandry," Vexyn said as he stepped onto the platform, escorted by Rumford and Yates. "You stand accused of high treason, obstruction of justice, and information brokering and espionage against the high crown. The consequence for even the least of these crimes…is death. How do you plead?”

Donivus finished his prayer and began hyperventilating.

“I did nothing, sir! S'il te plaît! Aies pitié! Mercy, please!”

Vexyn paused, looked at Varryn, who shook his head, and then continued. “If you will not cooperate with us, then you stand against us and jeopardize the safety of the imperial crown and all its subjects. Master Ebonheart…you may proceed.”

Corinth subconsciously clutched his rosary.

Ebonheart stepped forward and hoisted the guillotine blade before pulling a lever. The lever locked the blade in place, preventing it from dropping. He motioned to Axios, who made Donivus kneel and locked him in place. Ebonheart checked the apparatus once more, then walked over to Donivus and removed his hood. The young man’s eyes met with the Master Interrogators, and he began to shake and whimper.

“S'il te plaît! S'il te plaît! I will tell you anything, please! I promise, everything you want I will tell you, I swear!” Donivus wailed.

Ebonheart chuckled. The noise was like a cracking whip to Corinth’s ears. The Master Interrogator looked at Vexyn and nodded.

“He will cooperate.”

Vexyn looked at the Emperor, who nodded with a slight smirk forming on his stony face. “Unshackle him.”

Corinth released a breath he hadn’t known he’d been holding. He released his rosary and let it dangle, and saw blood on his hands where the points of the metal star had dug in. A drop dangled from the wound, accumulated into a tear, then plopped to the floor of the platform and slipped between the floorboards.

As if on cue, a loud shot rang out from somewhere within the crowd, and the lever that held the blade in place was broken.

The guillotine plummeted.

Odessa placed a hand over her mouth in shock, then screamed.

Corinth looked around, trying to find the shooter from his vantage point. He saw a black figure, a hundred yards across the square, sitting atop a roof. He watched it disappear as quickly as it came, crawling silently over the side of the roof, out of sight. Then, he looked at the guillotine.

Donivus Ballandry’s head rolled across the floor.

Pandemonium ensued.

Storm Peak was abuzz with chatter as more pirates sat in its rows than ever before. The whole island heard of the Immortal Captain's arrival. After five long years, their de-facto leader had returned.

"Order! I demand order in the court!" Lord Zakum shouted as he slammed his gavel down. The crowd slowly began to die down as the Brethren Court readied to address them.

"Where is he?" Lord Kryta whispered, leaning toward him.

"Only Zafuma knows…" Zakum sighed.

"If he doesn't show soon, we're goin' to have a riot on our hands," Firebeard added as he watched the pirates laugh and drink amongst themselves. Even as their lords, it was dangerous to have these many pirates in one place idle.

"He will come," Xin-Jun said with certainty.

"Oh? And how do you know that, pray tell?" Goldfang gave him a skeptical look.

"He is our leader. Why would he not show himself?" Lord Krait asked. She saw Captain Pate in the crowd, sitting with his two ships' worth of men. They locked eyes as he nodded to her.

"Perhaps he brings dire news?" Kryta suggested. "Pirates aren't known for taking bad news well…"

"He is here," Xin-Jun stated, pointing at the doorway in front of them, positioned underneath the rows of seats.

Approaching down the hall were six figures, lit by the torches that illuminated the long passageway. Zakum ordered all be quiet as the figures approached. Morgan was the first to come out into the parthenon. Followed by his remaining officers and Hanover. The crowd cheered immediately upon seeing him, and he waved at them like a king waving at a parade crowd. He stopped in front of the pirate lords, looking at his chair a moment. He thought to sit in it, but he felt that for what he was about to say next, it would be best if he stood in front of them.

"Welcome home, Lord Morgan. You have been gone overlong," Kryta addressed him immediately. She stood and bowed, as did the other pirate lords. Her greeting was left wanting. It was cordial, but uncertain. He sniffed the air and looked around. Something was off. The pirates were surprised, elated to see him, but there were murmurs in the crowd. He'd heard them as well when he walked through town.

"Greetings, Lord Kryta, Lord Zakum…Krait'Malai, Xin-Jun, Goldfang…and who could forget you, Lord Firebeard?" Morgan said, addressing each with his gaze. He saw mixed feelings in all of them. Anxiety, annoyance, perhaps even fear.

Why?

"I have the feeling that my return is unexpected, but also unwelcome. You did not anticipate my return. Fair enough. The sea is a dangerous place to wander for five years as an ordinary sailor, never mind a pirate with a bounty on his head. But now I am here, alive and…well, alive," Morgan said. He folded his arms behind his back and gestured to his bloody and battered crew behind him. "Though our enemies tried to ensure that wasn't the case."

Goldfang sniffed the air, an almost comical gesture for a man to do. Wuhlven are no ordinary men, however. "What became of your men and Azura, Lord Morgan? When you arrived, they were nowhere to be found. Almost three-hundred souls were with you."

Morgan scowled and turned to address the audience. "My crew and my ship are gone. Destroyed. What you see before you are all that remains."

The crowd went wild with gasps and speculation. Another powerful pirate had been brought to his knees; his crew vanished into thin air. What terrible beast could have done that to the Immortal Captain? Was it a rogue wave? An Alyria storm? A kraken? Had the navy sent a fleet after them and cornered them? He heard it all.

"Your ship…Azura is gone? How can that be? She was unstoppable! She's seen countless battles! She is a ship of legend!" Krait gasped, unable to contain her surprise.

"Yes, yes she was. But there's always a bigger fish, isn't there?" Morgan said, pivoting back to the lords in their seats.

Firebeard leaned forward. "Cap'n…what happened? Ye are far too crafty to be bested by the Bluecoats or the Sha'nav. What sank Azura?"

Morgan stroked his beard, leaving a long pause before his response. "An age ago, I killed a man that once used to be my friend. Some would argue that I saved our very world with that act. It sealed my name in history as the Immortal Captain. Unkillable, unbeatable, and unshakable. That's the funny thing about legends, though. They're just stories, and often do not do reality its humble justice. I am flesh and blood like any other, and it would seem that what I thought was dead and gone in my past is far from gone with the wind…"

"No, no he isn't. He found you, didn't he, my lord?" A man called out from behind him. Morgan turned.

Captain Pate stepped down from the stands and approached. He took off his hat and nodded to the older pirate. "My name is Edward Patron, sir. And I believe we have both experienced the same foe. One that came back from the dead, isn't it? With a coterie of Damned at his beck and call, glistening like gold and hungering for flesh? The Dread Captain…"

The crowd uproared again. People called him crazy, dismissing his warnings. They didn't want to believe that what he said was true. Morgan quieted them with a raise of his hand.

"…Edward Patron. I've heard of you on the wind, son. They say that you've become quite a force to be reckoned. When I was in the Emperor's study, yours was a face on his wall. Congratulations. You've made his Most Wanted list."

Pate gave a surprised smirk. The man he idolized knew his name. He hid it as quick as it came. "Is that so, my lord? Well, then I'd say this is a sorry state of affairs. I've earned my name but lost the reason for it. My men, and my fleet are gone. Your old friend, Felix Helregal saw to that."

Morgan's face darkened. "Aye…you met with the Dread Captain as well, did you?"

"Met with him? I nearly died to 'em," Pate stated.

Morgan nodded and faced the pirate lords once more. "Ladies and gentlemen of the Brethren Court, we stand at the precipice of a great and terrible threat. Soon, his shadow will descend upon us, and if we are not ready to combat him, then we risk losing all that we have accomplished in these past hundred years. What Edward Patron says is true. The Dread Captain has returned from the Dark Depths, and he will doubtless set his gaze upon us.

"If he is so bold as to destroy a pirate fleet and come after me, how long then will it be before he comes knocking at all your doors? Before he darkens the sky with smoke as he razes your ships and plunders your wealth? He has with him a host of Damned, men and women who have sold their souls to his service to escape damnation in the afterlife. And in return? He made them ravenous undead. How long before they gnaw upon your bones as they gnawed upon my men?

"As the oldest member of the Brethren Court, I, Lord Morgan Sarron of the Azura Pirates, motion to declare war on the Dread Captain, Felix Helregal, and all who follow him. Dread is upon us, brethren. We must destroy it before it consumes us all. And when it lays at our feet, we will plunder all the wealth it has robbed and remind those who stand against us why it is they fear to sail on our seas…"

The crowd went into a frenzy; they screamed for blood.

They screamed for war.

And they screamed for treasure.

Morgan smiled at the chaos he had caused and turned to face the other lords. He nodded to them and raised an open hand of invitation. They looked at the crowd, already brawling with one another and firing their guns into the air. They looked then, at Morgan, who silently waited for their decree, and then at each other.

Lord Zakum nodded and slammed his gavel. The lords stood in unison once more, and the words that Pate had been waiting to hear were uttered from his lips.

"Motion passed."

Brunt, Andrews, Jackson, Franklin, Smith…and yes, even you, Oculeth. This is for all of you…

Pate cheered and pumped his fist into the air.

*****

It was dark, here.

So very dark.

He couldn't see where he was, all he could see was himself, looking back at him in the mirror. Something was off about his reflection, however. He stepped closer, touching his face. His reflection did the same.

"How long have I had purple eyes?"

He covered his mouth. He could hear his thoughts aloud?

The purple-eyed version of himself smiled.

But he didn't feel himself smiling.

"So, you're finally awake. You slumbered so peacefully, Armen Hanover," the purple-eyed Hanover said. But it didn't have his voice, it had a deep, intoxicating woman's voice. He didn't know whether to be titillated or terrified.

"Why not both?" The clone said, morphing into someone completely different.

Before him stood a purple-eyed woman with pale skin, full lips, wide hips, and pert breasts. She was completely naked, her shaven body on full display. Her long, wild, raven black hair hung in curly tresses all about her. She had wings on her back, dark purple in pigment, reminiscent of bat wings… or demon wings.

"A demon, or an angel? It is all a matter of perception, is it not?" she posited.

"Who are you… where am I?" Hanover asked, looking around his new environment as light now poured into it from above. He was surrounded by a room of mirrors, all reflecting versions of himself at him.

"You wanted to help me, did you not? We made a bargain. I save you, and *you* save me…" the woman said, her voice now familiar.

"Atla…this is what you look like?" Hanover asked, stepping back from her as alarm bells rang in his head.

"I have…many…forms," she said. Her voice changed, as did her body. At once it was hard and masculine, then it turned soft and feminine again, then an androgenous mix of the two. It smiled at his confusion, then shifted into an elderly woman with purple irises and a furtive grin.

He recognized who she was, now.

"You're the woman. The woman who…" He rubbed at his wrist tattoo. It glowed purple.

"I thought you would remember me," the old woman tittered. Then, she turned back to the naked, bat-winged young woman. "I also go by many names. Atla was once one, now one of many. But I liked her name. Liked what she was, what she stood for. I think we'll use it again for a time, don't you think?" she asked in a giddy, playful tone.

He pressed his back to the glass, wanting to be as far away from her as possible.

"As for where you are, well. You're where she once was. Or I…or we, for that matter," Atla said, speaking in riddles.

"This is…this is the inside of the Eye of Atla?" Hanover asked, confused.

"Mmm, yes. Perceptive, aren't you?" she complimented him in that mocking, playful tone.

"Why am I here? Where are my friends? My brothers in black?" Hanover asked in a worried tone. The last he saw of Osiris, the Azura was a bloodbath. Had he survived? Had any of them survived?

"Rest assured, my friend. That boy you so admire breathes. Though…he probably wishes that he didn't, right about now," she said, wincing before smiling again. "That undead Drakkari saw to that."

"Is he hurt? How bad is it?!" Hanover panicked. "I should've been there to help him, I should've—"

"He will live. Though many of your other comrades cannot say the same. Of the eleven officers of Azura, seven remain. Of the two-hundred and sixty-three men that were aboard Azura at the outset of your *fated* voyage…only eight remain," Atla said coolly.

"Oh, Stars…" Hanover gasped, hyperventilating. "What happened? How did they—how did we—"

The reflections of Hanover in all the mirrored walls of the room began panicking. Some of them cried, some of them screamed, others grabbed at their hair, sobbed uncontrollably; screamed in rage, and everything in between.

"Be calm, child. I would recommend you learn to control your feelings in this place…" Atla said, motioning to the figures in the mirrors. "They will undo you, if you do not control them."

Hanover gasped at his reflections, twisted by their emotions. He pressed his back against one of the mirrors as he clutched at himself in fear. He gasped as a pair of arms formed out of the mirrored glass and wrapped around him, and a familiar face appeared next to his, smiling.

"No! Get off of me! Get away!" he shouted.

"Calm, child. We made a bargain, you, and I. You and your brother are mine. Body and soul…" Atla said, her voice morphing to that of the old woman again.

Hanover struggled. "Taren! Taren, save me! Brother, please! Osiris! Osiris help! Please—" a hand covered his mouth as he gazed at his screaming, struggling reflections.

"Sssshhhh…be calm," the old woman said.

She pulled him into the mirror.

*****

He heard unfamiliar voices all around him as he came to. His mind was an out of focus fog…

"Hanover…" he mumbled.

"He's waking!" he heard a woman gasp. "Go get Messanari!"

He opened his eyes slowly, and everything immediately came into focus as he saw several women standing around him. He bolted upright and went wide-eyed when he realized he was butt naked.

"Oh, sink me!" he cursed.

The woman fled as he got to his feet and futilely tried to cover his body from their view. "Fuck it. Where are my clothes? Where the *fuck* are my clothes?!"

He tore open baskets and dumped their contents on the floor, but none of it looked like his.

"Rega izvozvo! What are you doing?!" A woman shouted, grabbing his arm and stopping him dumping another basket onto the floor.

He looked at her sharply and was taken aback by her striking hazel eyes. "Where the…where the devil are my clothes?!" he barked, coming back to the moment.

"Your *clothes* are gone, iwe benzi! We had to make you new ones, now follow me!" she shouted.

He froze as she snatched the basket from him, sat it down, then led him into another room. The other women had come out of hiding and were gazing at him as he went. He tried yet again to cover himself, but realized there was no point.

"They've already seen what you have on offer. Your modesty is pointless, pirate," the woman said bluntly.

"Well blow me the fuck down," Osiris said incredulously. They'd taken his clothes, stripped him naked, and ogled him while he was unconscious. He wasn't sure whether he should be angry or paying them. "At least take me out for supper first."

"What?" the woman asked.

"Nothing. Where are my clothes, woman?"

"My name is Messanari, not woman. And I would suggest that you be more polite, considering you are outnumbered, naked, and in an environment unfamiliar to you. Alyrian or no," she said smugly.

He wanted to rebuke her, but she was right. "Aye…"

He absorbed his new surroundings as she led him through the house. He could tell that it wasn't of Kurzan origin. Judging by the brown-skinned women that were attending him, and the portraits of dark-skinned warriors with fur-lined armor and spears on the wall, he guessed that they were somewhere in Xalla. The house was decorated with black and yellow tapestries and wooden furniture. Whomever owned this place was well-off.

He looked at Messanari, walking a few paces in front of him. His eyes landed on her backside, and he caught himself staring as he watched her walk, admiring the subtle, confident swish of her hips as she strode.

"Where are we?" he finally asked, already guessing the answer.

"We are in Zambwali of the Luxon province," Messanari answered as she stopped at a door and opened it.

"Luxon? In Xalla?" Osiris asked.

"Do you know of any other provinces named Luxon?" Messanari asked as she led him into what appeared to be a bedroom. There were a pair of clothes laid out on the bed. "This is your new bedroom, and *these* are your new clothes."

"New clothes? What was wrong with my old ones?" Osiris asked.

"Bloody and torn to pieces. I had to cut them off from you in order to mend your wounds. You are welcome, by the way," Messanari said smartly.

Gone were his black vest, brown, button-up shirt, plain brown sash, black trousers and boots. In their place was a black, hooded coat, a white, long-sleeved shirt, a thick, bright red sash made of some sort of velvety silk, and baggy white pants. His new shoes were form-fitting and low-profile. He noticed that his bandana, which he normally wore tied around an arm, was still intact, though its fabric was frayed and faded from where Messanari had clearly been trying to scrub the blood from it.

"He told me that meant a lot to you, pirate," Messanari said, nodding to the bandana.

He picked it up and smelled it. It smelled clean and sanitized, but underneath he could still smell the smoke, gunpowder, and blood… he pushed the memory of that last, bloody night into the back of his mind.

"Aye."

"Well, how do you like your new clothes?" she asked, sounding hopeful.

Osiris shrugged as he tied the bandana back onto his arm. "Different from what I'm accustomed to. But I'm told Luxon is a lot hotter than up north, so I suppose that's to be expected. Good quality, though," he admitted.

"Yes, it is," she said. "Come. Uncle Yaman wanted to see you when you awoke."

"Yaman? Yaman Huasca? He yet lives? And he's your uncle?!" Osiris asked, surprised. He supposed it made sense. He'd had to have gotten here somehow. He suddenly felt bad about ogling his niece's backside.

"Are you surprised?" she asked.

"No. No, I suppose not."

They left the bedroom, veered to the left and went out the main door of the house, stepping out into the blindingly bright—and hot—sun. Osiris pulled the hood over his head to cover his eyes. Surprisingly, the black coat felt cool and airy on his skin. The grass was golden yellow, and he realized then that they were on some type of savannah plain. There wasn't another building in sight, just a large hilltop to the left, shaded by a tree, and a long road that went off into the distance. He could see a stable to his right where horses were likely kept. He supposed they rode them into town, wherever that was down that long dirt road.

"He is up there. Go to him," Messanari instructed.

He nodded, then started walking toward the hill. He paused and looked over his shoulder at her. "Aye, uh...thank ye for not lettin' me die, Miss Messanari. I know that must've been temptin'," he said, watching her smirk turn to a scowl.

"Indeed, it was. Next time, I'll be sure to let you bleed out on that table," Messanari huffed.

"Let's pray there isn't one then, ay?" he chuckled as she slammed the door shut behind him.

✶✶✶✶✶

Though it was only a few hundred yards away, Osiris had broken a sweat reaching the hilltop. The heat, and perhaps the untold amount of time he'd been unconscious, had gotten to him.

"Stars above...it's hot as a brahmak's nut sack out here," he gasped as he stood outside the hut at the top of the hill. While the house looked distinct, but still visibly modern, the hut was a primitive hay and mud structure sitting atop the hill like a blister. He was confused as to why Huasca used it. "You in there, old man?"

"Old man. Is that any way to speak to the man who saved your life, child?" Yaman Huasca asked as he stepped out from behind the straw curtain of the hut.

676

His clothing had changed drastically. Now, he really *did* look like a shaman. He wore a cloak made of some sort of animal fur, and a necklace of sharp teeth. He had feathers handing off his earrings, and small skulls dangling from a sash around his hips. His feet were bare, favored instead for a pair of fur leg wraps the same material as his cloak. He wore no shirt, instead he simply wore the cloak, and a skirt made of striped fur. The ritual scars covering his arms, chest, and everything else, were on full display.

"Ye act as though you haven't done that a hundred times before. Why would I start being proper now?" Osiris shrugged. "I see you've decided to dress the part now, ay?"

"It is my traditional attire. Now that I am back in the homeland, I must look my role," Huasca explained. He walked over to a large, flat rock overlooking the road that stretched into the distance. There was a stump sat next to it, and he nodded at it. "Sit."

Osiris shrugged and sat down on the stump as Huasca made himself comfortable on the rock. They sat there in silence for a while, watching the leaves and the grass blow with the wind, and watching a large, horned gazra feeding on the grasses. A red-feathered bird, perched on a nearby tree watched the horizon, cocking its head from side to side and letting out calls.

"You saved me…how and why?" Osiris asked.

"You act as though I have not saved you countless times since you were but a child. Why would I stop now?"

"There's the why. But how in Sheolhenna did you manage to fight off that…that monster?" Osiris asked, unable to hide the fear in his voice.

"I didn't. Not on my own. Bawon Samedi gave me back some of me power, and I used it to surprise the creature before a proper fight could ensue. Thank him."

"Bawon Samedi…is that the bastard that's been talkin' to me, in the back of my mind?" Osiris asked, putting the pieces together.

"Mmm. I did not expect him to be so overt so soon…" Huasca admitted.

"Yeah, well, fat lot of good he did. I was nearly torn to pieces and all he could do was tell me I cocked up," Osiris shook his head.

"Without him, you would have been a broken heap on the deck of Azura as she sank. The Dread Captain would have raised you, and you might very well be on the side of our enemy, now…"

The Dread Captain…

Osiris' expression hardened as he thought of him. The legends didn't do the man justice. He was a menace if ever there was one. "Who survived? Is it only us, now?"

Huasca shook his head. "I believe Morgan, Stone, Flint, Cutter, Cage, and Hanover are still alive. The rest…"

They sat in silence again. They did that for a long time. Thinking about all the friends they'd lost. All the adventures they'd been on, all the treasures they'd claimed. Together. All gone.

A shuzi—a black maned, sabretooth lion—was creeping closer to the gazra. It approached from downwind and behind the animal. The gazra, it seemed, hadn't noticed. The bird let out an alarmed call, and the gazra lifted its head, looking around. The lion froze and laid still on the ground.

"Why'd ye bring me here, old man? I'm exiled from this place."

"Around here? Nobody knows and nobody cares. Zambwali is far from the meccas of trade and power in Luxon. You are safe here, Assahj."

Osiris scowled. "I don't go by that name anymore. It's dead."

"So long as you live, it does as well. It is time to stop running," Huasca said.

"Best to leave it in the past," Osiris said.

"Often times, child, the past comes back to haunt the future," Huasca warned. "Every man cast a shadow. Every sun has a moon. Every fire has smoke. From the womb to the tomb…"

The shuzi was closing in, and the gazra was ignoring the frantic calls of the bird, trying to warn it. The gazra raised its head again and made an annoyed grunt at the bird before spotting the predator. Osiris froze. Huasca leaned forward. The gazra bleated loudly and tore off to the west. The shuzi exploded and sprinted after it. Its pride, camouflaged in the tall grass, rose and gave chase. The animal was tackled by one of them, which clung to it as the others piled in. The black-maned shuzi closed in and gave the creature a killing bite to the neck, evading its bucking horns.

"The gazra died because it did not heed the warning of the bird. The shuzi prevailed because it relied upon its family to aid it in the hunt. Which are you? The gazra, or the shuzi?" Huasca asked.

Osiris folded his arms. He watched the predator tear into its prey, and he couldn't help but think of that terrible night, when he watched his brethren get torn apart. The black-maned shuzi raised its head to the sky and let out a triumphant roar. It sounded like the roar that Black made as he stood over him, dying on the deck.

"…I don't know…"

"We can teach you, Assahj. But only if you are ready to learn…"

Osiris stood up, still watching the pride of shuzi feed on the dead gazra. He was ready, now. He knew that if he wanted to avenge Azura, he would have to learn.

"I am ready."

He was Assahj, now.

To Be Continued In...

Alyria II:

Shadow over oceanus

Index

El'wa Language/ Phrases

Da'nask: Damn, or a similar expletive.

Da'nem: A word meaning 'subordinate', or anyone considered to be beneath the speaker.

Fal'ren: A friendly term, meaning 'friend' or 'comrade'.

Fro'kal: 'Good friend', or 'old friend', depending on the context.

Ful'karin: Fuck, or a similar expletive.

Naq: No/ Don't.

Sha'nav: The navy. The word combines two root words, sha (meaning sea) and nav (meaning wayfarer).

Sohathin mel'dus: A phrase meaning 'good evening'. Sohathin is the el'wish word for moon, and mel'dus is the phrase 'greetings' or 'hello'.

Sul'ren: A formal term, meaning 'sir', 'ma'am', or 'superior'.

Tapo: Oh no!

Un'ghol: A derogatory term, usually meaning monster, or vermin.

Vash'a q'atra: Thank you!

Ver'mak: A catch-all term used by El'wa to describe any of the 'lesser' races.

Yaren el'kali: Rest in paradise.

Zamsk: 'Oh well' or 'fine' in a begrudging or reluctant manner.

Duwa Language/ Phrases

Ghunbeann: The mountain-less Duwa; those who do not live beneath the earth.

Manóg: A slang term for humans.

Pirate Terminology/ Phrases

Crack the kettle/ Crack jenny's cup: To have sex with someone, typically a prostitute.

Gasp to fishes: A phrase typically meaning "sure as the grave" or "on your/ my grave".

Imp: Short for 'Imperial', it's a common term used by pirates in reference to Kurzan imperial forces or officials.

Old Jack Ketch: A euphemism for the hangman.

Shiver me timbers!: A phrase often said during a battering storm, causing the ship to creak from the strain; also said out of surprise, or to make an oath.

Sink me!: An exclamation of surprise.

Common/ Colloquial Terms

Alcosav: A type of alcohol common amongst the humans of Hera in every region. A mix of several spirits in a dirty brew, alcosav can be very strong or weak depending on what was mixed into it and how much water and pure alcohol is in the brew. It is most common in rural areas where distillation is hard to come by, so multiple alcohols will often be poured together in large barrels to sit, then be poured out and bottled as needed.

Alyrian Slurs

Apostate: The term for all Alyrians who aren't collared: a brand applied to the neck of an Alyrian to suppress their powers. The brand is controlled by the Consortium, requiring a Brander to control it. The stronger the brand is, the more pronounced its appearance. Those without brands are instantly identifiable as apostates, as all Alyrians have tattoos across their body, marking their Alyrian gifts. Apostasy is punishable by death, and it is the duty of all magisters to seek out and either recruit, capture, or eliminate all apostates they find.

Devil-blood: A slur used by many to describe Alyrians, especially apostates. The term was coined to describe the glowing, fiery quality of Alyrian tattoos, with many believing the glow was due to the blood of demons flowing through their veins. Some Alyrians can summon demons.

Glow-stick: A term used to describe the often-glowing tattoos covering an Alyrian's body, resembling a glowing stick or shape in the dark.

Spark: A term referring to an Alyrian's ability to create sparks of light, electricity, or energy, typically a by-product of their magick.

CREATURES

Brahmak: Towering winged demons that occasionally serve as a powerful summons for masterful warlocks or, more often, as battlefield commanders, generals, and even shock troopers in demonick hosts and armies. The creatures are noted for their fearsome appearance, even by demon standards. They stand as tall as two-story buildings and, whether male or female, are powerfully built. They often sport a rack of ponderous horns, have dragon-like, skeletal faces, and a hateful grin or grimace constantly twisting their face. It is said that to gaze into the eyes of a Brahmak is to gaze into hell itself. Few who face them live to tell of it.

Cambion: Half-demons, born from the union of a mortal and a demon. Though they can be formed, technically, from any union of mortal and demon, the most common variants are the spawn of succubi and incubi. Cambions are vicious, feral creatures with the emotions of mortals and the power of demons. They are often used to infiltrate settlements prior to the arrival of a demonick host and relay information prior to their arrival.

Devil: A higher-ranking demon, devils are well-known and well-feared on Hera for their deceptive guile and formidable power when angered. Depending on their patron infernal, a devil can vary in appearance from darkly beautiful in appearance, to frighteningly hellish. They prefer to use their charisma and deceptive intelligence to corrupt and control mortals, but should they feel threatened, or should civility fail them, they are deadly fighters and Alyrians as well.

Drakkari: The race from which Officer Black hails. Subterranean in origin, they were once a powerful and vicious warrior race that ruled the subterranean hollows and warrens beneath Hera.

Drowner: A form of undead, drowners are what becomes of those unfortunate enough to die in the Alyria-tainted swamps of Sarx. A vestige of their soul remains, animating their corpse, now transformed into a water-logged, ugly imitation of life. Drowners prowl the moors, swamps, and wetlands of Sarx, and are especially active at night. They get their name from their preferred method of attack: bursting out from under the water's surface and grabbing hold of someone and drowning them.

Halghoul: A human in the process of becoming a ghoul. They like to feed on decaying flesh, and are known to rob graves.

Hydra: A large, multi-headed sea creature resembling a cross between a serpent and a dragon. They come in many different shapes and sizes and migrate across the seas of Hera. The creatures have a special organ in their abdomen that allows them to rapidly regenerate their heads when cut, spawning two more in their place. As a result, they can prove quite difficult to slay without special equipment.

Imp: The imp is a lowly demon resembling a horned, fiendish chimp or monkey. They can cast simple spells, however, and so while they may look comparatively weak, they are still more than capable of killing a mortal with a swipe of their claws or a toss of a fireball. They are a favorite summon for novice warlocks and demonologists, as they are easily manipulated and, admittedly, quite dull and craven.

Widow Crab: A large, scavenging crustacean who lurks about places of death, such as derelict ships at sea. The creatures are ponderous in size, easily reaching ten feet across and six feet tall when standing. They use their powerful legs and claws to scale up the sides of ships and attack their prey. Their carapace is typically black but can range from grey to white or even blue. Though well suited to attacking and killing humans and other small, two-legged creatures, they prefer to scavenge their food, eating detritus on the sea floor often, but are drawn by corpses dropped into the water and the fish that feed on them.

Kraken: Kraken are large, voracious, highly intelligent and predatory cephalopods that all but rule the ocean wherever they inhabit, often sitting comfortably at the top of the food chain and able to compete with even the largest and most dangerous creatures that inhabit the sea, save for perhaps in the black depths at its bottom. Though they prefer to feed on whales, sharks, and other large prey, they will, on occasion, attack ships, sometimes mistaking them for whales. They come in two major types: octos and coleos kraken.

Luxill: A type of levitating eel-like creature that is common in places with large amounts of Alyria. The creatures seem to be drawn to bodies of water and places that emanate Alyria. They are carnivorous but typically only prey on insects, invertebrates, and small vertebrate animals like rats. However, larger variants, which are sometimes reported in remote locations, can be quite hostile and have even been said to prey on kith if given the opportunity.

Taurox: Taurox are a breed of large bovine creatures, cousins to cows and bulls, but much larger and harder to tame. Taurox have ponderous, forward-facing horns used for jousting and defense from predators. That, combined with their enormous size (about fifteen feet in length from nose to tail), and cantankerous attitude, ensures that predators seldom hunt them. As a result, they graze and multiply with impunity in most areas and must be culled to ensure they do not over-graze pastures and lands needed for farming or for other wildlife. This is a difficult task, as taurox tend to travel in small herds of a dozen or so related individuals and can kill a man easily with a well-placed kick or goring. All but the hardiest, most foolish or desperate predators avoid them as a result.

Troll: Whether under a bridge, a mountain ridge, or a forest knoll. Trolls are an ever-present threat to travelers on Hera. Large, often times hairy, foul-smelling, and with a mean and violent disposition, trolls have claimed more lives than most other fae and forest creatures combined due to their intelligence and their love for well-traveled areas to lurk. Tall and lanky, trolls will often hide among trees or scrunch themselves down to blend in with the environment and hide under bridges and the like. From there, they plot and wait for unsuspecting prey. An arm reaching out from the darkness is often all an unfortunate victim will see before they are torn to pieces by its savage owner. Trolls are the bane of the civilized world and are often the subjects of fairytales and folklore.

Goblins: Small, squat, and mischievous fae, goblins are often a nuisance to the civilized races of Hera. Preferring to steal objects, food, and valuables from men to grow their wealth and status in their tribes, goblins are primitive creatures that lust for material wealth. A wealthy goblin chieftain will often lay claim to other goblins and use them as fighters, breeding stock, and anything else the greedy goblin desires. Goblins typically prefer to cower than fight when cornered, though they can be dangerous when in groups. Coordinated and organized goblins are rare, but they occasionally appear when their numbers have grown sufficiently, and a leader with some sense and purpose has taken the reigns. In groups, goblins can kill men and have been known to sack villages for slaves to sell (especially children) and goods to trade.

Nymphs: Capricious, mischievous, and lustful. Nymphs are elemental fae beings with a love for revelry. They will set themselves up in ruins and self-made encampments in forests, wiling away their days with drink, sex, music, and mischief. It is common for nymphs to play tricks on mortals, either to entice them into copulation or to satisfy their other urges and curiosities. Nymphs, being fae, are drawn to Alyria and its unpredictable winds.

Months of The Year

Hermora: 31 Days

Idollus: 31 Days

Aerona: 31 Days

Gofannon: 31 Days

Xallha: 30 Days

Brunnda: 30 Days

Thalla: 31 Days

Bramma: 30 Days

Sanguinar: 30 Days

Zylloth: 31 Days

Mordu: 30 Days

Druumas: 31 Days

Mourn: 29 Days

ACKNOWLEDGMENTS

This book would not be possible without the amazing people in my life who supported me through the struggles. My family: Uncle Fulton, Aunt Darleen, Jenay, and of course Jaret, and so many others who helped me and molded me through the years. This book is also for the amazing designers and editors who laid their hands on my work. Ellie, if you're reading this, you're a legend. I also want to thank the multi-talented CJ Monet for her work on the logo, as well as the numerous people who beta-read, advised, and gave me feedback on the multiple iterations of my work. And finally, I want to thank the author, Beatrice Loo, or Lacey as I know her, for coming up with the title of the book and helping to edit it. Without all your input, Alyria would have never made it to print. Thank you so very much.

About the Author

My name is Gerrod Rahman Thomas, but I go by SNRL Rocky. I was born and raised in Burlington Township, New Jersey. I lived there for almost twenty years. I went to school at Burlington Township High School and graduated with unremarkable grades. I barely got my yearbook signed, and by the end of my senior year, most people who knew me in my class probably wouldn't have had much of anything to tell you about me other than that I was marginally funny, quite chubby, and had a girlfriend that I'd been with for most of high school.

And that was it.

I wasn't a star athlete, or a student government member, or the class clown, or valedictorian, or anything or anybody of any real noteworthiness. I was average. I went to community college at Rowan College at Burlington County, or RCBC for short, and went for an Associate of the Arts degree that I'd planned to turn into a Game Design degree at the Art Institute of Philadelphia. Or it was until I dropped out. My grades were abysmal, I didn't really apply myself, and I spent all my free time playing video games with my friends online and generally just trying to act like the world outside didn't exist. I was, unsurprisingly, very depressed. All that changed when I came to Fayetteville, North Carolina, however.

I don't know why God gave me that chance and sent me down this path, but I am forever grateful. Because without Fayetteville, without my family there, without my cousin? I would have never become the man I am today.

I'm a business owner now. I don't know where I'd be without Blue Shades Publishing. I have my own podcast, Blue Shades Podcast. I'm starting to Twitch stream now. And, of course, I wrote the book you see before you. I can't wait to see where my life goes next. I am blessed and highly favored, and my dreams, slowly but surely, are coming true.

My life started out average, but it's turning into something exceptional. I am no different from you. Yours can, too.

If you'd like to keep up with what else I'm doing or message me, you can follow me on the social media handles listed below.

Instagram (Business): @blueshadesnc

Instagram (Personal): @snrl.rocky
TikTok (Business): @blueshades.pub
Tiktok (Personal): @snrlrocky
Twitch/ Kick: @snrlrocky/ @SNRLRocky